THE LEW ARCHER OMNIBUS

VOLUME 3

THE AUTHOR

Ross Macdonald was the pseudonym of Kenneth Millar. Born outside San Francisco in 1915, he grew up in Vancouver, British Columbia. He returned to the U.S. in 1938, earned a Ph.D at the University of Michigan, served in the Navy during World War II and published his first mystery novel in 1944. He served as president of the Mystery Writers of America and was awarded both the Silver Dagger award by the Crime Writers' Association of Great Britain and the Grand Master Award by the Mystery Writers of America. He was married to the novelist Margaret Millar. He died in 1983.

THE LEW ARCHER OMNIBUS

OMNIBUS

VOLUME 3

ROSS MACDONALD

This omnibus edition first published in Great Britain in 1997 by
Allison & Busby Ltd
114 New Cavendish Street
London W1M 7FD

A catalogue record for this book is available from the
British Library

ISBN 0 74900 340 5

Printed and bound in Great Britain by
Mackays of Chatham plc
Chatham, Kent

THE IVORY GRIN

To all HANDS

CHAPTER 1

I found her waiting at the door of my office. She was a stocky woman of less than medium height, wearing a blue slack suit over a blue turtleneck sweater, and a blue mink stole that failed to soften her outlines. Her face was squarish and deeply tanned, its boyish quality confirmed by dark hair cut short at the nape. She wasn't the type you'd expect to be up and about at eight thirty in the morning, unless she'd been up all night.

As I unlocked the door she stood back and looked up at me with the air of an early bird surveying an outsize worm. I said: "Good morning."

"Mr. Archer?"

Without waiting for an answer, she offered me a stubby brown hand. Her grip, armed with rings, was as hard as a man's. Releasing her hand, she placed it behind my elbow, ushered me into my own office, and closed the door behind her.

"I'm very glad to see you, Mr. Archer."

She had begun to irritate me already. "Why?"

"Why what?"

"Why are you glad to see me?"

1

"Because. Let's sit down and be comfortable so we can talk." Without charm, her petite willfulness was disquieting.

"About anything in particular?"

She seated herself in an armchair by the door and looked around the waiting-room. It was neither large nor expensively furnished, and she seemed to be registering those circumstances. Her only comment was to click her ringed fists together in front of her. There were three rings on each hand. They had good-sized diamonds in them, which looked real.

"I have a job for you," she said to the sagging green imitation-leather davenport against the opposite wall. Her manner had changed from girlish vivacity to boyish earnestness. "It's not what you'd consider a big job, but I'm willing to pay well. Fifty a day?"

"And expenses. Who sent you to me?"

"But nobody. Do sit down. I've known your name for ages, simply ages."

"You have the advantage of me."

Her gaze returned to me, tireder and older after its little slumming excursion around my antechamber. There were olive drab thumbprints under her eyes. Maybe she had been up all night, after all. In any case she looked fifty, in spite of the girlishness and the boyishness. Americans never grew old: they died; and her eyes had guilty knowledge of it.

"Call me Una," she said.

"Do you live in Los Angeles?"

"Not exactly. Where I live doesn't matter. I'll tell you what does, if you want me to be blunt."

"I couldn't bear it if you weren't."

Her hard dry glance went over me almost tangibly and rested on my mouth. "You look all right. But you sound kind of Hollywood to me."

I was in no mood to swap compliments. The ragged edge on her voice, and her alternation of fair and bad

2

manners bothered me. It was like talking to several persons at once, none of them quite complete.

"Protective coloration." I caught her glance and held it. "I meet a lot of different types."

She didn't flush. All that happened was that her face looked a little congested for a moment. It passed, and the incomplete boy in her came to the point:

"I mean, do you make a habit of cutting your clients' throats? I've had some pretty discouraging experiences."

"With detectives?"

"With people. Detectives are people."

"You're full of compliments this morning, Mrs. —"

"I said just call me Una. I'm not proud. Can I trust you to do what I want you to do and stop? Take your money and go about your business?"

"Money?"

"Here." She produced a crumpled bill from a blue leather pouch and tossed it to me as if it were an old piece of Kleenex and I were a wastebasket. I caught it. It was a hundred-dollar bill, but I didn't put it away.

"A retainer always helps to establish a bond of loyalty," I said. "I'll still cut your throat, of course, but I'll give you sodium pentothal first."

She addressed the ceiling, darkly: "Why does everybody in these parts work so hard for laughs? You haven't answered my question."

"I'll do what you want me to do so long as it's not illegal and makes some kind of sense."

"I'm not suggesting anything illegal," she said sharply. "And I promise you it makes sense."

"All the better." I tucked the bill into the bill compartment of my wallet, where it looked rather lonely, and opened the door to the inner office.

There were three chairs in it, and no room for a

fourth. After I had opened the Venetian blinds, I took the swivel chair behind the desk. The armchair I pointed out for her faced me across the desk. Instead, she sat down in a straight chair against the partition, away from the window and the light.

Crossing her trousered legs, she pushed a cigarette into a short gold holder and lit it with a squat gold lighter.

"About this job I mentioned. I want you to locate a certain person, a colored girl who used to work for me. She left my house two weeks ago, on the first of September to be exact. It was good riddance of bad rubbish as far as I was concerned, only she took along a few little knickknacks of mine. A pair of ruby earrings, a gold necklace."

"Insured?"

"No. Actually they're not very valuable. Their value is sentimental—you know? They mean a lot to me, sentimentally." She tried to look sentimental and failed.

"It sounds like a matter for the police."

"I don't think so." Her face closed up solid like brown wood. "You make your living tracing people, don't you? Are you trying to talk yourself out of a living?"

I took the hundred-dollar bill out of my wallet and dropped it on the desk in front of me. "Apparently."

"Don't be so touchy." She forced her grim little mouth into a smile. "The truth is, Mr. Archer, I'm a fool about people. Anybody that ever worked for me, even if they took advantage of me—well, I feel responsible for them. I had a very genuine affection for Lucy, and I guess I still have. I don't wish to make any trouble for her, nothing like that. I wouldn't dream of sicking the police on Lucy. All I really want is a chance to talk to her, and get my things back.

4

And I was so hoping that you would be able to help me?"

She lowered her short bristling lashes over her hard black eyes. Maybe she could hear the music of distant violins. All I could hear was the pushing and hooting of traffic on the Boulevard one story down.

"I think you said she was a Negro."

"I have no race prejudice—"

"I don't mean that. Black girls are unfindable in this city. I've tried."

"Lucy isn't in Los Angeles. I know where she is."

"Why don't you simply go and talk to her?"

"I intend to. First I'd like to get some idea of her movements. I want to know who she sees, before I talk to her, and after."

"That's a pretty elaborate way to go about recovering some jewelry. What's the purpose?"

"It's none of your business." She tried to say it gaily and girlishly, but the hostility showed through.

"I believe you're right." I pushed the bill across the desk towards her, and stood up. "In fact, it sounds like a wild-goose chase. Why don't you try the classified ads in the *Times*? There are plenty of investigators who live on a steady diet of wild goose."

"By God, I think the man's honest." She spoke to one side as if her alter ego was standing there. "All right, Mr. Archer, you have me, I guess."

The image didn't excite me, and I registered a suitable apathy.

"I mean I'm in a hurry. I haven't got time to shop around. I'll even admit that I'm in a spot of trouble."

"Which has nothing to do with petty theft or costume jewelry. You could have thought of a better story. But please don't try."

"I'm not. This is straight. When Lucy was working in my house she naturally got to know my family affairs. Well, there was bad feeling when she left, not

5

on my side, on hers. There are one or two things that
could embarrass me if she decided to spread them. So
I want to know who she's seeing. From that I can
draw my own conclusions."

"If I knew a little more about these embarrassing
facts—"

"I'm not going to tell you, that's definite. My whole
idea in coming to you is to keep them from getting
out. Now what could be franker than that?"

I still didn't like her story, but the second version
was an improvement over the first. I sat down again.
"What sort of work did she do for you?"

She hesitated briefly. "General housework. She's a
maid. Her full name is Lucy Champion."

"And where did she work for you?"

"In my house, naturally. There's no reason for you
to know where it is."

I swallowed my irritation. "Where is she now, or is
that another secret?"

"I know I seem unreasonable and suspicious," she
said. "Believe me, I've been burned. I take it you'll do
this job for me?"

"I might as well."

"She's in Bella City, up the Valley. You'll have to
hurry to make it before noon. It's a good two hours
from here."

"I know where it is."

"Good. A friend of mine saw her there yesterday, in
a restaurant on Main Street near the corner of Hidalgo. My friend talked to the waiter and found out that
Lucy eats her lunch there every day between twelve
and one. It's a combination café and liquor store
called Tom's. You can't miss it."

"A picture of Lucy would help."

"I'm sorry." She spread her hands in an automatic
gesture that placed her ancestry on the north shore of
the Mediterranean. "The best I can do is a descrip-

tion. She's a handsome girl, and so light she could pass for South American or California Spanish. She has nice big brown eyes, and not too much of a mouth, like some of them. A nice little figure, too, if she wasn't so skinny."

"How old?"

"Not old. Younger than me—than I." I noticed the self-correction, as well as the self-flattery in the comparison. "In her early twenties, I'd say."

"Hair?"

"Black, in a straight bob. She keeps it straight with oil."

"Height?"

"A couple of inches taller than I. I'm five foot two."

"Distinguishing characteristics?"

"Her legs are her best feature, as she well knows." Una couldn't pay another woman an unmixed compliment. "Her nose is sort of turned up—cute, if her nostrils didn't sort of stare at you."

"What was she wearing when your friend saw her?"

"A black-and-white checkered sharkskin suit. That's how I know it was her. I gave her the suit a couple of months ago. She altered it for herself."

"So you won't want the suit back."

That seemed to strike a nerve. She removed the butt that had gone out in her holder and crushed it violently in the ashtray beside her chair. "I've taken quite a bit from you, mister."

"We're about even now," I said. "I've been keeping score. I just wouldn't want you to think that you were buying very much for a hundred bucks. I have to watch that around here. You're suspicious. I'm touchy."

"You talk as if you were bitten by a bear. Do you have an unhappy home life, by any chance?"

"I was just going to ask you about yours."

7

"Don't start worrying about my home life. That's one thing—I don't want you talking to Lucy." She had a quick change of mood, or affected one. "Oh hell, it's my life and I live it. We're wasting time. Are you willing to do what I say, no more no less?"

"No more anyway. She mightn't turn up at the restaurant today. If she does, I tail her, keep a record of where she goes, who she sees. And report to you?"

"Yes. This afternoon if possible. I'll be registered at the Mission Hotel in Bella City. Ask for Mrs. Larkin." She glanced at the square gold watch on her right wrist. "You better get going. If she leaves town let me know immediately, and stay with her."

She moved deliberately and quickly to the outer door. Her walk was the shortest distance between things she wanted. The back of her neck was heavy under the cropped hair, swollen with muscle as if she had often used it for butting and rooting. Turning at the door to lift a flashing hand in good-bye, she hitched the mink stole higher. I wondered if she used it to conceal that telltale grossness.

I went back to my desk and dialed the switchboard of my answering service. Standing by the window, I could see the sidewalk below through the slats of the Venetian blind. It swarmed with a bright young crowd of guys and girls buzzing and fluttering in pursuit of happiness and the dollar.

Una emerged among them, dark and foreshortened by the height from which I was watching her. She turned uphill, her head thrust forward on her heavy neck, like an irresistible force searching for an immovable object. The switchboard answered in a youthful female gurgle on the fifth ring. I told it I was going out of town for the weekend.

8

CHAPTER 2

From the top of the grade I could see the mountains on the other side of the valley, leaning like granite slabs against the blue tile sky. Below me the road meandered among brown September hills spattered with the ink-blot shadows of oaks. Between these hills and the further mountains the valley floor was covered with orchards like vivid green chenille, brown corduroy ploughed fields, the thrifty patchwork of truck gardens. Bella City stood among them, a sprawling dusty town miniatured and tidied by clear space. I drove down into it.

The packing houses of the growers' associations stood like airship hangars on the edge of the green fields. Parched nurseries and suburban ranchos offered tomato plants and eggs and lima beans for sale. There was a roadside traffic of filling stations, drive-ins, motels slumping dejectedly under optimistic names. In the road the big trucks went by in both directions, trailing oil smoke and a long loud raspberry for Bella City.

The highway was a rough social equator bisecting the community into lighter and darker hemispheres.

Above it in the northern hemisphere lived the whites who owned and operated the banks and churches, clothing and grocery and liquor stores. In the smaller section below it, cramped and broken up by ice plants, warehouses, laundries, lived the darker ones, the Mexicans and Negroes who did most of the manual work in Bella City and its hinterland. I remembered that Hidalgo Street ran parallel to the highway and two blocks below it.

It was fairly hot and very dry. The dryness ached in my sinuses. Main Street was loud and shiny with noon traffic moving bumper to bumper. I turned left on East Hidalgo Street and found a parking space in the first block. Housewives black, brown, and sallow were hugging parcels and pushing shopping carts on the sidewalk. Above them a ramshackle house, with paired front windows like eyes demented by earthquake memories, advertised Rooms for Transients on one side, Palm Reading on the other. A couple of Mexican children, boy and girl, strolled by hand in hand in a timeless noon on their way to an early marriage.

Two privates appeared from nowhere, pale in their uniforms like young ghosts trapped by reality. I got out and followed them across Main and into a magazine shop near the corner. The unlit neon sign of Tom's Café was almost directly across the street. Beer on Tap. Steam Beer. Try Our Spaghetti Special.

The soldiers were inspecting a rack of comic books with the air of connoisseurs. They selected half a dozen each, paid for them and left.

"Milk sops," the clerk said. He was a gray-headed man with smeared spectacles. "They draft them in didees these days. Cradle to grave in one jump. When I was in the AEF."

I grunted, stood by the window looking out. Tom's Café had a varied clientele. Business suits and over-

10

alls, sport shirts and T-shirts and sweaters went in and came out. The women wore gingham dresses, sunsuits with halters, slacks and shirts, light topcoats over faded flowered silk. There were whites among them, but Negro and Mexican heads were in the majority. I didn't see a black-and-white sharkskin suit.

"When I was in the AEF," the clerk said softly and wistfully from behind the counter.

I picked up a magazine and pretended to read it, watching the changing crowd on the other side of the street. The light danced in standing waves on the car tops.

The clerk said in a changed tone: "You're not supposed to read them until you pay for them."

I tossed him a quarter, and he was mollified: "You know how it is. Business is business."

"Sure." I said it gruffly, to ward off the AEF.

Through the dusty window, the people resembled extras in a street scene in very early color. The faces of the buildings were depthless and so ugly that I couldn't imagine their insides. Tom's Café was flanked on one side by a pawnshop displaying violins and shotguns in its window, on the other side by a movie house plastered with lurid advertisements for *La Liga de Muchachos*. The crowd hurried faster, it seemed, and then the scene focused on the double swinging doors of Tom's Café. A light-skinned Negro girl with short black hair and a black-and-white checked suit came out, paused on the edge of the sidewalk and turned south.

"You forgot your book," the clerk called after me.

I was halfway across the street when she reached the corner of Hidalgo and Main. She turned left, walking quickly with short steps. The sun gleamed on her oiled hair. She passed within three feet of my

11

convertible. I slid behind the wheel and started the engine.

Lucy carried herself with an air. Her hips swayed pearlike from the narrow stem of her waist, and her stockingless tan legs worked pleasantly below the checked skirt. I let her cover the rest of the block, then followed her by fits and starts from parking place to parking place. In the second block I stopped in front of a frame Buddhist church. In the third, a pool hall where black and Mexican and Asian boys handled cues over green tables. In the fourth, a red-brick school in a yellow desert of playground. Lucy kept on walking due east.

The road degenerated from broken asphalt to dirt, and the sidewalk ended. She picked her way carefully among the children who ran and squatted and rolled in the dust, past houses with smashed windows patched with cardboard and scarred peeling doors or no doors at all. In the photographic light the wretchedness of the houses had a stern kind of clarity or beauty, like old men's faces in the sun. Their roofs sagged and their walls leaned with a human resignation, and they had voices: quarreling and gossiping and singing. The children in the dust played fighting games.

Lucy left Hidalgo Street at the twelfth intersection and headed north along the green board-fence of a baseball park. A block short of the highway she went east again into a different kind of street. It had a paved road and sidewalks, small green lawns in front of small well-kept houses, white frame and stucco. I parked at the corner, half hidden by the clipped eugenia hedge that surrounded the corner lot. The name of the street was stenciled on the curb. Mason Street.

About the middle of the block, a faded green Ford

coupé stood in a driveway under a pepper tree in front of a white bungalow. A Negro boy in yellow swimming trunks was hosing it down. He was very large and strong-looking. At a distance of half a block I could see the muscles shimmering in his wet black arms. The girl crossed the street toward him, walking more slowly and gracefully than she had been.

When he noticed her he smiled and flicked the spray from the hose in her direction. She dodged and ran toward him, forgetting her dignity. He laughed and shot the water straight up into the tree like a jet of visible laughter that reached me as sound a half second later. Kicking off her shoes, she scampered around the car one step ahead of his miniature rain. He dropped the hose and raced around after her.

She reappeared on my side and snatched up the nozzle. When he came around the car she turned the white stream full in his face. He came on dripping and laughing, and wrenched the nozzle out of her hands. Their laughter joined.

Face to face on the green grass, they held each other by the arms. Their laughter ended suddenly. The pepper tree shaded them in green silence. The water from the hose bubbled springlike in the grass.

A door slammed. I heard its delayed percussion like the sound of a distant ax-blow. The lovers sprang apart. A stout black woman had come out on the porch of the white bungalow. She stood with her hands clasped at her thick aproned waist and looked at them without speaking. At least her lips didn't move perceptibly.

The boy picked up a chamois and began to polish the car top like somebody wiping out the sins of the world. The girl stooped for her shoes with an air of earnest concentration, as if she'd been searching high and low for them. She passed the boy without turning

13

her head and disappeared around the side of the bungalow. The stout black woman went back into the house, closing the screen door soundlessly behind her.

CHAPTER 3

I circled three quarters of the block, left my car short of the intersection, and entered Mason Street from the other end, on foot. Under the pepper tree the Negro boy was still wiping down the Ford. He glanced at me as I crossed the road, but paid me no further attention.

His house was the fifth on the north side of the street. I opened the white picket-gate of the third house, a stucco cottage wearing a television aerial like a big metal feather in its cap. I knocked on its screen door and took a black notebook and a pencil out of my inside breast pocket.

The inner door was opened a few inches, the thin yellow face of a middle-aged Negro inserted in the aperture. "What do you want?" When they shut, his lips turned inward over his teeth.

I opened the notebook and held the pencil poised over it. "My firm is making a national survey."

"There's nothing we need." The ingrown mouth closed, and the door closed after it.

The door of the next house was standing open. I could see directly into a living-room crowded with

15

old Grand Rapids furniture. When I knocked on the door, it rattled against the wall.

The boy under the pepper tree looked up from the fender he was polishing. "Just walk right in. She'll be glad to see you. Aunty's glad to see anybody." He added: "Mister," as a deliberate afterthought and turned his wedge-shaped back on me.

The voice of the house spoke up from somewhere in the rear. It was old and faded but it had a carrying quality, like a chant: "Is that you, Holly? No, it wouldn't be Holly yet. Anway, come in, whoever you are. You must be one of my friends, and they visit me in my room now, now that I can't get out. So come on in."

The voice went on without a break, the words linked to each other by a pleasant deep-South slurring. I followed it like a thread across the living-room, down a short hallway, through the kitchen to a room that opened from it. "I used to have my visitors in the sitting-room, that wasn't so long ago. Just lately the doctor told me, you stay in bed now, honey, don't try to cook any more, let Holly do for you. So here I lie."

The room was small and bare, lit and ventilated by a single window, which was open. The source of the voice was a bed beside the window. Propped with pillows against the maple headboard, a Negro woman smiled from a sunken gray face, with great eyes like dark lanterns. Between the smiling blue lips the thread of talk unwound:

"It's a blessing for me, he said, that my joints are frozen solid with the arthritis, because if I tried to run around like I used to, my heart would give out sure. I told him he was a Job's comforter, what good is keeping my heart going like a watch that won't tell time if I can't get up and cook. He said I was one of the stiff-necked generations and I laughed right out in his face, I couldn't help it. That young doctor's a good friend of mine, I don't care what he says. Are you a doctor, son?"

The great eyes shone on me, and the blue lips smiled. I hated to lie when the human element cut across my work. I lied: "We're making a survey of radio users in southern California. I see you have a radio."

There was a small imitation-ivory table radio between her bed and the wall.

"I certainly have." She sounded disappointed. Her gray upper lip, faintly mustached, puckered in many vertical wrinkles.

"Is it working?"

"It certainly is working." The question revived her spirits by giving her a subject for conversation. "I wouldn't give house-room to a radio that wasn't working. I listen to it morning, noon and night, just shut it off the minute before you knocked on the door. I'll turn it on again when you go away. But don't hurry. Come in and sit down. I like to make new friends."

I sat in the room's only chair, a rocker near the foot of the bed. From there I could see the side of the white bungalow next door, with an open kitchen-window towards the rear.

"What's your name now, son?"

"Lew Archer."

"Lew Archer." She repeated it slowly, as if it were a short, eloquent poem. "Now that's a pretty name, a very pretty name. My name is Jones, after my last husband. Everybody calls me Aunty. I have three married daughters and four sons in Philadelphia and Chicago. Twelve grandchildren, six great-grandchildren, more on the way. See my pictures?" Above the radio, the wall was studded with thumbtacked snapshots. "It must be relieving to you to get off your feet for a little. This survey job, does it pay much, son?"

"Not much."

17

"You wear nice clothes, though, that's a comfort to you."

"This job is only temporary. I wanted to ask you, do your neighbors have radios? I couldn't get an answer out of the man next door."

"That Toby man? He's a surly one. They have radio *and* television." Her sigh expressed envy and resignation. "He owns himself a half block of income property down on Hidalgo Street."

I made a meaningless entry in my notebook. "What about the other side?"

"Not Annie Norris. I was as churchy as Annie Norris when I had the free use of my limbs but I was never as stiff-necked as Annie. Never could see the harm in a little radio music. Annie claims that it's a contraption of the devil, and I told her she's not moving with the times. She wouldn't even let that boy of hers go to the moving pictures, and I told her worse things could happen to a boy than a little innocent entertainment. Worse things could and worse things did." She fell silent. One of her gnarled hands struggled up from where it rested on the sheet that covered her knees. "Speak of the devil. Hear that?"

With a surge and lunge of her entire body, she turned her face away, towards the window. Behind the walls of the house next door, two female voices were arguing.

"She's carrying on with her boarder again. Listen."

One voice was a heavy contralto, easily identified with the stout black woman. I caught fragments of what she said: "You listen ... out of my house ... making eyes at my son ... get out ... my son."

The other voice was soprano, shrill with fear and anger. "I didn't. It's a lie. You rented me the room for a month—"

The heavy voice broke like a wave: "Get out. Pack up and get. You can have your money back for the

18

rest of the time. You'll be needing it to buy liquor, Miss Champion."

The screen door slammed again, and the boy's voice spoke inside: "What's going on in here? Mama, you leave Lucy alone."

"You stay out of this. It's none of your affair. Miss Champion is leaving."

"You can't throw her out like this." The boy's tones were high and hurt. "She's paid up to the end of the month."

"She's leaving, irregardless. Alex, you go to your room. What would your father think, he heard you talking to your mother the way you've been talking?"

"You do what your mother tells you," the girl said. "I wouldn't stay here anyway, after the insinuations."

"Insinuations!" The older woman gave the word a savage satiric twist. "These are facts I'm talking, Miss Champion, and they're not the only facts. I wouldn't soil my tongue with the other thing while Alex was listening—"

"What other thing?"

"You know what other thing. I didn't rent my good clean room for any such use as you put it to last evening. You entertained a man in your room last night and don't try to lie your way out of it."

If Lucy made any answer, it was too low to be heard. Mrs. Norris appeared suddenly at the kitchen window. I had no time to move back out of her line of sight, but she didn't raise her eyes. Her face was stony. She slammed the window down, and jerked the blind down after it.

Gasping and smiling, the old woman rolled back onto her pillows: "Well! It looks as if Annie's lost her boarder. I could have told her she was borrowing trouble, renting a room to that young Lucy creature with a grown boy in the house." She added with the candor of the very old, who have nothing but life to

19

lose: "Shucks, if she really goes, there won't be no more arguments to listen to."

I got up and touched her thin flannelette shoulder. "It was nice to meet you, Aunty."

"Same to you, son. I hope you get yourself a better job than that walking job you got. I know what it does to the feet. I cooked all my life in big houses. You take good care of your feet. . . ." The voice trailed me out like a cobweb spun endlessly into space.

I went back to my car and drove it forward a few yards into a position from which I could watch the Norris house. My job was a walking job and a driving job, but mainly a sitting and waiting job. It was hot under the top of my car, but I needed it for cover. I took off my coat and sat and waited. The seconds piled up slowly into minutes like rows of hot bright pennies.

At two by my dashboard clock, which was working, a yellow cab entered Mason Street from the other end. It slowed and honked in front of the Norris house, turned in the driveway behind the Ford coupé, and backed into the curb. Lucy Champion came down the driveway with a suitbox under her arm and a hat on her head. Behind her Alex Norris, fully clothed now, carried a pair of matched gray suitcases. The driver put them in the trunk and Lucy got into the back seat with a reluctant awkwardness. Alex Norris watched the cab out of sight. From the porch, his mother watched him.

I drove past them with my head averted, and followed the cab to Hidalgo Street, along Hidalgo to Main, then south on Main. The railway station lay in that direction, and I half expected Lucy to take a train. Her cab turned into the circular drive by the station, deposited her and her luggage on the platform. Lucy went into the station. I parked behind it and headed for the back door of the waiting-room. At

20

the same moment, Lucy came out. Her face was heavily powdered, and her hair tucked up under her hat. Without a glance at me, she walked to the taxi rank on the other side of the building and climbed into a black-and-white cab. While its driver was picking up her luggage from the platform, I turned my car.

The black-and-white cab went north on Main to the highway, then west along the highway for two blocks. It slowed and turned sharp left under a canvas sign stretched between two poles: MOUNTVIEW MOTEL AND TRAILER COURT. I drove by it, U-turned at the next intersection, and came back in time to see the black-and-white cab pull out with its back seat empty.

I parked short of the canvas sign and slid to the other side of the seat. The Mountview Motel and Trailer Court stood in the social badlands between the highway and the railroad tracks. It had a view of the mountains in the sense that every building in Bella City had. Through a wire-net fence to which vines clung halfheartedly, I could see twenty or thirty house-trailers lying like beached whales in the dusty court. Around and under them, children and dogs were playing. The near side of the court was half enclosed by an L-shaped building made of concrete blocks, pierced with twelve windows and twelve doors. The first door was marked Office. Lucy's suitcases stood on its low concrete stoop.

Lucy came out, followed by a fat man in a T-shirt. He picked up her suitcases and escorted her to the seventh door, in the corner of the ell. Even at a distance, she looked rigid with strain. The fat man unlocked the door and they went inside.

I drove into the court and parked in front of the office. It was a dismal cubicle, divided by an unpainted wooden counter. A frayed canvas settee stood by the door. On the other side of the counter there was a rolltop desk stuffed with papers, an unmade studio bed, an electric coffeemaker full of grounds, over all a sour coffee smell. A dirty printed card scotch-taped to the top of the counter announced: We Reserve the Right to Choose Our Clientele.

CHAPTER 4

The fat man came back to the office, his belly
rising and falling under the T-shirt. His forearms were
marked with blue tattooings like the printing on sides
of beef. One on the right arm said: I Love You Ethel.
His small eyes said: I love nobody.

"Any vacancies?"

"You kidding? Vacancies is what we got plenty of."
He looked around his office as if he suspected something the matter but couldn't exactly place it. "You
want a room?"

"Number six if it's empty."

"It ain't."

"How about number eight?"

"You can have eight." He rummaged in the desk for
a registration blank, which he pushed across the
counter. "You on the road?"

"Uh-huh." I signed my name illegibly, omitting my
license number and home address. "Hot today."

"You ain't seen nothing." His defensive tone was
accentuated by an asthmatic wheeze. "It's barely a
hundred. You should of been here around the first of
the month. It was darn near a hundred and ten.

23

That's what keeps the tourists away in droves. The room is two and a half single."

I gave him the money and asked to use the phone.

"Long distance?" he wheezed suspiciously.

"A local call. Private, if you don't mind."

He produced a telephone from under the counter and ambled out, slamming the screen door behind him. I dialed the number of the Mission Hotel. Una's voice answered immediately when the switchboard called her room:

"Who is it?"

"Archer speaking, from the Mountview Motel. Lucy Champion checked in here a few minutes ago. She was evicted by her landlady, a colored woman named Norris on Mason Street."

"Where is this motel?"

"On the highway two blocks west of Main. She's in room seven."

"All right, fine," on a rising note. "Keep a close watch on her. I'm going to pay her a visit. I want to know where she goes after I talk to her."

She hung up. I moved into room eight by placing my overnight bag in the middle of the worn rag rug and hanging my jacket on the one wire hanger in the cardboard wardrobe. The bed was covered with a sleazy green spread that failed to conceal the economic depression in its middle. I didn't trust the bed. I sat on a straight chair that I placed beside the front window and lit a cigarette.

The window gave me a view of Lucy's door and window across the inner corner of the ell. The door was closed, the green roller-blind drawn down over the window. The smoke from my cigarette rose straight up through the stagnant air to the yellow plaster ceiling. A woman groaned behind the wallboard partition in the next room, number nine.

A man's voice said: "Anything the matter?"

24

"Don't talk."

"I thought something was the matter."

"Shut up. There's nothing the matter."

"I thought I hurt you."

"Shut up. Shut up. Shut up."

My cigarette tasted like burning grass. I butted it in the lid of a coffee can which had been left in the room as an ashtray and thought of the people who had lain alone or in pairs on the iron bed and looked at the yellow ceiling. Traces of their dirt remained in the corners, their odors clung to the walls. They had come from all over the country to look at the yellow ceiling, stir in the iron bed, finger the walls and leave their indelible marks.

I moved across the floor to the partition between my room and Lucy's. She was sobbing. After a while she said something to herself that sounded like: "I won't." And after another while: "I don't know what to do."

People were always sobbing to themselves and saying that they didn't know what to do. Still, it was hard to listen to. I went back to my chair by the window and watched the door, trying to imagine I didn't know what was going on behind it.

Una appeared in front of it suddenly like a figure in a dream. A marijuana dream. She had on leopard-spotted slacks and a yellow silk shirt. Leaning towards the door like an eager fighter, she struck it two backhanded blows with her right fist.

Lucy opened the door. Her curled brown hands came up to her mouth and hooked on her lower lip. Una pushed in like a small garish battering-ram, and Lucy fell back out of my line of vision. I heard her staggering heels strike the floor. I moved to the partition.

"Sit down," Una said briskly. "No, you sit on the

bed. I'll take the chair. Well, Lucy. What have you been doing with yourself?"

"I don't want to talk to you." Lucy's voice might have been soft and pleasant if fear hadn't been playing tricks with it.

"You don't have to get excited."

"I'm not getting excited. What I do is my own business. It's no business of yours."

"I wonder about that. Just what does your business cover?"

"I've been looking for a job, a *decent* job. When I save a little money, I'm going back home. It's not your business, but I'm telling you anyway."

"That's a good thing, Lucy. Because you're not going back to Detroit, now or ever."

"You can't stop me!"

There was an interval of silence. "No, I can't stop you. I will tell you this. When you step off that train, there'll be a reception waiting for you. I phone Detroit long distance every afternoon."

Another, longer pause.

"So you see, Lucy, Detroit is out for you. You know what I think you should do, Lucy? I think you made a mistake leaving us. I think you should come back with us."

Lucy sighed very deeply. "No, I can't."

"Yes. You come back. It'll be safer for you and safer for us, safer for everybody." The bright clatter of Una's tone took on an illusive softness: "I'll tell you what the situation is, dearie. We can't just have you running around loose the way you have been. You'll get into trouble, or you'll have a teensy bit too much to drink in the wrong company, and then you'll blab. I know you people, you see. Blabbermouths every one of you."

"Not me," the girl protested. "I'd never blab, I

promise you faithfully. Please leave me go on the way I been, minding my own business, *please.*"

"I've got my duty to my brother. I'd like to leave you alone, Lucy. If you'd co-operate."

"I always co-operated before, before it happened."

"Sure you did. Tell me where she is, Lucy. Then I'll leave you alone, or you can come back to us on double the salary. We trust you. It's her we don't trust, you know that. Is she here in town?"

"I don't know," Lucy said.

"You know she's here in town. Now tell me where she is. I'll give you a thousand dollars cash on the barrelhead if you'll tell me. Come on now, Lucy. Tell me."

"I don't know," Lucy said.

"A thousand dollars cash on the barrelhead," Una repeated. "I have it right here."

"I won't take your money," Lucy said. "I don't know where she is."

"Is she in Bella City?"

"I don't know, mum. She brought me here and left. How do I know where she went? She never told me nothing."

"That's funny, I thought you were her regular little confidante." Harshly, with a sudden change of pace: "Was he hurt bad?"

"Yes. I mean, I don't know."

"Where is he? In Bella City?"

"I don't know, mum." Lucy's voice had sunk to a stolid monotone.

"Is he dead?"

"I don't know who you talking about, mum."

"Rotten little liar!" Una said.

I heard a blow. A chair scraped. Someone hiccuped once, loudly.

"You leave me be, Miss Una." The pressure of the situation had thrown Lucy back into sullen nonresistance, and slurred her speech. "I don't have to take nothing from you. I'll call the *po*llice."

"I'm sorry, honey. I didn't mean to hit you. You know my bad temper, Lucy." Una's voice was husky with false solicitude. "Did I hurt you?"

"You didn't hurt me. You couldn't hurt me. Just stay away from me. Go away and leave me be."

"Why should I?"

"Because you won't get nothing out of me."

"How much are you holding out for, honey?"

"And don't you call me honey. I'm no honey of yours."

"Five thousand dollars?"

"I wouldn't touch your money."

"You're getting pretty uppity for a nigger gal that couldn't get a job until I gave her one."

"Don't you call me that. And you know what you can do with your job. I wouldn't go back to it if I was starving to death."

"Maybe you will," Una said cheerfully. "I hope you do starve to death."

Her footsteps marched to the door, and the door slammed. In the hollow silence that ensued in the room, a series of slow dragging movements ended in the creak of bedsprings and another yawning sigh. I went back to my window. The sky blazed blue in my eyes. At the entrance Una was climbing into a taxi. It went away.

Two cigarettes later, Lucy came out and locked her door with a brass-tagged key. She wavered on the concrete stoop for a moment, gathering herself like an inexperienced diver for a plunge into cruel space. Thick powder clung like icing sugar to her face, imperfectly masking its darkness and its despair. Though she was wearing the same clothes, her body looked softer and more feminine.

She left the court and turned right along the shoulder of the highway. I followed her on foot. Her steps were quick and uncertain, and I was half afraid she might fall in front of a car. Gradually her stride took on the rhythm of some purpose. At the first traffic-lights, she crossed the highway.

I went ahead of her and ducked into the first store I came to, which happened to be an open-front fruit-and-vegetable market. Bent over a bin of oranges with my back to the street, I heard her heels on the pavement and felt her shadow brush me, like a cold feather.

CHAPTER 5

The street was one block west of Main and parallel to it. Its pitted asphalt was lined with Main Street's leavings: radio and shoe repair shops, reupholsterers, insect exterminators, flytrap lunchrooms. A few old houses survived among them as flats and boarding-houses.

Lucy paused in front of a house in the third block and looked up and down the street. A hundred yards behind her, I was waiting at a bus stop on the corner. In a sudden flurry of movement, she ran across the shallow yard of the house and up the veranda steps. I walked on.

The house she had entered leaned with an absent and archaic air between a mattress-cleaning plant and a one-chair barbershop. Three-storied and weird-ly gabled, it had been built before the invention of California architecture. Wavy brown watermarks streaked its gray frame sides. The lower panes of the ground-floor windows, painted white, faced the sun like a blind man's frosted glasses. Beside the double front-door there was a name on a board, printed in large black letters: SAMUEL BENNING, M.D. A card

30

above the bell-push said, in English and Spanish, Ring and Enter. I did.

The air in the hallway was a thin hospital-soup compounded of cooking odors, antiseptic, dimness. A face swam at me through it. It was a big man's face, too sharp and aggressive. I shifted my feet instinctively, then saw that it was my own face reflected in murky glass, framed in the tarnished curlicues of a wall mirror.

A door let light in at the end of the hall. A dark-haired woman came through it. She wore the gray striped uniform of a nurse's aide, and she was handsome in a plump and violent way. Her black eyes looked at me as if they knew it. "You wish to see the doctor, sir?"

"If he's in."

"Just go into the waiting-room, sir. He will take care of you presently. The door on your left."

She rolled away on smoothly revolving hips.

The waiting-room was unoccupied. Large and many-windowed, it had evidently been the front parlor of the house. Its present quality was a struggling lack of respectability, from the shredding carpet to the high discolored ceiling. Against the walls there were some wicker chairs that someone had recently brightened up with chintz. And the walls and floor were clean. In spite of this, it was a room in which the crime of poverty had left clues.

I sat down in one of the chairs with my back to the light and picked up a magazine from a rickety table. The magazine was two years old, but it served to mask my face. Across the room from me, in the inner wall, there was a closed door. After a while a tall black-haired woman wearing an ill-fitting white uniform opened the door. I heard a voice that sounded like Lucy's say something unintelligible and emotional, several rooms away. The woman who had opened the door closed it sharply behind her and came towards me:

"Do you wish to see the doctor?"

Her eyes were the color of baked blue enamel. Her beauty canceled the room.

I was wondering how the room had happened to deserve her when she interrupted me: "Did you wish to see the doctor?"

"Yes."

"He's busy now."

"Busy for how long? I'm in a hurry."

"I couldn't say how long."

"I'll wait for a while."

"Very well, sir."

She stood with perfect calm under the pressure of my stare, as if it were her natural element. Her beauty wasn't the kind that depended on movement or feeling. It was plastic and external like a statue's; even the blue eyes were flat and depthless. Her whole face looked as if it had been frozen with novocaine.

"Are you one of Dr. Benning's patients?"

"Not yet."

"Can I have your name, please?"

"Larkin," I said at random. "Horace Larkin."

The frozen face remained frozen. She went to the desk and wrote something on a card. Her tight, lumpy uniform made me restless. Everything about her bothered me.

A bald man in a doctor's smock jerked the inner door open. I raised the magazine in front of me and examined him over its edge. Large-eared and almost hairless, his head seemed naked, as if it had been plucked. His long face was dimly lit by pale worried eyes. Deep lines of sorrow dragged down from the wings of his large vulnerable nose.

"Come here," he said to the receptionist. "You talk to her, for heaven's sake. I can't make head or tail of it." His voice was high-pitched and rapid, furious with anger or anxiety.

The woman surveyed him coldly, glanced at me, and said nothing.

"Come on," he said placatingly, raising a bony red hand towards her. "I can't handle her."

She shrugged her shoulders and passed him in the doorway. His stringy body cringed away from hers, as if she radiated scorching heat. I left the house.

Lucy came out ten minutes later. I was sitting in the barber shop beside Dr. Benning's house. There were two men ahead of me, one in the chair having his neck shaved, the other reading a newspaper by the window. The newspaper-reader was an unstylish stout in a tan camel's-hair jacket. There were purple veins in his cheeks and nose. When Lucy passed the window heading south, he got up hurriedly, put on a soiled panama, and left the shop.

I waited, and followed him out.

"But you are next, sir," the barber cried after me. I looked back from the other side of the street, and he was still at the window, making siren gestures with a razor.

The man with the veined nose and the panama hat was halfway to the next corner, almost abreast of Lucy. She led us back to the railway station. When she reached it, a passenger train was pulling out towards the north. She stood stock-still on the platform until its smoke was a dissolving haze on the foothills. The man in the camel's-hair coat was watching her, slouched like a barely animate lump of boredom behind a pile of express crates under the baggage-room arch.

Lucy turned on her heel and entered the station. A narrow window under the arch gave me a partial view of the waiting-room. I moved to another window, ignoring the man behind the express crates but

33

trying to place him in my memory. Lucy was at the ticket window with green money in her hand.

The man edged towards me, his stout body wriggling along the wall as if the shade-latticed air offered solid resistance to its movement. He laid two soft white fingers on my arm:

"Lew Archer, *n'est-ce pas?*" The French was deliberate clowning, accompanied by a smirk.

"Must be two other people." I shook the fingers loose.

"You wouldn't brush me, boysie. I remember you but vividly. You testified for the prosecution in the Saddler trial, and you did a nice job too. I combed the jury panel for the defense. Max Heiss?"

He took off his panama hat, and a shock of red-brown hair pushed out over his forehead. Under it, clever dirty eyes shone liquidly like dollops of brown sherry. His little smile had a shamefaced charm, acknowledging that he had taken a running jump at manhood and still, at forty or forty-five, had never quite got his hands on it. —If it existed, the smile went on to wonder.

"Heiss?" he said coaxingly. "Maxfield Heiss?"

I remembered him and the Saddler trial. I also remembered that he had lost his license for tampering with prospective jurors in another murder trial.

"I know you, Max. So what if I do?"

"So we toddle across the street and I'll buy you a drink and we can talk over old times and such." His words were soft and insinuating, breaking gently like bubbles between his pink lips. His breath was strong enough to lean on.

I glanced at Lucy. She was in a telephone booth at the other end of the waiting-room. Her lips were close to the mouthpiece and moving.

"Thanks, not this time. I have a train to catch."

"You're kidding me again. There isn't another train

34

in either direction for over two hours. Which means you don't have to be anxious the girl will get away, *n'est-ce pas?* She can't possibly use that ticket she just bought for over two hours." His face lit up with a practical joker's delight, as if he had just palmed off an explosive cigar on me.

I felt as if he had. "Somebody's kidding. I'm not in the mood for it."

"Now don't be like that. You don't have to take offense."

"Beat it, Max."

"How can we do business if you won't even bat the breeze?"

"Go away. You're standing in my light."

He waltzed in a small circle and presented his smirk to me again: "*Avee atquee valee,* boysie, that means good-bye and hello. I'm on public property and you can't push me off. And you got no monopoly on this case. If the true facts were known, I bet you don't even know what case you're on. I got a priority on you there."

I couldn't help being interested, and he knew it. His fingers returned like a troupe of trained slugs to my arm:

"Lucy is my meat. I won her in a raffle by dint of sheer personal derring-do. Signed her up for a seven-year contract and just when I'm thinking of converting the deal into cash, lo and behold I stumble into you. In my alcoholic way."

"That was quite a speech, Max. How much truth is there in it?"

"Nothing-but-the-truth-so-help-me-God." He raised his palm in mock solemnity. "Not the whole truth, naturally. I don't know the whole truth and neither do you. We need an exchange of views."

Lucy came out of the telephone booth. Whenever she left an enclosed space her body huddled protectively into itself. She sat down on a bench and crossed her legs, leaning forward as if she had stomach cramps.

Heiss nudged me softly. His moist eyes shone. He might have been confiding the name of his beloved. "I do know there's a great deal of money in it."

"How much?"

"Five grand. I'd be willing to go fifty-fifty with you."

"Why?"

"Simple panic, chum." Unlike most natural liars, he could use the truth effectively. "Hit me and I black out. Shoot me and I bleed. Frighten me and I lose my controls. I'm not the courageous type. I need a partner who is, one that won't tear me off."

"Or a fall guy?"

"Perish the thought. This is strictly legal, believe me. You don't often pick up twenty-five hundred legally."

"Go on."

"In a minute. *Exchange* of views is what I said. You haven't told me a thing. What tale did the lady tell you, for example?"

"Lady?"

"Woman, dame, whatever she is. The one with the boyish bob and the diamonds. Didn't she hire you?"

"You know everything, Max. How can I tell you something you don't know?"

"You can try. What was her story to you?"

"Something about missing jewels. It wasn't very convincing even at the time."

"Better than the guff she handed me. Do you know what she gave me? That the girl was her late husband's servant, and when he died he left a legacy to her, and she was the executrix of the estate. And oh mercy me I owe it to my poor dead husband to find Lucy and pay off." With a nasty wit, he mimicked

36

Una's accents of false sentiment. "She must have thought she was dealing with an imbecile or something."

"When was this?"

"A week ago. I spent a good solid week picking that black girl up." He shot a vicious glance through the window at Lucy's impervious back. "So I found her, and what happened? I phoned up the good executrix and asked her for further instructions, and she fired me."

"What's she trying to cover up, Max?"

"Are we in business?"

"That depends."

"The hell. I offer you a half interest in a big deal, and you say that depends. *That depends.* I bare my bosom to you, and all you do is play clam. It isn't ethical."

"Is the five grand ethical?"

"I promised you it was. I've been burned, I lost my license once—"

"No blackmail involved?"

"Absolutely not. If you want the honest truth, the thing's so legal I'm afraid of it."

"All right, here's what I think. It isn't Lucy she wants at all. Lucy's a decoy duck for somebody else."

"You catch on rapidly. Do you know who the somebody else is, though?"

"I haven't identified her, no."

"Uh-uh. Not *her.*" He smiled with superior knowledge. "*Him.* I've got his name and description and everything else. And that black babe is going to lead us to him, watch."

Heiss was emotionally carried away. His sherry-brown eyes slopped round in their sockets, and his hands congratulated each other. To me, his story sounded too good to be true. It was.

Lucy straightened suddenly and jumped up from

37

the bench, heading for the back door of the waiting-room. I left Heiss standing. When I turned the rear corner of the station, Lucy was climbing into a green Ford coupé. Alex Norris was at the wheel. The Ford was rolling before the door slammed.

There was one taxi at the stand beside the station. Its driver was sprawled asleep in the front seat, his peaked cap over the upper part of his face, his mouth wide and snoring. Out of the tail of my eye, I saw the Ford turn north toward the highway.

I shook the driver awake. He was little and gray-haired, but he wanted to fight. "Take it easy, for Christ's sake. What goes on?"

I showed him money. "Follow that Ford coupé."

"All right, take it easy."

Max Heiss tried to get in beside me. I shut the door in his face, and the taxi pulled away. We were in the street in time to see the Ford turn left at the highway intersection, towards Los Angeles. At the intersection a red light stopped us. It was a long time before it turned green again. We drove fast out of town, pass-ing everything on the highway. No green Ford.

Five miles beyond the city limits, I told the driver to turn around.

"Sorry," he said. "I couldn't run that light with all the traffic going through. You have trouble with those people?"

"No trouble."

When I got back to the station, Max Heiss had gone. That suited me just as well. I ordered break-fast, always a safe meal, in the station lunchroom, and discovered when I started to eat it that I was hungry.

It was shortly after five o'clock when I finished my bacon and eggs. I walked back to the Mountview Motel.

CHAPTER 6

Lucy's key, with the numbered brass tag dangling from it, was in her door. I obeyed my impulse to knock. There was no answer. I looked around the court, which was sunk in the somnolence and heat of late afternoon. On its far side trailer children were chirping like crickets. I knocked again, listened to answering silence, turned the knob and stepped inside. Lucy was lying almost at my feet. I closed the door and looked at my watch. Five seventeen.

The roller blind was down over the window. Light slanted through the cracks in the blind, supporting a St. Vitus's dance of dust motes. There was a wall switch beside the door, and I jogged it with my elbow. The yellow walls sprang up around me and the ceiling pressed down from overhead, ringed with concentric shadows. The light radiated from a wall bracket directly over Lucy. Its paper-shaded bulb shone down into her face, which was gray as a clay death-mask in a pool of black blood. Her cut throat gaped like the mouth of an unspeakable grief.

I leaned on the door and wished myself on the

39

other side of it, away from Lucy. But death had tied me to her faster than any ceremony.

One of her arms was outflung. Beside the spread upturned hand something metal glinted. I stooped to look at it. It was a handmade knife with a curved six-inch blade and a black wooden handle ornamented with carved leaves. The blade was stained.

I stepped across Lucy towards the bed. It was identical with the bed in my room, its green rayon cover wrinkled where she had lain on it. At its foot her suitcases stood unopened. I opened one of them, using a clean handkerchief to mask my fingerprints. It was neatly packed with nurses' uniforms, crisp and starched from the laundry. Like the private compartment of a divided life, the contents of the other suitcase were a jumbled mess. It had been packed in a hurry with a tangle of stockings, wadded dresses, soiled blouses and underwear, an *Ebony* and a sheaf of romance magazines, an Ellington album wrapped in red silk pajamas. I found an envelope tucked among the powders and creams in a side pocket.

It was addressed to Miss Lucy Champion, c/o Norris, 14 Mason, Bella City; and postmarked Detroit, Mich., Sept. 9. The letter inside lacked date or return address:

DEAR LUCY

Am very sorry you lost your job we all thot you got youself fixed up for Life but you never know what is going to come, sure we want you back honey can you raze the fair am afraid we cant. You father is out of work agin and am the soul sport of the family agin, hard to make ends meat. Can always give you a bed to sleep in honey something to eat, come home things will be better. Brother is still in

40

school doing real good writting this for me (hi sis).
Hope you can raze fair stay off the roads.

MOTHER

P.S.—*How are you sis am fine, you know who.*

I put the letter back where I had found it, and closed the suitcase. Its catch clicked loudly, like a final tick of time.

Lucy's purse lay in a nest of dust in the corner behind her head. It contained lipstick and a handkerchief stained with it, a few ten- and five- and one-dollar bills and some change, a one-way ticket to Detroit, a social security card, and a newspaper clipping. The clipping was printed in old-fashioned type under a single-column head:

MOTHER OFFERS REWARD
FOR MISSING MAN

Arroyo Beach, Sept. 8 (Special to the BELLA CITY PRESS.) Mrs. Charles A. Singleton, socialite resident of this resort town, today posted a reward of $5,000 for information concerning the whereabouts of her son. The son, Charles A. Singleton, Jr., disappeared from the public rooms of a local hotel one week ago, on the evening of September 1st. His friends and relatives have not heard from him since that date.

Singleton, a Harvard graduate and wartime Air Force Lieutenant, is of medium height and athletic build, with curly brown hair, hazel eyes and a ruddy complexion. When last seen he was wearing a grey worsted suit, white shirt, dark red tie, and black shoes, without hat or topcoat. The missing man, son of the late Major Charles A. Singleton, is heir to the Singleton agricultural enterprises. His maternal grandfather was Colonel Isaac

Carlyle, who married Maria Valdes, daughter of the founder of the great Valdes land-grant estates.

Local police are inclined to reject suggestions of foul play, though Mrs. Singleton herself expresses fears for her son's safety. County Sheriff Oscar Lanson states: "Kidnapping seems out of the question. There has been no ransom note, for one thing. As for foul play, the evidence indicates that Mr. Singleton left Arroyo Beach under his own power, for his own reasons. It is to be remembered that he is a young, unattached man, with a background of travel. We are, however, doing everything we can to locate him, and will welcome any information from the public."

Anyone having information as to Singleton's whereabouts was urged to contact Capt. Kennedy of the Arroyo Beach sheriff's office.

I read the report twice, fixing the names, times, places, in my head, then replaced the clipping in the purse and the purse in the corner. In a way I knew less than before, as something written in a foreign language extends the range of your ignorance. I looked at my watch. Five twenty-four. Seven minutes since I had found Lucy.

In order to reach the door I had to step over her again. I looked down into the gray face before I switched off the light. Alienated and deeply sunk beyond time already, the face told me nothing. Then it was swallowed by shadows.

In the court, the yellow sunlight looked thin and faded, as if it had been late afternoon for an insupportable time. An old car turned in from the highway and rolled across the gravel to the trailers, leaving a feeble flurry of dust on the stagnant air. I waited for the dust to settle before I started across the court to the office. Before I reached it I saw that Alex Norris was watching me from the gate.

Moving with awkward speed in a pressed blue suit too small for him, he ran at me. I went to meet him and crouched for the onset. He was heavy and strong, and he knew how to use his weight. His shoulder took my midriff and laid me on the gravel on my back. I got up. He didn't know how to use his fists. I stepped inside a wild swing and bent him with a body-blow. It brought his head forward for an uppercut. Instead, to save my knuckles and his face, I locked his right arm and used it as a lever to turn him away.

"Let me go," he said. "Fight fair. I'll show you."

"You showed me. I'm too old to fight. Me and Joe."

"He could beat your brains out," the boy cried defiantly. "Turn me loose, I'll do it myself. What were you doing in Lucy's room?"

"Something's happened to her."

Bowed and immobilized by my hold, he had to crane his neck sideways to look at me. His black forehead was sprinkled with droplets of sweat, and his eyes were large and bright with expectations of disaster. "You're a liar. Let me go."

"Will you stand and talk to me, like a sensible man?"

"No." But the word lacked force. The brightness of his eyes was glazing, would turn to tears in a minute. He was a boy in a man's frame. I released him.

He straightened slowly, rubbing his cramped arm. Beyond him, on the other side of the court, a ragged line of spectators was moving slowly towards the lure of violence.

"Come into the office, Alex."

He stiffened. "Who's going to make me?"

"Nobody's going to make you. Come on, anyway."

"I don't have to."

"How old are you, Alex?"

43

"Nineteen, going on twenty."

"Ever been in trouble?"

"I never have. Ask my mother."

"Lucy your girl friend?"

"She's not my girl friend. We're going to get married." He added, with pathetic irrelevance: "I can support a wife."

"Sure you can."

His bright gaze was painful on my face. "Is something the matter? Why did you go in there?"

I groped back for the impulse that had made me knock on Lucy's door and go in. "To talk to her. To warn her to leave town."

"We are leaving, tonight. That's what I'm waiting for. She came to get her things." As if it were being turned by a long-handled wrench against his will, his head turned on his shoulders to look at the closed door of number seven. "Why doesn't she come out? Is she sick?"

I said: "She's not coming out."

The gallery of onlookers from the trailers was straggling across the court, uttering small sounds of menace and excitement. I pulled the office door open and held it for Alex. He went in past me, moving nothing but his legs.

The man who loved Ethel and nobody else was sitting on the studio bed with his back to the door, a half-empty Coke bottle in his fist. He rose and padded to the counter, casting a backward glance at the studio bed. From the cover of a magazine spread open on its pillow, a bare-bosomed woman screamed soundlessly for assistance.

Disregarding her pleas, the pink-haired man said: "What can I do for you?" Then his slow nerves reacted to the black boy: "What does he want?"

"The telephone," I said.

"Local call?"

44

"The police. Do you know the number?"

He knew it. "Trouble?"

"In number seven. Go and take a look. I wouldn't go in, though. Don't let the others, either."

He leaned on the counter, his belly oozing over its edge like cottage cheese in a bag. "What happened?"

"Look for yourself. Give me the telephone first."

He handed me the telephone, hustled to the door and out. Alex tried to follow him. I kept my right hand on the boy's arm and dialed with my left. When he heard what I had to say to the desk sergeant he fell forward across the counter, catching his weight on his forearms. The upper half of his body was shaken by an inaudible sobbing. The desk sergeant said that he would send a car right out.

I shifted my hand to the boy's back. He shied away from it as if I were trying to stab him.

"What were you doing out there, Alex?"

"Minding my own business."

"Waiting for Lucy?"

"If you know, you don't have to ask me."

"How long were you waiting?"

"Nearly half an hour. I drove around the block a couple of times and came back."

I looked at my watch: five thirty-one. "She went in about five o'clock?"

"It was just about five."

"Did she go in alone?"

"Yes. Alone."

"Did anybody else go in afterwards?"

"Not that I saw."

"Did anybody come out?"

"You did. I saw you come out."

"Besides me. Before me."

"I didn't see. I drove around the block."

"Did you go in?"

"No, sir. I didn't go in."

"Why not?"

"She said she'd only be five minutes. Her bags, they were still packed."

"You could have gone in."

"I didn't want to. She didn't want me to."

"Lucy was passing, wasn't she?"

"What if she was? There is no law against passing in this state."

"You're well informed," I said. "Going to school?"

"I just started junior college. But I'm quitting."

"To get married?"

"I'll never get married. I'll never marry anybody now. I'll run away and lose myself." With his head dejected below his shoulders, he was speaking to the scarred top of the counter.

"You're going to have to stick around and answer a lot of questions. Pull yourself together."

I shook him roughly by the shoulder. He wouldn't turn or move until the siren whooped on the highway. Then his head came up like an animal's at bay.

CHAPTER 7

A black patrol-car ground to a stop on the gravel outside the office. A plainclothesman got out, mounted the stoop, and filled the doorway. In spite of his gray fedora and baggy gray clothes, he looked as if he had always been a policeman—had teethed on handcuffs, studied his lessons in the criminal code, pounded out his career on broken pavements, in nocturnal alleys. Scarred and seamed by fifty years of sun and other weather, his face was a relief map of life in the valley.

"I'm Brake, lieutenant of detectives. You the one that phoned?"

I said I was. "She's in room seven, at the end of the court."

"Dead?"

"Very."

Alex let out a choked noise. Brake took a step towards him and looked him over closely. "What are you doing here?"

"Waiting for Lucy."

"She the one that's dead?"

"Yes, sir."

47

"You're going to have a long wait. Did you cut her?"

Alex looked at the detective as if he were a tree too thick to climb. "No, sir."

"You're Annie Norris's boy, aren't you?"

"Yes, sir."

"How's your mother going to like this?" Before Alex could answer, Brake turned to me: "Did he cut her?"

"I doubt it. He stayed around after it happened. They were on their way to get married, he says."

"He says."

"I didn't cut her," Alex said. "I wouldn't hurt a hair of Lucy's head." He was leaning slackly against the counter on his elbows, as if he no longer had a use for his body.

The fat key-clerk came in, letting the door close softly on his heel. He moved sideways along the wall and around the end of the counter to his world of paper bosoms, dirty sheets, silent screams for assistance. The sight of death had reminded him of the buried guilts in the graveyard of his mind, and he jumped when Brake said to his back:

"Are you the key-clerk?"

"Yes, sir."

"I want a key to number seven, all the keys in fact."

"They're both out, Mr. Brake." He came forward placatingly, offering his quivering body as a sacrifice. "I give her one when she rented the room, and then when she came back she asked me for the duplicate. She said she lost the other. I said she'd have to pay—"

I cut in: "The key's in the door, lieutenant."

"Why didn't you say so?"

Brake stepped outside and summoned his driver to keep an eye on Alex. A second police-car drew up behind the first. The ring of spectators broke and

48

re-formed around it. A uniformed sergeant pushed through them to join Brake. He had a folded tripod and camera under one arm and a fingerprint kit in the other hand. "Where's the stiff, lieutenant?"

"Over yonder. Call the deputy coroner?"

"He's on his way."

"She'll spoil before we get to her, at this rate. Now take it easy, folks. Gangway."

The crowd made way for them and surged in their wake.

Inside the office, Alex and his guard sat in glum intimacy on the settee. The guard was a large young cop in a blue traffic-officer's uniform. Beside his thick-chested frame Alex looked smaller and thinner. His gaze was turned inward. He seemed to be seeing himself for the first time as he was: a black boy tangled in white law, so vulnerable he hardly dared move a muscle.

Behind the counter, the key-clerk was comforting himself with the remnant of his Coke. I sat on the studio bed beside him:

"I'd like to get that straight about the keys."

"Questions!" He belched pathetically. Brown liquid trickled from the corner of his mouth into a red rash on his chin. "You prob'ly won't believe me, I look like a healthy constitution, only I got delicate nerves. I'm still on partial disability from the Army, and that's the proof of it. I can't take all this cross-questioning and stuff. The way the lieutenant looked at me, you'd think I done her in." He pouted like a bloated dilapidated imbecile little boy.

"When did you see her last?"

"Must of been around five o'clock, I didn't look at the time."

"She needed another key?"

"That's correct. I asked her what happened to the one I give her when she checked in. She said she

49

must of lost it. I said that would be fifty cents extra and she paid me the money right then. She said she was checking out. Little did I know she had a rendez-voose with murder."

"Did she seem disturbed?"

"I don't know. I didn't specially notice. I was the one that should of been disturbed. Why'd she want to come here to get herself chopped? They'd do it for her down on Hidalgo any day of the week."

"It certainly was tough on you," I said, "and inconsiderate of her."

"You're bloody right." Self-pity gurgled in his throat like a hemorrhage beyond the reach of irony or cautery. "How did I know she was passing herself for white? That she was going to bleed all over my floor? I got to clean it up."

On the other side of the counter Alex sat with his guard. All I could see of him was the top of his head, but I could hear him breathing.

"After the girl went into her room," I said, "did anybody else go in?"

"Not that I saw. I don't pay no attention half the time. They go and come." The phrase pleased him, and he repeated: "Go and come."

"You didn't see anybody?"

"Naw. I was sitting down in here passing the time. They come and go." A flash of anger galvanized him feebly: "I *wisht* I seen him. Just lemme get my hands on the guy that done it and mussed that floor—"

"You think it was a man?"

"Who said so?"

"You said 'guy.'"

"Only a manner of speaking. Anyway, why would a woman cut a woman?" Leaning towards me, he said in a loud stage whisper: "You want my honest opinion, I think that young buck done it. They're always cutting their wenches, you know that."

50

There was a scuffle of feet. Alex Norris came over the counter head first and lighted on all fours in front of us. Scrambling to his feet, he landed one backhanded blow on the side of the clerk's head. The clerk screamed gently and swooned across my legs.

Alex dived for the open window. Unable to get to my feet, I yelled: "Stop it, Alex! Come back!"

He kicked out the screen and hoisted one leg over the sill. The coat of his blue suit was split down the back.

His guard strode round the end of the counter, lifting the right side of his uniform blouse. His black police-holster snapped open and a revolver popped up in his hand like a lethal jack-in-the-box. Its safety clicked off. Alex was still in the window, struggling to force his other leg through the narrow opening. He was a sitting duck, and the range was almost point-blank.

I rolled the key-clerk off my knees to the floor and stepped across the line of fire. The trigger-happy guard cursed me and said: "Get out of the way."

Alex was out of the window. I went out after him. He was pounding across a field of tall dry grass towards the fence that ran along the highway. It was a seven-foot wire fence. He ran up it and vaulted over in a single fluid motion. His Ford coupé was parked on the shoulder of the highway.

I got over the fence and fell on the other side. A gun went off behind me. Alex was in his car, kicking the starter. A bullet struck the hood of the Ford with the plop of a heavy raindrop, leaving a hole. As if stung, the Ford jumped forward, its rear wheels churning the gravel. I ran for it and got one arm hooked through the open right window.

Alex didn't turn his head over the wheel, but he braked suddenly, swerved, and accelerated. I lost my precarious grip on the door. When I hit the ground, I rolled. The colored world spun into gray monochrome and blacked out for a second. The young traffic-cop with the gun hauled me to my feet. The Ford was out of sight.

"Listen, you." He cursed me unimaginatively a few times. "I could of pinked him, if you hadn't been in the way. What you trying to pull?" The revolver in his right hand seemed to be threatening me. His left hand was automatically brushing gravel off the back of my jacket.

"You wanted him alive. If you shot him you'd be in the soup. He wasn't under arrest."

His face went white under the tan, as if I had turned a valve on its blood supply. Almost furtively, he put the revolver away.

Brake came out through the gate of the court, running swiftly and cumbrously like a bear on its hind legs. He had grasped the situation before he reached us:

"You're wasting time, Trencher. Take after him. Use the other car. I'll get on the radio. What's his number?"

"I didn't get it, lieutenant."

"You're doing great work, Trencher." Brake waved him away.

I gave him the license number. Moving with alert impatience, Brake went back to the patrol-car and shut himself in to radio his headquarters. I waited for him beside it:

"What's the story, lieutenant?"

"General alarm. Roadblocks." He started for Lucy's room.

The crowd of trailer people, men and women and children, blocked his path. One of the men spoke up: "The boy get away from you, captain?"

"We'll get him back. Incidentally, I want all you people to stay home tonight. We'll talk to you later."

52

"Is it murder?" The question fell into a hush, which was broken by a sparrowlike twittering from women and children.

"I'll guarantee this:" Brake said, "she didn't cut herself shaving. Now break it up. You people go back to your houses."

The crowd drew back muttering. Advised by his glance to come along, I followed Brake to the door of number seven. Inside, the identification officer was taking measurements and photographs. Lucy lay under his ministrations with the bored expression of a hostess whose guests' antics were getting out of hand.

"Come in," Brake said. "Shut the door."

One of the suitcases was open on the bed, and he returned to his examination of it. I stayed by the door, watching his large practiced hands go through the white uniforms.

"Trained nurse, apparently." He added very casually: "How did you happen to find her?"

"I knocked on the door and she didn't answer. The door wasn't locked. I looked in."

"Why do that?"

"I'm in the room next door."

His narrow gray gaze came up to my face. "You know her?"

"Never met her."

"Hear any noise? See anybody?"

"No." I made a quick decision: "I'm a private detective from Los Angeles. I've been tailing her since noon."

"Well." The gray eyes clouded. "That makes it interesting. Why were you doing that?"

The identification man, who was dusting the second suitcase for fingerprints, turned his head to give me a sharp-faced look.

"I was hired to."

53

Brake straightened up and faced me. "I didn't think you were doing it for fun. Let's see your identification."

I showed him my photostat.

"Who hired you?"

"I don't have to answer that."

"You weren't hired to kill her, by any chance?"

"You'll have to do better than that, if you want any co-operation from me."

"Who said I wanted any co-operation from you? Who hired you?"

"You get tough very quickly, lieutenant. I could have blown when I found her, instead of sticking around to give you the benefit of my experience."

"Can the spiel." He didn't needle easily. "Who hired you? And for God's sake don't give me the one about you got your client's interests to protect. I got a whole city to protect."

We faced each other across the drying moat of blood. He was a rough small-city cop, neither suave nor persuasive, with an ego encysted in scar-tissue. I was tempted to needle him again, to demonstrate to these country cousins how a boy from the big city could be hard in a polished way. But my heart wasn't in the work. I felt less loyalty to my client than to the dead girl on the floor, and I compromised:

"A woman who gave her name as Una Larkin came to my office this morning. She hired me to tail this girl, and told me where to find her at lunchtime. Tom's Café on Main Street. I picked her up there and followed her home to Alex Norris's house, where she was a roomer—"

"Save the details for your statement," Brake said. "What was that about the client's name? You think it was a phony?"

"Yes. Am I going to make a statement?"

"We'll go downtown soon's we finish up here. Right now I want to know what she hired you for."

"She said Lucy worked for her, and left a couple of weeks ago with some of her jewelry—ruby earrings and a gold necklace."

Brake glanced at the identification man, who wagged his head negatively. He said to me: "You'll have to take it up with the County Administrator. Or is that story phony, too?"

"I think so."

"The woman live in town here?"

"I doubt it. She was very cagy about who she was and where she came from."

"You giving it straight, or suppressing information?"

"Straight." Una had bought that much with the hundred that was lonely in my wallet.

"It better be. Did you call us as soon as you found her?"

"There was a few minutes' time-lag. On my way across the court to the office, young Norris attacked me."

"Was he going or coming?"

"Neither. He was waiting."

"How do you know?"

"I held him and questioned him a little. He said he'd been waiting for Lucy to get her things since five o'clock. They were going away to be married. He didn't know she was dead until I told him."

"You read minds, huh?" Brake's face slanted, chin out, towards me, cracked and red like Bella Valley earth above the irrigation level. "What else do you do, Mister Experience?"

"When I make a statement, I try to keep the record straight. The physical facts are against Norris. It looks like consciousness of guilt, running out like that—"

"You don't tell me," Brake said heavily, and his

55

assistant snickered. "I never would have thought of that by myself."

"He ran because he was scared. He thought he was going to be railroaded, and maybe he was right. I've seen it happen to black boys, also to white boys."

"Oh sure, you've been around. You've had a lot of experience. Only I don't want the goddam benefit of your goddam experience. I want your facts."

"You're getting them. Maybe I'm going too fast for your powers of assimilation."

Brake's small eyes crossed slightly. His large face became congested with dark blood. The developing situation was interrupted by someone opening the door behind me, and singing out: "Break it up, boys. I have a date with a lady. Where's the lady?"

It was the deputy coroner, a plump young medical man bubbling with the excessive cheerfulness of those who handled death as a regular chore. He was accompanied by a white-coated ambulance driver and a black-coated undertaker who strove to outdo him in gaiety. Brake lost interest in me and my selection of facts.

Samples of blood were taken from the floor. The stained bolo knife and Lucy's smaller belongings were packed in evidence cases. Its position having been outlined with chalk, the body was lifted onto a stretcher and covered with canvas. The undertaker and the ambulance driver carried it out. Brake sealed the door.

It was twilight, and the courtyard was almost empty. Around a pole in its center, a group of women stood in the spill of light from a single arc-lamp. They were talking in loud self-righteous tones about murders they had seen or read or heard about or imagined. Their voices sank to an uneasy protesting murmur as Lucy's cortege went by them. Their eyes, bright-dark in faces splashed with white by the lamp on the pole, followed the covered stretcher to the back door of the waiting hearse. The sky was a dingy yellow ceiling.

CHAPTER 8

The Mission Hotel was the most impressive building on Main Street. It was a concrete cube pierced with four rows of windows and surmounted by a broadcasting mast that thrust a winking red light towards the stars. Its flat white façade was stained red by a vertical neon sign over the entrance.

The lobby was deep and gloomy, furnished with dark wrinkled-leather chairs. Those near the half-curtained windows at the front were occupied by old men sitting in stiff impromptu positions, as if a flood had lodged them there years ago and then receded forever. On the wall above their heads, an obscure mural depicted U.S. cavalrymen riding strange horses with human knees in pursuit of still stranger Indians.

The desk-clerk was a mouse-colored little man who was striving against heavy odds to confer distinction on himself and his surroundings. With hair and eye-brow-moustache scrupulously brushed, a cornflower in his buttonhole matching the delicate pin-stripe in his flannels, and at his languid elbow a vase of cornflowers to underline his point, he might have inspired a tone poem by Debussy. He answered my question in tones of careful elegance, implying that he hadn't always manned an outpost in the wilderness:

"I believe Mrs. Larkin is in her suite. I haven't seen her go out, sir. Whom shall I say is calling?"

"Archer. Don't bother announcing me. What's her room number?"

"One hundred and two, Mr. Archer. I think she's expecting you."

It was opposite the elevator on the second floor. At the end of the corridor a pair of curtained French doors had a red-lit sign above them: FIRE ESCAPE. I knocked on the door of 102. The elevator creaked and thumped behind me like an old heart running down.

A wan voice called through the door: "Who is it, anyway?"

"Archer."

"Come in."

The door was locked, and I said so.

"All right, all right, I'm coming." The door swung inward.

Una looked sick. The olive-drab patches under her eyes had darkened and spread. In red Japanese pajamas she looked less like a woman than a sexless imp who had grown old in hell.

She stood back to let me enter the room and closed the door softly behind me. It was the sitting-room of the bridal or gubernatorial suite, if honeymooners or politicians ever came there. The two tall windows that overlooked the street had drapes of dark-red plush. They were lit from outside by a red neon glow that competed with the light of a parchment-shaded floor lamp made of twisted black iron. The tall carved Spanish chairs looked unsat in and unsittable. The only trace of Una's occupancy was a leopard coat hanging over the back of a chair.

"What's the trouble?" I said to her back.

59

She seemed to be supporting herself on the doorknob. "No trouble. It's this foul heat, and the waiting and the uncertainty." She saw where that was leading her, into candor, and switched off the little-girl whine. "I have a migraine, God bless it. They hit me regularly."

"Too bad." I added, with deliberate tactlessness: "I have a headache myself."

She turned on me with a hypochondriac's fierce competitive smile. "Not migraine, I bet. If you haven't had migraine you don't know what it is. I wish I could have my head amputated. Wouldn't that be stylish, though, a headless torso strutting around?" She was making an effort to master her self-pity and carry it off as a joke. "Men wouldn't know the difference."

Una was flattering herself again. Even in lounging pajamas, her torso was no more interesting or curvilinear than a brick. I backed into one of the unsittable chairs, and said: "You're a great admirer of men."

"They're an admirable race. Well?" She stood above me, her changed tone indicating that there was no more time for comedy.

"I have a report to make. Why don't you sit down?"

"If you say so." The chair was too big for her, and her feet dangled clear of the floor. "Go ahead."

"Before I do, there are a couple of matters that need straightening out."

"What does that mean?" The pain behind her tongue gave it a vicious twang.

"You lied once to me this morning, about the theft of some jewelry. It's possible that you lied twice."

"Are you calling me a liar?"

"I'm asking you."

"You've been talking to her."

"Not exactly. Is that what I'd find out if I had? That you're a liar?"

"Don't put words into my mouth, I don't like it. I gave you the reason I had for wanting Lucy followed."

"The second time."

"The second time, then."

"You didn't say very much."

"Why should I? I've got a right to some privacy."

"You had this morning. Not any more."

"What is this?" she asked the room in perplexity. Her hands twisted, and their diamonds caught and reflected red light from the window. "I pay a man a hundred dollars to do a job for me, so he wants to know my grandfather's middle name. It was Maria, curiously enough."

"You're very frank about things that don't count. But you haven't given me your own name yet. I don't even know where you live."

"If it was any of your business, I'd tell you. Who do you think you are?"

"Merely an ex-cop trying to hustle a living. I sell my services on the open market. It doesn't mean I have to sell them to anybody."

"That's tall talk for a peeper. I can buy and sell you twenty times over—"

"Not me. You should have taken my advice and gone to the classifieds. There are bums you can hire for fifteen dollars a day to do anything short of murder. Murder comes higher."

"What about murder? Who said anything about murder?" Her voice had dwindled suddenly to a bodiless whisper that buzzed and wavered like a mosquito's flight.

"I did. I said it was expensive, in more ways than one."

"But why bring it up, what's the point? You haven't been talking to anybody? One of these bums you mentioned?"

She was thinking of Maxfield Heiss. I said I hadn't.

"Not Lucy?"

"No."

"But you have been staying close to her?"

"As close as possible."

"Where is she? Where did she go?"

"I don't know."

"You don't know! I paid you good money to tail her. That was the whole point."

She slid off the chair and faced me with clenched fists. I was ready to catch them if she flung herself on me. Instead, she used them on herself, beating her bony flanks in staccato rhythm. "Has everybody gone crazy?" she yelped at the ceiling.

"Settle down. You sound as if you have. I wouldn't put homicidal mania past you—"

"Homicidal mania!" Her voice rose to the narrow limit of its range, and broke. "What about homicidal mania? You *have* been talking to Lucy."

"No. I overheard you talking to her, though, this afternoon. I didn't like the sound of it. There's violence in my business but I don't like cold-blooded violence, or people who threaten other people with it."

"Oh. That." She looked relieved. "I slapped her face for her, not very hard. She had it coming."

"Tell me more."

"You can go to hell."

"Later, perhaps. Before I kiss you good-bye, I want some information. Who you are, where you came from, why you were after Lucy. Also what you were doing at five o'clock this afternoon. We'll start with that."

"Five o'clock? I was right here, in this room. Is it important?" The question was neither rhetorical nor defiant like most of her other questions. She knew or sensed what was coming.

"Never mind that. Can you prove it?"

"If I have to. I made a telephone call around five." Her hands were moving over and over each other, trying to warm themselves at the cold fire of the diamonds. "I wouldn't want to use that unless I have to. You haven't even told me what it is I need an alibi for."

"Who were you calling?"

"You wouldn't be interested. I said I can prove it if I have to. It was long distance. They keep a record." She retreated to a leather hassock and crouched uneasily on its edge.

"I'm interested in everything about you, Una. A little while ago I made a statement to the police, and I couldn't leave you out."

"You went to the cops?" Her voice was incredulous, as if I had leagued myself with the forces of evil.

"They came to me. I found Lucy with her throat cut shortly after five o'clock."

"Did you say throat cut?"

"I did. She was dead in her motel room. I had to explain what I was doing there. Naturally your name came up—the name you're using."

"Why aren't they here?"

"I didn't tell them you were in town. I thought, before I threw you to them, I'd give you a chance to level. I'm also a little curious about who I'm sticking my neck out for, and why."

"You sap! They might have followed you here."

"Sap is the word." I stood up. "I haven't thought of a word for you, but I will."

"Where are you going?"

"Down to the station to amplify my statement. The longer I wait, the more trouble it's going to make for me."

"No, you can't do that." She scrambled to her feet and ran jerkily to the door, spreading her arms across

63

it like a crucified marionette. "You're working for me. You can't turn me in."

I took the hundred from my wallet and tossed it at her feet. She stooped for it, watching me anxiously to see that I didn't escape:

"No. Please take it back. I'll give you more."

"You haven't got enough. Murder comes very high on my price-list."

"I didn't kill her, you—Mr. Archer. I told you my alibi."

"Telephone alibis are easy to fix."

"I didn't fix it. There's no way I could have fixed it. I was here in this room. Ask the switchboard. I haven't been out of here since early this afternoon."

"And that's why you're taking it so calmly, eh?" I reached for the doorknob.

"What are you going to do?"

Her cold hand closed over mine. The bill fell like a crumpled green leaf to the floor. Braced against the door, breathing with terrier quickness, she didn't notice it.

"I'll see the switchboard girl, if the same one's still on duty."

"It was the desk-clerk who handled the call. I recognized his voice."

"All right, I'll talk to the desk-clerk. Then you and I are going into this thing in detail."

"Not with cops?"

"It's up to you. We'll see how your story checks."

"No. Stay here. You can't do this to me." The words were punctuated by gasping breaths.

I turned the knob and pulled on it. She sat down against the door and began to scream wordlessly. The opening door pushed her sideways. Legs spraddled, mouth wide open, she looked up at me in the reddish murderous light and I looked down at her. She was making a steady unbearable sound like the screech of tearing metal. I closed the heavy door, cutting off the sound.

The desk-clerk beamed with pleasure at the sight of me. I was the fortunate traveler whose lady-friend in the expensive suite wore genuine leopardskin and probable diamonds.

"I'm looking after things for Mrs. Larkin," I said. "May I see her room account?"

"Certainly, sir." Plucking a large card from a filing drawer beside him, he leaned confidentially across the polished counter top. "I do hope Mrs. Larkin isn't checking out. She tips quite beautifully. It's good for general morale among the help." His voice sank to a bashful murmur: "She isn't a Hollywood personality, by any chance?"

"I'm surprised she told you."

"Oh, she didn't *tell* me. I deduced it. I recognize real class. Of course I did have a clue."

His polished oval fingernail pointed to the top of the card. Una had given the Hollywood-Roosevelt Hotel as her home address. Below it, only three items were listed on the account: twelve dollars for the suite, which had been paid in advance; a telephone charge of $3.35; and $2.25 for room service.

"She's been here less than one full day," I said in a penny-pinching way. "Three thirty-five seems like a lot of money for phone calls."

His small mustache rose towards his nostrils as if it was about to be inhaled. "Oh no, it's perfectly legitimate. It was all one call, long distance and person-to-person. I took care of it myself."

"Isn't that unusual?"

"I wish it were. The daytime operator goes off at five, and the night operator was a little late. I was at the switchboard myself when Mrs. Larkin called down."

"At five?"

65

"Maybe one or two minutes after. I'd just sat down in front of the board that minute. Switchboards have always fascinated me."

"You're sure it was Mrs. Larkin?"

"Oh, absolutely. Her voice is quite unique. Is she an actress of some kind, a character actress?"

"You're quite acute," I said. "She is also a character in her own right. It's hard to believe she'd spend that much money on a single phone call."

"Just ask her!" He was cut to the quick, which was very near the surface. "Go and ask her."

"Mrs. Larkin doesn't like to be bothered with these trivial details. She employs me to protect her from them, in fact. Now, if it was a call to Detroit, I could understand it."

"Ypsilanti," he said eagerly. "It was to the Tecumseh Tavern in Ypsilanti. That's right outside Detroit, isn't it?"

I assumed a thoughtful expression. "Let's see now, who does Mrs. Larkin know in Ypsilanti?"

"His name was Garbold. She asked for a man called Garbold, person-to-person." But his eagerness was beginning to fade at the edges. He looked down at his vase of cornflowers as if he suspected that noxious insects might be concealed among them.

"Of course. Garbold. Why didn't you say so? There's no trouble there. Mrs. Larkin will take care of it." I scrawled my initials at the bottom of the card and left him quickly.

Una had been quicker. I knocked once on her door and got no answer. What I got was the feeling you get when you go to a great deal of trouble to hit yourself a sharp blow at the base of the skull with a rubber hammer.

The door wasn't locked. The leopard coat was gone from the back of the chair. Bedroom and bathroom were as clean as a whistle. I left as Una had, by the fire escape.

In the alley behind the hotel, a woman in a shawl and a dragging black skirt was hunched over an open garbage-can. She looked up at me from an infinite network of wrinkles.

"Did a lady come down here? In a spotted coat?"

The ancient woman removed something from her mouth's eroded crater. I saw it was a red steak-bone she had been gnawing. "*Sí*," she said.

"Which way did she go?"

She raised the bone without speaking, and pointed up the alley. I dropped the change from my pocket into her mummified hand.

"*Muchas gracias, señor.*" Her black Indian gaze came from the other side of history, like light from a star a thousand years away.

The alley led to the hotel garage. Mrs. Larkin had taken her car out within the last five minutes. It was a new Plymouth station-wagon. No, they didn't keep track of license numbers. Probably she'd left a forwarding address at the desk. Try there.

CHAPTER 9

I climbed the oil-stained concrete ramp to the sidewalk and stood at its edge, undecided what to do. I
had no client, no good leads, not much money. Regret
for Una's hundred-dollar bill was gnawing at me already, like a small hungry stomach ulcer. The crowd
went by like a kaleidoscope continually stirred, in
which I only just failed to discern a pattern.

It was an early Saturday-night crowd. Farmhands
in jeans and plaid shirts, soldiers in uniforms, boys in
high-school windbreakers, roved singly and in pairs
and packs among women of all ages and all shades.
Hard-faced women in hats towed men in business
suits. Ranchers hobbling in high-heeled boots leaned
on their sun-faded wives. Under the winking yellow
lights at the intersection, long shiny cars competed for
space and time with pickup trucks, hot-rods, migrant
jalopies. My car was still in the court of the Mountview Motel. I stepped out into the crowd and let it
push me south, towards the highway.

Above the highway corner there was a cigar store
with a pay-telephone sign. Under the sign a quartet
of Mexican boys were watching the world go by.

They leaned in a row, one-legged like storks, their lifted heels supported by the windowsill of the shop, displaying mismatched fluorescent socks under rolled jeans. Keep Your Feet on the Sidewalk Please was lettered on the wall beside them in vain.

I detached myself from the crowd and went in through the shop to the telephone booth at the rear. Three taxi-drivers were shooting craps on the back counter. I looked up Dr. Samuel Benning's number in the local directory, and dialed it. At the other end of the line the phone rang twenty times. My nickel jangled in the coin return with the fanfare of a silver-dollar jackpot.

Before I reached the front door a young woman passed the window, walking south by herself. The four boys sprang into a burlesque routine. The one at the end pushed the one beside him, who almost caromed with the woman. He recovered his balance and rumpled the ducktail haircut of the third, who punched the fourth in the stomach. They staggered around in front of the entrance, breathless with simulated laughter.

I pushed out through them. The woman looked back in disdain. Though she had changed her striped gray uniform for a white batiste blouse and a white skirt, I recognized her face. She was the plump dark-eyed woman who had directed me into Dr. Benning's waiting-room. The back of my neck began to itch where the bitch goddess coincidence had bitten me before.

The woman walked on, switching her red-ribboned horsetail of black hair above the soft round rotation of her hips. I followed her, with compunction. She reminded me of Lucy for some reason, though she was wide and low-slung where Lucy had been lean and high-stepping. She walked, with a similar air of knowing where she was going, into the section in which I had first seen Lucy. When she crossed the street and entered Tom's Café, my compunction turned acute.

She paused inside the glass door to get her bearings. Then she set her course for one of the rear booths. A man was sitting in the booth with his back to the door. His panama hat showed above the low plyboard partition. He rose to greet her, buttoning his camel's-hair jacket, and stood above her in an attitude of delight while she inserted her hips between the seat and the table. As a final mark of devotion he removed his hat and smoothed his stubbly shock of brown hair with fat white fingers, before he sat down opposite her. Max Heiss was exerting charm.

I went to the bar, which covered the whole left wall of the café. The booths along the opposite wall were full, and the bar was packed with Saturday-night drinkers: soldiers and shrill dark girls who looked too young to be there, hard-faced middle-aged women with permanented hair, old men renewing their youth for the thousandth time, asphalt-eyed whores working for a living on drunken workingmen, a few fugitives from the upper half of town drowning one self to let another self be born. Behind the bar a hefty Greek in an apron dispensed fuel, aphrodisiac, opiate, with a constant melancholy smile.

I ordered a short rye and took it standing, keeping an eye on Heiss in the bar mirror. He was leaning far over the table towards the dark-eyed woman, and she was registering pleasant shock.

The booth behind him was vacated, and I crossed to it before the table was cleared. The room was surging with noise. A juke box bawled above the babel of tongues at the bar. An electric shuffleboard beside the liquor counter at the front gave out machine-gun bursts of sound at intervals. I propped myself in the corner of the seat with my ear pressed to the plyboard. A yard away, Heiss was saying:

"I been thinking about you all day, dreaming about those great big beautiful eyes. I been dreaming about those great big beautiful etcetera, too, sitting and dreaming about 'em. You know what an etcetera is, Flossie?"

"I can guess." She laughed, like somebody gargling syrup. "You're a great kidder. Incidently, my name isn't Flossie."

"Florie, then, what does it matter? If you were the only girl in the world, which is what you pradically are as far as I'm concerned, what does it matter? You're the girl for me. But I bet you've got plenty of boy friends." I guessed that Max had been drinking all day, and had reached the point where anything he said sounded like poetry set to music.

"I bet I have, not. Anyways, it's no business of yours, Mr. Desmond. I hardly know you." But she knew the game.

"Come on over on this side and get to know me better, kid. Florie. Sweet name for a sweet kid. Did anybody ever tell you you got a mouth like a flower, Florie?"

"You certny got a line, Mr. Desmond."

"Aw, call me Julian. And come on over. I warn you it isn't safe. When I get close up to a great big beautiful etcetera, I want to take a bite out of it, I warn you."

"You hungry or something?" I heard the rustle and creak of the girl's movement into the near seat. "Incidently, Julian, I'm kind of hungry. I could eat something."

"*I'm* going to eat *you*." Max's voice was muffled. "I guess I better fatten you up first, huh? You want a steak, and something to drink? After that, who knows? *Quien sabe,* isn't that how you say it?"

"I only talk American," she answered him severely.

71

Having established that, she relaxed again: "A steak will be swell, Julian. You're a real fun guy."

Heiss hailed the waitress. She crossed the room, a lank henna-head mincing on tender feet. "What'll it be?"

"A steak for the little lady. I've already dined myself."

"Let's see, you're drinking sherry."

"Very dry sherry," said Desmond-Heiss.

"Sure, very dry." She turned her head to one side and threw the line away: "Maybe you take it in powder form."

"An Alexander for me," the girl said.

"Sure, kiddie, have yourself a time." But there was an undertone in his voice, the no-expense-account blues. "Nothing's too good for Florie."

A woman came in from the street and walked quickly along the row of booths. Her wide-shouldered black coat swung out behind with the energy of her movement and showed the white uniform underneath. She didn't see me but I saw her and straightened up in my seat. She stopped beside Heiss and Florie, her blue eyes glittering in her cold porcelain face.

"Hello, Mrs. Benning. You want to see me?" Florie's voice was small and tinny.

"You didn't finish your work. You can come and finish it now."

"I did do my work, Mrs. Benning. Everything you said."

"Are you contradicting me?"

"No, but it's Saturday night. I got a right to my Saturday nights. When do I get a chance to have some fun?"

"Fun is one thing. What you're doing is peddling my private affairs to a dirty snooper."

72

"What's that?" Heiss put in brightly. "I beg your pardon, lady?"

"Don't 'lady' me. Are you coming, Florie?" The woman's voice was low, but it hummed like an overloaded electric circuit.

"I hope there ain't no trouble, ma'am," the waitress said briskly behind her.

Mrs. Benning turned to look at her. I didn't catch the look, because the back of her dark head was towards me. The waitress backed away, holding the menu card as if to shield her chest.

Heiss stood up, not quite so tall as she was. "I don't know who you are, lady. I can tell you this, you got no call to molest my girl friend in public." His face was groping for an attitude. Then his liquid gaze met hers and drooled away.

She leaned towards him, talking in a low buzzing monotone: "I know who you are. I saw you watching the house. I heard you talking to Florie on the office extension. I'm warning you: stay away from her, and especially stay away from me."

"Florie has a right to her friends." Heiss had found a manner, that of man-of-the-world, but it went bad immediately. "As for you, Mrs. Benning, if that's what you call yourself, I wouldn't touch you. I wouldn't buy you for cat's-meat—"

She laughed in his face: "You'd never have the chance, little man. Now crawl back down your hole. If I ever see you again, I'll knock you over with a stick the way I would a gopher. Come on, Florie."

Florie sat head down with her arms on the table, frightened and stubborn. Mrs. Benning took her by the wrist and hauled her to her feet. Florie didn't resist. With dragging feet, she followed Mrs. Benning to the door. There was a taxi waiting at the yellow curb outside. By the time I reached the street, it had pulled away and lost itself in the traffic.

73

I had a bad feeling that history was repeating it-self, in spades. The bad feeling got worse when Heiss came up behind me and touched my arm. He touched people whenever he could, to reassure him-self of his membership in the race.

"Go and take gopher poison," I said.

The veined nose stood out on his pale face. "Yeah, I saw you in there. I thought you run out on me, boysie. I was consoling my bereavement with a nice fresh chunk of Mexican cactus candy."

"Pumping her, you mean."

"You unnerestimate me. I pumped Florie dry long since! They can't resist me, boysie. What is it I got that they can't resist me, I wonder." His mobile mouth was working overtime, talking him back into his own good opinion.

"What's the pitch, Max?"

"No dice, Archer. You got your chance to cut in, this aft. You couldn't be bothered with me. Now I can't be bothered."

"You want to be coaxed."

"Not me. Lay a small pinkie on me and I scream my head off." He cast a smug eye on the crowds streaming past us, as if he was depending on them for protection.

"You don't know me well," I said. "Those aren't my methods."

"I know you as well as I want to," he said. "You gave me the quick old brush this aft."

"Forget it. What's the tieup with this missing man in Arroyo Beach?"

"Come again, boysie." He leaned against the corner post of the storefront. "I should give you something for nothing. Nobody ever gave me something for nothing. I got to roust and hustle for what I get." With a lipstick-stained handkerchief, he wiped his face.

"I'm not trying to take something from you, Max."

"That's jakeroo, then. Good night. Don't think it ain't been charming." He turned away.

I said: "Lucy's dead."

That stopped him. "What did you say?"

"Lucy had her throat cut this afternoon."

"You're stringing me."

"Go out to the morgue and take a look for yourself. And if you won't tell me what you know, tell it to the cops."

"Maybe I will at that." His eyes shone like brown agates lit from behind. "Well, *bon soir* again."

He moved away, with one or two furtive back-glances, and joined the northward stream of pedestrians. I wanted to go after him and shake the truth out of him. But I had just said those weren't my methods, and the words stood.

CHAPTER 10

I picked up my car at the Mountview Motel and drove to Dr. Benning's house. There were no lights behind its white painted windows. From the overgrown yard it looked like a house no one had lived in for a long time. Its tall gray front stood flimsily against the dark red sky like a stage set propped by scantlings from behind.

When I rang the door bell, the house resumed its dimensions. Far in its interior, behind walls, the buzzer sounded like a trapped insect. I waited and rang again and no one answered. There were old-fashioned glass panels, ground in geometric patterns, set in both of the double doors. I pressed my face to one of them and looked in and saw nothing. Except that the glass was cracked in one corner, and gave slightly under pressure.

I slipped on a driving-glove and punched out the cracked corner. It smashed on the floor inside. I waited and looked up and down the street and rang the bell a third time. When nobody answered and nobody passed on the sidewalk I eased my arm through the triangular hole and snapped the Yale lock.

I closed and relocked the door with my gloved hand. Broken glass crunched under my heel. Feeling along the wall, I found the door of the waiting-room. A little light fell through the windows from the street, lending the room a vague beauty like an old woman with good features, heavily veiled.

I located the filing cabinet behind the desk in the corner. Using my pocket flash and shielding its light with my body, I went through the Active Patient drawer of the file. Camberwell, Carson, Cooley. There was no card for Lucy Champion.

Dousing the light, I moved along the wall to the inner door, which was a few inches ajar. I pushed it open wider, slid through and closed it behind me. I switched on the flash again and probed the walls and furniture with its white finger of light. The room contained a flat-topped oak-veneer desk, a swivel chair and a couple of other chairs, an old three-tiered sectional bookcase not quite full of medical texts and journals. Above the bookcase on the calcimined wall, there was a framed diploma issued in June 1933 by a medical school I had never heard of.

I went through an open door into a room with figured oilcloth walls and a linoleum floor. Brownish stains on the far wall outlined the place where a gas range had once stood. An adjustable examination-table of brown-painted steel padded with black leatherette had taken its place. There were a battered white enameled instrument cabinet and a sterilizer against the wall beside it. On the other side of the room, under the blinded window, a faucet dripped steadily into a sink. I went to the closed door in the wall beyond it, and turned the knob. It was locked.

The second pass-key I tried opened the door. My light flashed on the ivory grin of death.

Six inches above the level of my eyes, a skeleton's shadowed sockets looked down hollowly. I thought in the instant of shock that it was a giant's bones, then saw that the long toe-bones dangled nearly a foot above the floor. The whole thing hung in the closet by wires attached to an overhead crossbar. Its joints had been carefully articulated with wire, and the movement of the door had set it swaying slightly. Its barred shadow wavered on the closet wall behind it.

It looked like a man's bones to me. I had an old brotherly feeling that I should take him by the unfleshed hand. He was lonely and desolate. I was afraid to touch him.

Somewhere in the house, no louder than a rodent squeak, a door or a floorboard creaked. It caused a croupy tightening in my breathing. I listened and heard the faint wheeze in my throat, and the dripping of the tap. Working with jumping fingers, I relocked the closet door and dropped the key in my pocket.

With the flash unlit in my hand, I retraced my steps by blind touch to the door of the consultation room. I had one foot across its metal-strip threshold when the light came on in my face. Dr. Benning's wife stood against the opposite wall with one hand on the light switch. She was so still that she might have been a figure in a frieze, part of the wall itself.

"What goes on in here?"

I squeezed out a husky answer: "The doctor wasn't here. I came in to wait."

"You a crib-smasher? Junkie? We've got no dope in this office."

"I came to ask a question. I thought the office might answer it for me."

"What question?" The small automatic steady in her hand was gun-metal blue, and her eyes had taken its color.

78

"Put the gun away, Mrs. Benning. I can't talk with iron in my face."

"You'll talk." She pulled herself away from the wall and moved towards me. Even in motion her body seemed still and frigid. But I could feel its power, like a land mine under a snowbank. "You're another lousy snooper, aren't you?"

"A fair-to-middling one. What happened to Florie?"

She stopped in the center of the room, her legs braced apart. The pupils of her gun-colored eyes were dark and empty like the muzzle of the gun at the center of her body.

I said: "If that gun went off and hurt me you'd be in a real jam. Put it away, it isn't needed."

She didn't seem to hear me. "I thought I saw you before. You were in the café. What happened to Florie is nobody's business but hers and mine. I paid her off and fired her. I don't approve of my servants stooling to scavengers. Does that take care of the question you had?"

"One of them."

"Fine. Now get out, or I'll have you arrested for burglary." The gun moved very little, but I felt it like a fingernail on my skin.

"I don't think you will."

"You want to stick around and find out?" She glanced at the telephone on the desk.

"I intend to. You're vulnerable, or you'd have called the cops right away. You don't talk like a doctor's wife, incidentally."

"Maybe you want to see my marriage license." She smiled a little, showing the tip of her tongue between white teeth. "I mean perchance you desire to peruse my connubial document. I can talk different ways, depending on who I'm talking to. To scavengers, I can also talk with a gun."

"I don't like the word scavenger."

79

"He doesn't like it," she said to nobody in particular.

"What do you think I want from you?"

"Money. Or are you one of the ones that gets paid off in the hay?"

"It's an idea. I'll take a rain check on it. Right now, I'd like to know what Lucy Champion was doing in this office. And if you won't put the gun away, set the safety."

She was still braced and tense, holding on to the gun the way a surfboarder clutches his stick. Muscular tension alone might squeeze the trigger and shoot me.

"The man's afraid." Her mouth was sullen and scornful, but she clicked the safety on with her thumb. "What about Lucy Champion? I don't know any Lucy Champion."

"The young colored woman who came here this afternoon."

"Oh. Her. The doctor has all kinds of patients."

"Do many of them get themselves killed?"

"That's a funny question. I'm not laughing, though, notice?"

"Neither is Lucy. She had her throat cut this afternoon."

She tried to swallow that without a tremor, but she was shaken. Her braced body was more than ever like a surfboarder's moving fast on troubled water.

"You mean she's dead," she said dully.

"Yes."

Her eyes closed, and she swayed without falling. I took one long step and lifted the gun from her hand and ejected the clip. There was no shell in the chamber.

"Did you know her, Mrs. Benning?"

The question brought her out of her standing trance. Her eyes opened, tile blue again and impermeable. "She was one of my husband's patients. Naturally he'll be shocked. That automatic belongs to him, by the way." She had assumed a mask of respectability and the voice that went with it.

I tossed the gun on the desk and kept the clip. "Is that his skeleton in the closet, too?"

"I don't know what you're talking about."

"Have it your way. You knew what I was talking about when I said that Lucy Champion was dead."

Her hand went to her forehead, white under dead-black hair. "I can't stand death, especially somebody's I know."

"How well did you know her?"

"She was a patient, I said. I've seen her a couple of times."

"Why isn't there a card for her?"

"A card?"

"In the active file."

"I don't know. Are you going to keep me standing here all night? I warn you, my husband will be back at any moment."

"How long have you been married, Mrs. Benning?"

"It's none of your damn business. Now get out of here or I *will* call the police."

She said it without conviction. Since I had told her Lucy was dead, there had been no force in her. She looked like a sleepwalker struggling to come awake.

"Go ahead and call them."

She looked at me with blank loathing. "Augh." It was a shallow retching sound. "Do your damnedest. Do your dirtiest. Only get out of my sight."

The upper faces of her breasts gleamed through the fabric of her uniform like cold trembling moons. I walked around her and let myself out.

CHAPTER 11

The state blacktop unwound like a used typewriter-ribbon under my headlights. It threaded the wilderness of stone that cut off Bella Valley from the ocean, clinging to the walls of precipitous canyons, looping across the shoulders of peaks that towered into darkness. After forty long mountain miles it dropped me down into the lap of the coastal range. A late moon was rising heavily on the sea.

Five minutes north of the junction with U.S. 101 Alternate, the lights of Arroyo Beach began to clutter the roadside. Motels, service stations, real-estate booths, chicken-steak pavilions were outlined in neon on the face of the darkness. I pulled up beside the pumps of a service station; while my car was being gassed I asked the attendant if he had a pay phone. He was a hammered-down elderly man in a uniform of gray coveralls and black leather bowtie, who looked and smelled as if he washed in crankcase oil. He jerked an oil-grained thumb towards the one-room office he had emerged from.

The local telephone directory was a thin pamphlet attached to the wall telephone by a chain. Mrs.

Charles Singleton was well represented in it. She lived at 1411 Alameda Topanga, and her telephone number was 1411. A second number was listed for the gatehouse, a third for the chauffeur's apartment, a fourth for the gardener's cottage, a fifth for the butler's pantry.

When the attendant brought me my change, I asked him where Alameda Topanga was.

"Who you looking for, brother?"

"Nobody in particular. I'm sightseeing."

"This is a funny time of the night to be sightseeing." He looked me over. "They got a private patrol, nights, on the Alameda, and you don't look like no member of no garden club."

"I'm interested in real estate. It's a good section, I heard."

"Good ain't the word for it, brother. Since they built the big hotel and the moneybags moved up here from Malibu, that property is worth its weight in gold. I only wisht I had a piece of it. I could of had. Before the war, if the old lady would of let me take a little money out of the sock, I could of had five acres at a steal. I could of been sitting pretty now, but she says save your money. The place is dead, she says, the rich set is pulling out for keeps." His laugh was bitter and compulsive, like an old cough.

"Too bad," I said. "Where is the Alameda?"

He gave me directions, pointing at the dark foothills as if they rose on the edge of the promised land. I turned towards them at the next intersection, and drove to the outskirts. Empty fields strewn with rubbish lay like a no-man's land between the suburban cottages and the country estates. I entered an avenue hemmed in on both sides by the gray trunks and overarched by the branches of eucalyptus trees. It went by a hedged polo field and across a golf course. Cars were massed around a lighted clubhouse in the distance, and gusts of music were blown my way by the wind.

The road ascended hills terraced like the steps of an easy manmade purgatory. I caught glimpses of glass-and-aluminum living-machines gleaming like surgical equipment in the clinical moonlight; Venetian palaces, Côte d'Azur villas, castles in Spain; Gothic and Greek and Versailles and Chinese gardens. There was a great deal of vegetable life, but no people. Perhaps the atmosphere of this higher region was too rare and expensive for the human breathing system. It was the earthly paradise where money begot plants upon property. People were irrelevant, unless they happened to have money or property.

The stone gateposts bearing the number 1411 were backed up by a Tudor cottage with dark leaded windows. The gates stood open. A sweeping drive conducted me through a line of yews like honorary pallbearers to a villa that faced the moon in white Palladian splendor.

I parked under the columned porte-cochere and rang the old-fashioned bell at the side entrance. Soft, doubtful footsteps approached the deep-paneled door from the other side. A key ground in the lock, and a young woman looked out, soft chestnut hair shadowing her face.

"What is it, sir?" Her voice was soft and doubtful.

"Is it too late to see Mrs. Singleton?"

I handed her my business card. She turned her profile to the light: soft chin, soft bee-stung mouth, straight and honest nose. Her eyes were still shadowed, but I saw how young she was.

"Investigator," she said. "Does this mean you're from the agency? It's late for Mrs. Singleton. She isn't terribly well."

"I run my own agency."

"I see. But it is about Charlie—Mr. Singleton?"

"He's still on the missing list, then."

"Yes. He is."

"I may have a lead for you."

"Really? You think you know where he is?"

"I haven't got that far. It's only today I stumbled across—this matter. I don't even know the circumstances of his disappearance. Or if the reward still stands."

"It does," she said with a faint, dubious smile. "If you'll tell me just what it is you stumbled across."

Late or not, I wanted to see Mrs. Singleton. I tossed the girl the heaviest answer I could think of: "A dead body."

Her hand went to her breast like a frightened bird. "Charlie's? Not Charlie's?"

"It was a young colored woman named Lucy Champion. She had her throat cut. Know her?"

Her answer was slow in coming. I guessed that it was going to be a lie, and that the lie came hard. "No. I don't know her. What possible connection—?" Her voice died.

"She was carrying a newspaper clipping about Singleton's disappearance and the reward. I thought she might have come here about it. The police will probably have the same idea, when they get around to it."

"Was she killed here, in Arroyo Beach?"

"In Bella City." She didn't recognize the name, and I added: "It's an inland town, in the valley, about thirty miles from here as the crow flies."

"Come in." She consulted my card again: "Mr. Archer. I'll ask Mrs. Singleton if she will see you."

She left me standing in the entrance hall and walked along it to a lighted doorway. She was clothed with expensive bad taste in a knitted rust-colored suit that made her look slightly overblown, at least from the rear. Her movements had an awkward innocence,

85

as if the sudden development of her body had embarrassed her with riches.

I put in several minutes looking at a sequence of Chinese paintings on the wall. A Chinese gentleman with giant earlugs denoting wisdom journeyed on foot through valleys and across rivers and mountains to a snow-line shrine. There were seven paintings, one for each stage of his journey.

The girl appeared in the doorway, her brown hair aureoled by the light behind her. "Mr. Archer. She'll see you."

The room had a lofty white ceiling supported by a Doric cornice. The walls were lined with cases of books uniformly bound in white calf. The cases were interspersed with paintings; one of them, of a laughing girl in a low-cut bodice, might have been a Watteau or a Fragonard. On a white sofa with a curved back, a heavy gray-haired woman sat.

She had the kind of face, square-jawed and heavy-eyebrowed, that unlucky women sometimes inherit from their fathers. It might have been handsome in a horsy way before age and ego had stiffened the bony framework and thrust it forward under the skin like concealed artillery. The slack body was encased in a black silk dress that would have served for mourning. In the monolithic black lap, the pale yellow hands were conspicuous. They had a constant tremor.

She cleared her throat: "Sit down, Mr. Archer, in this armchair here." And after I had done so: "Now tell me just who you are."

"I'm a licensed private detective. Most of my work is in Los Angeles, and I have my office there. Before the war I was a detective-sergeant on the Long Beach force. I gave the young lady my card."

"Sylvia showed it to me. She told me further that you had some rather shocking information, about a colored young woman?"

"Her name is Lucy Champion. I found her with her throat cut in a Bella City motel. There was a clipping in her purse from the Bella City paper, concerning your son's disappearance and the reward you offered. It occurred to me as a possibility that she was killed because she intended to claim the reward. She showed up in Bella City about the same time your son left here, two weeks ago. And I thought she might have approached you."

"Isn't that rather jumping to conclusions, on the very flimsiest grounds?" Mrs. Singleton's voice was low and cultivated. Her hands twitched and plucked at each other like nervous scorpions. "You're surely not implying that we had anything whatever to do with the girl's death? Or with her life."

"I didn't make myself clear." —Though I thought I had. "Assume that your son met with foul play. Assume that Lucy Champion knew what had happened and who was responsible for it. If she was intending to go to you or the authorities with that sort of information, it would explain what was done to her."

Mrs. Singleton gave no sign of having heard me. She looked down at her angry hands as if she'd have liked to disown them. "Light me a cigarette, Sylvia."

"Of course." Sylvia rose from her seat at the end of the sofa, took a cigarette from an ivory box, placed one end between the clamped blue lips, applied the flame of a table-lighter to the other.

Mrs. Singleton inhaled deeply, and exhaled from mouth and nostrils. The smoke crawled like fog in the crannies of her head. Even her eyes looked smoky. "You're not implying, I trust, that my son ran off to Bella City with a colored girl."

"Oh no, Mrs. Singleton!" the girl cried out. "He doesn't mean that." Then she remembered her place, which was to be seen and not heard. She sat down in her corner, looking as if she had given herself a fright.

Mrs. Singleton persisted: "What possible connection could there be between such a person and my son?"

"I'd like to know myself. In fact I'm interested enough to be willing to work on this case on a contingent basis."

"You mean, no doubt, that if you were to qualify for the reward, it would be paid to you. That can be taken for granted."

"Something more definite. Reward money has a way of slipping into policemen's pockets. It has a homing instinct for authority. And I'd like to be sure of my fifty a day and expenses."

"Naturally you would." She exhaled smoke, purring behind it like a cat in a curtain. "What I fail to see is any particular reason why I should underwrite your activities."

"I can't afford to work for fun. It would also be useful to be able to name you as a client.".

"That I can understand." Her iron-gray head struck an imperious pose, a little like a late Roman emperor's. Her low voice rose in volume and pitch as if it were preparing to dominate a tea party or repel a barbarian assault. "I do *not* understand why you must interest yourself at all in my affairs. I am employing a detective agency now. They've already cost me more than I can easily afford, and in value received they've given me absolutely nothing. I'm not a wealthy woman." Which probably meant, in her circle, that she could count her millions on the fingers of one hand. She added breathlessly in the ebb of her self-pity: "I'm not unwilling to pay for helpful information, but if a large agency has failed to restore my son to me, as it has, I see no reason to suppose that one man alone might succeed, do you?"

The cigarette in the corner of her mouth was burning short. Sylvia removed it without being asked, and crushed it out in an ashtray.

I said: "Let me kick it around and see what I can do. I intend to find out why Lucy Champion was killed. If and when I do, it may lead to your son. That's my hunch, at least."

"Your hunch," she said contemptuously. "If Charles were being held under duress, for ransom, your visit to me tonight under these circumstances could be interpreted as an overture, from whoever was holding him. Did you know this Negress, the one you claim was murdered?"

"She was murdered. Did you know her?"

Her face radiated a dull white glow of anger. "I warn you not to be insolent, young man. I know how to deal with insolence."

I glanced at Sylvia, who smiled bleakly and almost imperceptibly shook her head:

"You must be very tired, Mrs. Singleton. It's very late."

The older woman paid no attention to her. She leaned towards me, her black silk lap wrinkling stiffly like iron under pressure:

"Only this morning, under circumstances similar to these, a man came here representing himself as a private detective, like you. He claimed that he could find Charles for me, if I would pay him part of the reward in advance. I naturally refused. Then he wasted a full hour of my time, asking me questions. When I tried to ask him a question or two in my turn, he had nothing to say, not a constructive word. What was his name, Sylvia?"

"Heiss."

"Heiss," the older woman repeated vehemently, as if she had invented the name on the spur of the moment. She rolled her eyes towards me. They had been pickled in tears, glassed in grief, but they were still shrewd. "Do you know *him*?"

"I don't think so."

"A most repugnant creature. Eventually he dared to suggest that I sign a contract to pay him five thousand dollars if he should produce my son, alive or dead. He boasted of his connections among the criminal element. I arrived at the conclusion that he was either conspiring to defraud me, or representing a criminal organization of some sort. I ordered him out of my house."

"And you've cast me in the same role?"

"Oh no," the girl said softly from her corner.

Mrs. Singleton subsided backward, her energy spent. Her head rolled on the curved back of the sofa, exposing a slack throat to an invisible knife. Rising words palpitated feebly in her throat: "I don't know what to think. I'm sick, old, exhausted, bereft. In a world of liars. No one will tell me anything."

Sylvia rose, her soft and anxious look shepherding me to the door. Mrs. Singleton called out with sudden eagerness:

"Mr. Archer. Did Charles send you to me? Is that it? Does he need money?" The change in her voice was startling. She sounded like a frightened girl. I turned to look at her face, and saw the same false girlishness touch it with beauty for an instant. The beauty passed like the beam of a searchlight moving across time. It left her mouth curled in a cynical parody of mother-love.

The situation was too complicated for me to understand or try to deal with. I didn't know whether the umbilical cord between Mrs. Singleton and her son had stretched and broken and snapped back in her face and knocked her silly. Or whether she knew he was dead and was talking against despair. Whichever it was, she was ready to believe almost anything and suspicious of nearly everybody. Reality had betrayed her.

"I've never met Charles," I said. "Good night. Good luck."

She didn't answer.

CHAPTER 12

Sylvia went with me to the end of the hall. "I'm sorry, Mr. Archer. The last two weeks have been terribly hard on her. She's been under drugs for days. When things don't fit in with her ideas, she simply doesn't hear them, or she forgets them. It isn't that her mind is affected, exactly. She's suffered so much, she can't bear to talk about the facts, or even think about them."

"What facts?"

She said surprisingly: "Can we sit in your car? I think she really wants me to talk to you."

"You'd have to be psychic to know it."

"I am a bit psychic where Mrs. Singleton is concerned. When you're under a person's thumb, you know."

"You get to know the thumbprint. How long have you worked for her?"

"Only since June. But our families have known each other for a great many years. Charles's father and mine went to Harvard together." She opened the door, leaning across me to reach the knob. "Excuse me, I need some fresh air."

"Is she all right by herself?"

"There are servants on duty. They'll put her to bed." She started towards my car.

"Just a minute, Sylvia. Do you have a picture of Charles? A recent snapshot would be good."

"Why, yes, I do."

"Get it for me, will you?"

"I have one here," she said without embarrassment. She took a red leather wallet from the pocket of her suit and extracted a small snapshot that she handed me: "Is it big enough, clear enough?"

The picture showed a young man in tennis shorts and an open-necked short-sleeved shirt, smiling into the sun. The strength and leanness of his features were emphasized by a short service crew-cut. He was strongly built, with wide sloping shoulders and muscular forearms. But there was an unreal, actorish quality about him. His pose was self-conscious, chest pouting, stomach sucked in, as if he feared the cold eye of the Leica or the hot eye of the sun.

"It's clear enough," I said. "May I keep it?"

"For as long as you need it. It's very like him."

Climbing into my car, she showed a fine round leg. I noticed when I slid behind the wheel that she filled the interior with a clean springlike smell. I offered her a cigarette.

"Thanks, I never smoke."

"How old are you, Sylvia?"

"Twenty-one." She added with apparent irrelevance: "I just received the first quarterly check from Mother's trust fund."

"Good for you."

"About the check, I mean, it's nearly a thousand dollars. I can afford to employ you, if you'll work for me instead of Mrs. Singleton."

"I couldn't promise anything definite. You want him found pretty badly, don't you?"

"Yes." The word had the pressure of her life behind it. "How much money should I give you?"

"Don't bother about it now."

"Why should you trust me?"

"Anybody would. What's more surprising is that you trust me."

"I know something about men," she said. "My father is a good man. You're not like that man Heiss."

"You talked to him?"

"I was in the room. All he wanted was money. It was so—naked. I had to threaten him with the police before he'd leave. It's really a pity. Mrs. Singleton might have opened out to you if he hadn't spoilt things."

"Are there things she could have told me, that she didn't?"

"Charlie's whole life," she said obscurely. "What did this Negro woman look like?"

I gave her a thumbnail description of Lucy Champion.

She interrupted me before I finished: "It's the same one." She opened the door on her side and began to get out. Everything she did was done gently, almost regretfully, as if an action was a dangerous gamble.

"Do you know her?"

"Yes. I want to show you something." And she was gone.

I lit a cigarette. Before I had smoked a half inch of it, Sylvia came out of the house and climbed in beside me again. "I believe this is hers."

She handed me a soft dark object. I turned on the overhead light to examine it. It was a woman's turban, knitted of black wool and gold thread. Inside, there was a maker's label: Denise.

"Where did you get this?"

"She was here, the day before yesterday."

"To see Mrs. Singleton?"

94

"I think now that must have been it. She drove up here in a taxicab in the middle of the afternoon. I was cutting flowers in the garden, and I saw her sitting in the back of the cab as if she couldn't make up her mind. Finally she got out, and the cab-driver started away. She stood in the drive and looked at the house for a moment. Then I think she lost her nerve."

"I can understand that."

"It is imposing, isn't it? I called out to her, to ask her what she wanted, and when she saw me coming towards her she literally ran. I felt like some sort of an ogress. I called to her not to be frightened, but she only ran faster down the drive. Her hat fell off, and she didn't even stop to pick it up. Which is how I happen to have it."

"You didn't follow her?"

"How could I? I had an enormous bunch of 'mums in my arms. The driver saw her running after him, and backed up for her. I had no right to stop her, in any case."

"You'd never seen her before?"

"Never. I thought perhaps she was a sightseer. She was quite smartly dressed, and this is a good hat. The fact that she didn't come back for it made me wonder, though."

"Did you go to the police?"

"Mrs. Singleton disapproved. I thought of asking Denise, but Mrs. Singleton was opposed to that, too."

"You know the woman who made this?"

"I know of her. She has a shop on the ocean boulevard, near the hotel."

"Here in Arroyo Beach?"

"Of course. Isn't it possible, if you questioned her, that she might know something more about Miss Champion?"

"It's very likely. Why didn't you see Denise yourself? You're not that much afraid of Mrs. Singleton."

"No." She was silent for a time. "Perhaps I was afraid of what I might find out. I'm not any more. Charles ran away with a woman, you see." She spoke with reluctance, but she got it out: "I think I was afraid that the Negro girl was—another of his women."

"His mother seems to have shared that idea. Any particular reason for it?"

"I don't know. She knows so much about him, more than she's ever admitted to herself."

"That's a hard saying."

"It's true. These pre-Freudian women know it all, but they never say it, even in their thoughts. Their whole lives are dressing for dinner in the jungle. That's my father's phrase. He teaches philosophy at Brown."

"Who was this woman, the one Charles ran away with?"

"A tall woman with yellow hair, and very beautiful. That's all I know about her. They were seen together in the bar at the hotel, the night he left. The parking lot attendant saw them drive away in his car."

"It doesn't necessarily mean he ran away with her. It sounds more like a pickup."

"No. They had been living together all summer. Charles has a mountain cabin on the Sky Route, and the woman was seen there with him nearly every weekend."

"How do you know?"

"I talked to a friend of Charles's who lives in the same canyon. Horace Wilding, the painter—you may have heard of him. He was very reticent, but he did tell me that he'd seen the woman there with Charlie. Perhaps if you talked to him? Since you're a man?"

I turned up the dash-lights and took out my notebook: "Address?"

"Mr. Wilding's address is 2712 Sky Route. He has no telephone. He said she was beautiful, too."

I turned to look at Sylvia, and saw that she was crying. Sitting quietly with her hands in her lap and tear-tracks bright on her cheeks. "I never cry!" she said fiercely. And then, not fiercely at all: "I wish I were beautiful, like her. I wish I had yellow hair."

She looked beautiful to me, and soft enough to put a finger through. Past the gentle outline of her body, I could see the lights of Arroyo Beach. Between the highway neons and the dotted line of lights hem-stitching the shore, the spotlit dome of the great hotel swelled like a captive balloon. Beyond it the moon was rising like a smaller white balloon dragging a cable of light across the sea's surface.

"If you want to be a blonde," I said, "why don't you bleach your hair like all the other girls?"

"It wouldn't do any good. He wouldn't even notice."

"You're in love with Charlie."

"Of course I am," as if every young girl in her senses fell in love with Charlie. I waited for her to go on, and she did: "From the first time I saw him. When he came back to Harvard after the war, he spent a weekend with us in Providence. I fell in love with *him*, not he with me. I was only a child. He was nice to me, though." Her voice sank to a confidential murmur: "He read Emily Dickinson with me. He told me he wanted to be a poet, and I thought I *was* Emily, I really did. All through college I let myself imagine that Charles would come for me and marry me. Of course he never did.

"I saw him a few times, once for lunch in Boston, and he was charming to me and that was all. Then he went home, and I never heard from him. Last spring when I graduated, I decided to come west and see him. Mrs. Singleton was looking for a companion, and my father secured the position for me. I thought if I was in the house with Charles he might fall in love with me. Mrs. Singleton rather approved. If Charles had to marry anyone, she preferred someone she could manage."

I looked into her face and saw that she was perfectly sincere. "You're a strange girl, Sylvia. Did you really talk it over with Mrs. Singleton?"

"I didn't have to. She left us together whenever it was possible. I can recognize a fact. Father says that a woman's chief virtue is the ability to see what is under her nose. And when she tells the truth about what she sees, that is her crowning glory."

"I take it back. You're not strange. You're unique."

"I think I am. But Charles didn't. He wasn't even at home very much, so I had no decent chance to make him fall in love with me by propinquity. He spent most of his time in his cabin, or driving around the state. I didn't know about the woman then, but I think she fits in with what he was trying to do. He was trying desperately to break away from his mother and her money and create a life of his own. Mrs. Singleton had all the money, you see, even before her husband died. *He* was the old-fashioned type of rich woman's husband: yachtsman and polo player, and errand boy for his wife. Charles had different ideas from his father. He believed that he and his class were out of touch with reality. That they had to save their individual souls by going down to the bottom of things and starting all over."

"Did he?"

"Save his soul, you mean? He tried. It turned out to be harder than he thought. This summer, for instance, he worked as a tomato-picker in the valley. His mother offered him the managership of a ranch, but he wouldn't take it. Of course he didn't last very long. He had a fight with a foreman and lost his job, if you could call it a job. Mrs. Singleton almost died when he came home with his face all swollen and blue. I almost died, too. But Charles seemed to take a certain satisfaction from it."

"When was this?"

"In July, a few weeks after I came. The middle of July."

"Where did the fight take place?"

"On a ranch near Bakersfield. I don't know exactly."

"After that, did he stay here until the first of September?"

"Off and on. He was often away on trips for two or three days at a time."

"Do you think he's off on another trip this time?"

"He may be. If he is, I don't believe he's coming back this time. Not ever. Not of his own accord."

"Do you think he's dead?" The question was blunt, but Sylvia could take it. Under her air of gentle bewilderment, she had strong reserves.

"I'd know it if he were dead. I don't believe he's dead. I believe he's made his final break with his mother, and the money from his great-grandfather's land grant."

"Are you sure you want him to come back?"

She hesitated before she spoke: "At least I must know that he's safe and living a kind of life that won't destroy him. For a man who shot down enemy planes during the war, he's such a child, such a dreamer. The wrong woman could break him." She drew in her breath sharply. "I hope I don't sound melodramatic."

"You sound very good to me. But you may be letting your imagination run away with you." I saw that she wasn't listening, and stopped.

Her mind was moving on a remote curve that she was trying to plot in words: "He felt so guilty about the money he'd never worked for, and doubly guilty because he was disappointing his mother. Charles

99

wanted to suffer. He saw his whole life as an expiation. He would choose a woman who would make him suffer."

Against the moonlight her face had a virgin bleakness. The softness of her mouth and chin was broken by angular shadows.

"You know what sort of woman she was, then."

"Not really. All my information is third-hand. A detective interviewed the bartender at the hotel, and told Mrs. Singleton about the woman. She told me."

"Come down there with me," I said. "I'll buy you a drink. I think you could use a drink."

"Oh no. I've never been in a bar."

"You're twenty-one."

"It isn't that. I have to go in now. I always read her to sleep. Good night."

When I leaned across to open the door for her, I could see the tears on her face like spring rain.

CHAPTER 13

A pair of Filipino bell-hops in maroon uniforms gave me an interested look as I went in, and lost interest immediately. Under a Moorish arch opposite the hotel entrance, an assistant manager stood behind the reservations desk like a tuxedoed saint in a niche. Over an arch in the far corner, a neon sign spelled out *Cantina* in red script. I made my way through the potted-palm formality of the lobby and out to a patio planted with banana trees. Couples loitered in their shade. I crossed to the bar in a hurry.

It was a large L-shaped room decorated with bullfight posters, blue with smoke, pounding with monkeyhouse din. White female shoulders, dinner jackets black, blue, and plaid, swayed and gesticulated three deep at the long bar. The men had the unnaturally healthy, self-assured faces of sportsmen who had never really had to take a chance. Except perhaps on their women. The women's bodies looked more conscious than their heads. Somewhere behind the walls, an orchestra started a samba rhythm. Some of the shoulders and dinner jackets were lured away from the bar.

101

There were two bartenders working, an agile Latin youth and a thin-haired man who kept a sharp eye on the other. I waited until their business had slacked off, and asked the thin-haired man if he was the regular bartender. He gave me the impervious stare of his trade.

"Sure thing. What are you drinking?"

"Rye. I'd like to ask you a question."

"Go ahead, if you can think of a new one." His hands went on working of their own accord, filling a shot-glass for me and setting it out on the bar.

I paid him. "About Charles Singleton, Junior. You saw him the night he disappeared?"

"Oh, no." He glanced up at the ceiling in mock despair. "I tell it to the sheriff. I tell it to the reporters. I tell it to the private dicks." His eyes returned to my level, gray and opaque. "You a reporter?"

I showed him my identification.

"Another private dick," he lamented imperturbably. "Why don't you go back and tell the old lady she's wasting your time and her money? Junior blew with as stylish a blondie as you could hope to see. So why would he want to come back?"

"Why did he go away?"

"You didn't see her. The dame had everything." His hands illustrated his meaning. "That beast and junior are down in Mexico City or Havana having themselves a time, mark my words. Why would he come back?"

"You had a good look at the woman?"

"Sure. She bought a drink from me while she was waiting for junior. Besides, she was in with him a couple of times before."

"What was her drink?"

"Tom Collins."

"How was she dressed?"

"Dark suit, nothing flashy. Smart. Not the real

102

class, but the next thing to it. She was a natural blonde. I could say this in my sleep." He closed his eyes. "Maybe I am."

"What color were her eyes?"

"Green or blue, or something in between."

"Turquoise?"

He opened his own eyes. "One question covers a lot of ground in your book, friend. Maybe we should collaborate on a poem, only some other day. You like turquoise, I'll say turquoise. She looked like one of those Polish kids I used to see in Chicago, but she was a long way off of West Madison, I can tell you that."

"Does anything ever happen that you miss?"

That bought me another thirty seconds of him. "Not around here it doesn't."

"And junior definitely wanted to go with her?"

"Sure. You think she held a gun on him? They were stuck on each other. He couldn't peel his eyes off of her."

"How did they leave? By car?"

"So I understand. Ask Dewey in the parking lot. Only you better slip him a little change first. He doesn't enjoy the sound of his own voice the way I do." Recognizing a good cue-line, he moved out of my range.

I drank up, and went outside. The hotel faced the sea, across a palm-lined boulevard. The parking lot lay behind a row of small expensive shops on its landward side. Moving along the sidewalk, I passed a display of silver and raw-hide pendants, two wax mannequins in peasant skirts, a window full of jade; and was hit between the eyes by the name Denise. It was printed in gold leaf on the plate-glass window of a hat shop. Behind the window a single hat hung on a stand by itself, like a masterpiece of sculpture in a

103

museum. The shop was dark, and after a second's hesitation, I went on.

Under an arc light at the corner of the parking lot there was a small green-painted shack like a sentry-box. A sign attached to its wall stated: *The sole income of attendants consists of tips.* I stood beside the sign and held a dollar in the light. From somewhere among the sardined ranks of cars, a little man appeared. He was thin and gray. Under his old Navy turtleneck the shoulder-bones projected like pieces of waterworn driftwood. He moved silently in canvas sneakers, leaning forward as if he were being dragged by the tip of his long sharp nose.

"Make and color? Where's your ticket, mister?"

"My car's parked around the corner. I wanted to ask you about another car. I guess you're Dewey."

"I guess I am." He blinked his faded eyes, innocently contemplating his identity. The top of his uncombed gray head was on a level with my shoulder.

"You know a lot about cars, I bet."

"I bet. People, too. You're a cop, or I miss my guess. I bet you want to ask me about young Charlie Singleton."

"A private cop," I said. "How much do you bet?"

"One buck."

"You win, Dewey." I passed the money to him.

He folded it up small and tucked it in the watch pocket of the dirtiest gray flannels in the world. "It's only fair," he said earnestly. "You take up my valuable time. I was polishing windshields and I pick up plenty money polishing windshields on a Saturday night."

"Let's get it over with, then. You saw the woman he left with?"

"Absotively. She was a pipperoo. I seen her coming and going."

104

"Say again."

"Coming and going," he repeated. "The blonde lady. She druv up about ten o'clock in a new blue Plymouth station-wagon. I seen her get out in front of the hotel. I was around in front picking up a car. I seen her get out of the station-wagon and go inside the hotel. She was a pipperino." His gray-stubbled jaw hung slack and he closed his eyes to concentrate on the memory.

"What happened to the station-wagon?"

"The other one druv it away."

"Other one?"

"The other one that was driving the station-wagon. The dark-complected one that dropped the blonde lady off. She druv it away."

"Was she a colored woman?"

"The one that was driving the station-wagon? Maybe she was. She was dark-complected. I didn't get a good look at her. I was watching the blonde lady. Then I come back here, and Charlie Singleton druv in after a while. He went inside and come out with the blonde lady and then they druv away."

"In his car?"

"Yessir. 1948 Buick sedan, two-tone green."

"You're very observant, Dewey."

"Shucks, I often seen young Charlie riding around in his car. I know cars. Druv my first car back in 1911 in Minneapolis, Minnesota."

"When they left here, which way did they go?"

"Sorry, chum, I can't say. I didn't see. That's what I told the other lady when she asked me, and she got mad and didn't give me no tip."

"What other lady was that?"

His faded eyes surveyed me, blinking slow signals to the faded brain behind them. "I got to get back to those windshields. My time is valuable on a Saturday night."

"I bet you can't remember about the other lady."

"How much you want to bet?"

"A dollar?"

"Double it?"

"Two dollars."

"Taken. She come blowing in a few minutes after they left, driving that blue Plymouth station-wagon."

"The dark-complected one?"

"Naw, this was another one, older. Wearing a leopardskin coat. I seen her around here before. She asked me about the blonde lady and young Charlie Singleton, which way they went. I said I didn't see. She called me a iggoramus and left. She looked like she was hopping mad."

"Was anybody with her?"

"Naw. I don't remember."

"The woman live around here?"

"I seen her before. I don't know where she lives."

I put two ones in his hand. "Thanks, Dewey. One more thing. When Charlie drove away with the blonde, did he seem to be happy about it?"

"I dunno. He tipped me a buck. Anybody would be happy, going off with that blonde lady." A one-sided grin pulled at his wrinkled mouth. "Me, fr instance. I ain't had nothing to do with female flesh since I left my old lady in the depression. Twenty years is a long time, chum."

"It certainly is. Good night."

Sniffing lonesomely, Dewey pointed his nose toward the rank of cars and followed it out of sight.

CHAPTER 14

I went back to the hotel and found a public telephone. According to the directory, the Denise Hat
Shop was run by a Mrs. Denise Grinker whose residence was at 124 Jacaranda Lane. I called her home
number, got an answer, and hung up.

The street twisted like a cowpath between the
highway and the shore. Jacaranda and cypress trees
darkened the road and obscured the houses along it. I
drove slowly, in second gear, turning my flashlight on
the house-fronts. It was a middle-class neighborhood
subsiding into bohemian defeat. Weeds were rampant
in the yards. Signs in dingy window corners advertised Handmade Pottery, Antiques, Typing: We Specialize in Manuscripts. The numerals 124 were painted in a vertical row, by hand, on the doorpost of a
graying redwood bungalow.

I parked, and walked in under a shaggy eugenia
arch. There was a rusty bicycle leaning against the
wall on the front porch. The porch light came on
when I knocked, and the door opened. A large woman wrapped in a flannel bathrobe appeared in the
opening, one hip out. Because her hair was caught up

107

in metal curlers, her face looked naked and very broad. In spite of that, it was a pleasant face. I could feel my frozen smile thaw into something more comfortable.

"Mrs. Grinker? My name is Archer."

"Hello," she said good-humoredly, looking me over with large brown eyes a little the worse for wear. "I didn't leave the darn shop unlocked again, touch wood?"

"I hope not."

"Aren't you a policeman?"

"More or less. It shows when I'm tired."

"Wait a minute." She brought a leather case out of the pocket of her bathrobe and put on tortoise-shell spectacles. "I don't know you, do I?"

"No. I'm investigating a murder that occurred in Bella City this afternoon." I produced the rolled-up turban from my pocket and held it out to her. "This belonged to the victim. Did you make it?"

She peered at it. "It's got my name inside. What if I did?"

"You should be able to identify the customer you sold it to, if it's an original."

She leaned closer under the light, her glance shifting from the hat to me. The dark-rimmed spectacles had gathered her face into a shrewd hard pattern. "Is it a question of identification? You said it belonged to the victim. So who was the victim?"

"Lucy Champion was her name. She was a colored woman in her early twenties."

"And you want to know if I sold her this turban?"

"I didn't say that exactly. The question is who you sold it to."

"Do I have to answer that? Let me see your badge."

"I'm a private detective," I said, "working with the police."

108

"Who are you working *for*?"

"My client doesn't want her name used."

"Exactly!" She blew me a whiff of beer. "Professional ethics. That's how it is with me. I can't deny I sold that hat, and I won't deny it was an original. But how can I say who bought it from me? I made it away back last spring some time. I do know one thing for certain, though, it wasn't a colored girl bought it. There's never been one in my shop, except for a few brownskins from India and Persia and places like that. They're different."

"Born in different places, anyway."

"Okay, we won't argue. I have nothing against colored people. But they don't buy hats from me. This girl must have found the hat, or stolen it, or had it given to her, or bought it in a rummage sale. So even if I could remember who bought it from me, it wouldn't be fair to drag my client's name into a murder case, would it?" Her voice contained a hint of phoniness, an echo of the daytime palaver in her shop.

"If you worked at it, Mrs. Grinker, I think you could remember."

"Maybe I could and maybe I couldn't." She was troubled, and her voice grew shallower. "What if I did? It would be violating a professional confidence."

"Do milliners take an oath?"

"We have our standards," she said hollowly. "Oh hell, I don't want to lose customers if I can help it. The ones who can pay my prices are getting as scarce as eligible men."

I tried hard to look like an eligible man. "I can't give you my client's name. I will say that she's connected with the Singleton family."

"The Charles Singletons?" She pronounced the syllables slowly and distinctly, like a quotation from a poem she had always loved.

109

"Uh-huh."

"How is Mrs. Singleton?"

"Not very well. She's worried about her son—"

"Is this murder connected with him?"

"I'm trying to find fhat out, Mrs. Grinker. I never will find out unless I get some co-operation."

"I'm sorry. Mrs. Singleton isn't a customer of mine— I'm afraid she buys most of her hats in Paris—but of course I know *of* her. Come in."

The front door opened directly into a redwood-paneled living-room. A gas heater burned low in a red-brick fireplace. The room was warm and shabby and smelled of cats.

She waved a hospitable hand towards a studio couch covered with an afghan. A glass of beer was bubbling its life away on a redwood coffee-table beside the couch. "I was just having a beer for a nightcap. Let me get you one."

"I don't mind if you do."

She went into another room, closing the door behind her.

When I sat down on the studio couch, a fluffy gray cat came out from under it and jumped onto my knee. Its purring rose and fell like the sound of a distant plane. Somewhere in the house, I thought I heard a low voice talking. Denise was a long time coming back.

I set the cat on the floor, and moved across the room to the door she had closed. On the other side of it, she was saying, in clipped telephone accents: "He claims to be employed by Mrs. Charles Singleton." A silence, lightly scratched by the sound of the telephone. Then: "I absolutely won't, I promise you. Of course, I understand perfectly. I *did* want to get your view of the matter." Another scratchy silence. Denise intoned a saccharine good-night, and hung up.

I tiptoed back to my seat, with the gray cat weav-

110

ing between my legs. It paraded back and forth in front of me, rubbing its sides on my trousers and looking up at my face with remote female disdain.

I said: "Scat."

Denise re-entered the room with a foaming glass in each hand. She said to the cat: "Doesn't the nasty mans like kitty-witties?"

The cat paid no attention.

I said: "There's a story about Confucius, Mrs. Grinker. He was a pre-Communist Chinaman."

"I know who Confucius is."

"It seems a stable burned down in a neighboring village, call it Bella City. Confucius wanted to know if any men were hurt. He didn't ask about the horses."

It hit her. The foam slopped over the rims of the beer-glasses and down across her fingers. She set the glasses on the coffee-table. "You can like cats and people, too," she said doubtfully. "I have a son in college, believe it or not. I even had a husband at one time. Whatever happened to him?"

"I'll look for him when I finish the case I'm on."

"Don't bother. Aren't you going to drink your beer?" She sat on the edge of the couch, wiping her wet fingers with a piece of Kleenex.

"The case I'm on," I said, "involves one dead woman and one missing man. If your cat had been run over by a hit-run driver, and somebody knew his license number, you'd expect to be told it. Who were you telephoning just now?"

"Nobody. It was a wrong number." Her fingers were twisting the damp Kleenex into a small cup-shaped object, roughly the shape of a woman's hat.

"The telephone didn't ring."

She looked up at me with pain on her large face. "This woman is one of my customers. I can vouch for her." The pain was partly economic and partly moral.

111

"How did Lucy Champion get the hat? Does your customer explain that?"

"Of course. That's why it's so utterly pointless to bring her name into it. Lucy Champion used to be her maid. She ran away some time ago, without giving notice. She stole the hat from her employer, and other things as well."

"What other things? Jewelry?"

"How did you know that?"

"I got it from the horse's mouth. Maybe horse isn't the right word. Mrs. Larkin is more of the pony type."

Denise didn't react to the name. Her quick unconscious fingers had moulded the Kleenex hat into a miniature replica of the black-and-gold turban. She noticed what her fingers had been making, and tossed it in front of the cat. The cat pounced.

The woman wagged her head from side to side. The metal curlers clicked dully like disconnected thoughts. "All this is very confusing. Oh well, let's drink up." She raised her glass. "Here's to confusion. And universal darkness covers all."

I reached for my beer. The sagging springs of the studio couch threw us together, shoulder to shoulder. "Where did you pick that up?"

"I went to school once, strangely enough. That was before I came down with a bad case of art. What did you say the name was?"

"Archer."

"I know *that*. The woman's name, who told you about the stolen jewelry."

"Mrs. Larkin. It's probably an alias. Her first name is Una."

"Small and dark? Fiftyish? Mannish type?"

"That's Una. Was she your customer?"

Denise frowned into her beer, sipped meditatively, came up with a light foam mustache. "I shouldn't be

112

talking out loud like this. But if she's using an alias, there must be something fishy." Her dubious expression hardened into self-concern: "You wouldn't quote me, to her or anybody else? My business is on the edge of nothing, I have a boy to educate, I can't afford any sort of trouble."

"Neither can Una, or whatever her name is."

"It's Una Durano, *Miss* Una Durano. At least that's what she goes by here. How did *you* happen to know her?"

"I worked for her at one time, briefly." The afternoon seemed very long ago.

"Where does she come from?"

"I wouldn't know. I'm much more interested in where she is now."

"I might as well tell all," Denise said wryly. "She lives on the Peppermill estate, leased it early last spring. I heard she paid a fantastic sum: a thousand dollars a month."

"The diamonds are real, then?"

"Oh yes, the diamonds are real."

"And just where is the Peppermill estate?"

"I'll tell you. But you won't go and see her tonight?" She pressed my arm with strong fingers. "If you do, she'll realize I told tales out of school."

"This is real life, Denise."

"I know it. It's my personal real life. The hundred dollars she paid me for that hat took care of the rent that month."

"What month was it?"

"March, I think. It was the first one she bought in my shop. She's been back a couple of times since."

"It must have looked good on her, if anything could."

"Nothing could. She has no feminine quality. Anyway, she didn't buy the turban to wear herself. She paid for it, with a hundred-dollar bill. But it was the

113

other woman with her tried it on and wore it out of the shop." Her hand was still on my arm, like a bird that had settled on a comfortable roost for the night. She felt my muscles tense. "What's the matter?"

"The other woman. Describe her."

"She was a lovely girl, much younger than Miss Durano. A statuesque blonde, with the most wonderful blue eyes. She looked like a princess in my hat."

"Did she live with Miss Durano?"

"I can't say, though I saw them together several times. The blonde woman only came into my shop that once."

"Did you catch her name?"

"I'm afraid not. Is it important?" Her fingers were sculpturing the muscle patterns in my forearm.

"I don't know what's important and what isn't. You have been helpful, though." I stood up out of her grasp.

"Aren't you going to finish your beer? You can't go out there tonight. It's after midnight."

"I think I'll have a look at the place. Where is it?"

"I wish you wouldn't. Promise me anyway you won't go in and talk to her, not tonight."

"You shouldn't have phoned her," I said. "But I'll make you a better promise. If I find Charlie Singleton, I'll buy the most expensive hat in your store."

"For your wife?"

"I'm not married."

"Oh." She swallowed. "Well. To get to the Peppermill house, you turn left at the ocean boulevard and drive out to the end of town, past the cemetery. It's the first big estate beyond the cemetery. You'll know it by the greenhouses. And it has its own landing field."

She rose heavily and crossed the room to the door. The cat had torn the Kleenex hat into shreds that littered the carpet like dirty snowflakes.

CHAPTER 15

I drove back to the ocean boulevard and turned south. A fresh breeze struck the windwing and was deflected into my face, carrying moisture and smells. Behind the whizzing palm trees on the margin of my headlights, the sea itself streamed silver under the moon.

The boulevard curved left away from the beach. It climbed a grade past wind-tormented evergreens huddled arthritically on the hillside. A stone wall sprang up beside the road, amplifying the hum of the tires and the mutter of the engine. Beyond the wall, stone angels pointed at the sky; saints spread their arms in iron benediction.

The cemetery wall ended abruptly, and its place was taken by a spear-pointed iron fence. I caught glimpses through it of a great lawn returning to wilderness, beyond it a flat field with a corrugated-iron hangar at one end, a wind-sock blowing from its roof. I slowed down.

A heavy wrought-iron gate hung between obelisk-shaped gateposts, one of which had a large FOR SALE sign bolted to it. I got out and tried the gate. It was chained and padlocked. Through its bars I could see a long straight drive lined with coconut palms, at its end a massive house surrounded with outbuildings. The sloping glass roof of a conservatory glinted at the end of one wing.

The gate was climbable. Iron leaves between the bars provided foot- and hand-holds. I switched off my headlights and went over it. Circling wide on the lawn away from the drive, I struggled through the waist-high grass and weeds. The traveling moon accompanied me to the house.

The building was Spanish Renaissance with a strong Inquisition hangover. Narrow windows barred with ornamental ironwork were set deep in its wide flat concrete face. A lighted window on the second floor formed a tall yellow rectangle striped with vertical bars. I could see part of the ceiling of the room, vague shadows dancing on it. After a while the shadows approached the window, grouping and solidifying into human form. I lay down flat on my back and pulled my jacket together over my shirt-front.

A man's head and shoulders appeared at the bottom of the tall yellow rectangle. I made out dark eyes in a moony blur of face under a tangle of hair. The eyes were raised to the sky. I looked straight up into its dark blue well, moonwashed and dripping with stars, and wondered what the man at the window was seeing there, or looking for.

He moved. Two pale hands sprang out from his dark silhouette and gripped the bars framing his face. He swayed from side to side, and I saw the white blaze on one side of his tangled head. His shoulders writhed. He seemed to be trying to wrench the bars out of their concrete sockets. Each time he tried and failed, he said one word in a low growling guttural.

"Hell," he said. "Hell. Hell."

The word fell heavily from his mouth forty or fifty

116

times while his body tugged and heaved, flinging itself violently from side to side. He left the window then, as suddenly as he had appeared in it. I watched his slow shadow retreat across the ceiling and dissolve out of human shape.

Moving closer to the wall, I worked along it to the ground-floor window in which a faint light showed. This opened into a long hallway with a rounded ceiling. The light came from an open door at its far end. Listening closely, I heard some kind of music, a thin jazz scrabbling and tapping on the lid of silence.

I circled the house to the left, past a row of closed garage-doors, a clay tennis-court patchily furred with twitch grass, a sunken garden overgrown with succulents. From its end a *barranca* widened down to a bluff that overhung the sea. Below the bluff, the sea slanted up like a corrugated-metal roof to the horizon.

I turned back to the house. Between it and the sunken garden there was a flagged patio walled with flowerboxes. Its tables and chairs were sand-blown and rusting, old iron relics of dead summers. Light fell among them from a picture window in the wall overhead. The jazz was louder behind the wall, like music at a dance to which I hadn't been invited.

The window was uncurtained but set too high to give me a view of the room. The black-beamed ceiling was visible, and the upper part of the far wall. Its oak panels were crowded with paintings of pigeon-breasted women in lace caps and mutton-chop-whiskered men, narrow-shouldered in black Victorian coats. Somebody's ancestors, not Una's. She had been stamped out by a machine.

Standing on my toes, I could see the top of Una's head covered with short black curls like caracul. She was sitting perfectly still beside the window. A young man was sitting opposite her, his profile visible from

117

the neck up. It was a heavy and amorphous profile, whatever strength it had concealed by pads of flesh under the chin, around the mouth and eyes. He had light brown hair bristling in an unkempt crew-cut. The focus of his attention was somewhere between him and Una, below the level of the windowsill. I guessed from the movement of his eye that they were playing cards.

The music behind the wall stopped and started again. It was the same old record, *Sentimental Lady*, being played over and over. Sentimental Una, I said to myself, just as the howling began. Distant and muted by intervening walls, the howling rose and fell like a coyote baying the moon. Or a man. The hair on the back of my neck prickled.

Una said, loudly enough to be heard through the plate-glass window: "For Christ's sake shut him up."

The man with the crew-cut rose into half-length view. He wore the white-drill smock of a nurse or orderly, but he had none of their air of efficiency. "What do I do, bring him down here?" He clenched his hands together in a womanish gesture.

"It looks as if you'll have to."

The howling rose again. The orderly's head turned towards it and then his body followed. He walked away from the window, out of my sight. Una got up and marched in the same direction. Her shoulders were trim in a tailored black pajama-jacket. She turned the music louder. It poured through the house like a dark intangible surf, and like a drowning person's, the man's cry rose above it. His howling was stilled suddenly. The music went on, washing over the human echo.

Then there were voices in the room, Una's voice weaving jerkily through the music: "Headache ... get some peace ... sedation"; and the growling guttural I had heard before, starting below the music and rising above it:

"I can't. It is terrible. Terrible things going on. I got to stop them."

"Old man Stopper himself. You're the one to stop them all right." It was the younger man's mezzo, with a titter running through it.

"Leave him alone!" Una cried savagely. "Let him have his say. You want him to yell all night?"

There was silence again, except for the swirling music. I stepped across a flowerbox into the patio and leaned my weight on one of the rusted tables. It held firm. Using a chair as a step, I got up onto the tabletop. The table teetered on its base, and I had a bad moment before it leveled back. When I straightened up, my head was almost even with the window-sill ten feet away.

On the far side of the room, Una was standing over a radio-phonograph. She turned it low and walked directly towards the window. I ducked instinctively, but she wasn't looking at me. With an expression in which outrage and tolerance were combined, she was watching the man who stood in the center of the room. The man with the blaze of white like a lightning scar on the side of his head.

His small body was wrapped in a robe of red brocaded silk which hung in folds as if he had borrowed it from a larger man. Even his face seemed to have shrunk inside its skin. Instead of jowls he had pale loose wattles that flapped with the movement of his mouth.

"Terrible things." His broken growl was loud in the silence. "Going on all the time. I caught the dogs at my mamma. They crucified my daddy. I climbed up out of the culvert up on the hill and saw the nails in his hands and he said kill them all. Kill them all. Those were his last streetcar I went down into the

119

tunnel under the river and the dead boys lying the ragpickers strutting around with the rods in their pants." He trailed off into an obscene medley of Anglo-Saxon and Italian.

The white-smocked orderly was sitting on the arm of a leather chair. The light from a standing lamp beside him gave him the unreality of a pink elephant. He called out like a rooter from the sidelines:

"You tell 'em, Durano. You got a beautiful engram, old boy."

Una darted towards him, angry face thrust forward: "*Mister* to you, you lump of dough. Call him *mister!*"

"*Mister* Durano, then. Sorry."

The man who bore the name raised his face to the light. The black eyes were flat and shiny, deep-sunk, like bits of coal pressed into soft snow brows. "*Mister* District Attorney," he cried earnestly. "He said there was rats in the river, rats in the Rouge Plant. He said kill them off. Rats in the drinking-water, swimming in my blood-veins, Mr. Doctor Attorney. I promised to clean them out."

"Give him the gun, for Christ's sake," Una said. "Get it over with."

"For Christ's sweet sake," Durano echoed her. "I seen him on the hill when I come up out of the culvert. Horseshoe nails in his hands, and the dogs at my mother. He give me the gun, said keep it in your pants boy, you get rats in the bloodstreams. I said I would clean them out." His thin hand dove like a weasel for the pocket of his bathrobe. It came out empty. "They took my gun. How can I clean them out when they took my rod away?" He raised his doubled fists in an agony of rage and beat his forehead with them. "Give me my gun!"

Una went to the record-player, almost running, as if a wind were hurrying her along. She turned it loud

120

and came back to Durano, struggling step by step against the psychic wind that was blowing in the room. The fat orderly hitched up his smock and took a black automatic from under his belt. Durano pounced on him feebly. The orderly offered no resistance. Durano wrenched the automatic from his hands and backed away a few feet.

"Now!" he said with authority. He uttered a string of obscenities as if his mouth was full of them and he was spitting them out to be rid of them. "Now, you two, hands on the heads."

The orderly did as he was told. Una lined up beside him with her hands in the air, rings flashing. Her face was expressionless.

"This is it," Durano said thickly. There were red welts on his forehead where he had struck himself. His slack mouth continued moving but I couldn't hear what he said under the music. He leaned forward, strained white fingers around the gun. It looked as if it were holding him up in the beating ocean of noise.

Una said something in a low voice. The orderly glanced down with a faint fat smile. Durano took a skipping little step and shot him three times point-blank. The orderly lay down on the floor and pillowed his head on an upflung arm, the faint smile still on his face.

Durano shot Una, three times. She doubled over, grimacing histrionically, and collapsed on a divan. Durano looked around the room for other possible victims. Finding none, he dropped the gun in the pocket of his bathrobe. I had noticed when he began to shoot with it that it was a toy cap-pistol.

Una rose from the divan and turned the music down. Durano watched her without surprise. The man in white hoisted himself to his feet and escorted Durano across the room. Durano looked back from the doorway with a dreaming smile. The self-inflicted bruises on his forehead were swelling and turning blue.

Una waved to him, exaggeratedly, like a mother to a child, before the orderly hustled him out. Then she sat down at the card table by the window and began to shuffle the deck. Sentimental Una.

I climbed down from my perch. Away down below on the beach I could hear the waves playing pattycake in the sand, sucking and gurgling rhythmically like idiot children.

I went around to the front of the house. The barred window on the second floor was still lit, and I could see the shadows on the ceiling. I moved in closer to the front door, which was made of carved black oak and about twelve feet high. It was the kind of door that demanded to be knocked on with the butt end of a gun. I stood in a weed-grown flowerbed, leaned my chin on the iron railing of the portico, fingered the butt of the gun in my jacket pocket. And decided to call it a day.

I lacked the evidence and the power to put Una under arrest. Until I had one or the other, it would be better to leave her where I could find her again, safe in the bosom of her family.

CHAPTER 16

The signpost at the mountain crossroads was splintered by the bullets of trigger-happy hunters. Four painted white boards projected from it. One pointed back the way I had come: ARROYO BEACH 7 MIS. One pointed forward: BELLA CITY 34 MIS. The one to the right said: EAGLE LOOKOUT 5 MIS; the one to the left: SKY ROUTE. The fifth direction, unmarked, was straight up to where a hawk wheeled on banked blue curves of air. It was bright early morning.

I got back behind the wheel of my car and turned onto the Sky Route. It was a hairpinning gravel road that traced the contours of the mountainside. On my left the mountain fell away into a canyon in which occasional rooftops were visible. Beyond the canyon's far edge the sea lay smoothed by distance like wine in a teacup, rimmed by the thin white curve of Arroyo Beach.

I passed a few rural mailboxes standing on posts at the entrances to steep lanes. The mailbox numbered 2712 also bore the legend HIGHHOLME, H. WILDING, ESQ., in bold red block-capitals. Wilding's lane widened into a clearing near the bottom of the canyon. A small stone house sat between white oaks at the back of the clearing.

There were bantam chickens scratching in the yard. An old hound cocked a grizzled snoot at me and lifted one eyebrow, refusing to move out of the path of the car. I set the emergency brake and got out. He growled at me apathetically, still without moving. A gray gander ran at me hissing and flapping, veered at the last moment into the trees. Somewhere in the wooded canyon below, a gang of kids were talking back and forth in Indian war-whoops.

The man who came out of the stone house could have passed for an Indian. He was dressed in a pair of dirty canvas shorts, and the rest of him was burned almost black by the sun. His straight black hair, grayed in streaks, hung down over his ears.

"Hello," he said, strumming a silent overture on his washboard ribs. "Isn't it a fine clear day? I hope you noticed the quality of the light. It's rather special. Whistler might have been able to snare it in paint, not I."

"Mr. Wilding?"

"Of course." He extended a paint-stained hand. "Delighted to see you. Delighted to see anybody and anything. Did it ever occur to you that light creates landscape, so that the world itself is created daily, in a sense? In my sense."

"It never has."

"Well, think about it," he said earnestly. "Light creates landscape out of old black chaos. We painters recreate it. I can't step outside in the morning without feeling like God himself on the second day. Or was it the third? It doesn't matter really. I've divested myself of time. I live in pure space."

"My name is Archer," I said, before I drowned in a mountain torrent of words. "Two weeks ago—"

"I'm sorry, I've been rude. I so seldom see people,

124

I'm a veritable gramophone when I do. Archer, you say? Were you born under Sagittarius by any chance, the sign of the Archer? If you were," he concluded rather lamely, "that would be fun."

"Sagittarius is my first name, curiously enough. It's more fun than you can imagine."

Wilding uttered a high loud laugh like a mockingbird's imitation of human mirth. A hooting echo of his laughter came back from the children in the woods.

"Who are you anyway?" he said. "Come in and have a cup of tea. I've only just brewed some."

"I'm a detective."

"On the Singleton case?"

"Yes."

"Oh." He didn't renew his invitation to tea. "There's really nothing I can tell you that I haven't told the others."

"I'm working alone. I haven't talked to the others, and I don't know what they know or what they think. My own feeling is that he's dead."

"Charles dead?" Surprise or some other emotion pulled like a drawstring through his cordovan face and left it wrinkled. "That would be a waste. He was only twenty-nine. Why do you feel that he is dead, Mr. Archer?"

"Analogy. A woman was killed yesterday, apparently because she knew what happened to him."

"The blonde woman, was she killed?"

"A colored woman." I told him about Lucy.

He squatted Indian-fashion, resting one elbow on his folded bare knees, and drew a design in the dust with his forefinger. It was a long-faced mask in the shape of a coffin, which looked a little like his own face. A bantam rooster came and pecked at his hand.

Wilding stood up, and struck himself lightly over the eyes with the hand that had drawn the coffin. "There's your symbol-making faculty at work in its crudest form. I wonder sometimes if my sainted mother didn't deceive my father with a Navajo." He obliterated the dust-drawing with his sandaled feet, talking on without a pause: "The painter makes objects out of events, the poet makes words out of events. What does the man of action do, Mr. Archer? Suffer them?"

"Your friend Singleton did, I think. I take it he was your friend, or is."

"Certainly he was. I've known Charles since he was a schoolboy. I taught at Arroyo Prep School for a while, before my pictures sold. And he's been coming up here in the summers for nearly ten years. You can see his place from here."

He pointed north along the canyon. Near its head, a half mile or more away, a squat structure of brown oiled logs gleamed dully among the live oaks. "I helped him to build it myself, in the summer of 1941. It's only a one-room affair, but Charles always called it his studio. He came back from his freshman year at Harvard with ideas of becoming a poet. His mother's house on the Hill made him feel cramped and stuffy. Both she and her house—I don't know whether you know them—are crusty with tradition, *not* the kind of tradition that a budding poet could use. Charles came up here to escape from it. He called this canyon his private vale of soul-making."

"I'd like to have a look at his cabin."

"I'll go over with you."

Wilding moved impulsively towards my car, and I followed him. I drove up the lane in low gear and turned left on the gravel road cut into the canyon wall. The second mailbox we came to was stenciled with the name Singleton. I turned left again into a lane that slanted down the side of the canyon. About halfway to the bottom, the log house stood on a natural shelf between the canyon's converging

126

walls. When I parked in front of it and got out, I saw that the front door was sealed with official paper.

I turned to Wilding: "You didn't tell me the place was sealed. Does the sheriff suspect violence?"

"He doesn't confide in me," Wilding said wryly. "When I told him about the shot I heard, he didn't seem to take it too seriously."

"The shot?"

"Sorry, I imagined that you knew. I heard a shot from this direction, late that Saturday night. I didn't think twice about it at the time, for the simple reason that I hear a great many shots, in and out of hunting season. When they questioned me the following week, I mentioned it of course. I believe they went over the premises quite thoroughly after that. They didn't find a bullet or anything of the sort."

"They wouldn't, if the slug went into Singleton."

"Mercy upon us," he said. "Do you really suppose that Charles was shot up here in his own cabin?"

"They must think something happened here, or they wouldn't have sealed it up. What else did you hear that Saturday night?"

"Nothing, absolutely nothing. A single shot around eleven o'clock, and that was all. A few cars went by, but there's always late night traffic on the road."

Wilding went to the large window that balanced the door in the front wall of the cabin. Standing on tiptoe, he peered in past the brown monk's-cloth drapes partly drawn across it. I looked over his shoulder into a square beamed room furnished in primitive luxury with polished wood, homespun fabrics, copper. Everything seemed to be in order and place. Above the copper-vented fireplace opposite the window, a handsome boy in oils looked out of a bleached wooden frame, over our heads, down five miles of sunlit canyon.

"That's Charles," Wilding said in a whisper, as if

the boy in the frame might overhear him. "I painted it myself, and gave it to him. He looked like a young Shelley when he was twenty. I'm afraid he doesn't any more. Charles lost his ethereal quality during the war, when he took up with that woman. Or it may have been the war itself that did it. I suppose I have a prejudice against women. I'm a confirmed bachelor myself."

"Is she the blonde you mentioned?"

"Did I mention her? I didn't mean to." He turned and laid a brown hand on my shoulder. "Look here, old chap, are you one of the old lady's investigators? If you are, I don't want to say any more. Naturally I told the whole thing to the sheriff."

"Anything you tell me is between us."

His bright black eyes explored my face like foraging beetles. "What is your interest in Charles, just while we're on the subject?"

"Mrs. Singleton's paid companion hired me."

"Sylvia Treen? She's a lovely child, very much in love with Charles, I think. But I had no idea—"

"She knows about the blonde."

"Yes. I told her. I thought it might be for the best, in the long run. Whatever happened, Charles would never marry Sylvia. He's not the marrying sort. I *didn't* let Sylvia know how long the affair had lasted."

"She said it was just this summer."

"I let her imagine that. Actually, it's been going on for seven or eight years. Charles introduced me to her the year he entered the Air Force. Her name was Bess, I don't recall her surname. She was very young and quite exciting, marvelously colored. Perfect in every way, until she opened her mouth—but I mustn't tattle." He continued to tattle: "Charles always did have a proletarian penchant, you know. In spite of that or because of it, it was clearly a case of true

128

love. The children were mad about each other. I shouldn't say children. *She* wasn't a child. She was already married, I understand. Which doubtless suited Charles." He added reflectively: "Perhaps he should have married her."

"You think she shot him?"

"I have no reason to think so. Certainly it's possible. Seven years is a long time for a young lady to wait for a young man to make up his mind."

"Was she here the night he disappeared?"

"I have no way of knowing. I did see a light in the cabin. Actually I haven't seen her for weeks. I do have the impression that they came up here together quite often during the summer, practically every Saturday night."

"And before that?"

He leaned against the sealed door and thought for a while, his thin brown arms folded on his chest. "Their visits haven't been continuous, I know that. Bess first appeared in the summer of 1943, and that was when I met her. I wanted to paint her. Charles was excessively possessive, and he never again asked me back when she was here. After that summer, I didn't set eyes on her again until 1945, when Charles left the Air Force. For the next two or three years I saw her at a distance quite often. Then Charles went back to Harvard in the fall of 1948 to study law, and I didn't see them again until this spring. It's possible that she followed him to Cambridge. I've never asked him about her."

"Why?"

"He's jealous, as I said, and secretive about his private affairs. It's partly his mother's doing. Mrs. Singleton's attitude towards the human libido is austere, to say the least."

"So you don't know where she came from, where

she went, what she was doing in Arroyo Beach, who she was married to?"

"To all of those questions, I have to answer no."

"You can describe her?"

"If I can find the words. She was a young Aphrodite, a Velasquez Venus with a Nordic head."

"Try me again, Mr. Wilding, in simple language."

"A Nordic Aphrodite rising from the Baltic." He smiled reminiscently. "She was perfect until she opened her mouth. Then it was painfully clear that she had learned to speak English, if English is the word, in shall we say a rather barbarous milieu."

"I take it she was a blue-eyed blonde, and no lady."

"*Baltic* blue eyes," he insisted. "Hair like pale young cornsilk. Almost too dramatic to paint seriously, though I dearly should have loved to do a nude." His eyes were burning a figure into the air. "Charles wouldn't hear of it."

"Can you draw her from memory?" I said.

"I could if I wished." He kicked at the dirt like a rebellious boy. "I haven't really bothered with human material for years. My present concern is pure space, lit by the intelligible radiance of nature, if you follow me."

"I don't."

"In any case, I never use my art, or allow it to be used."

"Uh-huh. Very high-minded. You've divested yourself of time. It happens a friend of yours has done it the hard way, probably. Most people would climb down off their high horse and do what they can to help."

He gave me a bitter, wrinkled look. I thought he was going to cry. Instead he let out another of his high inhuman laughs, which echoed like the cry of a lost gull down the canyon. "I do believe you're right,

130

Mr. Sagittarius. If you'll take me home, I'll see what I can do."

He came out of his house a half hour later, waving a piece of drawing paper:

"Here you are, as representational as I can make her. It's pastel chalk sprayed with fixative, so don't try to fold it."

I took the drawing from his hand. It was a colored sketch of a young woman. Her pale blonde braids were coroneted on her head. Her eyes had the dull gleaming suavity of tile. Wilding had caught her beauty, but she was older in time than in the picture.

He seemed to sense what I was thinking: "I had to sketch her as I first saw her. That was my image of her. She'll be seven or eight years older."

"She's changed the color of her hair, too."

"You know her, then."

"Not well. I'll get to know her better."

CHAPTER 17

I climbed the front steps of Dr. Benning's house and rang the doorbell. The hole I had punched in the corner of the pane had been mended with cardboard and scotch tape. Dr. Benning came to the door in shirtsleeves, with suspenders dragging. His uncombed hair was a fringe of withering grass around the pink desert of his scalp. He had the air of a beaten old man, until he spoke. His voice was crisp and impatient:

"What can I do for you? Weren't you in my waiting-room yesterday afternoon?"

"This isn't a professional call, doctor."

"What kind of call is it? I'm just getting up."

"Haven't the police contacted you?"

"They have not. Are you a policeman?"

"A private detective, working with the police." I showed him my photostat. "We're investigating the murder of a colored girl named Lucy Champion. She visited your office yesterday afternoon."

"You followed her here?"

"I did."

132

"Do you care to tell me why?" In the harsh morning light his eyes were pale and strained.

"I was hired to."

"And now she's dead?"

"She got away from me. When I found her again, late yesterday afternoon, her throat had been cut."

"It's curious you didn't get in touch with me before. Since she was my patient, and I was apparently one of the last persons to see her alive."

"I tried to last night. Didn't your wife tell you?"

"I haven't had a chance to speak with her this morning. She isn't well. Come in, though, won't you? If you'll just give me a chance to finish dressing, I'll be glad to help you in any way I can."

He ushered me into the waiting-room. I heard his slippered feet diminuendo up the stairs to the second floor. Ten minutes later he came down, dressed in a creased blue store suit, and freshly shaved. Leaning on the receptionist's desk in the corner, he lit a cigarette and offered me the package.

"Not before breakfast, thanks."

"I'm foolish to do it myself. I warn my patients about smoking on an empty stomach. But that's the way of us doctors. Preventive medicine is our watchword nowadays, and half of us are still dying prematurely of overwork. Physician, heal thyself." Benning had put on a professional manner along with his clothes.

"Speaking of premature death," I said.

"I shouldn't be chattering." His quick smile held remnants of boyish charm. "It's a bad habit I've fallen into, from trying to establish *rapport* with my patients. Now about this patient, Miss Champion. You say her throat was cut, Mr.—is it Archer?"

"Her throat was cut, and it's Archer."

"Exactly what sort of information do you want from me?"

133

"Your observations, personal and professional. Was yesterday the first time she came here to your office?"

"I believe it was the third time. I have to apologize for the condition of my records. I haven't had trained help recently. And then so many of my patients are one-time cash patients. It's in the nature of a general practice among, well, poor people. I don't always keep full records, except in the cash-book. I do recall that she was in twice before: once in the middle of last week I think, and once the week before that."

"Who referred her?"

"Her landlady, Mrs. Norris."

"You know Mrs. Norris?"

"Certainly. She's often done practical nursing for me. Anna Norris is the finest type of Negro woman, in my opinion. Or dark-complected woman, as she would say."

"Her son is suspected of this murder."

"Alex is?" He swung one nervous leg, and his heel rapped the side of the desk. "Why on earth should he be under suspicion?"

"He was on the scene. When they arrested him, he panicked and ran. If he hasn't been caught, he's probably still going."

"Even so, isn't Alex an unlikely suspect?"

"I think so. Lieutenant Brake doesn't. Alex was intimate with the girl, you know. He was going to marry her."

"Wasn't she much older?"

"How old was she?"

"I'd say in her middle twenties. She was a registered nurse, with several years of experience."

"What was the matter with her?"

A length of ash fell from his untended cigarette. Absently, he ground it into the carpet with the toe of his worn black shoe. "The matter with her?"

"What were you treating her for?"

"It amounted to nothing really," he answered after a pause. "She had an intestinal complaint which I think was caused by a slight colonic spasm. Unfortunately she knew too much about illness, and too little. She magnified her trouble into a malignant disease. Of course she had nothing of the sort, nothing more than a mild psychosomatic ailment. Do you follow me?"

"Partly. Her symptoms were caused by nerves."

"I wouldn't say nerves." Benning was expanding in the glow of his superior knowledge. "The total personality is the cause of psychosomatic ills. In our society a Negro, and especially a highly trained Negro woman like Miss Champion, is often subjected to frustrations that could lead to neurosis. A strong personality will sometimes convert incipient neurosis into physical symptoms. I'm stating it crudely, but that's what Miss Champion did. She felt cramped by her life, so to speak, and her frustration expressed itself in stomach cramp." He paused for breath.

"What was she doing here in Bella City?"

"I'd like to know myself. She claimed to be looking for a job, but I don't think she was registered in California. I'd give a good deal for a social history on her."

"She was from Detroit. Her family is poor and pretty ignorant. Does that help?"

"It doesn't tell me much about her psychic life, does it?"

"Why is her psychic life important?"

"I could see that fear of illness wasn't her only phobia. She had a deeper and more general fear which expressed itself in various ways. I tried to explain that to her, to give her some insight, but she wasn't equal to it. She broke down and cried on my shoulder. Then it came out about her other fears."

"What was she afraid of?"

He spread his hands like a lecturer. "It's hard to say.

135

I'm not a psychiatrist, though I do try to keep up with the literature." He looked around his shabby waiting-room, and an obscure impulse made him add: "Which is more than you can say for my colleagues in this desolate town."

"Was her fear real or imaginary?"

"Precisely the question I can't answer, without knowing more about her." His eyes clouded with thought. "Fear is always real subjectively. The true question about fear is whether it's relevant, justified by the situation. In this case it seems to have been. Miss Champion believed that she was being hunted, that she was marked for death."

"Did she give you any details?"

"No. I didn't have time to gain her confidence. She failed to mention these persecution fears at all until her last visit, yesterday. You've been investigating her life and death, Mr. Archer. Was she really being hunted down by someone? Someone who finally caught her?"

"I don't know. I was trailing her myself, and I did a poor job of it and she caught on. If she was full of fear, that might have been enough to set her off." I asked a question I didn't want to ask: "You don't think she could have killed herself out of pure funk?"

Dr. Benning began to pace back and forth along a worn path that cut across the carpet from one door to the other. When he stopped and faced me, he looked ill at ease: "I'll be frank with you. I was concerned about her in that sense, which is why I did my best to allay her fears."

"You thought she had suicidal tendencies?"

"I took it into account as a possibility. That's all I can say. I'm no psychiatrist." He spread his hands palms upward in a gesture of awkward helplessness. "Was the wound consistent with suicide?"

"It was pretty deep to be self-inflicted. Brake or the

136

deputy coroner can answer that question better than I can. And Brake will want your statement."

"I'm ready now, if you're going to the station."

I said I was. Benning went into the hall and got his hat. With his bald head covered he looked a good deal younger, but neither handsome nor well-heeled enough to be married to the woman he was married to.

He called up the stairs before we left: "I'm going out, Bess. Do you want anything?"

There was no answer.

CHAPTER 18

The dirty-white brick city hall was distinguished from the surrounding store- and office-buildings by a flagless flagpole standing in its patch of scorched grass. At the rear a concrete ramp sloped down from a paved parking lot to the scuffed green door of the police department. Benning turned at the door, smiling a sour private smile.

"The descent into Avernus," he said.

Inside, in a green-walled corridor, a few wire-netted ceiling-bulbs maintained a bilious twilight. Under the brisk odors of floor oil and metal polish, the smells of fear and germicide, poverty and old sweat, kept up a complicated human murmur. In the furthest, dimmest corner, opposite a door marked DESK SERGEANT, a monumental shape sat on a wooden bench against the wall.

It belonged to a large Negro woman in a black cloth coat. The hair that showed under the side of her black felt hat was the color and texture of steel wool. I recognized her when she turned to look at us.

Benning spoke first—"Mrs. Norris!"—and went to her with his hands out.

She took them, raising her heavy, dark face to his. "I'm glad to see you, doctor." Cross-hatched by shadow, her nose and mouth and chin looked like black stone rounded by years of weather. Only her eyes gleamed sorrowfully with life. "They've arrested Alex. They're accusing him of murder."

"It must be a mistake," he said in a low bedside voice. "I know he's a good boy."

"He is a good boy." She looked questioningly at me.

"This is Mr. Archer, Mrs. Norris. He's working on the case. Mr. Archer has just been telling me that he thinks Alex is innocent."

"Thank you, Mr. Archer, and pleased to make your acquaintance."

"When was he arrested?"

"Early this morning, in the desert. He was trying to get out of the state. The car broke down. He was a young fool to run away in the first place. It's twice as bad for him, now that they've brought him back."

"Did you get him a lawyer?" Benning said.

"Yes, I'm having Mr. Santana. He's up in the Sierra for the weekend, but his housekeeper got in touch with him."

"He's a good man, Santana." Patting her shoulder, he moved towards the desk sergeant's door. "I'll talk to Brake, and see what I can do for Alex."

"I know Alex has a good friend in you, doctor."

Her words were hopeful, but her back and shoulders sloped in resignation. When she saw my intention of sitting down, she gathered her coat and shifted her body to one side, an involuntary sigh escaping from its concertina folds. I sat on a scrambled alphabet of initials carved in the soft wood of the bench.

"Do you know my son, Mr. Archer?"

"I talked to him a little last night."

"And you don't believe he's guilty?"

"No. He seemed very fond of Lucy."

She pursed up her heavy lips suspiciously, and said in a smaller voice: "Why do you say that?"

"He said it himself. Also, it showed in his actions."

That silenced her for a while. Her diffident black hand touched my arm very softly and retreated to her bosom. A thin gold wedding-band was sunk almost out of sight in the flesh of its third finger. "You are on our side, Mr. Archer?"

"The side of justice when I can find it. When I can't find it, I'm for the underdog."

"My son is no underdog," she said with a flash of pride.

"I'm afraid he'll be treated like one. There's a chance that Alex may be railroaded for this murder. The only sure way to prevent that is to pin it on the murderer. And you may be able to help me do that." I took a deep breath.

"I believe that you are a righteous man, Mr. Archer."

I let her believe it.

"You're welcome to anything I can say, or do," she continued. "It is true, what you said before. My boy was crazy for that woman. He wanted to marry her. I did my best to prevent it, every way I could. Alex is only nineteen, much too young to think about getting married. I planned an education for him. I tried to tell him that a dark-complected man is nothing in this country without an education to stand on. And Lucy wasn't the wife for him. She was older than Alex, five or six years older, and she was fast in her habits. I sent her away from my house yesterday, and then she got herself killed. I confess I made a mistake. I rose up in anger against her. She had no safe place to go. If I'd known what was going to come to her, she could have stayed on with us."

"You don't have to blame yourself. I think what happened to her was bound to happen."

"Do you think that?"

"She was carrying something too heavy for her."

"I had that feeling. Yes. She was afraid." Mrs. Norris leaned towards me with heavy confiding charm: "I had the feeling from the beginning that Lucy Champion was bad luck to me and my house. She was from Detroit, and I lived there myself when Alex was an infant. Last night when they came to me and said that she was killed, it was like all the things I'd dreaded for myself and Alex, when we were moving from city to city trying to find a living in the depression. Like those things had suddenly come true for us at last, here in this valley. After all those years I worked and planned, keeping my name respectable."

Looking into her eyes, deep black springs tapping the deep black past, I couldn't think of anything to say.

"I misstated myself," she said with renewed energy. "It is not my name I care for. It's my son. I believed if we could get out of those big cities in the North and live in a decent place of our own, I could bring him up straight as his father wished for him. Now he has been arrested."

"Where is his father? It would be a good thing if he stood by."

"Yes, it would be a good thing. Alex's father died in the war. Mr. Norris was a chief petty officer in the United States Navy." She blew her nose with the force and effect of an exclamation mark, and dabbed at her eyes.

I waited a while, and said: "When did Lucy Champion come to your house?"

"She drove up in a taxi on a Sunday morning before church. It must have been two weeks ago today. I never like to do business on the Sabbath, but then I had no right to turn her away just for my private indulgence. The decent hotels were closed to

141

her in this city, and most of the houses where our people can rent are not fit for dogs to inhabit. She was well spoken and well dressed. She told me she was on a vacation from her work, and she wanted to stay in a private house. I had the side room empty since the spring, and with Alex commencing college I needed the money.

"She seemed a peaceable little soul, though she was nervous and shy. She scarcely ever went out at all except to get herself lunch. She made her own breakfast, and ate her dinners with us. We had a boarding arrangement."

"Did she eat well?"

"Now that you mention it, she didn't. Picked at her food like a bird. I asked her once or twice if my food was not agreeing with her, but she was vague in her answers."

"Did she mention any illness to you?"

"She never did, Mr. Archer. Excuse me, now, she did. There was some trouble with her stomach. Nervous stomach."

"And you sent her to Dr. Benning?"

"I didn't send her. I said if she needed a doctor, he was a good man to go to. Whether she went to him or not, that I can't say."

"She went to him all right. But she never spoke of Dr. Benning to you?"

"Not that I recollect, except for that one time I recommended him."

"Did she mention Mrs. Benning?"

"Mrs. Benning? Dr. Benning has no wife that I know of."

"I met her last night, in his house. At least I met a woman who calls herself Mrs. Benning."

"You must refer to Florida Gutierrez. She works for the doctor. He wouldn't marry her. Dr. Benning

142

wouldn't marry any woman, not after the bad trouble
he had with his first wife."

"Was he a widower?"

"Divorced," she said flatly, unable to conceal her
disapproval. She added quickly: "Not that I blame
the doctor, except for his foolishness marrying a woman so much younger than him—than he. She was a
Jezebel to him, a blonde Jezebel mistreating him
without shame. It ended as I expected, with her
running off and divorcing him. At least that was the
story I heard." She pulled herself up sharp. "I ought
to wash out my mouth, repeating gossip and scandal
on the Lord's Day."

"What was her name, Mrs. Norris?"

"Elizabeth Benning. Doctor called her Bess. I don't
know her maiden name. He married her in the war,
when he was a medical officer in the United States
Navy. That was before we moved here from the
North."

"And how long ago did she leave him?"

"Nearly two years, it was. He was better off without
her, though I never dared tell him so."

"She seems to have come back."

"Now? In his house?"

I nodded.

Her mouth pursed up tight again. Her whole face
closed against me. Distrust of white men lay deep
and solid in her like stone strata deposited through
generations of time. "You won't repeat that which I
have been saying? I have an evil tongue and I've still
not learned to curb it."

"I'm trying to get you out of trouble, not deeper
in."

She answered slowly, after a time: "I do believe
you. And it's true, she returned to him?"

"She's there in the house. Didn't Lucy mention her

143

at all? She went to the doctor three times, and Mrs. Benning has been working as his receptionist."

She answered positively: "Lucy never did."

"The doctor told me you've had nursing experience. Did Lucy show any signs of illness, physical or mental?"

"She seemed a well woman to me, apart from her eating habits. Of course when they drink, often they don't eat."

"She drank?"

"I learned to my sorrow and shame she was a drinker. And now that you ask me about her health, Mr. Archer, there is this thing has been puzzling me."

She opened the clasp of her black purse and groped for something inside. It turned out to be a clinical thermometer in a black leatherette carrying case, which she handed to me.

"I found this after she left, in the medicine cabinet over the sink in her room. Don't shake it down now. I want you to look at the temperature."

I opened the case and turned the narrow glass stem until I could see the column of mercury. It registered 107° F.

"Are you sure this was Lucy's?"

She pointed to the initials, L.C., inked on the case. "Certainly it belonged to her. She was a nurse."

"She couldn't have had a temperature like that, could she? I thought 107 was fatal."

"It is, for adults. I don't understand it myself. Do you think I should show it to the police?"

"I will, if you like. In the meantime, can you tell me anything more about her habits? You say she was quiet and shy?"

"Very much so, at first, keeping herself to herself. Most of her evenings she just plain sat in her room with a little portable gramaphone she brought along with her. I thought it was a peculiar way for a young

144

woman to spend her vacation, and I said so. She laughed at that, but not in a humorous way. She became hysterical, and that was when I realized the strain that she was under. I began to feel the strain in the atmosphere when she was in the house. She was *in* the house twenty-three hours out of the twenty-four, it seemed like."

"Did she have any visitors?"

She hesitated. "No, she had never a one. She sat in her room and kept that jazzy music playing on the radio. Then I discovered her drinking. I was cleaning her room one day when she was out to buy her lunch downtown. I opened up a drawer to put fresh paper in the bottom, and it had whisky bottles in it, three or four empty pint bottles." Her voice was hushed with outrage.

"Maybe it helped her nerves."

She looked at me shrewdly: "Alex said just those words to me when I mentioned it to him. He defended her, which set me to thinking about the two of them living together in the same house. That was the end of last week. Then the middle of this week, late Wednesday night it was, I heard her tromping around in her room. I knocked on her door, and she responded in silk pajamas and there was Alex with her in her room. He said she was teaching him to dance. To all appearances, she was teaching my son the wicked ways of the world, in red silk pajamas, and I told her that to her face."

Her bosom heaved with remembered anger, like the aftershock of an earthquake:

"I told her she was degenerating my God-fearing household into a dance-hall, she must let my son alone. She said it was Alex's choice and he backed her up, he said he loved her. Then I was harsh with her. The red silk pajamas over her insolent flesh, they blinded my eyes to charity. My evil anger rose up and I said she must let Alex alone or leave my house in her nightclothes as she was. I said that I was planning better things for my son than she could give him. Alex spoke up then, saying if Lucy Champion went he would go along with her."

Now in a sense, he had. His mother's gaze seemed to be following his image into the shadows where Lucy had preceded him.

"You let her stay, though," I said.

"Yes. My son's wish is powerful with me. Lucy herself went away next morning, but she left her things behind. I don't know where she spent the day. I know she took a bus somewhere because she complained about the service that night when she came back. She was very excited in her manner."

"Thursday night?"

"Yes, it was Thursday night. All day Friday she was quiet and meek, though worried under the surface. I guessed she was planning something, and I was fearful she intended to run away with Alex. That night there was more trouble. I saw there was going to be trouble on top of trouble if she stayed."

"What was the Friday night trouble?"

"I'm ashamed to speak of it."

"It may be important." Casting back over the quarrel I had eavesdropped on, I guessed what Mrs. Norris was holding back: "She did have a visitor, didn't she?"

"Perhaps it is best for me to tell you, if it will help Alex." She hesitated. "Yes, Lucy had a visitor Friday night. I heard him go in by her side entrance and I watched for him and saw him when he left. She entertained a man in her room, a white man. I didn't speak of it that night, mistrusting my anger so. I promised myself to sleep and pray on it, but I slept very little. Lucy slept late and then she went out for lunch when I was at the store. When she came back,

146

she tempted my son. She kissed him in full sight on the public street. It was wanton and shameless. I said she had to go, and she went. My boy wanted to leave me and go with her. I had to tell him then about the man in her room."

"You shouldn't have."

"I know it. I confess it. It was rash and scornful of me. And it failed to turn him from her. The same afternoon she telephoned for him and he went to her call. I asked him where he was going. He wouldn't say. He took the car without asking for my permission. I knew then he was lost to me, whatever happened. He never before refused to do my bidding."

She bowed suddenly, sobbing into her hands, a black Rachel lamenting the wrecked hopes of all mothers for their sons, black and white and tan. The desk sergeant appeared in his doorway and watched her in silence for a while before he spoke:

"Is she all right?"

"She's worried about her son."

"She has a right to be," he said indifferently. "You Archer?"

I said I was.

"Lieutenant Brake will see you in his office now, if you're waiting."

I thanked him, and he retreated quickly.

Mrs. Norris's fit of grief had subsided as suddenly as it rose. She said: "I'm truly sorry."

"It's all right. You've got to remember that Alex can still be decent, even if he did disobey you. He's old enough to make decisions."

"I can accept that," she said. "But that he should leave me for a light, common woman, it was cruel and it was wrong. She led him straight into jail."

"You shouldn't have worked on his jealousy," I said.

"Have you lost your faith in him because of that?"

"No, but it gives him a motive. Jealousy is danger-

147

ous stuff to fiddle with, especially when you're not sure of your facts."

"There was no doubt what she was, with a white man with her late at night in her room."

"She had only one room."

"That's true."

"Where else could she have a visitor?"

"In my good front parlor," she said. "I gave her free use of the parlor."

"Maybe she wanted privacy."

"Why, I'd like to know." The question implied its own answer.

"There are plenty of reasons for a man to visit a woman. What did this man look like?"

"I saw him only a second, under the street light at the corner. He was an ordinary-looking man, middle size, middle age. At least he seemed slow in his movements. I didn't lay eyes on his face, not to *see* it."

"Did you notice his clothes?"

"I did. He wore a panama straw hat, and a light-colored jacket. His trousers were darker in color. He did not appear respectable to me."

"He probably isn't respectable, Mrs. Norris. But I can assure you he visited her for business purposes."

"Do you know him?"

"His name is Max Heiss. He's a private detective."

"Like you?"

"Not exactly." I rose to go.

She laid a detaining hand on my arm: "I said too much, Mr. Archer. You do still believe that Alex is innocent?"

I said: "Of course." But I was bothered by the motive she had provided.

Mrs. Norris sensed my doubt, and thanked me sadly, withdrawing her hand.

CHAPTER 19

Brake's office was a bare cubicle walled with the same green plaster as the corridor. Close up under the ceiling, heating-pipes like sections of iron viscera hung from metal supports. A single small window, high in the wall, flyspecked a square of sky.

Dr. Benning was sitting uncomfortably with his hat on his knees, in a straight chair against the wall. Brake, with his usual air of alert stolidity, was talking into the telephone on his desk:

"I'm busy or haven't you heard. Let the HP handle it. I haven't been a traffic cop for twenty years."

He hung up, and ran a hand like a harrow through his dust-colored hair. Then he pretended to be noticing my presence in the doorway for the first time: "Oh. It's you. You decided to favor us with a visit. Come in and sit down. The doc here tells me you're taking a pretty active interest in this case."

I sat beside Benning, who smiled deprecatingly and opened his mouth to speak. Before he had a chance to, Brake went on:

"Since that's the situation, let's get a couple of things straight. I'm no one-man team. I like help, from

149

private cops or citizens or anybody. I'm glad you sent the doc in to fill me in on the stiff, for instance."

"What do you think about suicide?"

Brake pawed my question away. "I'll come to that, I got a point to make first. If you're going to be in on this case, talking to my witnesses and messing around in general, I got to know where you stand and where your client stands."

"My original client ran out on me."

"So what's your interest? The doc here tells me you think we're trying to frame the Norris boy."

"I didn't put it so strongly," Benning said. "I also happen to agree with Mr. Archer, that the lad is probably innocent."

"Is that your opinion, Archer?"

"It is. I'd like to talk to Alex—"

"Sure you would. Did his mother hire you, by any chance? To cross me up, by any chance?"

"Having delusions of persecution, lieutenant?"

Hostility darkened his face for a slow instant, like a cloud-shadow crossing a hillside. "You admit it's your opinion that Norris ain't guilty. Before we do any talking, I want to know if you're looking for evidence to hang an opinion on, like a bloody lawyer. Or looking for evidence period."

"Evidence period. I was hired last night by a Miss Sylvia Treen. She's Mrs. Charles Singleton's companion."

Benning leaned forward at the sound of the second name: "Isn't she the woman whose son is missing?"

"That's right," Brake said. "We got a routine circular on him last week. Then we find this clipping about him in Champion's things. I been trying to figure how a missing high-lifer like Singleton fits in with a dinge cutting in the valley here. You got any ideas on the subject, doc?"

"I haven't really thought about it." He thought about

150

it. "At first glance it does appear that the connections may be accidental. I know some of my patients carry all sorts of unconnected things around with them, clippings and whatnot. Women who are emotionally disturbed often identify themselves with people in the newspapers."

Brake turned to me impatiently: "What about you, Archer? You got any opinions?"

I glanced at Benning's long conscientious face, wondering how much he knew about his wife. It wasn't my job to fill him in on her background.

"None that you couldn't shoot full of holes with a pea-shooter."

"I favor a .45 myself," Brake said. "What about your client? Miss Treen, is that her name?"

"Miss Treen gave me some of the details of Singleton's disappearance." I passed them on to Brake, or at least enough of them to hold his co-operation in Bella City without being embarrassed by it in Arroyo Beach. I left the blonde woman out of it entirely.

Bored with my expurgated version, Brake snapped his metal armbands and fiddled with the papers in his "In" basket. Benning listened with close and nervous attention.

When I finished, the doctor rose abruptly, turning his hat in his hand: "If you'll excuse me, men, I should look in at the hospital before church."

"Appreciate you coming in," Brake said. "Give the stiff a once-over if you like, but I don't think you'll find any hesitation marks. I never seen a suicide with a cut throat that didn't have hesitation marks. Or one that was cut so deep."

"Is she in the hospital morgue?"

"Yeah, waiting for autopsy. Just go right in and tell the guard I sent you."

"I'm on the staff of the hospital," Benning said with his sour private smile. He jammed his hat on his head and moved sideways to the door, his long legs scissoring awkwardly.

"Just a minute, doctor." I stood up and handed him the thermometer Mrs. Norris had given me. "This belonged to Lucy Champion. I'd like to see what you make of it."

He took the thermometer out of its case and held it to the light. "A hundred and seven, that's quite a temperature."

"Did Lucy have a fever yesterday?"

"Not to my knowledge."

"Isn't it standard practice to take a patient's temperature?"

He answered after a pause: "Yes, I remember now, I took Miss Champion's. It was in the normal range. She wouldn't have lasted long with a temperature of 107."

"She didn't last long."

Brake came around his desk and took the thermometer from Benning's hand. "Where did you get this, Archer?"

"From Mrs. Norris. She found it in Lucy's room."

"She could of hotted it up with a lighted match. Eh, doc?"

Benning looked puzzled. "That wouldn't make much sense."

"It does to me. She might of been trying to prove that Champion was delirious, killed herself when she was out of her head."

"I don't think so," I said.

"Wait a minute. Hold it." Brake banged his desk with a gavel-heavy palm. "Didn't Champion come here around the first of the month?"

"Two weeks ago today."

"That's what I thought. You know what the heat was here in the valley weekend before last? A hun-

152

dred and seven. It wasn't Champion who had the
fever, it was this bloody town."

"Is that right, doctor?" I said. "Does a mercury
thermometer hold a reading like that?"

"If it's not disturbed. It happens to mine all the
time, I should have remembered."

"There goes your clue," Brake said.

"And here go I," Benning added with lame
whimsy.

When the door had closed behind him, Brake
leaned back in his chair and lit a cigar. "You think
there's anything in the doc's idea that Champion had
a phobia?"

"He seems to know his psychology."

"Sure he does. He told me he wanted to specialize
in it at one time, only he couldn't afford another five
years of training. If he tells me the girl was psycho,
I'm willing to take his word for it. He knows what he's
talking about. The trouble is I don't." He blew a
smoke ring and speared it with an obscene middle
finger. "I'm all for physical evidence myself."

"Have you got much in that line?"

"Enough. You keep it under your hat and not go
running to the defense?"

I caught him up on the word. "Aren't you jumping
ahead of yourself a little?"

"I learned in this job to look a long way ahead."

He lifted a black-steel evidence case from the bottom drawer of his desk, and raised the lid. It contained the bolo knife with the carved black wooden
handle. The bloodstains on the curved blade had
dried dark brown.

"I've seen that."

"You don't know who it belongs to, though."

"Do you?"

"I showed this bolo to Mrs. Norris last night, before
she knew how Champion got killed. She identified it

153

right off. Her husband sent it to Alex from the Philippines, about seven years ago. It's been in the kid's possession ever since. He had it mounted on his bedroom wall, and she saw it every morning when she went in to make his bed, right up to yesterday morning."

"Did she say that?"

"She did. So maybe Champion had hot psychological flashes like the doc said. Maybe there's a tie-up with the Singleton case that we don't know about. I'm not going to lose any sleep over it. I got enough right here to arraign *and* convict." He shut the lid of the evidence box, relocked it and replaced it in the drawer.

I had been trying to decide all morning whether to give Brake everything I knew. I decided not to. The frayed ends of several lives, Singleton's and his blonde's, Lucy's, and Una's, were braided into the case. The pattern I was picking out strand by strand was too complicated to be explained in the language of physical evidence. Brake's understanding was an evidence box holding the kinds of facts that could be hammered through the skulls of a back-country jury. It wasn't a back-country case.

I said: "Have you got the boy's side of it yet? He isn't stupid. He must have known the bolo could be traced to him. Would he use it to do a murder and leave it lying there?"

"He didn't leave it lying. He started back for it. You saw him coming back. He even jumped you."

"That's not important. He thought I was messing with Lucy, and he got mad. The boy was under a strain."

"Sure he was. That's part of my case. He's the emotional type. I'm not claiming premeditation, see. I say it's a crime of passion, second degree. He got hot pants and busted in on her. Or maybe he lifted the key from her purse when they were out riding. Anyway she wasn't having any. He ran wild and cut her and took off. Then he remembered the knife and came back for it."

"Your story fits the external facts. It doesn't fit your suspect." But I was thinking that if and when Brake discovered the jealousy motive, he would have a steamroller case.

"You don't know these people the way I do. I deal with them every day." He unbuttoned his left shirtcuff and bared a heavy freckled forearm. A white scar ran jaggedly from the wristbone to the elbow. "The buck that gave me this was trying for my throat."

"So that makes Norris a slasher."

"There's more to it than that." Brake was on the defensive in spite of his honorable scar. The violent world he fought for and against didn't suit him or anybody else, and he knew it.

"I think there is more to it. Too many people were interested in Lucy. I wouldn't settle for the first suspect we stumble across. It isn't that easy."

"You took me up wrong," he said. "What I mean, the boy acts guilty. I been looking at their faces for thirty years, listening to them talk." He didn't have to tell me. The thirty years were marked clearly on him, like fire-traces on an old tree. "All right, I'm still in the minor leagues. All right. This is my league. Champion is a minor league killing."

"Consciousness of guilt is pretty tricky stuff. It's psychological, for one thing."

"Psychological hell. It's a plain fact. We try to hold him for questioning, he runs out. We catch him and bring him back and he won't talk. I tried to talk to him. He's sullen. Tell him the world was flat, he wouldn't answer yes or no or maybe."

"How have you been treating him?"

"Never laid a finger on him, neither did anybody

155

else." Brake pulled down his shirt-sleeve and rebuttoned the cuff. "We got our own brand of psychology."

"Where is he?"

"Out at the morgue."

"Isn't that a little unusual?"

"Not by me. I get a killing a month in this town, sometimes two. And I solve them, see? Most of them. The atmosphere at the morgue will loosen a killer up faster than anything I know."

"Psychology."

"That's what I said. Now, you playing on my team or you want a crying towel to cry into? If you're on my team, we'll go on out there and see if he's ready to talk."

CHAPTER 20

The door was numbered 01. The room behind the
door was windowless, low-ceilinged, concrete-walled.
When the door sucked shut behind us, we might have
been in a sepulcher far down under the earth. Brake's
heel struck dully on the composition floor. His shadow
spread across me as he approached the only light in
the room.

It was a cone-shaded bulb that hung low on an
adjustable pulley over a rubber-wheeled stretcher.
Lucy's sheeted body lay on the stretcher under its
white glare. Her head was uncovered and turned
towards Alex Norris. He was sitting in a chair on the
far side of the stretcher, looking steadfastly into the
dead woman's face. His right wrist was linked to hers
by twin rings of blue steel. The pumps of a cooling
system hummed and throbbed like time running
down in the concrete walls. Behind the paired glass
doors of the refrigerator, the other sheeted bodies
might have been waiting for judgment, dreaming a
preview of hell. It was as cold as hell.

The uniformed policeman who had been sitting

opposite Alex got to his feet, raising his hand in a slovenly salute. "Morning, lieutenant."

"What's good about it? You running a wake in here, Schwartz?"

"You told me not to mark him. Like you said, I been letting nature take its course."

"Well? Did nature take its course?" Brake stood over Alex, wide and impermeable against the light. "You want to make a statement now?"

Moving to one side, I saw Alex look up slowly. His face had thinned. The passage of the night had pared flesh from his temples and cheekbones. His wide carved lips drew back from his teeth and closed again without making any sound.

"Or you want to sit all day and hold hands?"

"You heard what the man said," Schwartz growled. "He ain't fooling. You sit here until you talk. In an hour or so the deputy coroner's gonna cut her up, finish the job you done. Maybe you want a ringside seat?"

Alex paid no attention to Brake or his subordinate. His gaze, incredulous and devoted, returned to the dead woman's head. Under the pitiless glare her hair shone like coiled steel shavings.

"What's the matter with you, Norris? You got no human feelings?" Brake sounded almost querulous in the subterranean stillness, almost feeble, as if the boy by accepting everything had turned the tables on him.

I said "Brake." The word had more force behind it than I intended.

"What's eating you?" He turned with a bewildered frown. The dead cigar in the corner of his mouth was like a black finger pulling one side of his face crooked. I retreated to the door, and he followed his own diminishing shadow towards me: "You want that crying towel?"

I said in a low voice, but not too low for Alex to overhear: "You're handling him wrong. He's a sensitive kid. You can't treat him like a punchy thug."

"Him sensitive?" Brake removed his cigar and spat on the floor. "He's got a hide like a rhinoceros."

"I don't think so. Give me a chance at him anyway. Uncouple him and let me talk to him alone."

"My wife and me were going up in the mountains today," Brake said irrelevantly. "We promised the kids a picnic."

He sneered at the dead cigar in his hand, dropped it suddenly, and ground it under his heel. "Schwartz! Turn him loose. Bring him over here."

The click of the handcuffs opening was tiny but very important, like the sound of a moral weight shifting on its fulcrum.

Schwartz pulled Alex to his feet. They crossed the room together, Alex round-shouldered and hanging back, Schwartz roughly urging him. "Taking him back to the cell, lieutenant?"

"Not yet." Brake addressed the boy: "Mr. Archer here is a friend of yours, Norris. He wants a little chinfest with you. Personally I think he's wasting all our time, but it's up to you. Will you talk to Mr. Archer?"

Alex looked from Brake to me. His smooth young face had the same expression I had seen on the ancient Indian face of the woman in the alley, beyond the reach of anything white men could do or say. He nodded wordlessly, and looked back at Lucy.

Brake and Schwartz went out. The door pulled shut. Alex started back across the room. He walked uncertainly with his legs spraddled like an old man's. The concrete floor sloped gently to a covered drain in the center of the room. He staggered down the barely perceptible slope and labored up the other side to the stretcher.

Standing over Lucy with his head bowed, he asked her: "Why did they do it?" in a dry hard voice.

I reached past him and pulled the sheet up over her head. I took him by the shoulders, turned him to face me. Part of his weight hung on me for a moment, until his muscles tightened. "Straighten up," I said.

He was as tall as I was, but his head was drooping on his undeveloped neck. I pushed my closed right hand under his chin. "Straighten up, Alex. Look at me."

He flinched away. I held him with my other hand on his shoulder. Suddenly he tensed and knocked my hand away from his chin.

"Steady, boy."

"I'm not a horse," he cried. "Don't you talk to me like I was a horse. Keep your hands off of me."

"You're worse than a horse. You're a stubborn mule. Your girl is lying dead, and you won't open your mouth to tell me who did it to her."

"They think I did it."

"It's your own fault if they do. You shouldn't have run out. You're lucky you didn't get shot."

"Lucky." The word was as blank as a hiccup.

"Lucky not to be dead. That's the one situation nobody can reverse. You think you've got it tough now, and you have, but that's no reason for turning into a dummy. One of these days you're going to snap out of it and really care what happened to Lucy. Only it'll be too late for you to do anything about it. You've got to help now."

I let go of him. He stood shakily, pulling at his fleshy lower lip with a bitten forefinger. Then he said: "I tried to tell them things at first, this morning when they brought me in. But him and the deputy D.A., they only had the one thing on their minds, to make me say I did it. Why would I kill my own fiancée?"

The question rose up hard from his working chest. His face was blind with the effort of speaking, the more terrible effort of speaking as a man. He couldn't sustain it: "I wish I was dead like Lucy."

"If you were, you couldn't help us."

"Nobody asked for any help from me. Who wants any help from me?"

"I do."

"You don't believe I killed her?"

"No."

He looked at me for maybe half a minute, his gaze shifting in heartbeat rhythm from one of my eyes to the other. "She didn't do it to herself, did she? Mister? You don't think Lucy—cut her own throat?" He whispered the question so as not to embarrass the dead woman behind him.

"It isn't likely. The suggestion has been made. What made you think of it?"

"No reason, except she was scared. She was awful scared yesterday. That's why I loaned her the knife, when she left our house. She asked me for something to protect herself with. I had no gun or anything to give her." His voice dropped apologetically. "I gave her the knife."

"The one she was killed with?"

"Yes. They showed it to me this morning. It was a little bolo knife that my father sent me from the South Pacific."

"She was carrying the knife?"

"Yessir, in her purse. She had a big purse. She put it in her purse when I gave it to her, before she went away from our house. If they caught her, she said she would leave her mark on them." A frown of grief knitted his eyebrows.

"Who was she afraid of?"

"Men following her. It started Thursday, when she came back on the bus from Arroyo Beach. She said

161

this man got off the bus and trailed her home. I thought at first she was spinning me a tale, trying to be mysterious. Then the next day I saw him myself when she came home from lunch. He was lurking around our street, and that night he came and visited her right in our house. I asked her about him yesterday, and she said that he was a crooked detective. That he was trying to make her do something against her will, but she wouldn't do it."

"Did she mention his name?"

"She said his name was Desmond, Julian Desmond. The next day another man was after her. I didn't see him. Lucy saw him, though. And there was the trouble at our house, and she moved out."

I swallowed the bitter taste of guilt in my mouth. "Was she planning to leave town?"

"She couldn't make up her mind before she left. She said she'd phone me. Then when she did phone, she was at the station. There was no train out for a couple of hours, and men there were spying on her. She said I should come with the car. I picked her up at the station and we got away from them, on the old airport road. We parked behind the airport fence, and we talked. She was shivering scared. Right there and then we decided to get married. I thought if we stayed together, I could defend her." His voice sank deep into his chest, almost out of hearing. "I didn't do so good."

"None of us did."

"She wanted to leave town right away. First we had to go back to the Mountview Motel to get her bags."

"Did she have her motel-key?"

"She said she lost it."

"Didn't give it to you?"

"Why would she give it to me? I couldn't go in there with her. Even if I was light enough to pass,

162

like her, I wouldn't do it. She went in there by herself. She never came out again. Somebody was waiting in there for her, and took the knife away from her and used it on her."

"Who was waiting?"

"Julian Desmond maybe. She wouldn't do what he wanted. Or the other one that was after her."

I was ashamed to tell him that I was the other one. His shoulders were slumped, and the flesh around his mouth hung almost stupidly. His moral strength was running out again. I placed Schwartz's chair for him and eased him into it:

"Sit down, Alex. You've covered the big points against you. There are a few little points left. Money is one of them. What were you intending to marry on?"

"I have some money of my own."

"How much?"

"Forty-five dollars. I made it picking tomatoes."

"Not much to get married on."

"I aimed to get a job. My back is strong." There was a sullen pride in his voice, but he wasn't meeting my eyes. "Lucy could work too. She worked as a nurse before."

"Where?"

"She didn't tell me where."

"She must have told you something."

"No sir. I never asked her."

"Did she have some money?"

"I didn't ask her. I wouldn't take money from a woman anyway."

"If you earned it, though," I said. "Didn't she say she'd cut you in if you got her safe out of town?"

"Cut me in?"

"On the reward," I said. "The Singleton reward."

His black gaze climbed slowly to the level of my

eyes, and quickly dropped. He said to the floor: "Lucy didn't have to pay me money to marry her."

"Where were you going to get married? Where were you going to drive to yesterday?"

"Las Vegas or someplace. It didn't matter. Anyplace."

"Arroyo Beach?"

He didn't answer. I had pushed him too fast and too far. Looking down at the locked round impenetrable skull, I understood Brake's routine and desperate anger after thirty years of trying to fit human truth into the square-cut legal patterns handed down for his use by legislators and judges. And thinking of Brake's anger, I lost my own.

"Listen, Alex. We're going back to the beginning again. Lucy was murdered. We both want to find the murderer and see him punished. You have more reason than I have to want that. You claim you were in love with her."

"I was!" The drill had struck the nerve.

"That's one reason, then. You have another reason: Unless we find the real killer, you'll be spending years of your life in jail."

"I don't care what happens to me now."

"Think about Lucy. When you were waiting for her at the motel, somebody took that knife and cut her throat with it. Why?"

"I don't know why."

"What did Julian Desmond want her to do?"

"Be a witness for him," he answered slowly.

"A witness to what?"

"I don't know what."

"A murder," I said. "Was it a murder?"

"Maybe. I don't know."

"It was a murder, wasn't it? He wanted her to help him collect the reward. But she thought she could go it alone, and get the reward money for herself. Isn't that the reason she was killed?"

"I didn't think it out, mister."

"But you knew about the reward money? You knew she hoped to collect it."

"I never hoped to share in it," he said doggedly.

"She went to Arroyo Beach on Thursday to see his mother, and lost her nerve at the last minute. Isn't that the truth?"

"Yes, sir. I gathered that."

"She was going to try again yesterday."

"Maybe she was. I had nothing to do with any murder. Lucy didn't either."

"But she knew what happened to Singleton."

"She knew something."

"And you know something, too."

"She let on about it to me. I didn't ask her. I didn't want to have any part of it. She told it to me anyway."

"What did she tell you, Alex?"

"A man shot him. A crazy man shot him and he died. She told me that."

CHAPTER 21

Schwartz was alone in the corridor. I asked him where Brake was.

"In his car. He got a radio call."

I started for the ambulance entrance, and met Brake coming in.

"Norris do any talking?"

"Plenty."

"Confess?"

"Hardly. He's ready to make a statement."

"When I'm ready. I got more important things right now. I'm going on a barbecue picnic in the mountains." He smiled grimly, and called along the corridor to Schwartz: "Take Norris back to his cell. Get Pearce in the D.A.'s office, if he wants to make a statement. I'll be back as soon as I can."

"Barbecue picnic?" I said.

"Yeah." He pushed out through the white metal-sheathed door and let it swing back in my face. I followed him out to his car and got in the right side as he got in the left.

"I thought you'd be interested, Archer." The car leaped forward under us, its tires whistling in the

166

gravel of the hospital parking lot. "It was a man that got himself barbecued. A man."

"Who is it?"

"Not identified yet. His car went over the side of Rancheria Canyon early this morning, and caught fire. When they found it they didn't even know there was a body in it at first. Couldn't get into it until they brought up a pump-truck from the ranger station. By that time the guy inside was nothing more than a clinker."

"Torch murder?"

"Hallman seems to think so. He's the CHP Captain. They had it tabbed as an accident until they thought to take a look at the gas tank. It's intact, and that means the gasoline for the fire came from somewhere else."

"What kind of car?"

"1948 Buick sedan. Registration destroyed. They're checking the license and engine number for ownership."

The last few jerry-built bungalows of the suburbs dropped behind. The speedometer needle moved steadily clockwise past fifty, sixty, and seventy, and hesitated near eighty. Brake flipped the siren switch. The siren began to moan in a low register.

I said before it drowned me out: "The car isn't two-tone green, is it? Singleton's car was a 1948 Buick. Is this one two-tone green?"

Brake pulled his hat off, leaving a red crimped line across his forehead, and tossed it into the back seat. "You've got Singleton on the brain. They didn't tell me the color. But where does he come in?"

"Norris said he was murdered," I shouted above the siren.

Brake switched it off. "What does Norris know about it?"

"Lucy Champion told him Singleton was shot."

167

"Only she don't make a very good witness. Don't let him string you, man. He'd tell you anything to wiggle his black neck out of the noose it's in."

The speedometer needle pushed on past eighty. At the top of a slight rise, the car lifted under us and almost took flight. I felt as if the speed had lifted us out of the world, pulled Brake loose from his roots in Bella City's broken pavements.

"Don't you think it's about time you admitted you made a mistake?"

He looked at me narrow-eyed. The speeding car wavered slightly with his attention before he turned back to the road. "When I got the weapon, his own knife?"

"She borrowed it from him for self-protection. She had it in her purse."

"Can he prove that?"

"He doesn't have to. You're the proof department."

"Hell, you're talking like a shyster lawyer. I hate those mealy-mouthed shysters that try to block the law."

"That's quite a mouthful."

"Chew on it."

The county blacktop we were on curved in to join a concrete highway running east and west across the valley. Brake went through a red sign and took the turn on squealing tires.

"What do I do when they go around cutting each other with knives, setting fire to each other? Pat them on the back and tell them to go to it? I say stop them, put them away."

"Put the right one away, though. You can't solve these killings separately, hang Lucy's on Alex and this new one on somebody else."

"I can if they're not connected."

"I think they are connected."

"Show me proof."

"I'm not going up for the fresh air."

The road had begun to climb through dried clay cutbanks marked with yellow Slide Area warnings. Even with the gas-pedal floorboarded under Brake's toe, the speedometer needle stuck at seventy like the hand of a stopped clock. The folded blue slopes of the eastern range were framed in steep perspective by the windshield. They looked near enough to touch. A minute later, a mile nearer, they looked just as far away. I began to feel the altitude in my ears. As we rose into new perspectives, a few small white clouds burst out like ripe cotton behind the peaks. Away behind and down, Bella City stood in its fields like carelessly grouped chesspieces on a dusty board.

Five miles farther on, a thousand feet higher, we came to a semicircular gravel turnout on the left side of the highway. Several cars, a tow-truck and a red pump-truck were parked in the turnout. A group of men stood at its outer edge, looking down. Brake pulled up behind a new Ford with Highway Patrol markings. An officer in olive-drab whipcord detached himself from the group and came toward us:

"Hello, Brake. I told the boys to leave everything the way it was down there after they put out the fire. We even took pictures for you."

"You people are learning. I'd paste a gold star on your forehead if I had one. Like you to meet Lew Archer here, the thinker. Captain Hallman."

The captain gave me a puzzled look and a hard hand. We moved to the low log fence that rimmed the edge of the turnout. Below it the canyon-side slanted down to a gravel creek-bed overgrown with live oaks. From our height the September creek looked like a winding pebble-path dotted with occasional mud-puddles. A toy automobile lying on its bank sent up tendrils of steam to vanish in the sun. It was a Buick, painted two shades of green.

A trail of broken bushes, some of them charred, showed where the Buick had left the road and rolled down into the gorge. Brake said to Hallman:

"Find anything on the road?"

"The tireprints on the shoulder. It wasn't rolling fast, and that's what made me suspicious in the first place. No skid marks. Somebody set fire to it and just took off the emergency and let her roll." Hallman added in dead earnest: "Whoever poured that gasoline and ignited it out here has got more than murder against him. It was just good luck it didn't start a forest fire. No wind."

"When did it happen?"

"Must have been before light this morning. The headlights were turned on. I didn't get a report until after eight o'clock. Then when I figured it for murder, I left the guy for you the way we found him."

"You still don't know who he is?"

"Wait until you see him. Like looking for a brand on a cooked hamburger. We should get a fast answer on the engine number, though."

"It's Singleton's car," I said to Brake.

"You might be right at that." He sighed. "Well, if I got to go down there, I got to go down."

"Feeling your age?" Hallman said. "You've packed a buck out of deeper holes than this. I'd go with you, but I been down twice already. I left a couple of the boys on guard."

I could see them sitting on a boulder behind the smashed car. In the telescopic air it was almost possible to read the conversation off their moving lips.

Brake stepped over the log barrier and started down. I followed him, using the zigzag trail he improvised and braking my descent by holding on to the branches of stunted trees. We were both breathing hard when we reached the bottom. The two highway patrolmen led us along the creekbed to the wreck.

It rested on its right side. The hood and top and radiator grille looked as if a sledgehammer crew had been working on them. All four tires had blown out. The left door was sprung.

"I'm afraid it isn't salvageable," one of the patrolmen said. "Even if there was any way of getting it out."

Brake turned on him savagely: "That's too bad. I was planning to take it for a spin."

He climbed onto the upper side of the car and wrenched the sprung door open as wide as it would go. I looked past him into the fire-gutted, water-soaked interior. Against the right front boor, which rested on the ground, a human shape lay curled with its face hidden.

Brake lowered himself through the opening. Supporting himself with one hand on the steering column, he reached for the black shape with his other hand. Most of the clothes had burned away, but there was still a belt around the middle. When Brake took hold of the belt and heaved, it snapped in his hand. He passed it up to me. The blackened silver buckle bore the initials C A S.

CHAPTER 22

I rang three times at long intervals. Sunday bells tolled antiphonally in the silences. Mrs. Benning finally came to the door. A bathrobe of rough brown wool was pulled high around her throat. He face was marked by sleep, as if she had been battling dreams all morning.

"You again."

"Me again. Is the doctor in?"

"He's at church." She tried to shut the door.

My foot prevented her. "That's fine. I want to talk to you."

"I'm not even dressed."

"You can dress later. There's been another killing. Another friend of yours."

"Another?" Her hand covered her mouth, as if I had slapped her.

I pushed into the hallway with her and closed the door. Sealed off from the noon glare and the slow Sunday noises, we stood close and looked into each other's faces. It seemed to me that we shared a twilight understanding. She turned away, her long back swaying from the waist. I kept my hands from reaching out to hold her still.

She spoke to the mirror: "Who was killed?"

"I think you know."

"My husband?" In the mirror, her face was mask-like.

"That depends on who you're married to."

"Sam?" She whirled, in a dancer's movement, ending plumb. "I don't believe it."

"It occurred to me as a possibility that you were married to Charles Singleton."

She laughed unexpectedly. It wasn't pleasant laughter, and I was glad when it broke off.

"I've never even heard of Singleton. Is that the name—Singleton? I've been married to Sam Benning for over eight years."

"That wouldn't prevent you from knowing Singleton, knowing him intimately. I have evidence that you did. He was murdered this morning."

She recoiled from me, breathing hard. Between breaths, she said: "How was he killed?"

"Somebody hit him with a hammer or some other heavy weapon. It made an inch-deep dent in his skull, but it didn't kill him. Then he was driven up into the mountains in his own car, soaked with gasoline, and set fire to. The car was pushed over a three-hundred-foot bank and left to burn, with Singleton inside it."

"How do you know it was his car?"

"It's a 1948 Buick two-door with a dark green body and a light green top."

"You're sure it was him inside?"

"He's been identified. Most of his clothes were burned off him, but his belt-buckle has his initials engraved on it. Why don't you come down to the morgue and make a formal identification?"

"I told you I don't even know him."

"You're showing a lot of interest in a stranger."

"Naturally, when you come here and practically accuse me of murdering him. When did all this happen, anyway?"

"Before dawn this morning."

"I've been in bed all night and all morning. I took a couple of nembutals, and I'm still groggy. Why come to me?"

"Lucy Champion and Charles Singleton were both friends of yours. Weren't they, Bess?"

"They were not." She caught herself. "Why did you call me Bess? My name is Elizabeth."

"Horace Wilding calls you Bess."

"I never heard of him, either."

"He lives on the Sky Route near Singleton's studio. He says Singleton introduced him to you in 1943."

"Wilding is a liar, he always has been a liar." She caught her lower lip in white teeth and bit it hard.

"You said you didn't know him."

"You're doing the talking. Talk yourself to death."

"Is that what Lucy did?"

"I don't know what Lucy did."

"She was a friend of yours. She came here to this office to see you."

"Lucy Champion was my husband's patient," she said flatly. "I told you that last night."

"You were lying. This morning your husband lied to cover you. He went into an explanation of why he had no records on her, and then he had to explain what he was treating her for. Any real disease would show up in an autopsy, and he knew that. So he had to make her a hypochondriac, a patient whose sickness was caused by fear. There's no post-mortem test for a phobia."

"She was a hypochondriac. Sam told me she was."

"I never knew a hypochondriac who didn't take his

174

temperature once a day at least. Lucy hadn't touched her thermometer in two weeks."

"Wouldn't that sound good in court, though, against the word of a professional man and his wife?"

"It's good enough for me. And this is as close to court as you want to get."

"I see. You're judge and jury and everything else. Those are a lot of things for one little man to be."

"Don't stretch my patience. If I get tired of this, what happens to you? See what kind of a judge you draw downtown. I'm giving you a chance to talk before I hand my evidence to the cops."

"Why?" Deliberately, she made me conscious of her body. She turned slightly and raised one hand to her head so that one of her breasts was lifted asymmetrically under the wool. The wide sleeve fell away from her round white forearm, and her white face dreamed upward. "Why go to all that trouble for poor little me? Poor little old incendiary me?"

"It's no trouble at all," I said.

She laid a cool hand on my cheek and let it trail onto my shoulder before she withdrew it. "Come out to the kitchen. I was making coffee. We can talk there."

I followed her, not certain which of us was doing what the other wanted him to do. The kitchen was large and poorly lit by a window over the sink. The sink was piled with dishes. I sat down at a chipped enamel table and watched her pour two cups of coffee from an automatic glass maker. When she had finished pouring, I pushed my full cup across the table to her and took hers.

"You don't trust me as far as you can see me, Mr. Man. What did you say your name was?"

"Archer. I'm the last of my branch of the Archer family. I'd hate to see it die out suddenly by poison."

"No children? Wife?"

"None of those things. Are you interested?"

"I could be." She pushed out her lips, which were fleshy and well-molded. "It happens I'm already fixed up with a very satisfactory—husband."

"You find him satisfactory?"

Her eyes, which had not gone soft with the rest of her face, narrowed to cool blue slits. "Leave him out of it."

"Because you've been playing him for a sucker?"

"I said leave him out of it. Unless you want hot coffee in the face." She reached for her cup.

"What about hot gasoline?"

Her cup rattled on the table, slopping some of its contents over the rim. "Do I look like a murderer to you?"

"I've seen some fine-looking ones. You can't deny that you're a hard girl."

"I came out of a hard school," she said. "Do you know the mill section of Gary, Indiana?"

"I've passed through."

"I graduated from it with honors." A queer pride glinted in her smile. "That doesn't make me a criminal, though. I might have turned into one if Sam hadn't taken me out of it. I was on probation when he married me."

"What for?"

"Nothing much. I guess I was what you call a juvenile delinquent. I didn't feel like one. My old man was a hunkie, see, a real old-country hunkie. He had the grand old hunkie idea of tying one on and beating the womenfolk every Saturday night. I got tired of hiding under the bed, so I went out on my own. Out into the great world, ha. I waited table for a while and then I made a connection. My connection gave me a hat-check concession in one of the east side clubs. It wasn't much of a joint but by the time I was sixteen I was making more in tips than my old

176

man ever made sweating it out in the mills. Only my luck went sour. There was gambling in the place I worked, somebody fluffed the protection, and I got picked up in a raid. I copped a plea and they put me on probation. The sourpuss judge set it up so I couldn't work in the clubs any more. That wasn't the worst of it. I had to go home and live with the family."

The dreams she had been battling in her sleep were taking over her waking mind. I didn't say a word.

"Naturally I took the first chance I had to get out of that stinking flat with the arguments. The social workers were snooping on me, making me stay in nights where the old man could get at me. Sam saved my life. He picked me up in a movie one day. I thought he was a wolf at first, but he was innocent. It was really funny to see a doctor so innocent. Sam was a Navy medico then, stationed at Great Lakes. He was the first man that wanted to marry me, and I took him up on it. He had his orders to California and he was leaving the next week. We came out here together."

"Did he know what he was getting?"

"He could see me," she said levelly. "I admit I didn't tell him I was jumping probation. But let's get one thing straight about Sam and me, before we drop the subject. I was the one that was doing him the favor. I always have been."

Looking at her and thinking of her husband, I believed her. "It's a pretty colorful background for a small-town doctor's wife. And I don't imagine you've told me the half of it."

"I don't imagine I have. More coffee?"

"More information. When did you and Benning come out here?"

"The spring of 1943. They gave him duty at Port Hueneme because it was near his home here. We

177

rented a cottage in Arroyo Beach for six months. Then he was shipped out. The next two years he was at sea, medical officer on a big transport. I saw him a few times when it came into San Francisco."

"Who else were you seeing?"

"That's a hell of a question."

"A hell of an answer. Why did you leave Benning two years ago?"

"You've really been snooping, eh? I had my private reasons."

"You ran away with Singleton, didn't you?"

She had started to rise from the table, and froze for an instant, leaning on it, with her face averted. "Why don't you mind your own business?"

"Singleton was incinerated this morning. I've made it my business to find out who struck the match. It's a queer thing you're not interested."

"Is it?"

She poured herself another cup of coffee, with steady hands. Somewhere in the Chicago wilderness, or beating around the country in wartime and peacetime, she had gathered strength and learned balance. I looked at her firm white legs. She caught my look and returned it in a slow curve. To a window-peeper it would have seemed like a pleasant domestic scene on a Sunday morning. I almost wished it was.

I got up and looked out of the window. The backyard was overgrown with brown weeds and cluttered with the detritus of years. At its rear a small ramshackle barn sagged in the shade of a pepper tree.

She came up behind me. I felt her breath on my neck. Her body touched my back:

"You don't want to make trouble for me, Archer. I've had plenty of trouble. I could use a little peace in my old age."

178

I turned, softly ambushed by her hips. "How old are you?"

"Twenty-five. Church lasts a long time in these parts. He usually stays for Sunday school, too."

I took her head in my hands. Her breasts were full and strong between us. Her hands moved on my back. I was looking at the part-line that ran white through her dull black hair. Where the part divided it there were narrow vestiges of blondeness at the roots.

"I've never trusted blondes, Bess."

"I'm a natural brunette," she said thickly.

"You're a natural liar, anyway."

"Maybe I am," she said in a different voice. "I feel like nothing at all. This business has torn me in half, if you want the truth. I'm only trying to hold myself together and stay on this side of the walls."

"And keep your friends out of trouble."

"I have no friends."

"What about Una Durano?"

Her face went stupid, with ignorance or surprise.

"She bought you a hat last spring. I think you know her well."

Her mouth twisted in a grimace which threatened to turn to crying. She was silent.

"Who killed Singleton?"

She wagged her head from side to side. The short black hair fell over her face. Her face was gray and wretched. I felt ashamed of what I was doing to her, and went on doing it:

"You were with Singleton when he left Arroyo Beach. Was it a snatch? Did you finger him for a mob, and then have to kill him? Did you have to kill him because Lucy got big ideas? Did Lucy dream a five-grand dream and have to die before it came true?"

"You've got it all wrong. I didn't finger Charlie Singleton. I wouldn't do anything to hurt him, or

179

Lucy either. She was a friend of mine, like you said."

"Go on."

"I can't," she said. "I'm not a squealer. I can't."

"Come down to the morgue and have a look at Charlie. You'll talk then."

"No." The word was like a retching in her insides. "Lay off me a little. Promise to lay off me, and I'll tell you something you don't know. Something important."

"How important?"

"Will you lay off me? I swear I'm absolutely clean."

"Let's have the one big fact."

Her head was down, but her slant blue gaze was on my face. "It isn't Charlie Singleton in the morgue."

"Who is it?"

"I don't know."

"Where is Singleton?"

"I can't answer any more questions. You promised you'd let me alone."

"How do you know it isn't Singleton?"

"That wasn't in the bargain," she said faintly. Behind fluttering eyelids, her blue gaze jumped like an unsteady gas flame.

"I'll put it as a hypothetical question. You know it wasn't Singleton this morning, because he was killed two weeks ago. He was shot, and you saw it happen. Yes or no?"

She didn't answer at all. Instead she fell forward against me, heavily. Her breath came fast as a small animal's. I had to hold her up.

CHAPTER 23

A high-pitched voice flicked at my back: "Take your hands off my wife."

Dr. Benning was standing just inside the kitchen door, with one hand on the knob. A black leather Bible was under his arm and his hat was on his head. I moved between him and his wife. "I was waiting to see you, doctor."

"Filth," he cried. "Ordure. I come home from the House of God—" The trembling of his mouth ruined the sentence.

"Nothing happened," the woman said behind me.

Benning had the eyes of a pole-axed steer. His hand on the doorknob and his shoulder against the jamb were supporting his weight. His body vibrated grossly like a tuning fork: "You're lying to me, both of you. You had your hands on her. Carnal knowledge—" The words knotted in his throat and almost choked him. "Like dogs. Like two dogs in the kitchen of my home."

"That's enough." The woman stepped around me. "I've heard enough from you, after I told you nothing happened. What would you do if it had?"

181

He answered disconnectedly: "I gave you a helping hand. I lifted you out of the gutter. You owe everything to me." The shock had sprung a booby-trap of clichés in his head.

"Good gray doctor Good-Samaritan! What would you do if anything had happened?"

He choked out: "A man can take so much from a woman. I have a gun in my desk—"

"So you'll shoot me down like the dog I am, eh?" She planted herself firmly on braced legs. Leaning towards him in a fishwife attitude, her body seemed to be reveling in its power, drawing terrific energy from his weakness.

"I'll kill myself," he cried on a high note.

A few tears squeezed from his eyes and ran down into the failure marks that dragged from the wings of his nose. He was the suicidal man who never quite nerved himself to suicide. I realized suddenly why his description of Lucy's fears had sounded so convincing. They were his own.

His wife said: "Go ahead. Don't let me stop you. Maybe that isn't such a bad idea." She moved in on him with her hands on her hips, flailing him with words.

He cringed away from her with one hand stretched towards her, asking for mercy. His hat caught on the end of a towelrack and fell to the floor. He looked as if he were disintegrating.

"Don't, Bess," he said so rapidly that I could barely catch the words. "I didn't mean it. I love you. You're all I've got."

"Since when have you got me?"

He turned to the wall, stood with his face against the rough plaster, his shoulders heaving. His Bible dropped to the floor.

I took her by the elbows from behind: "Leave him alone."

"Why should I?"

"I hate to see any man broken down by any woman."

"You can leave."

"You're the one that's leaving."

"Who do you think you're talking to?" She was still showing fire, but it was warmed-over fire.

"Singleton's girl friend," I said into her ear. "Now get out of here. I want to ask your husband a couple of questions."

I pushed her through the doorway and closed it after her. She didn't try to come back into the kitchen, but I could feel her presence behind the door.

"Dr. Benning."

He was quieting down. After a while he turned to face me. In spite of his baldness, his middle age, his beaten air, he looked like a heartbroken adolescent in disguise.

"She's all I've got," he said. "Don't take her away from me." He was slipping rung by rung into a hell of self-abasement.

I lost patience: "I wouldn't take her as a gift. Now if you can concentrate for a minute, where was your wife between five and six yesterday afternoon?"

"Right here, with me." A grief-stricken hiccup made a cæsura between the phrases.

"Where was she between twelve last night and eight this morning?"

"In bed, of course."

"Will you swear to it, on the Bible?"

"Yes, I will." He picked up the Bible and held it with his right hand flat on the cover: "I swear that my wife Elizabeth Benning was in this house with me yesterday afternoon between five and six and all last night from midnight until morning. Does that satisfy you?"

"Yes. Thank you." I wasn't satisfied, but this was

183

the best I could hope for until I found more evidence.

"Is that all?" He sounded disappointed. I wondered if he was afraid to be left alone in the house with her.

"Not quite. You had a servant until yesterday. Florie?"

"Florida Gutierrez, yes. My wife discharged her for incompetence."

"Do you know her address?"

"Of course. She'd been in my employ for nearly a year. 437 East Hidalgo Street, Apartment F."

Mrs. Benning was standing outside the door. She flattened herself against the wall to let me go by. Neither of us spoke.

The long one-storied frame building stood at right angles to Hidalgo Street, facing a littered alley. Across the alley, a high wire fence surrounded a yard of piled lumber. I could smell cut white pine when I got out of my car.

At the head of the roofed gallery that ran along the building, a very fat Mexican was propped in a chair against the wall. He had on a bright-green rayon shirt that showed every fold of his stomach and chest.

I said: "Good morning."

"Good afternoon, I think."

He removed a brown cigarette from his mouth and shifted his weight, bringing his slippered feet onto the floor. There was a grease-spot on the wall where his iron-gray head had rested. The open door beside him was lettered amateurishly with a large red A.

"Good afternoon then. Where is Apartment F?"

"Second last door." He gestured with his cigarette towards the rear, where a few dark men and women in their Sunday clothes were sitting in the shadow of the gallery, watching the lumberyard. "Florida ain't here, if it's her you're looking for."

184

"Florida Gutierrez?"

"Gutierrez." He repronounced the name for me, with the accent on the second syllable. "She went away."

"Where to?"

"How do I know where to? She told me she was going to live with her sister in Salinas." His brown eyes were gently cynical.

"When did she go?"

"Last night, about ten o'clock. She was five weeks behind in her rent. She came in with a handful of bills and said: 'How much do I owe? I am moving out, to live with my sister in Salinas.' I saw the man waiting outside in the big automobile and I said: 'Florida, your sister has changed in appearance.' She said: 'He is my brother-in-law.' And I said: 'You're a lucky young woman, Florida. Ready to join the starvation army this morning, and tonight driving off with your brother-in-law in a Buick automobile.'" He set the cigarette between his smiling white teeth and blew a plume of smoke.

"Did you say Buick?"

"A fine big Buick," he said, "with holes in the side. And a foolish girl riding away in it, with holes in her head. What could I do?" He spread his hands in cheerful resignation. "She is not a member of the Martinez family. *Gracias á Dios*," he added under his breath.

"Did you notice the color of the car?"

"I couldn't tell for sure. It was dark night. Blue or green, I would say."

"And the man?"

He studied me with noncommittal eyes. "Florida is in trouble? You are from the police?"

I showed him my photostat and listened to him spell it out. "I thought it was trouble," he said quietly.

"Was the man young and good-looking?"

"He was a man of middle age. He didn't leave the automobile, even when Florida carried out her bags. No manners! I didn't like his looks."

"Can you describe him?"

"I didn't see him too well."

"I have a man in mind," I said. "Short brown hair, fattish, shifty-looking, wino eyes, panama hat, light tan jacket. Calls himself Julian Desmond."

He snapped his fingers. "That is the man. Florida called him Julian. Is he truly her brother-in-law?"

"No. You were right about him. I guess you know this town pretty well, Mr. Martinez."

The suggestion seemed to exhilarate him. "For sixty-three years! My father was born here."

"Here's a question you should be able to answer. If you were Julian, and you wanted to take Florida to a hotel for the night, which one would you go to?"

"Any of them in the lower town, I guess."

"Name the most likely ones, will you?" I took out my notebook.

He regarded it unhappily, disturbed by the notion of having anything he said committed to writing. "This trouble, is it serious?"

"Not for her. She's needed as a witness."

"A witness? Is that all? What kind of a witness?"

"The Buick she left in was involved in an accident this morning. I'm trying to identify the driver."

The old man sighed with relief. "I will be glad to help."

When I left him, I had the addresses of several hotels: the Rancheria, the Bella, the Oklahoma, the California, the Great West, the Pacific, and the Riviera. I was lucky on my third try, which happened to be the Great West.

CHAPTER 24

It was an old railroad hotel on Main Street between the tracks and the highway. Its narrow-
windowed brick face was lugubrious, as if the big
trucks going by for years had broken its steam-age
spirit. There were battered brass spittoons on the floor
of the lobby, old Union Pacific photogravures on the
walls. Four men were playing contract at a card table
near the front window. They had the still faces and
satisfied hands of veteran railroaders growing old on
schedule.

The clerk was a skinny old man in a green eyeshade and a black alpaca coat. Yes, Mr. and Mrs.
Desmond were registered: 310, on the third floor. No
phone, I could just go up. The bell-hop was off on
Sundays, he added whiningly.

I started for the elevator. The clerk called me back:
"Wait a minute, young fellow, since you're going up
anyways. This wire came in for Mr. Desmond this
morning. I didn't like to disturb him." The eyeshade
suffused his face with a green cadaverous flush.

I took the sealed yellow envelope. "I'll give it to
Mr. Desmond."

"The elevator isn't working," he whined. "You'll have to use the stairs."

The second floor was hotter than the first. The third floor was stifling. At the end of a windowless corridor lit by twenty-watt bulbs I found the door I was looking for. A cardboard DO NOT DISTURB sign dangled from the knob.

I knocked. Bedsprings groaned. A woman called out drowsily: "Who is it? Julian?"

I said: "Florie?"

Unsteady footsteps approached the door. She fumbled at the lock. "Just a minute. I'm blind this morning."

I slipped the telegram into the breast pocket of my jacket. The door opened inward and I went in with it. Florie looked at me dumbly for five or six long seconds. Her black hair was matted and frizzled. Her eyes hung heavy and dark under heavy lids. In the frightened attitude her body had assumed, her hips and breasts seemed strangely irrelevant. The rouge-stained mouth in her sallow face was like a wilted red rose stuck in plasticine.

She made an erratic rush for the bed, and covered herself with a sheet. Her mouth fell open. I could see her pale lower gums. She brought it closed with an effort. "What do you want?"

"Not you, Florie. Don't be scared."

The air in the room was stale, spiked with cheap alcohol and perfume. A half-empty half-gallon jug of muscatel stood on the floor by her bed. Her clothes were scattered on the floor and chair and dresser. I guessed she had taken them off in a staggering fury before she passed out.

"Who are you? Did Julian send you?"

"I was hired by the hotel association to check on false registrations." I didn't mention that my work in that field had ended ten years ago.

188

She chattered over the taut edge of the sheet: "I didn't register. He did. It was all his fault. Besides, we didn't do nothing. He brought me up here last night and parked me with a jar of muscadoodle. Then he went away and I haven't seen him since. I waited up for him half the night. He never did come back. So how do you have anything on me?"

"I'll make a bargain with you. No charges if you co-operate."

Suspicion darkened her face. "How do you mean, co-operate?" Her body wriggled uneasily under the sheet.

"Just answer my questions. Desmond's the one I want. It looks as if he ran out on you."

"What time is it?"

"One thirty."

"Sunday afternoon?"

"Uh-huh."

"He did run out! He promised to take me on a trip." She sat up on the bed, holding the sheet across her excessive bosom.

"How did you meet him?"

"I didn't meet him. He come to the office one night last week, Thursday night it was. I was just finishing up my cleaning. The doctor was out already, over at the library or someplace, and I was all alone in the office."

"Where was Mrs. Benning?"

"She was upstairs, I guess. Yeah, she was upstairs with that colored girl friend of hers."

"Lucy Champion?"

"That's the one. Some people have funny friends. This Lucy woman come to visit her and they went upstairs to talk. Julian Desmond said it was me he wanted to see. He fed me a line how he was recruiting nurse's aides for Hawaii at four hundred dollars a month! I was a sucker, I guess. I let him pump me

189

about who I worked for and he took me out that night and got me plastered and asked me a bunch of questions about Mrs. Benning and that Lucy. I told him I didn't know Lucy from a hole in the ground, or Mrs. Benning either for that matter. He wanted to know when she came back to her husband, and if her hair was dyed and if they were really married, stuff like that."

"What did you tell him?"

"I told him how she came back over the weekend, two weeks ago it was. When I walked in on Monday morning there she was. Doctor says: 'Meet my wife. She's been in a sanitarium.' She didn't look like san stuff to me—" Florie broke off suddenly. Her mouth clamped shut. "That was all I said. I caught on what he was up to, and you don't catch me playing blackmailers' games."

"I can see that. What else was there to tell?"

"Nothing else, not a thing. I don't know nothing about Mrs. Benning. She's a mystery woman to me."

I changed the direction of my approach: "Why did she fire you last night?"

"She didn't fire me."

"Why did you leave?"

"I didn't want to work for her any more."

"You worked for her yesterday, though."

"Yeah, sure, that was before she fired—I mean I left."

"Were you in the house all Saturday afternoon?"

"I was until six. I get off at six unless there's extra cleaning. I mean I did."

"Was Mrs. Benning there all afternoon?"

"Most of it. She went out in the late afternoon, said she was going to shop for Sunday."

"What time did she go out?"

"Around five, a little before five."

"What time did she come back?"

190

"I left before she came back."

"And the doctor?"

"He was there, far as I know."

"He didn't go out with her?"

"No, he said he was going to take a siesta."

"When did you see her after that?"

"I didn't."

"You saw her in Tom's Café around eight."

"Yeah. Yeah, I forgot about that." Florie was getting rattled.

"Did she give you money?"

She hesitated. "No." But she had to turn and look at the red plastic purse on the dresser.

"Why did she give you money?"

"She didn't."

"How much money?"

"Just my back pay," she stammered. "They owed me back pay."

"How much back pay?"

"Three hundred dollars."

"That's a lot of back pay. Isn't it?"

She lifted her heavy gaze to the ceiling and brought it down again to the red purse on the dresser. She watched the purse intently, as if it was alive and struggling to take flight. "It was a bonus." She had found a word. "She gave me a bonus."

"What for? She didn't like you."

"*You* don't like me anyway," she said in a childish voice. "I didn't do anything bad. I don't see how you have to jump on me."

"I like you fine," I lied. "Only it happens I'm trying to solve some murders. You're an important witness."

"Me?"

"You. What did she pay you to keep quiet about?"

"If I'm a witness, do I have to give the money back? The bonus?"

"Not if you keep your mouth shut about it."

191

"You won't tell?"

"I couldn't be bothered. What did she buy from you, Florie?"

I waited, listening to her breathing.

"It was the blood," she said. "I found some dried drops of blood on the floor of the examination room. I cleaned it up."

"When?"

"Monday two weeks ago, the first day I saw Mrs. Benning. I asked doctor about the blood and he said he had an emergency over the weekend—a tourist that cut his finger. I didn't think of it again until Mrs. Benning brought it up last night."

"Like the woman who urged her children not to put peas in their noses."

"Who was she?" Florie asked almost brightly.

"It's a story. The point is that the children put peas in their noses as soon as she turned her back. I'll bet a nickel you told Desmond about the blood the minute Mrs. Benning turned hers."

"I did not," she said, with that peculiar whining intonation which means guilty as charged but I can't help it if people are always leading me astray.

She introduced a diversion:

"Anyway, his name isn't Desmond. It's Heist or something like that. I caught a glimpse of his driver's license."

"When?"

"Last night in the car."

"The Buick?"

"Yeah. Personally I think he stole it. I had nothing to do with it. He already had it when he came to move me out of the apartment. He tried to tell me he *found* it, can you imagine. He said it was worth five thousand, probably more. I told him that was a lot of money for a secondhand Buick, but he just laughed."

"Was it a green 1948 two-door sedan?"

"I don't know the years. It was a two-door Buick, and that was the color. He stole it, didn't he?"

"I think he found it all right. Did he say where?"

"No. It must have been in town, though. He had no car at suppertime and then at ten o'clock when he picked me up at the apartment, he was driving this Buick. Where would a guy find a Buick?"

"It's a good question. Put on your clothes, Florie. I'll look away."

"You're not going to arrest me? I didn't do nothing wrong—anything wrong."

"I want you to try to identify somebody, that's all."

"Who?"

"That's another good question."

I went to the window and tried to open it. I could hardly breathe the hot foul air sealed in the little room. The window rose four inches and stuck forever. It faced north towards the City Hall and the Mission Hotel. In the sun-stopped streets a few pedestrians trudged, a few cars crawled and snored. Behind me I heard the twang of a snagged comb, Florie's quiet swearing, the pull and snap of a girdle, the slither of silk stockings, heels on the floor, water running in the sink.

At the rear of a bus depot below the window, a dusty blue bus was loading passengers: a pregnant Mexican woman herding half-naked brown children, a fieldworker in overalls who might have been the father of the children, an old man with a cane casting a tripod shadow on the asphalt, two young soldiers looking bored with any possible journey through any valley under any sky. The line moved forward slowly like a colored snake drunk with sun.

"Ready," Florie said.

She had on a bright red jacket over the batiste blouse. Her hair was combed back from her face, which looked harder under a white and red cosmetic

193

mask. She peered at me anxiously, clutching the red plastic purse.

"Where are we going?"

"To the hospital."

"Is he in the hospital?"

"We'll see."

I carried her cardboard suitcase down to the lobby. Heiss had paid for the room in advance. The aged clerk didn't ask me about the telegram. The contract players followed our progress across the lobby to the street with knowing looks.

In my car, Florie relaxed into hangover somnolence. I drove across town to the county hospital. Obscured by the dust and insect splashes on the windshield, wavering in the heat, the streets and buildings were like an image of a city refracted through Florie's mind. The asphalt was soft as flesh under the wheels.

It was cold enough in the morgue.

CHAPTER 25

She came out shivering, holding the red purse against her breast like an external heart that wouldn't hold still. I supported her elbow. At the ambulance door she pulled away from me and went out by herself to the car. She stumbled on high heels across the gravel, dazed by too much light.

When I got in behind the wheel she looked at me with horror as if my face had been scorched, and slid far over against the opposite door. Her eyes were like large marbles made of black glass.

I took the yellow Western Union envelope out of my inside pocket: Mr. Julian Desmond, c/o Great West Hotel, Bella City, California. As long as Heiss was alive, it was a crime to open it. Since he was dead, it was legitimate evidence.

It contained a night letter sent from Detroit by someone who signed himself "Van":

ONCEOVER LIGHTLY DURANOS AIRMAIL REPORT FOLLOWS. LEO ARRESTED FELONIOUS ASSAULT 1925 AGE TWENTY SERVED SIX ARRESTED 1927 KIDNAPPING NO CASE ALLEGED MEMBER OR PROTECTEE PURPLE GANG

195

ARRESTED 1930 SUSPICION MURDER NOLLE PROSSED
NO WITNESSES 1932 MURDER AIRTIGHT ALIBI AC-
QUITTED. BREAKUP PURPLE GANG LEO TO CHICAGO
RAN GOON SQUAD THREE-FOUR YEARS THEN SYN-
DICATE TIEUP LEGIT FRONT HATCHECK CONCESSIONS.
ARRESTED CONTRIBUTING DELINQUENCY MINOR EARLY
1942 COMMITTED STATE HOSPITAL DIAGNOSIS UN-
KNOWN RELEASED OCTOBER 1942 GUARDIANSHIP SIS-
TER UNA PUBLIC STENOGRAPHER AND BOOKKEEPER.
ENFORCER FOR NUMBERS RING ATTEMPTING TAKE
OVER ROUGE AND WILLOW RUN PLANTS BROKEN UP
1943. 1944 LEO AND UNA ORGANIZED DETROIT-BASED
NUMBERS RING STILL GOING GOOD PROTECTION ESTI-
MATED WEEKLY NET TWO TO THREE GEES. LEO AND
UNA NOT SEEN MICHIGAN SINCE JANUARY YPSILANTI
HOUSE CLOSED BANKS BEING RUN BY WILLIAM
GARIBALDI ALIAS GARBOLD OLDTIME PURPLE ALUM-
NUS. NO RECORD ELIZABETH BENNING LEO LIVING
WITH BESS WIONOWSKI PRIOR DEPARTURE MICHIGAN.
DO I DIG DEEPER.

"I should go some place and lie down," Florie said
in a small voice. "You didn't tell me he was dead. You
didn't tell me they blowtorched him. A shock like that
is enough to kill a girl."

I put the telegram away. "I'm sorry. I didn't know
who it was until you identified him. What makes you
so positive?"

"I worked for a dentist one time. I notice teeth.
Julian had bad teeth. I could tell it was him by the
fillings." She covered her glassy black eyes with her
hand. "Won't you take me where I can lie down?"

"First the police."

Brake was sitting at his desk with a deeply bitten
sandwich in his hand. The bite he had taken was
pouched in his cheek, rolling rhythmically with his
chewing. He said around it:

"The wife put up enough sandwiches to feed an army before I remembered to call off the picnic. I told her to bring some down here, save me lunch money. Lunch money mounts up."

"Even with all this overtime?"

"I'm saving the overtime to buy a yacht." Brake knew I knew that no cop ever was paid for overtime.

"Miss Gutierrez here has just made a positive identification on your torch victim." I turned to her. "This is Lieutenant Brake."

Florie, who had been hanging back in the doorway, took a timid step forward. "Pleased to meet you. Mr. Archer convinced me to do my duty."

"Good for him." Brake popped the remnant of his sandwich into his mouth. Whatever was about to happen or be said, he would have finished his sandwich. "Does she know Singleton?"

"No. It isn't Singleton."

"The hell it isn't. The license was issued to Singleton, and the engine-number checks." He tapped a yellow teletype flimsy on top of the pile in his "In" basket.

"It's Singleton's car but not his body in it. The body belongs to Maxfield Heiss. He was a Los Angeles detective. Florie knew him well."

"I didn't know him so well. He made advances to me, trying to pump me about my bosses."

"Come inside, Miss Gutierrez, and shut the door behind you. Now tell me, who are your bosses?"

"Dr. and Mrs. Benning," I said.

"Let her do her own talking. What was he trying to find out about them, Miss Gutierrez?"

"When Mrs. Benning came back and if she dyed her hair and all like that."

"Anything about murder?"

"No, sir. Julian didn't say nothing about a murder."

"Julian who?"

"Heiss was using an alias," I said. "We should get over to Benning's."

I turned to the door. There was a cork bulletin board beside it, with a number of frayed Wanted circulars thumbtacked to it. I wondered how Mrs. Benning would look in that crude black-and-white.

Brake said: "Can you swear to the identification, Miss Gutierrez?"

"I guess, if you insist."

"What do you mean, you guess?"

"I never like to swear, it ain't ladylike."

Brake snorted and stood up and left me standing in the room with Florie. He returned with a uniformed police-woman, white-haired and granite-eyed:

"Mrs. Simpson will stay here with you, Miss Gutierrez, until I get back. You're not in custody, understand."

Brake and I climbed the ramp to the parking lot.

"We'll take my car. There's something I want you to read." I handed him the night letter from Detroit.

"I hope it makes more sense than that little dame. She's a moron."

"She can see and remember."

He grunted as he climbed into the car. "What did she see?"

"Blood. Dried blood on the floor of Benning's examination room. It was her job to clean it."

"When? Yesterday?"

"Two weeks ago. The Monday after the weekend that Singleton was shot."

"You definitely think he was shot?"

"Read the telegram. See what it means to you." I started the car, and turned on a crosstown street in the direction of Benning's house.

Brake looked up from the yellow paper. "It don't mean a great deal to me. It's mostly a rap sheet on a mobster I never heard of. Who is this Durano?"

"A Michigan numbers racketeer. He's in California now. His sister Una is the one who hired me in the first place."

"Why?"

"I think her brother shot Singleton. Lucy was a witness, and Una Durano was trying to find her and silence her."

"Where is he now?"

"I wouldn't know." But the blasted man with the toy gun was vivid behind my eyes.

"Funny you didn't pass on this stuff to me."

I said, a little disingenuously: "I couldn't tell you what I didn't know. I just got hold of the telegram, at the hotel where Heiss was staying."

"You're building a pretty big story out of a little bit of a telegram. And it ain't even evidence, unless you have your mitts on the guy that sent it. Who's this Van?"

"Sounds like an undercover man for a Detroit agency."

"Agency work costs money. Was Heiss a bigtimer?"

"Hardly, but he kept hoping. He thought he saw big money in this case, starting with the Singleton reward."

"What was he doing with Singleton's car?"

"He told Florie he found it. It was evidence, to help him collect the reward. Before that he tried to get Lucy to be a witness for him. But the Singleton reward was only a beginning for him. He had bigger money on his mind."

"Blackmail? From Durano?"

"It's possible."

"So you think those mobsters torched him."

"That's possible, too."

We had reached Benning's block. I parked in front of the barber shop beside his house. Brake made no move to get out of the car. "Do you know any of these things that you say are possible?"

"I don't know anything for sure. It's a peculiarity of this case. We've got damn little physical evidence and damn few honest witnesses. There's no single detail strong enough to hang your hat on. But I have got a *Gestalt* on the whole picture."

"A what?"

"Call it a hunch, about how the case hangs together. There are a lot of people in it, so it can't be simple. Even with two people, actions are never simple."

"Cut the philosophy. Come down to cases again. If these are gang killings, what are we doing here? Mrs. Benning doesn't come into it at all."

"Mrs. Benning is the central figure in the picture," I said. "She had three men on the string: Durano, Singleton, Benning. Durano shot Singleton over her. She couldn't face an investigation so she skipped out and came back to Benning for help."

"What did she do with Singleton?"

"We better ask her."

CHAPTER 26

Blinded and gray-sided, Benning's house seemed to exhale its own shabby twilight. The doctor was pale and blinking like a twilight creature when he came to the door:

"Good afternoon, lieutenant."

He looked at me without speaking. Brake flashed his buzzer to indicate this wasn't a social call. Benning backed up abruptly, reaching for his hat on the hall rack and setting it on his head.

"You going somewhere, doctor?"

"Why no, I wasn't. I often wear a hat in the house." He gave Brake a sheepish smile.

The hallway was dim and chilly. An odor of rotting wood, which I hadn't noticed before, underlay the other odors. Men with a sense of failure like Benning had a knack of choosing the right environment for failure, or creating it around them. I listened for the sound of the woman in the house. There was no sound except the drip of a tap somewhere like a slow internal hemorrhage.

Brake said in formal tones: "I want to see the lady known as Mrs. Benning."

"Do you mean my wife?"

"I do."

"Then why not say so?" Benning spoke with acerbity. He was pulling himself together under the hat.

"Is she here?"

"Not at the moment, no." Biting at the inside of his long upper lip, the doctor resembled a worried camel chewing a bitter cud. "Before I answer any questions, no matter how charmingly phrased, I'd like to know if you're here in an official capacity. Or do you simply derive a puerile pleasure from displaying your badge?"

Brake turned dull red. "There's no pleasure in it, doctor. I got two murders on the book, another one floating."

Benning swallowed several times, his adam's-apple bobbing like a distorted yo-yo in his throat. "You're not seriously suggesting that there's any connection." The words fell into a silence that seemed to disturb him. He filled it by adding: "Between my wife and these murders?"

"I'm asking for your co-operation, doctor. You gave it to me this morning. I can't keep down crime without the co-operation of the citizenry."

The two men faced each other in silence for a minute. Brake's silence was heavy, persistent, thick, like a tree-stump's. Benning's was tense and alert. He might have been listening to a sound too high for our ears to catch.

He cleared his throat. The distorted yo-yo bobbed. "Mrs. Benning has gone to San Francisco for a few days. It's been hard for her to readjust to Bella City and—marriage. After the unpleasantness of the last two days—well, we both thought she needed a rest. She left about an hour ago."

I said: "Where is she going to stay in San Francisco?"

"I'm sorry, I don't know the address. Bess makes a point of enjoying the utmost personal freedom, and I make a point of allowing it." His pale eyes were watching me, daring me to mention our last meeting.

"When is she coming back?"

"I assume in a week or so. It will depend partly on the friends she's staying with."

"What friends?"

"I can't help you there, either. I don't really know my wife's friends. We've been living apart for the past two years."

He was choosing his words very carefully, as if the slightest mishandling might jar out of them a blast of meaning that would destroy him and his house. It struck me that Bess had left him and wasn't coming back. This was the fact he was concealing from me and Brake, and possibly from himself.

"Why did she come back after those two years?"

"I believe she realized that she had made a mistake in leaving me. Not that you have any license to ask me."

"The doctor's right," Brake said. "Absolutely right. How's she traveling, by the way?"

"By car. She took my car." He added stiffly: "She had my permission to take it."

"Let's see, that's a Chevvie sedan, isn't it, doctor?"

"A 1946 blue Chevrolet sedan."

"And the license?"

"5T1381."

Brake made a note of it. "What route is she taking?"

"I have no idea. Surely you're not proposing to have Mrs. Benning picked up on the highway?"

"First I want to make sure she isn't here."

"You think I've been lying to you?"

"Not a bit. I'm just doing my job. May I have your permission to look through the house?"

203

"Do you have a search warrant?"

"I do not. I took it for granted you had nothing to hide."

Benning managed to smile. "Of course. I was merely curious." He swung his arm in a quarter circle that ended with his knuckles thumping the wall. "Make free with my demesne, gentlemen."

Brake started up the stairs that rose at the end of the hallway. I went through the outer rooms with Benning, and paused in the examination room. He spoke quietly from the doorway:

"I know my enemies, Mr. Archer, and my wife's enemies. I understand your type, the appetitive man. What you can't have you seek to destroy." His voice was rising like an ill wind, carrying echoes of our previous meeting.

"Why did your wife come back to you?" I said.

"She loved me."

"Then why did she leave you again today?"

"She was afraid."

"Afraid of the Duranos? The police?"

"She was afraid," he repeated.

I looked around the shabby oilcloth walls and the scrubbed linoleum floor. The faucet was still leaking drop by drop into the sink.

"Is this the room where Florie found the blood, doctor?"

"Blood?" he said. "Blood?"

"The day after your wife came back there were spots of blood on the floor. According to Florie."

"Oh, yes. I had an emergency patient that Sunday. Cut finger."

"I suggest that your emergency patient came here late Saturday night. Mrs. Benning brought him to you for treatment. He had a slug in his body instead of a cut finger. His name was Singleton. What happened to him, doctor, did he die on your hands?"

"I had no such patient."

"I suggest that you performed an unreported operation on a dying man, and couldn't save him."

"Have you made that suggestion to Brake?"

"No. I'm not your enemy. I'm not interested in breaches of medical ethics. I'm after a murderer. But I haven't even been able to prove that Singleton was murdered. Was he?"

Our glances met and locked, until Benning disengaged his. "It's not myself I'm concerned about," he said falteringly.

"Your wife? Did she do the shooting?"

He failed to meet my eyes again. Both of us were listening to Brake's unaccompanied footsteps coming down the stairs and through the house.

Brake saw the tension between us as soon as he entered the room:

"What goes on?"

"Very little," I said.

Benning looked at me with gratitude, and drew himself up visibly. "Did you look under all the beds, lieutenant?"

"I did. No women's clothes in the closets, either. You sure your wife isn't planning to stay away?"

"She hasn't many clothes."

Brake crossed the room to the locked closet which I had broken into the night before. He shook the knob with the violence of frustration. "You check this room in here, Archer?"

"It's only a closet," Benning said. "There's nothing inside but my skeleton."

"Your what?"

"It's an anatomical specimen."

"Open up."

Benning went to the closet door with a key-ring jingling in his hand. As he unlocked it, he gave us a

205

bright bitter smile over his shoulder. "You don't seriously think I've locked my wife in here?"

He swung the door open. The sparse head grinned steadfastly, superciliously, from its refuge beyond time. Benning stood back, watching us for signs of shock or surprise. He seemed disappointed when we showed none.

"Mr. Macabre," I said. "Where did he come from?"

"I got him from a medical-supply house." He pointed out a rectangular brass tag attached to one of the ribs: Sunset Hospital Equipment Co., Ltd. I had missed it the night before.

"Not many doctors have these any more, do they?"

"I keep him for a special reason. I worked my way through medical school, and I never received an adequate grounding in anatomy. I've been studying it on my own, with the help of this old boy." He poked the varnished cage of ribs with his finger, and set the whole thing swaying. "Poor old boy. I've often wondered who or what he was. A convicted felon, or a pauper who died in a charity ward? *Memento mori.*"

Brake had been fidgeting. "Let's go," he said suddenly. "I've got work to do."

"There are a couple of other points I want to take up with Dr. Benning."

"Make it fast, then." Brake seemed to have broken through the thin ice, and contracted a case of cold feet. He moved out through the waiting-room as if to detach his authority from me.

The doctor followed Brake, emphasizing the realignment that was taking place. It had been two against him. Now it was two against me.

"I don't really mind, lieutenant. I'd like to satisfy Mr. Archer completely and have it over with. If Mr. Archer can be satisfied." Benning turned to face me in the waiting-room like an actor who has been groping for his part and finally begun to live it.

206

"There's a conflict of testimony," I said. "Florie Gutierrez says that your wife and Lucy Champion were friends. You claim they weren't. Florie says your wife was out of the house when Lucy was killed yesterday afternoon. You claim she was here with you."

"I can't pretend to be objective in this matter, with my wife's reputation at stake. I'll tell you my own experience of Florida Gutierrez. She's an unmitigated liar. And when my wife discharged her last night—"

"Why did your wife discharge her?"

"Incompetence. Dishonesty and incompetence. The Gutierrez woman threatened to get even, as she put it. I knew she'd go to almost any lengths to damage us. But the lengths she's gone to have surprised even me. There seems to be no limit to human malice."

"Was your wife in the house between five and six yesterday?"

"She was."

"How do you know? You were taking a siesta."

He was silent for nearly half a minute. Brake was watching from the doorway with the air of a disinterested spectator.

"I didn't sleep," Benning said. "I was conscious of her presence in the house."

"But you couldn't see her? It might have been Florie? You can't swear it was your wife?"

Benning took off his hat and inspected its interior as if for a missing idea. He said slowly and painfully: "I don't have to answer that question, or any other question. Even if I were in court—you can't force a man to testify against his wife."

"You volunteered an alibi for her. Incidentally, you haven't proved she is your wife."

"Nothing could be easier." He strode into his consultation room and came back with a folded document that he handed to Brake.

Brake glanced at it, and passed it to me. It was a marriage certificate issued in the State of Indiana on May 14, 1943. It stated that Samuel Benning, aged 38, had been married on that date to Elizabeth Wionowski, aged 18.

Benning took it out of my hands. "And now, gentlemen, it's about time I insisted that my private life, and my wife's, is no affair of yours. Since she isn't here to defend herself, I'll remind you that there are libel laws, and false arrest is actionable in the courts."

"You don't have to remind me." Brake stressed the personal pronoun. "There's been no arrest, no accusation. Thank you for your co-operation, doctor."

Brake slung a look from the door which tightened on me like a rope. We left Benning in the hallway, leaning like a flimsy buttress against the rotting wall. He was pressing the marriage certificate to his thin chest as if it was a love token or a poultice or a banknote, or a combination of all three.

The interior of my car was furnace-hot. Brake pulled off his coat and folded it on his knees. His shirt was blotched with sweat.

"You went too far, Archer."

"I think I didn't go far enough."

"That's because you don't have my responsibility."

I admitted that that was true.

"I can't take chances," he went on. "I can't act without evidence. I got nothing to justify a warrant for Mrs. Benning."

"You've got just as much on her as you have on Alex Norris. He's still in jail."

Brake answered doggedly: "He's being held without charge for twenty-four hours. It's legal. But you can't do that with people like Mrs. Benning. She's a doctor's wife, remember. I stuck my neck out going to Benning at all. He's lived all his life in this town. His father was the high-school principal for twenty years."

He added defensively: "Anyway, what have we got on her?"

"You noticed her maiden name in the marriage certificate? Elizabeth Wionowski. The same name as the one in the telegram. She was Durano's woman."

"That don't prove anything about Singleton, even if it was evidence, which it isn't. What I don't see in your story is this idea of a woman changing partners back and forth like a bloody square dance. It don't happen."

"Depends on the woman. I've known women who kept six men on the string at the same time. Mrs. Benning has been alternating three. I have a witness who says she was Singleton's mistress for seven years, off and on. She came back to Benning because she needed help—"

Brake brushed the words like mosquitoes away from his head. "Don't tell me any more. I got to take this careful and slow or I'm up the crick without a paddle."

"You or Norris."

"And don't needle me. I'm handling this case the way I have to. If you can bring in Mrs. Benning to make a statement, okay, I'll listen. But I can't go out and bring her in myself. I can't do anything to the doctor just because his wife went on a trip. Nobody told her not to."

The sweat was running down his slant low forehead, gathering in his eyebrows like dew in a thicket. His eyes were bleak.

"It's your town, lieutenant."

I dropped him at the rear of the City Hall. He didn't ask me what I intended to do next.

CHAPTER 27

It was late afternoon when I drove through Arroyo Beach to the ocean boulevard. The palm-lined sand was strewn with bodies like a desert battlefield. At the horizon sea and sky merged in a blue haze from which the indigo hills of the channel islands rose. Beyond them the sun's fire raged on the slopes of space.

I turned south into traffic moving bumper to bumper, fender to fender, like an army in retreat. The arthritic trees cast long baroque shadows down the cemetery hill. The shadow of Durano's house reached halfway across its wilderness of lawn towards the iron fence. I pulled out of the traffic into the entrance to the drive.

The gate was still chained and padlocked. There was a button set in the gatepost under a small weathered sign: RING FOR GARDENER PLEASE. I rang three times, without audible effect, and went back to my car to wait. After a while a small figure came out of the house. It was Una. She moved impatiently down the drive, chunky and squat between the slender coconut palms.

Her gold lamé coat gleamed like mail through the bars of the gate. "What do you want, you?"

I got out of the car and approached her. She looked at me, and at the house, as if invisible wires were jerking at her alternately from each direction. Then she right-about-faced and started away.

"I want to talk about Leo," I said above the traffic noises.

Her brother's name pulled her back to the gate: "I don't understand you."

"Leo Durano is your brother?"

"What if he is? I thought I fired you yesterday. How many times do I have to fire you before you stay fired?"

"Was that the trouble with Max Heiss, that he wouldn't stay fired?"

"What about Max Heiss?"

"He was killed this morning, murdered. Your labor turnover is rapid, and all of your ex-employees are ending the same way."

Her expression didn't change, but her diamonded right hand reached for one of the bars and gripped it. "Heiss had a lot of drunky ideas. If somebody cut him down, it's no affair of mine. *Or* my brother's."

"It's funny," I said, "when I saw Heiss in the morgue I thought of you and Leo. Leo has quite a record in that line."

Her hand left the bar and jumped like a brilliant crustacean to her throat. "You've seen Bess Wionowski."

"We had a little chat."

"Where is she?" Una spoke as if her throat was hurting her.

"Blown again," I said. "You might as well open the gate. We can't talk here."

"I might as well."

She groped in the wide square pocket of her gold

coat. I had my finger hooked in the trigger guard of my gun. All she brought out was a key, with which she opened the padlock. I unchained the gate and pushed it open.

Her hand closed on my arm: "What happened to Max Heiss? Did he get sliced, like Lucy?"

"He was put to the torch like Joan of Arc."

"When?"

"Early this morning. We found him in the mountains, in a wrecked car. The car belonged to Charles Singleton, and Heiss was wearing Singleton's clothes."

"Whose clothes?"

Her fingers were biting into me. Contact with her was unpleasant and strange, like being grabbed by the branch of a small spiny tree. I shook her hand off.

"You know him, Una, the golden boy Bess was running with. Somebody blowtorched Heiss and dressed him in Singleton's clothes to make it look as if Singleton died this morning. But we know better, don't we?"

"If you think Leo did it, you're crazy."

"I'm surprised you still use that word in your family."

Her gaze, which had been steady on my face, swerved away. She said with her head down: "Leo was home in bed this morning. I can prove it by his nurse. Leo is a very sick man."

"Paranoia?" I said distinctly. "G.P.I.?"

Her rigid calm tore like a photograph. "Those lying sawbones at the clinic! They promised me they kept professional secrets. I'll professional-secret them when they send me their next bill."

"Don't blame the clinic. I've seen enough commitment trials to recognize paranoid symptoms."

"You've never seen my brother."

I didn't answer the unasked question. "I'm going to see him now, with you."

"I've taken good care of Leo," she cried suddenly, "with trained nurses all the time, the best of care! The doctor comes every day to see him. I work and slave for that man, making him things he likes to eat, spumoni, minestrone. When I have to, I feed him with my own hands." She choked back the running words and turned away from me, ashamed of the solicitous old woman jostling her other selves.

I put one hand on her stiff elbow and propelled her towards the house. Its red-tiled upper edge cut off the sun. I looked up at the barred window behind which Leo Durano had been receiving the best of care, and heard a silent word repeated like an echo from the wall many times.

Inside the front door, an iron stairway curved in a spiral to the second floor. Una climbed it and preceded me along a dust-littered hallway. Near its end, the large young man in the white smock sat in an armchair beside a closed door.

My presence startled him. "Doctor?" he said to Una.

"Just a visitor."

He shook his cheeks at her. "I wouldn't do it, Miss Durano. He's been hard to handle this afternoon. I had to restrain him."

"Open the door, Donald," Una said.

He produced a key from his tentlike smock. The room contained a bare iron cot and a disemboweled platform-rocker bolted to the floor. A few shreds remained of the drapes that had hung at the barred window. Beside the window, the plaster wall showed handprints, and indentations that could have been made by fists. The inner side of the oak door had been splintered, and repaired with bare oak boards.

Durano was sitting on the floor against the wall in the far corner by the window. His arms, folded in his lap, were sheathed in a brown leather restrainer on

213

which toothmarks were visible. He looked up at us through soiled black hair that straggled over his forehead. His bleeding mouth opened and closed, trying to trap a word.

The word sounded like: "Forgive."

Una ran across the room to him and went down clumsily on her trousered knees. "We don't treat you good, Leo. Forgive me." She drew his head against her metal torso.

"Forgive," he answered brokenly. "I forgive me. Released without charge. I told the ragpickers you can't vag an honest man or the son of an honest man, told them I was doing my father's business."

Clasping the mumbling head in both arms, Una looked up at me scornfully. "This is the poor little fellow who committed a murder this morning, eh? Tell him, Donald, where was Leo this morning?"

Donald swallowed painfully. "Police?"

"Close enough," I said.

"He was right in this room. All night and all morning. Every night and morning. Durano don't get around much any more."

"Shut up, you." Una left her brother and advanced on Donald. "No smart cracks, fat boy. He's a better man right now than you'll ever be. You'd still be emptying bedpans for sixty a month if it wasn't for Leo Durano. Mister to you."

He backed away from her, flushed and cowering like a browbeaten German wife. "You ask me a question, Miss Durano."

"Shut up." She passed him like a small cold wind, and hustled off down the corridor.

I said: "Donald. What about Saturday night two weeks ago? Was Durano in his room?"

"I wasn't here. We usually get Saturday nights off."

"We?"

214

"Me and Lucy before she left. Miss Durano paid me extra to stay last night. He was bad last night."

"You coming?" Una called from the head of the stairs.

She took me to the room with the picture window at the rear of the house. The sun's fires had blazed out of control across the whole western sky and were eating at the sea's edges. Along the shore where the beach curved, a few late swimmers were tossed like matchsticks in a bloody froth of surf. I sat down in a chair against the side wall where I could watch the whole room and its doors and windows.

Seen from inside by daylight, the room was spacious and handsome in an old-fashioned way. Kept up, it might have been beautiful. But the carpets and the surfaces of the furniture were gray with dust, strewn with the leavings of weeks: torn magazines and crumpled newspapers, cigarette butts, unwashed dishes. A bowl of rotting fruit was alive with insects. The wall plants had drooped and died. Cobwebs hung in shaggy strands from the ceiling. It was a Roman villa liberated by Vandals.

Una sat down at the card-table by the big window. The cards with which she and Donald had been playing the night before lay scattered across the table, mixed with a confetti of potato chips. A pair of clouded glasses sat on its edge. Una's hand crept out onto the table and began to gather the cards.

"How long has Leo been insane?" I said.

"What does it matter? You know he didn't kill Heiss."

"Heiss isn't the only one."

"Lucy Champion, then. He wouldn't hurt Lucy. They got along swell till she left. She was a damn good nurse, I'll give her that."

"That isn't why you were so anxious to get her back."

215

"Isn't it?" She smiled a keen half-smile, as bitter as wormwood.

"How long has he been insane, Una?"

"Since the first of the year. He blew his top for keeps at a New Year's party in the Dial, that's a night-spot in Detroit. He was trying to make the orchestra play the same piece over and over, some piece from an opera. They played it three times and quit. Leo said they were insulting a great Italian composer. He was going to shoot the orchestra leader. I stopped him.

"It was New Year's Eve and everybody thought he was loaded. I knew different. I'd been watching him since summer. He had bad headaches all last year, and along in the fall he was flying off the handle every day. It was Bess set him off, he never should have taken her back. They fought like wildcats all the time. Then he started to lose his memory. He got so he didn't even know his collectors' names."

"Collectors?"

Her hand became still among the half-gathered cards. She uncrossed and recrossed her legs. "He runs a collection agency."

"With a gun?"

"Leo always carried large sums. The gun was for protection. I didn't realize he was dangerous until he tried to use it on that musician. The doctor in Detroit said he was in a hopeless state, he wouldn't live long. I saw I had to get him out of Michigan. I wasn't going to have my brother committed."

"Again."

"*Again*, God damn you, if you know so much."

"So you hired a couple of nurses and moved to California. No doubt reasoning that Californians were expendable, in case he tried to shoot somebody else."

She turned from the card-table to look at my face, try to assess my meaning. "California was *her* idea.

Anyway, I don't see why you go on about killing. I keep him under close guard. The idea that Leo did these murders is ridiculous."

"You didn't take it so lightly when I brought it up. You've worked like a dog since I got here to build up his alibi. On top of that you've outlined his defense on a plea of not guilty by reason of insanity, complete with medical witnesses."

"I've been showing you that Leo can't be tried for murder, let alone convicted."

"Why go to all that trouble if the idea is ridiculous?"

She bent forward stiffly in her chair, planting her feet on the floor: "You wouldn't want to harass a poor sick guy. What happens if you tip the cops in? They'll pin a bum rap on him, with his record, or if that doesn't work they'll send him away."

"There are worse places than a state hospital." I was sitting in one.

"I can't face it," she said. "He was in before and I saw how they treated him. He's got a right to spend his last days with somebody that loves him."

Though she said them with great intensity, the words fell flat. I studied her head, slanting square and hard out of the gold coat. On the window side the sun cast her face in rosy relief. Its other side was in shadow so deep by contrast that she looked like half a woman. Or a woman composed half of flesh and half of darkness.

"How long do the doctors give him?"

"Not more than a year. You can ask them at the clinic. Two years at the outside."

"Anywhere from one hundred to three hundred grand."

"What the hell do you mean by that?"

"My information is that Leo draws two to three grand a week from a numbers ring in Michigan. That

217

adds up to a possible total of three hundred grand in two years, before taxes if you pay taxes."

"I don't know what you're talking about."

"Money," I said. "Don't tell me you're not handling Leo's money. I wouldn't believe it."

An irrepressible faint smile appeared on her mouth, as if I had flattered her subtly. "I have big expenses, very big expenses."

"Sure you have. Mink, diamonds, an ocean-front estate. They all cost money."

"Medical expenses," she said, "you wouldn't believe."

"Sure. You've got to keep him alive. The income lasts as long as he does. As long as you keep him under wraps, he's a boss racketeer on Sabbatical leave drawing his weekly take. But when he dies, or the cops lock him up, or news of his condition gets back to Michigan, it's finished for you. You're a pretty hard type but I don't see you going back to Michigan and fighting a war of succession with his mob. If you could do that, you wouldn't have come to me in the first place."

She sat in silence, shivering a little inside the metal coat. Then she took up the gathered half of the deck and flung it down at random on the table. Brushed by her sleeve, a glass fell to the floor and broke.

"You didn't figure this out for yourself," she said in cold still anger. "It was Bess Wionowski put you onto it."

"She may have helped."

"That's Wionowski's gratitude." A hard pulse kicked like a tiny animal tangled in the veins of her left temple. "She was on her uppers, last year when Leo took her back. We ransomed her out of a cell in Detroit city jail and treated her like a queen. When we came out here to Cal, we even let her choose the town to live in. I might of known she had a reason for picking this place."

"Singleton," I said.

The name acted on Una like an electric shock. She jumped to her feet, kicking out at the shards of glass on the floor as if she hated everything actual. "The filthy disloyal filly. Where is she now? Where is she? If you got her hid out waiting for her cut, you can go back and tell her I don't pay off to squealers."

She stood above me in a spiteful rage, less than half a woman now, a mean little mannish doll raving ventriloquially.

"Come down to earth," I said. "You'll give yourself a migraine. Neither of us wants your dirty money."

"If my money's so dirty, what are you sucking around for?"

"Just the truth, sweetheart. You know what happened to Singleton, if anybody does. You're going to tell me."

"And if I don't?"

"You tell the cops. I'll have them here before dark."

She sat on the edge of her chair and looked out at the setting sun. Half down on the horizon, its red hemisphere was like a bird's giant eye on which the inflamed blue underlid was shutting slowly.

"How did it happen?" I said.

"Give me a chance to think—"

"You've had two weeks. Now talk."

"It was all Bess Wionowski's fault. The big estate and the high living weren't good enough for that Chicago chippie. Way last spring she started dating this guy from the Hill, this Singleton scion. I figured she knew him from when she lived here during the war. Before long she was spending nights with him. I tried to keep it from Leo but he found out about it some way. He has his lucid times, anyway he had until two weeks ago. It was a Saturday night, and Bess

219

was up the mountain with her highfalutin boy friend, set to make beautiful music. Leo found out where she was, from Lucy Champion, I guess. Lucy was supposed to be looking after him that night. When he blew off, she couldn't handle him. Lucy called a taxi and went up the hill to warn the—lovers." The word had an obscene sound in Una's mouth.

"Where were you?"

"Downtown. When I got back Leo was waiting for me with a gun. He'd taken the springs off his bed and broken the door down and found the gun in my room. He made me drive him up to Singleton's studio, forced me at gunpoint to do it. Singleton came out of the door, and Leo shot him in the guts. I grabbed Leo from behind as soon as he turned that gun away from me. It took all four of us to tie him."

"All four?"

"Me and Bess and Lucy. Lucy was there. And Singleton."

"Singleton was shot, you said."

"He could still navigate, the last I saw of him. I left right away when we got Leo under control. I had to get Leo home."

"So you don't know what happened to Singleton?"

"No. They all three dropped out of sight. I hired Max Heiss to find out if Singleton was alive or dead. He watched the Singleton house all last week. On Thursday Lucy turned up there, sniffing around for the reward I guess. Heiss rode the bus back to Bella City with her and found out more than he ever turned in to me. Friday night he reported to me and claimed he lost Lucy in Bella City. I knew he was crossing me because he dropped a hint about the shooting. He was going to let me buy him off and then collect the Singleton reward besides."

"So you killed him for being greedy."

"Think again."

"You were the one with everything to lose. Lucy and Heiss were the ones to lose it for you."

"I still have everything to lose. Would I hand you all this on a silver platter if I wasn't clear?"

"Who else had a reason to kill them?"

"Bess," she said harshly. "Lucy was in touch with Bess in Bella City, I could tell by talking to Lucy. Max Heiss was on her track. How do I know what Bess did with Singleton? Maybe he died on her hands and that made her accessory. Bess couldn't stand a police investigation. Bess has a record going back ten years."

I stood up and moved towards her and stood over her: "Did you remind Bess of her record, up at Singleton's cabin, after your brother shot him? Is that why she dropped out of sight and took Singleton into hiding?"

"Figure it out for yourself."

"You scared her into hushing it up, didn't you? Purely out of sisterly devotion, of course, to protect your brother, and his income."

She shifted restlessly in the chair, doubling her legs under her to tighten her defenses. "What other reason would I have?"

"I've been casting around for one," I said. "I thought of something that happened in Los Angeles about fifteen years ago, to a man and his wife and their son. The son was a Mongoloid idiot, and the man hated his wife for giving him that son. When the boy was ten or twelve years old, his father bought a shotgun and took him out on the desert and taught him to shoot. The boy had brains enough to pull the trigger of a shotgun. One night the father handed him the gun and told him to shoot his mother. She was asleep in bed. The boy blew her head off, being eager to please. He wasn't prosecuted. But his father was, though he hadn't physically committed the murder.

221

He was convicted on a first-degree charge and put away with cyanide."

"Too bad for him."

"Too bad for anybody who tries to do murder by proxy. If you incite an insane person to commit a crime you're legally guilty of it. Did you know that was the law when you drove your brother up the mountain to Singleton's cabin and handed him a gun?"

She looked up at me with loathing, the muscles weaving and dimpling around her mouth. On the left side of her head where the knotted veins jerked, her face had swelled lopsided, as if moral strain had pushed or melted it out of shape. The light from the window fell on her like visible heat from an open furnace-door.

"You'll never bum-rap me," she said. "You haven't even got a body. You don't know where golden boy is any more than I do."

Her statement turned at the end into a question. I left the question turning like a knife in her brain.

CHAPTER 28

Lights shone like wit in a dowager behind the windows of the Palladian villa. The green spectrum of its lawns and trees was deepening around it into solid green darkness. I parked under the porte-cochere and yanked at the old-fashioned bell-pull that hung by the side entrance.

A stout woman in an apron opened the door. Her hand left a deposit of white flour on the doorknob. "What is it?"

"Is Miss Treen in?"

"I think she's busy. Who shall I say is calling?"

"Mr. Archer."

She permitted me to enter the hallway. I started to sit down on an elegant bowlegged chair, caught her backward look of disapproval, and remained standing. The Chinese gentleman with the wise earlobes was pursuing his timeless journey along the wall, from the lowlands across a river valley into the highlands and up the snowcapped mountain to his shrine. There were seven of him, one for each stage of the journey. There was only one of me, and my earlobes felt inadequate.

Sylvia appeared at the end of the hall, pale and absent-looking in a black suit like a uniform. "I'm so relieved you've come."

"How's Mrs. Singleton?"

"Not well, I'm afraid. This afternoon was too much for her. The police phoned from Bella City to say that Charles's car had been found with his body in it. They wanted her to make a formal identification. Before she was ready to leave, they called again. The body had been identified as someone else, some detective. I'm so glad it wasn't you."

"So am I. It was Max Heiss."

"Yes. I found that out. Why was he killed, do you know? Why was he dressed in Charles's clothes?"

"Somebody wanted to have it appear that Charles died in an accident this morning. The body was burned to make it hard to identify."

Her mouth was pulled thin across her teeth in horror. "There are such dreadful things in the world. Why?"

"There are dreadful things in people's heads. This one is easier to explain than some. If Charles died in an accident this morning, he couldn't have died in a shooting two weeks ago."

"You mean that he did die two weeks ago? You can't mean that," she softly prompted the irreversible facts.

"Charles is probably dead, Sylvia. I know he was shot. I think he died of it."

"Who would shoot Charles?"

"He was mixed up with a woman named Bess. She had other lovers. One of them caught Charles with her in his studio, and shot him. Bess had a police record, and she was forced to cover up the shooting. She took Charles to her husband, who is a doctor in Bella City. Charles died, apparently. No one has seen him since."

"*She* has," Sylvia whispered.

"Who?"

"The woman, Bess. She phoned here a little while ago. I'm certain it was the same woman."

"You spoke to her?"

"Yes. She insisted on talking to Mrs. Singleton, but Mrs. Singleton was in no condition. The woman didn't identify herself. She didn't have to. I knew from what she said that she was—Charles's mistress."

"What did she say?"

"That she could give us information."

"Five thousand dollars' worth?"

"Yes. She claimed to know where Charles is."

"Did you arrange to meet her?"

"I invited her to come here, but she wouldn't. She said she'd phone again at seven to fix a meeting-place. We must have the money ready for her in cash, in unmarked bills. Fortunately Mrs. Singleton has the cash on hand. She's been holding it in readiness ever since she posted the reward."

"Mrs. Singleton is going through with this, then."

"Yes, I advised her to. I may be quite wrong. I've had no one to turn to. The woman particularly warned me not to call in the police or Mrs. Singleton's detective agency or her lawyers. She said that if we did, the deal was off."

"She didn't mention me, though."

"If only you would stand by, Mr. Archer. I'm not equipped to handle this kind of—transaction. I wouldn't even know what to ask for in the way of proof."

"What sort of proof did she offer?"

"Proof that she knows where Charles is. She didn't describe its nature and I hadn't the presence of mind to question her about it. The whole thing took me by surprise. I lacked the wit, even, to ask her if Charles was dead." She hesitated, then said in a rush of feeling: "Of course I meant to ask her. I was afraid to, I suppose. I put it off. Then the operator asked her to deposit more money, and she hung up."

"It was a long distance call?"

"I had the impression it was from Los Angeles."

"How much did the operator ask for?"

"Forty cents."

"Probably Los Angeles. Bess didn't give her name?"

"No, but she called him Charlie. Not many people did. And she knew my name. Charles told her about me, I guess." She bit her lip. "When I realized that, I felt sort of let down. It wasn't simply her calling me by my first name. She *condescended* to me, as if she knew all about me—how I felt about Charles."

"You'd feel better if you knew all about her."

"Do you?"

"Nobody does. She's crowded several lives into her first twenty-five years."

"Is that all she is, twenty-five? I imagined she was much older, older than Charles."

"Bess grew up early and fast. She was married in her teens to a man twice her age. He brought her out here during the war. She met Charles here in 1943."

"So long ago," she said desolately. Her loss of Charles was final, and retroactive. "Long before I knew him."

"Wilding saw her with Charles in 1943."

"He didn't tell me."

"He wouldn't. Since then she's been back and forth across the country, in and out of jail—"

"You said she had a husband. What about him?"

"She broke his spirit years ago. She uses him when she has to, when she has nothing better to do with herself."

"I don't—I can't understand—Charles's taking up with such a woman."

"She's a fine-looking wench. And she was safely married to a man who wouldn't divorce her."

"But he's such an idealist. His standards are so high. Nothing was ever good enough for Charles."

"It's possible he was out of touch with his own standards. I never met Charles, but he sounds flawed to me—a man trying all his life to get hold of something real and not succeeding." I didn't know for sure whether my candor came from concern for the living girl or jealousy of the dead man. "That bullet in the guts was probably the realest thing that ever happened to him."

Her hazel eyes were troubled, but transparent as water in a well. "You mustn't speak of him in that way."

"Speak no ill of the dead?"

"You don't know that he is dead." She cupped her left breast gravely in her right hand. "I feel, here, that he is alive."

"I interviewed a witness today who saw him shot."

"How can I feel so strongly that he is alive?"

"He may be," I said without conviction. "My evidence isn't conclusive."

"Yet you won't let me have any hope. I think you wish him dead."

I touched the back of her hand, which still lay over her breast. "I never saw a girl with more goodness. I'd hate to see you waste it all on the memory of a guy who never gave a thought to anybody but himself."

"He wasn't like that!" She was flushed and radiant with anger. "He was beautiful."

"Sorry," I said. "I'm tired. I shouldn't try to mastermind other people's lives. It never works out." I sat down in the bowlegged chair and let the thoughts in my head string off in whirling darkness.

Her touch on my shoulder straightened me up. She looked down at me with a smile of wise innocence:

"Don't be sorry, and don't be angry with me. I wasn't exactly nice."

Nice was her middle name, but I kept that to myself. I looked at my wristwatch:

"It's nearly seven now. What are you going to say to her?"

"Whatever you think. Won't you take the call?"

"She knows my voice. You talk to her. Tell her you have the money. You'll buy her information, provided it's backed up by proof. If she's in Los Angeles or within driving distance, make an appointment for ten tonight, later if she insists. She's to go to West Hollywood and park in front of 8411½ Sunset Boulevard. You'll contact her there."

"I?"

"We both will." I printed the address in my notebook, and tore the leaf out for her. "No matter how she gripes, don't let her choose the meeting-place."

"Why not?"

"You're going to be with me. Bess may or may not be dangerous herself, but she has dangerous friends."

She read the address I had printed. "What place is this?"

"My office. It's a good safe place to talk to her, and I have built-in mikes. I don't suppose you take shorthand?"

"*Pas trop.* I can take some sort of notes."

"How's your memory? Repeat the instructions I gave you."

She did, without an error, and said with the air of a child remembering her manners:

"Come into the library, Mr. Archer. Let me make you some tea while we're waiting. Or a drink?"

I said that tea would be fine. The telephone rang before I got a taste of it. It was Bess calling from Los Angeles.

CHAPTER 29

At half past nine we were in my West Hollywood office. I called my answering service and was informed that a Mr. Elias McBratney of Beverly Hills had phoned twice on Saturday and would phone again on Monday. James Spinoza, Jr., of Spinoza Beach Garb, wished me to call him back as soon as possible about those shortages. A lady who declined to give her name had tried to reach me four times between eight ten and nine twenty. I thanked the operator and said I would take my own calls until further notice.

I turned out the desk lamp. The inner office was dimly lit by the rectangular white beam that fell from the outer room through the one-way panel in the glass door. A changing light thrown up from the Boulevard silhouetted the girl against the window.

"Look at the lights all up the sides of the hills," she said. "I've never seen this city at night. It's so new and aspiring."

"New anyway."

I stood behind her watching the cars run by in the road. I felt very close to Sylvia in the half-dark, and very conscious of time. The headlights flashed and disappeared like a bright succession of instants plunging out of darkness into darkness.

"Some day we'll have to jack it up and put a foundation under it."

"I like it the way it is," she said. "New England is all foundation and nothing else. Who cares about foundations?"

"You do, for one."

She turned, and her shoulder brushed me like a friendly movement of the darkness itself. "Yes, I do. You have foundations, Archer, don't you?"

"Not exactly. I have a gyroscope arrangement. I'm afraid to let it stop spinning."

"That's better than foundations. And I don't believe you're afraid of anything at all."

"Am I not." I emitted a cynical-uncle chuckle which turned into a real laugh. Sylvia didn't join in.

The telephone on the desk rang sharply. I reached for it and spoke into the mouthpiece:

"Hello."

No answer. Only a faint electric murmur, the sound of thin wire in thin space. A click at the other end. Dead line.

I dropped the telephone into its cradle. "Nobody there."

"Perhaps it was the woman. Bess." Sylvia's face in the upward light from the window was white and enormous-eyed.

"I doubt it. She has no way of knowing this is my address."

"Will she come, do you think?"

"Yes. She needs the money for a getaway." I patted my fat breast-pocketful of bills.

"Getaway," Sylvia said, like a tourist picking up a foreign word. "What a wretched life she must have led, and still be leading. Oh, I hope she comes."

230

"Is it so important?"

"I have to know about Charles, one way or the other." She added under her breath: "And I want to see her."

"You'll be able to." I showed her the one-way panel in the door, and the earphones wired to the mike in the outer room. "You stay in here and take your notes. I'll keep her in the other room. I don't expect any trouble."

"I'm not afraid. I was afraid of everything for so very long. I've suddenly got over it."

At eight minutes to ten, a blue Chevrolet sedan passed slowly on the far side of the road, in the direction of Los Angeles. The face of the woman behind the wheel was caught in a photoflash of approaching headlights.

"That was Bess. You stay in here now and be still. Away from the window."

"Yes."

Closing doors behind me, I ran downstairs to the street. At two minutes to ten the Chevrolet came back and pulled up to the curb directly opposite the doorway where I was waiting. I crossed the sidewalk in three steps, opened the car door, pushed my gun into the woman's side. She released the emergency brake and raced the engine. I plucked the key out of the ignition switch. She tried to scratch my face. I locked her fingers.

"Calm down, Bess. You're caught."

"When haven't I been." She drew a long sighing breath. "I could stand it better before I started bumping into you. Well, little man, what now?"

"The same as before, except that you're going to do your talking to me."

"Who says I am?"

"Five grand says it."

"You mean you've got the money for me?"

231

"When you earn it."

"And I can go free?"

"If you're reasonably clean, and I don't mean vice-squad stuff."

She leaned close to study my eyes as if her future lay behind them. I leaned away.

"Let me see the money."

"Upstairs in my office."

"What are we waiting for then?"

She came out of the car, her body full and startling in a yellow jersey dress with a row of gold buttons down the front. I frisked her on the stairs and found no gun and burned my hands a little. But in the lighted room I saw that she was losing what she had had. Her past was coming out on her face like latent handwriting. Her powder and lipstick, alkali and orange in the fluorescent light, were cracking and peeling off. Grime showed in the pores of her nose and at the sides of her neck. Dissolution was working in her rapidly like a fatal disease she had caught from her husband that day.

She felt my look cold against her, and reached up automatically to straighten her hair. It was streaked greenish yellow and black. I guessed she had been working on it with peroxide half the afternoon, trying to reconstruct her image in a cheap hotel mirror. And I wondered what the girl behind the one-way panel was thinking.

"Don't look at me," Bess said. "I've had a bad day."

She sat in a chair by the outer door, as far from the light as possible, and crossed her legs. Nothing could happen to legs.

"You've had a bad day coming," I said. "Now talk."

"Don't I get a peek at the money?"

I sat down facing her and placed the five brown-paper-wrapped packages on the table between us.

There was a microphone built into the table lamp, and I switched it on.

"Five grand, you said?"

"You're dealing with honest people. You can take my word for it."

"How much do I have to give you?"

"The whole thing. All you know."

"That would take years."

"I wonder. We'll start with something simple. Who killed Singleton?"

"Leo Durano blasted him." Her clouded blue gaze had returned to the packages of money. "Now I guess you want to know who Leo Durano is."

"We've met. I know his record."

She was beyond surprise. "You don't know Leo like I know Leo. I wish I never set eyes on him."

"He was picked up for contributing about ten years ago. Were you the minor?"

"Uh-huh. He was the connection I told you about, the one with the hat-check concessions in the clubs. We both got sneezed the same night, and they found out we lived in the same hotel room. He got off easy. The court doctor said he was batty, I could of told them that. They stuck him away in the booby-hatch for a spell, until Una talked him out of there. She's been talking him out of jams since he was a kid."

"Not this one," I said. "Now what about Singleton?"

"Me and Charlie?"

"You and Charlie."

"He was the one big love of my life," her cracked lips said. Her bleached hands moved down her smooth jersey body from breasts to thighs, wiping out a memory, or reviving it. "I met him too late, after I married Sam. Sam and I were living together in Arroyo Beach, and Sam was all work and no play, and that was never for me. Charlie picked me up in a bar. He had everything, looks and class and an Air Force

233

officer's uniform. Real class. Class was the one thing I really wanted. I went with him the first night and it worked like magic. I didn't know what it was before Charlie showed me. Leo and Sam and the others never even scratched my surface.

"Charlie had to go back to Hamilton Field but he'd fly down weekends. I waited for those weekends. Then Sam went to sea and I couldn't even remember what he looked like. I can't remember now. It was different when Charlie went. He went all the way to Guam. He couldn't fly back from there. The waiting stretched out, and he didn't write.

"Sam wrote though, and Sam was the first to come back. I made the best of a bad job. After all I was married to the guy. We settled down in Bella City and I cooked his chops for him and said hello how are you to the cheesy patients he had. I never mentioned Charlie to him but I guess he figured it out from the things I didn't say. It wasn't any good at all after Sam came back. I stuck it for one year, keeping track of Charlie in the Arroyo newspaper and marking off the days on the calendar. I crossed off every day for a year. I got up early in the morning to cross them off and then I went back to bed.

"One Saturday morning I didn't go back to bed. I got on a bus and rode to Arroyo Beach and phoned Charlie and we started over again, nearly every weekend. That was the summer of forty-six, I guess. It didn't last. He said good-bye in September and went back to Boston to take a course at Harvard Law School. I stayed with Sam that winter. It was a long winter. Summer was good when it came but it didn't last. It never lasted. Next year when the rains came in the valley and I saw that green stuff on the hills I couldn't stick it. I couldn't even hear what Sam was saying any more; it went through my head like wind.

"I got on a train for New York and from there to

Boston, Massachusetts. Charlie was living in his own apartment in Belmont, but he wasn't glad to see me. He said I was part of his California vacations, I didn't fit into his Boston life. Scat. I told him what he was, and I walked out of there with nothing on but a dress. It was March, and it was snowing. I was going to walk into the river because the name of it was the Charles River and that would drive him crazy. I hoped.

"I looked at the river for a while with the snowflakes falling into it. Then I walked to the end of the subway and rode downtown. I didn't even rate a cold out of it. For a long time then I lived on Scollay Square, getting back at Charlie. I phoned him once to tell him what I was doing. He hung up on me. That night it was the third rail in the subway I looked at. I stood and looked at it for over an hour, and I couldn't move forward or back.

"A character in a boiled shirt saw me watching the third rail and picked me up. He turned out to be an unemployed ballroom-dancer from Montreal. Paul Theuriet. I supported him the rest of that year while we tried to work up an act together. Ever hear of Lagauchetière Street in Montreal?"

"I never did."

"It's rugged, and so was the act. Paul said I could make a dancer out of myself. God knows I tried. I was too clumsy or something. *He* was old and gouty in the joints. We did get ourselves booked into a few third-string clubs in Niagara Falls, Buffalo, Toledo. Then we were stranded in Detroit. I was waiting table in a beer joint, trying to raise enough money for limber-legs to open a dance studio, getting nowhere. We tried the old badger a couple of times. Paul fumbled it and ran out to Canada, left me holding the bag. That was where Leo came into my life again."

"It's about time."

"You asked for all of it," she said with a wry stubborn smile. This was her saga, all she had to show for her life, and she was going to tell it her own way:

"Leo heard that I was in the Detroit clink for extortion. He was going good again, a medium big gun in Michigan numbers. He had pull with the cops, and he hadn't forgotten me. He sprung me out of that rap. After all those years, I moved back in with Leo and his sister. No class, but the chips. I was in the chips."

"So you lived happily ever after, and that's why you're not here."

"It isn't funny," she said. "Leo started to have the fantods, worse than ever. It got so bad I sent some money to Sam, for an insurance policy. I thought if it got too bad I could come out here and retire on Sam. They didn't know about Sam."

"They?"

"Leo and his sister. She handled the money for Leo after his memory faded. Leo blew his top the end of last year. He tried to gun an orchestra leader for no good reason at all. We took him to a doctor and the doctor said he'd been sick for twenty years and was in the final stage of paresis. We couldn't keep him in Michigan after that. He had enemies in the organization. The money boys and the underdogs with the irons were both turning against him. Leo never laid anything on the line for his share of those banks. All he ever put up was his hard-nose reputation and his connections. If they knew he lost his mind they'd cut him out, or cut him down. So it was California here we came. I sold Una on Arroyo Beach.

"Ever since Boston, when Charlie Singleton kicked me out of his life, I had this certain idea busting my brain. He thought I was from hunger, and I thought if I went back to Arroyo Beach with money on my back I'd make him squirm. Pass him on the street and pretend I didn't know him. Anyway, that was my idea. When I did see him again, I did a quick reverse and there I was back at the old stand, Saturday nights in his studio. I didn't care about anything he did to me in the past. He was the only man I liked to be with. It went along like old times until a couple of weeks ago the lid blew off. When Leo found out about Charlie and me." She paused, her eyes like fogged blue steel.

"Did he find out from Lucy?"

"Not a chance. Lucy was my one real friend in that house. Besides, she was a nurse. She had psychic—psychiatric training. She wouldn't pull a raw deal like that on one of her patients. She was the one who warned us Leo was on the warpath. She came up the mountain in a cab one jump ahead of him."

"Who sent Leo on the warpath?"

"Una did, at least that's what we figured afterwards. Lucy drove me over to the hotel to keep my date with Charlie. When Lucy got back to the house, Una cross-questioned her about where I was and who I was with. Lucy wouldn't talk, and Una fired her. I guess Una knew all about it already. She turned Leo loose and sicked him on us.

"Maybe the fantods ran in the family. Anyway, she must have been far gone with whatever it was she had, to give Leo a loaded gun and a green light. I didn't understand it at the time. I was in the studio with Lucy when it happened. I looked out the window and saw Leo in the station-wagon with Una, and Charlie walking out to him, not realizing the danger. Charlie went right up to the station-wagon, and Leo shot him. Charlie fell down and got up again. Una took Leo's gun away from him. We all stepped in and got him under control. Then Una put on an act about how Leo forced her to bring him there. I believed her, then. I was scared not to believe her. I've always been scared of Una.

237

"She said the shooting had to be hushed up, or else. It had to be as if nothing happened. No hospital for Charlie, and him doubled up in his car. I was afraid to argue with Una. I took what clothes I had in the studio and drove Charlie and Lucy over the pass to Bella City.

"I'd been to see Sam Benning a couple of times in the spring and summer, in case I ever needed him. He thought I was working in L.A., modeling clothes. We were on pretty good terms, but I couldn't tell Sam the truth: that one boy-friend shot the other and Sam was to make it all come right in the end. I played it as strong as I could with Sam. I told him Charlie had made a rough pass and I shot him myself. Lucy backed me up. Charlie was past talking by then.

"Sam believed me. He made me promise if he fixed Charlie up I had to stick with him in Bella City from then on and be a wife to him. I promised. He had me over a barrel.

"Maybe the wound was worse than it looked at first, or Sam isn't much of a surgeon. He blamed Lucy for what happened, said she fouled up the operation trying to assist him. Sam was always a man to shift blame onto other people's shoulders. Anyway Charlie died that night, right on the table in the examination room, before he came out of the ether."

"Who gave him the anesthetic?"

"I don't know, I wasn't there. I couldn't stand to see him bleeding."

"You're a strange woman, Bess."

"I don't think so. How could I watch Sam cutting into him? Charlie was my boy. I loved him."

"I'll tell you what's really strange," she added after an interval: "The people you love are never the ones that love you. The people that love you, the way Sam loved me, they're the ones you can't love. Sam was a good man when I first knew him. But he was too

238

crazy about me. I couldn't love him, ever, and he was too smart to fool. It ruined him.

"He did a wild thing that Sunday morning. There was Charlie dead in his house, and Sam thinking I had shot him. I couldn't change my story at that late date. Sam was afraid he was going to lose me again, and it pushed him over the edge. He butchered Charlie, cut him up into pieces like a butcher. He locked the cellar door on me, wouldn't let me down there. I could tell from the noises what he was doing. There was a laundry tub and an old gas stove down there that his mother left behind her when she died. When he was through, there was nothing but bones left. He spent the next three nights working on them, putting them together with wire. Sam always was good with his hands. When it was all wired together and varnished and dried, he riveted on a tag from a medical-supply house and hung the thing in a closet. He said that was the skeleton in my closet and if I ever left him—" She drew a fingernail across her throat.

There was a muffled cry from the inner room.

"And that's your proof?" I said loudly.

"You'll find it in the closet off his examination room. Unless you already did?"

"What did he do with Charlie's car?"

"Hid it in the barn, under some old boards and tarpaulins. I helped him."

"Did you help him burn Max Heiss, when Max found the car?"

Bess didn't hear me. An intermittent sobbing and gasping rose and fell in the inner room. Bess was listening to it, the flesh haggard on the bones of her face like wet clay drooping on an armature.

"You crossed me, you," she said.

Something fell softly and heavily against the inside of the glass-paneled door. I went to it. The door was hard to open because Sylvia had fainted against it. I

239

reached around its edge and turned her onto her back. The metal earphones pincered her closed white face. Her eyes came open:

"I'm sorry. I'm such a fool."

I started for the water cooler. Bess was at the outer door, fumbling with the Yale lock. The packages of bills were gone from the table.

"Sit down," I said to her straining yellow back. "I haven't finished with you."

She didn't answer. All her remaining energy was focused on escape. The lock snapped back. The door opened inwards with Una pushing behind it from the hallway.

Una's mouth was wet. Her eyes were blind with the same darkness I had seen on her brother's face. The gun in her hand was real.

"I thought you'd be here with him. This is the payoff, Wionowski, to squealers and false friends."

"Don't do it." Bess was leaning off balance against the opening door, still bent on escape.

I moved sideways to the wall, bringing my gun out fast, not fast enough. Bess staggered backwards under the blow of the first shot from Una's gun and went down under the second. The twin explosions smashed like bones in my head.

I shot to kill. Una died on her feet, of a smudged hole in the temple, and thumped the floor. I held Sylvia's hand until the police arrived. Her hand was ice cold at first. After a while it was a little warmer, and I could feel her blood beating.

CHAPTER 30

The starred sky arched like a crystal roof over the town. The valley floor was like the floor of a cave, the mountains blunt stalagmites against its glimmering walls. Once I got off the highway, the streets of Bella City were deserted. Its midnight buildings, leached of color by the alkali moonlight, stood like gray shadows on their own black shadows.

Parking at Benning's curb, I rang the bell and heard its complaint inside the house. A door creaked open at the rear of the hallway. Benning passed through its widening shaft of light and shut the door behind him. His face appeared above the cardboard patch in the corner of the window. It was crumpled and streaked like a discarded charcoal-sketch of it-self.

He opened the front door. "What is it? Why have you come here?"

"Let me see your hands, doctor." I showed him the gun in mine.

He stepped out onto the porch, bulky in a zippered blue coverall, and held out his empty hands.

"They're dirty," he said. "I've been doing some cleaning in the house."

"Your wife is dead."

"Yes. I know. They phoned me from Los Angeles. I'm getting ready to go." He glanced down at my gun as if it were an obscenity that shouldn't be mentioned. "Perhaps they sent you to fetch me?"

"I came on my own."

"To spy on my grief, Mr. Archer?" he asked with broken irony. "You'll be disappointed. I can't feel grief, not for her. I've suffered too much for her." He turned up his dirty palms and looked down into them. "I have nothing." His fists closed slowly on moonlight. "Who is this woman who murdered her?"

"Una Durano. She's dead, too. I shot her."

"I'm grateful to you for that." His words were as insubstantial as his double fistful of moonlight. "Why did she do it to Bess?"

"She had various reasons. Your wife was a witness to the Singleton shooting, for one."

"Bess? A witness?"

"She was there when Singleton was shot."

"Who on earth was Singleton?"

"You know as well as I do, doctor. He was your wife's lover almost as long as you were married to her."

Benning looked up and down the empty street. "Come inside," he said nervously. "I only have a few minutes, but we can talk there."

He stood aside to let me enter first, maintaining a formal politeness like a wire-walker afraid to look down. I waved him in with my gun and followed him through the waiting-room into the consultation room. The inside of the house was suffocating after the chilly night air.

I pulled his swivel chair into the middle of the room. "Sit down, away from the desk."

"You're very hospitable," he said with his down-dragging smile. "Bess was, too, in her way. I won't deny that I knew of her affair with Singleton. Or that I was glad she shot him. It seemed fitting that she should be the one to destroy that arrogant young man."

"Bess didn't destroy him."

"I'm afraid you're mistaken. Now that Bess is dead, I'm free to tell you the truth. She confessed to me that she shot him."

"She was lying to you."

He stood wide-legged and stubborn under the light, shaking his long head from side to side. "She couldn't have been lying. No one would lie about such a thing."

"Bess did. It was the only way she could persuade you to take care of him. The crime was actually committed by Una Durano. Bess was a witness, as I said."

He slumped into the chair. "Do you know that, for a fact?"

"I couldn't prove it in court. I don't have to. Una is dead, along with the competent witnesses, Singleton and Lucy and Bess."

"Did this woman murder them all? What kind of a woman was she?"

"As hard and nasty as they come. But she didn't kill them all. Bess was the only one she killed. She thought Bess had turned informer against her."

"You said she murdered Singleton."

"Not exactly."

"You said she committed the crime," he insisted.

"The crime was attempted murder, done by proxy, but you finished Singleton off. I think he'd still be alive if you hadn't got your knife into him."

Benning's body jerked backwards. His large grimy hands moved towards each other across his denim-

243

covered abdomen. The thumb and forefinger of one hand plucked at the coverall zipper as if it were a sutured incision in his flesh.

He found his voice: "This is utter nonsense. You can't prove either the fact or the intent. Singleton's death was pure accident. I couldn't stop the internal hemorrhage."

"You destroyed the body. That carries a lot of weight."

"If you could prove it. But there is no body. You have nothing." It was an echo of what he had said about himself.

"Singleton's bones will do."

"Bones?"

"The skeleton you rigged to hold Bess in line. It's turned into a booby trap."

"You've left me far behind."

I moved the gun in my hand, drawing his attention to it. "Open the closet in the examination room."

He rose, still holding his middle where my accusation had hit him. I thought he was too willing. The closet was empty. He shut the door and leaned against it. His long-toothed melancholy grin mimicked the grin of the absent skull.

"Where is it, doctor?"

"I suppose Bess took it with her. That would be fitting, too."

There was an iron grate set in the baseboard beside the closet door. Benning's glance rested on it involuntarily, a second too long. The grate was the closed outlet of an old-fashioned hot-air system. Holding my gun on Benning, I stooped to touch it. It was warm, and under it I could sense the minute vibrations of fire.

"Show me the furnace."

Benning stood flat against the door, his eyes gleaming palely, as though they belonged to a tormented animal crouched inside of him. He drooped suddenly, but I distrusted his docility. It was taut and dangerous. I held my gun close to his back as we went through the house and down the basement stairs.

The light was still on in the basement. A naked bulb suspended on a wire cast a dingy yellow glare on shelves of empty jars, broken furniture, newspapers and magazines, generations of cobwebs. A rusty three-burner gas plate squatted on a bench beside the stairs, and a copper boiler, dented and green with age, hung on the wall above it. Benning avoided that corner of the basement.

In the far corner, behind a rough board partition, an old cast-iron furnace was breathing like a bull. I used my toe to open the fire door, and saw what lay in the heart of the fire: a skull licked by flames in a phœnix nest of bones.

Beside me, Benning was lost in contemplation. The orange light of the fire played feebly on the lower part of his face. He seemed for an instant to be young and smiling.

"Put it out."

He came to himself with a start. "I can't. I don't know how."

"Find a way, and be quick about it. Those bones are worth money to me."

He attached a garden hose to a tap in the hot water tank, and turned its stream on the fire. Steam sizzled and gushed from the furnace door. He emerged from it coughing, and sat down on a pile of kindling against the board partition. I looked into the blackened fire-box at five thousand dollars' worth of charred bones, all that remained of the golden boy. It was a hell of a way to make money, selling dead men's bones. I kicked the iron door shut.

With his eyes closed, his head lolling back against the boards, Benning looked like another dead man.

"Are you ready to give me a full confession?"

"Never," he said. "They can't convict me."

"They have three tries, remember."

"Three?"

"If it was only Singleton, there'd be some room for doubt, even for sympathy. He took Bess away from you. You had some justification for letting the scalpel slip in his bowels."

He said in a deeper voice: "My enemy was delivered into my hands." Then opened his eyes in bewilderment, as if he had talked in his sleep and waked himself from nightmare.

"That doesn't apply to Lucy. She tried to help you."

Benning laughed. With a great effort, he throttled the laugh and imposed silence on himself.

"Before Bess was killed tonight, she told me Lucy assisted at the operation. Lucy was in a position to know who and what killed Singleton. When things closed in on her—landlady trouble, no job, detectives tailing her—she thought of selling her knowledge to Singleton's family. But she made the mistake of coming to you yesterday and giving you a chance before she did anything final.

"If she could get money from you, she wouldn't have to sell you out or involve herself in a murder case. You gave her the money you had on hand, enough to buy a train ticket and get out of town. You also hedged against the chance that she wouldn't take that train, by filching her motel-key out of her purse. Lucy missed the train, in every sense. When she went back to the motel, you were waiting in her room. She tried to defend herself with a knife. You were too strong for her."

"You can't prove it," Benning said. Bowed far forward, he was staring down at the wet concrete floor.

"A witness will turn up. Somebody must have seen

246

you go out, even if Florie didn't. You must have passed somebody who knows you between here and the Mountview Motel, going or coming. If I have to, I'm going to canvass the whole population of the town."

His head came up as if I had tightened a knot under his jaw. He knew he had been seen. "Why do you want to do this? Why do you hate me?" He wasn't asking me alone. He was asking all the people who had known him and not loved him in his life.

"Lucy was young," I said. "She had a boy friend who wanted to marry her. They honeymooned in the morgue, and Alex is still in jail, sweating out your rap for you. Do you think you're worth the trouble you've caused?"

He didn't answer me.

"It's not just the people you've killed. It's the human idea you've been butchering and boiling down and trying to burn away. You can't stand the human idea. You and Una Durano don't stack up against it, and you know it. You know it makes you look lousy. Even a dollar-chaser like Max Heiss makes you look lousy. So you have to burn his face off with a blowtorch. Isn't that what you did?"

"It's not true. He demanded money. I had no money to give him."

"You could have taken your medicine," I said. "That never occurred to you. It hasn't yet. When Max found the Buick in your barn, that made him your enemy. Naturally he had to die. And when he came back for his money, you were ready for him, with Singleton's clothes and a blowtorch and a can of gasoline. It must have seemed like a wonderful plan, to get rid of Heiss and in the same motion establish Singleton's death by accident. But all it accomplished was to tip Bess off on what you'd done. As soon as I

247

told her about the car he was found in, she realized you killed Max. And she left you."

"She left me, yes. After all I'd done for her."

"Not for her. For you. You've killed two men and a woman because they threatened your security. You'd have killed Bess if she hadn't got out fast. She didn't tell me that, but I think she knew it. She was the one you wanted to kill from the start, if you hadn't been afraid."

He shuddered, covering his eyes with his spread fingers. "Why are you torturing me?"

"I want a confession."

It took him several minutes to bring himself under control. When he lowered his hands, his face had smoothed and thinned. His eyes seemed smaller and darker. No animal was using them.

He got up awkwardly from the pile of wood and took a halting step towards me:

"I'll give you a confession, Mr. Archer. If you'll let me have access to my drug cabinet, for just a moment?"

"No."

"It will save time and trouble, for all of us."

"It's too easy. I've promised myself one satisfaction out of this case. To see you go in and Alex Norris come out."

"You're a hard man."

"I hope so. It's the soft ones, the self-pity boys like you, that give me bad dreams." I had had enough of that basement, cluttered with broken objects, wet and hot and squalid with broken desires. "Let's go, Benning."

Outside, the flawed white moon was higher among the stars. Benning looked up at them as if the night had really become a cave of shadows, the moon a clouded port and the stars peepholes into a terrible brightness:

"I do feel grief for her. I loved her. There was nothing I wouldn't do."

He started down the veranda steps, his short black shadow dragging and jerking at his heels.

THE GALTON CASE

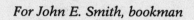

For John E. Smith, bookman

chapter

1

THE law offices of Wellesley and Sable were over a savings bank on the main street of Santa Teresa. Their private elevator lifted you from a bare little lobby into an atmosphere of elegant simplicity. It created the impression that after years of struggle you were rising effortlessly to your natural level, one of the chosen.

Facing the elevator, a woman with carefully dyed red hair was toying with the keyboard of an electric typewriter. A bowl full of floating begonias sat on the desk in front of her. Audubon prints picked up the colors and tossed them discreetly around the oak walls. A Harvard chair stood casually in one corner.

I sat down on it, in the interests of self-improvement, and picked up a fresh copy of the *Wall Street Journal*. Apparently this was the right thing to do. The red-headed secretary stopped typing and condescended to notice me.

"Do you wish to see anyone?"

"I have an appointment with Mr. Sable."

"Would you be Mr. Archer?"

"Yes."

She relaxed her formal manner: I wasn't one of the chosen after all. "I'm Mrs. Haines. Mr. Sable didn't come into the office today, but he asked me to give you a message when you got here. Would you mind going out to his house?"

"I guess not." I got up out of the Harvard chair. It was like being expelled.

"I realize it's a nuisance," she said sympathetically. "Do you know how to reach his place?"

"Is he still in his beach cottage?"

"No, he gave that up when he got married. They built a house in the country."

"I didn't know he was married."

"Mr. Sable's been married for nearly two years now. Very much so."

The feline note in her voice made me wonder if she was

1

married. Though she called herself Mrs. Haines, she had the air of a woman who had lost her husband to death or divorce and was looking for a successor. She leaned toward me in sudden intimacy:

"You're the detective, aren't you?"

I acknowledged that I was.

"Is Mr. Sable hiring you personally, on his own hook? I mean, the reason I asked, he didn't say anything to me about it."

The reason for that was obvious. "Me, either," I said. "How do I get to his house?"

"It's out in Arroyo Park. Maybe I better show you on the map."

We had a brief session of map-reading. "You turn off the highway just before you get to the wye," she said, "and then you turn right here at the Arroyo Country Day School. You curve around the lake for about a half a mile, and you'll see the Sables' mailbox."

I found the mailbox twenty minutes later. It stood under an oak tree at the foot of a private road. The road climbed a wooded hill and ended at a house with many windows set under the overhang of a flat green gravel roof.

The front door opened before I got to it. A man with streaked gray hair growing low on his forehead came across the lawn to meet me. He wore the white jacket of domestic service, but even with this protective coloration he didn't fit into the expensive suburb. He carried his heavy shoulders jauntily, as if he was taking his body for a well-deserved walk.

"Looking for somebody, mister?"

"Mr. Sable sent for me."

"What for?"

"If he didn't tell you," I said, "the chances are that he doesn't want you to know."

The houseman came up closer to me and smiled. His smile was wide and raw, like a dog's grin, and meaningless, except that it meant trouble. His face was seamed with the marks of the trouble-prone. He invited violence, as certain other people invite friendship.

Gordon Sable called from the doorway: "It's all right, Peter. I'm expecting this chap." He trotted down the flagstone path and gave me his hand. "Good to see you, Lew. It's been several years, hasn't it?"

"Four."

2

Sable didn't look any older. The contrast of his tanned face with his wavy white hair somehow supported an illusion of youth. He had on a Madras shirt cinched in by form-fitting English flannels which called attention to his tennis-player's waistline.

"I hear you got married," I said.

"Yes. I took the plunge." His happy expression seemed a little forced. He turned to the houseman, who was standing there listening: "You'd better see if Mrs. Sable needs anything. And then come out to my study. Mr. Archer's had a long drive, and he'll be wanting a drink."

"Yaas, massuh," the houseman said broadly.

Sable pretended not to notice. He led me into the house, along a black-and-white terrazzo corridor, across an enclosed court crowded with tropical plants whose massed colors were broken up and reflected by an oval pool in the center. Our destination was a sun-filled room remote from the rest of the house and further insulated by the hundreds of books lining its walls.

Sable offered me a leather chair facing the desk and the windows. He adjusted the drapes to shut off some of the light.

"Peter should be along in a minute. I'm afraid I must apologize for his manners, or lack of them. It's hard to get the right sort of help these days."

"I have the same trouble. The squares want security, and the hipsters want a chance to push people around at fifty dollars a day. Neither of which I can give them. So I still do most of my own work."

"I'm glad to hear that." Sable sat on the edge of the desk and leaned toward me confidentially: "The matter that I'm thinking of entrusting to you is a rather delicate one. It's essential, for reasons that will emerge, that there should be no publicity. Anything you find out, if you do find anything out, you report to me. Orally. I don't want anything in writing. Is that understood?"

"You make it very clear. Is this your personal business, or for a client?"

"For a client, of course. Didn't I say so on the telephone? She's saddled me with a rather difficult assignment. Frankly, I see very little chance of satisfying her hopes."

"What does she hope for?"

Sable lifted his eyes to the bleached beams of the ceiling. "The impossible, I'm afraid. When a man's dropped out of sight for over twenty years, we have to assume that he's dead and buried. Or, at the very least, that he doesn't want to be found."

"This is a missing-persons case, then?"

"A rather hopeless one, as I've tried to tell my client. On the other hand, I can't refuse to make an attempt to carry out her wishes. She's old, and ill, and used to having her own way."

"And rich?"

Sable frowned at my levity. He specialized in estate work, and moved in circles where money was seen but not heard.

"The lady's husband left her excellently provided for." He added, to put me in my place: "You'll be well paid for your work, no matter how it turns out."

The houseman came in behind me. I knew he was there by the change in the lighting. He wore old yachting sneakers, and moved without sound.

"You took your time," Sable said.

"Martinis take time to mix."

"I didn't order Martinis."

"The Mrs. did."

"You shouldn't be serving her Martinis before lunch, or any other time."

"Tell her that."

"I intend to. At the moment I'm telling you."

"Yaas, massuh."

Sable reddened under his tan. "That dialect bit isn't funny, you know."

The houseman made no reply. His green eyes were bold and restless. He looked down at me, as if for applause.

"Quite a servant problem you have," I said, by way of supporting Sable.

"Oh, Peter means well, don't you, old boy?" As if to foreclose an answer, he looked at me with a grin pasted on over his embarrassment. "What will you drink, Lew? I'm going to have a tonic."

"That will do for me."

The houseman retreated.

"What about this disappearance?" I said.

"Perhaps disappearance isn't exactly the right word. My client's son walked out on his family deliberately. They made no attempt to follow him up or bring him back, at least not for many years."

"Why not?"

4

"I gather they were just as dissatisfied with him as he was with them. They disapproved of the girl he'd married. 'Disapproved' is putting it mildly, and there were other bones of contention. You can see how serious the rift was from the fact that he sacrificed his right to inherit a large estate."

"Does he have a name, or do we call him Mr. X?"

Sable looked pained. It hurt him physically to divulge information. "The family's name is Galton. The son's name is, or was, Anthony Galton. He dropped out of sight in 1936. He was twenty-two at the time, just out of Stanford."

"That's a long time ago." From where I sat, it was like a previous century.

"I told you this thing was very nearly hopeless. However, Mrs. Galton wants her son looked for. She's going to die any day herself, and she feels the need for some sort of reconciliation with the past."

"Who says she's going to die?"

"Her doctor. Dr. Howell says it could happen at any time."

The houseman loped into the room with a clinking tray. He made a show of serviceability as he passed us our gin-and-tonics. I noticed the blue anchor tattoo on the back of his hand, and wondered if he was a sailor. Nobody would mistake him for a trained servant. A half-moon of old lipstick clung to the rim of the glass he handed me.

When he went away again, I said:

"Young Galton got married before he left?"

"Indeed he did. His wife was the immediate cause of the trouble in the family. She was going to have a child."

"And all three of them dropped out of sight?"

"As if the earth had opened and swallowed them," Sable said dramatically.

"Were there any indications of foul play?"

"Not so far as I know. I wasn't associated with the Galton family at the time. I'm going to ask Mrs. Galton herself to tell you about the circumstances of her son's departure. I don't know exactly how much of it she wants aired."

"Is there more to it?"

"I believe so. Well, cheers," he said cheerlessly. He gulped his drink standing. "Before I take you to see her, I'd like some assurance that you can give us your full time for as long as necessary."

"I have no commitments. How much of an effort does she want?"

"The best you can give, naturally."

5

"You might do better with one of the big organizations."

"I think not. I know you, and I trust you to handle this affair with some degree of urbanity. I can't have Mrs. Galton's last days darkened by scandal. My overriding concern in this affair is the protection of the family name."

Sable's voice throbbed with emotion, but I doubted that it was related to any deep feeling he had for the Galton family. He kept looking past me or through me, anxiously, as if his real concerns lay somewhere else.

I got some hint of what they were when we were on our way out. A pretty blond woman about half his age emerged from behind a banana tree in the court. She was wearing jeans and an open-necked white shirt. She moved with a kind of clumsy stealth, like somebody stepping out of ambush.

"Hello, Gordon," she said in a brittle voice. "Fancy meeting you here."

"I live here, don't I?"

"That was supposed to be the theory."

Sable spoke carefully to her, as if he was editing his sentences in his head: "Alice, this is no time to go into all of it again. Why do you think I stayed home this morning?"

"A lot of good it did me. Where do you think you're going now?"

"Out."

"Out where?"

"You have no right to cross-examine me, you know."

"Oh yes I have a right."

She stood squarely in front of him in a deliberately ugly posture, one hip out, her breasts thrust forward under the white shirt, and at the same time sharp and tender. She didn't seem to be drunk, but there was a hot moist glitter in her eyes. Her eyes were large and violet, and should have been beautiful. With dark circles under them, and heavy eyeshadow on the upper lids, they were like two spreading bruises.

"Where are you taking my husband?" she said to me.

"Mr. Sable is doing the taking. It's a business matter."

"What sort of business, eh? Whose business?"

"Certainly not yours, dear." Sable put his arm around her. "Come to your room now. Mr. Archer is a private detective working on a case for me—nothing to do with you."

"I bet not." She jerked away from him, and swung back

6

to me. "What do you want from me? There's nothing to find out. I sit in this morgue of a house, with nobody to talk to, nothing to do. I wish I was back in Chicago. People in Chicago *like* me."

"People here like you, too." Sable was watching her patiently, waiting for her bout of emotion to wear itself out.

"People here hate me. I can't even order drinks in my own house."

"Not in the morning, and this is why."

"You don't love me at all." Her anger was dissolving into self-pity. A shift of internal pressure forced tears from her eyes. "You don't care a thing about me."

"I care very much. Which is why I hate to see you fling yourself around the landscape. Come on, dear, let's go in."

He touched her waist, and this time she didn't resist. With one arm holding her, he escorted her around the pool to a door which opened on the court. When he closed the door behind them, she was leaning heavily on him.

I found my own way out.

chapter

2

SABLE kept me waiting for half an hour. From where I sat in my car, I could see Santa Teresa laid out like a contour map, distinct in the noon light. It was an old and settled city, as such things go in California. Its buildings seemed to belong to its hills, to lean with some security on the past. In contrast with them, Sable's house was a living-machine, so new it hardly existed.

When he came out, he was wearing a brown suit with a wicked little red pin stripe in it, and carrying a cordovan dispatch case. His manner had changed to match his change in costume. He was businesslike, brisk, and remote.

Following his instructions and his black Imperial, I drove into the city and across it to an older residential section. Massive traditional houses stood far back from the street, behind high masonry walls or topiary hedges.

Arroyo Park was an economic battleground where managers and professional people matched wits and incomes. The people on Mrs. Galton's street didn't know there had been a war. Their grandfathers or great-grandfathers had won it for them; death and taxes were all they had to cope with.

Sable made a signal for a left turn. I followed him between stone gateposts in which the name Galton was cut. The majestic iron gates gave a portcullis effect. A serf who was cutting the lawn with a power-mower paused to tug at his forelock as we went by. The lawn was the color of the ink they use to print the serial numbers on banknotes, and it stretched in unbroken smoothness for a couple of hundred yards. The white façade of a pre-Mizener Spanish mansion glared in the green distance.

The driveway curved around to the side of the house, and through a porte-cochere. I parked behind a Chevrolet coupé displaying a doctor's caduceus. Further back, in the shade of a great oak, two girls in shorts were playing badminton. The bird flew back and forth between them in flashing repartee. When the dark-headed girl with her back to us missed, she said:

"Oh, damn it!"

"Temper," Gordon Sable said.

She pivoted like a dancer. I saw that she wasn't a girl, but a woman with a girl's body. A slow blush spread over her face. She covered her discomfiture with an exaggerated pout which made the most of her girlishness:

"I'm off my form. Sheila *never* beats me."

"I do so!" cried the girl on the other side of the net. "I beat you three times in the last week. Today is the fourth time."

"The set isn't over yet."

"No, but I'm going to beat you." Sheila's voice had an intensity which didn't seem to go with her appearance. She was very young, no more than eighteen. She had a peaches-and-cream complexion and soft doe eyes.

The woman scooped up the bird and tossed it over the net. They went on playing, all out, as if a great deal depended on the game.

A Negro maid in a white cap let us into a reception room. Wrought-iron chandeliers hung like giant black bunches of withered grapes from the high ceiling. Ancient black furniture stood in museum arrangements around the walls under old dark pictures. The windows were narrow and deep in the thick walls, like the windows of a medieval castle.

"Is Dr. Howell with her?" Sable asked the maid.

"Yes, sir, but he ought to be leaving any time now. He's been here for quite a while."

"She didn't have an attack?"

"No, sir. It's just the doctor's regular visit."

"Would you tell him I'd like to see him before he leaves?"

"Yes, sir."

She whisked away. Sable said in a neutral tone, without looking at me: "I won't apologize for my wife. You know how women are."

"Uh-huh." I didn't really want his confidences.

If I had, he wouldn't have given them to me. "There are certain South American tribes that segregate women one week out of the month. Shut them up in a hut by themselves and let them rip. There's quite a lot to be said for the system."

"I can see that."

"Are you married, Archer?"

"I have been."

"Then you know what it's like. They want you with them all the time. I've given up yachting. I've given up golf. I've practically given up living. And still she isn't satisfied. What do you do with a woman like that?"

I'd given up offering advice. Even when people asked for it, they resented getting it. "You're the lawyer."

I strolled around the room and looked at the pictures on the walls. They were mostly ancestor-worship art: portraits of Spanish dons, ladies in hoop skirts with bare monolithic bosoms, a Civil War officer in blue, and several gentlemen in nineteenth-century suits with sour nineteenth-century pusses between their whiskers. The one I liked best depicted a group of top-hatted tycoons watching a bulldog-faced tycoon hammer a gold spike into a railroad tie. There was a buffalo in the background, looking sullen.

The maid returned with a man in Harris tweeds. Sable introduced him as Dr. Howell. He was a big man in his fifties, who carried himself with unconscious authority.

"Mr. Archer is a private investigator," Sable said. "Did Mrs. Galton mention what she has in mind?"

"Indeed she did." The doctor ran his fingers through his gray crewcut. The lines in his forehead deepened. "I thought that whole business of Tony was finished and forgotten years ago. Who persuaded her to drag it back into the light?"

"Nobody did, so far as I know. It was her own idea. How is she, Doctor?"

"As well as can be expected. Maria is in her seventies. She

has a heart. She has asthma. It's an unpredictable combination."

"But there's no immediate danger?"

"I wouldn't think so. I can't say what will happen if she's subjected to shock or distress. Asthma is one of those things."

"Psychosomatic, you mean?"

"Somatopsychic, whatever you want to call it. In any case it's a disease that's affected by the emotions. Which is why I hate to see Maria getting all stirred up again about that wretched son of hers. What does she hope to gain?"

"Emotional satisfaction, I suppose. She feels she treated him badly, and wants to make up for it."

"But isn't he dead? I thought he was found to be legally dead."

"He could have been. We had an official search made some years ago. He'd already been missing for fourteen years, which is twice the time required by the law to establish presumption of death. Mrs. Galton wouldn't let me make the petition, however. I think she's always dreamed of Anthony coming back to claim his inheritance and all that. In the last few weeks it's become an obsession with her."

"I wouldn't go that far," the doctor said. "I still think somebody put a bee in her bonnet, and I can't help wondering why."

"Who do you have in mind?"

"Cassie Hildreth, perhaps. She has a lot of influence on Maria. And speaking of dreams, she had a few of her own when she was a kid. She used to follow Tony around as if he was the light of the world. Which he was far from being, as you know." Howell's smile was one-sided and saturnine.

"This is news to me. I'll talk to Miss Hildreth."

"It's pure speculation on my part, don't misunderstand me. I do think this business should be played down as much as possible."

"I've been trying to play it down. On the other hand I can't downright refuse to lift a finger."

"No, but it would be all to the good if you could just keep it going along, without any definite results, until she gets interested in something different." The doctor included me in his shrewd glance. "You understand me?"

"I understand you all right," I said. "Go through the motions but don't do any real investigating. Isn't that pretty expensive therapy?"

10

"She can afford it, if that's what worries you. Maria has more coming in every month than she spends every year." He regarded me in silence for a moment, stroking his prow of a nose. "I don't mean you shouldn't do your job. I wouldn't ask any man to lie down on a job he's paid to do. But if you find out anything that might upset Mrs. Galton—"

Sable put in quickly: "I've already taken that up with Archer. He'll report to me. I think you know you can rely on my discretion."

"I think I know I can."

Sable's face changed subtly. His eyelids flickered as though he had been threatened with a blow, and remained heavy over his watchful eyes. For a man of his age and financial weight, he was very easily hurt.

I said to the doctor: "Did you know Anthony Galton?"

"Somewhat."

"What kind of person was he?"

Howell glanced toward the maid, who was still waiting in the doorway. She caught his look and withdrew out of sight. Howell lowered his voice:

"Tony was a sport. I mean that in the biological sense, as well as the sociological. He didn't inherit the Galton characteristics. He had utter contempt for business of any kind. Tony used to say he wanted to be a writer, but I never saw any evidence of talent. What he was really good at was boozing and fornicating. I gather he ran with a very rough crowd in San Francisco. I've always believed myself that one of them killed him for the money in his pockets and threw him in the Bay."

"Was there any indication of that sort of thing?"

"Not to my certain knowledge. But San Francisco in the thirties was a dangerous place for a boy to play around in. He must have dredged pretty deep to turn up the girl he married."

"You knew her, did you?" Sable said.

"I examined her. His mother sent her to me, and I examined her."

"Was she here in town?" I said.

"Briefly. Tony brought her home the week he married her. I don't believe he had any notion the family would accept her. It was more a case of flinging her in their faces. If that was his idea, it succeeded very well."

"What was the matter with the girl?"

11

"The obvious thing, and it was obvious—she was seven months' pregnant."

"And you say they'd just been married?"

"That's correct. She hooked him. I talked with her a little, and I'd wager he picked her up, hot off the streets. She was a pretty enough little thing, in spite of her big belly, but she'd had a hard life. There were scars on her thighs and buttocks. She wouldn't explain them to me, but it was evident that she'd been beaten, more than once." The cruel memory raised faint traces of scarlet on the doctor's cheekbones.

The doe-eyed girl from the badminton court appeared in the doorway behind him. Her body was like ripening fruit, only partly concealed by her sleeveless jersey and rolled shorts. She glowed with healthy beauty, but her mouth was impatient:

"Daddy? How much longer?"

The color on his cheekbones heightened when he saw her. "Roll down your pants, Sheila."

"They're not pants."

"Whatever they are, roll them down."

"Why should I?"

"Because I'm telling you to."

"You could at least tell me in private. How much longer do I have to wait?"

"I thought you were going to read to your Aunt Maria."

"Well, I'm not."

"You promised."

"You were the one who promised for me. I played badminton with Cassie, and that's my good turn for the day."

She moved away, deliberately exaggerating the swing of her hips. Howell glared at the chronometer on his wrist, as if it was the source of all his troubles. "I must be getting along. I have other calls to make."

"Can you give me the wife's description?" I said. "Or her name?"

"I don't recall her name. As for appearance, she was a little blue-eyed brunette, rather thin in spite of her condition. Mrs. Galton—no, on second thought I wouldn't ask her about the girl unless she brings the matter up herself."

The doctor turned to go, but Sable detained him: "Is it all right for Mr. Archer to question her? I mean, it won't affect her heart or bring on an asthmatic attack?"

"I can't guarantee it. If Maria insists on having an attack,

12

there's nothing I can do to prevent it. Seriously, though, if Tony's on her mind she might as well talk about him. It's better than sitting and brooding. Good-by, Mr. Archer, nice to meet you. Good day, Sable."

chapter
3

THE maid took Sable and me to a sitting-room on the second floor where Mrs. Galton was waiting. The room smelled of medicine, and had a hushed hospital atmosphere. The heavy drapes were partly drawn over the windows. Mrs. Galton was resting in semi-twilight on a chaise longue, with a robe over her knees.

She was fully dressed, with something white and frilly at her withered throat; and she held her gray head ramrod straight. Her voice was reedy, but surprisingly resonant. It seemed to carry all the remaining force of her personality:

"You've kept me waiting, Gordon. It's nearly time for my lunch. I expected you before Dr. Howell came."

"I'm awfully sorry, Mrs. Galton. I was delayed at home."

"Don't apologize. I detest apologies, they're really just further demands on one's patience." She cocked a bright eye at him. "Has that wife of yours been giving you trouble again?"

"Oh, no, nothing of that sort."

"Good. You know my thoughts on the subject of divorce. On the other hand, you should have taken my advice and not married her. A man who waits until he's nearly fifty to get married should give up the idea entirely. Mr. Galton was in his late forties when we were married. As a direct consequence, I've had to endure nearly twenty years of window-hood."

"It's been hard, I know," Sable said with unction.

The maid had started out of the room. Mrs. Galton called her back: "Wait a minute. I want you to tell Miss Hildreth to bring me my lunch herself. She can bring up a sandwich and eat it with me if she likes. You tell Miss Hildreth that."

"Yes, Mrs. Galton."

The old lady waved us into chairs, one on each side of her, and turned her eye on me. It was bright and alert but somehow inhuman, like a bird's eye. It looked at me as if I belonged to an entirely different species:

"Is this the man who is going to find my prodigal son for me?"

"Yes, this is Mr. Archer."

"I'm going to give it a try," I said, remembering the doctor's advice. "I can't promise any definite results. Your son has been missing for a very long time."

"I'm better aware of that than you, young man. I last set eyes on Anthony on the eleventh day of October 1936. We parted in bitter anger and hatred. I've lived ever since with that anger and hatred corroding my heart. But I can't die with it inside of me. I want to see Anthony again, and talk to him. I want to forgive him. I want him to forgive me."

Deep feeling sounded in her voice. I had no doubt that the feeling was partly sincere. Still, there was something unreal about it. I suspected that she'd been playing tricks with her emotions for a long time, until none of them was quite valid.

"Forgive you?" I said.

"For treating him as I did. He was a young fool, and he made some disastrous mistakes, but none of them really justified Mr. Galton's action, and mine, in casting him off. It was a shameful action, and if it's not too late I intend to rectify it. If he still has his little wife, I'm willing to accept her. I authorize you to tell him that. I want to see my grandchild before I die."

I looked at Sable. He shook his head slightly, deprecatingly. His client was just a little out of context, but she had quick insight, at least into other people:

"I know what you're both thinking. You're thinking that Anthony is dead. If he were dead, I'd know it here." Her hand strayed over the flat silk surface of her breast. "He's my only son. He must be alive, and he must be somewhere. Nothing is lost in the universe."

Except human beings, I thought. "I'll do my best, Mrs. Galton. There are one or two things you can do to help me. Give me a list of his friends at the time of his disappearance."

"I never knew his friends."

"He must have had friends in college. Wasn't he attending Stanford?"

"He'd left there the previous spring. He didn't even wait to graduate. Anyway, none of his schoolmates knew what happened to him. His father canvassed them thoroughly at the time."

"Where was your son living after he left college?"

"In a flat in the slums of San Francisco. With that woman."

14

"Do you have the address?"

"I believe I may have it somewhere. I'll have Miss Hildreth look for it."

"That will be a start, anyway. When he left here with his wife, did they plan to go back to San Francisco?"

"I haven't any idea. I didn't see them before they left."

"I understood they came to visit you."

"Yes, but they didn't even stay the night."

"What might help most," I said carefully, "would be if you could tell me the exact circumstances of their visit, and their departure. Anything your son said about his plans, anything the girl said, anything you remember about her. Do you remember her name?"

"He called her Teddy. I have no idea if that was her name or not. We had very little conversation. I can't recall what was said. The atmosphere was unpleasant, and it left a bad taste in my mouth. *She* left a bad taste in my mouth. It was so evident that she was a cheap little gold-digger."

"How do you know?"

"I have eyes. I have ears." Anger had begun to whine in the undertones of her voice. "She was dressed and painted like a woman of the streets, and when she opened her mouth —well, she spoke the language of the streets. She made coarse jokes about the child in her womb, and how"—her voice faded almost out—"it got there. She had no respect for herself as a woman, no moral standards. That girl destroyed my son."

She'd forgotten all about her hope of reconciliation. The angry wheezing in the passages of her head sounded like a ghost in a ruined house. Sable was looking at her anxiously, but he held his tongue.

"Destroyed him?" I said.

"Morally, she destroyed him. She possessed him like an evil spirit. My son would never have taken the money if it hadn't been for the spell she cast on him. I know that with utter certitude."

Sable leaned forward in his chair. "What money are you referring to?"

"The money Anthony stole from his father. Haven't I told you about it, Gordon? No, I don't believe I have. I've told no one, I've always been so ashamed." She lifted her hands and dropped them in her robed lap. "But now I can forgive him for that, too."

"How much money was involved?" I said.

15

"I don't know exactly how much, to the penny. Several thousand dollars, anyway. Ever since the day the banks closed, Mr. Galton had had a habit of keeping a certain amount of cash for current expenses."

"Where did he keep it?"

"In his private safe, in the study. The combination was on a piece of paper pasted to the inside of his desk drawer. Anthony must have found it there, and used it to open the safe. He took everything in it, all the money, and even some of my jewels which I kept there."

"Are you sure he took it?"

"Unfortunately, yes. It disappeared at the same time he did. It's why he hid himself away, and never came back to us."

Sable's glum look deepened. Probably he was thinking the same thing I was: that several thousand dollars in cash, in the slums of San Francisco, in the depths of the depression, were a very likely passport to oblivion.

But we couldn't say it out loud. With her money, and her asthma, and her heart, Mrs. Galton was living at several removes from reality. Apparently that was how it had to be.

"Do you have a picture of your son, taken not too long before his disappearance?"

"I believe I have. I'll ask Cassie to have a look. She should be coming soon."

"In the meantime, can you give me any other information? Particularly about where your son might have gone, who or where he might have visited."

"I know nothing of his life after he left the university. He cut himself off from all decent society. He was perversely bound to sink in the social scale, to declass himself. I'm afraid my son had a *nostalgie de la boue*—a nostalgia for the gutter. He tried to cover it over with fancy talk about re-establishing contact with the earth, becoming a poet of the people, and such nonsense. His real interest was dirt for dirt's own sake. I brought him up to be pure in thought and desire, but somehow—somehow he became fascinated with the pitch that defileth. And the pitch defiled him."

Her breathing was noisy. She had begun to shake, and scratch with waxy fingers at the robe that covered her knees.

Sable leaned toward her solicitously. "You mustn't excite yourself, Mrs. Galton. It was all over long ago."

"It's not all over. I want Anthony back. I have nobody. I have nothing. He was stolen away from me."

16

"We'll get him back if it's humanly possible."

"Yes, I know you will, Gordon." Her mood had changed like a fitful wind. Her head inclined toward Sable's shoulder as though to rest against it. She spoke like a little girl betrayed by time and loss, by fading hair and wrinkles and the fear of death: "I'm a foolish angry old woman. You're always so good to me. Anthony will be good to me, too, won't he, when he comes? In spite of all I've said against him, he was a darling boy. He was always good to his poor mother, and he will be again."

She was chanting in a ritual of hope. If she said it often enough, it would have to come true.

"I'm sure he will, Mrs. Galton."

Sable rose and pressed her hand. I was always a little suspicious of men who put themselves out too much for rich old ladies, or even poor ones. But then it was part of his job.

"I'm hungry," she said. "I want my lunch. What's going on downstairs?"

She lunged half out of her long chair and got hold of a wired bellpush on the table beside it. She kept her finger pressed on the button until her lunch arrived. That was a tense five minutes.

chapter
4

IT CAME on a covered platter carried by the woman I'd seen on the badminton court. She had changed her shorts for a plain linen dress which managed to conceal her figure, if not her fine brown legs. Her blue eyes were watchful.

"You kept me waiting, Cassie," the old woman said. "What on earth were you doing?"

"Preparing your food. Before that I played some badminton with Sheila Howell."

"I might have known you two would be enjoying yourselves while I sit up here starving."

"Oh come, it's not as bad as all that."

"It's not for you to say. You're not my doctor. Ask August Howell, and he'll tell you how important it is that I have my nourishment."

"I'm sorry, Aunt Maria. I thought you wouldn't want to be disturbed while you were in conference."

17

She stood just inside the doorway, still holding the tray like a shield in front of her. She wasn't young: close up, I could see the fortyish lines in her face and the knowledge in her blue eyes. But she held herself with adolescent awkwardness, immobilized by feelings she couldn't express.

"Well, you needn't stand there like a dummy."

Cassie moved suddenly. She set the tray on the table and uncovered the food. There was a good deal of food. Mrs. Galton began to fork salad into her mouth. The movements of her hands and jaws were rapid and mechanical. She was oblivious to the three of us watching her.

Sable and I retreated into the hallway and along it to the head of the stairs which curved in a baronial sweep down to the entrance hall. He leaned on the iron balustrade and lit a cigarette.

"Well, Lew, what do you think?"

I lit a cigarette of my own before I replied. "I think it's a waste of time and money."

"I told you that."

"But you want me to go ahead with it anyway?"

"I can't see any other way to handle it, or handle her. Mrs. Galton takes a good deal of handling."

"Can you trust her memory? She seems to be reliving the past. Sometimes old people get mixed up about what actually happened. That story about the money he stole, for example. Do you believe it?"

"I've never known her to lie. And I really doubt that she's as confused as she sounds. She likes to dramatize herself. It's the only excitement she has left."

"How old is she?"

"Seventy-three, I believe."

"That isn't so old. What about her son?"

"He'll be about forty-four, if he's still extant."

"She doesn't seem to realize that. She talks about him as if he was still a boy. How long has she been sitting in that room?"

"Ever since I've known her, anyway. Ten years. Occasionally, when she has a good day, she lets Miss Hildreth take her for a drive. It doesn't do much to bring her up to date, though. It's usually just a quick trip to the cemetery where her husband is buried. He died soon after Anthony took off. According to Mrs. Galton, that was what killed him. Miss Hildreth says he died of a coronary."

"Is Miss Hildreth a relative?"

"A distant one, second or third cousin. Cassie's known the family all her life, and lived with Mrs. Galton since before the war. I'm hoping she can give you something more definite to go on."

"I can use it."

A telephone shrilled somewhere, like a cricket in the wall. Cassie Hildreth came out of Mrs. Galton's room and moved briskly toward us:

"You're wanted on the telephone. It's Mrs. Sable."

"What does she want?"

"She didn't say, but she seems upset about something."

"She always is."

"You can take it downstairs if you like. There's an extension under the stairs."

"I know. I'll do that." Sable treated her brusquely, like a servant. "This is Mr. Archer, by the way. He wants to ask you some questions."

"Right now?"

"If you can spare the time," I said. "Mrs. Galton thought you could give me some pictures, perhaps some information."

"Pictures of Tony?"

"If you have them."

"I keep them for Mrs. Galton. She likes to look at them when the mood is on her."

"You work for her, do you?"

"If you can call it work. I'm a paid companion."

"I call it work."

Our eyes met. Hers were dark ocean blue. Discontent flicked a fin in their depths, but she said dutifully: "She isn't so bad. She's not at her best today. It's hard on her to rake up the past like this."

"Why is she doing it?"

"She had a serious scare not long ago. Her heart almost failed. They had to put her in an oxygen tent. She wants to make amends to Tony before she dies. She treated him badly, you know."

"Badly in what way?"

"She didn't want him to live his own life, as they say. She tried to keep him all to herself, like a—a belonging. But you'd better not get me started on that."

Cassie Hildreth bit her lip. I recalled what the doctor had said about her feeling for Tony. The whole household seemed to revolve around the missing man, as if he'd left only the day before.

19

Quick footsteps crossed the hallway below the stairs. I leaned over the balustrade and saw Sable wrench the front door open. It slammed behind him.

"Where's he off to?"

"Probably home. That wife of his—" She hesitated, editing the end of the sentence: "She lives on emergencies. If you'd like to see those pictures, they're in my room."

Her door was next to Mrs. Galton's sitting-room. She unlocked it with a Yale key. Apart from its size and shape, its lofty ceiling, the room bore no relation to the rest of the house. The furniture was modern. There were Paul Klee reproductions on the walls, new novels on the bookshelves. The ugly windows were masked with monks-cloth drapes. A narrow bed stood behind a woven wood screen in one corner.

Cassie Hildreth went into the closet and emerged with a sheaf of photographs in her hand.

"Show me the best likeness first."

She shuffled through them, her face intent and peaked, and handed me a posed studio portrait. Anthony Galton had been a handsome boy. I stood and let his features sink into my mind: light eyes set wide apart and arched over by intelligent brows, short straight nose, small mouth with rather full lips, a round girlish chin. The missing feature was character or personality, the meaning that should have held the features together. The only trace of this was in the one-sided smile. It seemed to say: to hell with you. Or maybe, to hell with me.

"This was his graduation picture," Cassie Hildreth said softly.

"I thought he never graduated from college."

"He didn't. This was made before he dropped out."

"Why didn't he graduate?"

"He wouldn't give his father the satisfaction. Or his mother. They forced him to study mechanical engineering, which was the last thing Tony was interested in. He stuck it out for four years, but he finally refused to take his degree in it."

"Did he flunk out?"

"Heavens, no. Tony was very bright. Some of his professors thought he was brilliant."

"But not in engineering?"

"There wasn't anything he couldn't do, if he wanted to. His real interests were literary. He wanted to be a writer."

"I take it you knew him well."

"Of course. I wasn't living with the Galtons then, but I used to visit her, often, when Tony was on vacation. He used to talk to me. He was a wonderful conversationalist."

"Describe him, will you?"

"But you've just seen his picture. And here are others."

"I'll look at them in a minute. Right now I want you to tell me about him."

"If you insist, I'll try." She closed her eyes. Her face smoothed out, as if years were being erased: "He was a lovely man. His body was finely proportioned, lean and strong. His head was beautifully balanced on his neck, and he had close fair curls." She opened her eyes. "Did you ever see the Praxiteles Hermes?"

I felt a little embarrassed, not only because I hadn't. Her description of Tony had the force of a passionate avowal. I hadn't expected anything like it. Cassie's emotion was like spontaneous combustion in an old hope chest.

"No," I said. "What color were his eyes?"

"Gray. A lovely soft gray. He had the eyes of a poet."

"I see. Were you in love with him?"

She gave me a startled look. "Surely you don't expect me to answer that."

"You just did. You say he used to talk to you. Did he ever discuss his plans for the future?"

"Just in general terms. He wanted to go away and write."

"Go away where?"

"Somewhere quiet and peaceful, I suppose."

"Out of the country?"

"I doubt it. Tony disapproved of expatriates. He always said he wanted to get *closer* to America. This was in the depression, remember. He was very strong for the rights of the working class."

"Radical?"

"I guess you'd call him that. But he wasn't a Communist, if that's what you mean. He did feel that having money cut him off from life. Tony hated social snobbery—which was one reason he was so unhappy at college. He often said he wanted to live like ordinary people, lose himself in the mass."

"It looks as if he succeeded in doing just that. Did he ever talk to you about his wife?"

"Never. I didn't even know he was married, or intended to get married." She was very self-conscious. Not knowing what to do with her face, she tried to smile. The teeth between her parted lips were like white bone showing in a wound.

21

As if to divert my attention from her, she thrust the other pictures into my hands. Most of them were candid shots of Tony Galton doing various things: riding a horse, sitting on a rock in swimming trunks, holding a tennis racket with a winner's fixed grin on his face. From the pictures, and from what the people said, I got the impression of a boy going through the motions. He made the gestures of enjoyment but kept himself hidden, even from the camera. I began to have some glimmering of the psychology that made him want to lose himself.

"What did he like doing?"

"Writing. Reading and writing."

"Besides that. Tennis? Swimming?"

"Not really. Tony despised sports. He used to jeer at me for going in for them."

"What about wine and women? Dr. Howell said he was quite a playboy."

"Dr. Howell never understood him," she said. "Tony did have relations with women, and I suppose he drank, but he did it on principle."

"Is that what he told you?"

"Yes, and it's true. He was practicing Rimbaud's theory of the violation of the senses. He thought that having all sorts of remarkable experiences would make him a good poet, like Rimbaud." She saw my uncomprehending look, and added: "Arthur Rimbaud was a French poet. He and Charles Baudelaire were Tony's great idols."

"I see." We were getting off the track into territory where I felt lost. "Did you ever meet any of his women?"

"Oh, no." She seemed shocked at the idea. "He never brought any of them here."

"He brought his wife home."

"Yes, I know. I was away at school when it happened."

"When what happened?"

"The big explosion," she said. "Mr. Galton told him never to darken his door again. It was all very Victorian and heavy-father. And Tony never did darken his door again."

"Let's see, that was in October 1936. Did you ever see Tony after that?"

"Never. I was at school in the east."

"Ever hear from him?"

Her mouth started to shape the word "no," then tightened. "I had a little note from him, some time in the course of the winter. It must have been before Christmas, because I got it at school, and I didn't go back after Christmas. I think it was in the early part of December that it came."

"What did it say?"

"Nothing very definite. Simply that he was doing well, and had broken into print. He'd had a poem accepted by a little magazine in San Francisco. He sent it to me under separate cover. I've kept it, if you'd like to look at it."

She kept it in a manila envelope on the top shelf of her bookcase. The magazine was a thin little publication smudgily printed on pulp paper; its name was *Chisel*. She opened it to a middle page, and handed it to me. I read:

"LUNA, by John Brown

"White her breast
As the white foam
Where the gulls rest
Yet find no home.

"Green her eyes
As the green deep
Where the tides rise
And the storms sleep.

"And fearful am I
As a mariner
When the sea and the sky
Begin to stir.

"For wild is her heart
As the sea's leaping:
She will rise and depart
While I lie sleeping."

"Did Tony Galton write this? It's signed 'John Brown.'"

"It was the name he used. Tony wouldn't use the family name. 'John Brown' had a special meaning for him, besides. He had a theory that the country was going through another civil war—a war between the rich people and the poor people. He thought of the poor people as white Negroes, and he wanted to do for them what John Brown did for the slaves. Lead them out of bondage—in the spiritual sense, of course. Tony didn't believe in violence."

"I see," I said, though it all sounded strange to me. "Where did he send this from?"

"The magazine was published in San Francisco, and Tony sent it from there."

"This was the only time you ever heard from him?"

"The only time."

"May I keep these pictures, and the magazine? I'll try to bring them back."

"If they'll help you to find Tony."

"I understand he went to live in San Francisco. Do you have his last address?"

"I had it, but there's no use going there."

"Why not?"

"Because I did, the year after he went away. It was a wretched old tenement, and it had been condemned. They were tearing it down."

"Did you make any further attempt to find him?"

"I wanted to, but I was afraid. I was only seventeen."

"Why didn't you go back to school, Cassie?"

"I didn't especially want to. Mr. Galton wasn't well, and Aunt Maria asked me to stay with her. She was the one sending me to school, so that I couldn't very well refuse."

"And you've been here ever since?"

"Yes." The word came out with pressure behind it.

As if on cue, Mrs. Galton raised her voice on the other side of the wall: "Cassie! Cassie? Are you in there? What are you doing in there?"

"I'd better go," Cassie said.

She locked the door of her sanctuary, and went, with her head down.

After twenty-odd years of that, I'd have been crawling.

chapter

5   I MET the doctor's daughter on the stairs. She gave me a tentative smile. "Are you the detective?"

"I'm the detective. My name is Archer."

"Mine's Sheila Howell. Do you think you can find him for her?"

"I can try, Miss Howell."

"That doesn't sound too hopeful."

"It wasn't meant to."

24

"But you will do your best, won't you?"

"Is it important to you? You're too young to have known Anthony Galton."

"It's important to Aunt Maria." She added in a rush of feeling: "She needs somebody to love her. I try, honestly, but I just can't do it."

"Is she a relative of yours?"

"Not exactly. She's my godmother. I call her aunt because she likes me to. But I've never succeeded in feeling like a niece to her."

"I imagine she makes it hard."

"She doesn't mean to, but she simply doesn't know how to treat *people*. She's had her own way for so long." The girl colored, and compressed her lips. "I don't mean to be *critical*. You must think I'm an awful person, talking about her to a stranger like this. I really do wish her well, in spite of what Dad thinks. And if she wants me to read *Pendennis* to her, I will."

"Good for you. I was on my way to make a phone call. Is there a telephone handy?"

She showed me the telephone under the stairs. It was an ancient wall telephone which nobody had ever bothered to change for a modern one. The Santa Teresa directory lay on a table under it. I looked up Sable's number.

He was a long time answering. Finally, I heard the receiver being lifted at the other end of the line. After another wait, I heard his voice. I hardly recognized it. It had a blurred quality, almost as if Sable had been crying:

"This is Gordon Sable."

"Archer speaking. You took off before we could make definite arrangements. On a case like this I need an advance, and expense money, at least three hundred."

There was a click, and then a whirring on the wire. Someone was dialing. A woman's voice said: "Operator! I want the police."

"Get off the line," Sable said.

"I'm calling the police." It was his wife's voice, shrill with hysteria.

"I've already called them. Now get off the line. It's in use."

A receiver was fumbled into place. I said: "You still there, Sable?"

"Yes. There's been an accident, as you must have gathered." He paused. I could hear his breathing.

"To Mrs. Sable?"

"No, though she's badly upset. My houseman, Peter, has been stabbed. I'm afraid he's dead."

"Who stabbed him?"

"It isn't clear. I can't get much out of my wife. Apparently some goon came to the door. When Peter opened it, he was knifed."

"You want me to come out?"

"If you think it will do any good. Peter is past help."

"I'll be there in a few minutes."

But it took me longer than that. The Arroyo Park suburb was new to me. I took a wrong turning and got lost in its system of winding roads. The roads all looked alike, with flat-roofed houses, white and gray and adobe, scattered along the terraced hillsides.

I went around in circles for a while, and came out on top of the wrong hill. The road dwindled into a pair of ruts in a field where nothing stood but a water tower. I turned, and stopped to get my bearings.

On a hilltop a mile or more to my left, I could make out a flat pale green roof which looked like the Arizona gravel roof of Sable's house. On my right, far below, a narrow asphalt road ran like a dark stream along the floor of the valley. Between the road and a clump of scrub oaks an orange rag of flame came and went. Black smoke trickled up from it into the still blue air. When I moved I caught a flash of sunlight on metal. It was a car, nose down in the ditch, and burning.

I drove down the long grade and turned right along the asphalt road. A fire siren was ululating in the distance. The smoke above the burning car was twisting higher and spreading like a slow stain over the trees. Watching it, I almost ran down a man.

He was walking toward me with his head bent, as if in meditation, a thick young man with shoulders like a bull. I honked at him and applied the brakes. He came on doggedly. One of his arms swung slack, dripping red from the fingers. The other arm was cradled in the front of his sharp flannel jacket.

He came up to the door on my side and leaned against it. "Can you gimme a lift?" Oily black curls tumbled over his hot black eyes. The bright blood on his mouth gave him an obscene look, like a painted girl.

"Smash up your car?"

He grunted.

"Come around to the other side if you can make it."

"Negative. This side."

I caught the glint of larceny in his eyes, and something worse. I reached for my car keys. He was ahead of me. The short blue gun in his right hand peered at the corner of the open window:

"Leave the keys where they are. Open the door and get out."

Curlyhead talked and acted like a pro, or a least a gifted amateur with a vocation. I opened the door and got out.

He waved me away from the car. "Start walking."

I hesitated, weighing my chances of taking him.

He used his gun to point toward the city. "Get going, Bud. You don't want a calldown with me."

I started walking. The engine of my car roared behind me. I got off the road. But Curlyhead turned in a driveway, and drove off in the other direction, away from the sirens.

The fire was out when I got to it. The county firemen were coiling their hose, replacing it on the side of the long red truck. I went up to the cab and asked the man at the wheel:

"Do you have two-way radio?"

"What's it to you?"

"My car was stolen. I think the character who took it was driving the one in the ditch there. The Highway Patrol should be notified."

"Give me the details, I'll shoot them in."

I gave him the license number and description of my car, and a thumbnail sketch of Curlyhead. He started feeding them into his mike. I climbed down the bank to look at the car I'd traded mine in on. It was a black Jaguar sedan, about five years old. It had slewed off the road, gouging deep tracks in the dirt, and crumpled its nose against a boulder. One of the front tires had blown out. The windshield was starred, and the finish blistered by fire. Both doors were sprung.

I made a note of the license number, and moved up closer to look at the steering-post. The registration was missing. I got in and opened the dash compartment. It was clean.

In the road above, another car shrieked to a halt. Two sheriff's men got out on opposite sides and came down the bank in a double cloud of dust. They had guns in their hands, no-nonsense looks on their brown faces.

"This your car?" the first one snapped at me.

"No."

I started to tell him what had happened to mine, but he didn't want to hear about it:

"Out of there! Keep your hands in sight, shoulder-high."

I got out, feeling that all this had happened before. The first deputy held his gun on me while the second deputy shook me down. He was very thorough. He even investigated the fuzz in my pockets. I commented on this.

"This is no joke. What's your name?"

The firemen had begun to gather around us. I was angry and sweating. I opened my mouth and put both feet in, all the way up to the knee.

"I'm Captain Nemo," I said. "I just came ashore from a hostile submarine. Curiously enough, we fuel our subs with seaweed. The hull itself is formed from highly compressed seaweed. So take me to your wisest man. There is no time to be lost."

"He's a hophead," the first deputy said. "I kind of figured the slasher was a hophead. You heard me say so, Barney."

"Yeah." Barney was reading the contents of my wallet. "He's got a driver's license made out to somebody name of Archer, West Hollywood. And a statewide private-eye ducat, same name. But it's probably a phony."

"It's no phony." Vaudeville had got me nowhere except into deeper trouble. "My name is Archer. I'm a private investigator, employed by Mr. Sable, the lawyer."

"Sable, he says." The deputies exchanged significant looks. "Give him his wallet, Barney."

Barney held it out to me. I reached for it. The cuffs clinked snug on my wrist.

"Other wrist now," he said in a soothing voice. I was a hophead. "Let's have the other wrist now."

I hesitated. But rough stuff not only wouldn't work. It would put me in the wrong. I wanted them to be in the wrong, falling on their faces with foolishness.

I surrendered the other wrist without a struggle. Looking down at my trapped hands, I saw the dab of blood on one of my fingers.

"Let's go," the first deputy said. He dropped my wallet in the side pocket of my jacket.

They herded me up the bank and into the back of their car. The driver of the fire truck leaned from his cab:

"Keep a close eye on him, fellows. He's a cool customer.

28

He gave me a story about his car getting stolen, took me in completely."

"Not us," the first deputy said. "We're trained to spot these phonies, the way you're trained to put out fires. Don't let anybody else near the Jag. Leave a guard on it, eh? I'll send a man as soon as we can spare one."

"What did he do?"

"Knifed a man."

"Jesus, and I thought he was a citizen."

The first deputy climbed into the back seat beside me. "I got to warn you anything you say can be used against you. Why did you do it?"

"Do what?"

"Cut Peter Culligan."

"I didn't cut him."

"You got blood on your hand. Where did it come from?"

"Probably the Jaguar."

"Your car, you mean?"

"It isn't my car."

"The hell it isn't. I got a witness saw you drive away from the scene of the crime."

"I wasn't in it. The man who was in it just stole my car."

"Don't give me that. You can fool a fireman with it. I'm a cop."

"Was it woman trouble?" Barney said over his shoulder. "If it was a woman, we can understand it. Crime of passion, and all. Shucks," he added lightly, "it wouldn't even be second-degree, probably. You could be out in two-three years. Couldn't he, Conger?"

"Sure," Conger said. "You might as well tell us the truth now, get it over with."

I was getting bored with the game. "It wasn't a woman. It was seaweed. I'm a seaweed-fancier from way back. I like to sprinkle a little of it on my food."

"What's that got to do with Culligan?"

Barney said from the front seat: "He sounds to me like he's all hopped up."

Conger leaned across me. "Are you?"

"Am I what?"

"All hopped up?"

"Yeah. I chew seaweed, then I orbit. Take me to the nearest launching pad."

Conger looked at me pityingly. I was a hophead. The pity

29

was gradually displaced by doubt. He had begun to grasp that he was being ragged. Very suddenly, his face turned dusky red under the tan. He balled his right fist on his knee. I could see the packed muscles tighten under the shoulder of his blouse. I pulled in my chin and got ready to roll with the punch. But he didn't hit me.

Under the circumstances, this made him a good cop. I almost began to like him, in spite of the handcuffs. I said:

"As I told you before, my name is Archer. I'm a licensed private detective, retired sergeant from the Long Beach P.D. The California Penal Code has a section on false arrest. Do you think you better take the jewelry off?"

Barney said from the front seat: "A poolroom lawyer, eh?"

Conger didn't say anything. He sat in pained silence for what seemed a long time. The effort of thought did unexpected things to his heavy face. It seemed to alarm him, like a loud noise in the night.

The car left the county road and climbed Sable's hill. A second sheriff's car stood in front of the glass house. Sable climbed out, followed by a heavy-set man in mufti.

Sable looked pale and shaken. "You took your time about getting here." Then he saw the handcuffs on my wrists. "For heaven's sake!"

The heavy-set man stepped past him, and yanked the car door open. "What's the trouble here?"

Conger's confusion deepened. "No trouble, Sheriff. We picked up a suspect, claims he's a private cop working for Mr. Sable."

The Sheriff turned to Sable. "This your man?"

"Of course."

Conger was already removing the handcuffs, unobtrusively, as if perhaps I wouldn't notice they'd ever been on my wrists. The back of Barney's neck reddened. He didn't turn around, even when I stepped out of the car.

The Sheriff gave me his hand. He had a calm and weathered face in which quick bright eyes moved with restless energy. "I'm Trask. I won't apologize. We all make mistakes. Some of us more than others, eh, Conger?"

Conger didn't reply. I said: "Now that we've had our fun, maybe you'd like to get on the radio with the description of my car and the man that took it."

"What man are we talking about?" Trask said.

I told him, and added: "If you don't mind my saying so,

30

Sheriff, it might be a good idea for you to check with the Highway Patrol yourself. Our friend took off in the direction of San Francisco, but he may have circled back."

"I'll put out the word."

Trask started toward his radio car. I held him for a minute: "One other thing. That Jaguar ought to be checked by an expert. It may be just another stolen car—"

"Yeah, let's hope it isn't."

chapter
6
THE dead man was lying where he had fallen, on a patch of blood-filmed grass, about ten feet from Sable's front door. The lower part of his white jacket was red-stained. His upturned face was gray and impervious-looking, like the stone faces on tombs.

A Sheriff's identification man was taking pictures of him with a tripod camera. He was a white-haired officer with a long inquisitive nose. I waited until he moved his camera to get another angle:

"Mind if I have a look at him?"

"Long as you don't touch him. I'll be through here in a minute."

When he had finished his work, I leaned over the body for a closer look. There was a single deep wound in the abdomen. The right hand had cuts across the palm and inside the curled fingers. The knife that had done the damage, a bloody five-inch switch-blade, lay on the grass in the angle between the torso and the outstretched right arm.

I took hold of the hand: it was still warm and limp: and turned it over. The skin on the tattooed knuckles was torn, probably by teeth.

"He put up quite a struggle," I said.

The identification officer hunkered down beside me. "Yeah. Be careful with those fingernails. There's some kind of debris under 'em, might be human skin. You notice the tattoo marks?"

"I'd have to be blind to miss them."

"I mean these." He took the hand away from me, and pointed out four dots arranged in a tiny rectangle between the first and second fingers. "Gang mark. He had it covered up later with a standard tattoo. A lot of old gang members do that. I see them on people we vag."

"What kind of gang?"

"I don't know. This is a Sac or Frisco gang. I'm no expert on the northern California insignia. I wonder if Lawyer Sable knew he had an old gang member working for him."

"We could ask him."

The front door was standing open. I walked in and found Sable in the front sitting-room. He raised a limp arm, and waved me into a chair:

"Sit down, Archer. I'm sorry about what happened. I can't imagine what they thought they were pulling."

"Eager-beavering. Forget it. We got off to a poor start, but the local boys seem to know what they're doing."

"I hope so," he said, not very hopefully.

"What do you know about your late houseman?"

"Not a great deal, I'm afraid. He only worked for me for a few months. I hired him originally to look after my yacht. He lived aboard the yacht until I sold it. Then he moved up here. He had no place to go, and he didn't ask for much. Peter wasn't very competent indoors, as you may have noticed. But it's hard for us to get help out in the country, and he was an obliging soul, so I let him stay on."

"What sort of a background did he have?"

"I gathered he was pretty much of a floater. He mentioned various jobs he'd held: marine cook, longshoreman, house-painter."

"How did you hire him? Through an employment agency?"

"No. I picked him up on the dock. I think he'd just come off a fishing-boat, a Monterey seiner. I was polishing brass, varnishing deck, and so on, and he offered to help me for a dollar an hour. He did a good day's work, so I took him on. He never failed to do a good day's work."

A cleft of pain, like a knife-cut, had appeared between Sable's eyebrows. I guessed that he had been fond of the dead man. I hesitated to ask my next question:

"Would you know if Culligan had a criminal record?"

The cleft in his brow deepened. "Good Lord, no. I trusted him with my boat and my house. What makes you ask such a question?"

"Two things mainly. He had a tattoo mark on his hand, four little black dots at the edge of the blue tattoo. Gangsters and drug addicts wear that kind of mark. Also, this has the look of a gang killing. The man who took my car is almost certainly the killer, and he has the earmarks of a pro."

Sable looked down at the polished terrazzo as if at any moment it might break up under his feet. "You think Peter Culligan was involved with criminals?"

"Involved is putting it mildly. He's dead."

"I realize that," he said rather shrilly.

"Did he seem nervous lately? Afraid of anything?"

"If he was, I never noticed. He didn't talk about himself."

"Did he have any visitors, before this last one?"

"Never. At least, not to my knowledge. He was a solitary person."

"Could he have been using your place and his job here as a sort of hide-out?"

"I don't know. It's hard to say."

An engine started up in front of the house. Sable rose and moved to the glass wall, parting the drapes. I looked out over his shoulder. A black panel truck rolled away from the house and started down the hill.

"Come to think of it," Sable said, "he certainly kept out of sight. He wouldn't chauffeur for me, said he'd had bad luck with cars. But he may have wanted to avoid going to town. He never went to town."

"He's on his way there now," I said. "How many people knew he was out here?"

"Just my wife and I. And you, of course. I can't think off-hand of anyone else."

"Have you had visitors from out of town?"

"Not in the last few months. Alice has been having her ups and downs. It's one reason I took Peter on out here. We'd lost our housekeeper, and I didn't like to leave Alice by herself all day."

"How is Mrs. Sable now?"

"Not so good, I'm afraid."

"Did she see it happen?"

"I don't believe so. But she heard the sounds of the struggle, and saw the car drive away. That was when she phoned me. When I got here, she was sitting on the doorstep in a half daze. I don't know what it will do to her emotional state."

"Any chance of my talking to her?"

"Not now, please. I've already spoken to Dr. Howell, and he told me to give her sedation. The Sheriff has agreed not to question her for the present. There's a limit to what the human mind can endure."

Sable might have been talking about himself. His shoulders drooped as he turned from the window. In the harsh sunlight his face was a grainy white, and puffy like boiled rice. In murder cases, there are usually more victims than one.

Sable must have read the look on my face. "This is an unsettling thing to me, too. It can't conceivably relate to Alice and me. And yet it does, very deeply. Peter was a member of the household. I believe he was quite devoted to us, and he died in our front yard. That really brings it home."

"What?"

"*Timor mortis*," he said. "The fear of death."

"You say Culligan was a member of your household. I take it he slept in."

"Yes, of course."

"I'd like to have a look at his room."

He took me across the court and through a utility room to a back bedroom. The room was furnished with a single bed, a chest of drawers, a chair, and a reading-lamp.

"I'll just look in on Alice," Sable said, and left me.

I went through Peter Culligan's meager effects. The closet contained a pair of Levis, a couple of workshirts, boots, and a cheap blue suit which had been bought at a San Francisco department store. There was a Tanforan pari-mutuel stub in the outside breast pocket of the suit coat. A dirty comb and a safety razor lay on top of the chest of drawers. The drawers were practically empty: a couple of white shirts, a greasy blue tie, a T-shirt and a pair of floral shorts, socks and handkerchiefs, and a cardboard box containing a hundred shells for a .38-caliber automatic. Not quite a hundred: the box wasn't full. No gun.

Culligan's suitcase was under the bed. It was a limp old canvas affair, held together with straps, which looked as if it had been kicked around every bus station between Seattle and San Diego. I unstrapped it. The lock was broken, and it fell open. Its contents emitted a whiff of tobacco, sea water, sweat, and the subtler indescribable odor of masculine loneliness.

It contained a gray flannel shirt, a rough blue turtle-neck sweater, and other heavier work clothes. A broad-bladed fisherman's knife had fish scales still clinging like faded sequins to the cork handle. A crumpled greenish tuxedo jacket was preserved as a memento from some more sophisticated past.

A union card issued in San Francisco in 1941 indicated

34

that Culligan had been a paid-up active member of the defunct Marine Cooks' Union. And there was a letter, addressed to Mr. Peter Culligan, General Delivery, Reno, Nevada. Culligan hadn't been a loner all his life. The letter was written on pink notepaper in an unformed hand. It said:

Dear Pete,

Dear is not the word after all I suffered from you, which is all over now and I'm going to keep it that way. I hope you realize. Just so you do I'll spell it out, you never realized a fact in your life until you got hit over the head with it. So here goes, no I don't love you anymore. Looking back now I don't see how I ever did love you, I was "infatuated." When I think of all you made me suffer, the jobs you lost and the fights and the drinking and all. You certainly didn't love me, so don't try to "kid" me. No I'm not crying over "spilt milk." I had only myself to blame for staying with you. You gave me fair warning plenty of times. What kind of person you were. I must say you have your "guts" writing to me. I don't know how you got hold of my address. Probably from one of your crooked cop friends, but they don't scare me.

I am happily married to a wonderful man. He knows that I was married before. But he does not know about "us." If you have any decency, stay away from me and don't write any more letters. I'm warning you, don't make trouble for me. I could make trouble for you, double trouble. Remember L. Bay.

Wishing you all success in your new life (I hope you're making as much money as you claim),

> *Marian*

Mrs. Ronald S. Matheson (and bear it in mind). Me come back to you? Don't ever give it another thought. Ronald is a very successful business exec! I wouldn't rub it in, only you really put me through the "wringer" and you know it. No hard feelings on my part, just leave me alone, please.

The letter had no return address, but it was postmarked San Mateo, Calif. The date was indecipherable.

35

I put everything back and closed the suitcase and kicked it under the bed.

I went out into the court. In a room on the other side of it, a woman or an animal was moaning. Sable must have been watching for me. The sound became louder as he opened a sliding glass door, and was shut off as he closed it. He came toward me, his face tinged green by the reflected light from the foliage:

"Find anything significant?"

"He kept shells for an automatic in his drawer. I didn't come across the automatic."

"I didn't know Peter had a gun."

"Maybe he had, and sold it. Or it's possible the killer took it away from him."

"Anything else?"

"I have a tentative lead to his ex-wife, if you want me to explore his background."

"Why not leave it to the police? Trask is very competent, and an old friend of mine into the bargain. I wouldn't feel justified in taking you off the Galton case."

"The Galton case doesn't seem so very urgent."

"Possibly not. Still, I think you should stay with it for the present. Was Cassie Hildreth any help?"

"Some. I can't think of much more to be done around here. I was planning to drive to San Francisco."

"You can take a plane. I wrote you a check for two hundred dollars, and I'll give you a hundred in cash." He handed me the check and the money. "If you need any more, don't hesitate to call on me."

"I won't, but I'm afraid it's money down the drain."

Sable shrugged. He had worse problems. The moaning behind the glass door was louder, rising in peaks of sound which pierced my eardrums.

chapter

7

I HATE coincidences. Aboard the plane, I spent a fruitless hour trying to work out possible connections between Maria Galton's loss of her son and Peter Culligan's loss of life. I had a delayed gestalt after I'd given up on the subject.

I was flipping through the smudged pages of *Chisel*, the little magazine that Cassie Hildreth had given me. Somebody named Chad Bolling was listed on the masthead as editor and publisher. He also had a poem in the magazine, "Elegy on the Death of Bix Beiderbecke." It said that the inconsolable cornet would pipe Eurydice out of Boss Pluto's smoke-filled basement. I liked it better than the poem about Luna.

I reread Anthony Galton's poem, wondering if Luna was his wife. Then the gestalt clicked. There was a town named Luna Bay on the coast south of San Francisco. From where I sat, a few thousand feet above the Peninsula, I could practically spit on it. And Culligan's ex-wife had referred to an "L. Bay" in her letter to him.

When the plane let down at International Airport, I headed for a telephone booth. The woman had signed herself Mrs. Ronald S. Matheson; the envelope had been postmarked in San Mateo.

I hardly expected a hit on such a random shot, after an indefinite lapse of time. But the name was in the directory: Ronald S. Matheson, 780 Sherwood Drive, Redwood City. I dialed the Emerson number.

I couldn't tell if it was a girl or a boy who answered. It was a child, pre-pubic: "Hello?"

"Is Mrs. Matheson there?"

"Just a minute, please. Mummy, you're wanted on the phone."

The child's voice trailed off, and a woman's took its place. It was cool and smooth and careful:

"Marian Matheson speaking. Who is calling, please?"

"My name is Archer. You've never heard of me."

"That's right, I haven't."

"Ever hear of a man named Culligan?"

There was a long pause. "Come again? I didn't catch the name."

"Culligan," I said. "Peter Culligan."

"What about him?"

"Did you ever know him?"

"Maybe I did, a long time ago. So what? Maybe I didn't."

"Let's not play games, Mrs. Matheson. I have some information, if you're interested."

"I'm not. Not if you're talking for Pete Culligan." Her voice had become harsher and deeper. "I don't care anything about him, as long as he leaves me alone. You can tell him that for me."

"I can't, though."

"Why not?"

"Because he's dead."

"Dead?" Her voice was a leaden echo.

"I'm investigating his murder." I'd just decided I was. "I'd like to talk to you about the circumstances."

"I don't see why. I had nothing to do with it. I didn't even know it happened."

"I'm aware of that. It's one reason I called."

"Who killed him?"

"I'll tell you when I see you."

"Who says you're seeing me?"

I waited.

"Where are you now?" she said.

"At the San Francisco Airport."

"I guess I can come there, if it has to be. I don't want you coming to the house. My husband—"

"I understand that. It's good of you to come at all. I'll be in the coffee shop."

"Are you in uniform?"

"Not at the moment." Or for the last ten years, but let her go on thinking I was law. "I'm wearing a gray suit. You won't miss me. I'll be sitting beside the windows close to the entrance."

"I'll be there in fifteen minutes. Did you say Archer?"

"Yes. Archer."

It took her twenty-five. I passed the time watching the big planes circling in, dragging their late-afternoon shadows along the runways.

A woman in a dark cloth coat came in, paused at the doorway, and looked around the huge room. Her eye lighted on me. She came toward the table, clutching her shiny leather purse as if it was a token of respectability. I got up to meet her:

"Mrs. Matheson?"

She nodded, and sat down hurriedly, as if she was afraid of being conspicuous. She was an ordinary-looking woman, decently dressed, who would never see forty again. There were flecks of gray in her carefully waved black hair, like little shards of iron.

She had once been handsome in a strong-boned way. Maybe she still was, under favorable lighting and circumstances. Her black eyes were her best feature, but they were hard with tension:

38

"I didn't want to come. But here I am."

"Will you have some coffee?"

"No, thanks. Let's have the bad news. I'll take it straight."

I gave it to her straight, leaving out nothing important. She began to twist the wedding ring on her finger, round and round.

"Poor guy," she said when I finished. "Why did they do it to him, do you know?"

"I was hoping you could help me answer that."

"You say you're not a policeman?"

"No. I'm a private investigator."

"I don't see why you come to me. We haven't been married for fifteen years. I haven't even seen him for ten. He wanted to come back to me, I guess he finally got tired of bucketing around. But I wasn't having any. I'm happily married to a good man—"

"When was the last time you heard from Culligan?"

"About a year ago. He wrote me a letter from Reno, claimed he'd struck it rich, that he could give me anything I wanted if I'd come back. Pete was always a dreamer. The first while after we were married, I used to believe in his dreams. But they all went blooey, one after another. I caught onto him so many years ago it isn't funny. I'm not laughing, notice."

"What kind of dreams did he dream?"

"Great big ones, the kind that never come off. Like he was going to open a chain of restaurants where food of all nations would be served. He'd hire the best chefs in the country, French, Chinese, Armenian, and so on. At which time he was a short-order cook on lower Market. Then there was the time he worked out a new system to beat the ponies. He took every cent we possessed to try it out. He even hocked my furniture. It took me all that winter to work it off." Her voice had the driving energy of old anger that had found an outlet. "That was Pete's idea of a honeymoon, me working and him playing the ponies."

"How did you get hooked up with him?"

"I was a dreamer, too, I guess you'd say. I thought I could straighten him out, make a man of him. That all he needed was the love of a good woman. I wasn't a good woman, and I don't pretend to be. But I was better than he was."

"Where did you meet?"

"In the San Francisco Hospital where I was working. I was a nurse's aide, and Pete was in the ward with a broken nose and a couple of broken ribs. He got beaten up in a gang fight."

"A gang fight?"

"That's all I know. Pete just said it was some rumble on the docks. I should have taken warning, but after he got out of the hospital I went on seeing him. He was young and good-looking, and like I said I thought he had the makings of a man. So I married him—the big mistake of my life, and I've made some doozies."

"How long ago was that?"

"Nineteen-thirty-six. That dates me, doesn't it? But I was only twenty-one at the time." She paused, and raised her eyes to my face. "I don't know why I'm telling you all this. I've never told a living soul in my life. Why don't you stop me?"

"I'm hoping you'll tell me something that will help. Did your husband go in for gambling?"

"Please don't call him that. I married Pete Culligan, but he was no husband to me." She lifted her head. "I have a real husband now. Incidentally, he'll be expecting me back to make his dinner." She leaned forward in her chair and started to get up.

"Can't you give me a few minutes more, Mrs. Matheson? I've told you all I know about Peter—"

She laughed shortly. "If I told you all *I* know, it would take all night. Okay, a few more minutes, if you promise me there won't be any publicity. My husband and me have a position to keep up. I'm a member of the PTA, the League of Women Voters."

"There won't be any publicity. Was he a gambler?"

"As much as he could afford to be. But he was always small-time."

"This money he said he made in Reno—did he tell you how he made it?"

"Not a word. But I don't think it was gambling. He was never that lucky."

"Do you still have his letter?"

"Certainly not. I burned it, the same day I got it."

"Why?"

"Because I didn't want it around the house. I felt like it was dirt tracked into the house."

"Was Culligan a crook, or a hustler?"

"Depends what you mean by that." Her eyes were wary.

"Did he break the law?"

"I guess everybody does from time to time."

"Was he ever arrested?"

"Yeah. Mostly for drunk and disorderly, nothing serious."

"Did he carry a gun?"

"Not when I was with him. I wouldn't let him."

"But the issue came up?"

"I didn't say that." She was becoming evasive. "I meant I wouldn't let him even if he wanted to."

"Did he own a gun?"

"I wouldn't know," she said.

I'd almost lost her. She wasn't talking frankly or willingly any more. So I threw her the question I didn't expect her to answer, hoping to gather something from her reaction to it:

"You mentioned an L. Bay in your letter to Culligan. What happened there?"

Her lips were pushed out stiff and pale, as if they were made of bone. The dark eyes seemed to shrink in her head:

"I don't know what makes you ask that." The tip of her tongue moved along her upper lip, and she tried again: "What was that about a bay in my letter? I don't remember any bay in my letter."

"I do, Mrs. Matheson." I quoted: " 'I could make trouble for you, double trouble. Remember L. Bay.' "

"If I said that, I don't know what I meant."

"There's a place called Luna Bay about twenty-five or thirty miles from here."

"Is there?" she said stupidly.

"You know it. What did Pete Culligan do there?"

"I don't remember. It must have been some dirty trick he played on me." She was a poor liar, as most honest people are. "Does it matter?"

"It seems to matter to you. Did you and Pete live in Luna Bay?"

"I guess you could call it living. I had a job there, doing practical nursing."

"When?"

"Way back when. I don't remember what year."

"Who were you working for?"

"Some people. I don't remember their name." She leaned toward me urgently, her eyes pointed like flints. "You have that letter with you?"

"I left it where I found it, in Culligan's suitcase in the house where he worked. Why?"

"I want it back. I wrote it, and it belongs to me."

"You may have to take that up with the police. It's probably in their hands by now."

"Will they be coming here?" She looked behind her, and all around the crowded restaurant, as if she expected to find a policeman bearing down on her.

"It depends on how soon they catch the killer. They may have him already, in which case they won't bother with secondary leads. Do you have any idea who it was, Mrs. Matheson?"

"How could I? I haven't seen Pete in ten years, I told you."

"What happened in Luna Bay?"

"Change the record, can't you? If anything happened, which I can't remember, it was strictly between me and Pete. Nothing to do with anybody else, understand?"

Her voice and looks were altering under pressure. She seemed to have broken through into a lower stratum of experience and a coarser personality. And she knew it. She pulled her purse toward her and held on to it with both hands. It was a good purse, beautifully cut from genuine lizard. In contrast with it, her hands were rough, their knuckles swollen and cracked by years of work.

She raised her eyes to mine. I caught the red reflection of fear in their centers. She was afraid of me, and she was afraid to leave me.

"Mrs. Matheson, Peter Culligan was murdered today—"

"You expect me to go into mourning?"

"I expect you to give me any information that might have a bearing on his death."

"I already did. You can leave me alone, understand? You're not getting me mixed up in no murder. Any murder."

"Did you ever hear of a man named Anthony Galton?"

"No."

"John Brown?"

"No."

I could see the bitter forces of her will gathering in her face. She exerted them, and got up, and walked away from me and her fear.

chapter

8

I WENT back to the telephone booths and looked up the name Chad Bolling in the Bay Area directories. I didn't expect to find it, after more than twenty years, but I was still running in luck. Bolling had a Telegraph Hill address. I immured myself in one of the booths and called him.

A woman's voice answered: "This is the Bolling residence."

"Is Mr. Bolling available?"

"Available for what?" she said abruptly.

"It has to do with magazine publication of a poem. The name is Archer," I added, trying to sound like a wealthy editor.

"I see." She softened her tone. "I don't know where Chad is at the moment. And I'm afraid he won't be home for dinner. I do know he'll be at The Listening Ear later this evening."

"The Listening Ear?"

"It's a new night club. Chad's giving a reading there tonight. If you're interested in poetry, you owe it to yourself to catch it."

"What time does he go on?"

"I think ten."

I rented a car and drove it up Bayshore to the city, where I parked it under Union Square. Above the lighted towers of the hotels, twilight had thickened into darkness. A damp chill had risen from the sea; I could feel it through my clothes. Even the colored lights around the square had a chilly look.

I bought a pint of whisky to ward off the chill and checked in at the Salisbury, a small side-street hotel where I usually stayed in San Francisco. The desk clerk was new to me. Desk clerks are always moving up or down. This one was old and on his way down; his sallow face drooped in the pull of gravity. He handed me my key reluctantly:

"No luggage, sir?"

I showed him my bottle in its paper bag. He didn't smile. "My car was stolen."

"That's too bad." His eyes were sharp and incredulous behind fussy little pince-nez. "I'm afraid I'll have to ask you to pay in advance."

"All right." I gave him the five dollars and asked for a receipt.

The bellhop who took me up in the old open ironwork elevator had been taking me up in the same elevator for nearly twenty years. We shook hands. His was crumpled by arthritis.

"How are you, Coney?"

"Fine, Mr. Archer, fine. I'm taking a new pill, phenylbuta-something. It's doing wonders for me."

He stepped out and did a little soft-shoe step to prove it. He'd once been half of a brother act that played the Orpheum circuit. He danced me down the corridor to the door of my room.

"What brings you up to the City?" he said when we were inside. To San Franciscans, there's only one city.

"I flew up for a little entertainment."

"I thought Hollywood was the world's center of entertainment."

"I'm looking for something different," I said. "Have you heard of a new club called The Listening Ear?"

"Yeah, but you wouldn't like it." He shook his white head. "I hope you didn't come all the way up here for *that*."

"What's the matter with it?"

"It's a culture cave. One of these bistros where guys read poems to music. It ain't your speed at all."

"My taste is becoming more elevated."

His grin showed all his remaining teeth. "Don't kid an old man, eh?"

"Ever hear of Chad Bolling?"

"Sure. He promotes a lot of publicity for himself." Coney looked at me anxiously. "You really going in for the poetry kick, Mr. Archer? With music?"

"I have long yearned for the finer things."

Such as a good French dinner at a price I could pay. I took a taxi to the Ritz Poodle Dog, and had a good French dinner. When I finished eating, it was nearly ten o'clock.

The Listening Ear was full of dark blue light and pale blue music. A combo made up of piano, bass fiddle, trumpet, and drums was playing something advanced. I didn't have my slide rule with me, but the four musicians seemed to understand each other. From time to time they smiled and nodded like space jockeys passing in the night.

The man at the piano seemed to be the head technician. He smiled more distantly than the others, and when the melody had been done to death, he took the applause with more

44

exquisite remoteness. Then he bent over his keyboard again like a mad scientist.

The tight-hipped waitress who brought my whisky-and-water was interchangeable with nightclub girls anywhere. Even her parts looked interchangeable. But the audience was different from other nightclub crowds. Most of them were young people with serious expressions on their faces. A high proportion of the girls had short straight hair through which they ran their fingers from time to time. Many of the boys had longer hair than the girls, but they didn't run their fingers through it so much. They stroked their beards instead.

Another tune failed to survive the operation, and then the lights went up. A frail-looking middle-aged man in a dark suit sidled through the blue curtains at the rear of the room. The pianist extended his hand and assisted him onto the bandstand. The audience applauded. The frail-looking man, by way of a bow, allowed his chin to subside on the big black bow tie which blossomed on his shirt front. The applause rose to a crescendo.

"I give you Mr. Chad Bolling," the pianist said. "Master of all the arts, singer of songs to be sung, painter of pictures, hepcat, man of letters. Mr. Chad Bolling."

The clapping went on for a while. The poet lifted his hand as if in benediction, and there was silence.

"Thank you, friends," he said. "With the support of my brilliant young friend Fingers Donahue, I wish to bring to you tonight, if my larynx will permit, my latest poem." His mouth twisted sideways as if in self-mockery. "It ain't chopped liver."

He paused. The instruments began to murmur behind him. Bolling took a roll of manuscript out of his inside breast pocket and unrolled it under the light.

" 'Death Is Tabu,' " he said, and began to chant in a hoarse carrying voice that reminded me of a carnival spieler. He said that at the end of the night he sat in wino alley where the angels drink canned heat, and that he heard a beat. It seemed a girl came to the mouth of the alley and asked him what he was doing in death valley. " 'Death is the ultimate crutch,' she said," he said. She asked him to come home with her to bed.

He said that sex was the ultimate crutch, but he turned out to be wrong. It seemed he heard a gong. She fled like a ghost, and he was lost, at the end of the end of the night.

While the drummer and the bass fiddler made shock waves

on the roof, Bolling raised his voice and began to belt it out. About how he followed her up and down and around and underground, up Russian Hill and Nob Hill and Telegraph Hill and across the Bay Bridge and back by way of the Oakland ferry. So he found the sphinx on Market Street cadging drinks and they got tight and danced on the golden asphalt of delight.

Eventually she fell upon her bed. "I'm star-transfixed," she said. He drank the canned hell of her lips, and it went on like that for quite a while, while the music tittered and moaned. She finally succeeded in convincing him that death was the ultimate crutch, whatever that meant. She knew, because it happened she was dead. "Good night, mister," she said, or he said she said. "Good night, sister," he said.

The audience waited to make sure that Bolling was finished, then burst into a surge of clapping, interspersed with *bravos* and *ole*'s. Bolling stood with pursed lips and absorbed it like a little boy sucking soda pop through a straw. While the lower part of his face seemed to be enjoying itself, his eyes were puzzled. His mouth stretched in a clownish grin:

"Thanks, cats. I'm glad you dig me. Now dig this."

He read a poem about the seven blind staggers of the soul, and one about the beardless wonders on the psycho wards who were going to be the *gurus* of the new truth. At this point I switched off my hearing aid, and waited for it to be over. It took a long time. After the reading there were books to be autographed, questions to be answered, drinks to be drunk.

It was nearly midnight when Bolling left a tableful of admirers and made for the door. I got up to follow him. A large girl with a very hungry face cut in in front of me. She attached herself to Bolling's arm and began to talk into his ear, bending over because she was taller than he was.

He shook his head. "Sorry, kiddie, I'm a married man. Also I'm old enough to be your father."

"What are years?" she said. "A woman's wisdom is ageless."

"Let's see you prove it, honey."

He shook her loose. Tragically clutching the front of her baggy black sweater, she said: "I'm not pretty, am I?"

"You're beautiful, honey. The Greek navy could use you for launching ships. Take it up with them, why don't you?"

He reached up and patted her on the head and went out. I caught up with him on the sidewalk as he was hailing a taxi.

"Mr. Bolling, do you have a minute?"

46

"It depends on what you want."

"I want to buy you a drink, ask you a few questions."

"I've had a drink. Several, in fact. It's late. I'm beat. Write me a letter, why don't you?"

"I can't write."

He brightened a little. "You mean to tell me you're not an unrecognized literary genius? I thought everybody was."

"I'm a detective. I'm looking for a man. You may have known him at one time."

His taxi had turned in the street and pulled into the curb. He signaled the driver to wait:

"What's his name?"

"John Brown."

"Oh sure, I knew him well at Harper's Ferry. I'm older than I look." His empty clowning continued automatically while he sized me up.

"In 1936 you printed a poem of his in a magazine called *Chisel.*"

"I'm sorry you brought that up. What a lousy name for a magazine. No wonder it folded."

"The name of the poem was 'Luna.' "

"I'm afraid I don't remember it. A lot of words have flowed under the bridge. I did know a John Brown back in the thirties. Whatever happened to John?"

"That's what I'm trying to find out."

"Okay, buy me a drink. But not at the Ear, eh? I get tired of the shaves and the shave-nots."

Bolling dismissed his taxi. We walked about sixty feet to the next bar. A pair of old girls on the two front stools flapped their eyelashes at us as we went in. There was nobody else in the place but a comatose bartender. He roused himself long enough to pour us a couple of drinks.

We sat down in one of the booths, and I showed Bolling my pictures of Tony Galton. "Do you recognize him?"

"I think so. We corresponded for a while, but I only met him once or twice. Twice. He called on us when we were living in Sausalito. And then one Sunday when I was driving down the coast by Luna Bay, I returned the visit."

"Were they living at Luna Bay?"

"A few miles this side of it, in an old place on the ocean. I had the very devil of a time finding it, in spite of the directions Brown had given me. I remember now, he asked me not to tell anyone else where he was living. I was the only one who knew. I don't know why he singled me out, except that he was keen to have me visit his home, and see his son. He may have had some sort of father feeling about me, though I wasn't much older than he was."

"He had a son?"

"Yes, they had a baby. He'd just been born, and he wasn't much bigger than my thumb. Little John was the apple of his father's eye. They were quite a touching little family."

Bolling's voice was gentle. Away from the crowd and the music he showed a different personality. Like other performers, he had a public face and a private one. Each of them was slightly phony, but the private face suited him better.

"You met the wife, did you?"

"Certainly. She was sitting on the front porch when I got there, nursing the baby. She had lovely white breasts, and she didn't in the least mind exposing them. It made quite a picture, there on the bluff above the sea. I tried to get a poem out of her, but it didn't come off. I never really got to know her."

"What sort of a girl was she?"

"Very attractive, I'd say, in the visual sense. She didn't have too much to say for herself. As a matter of fact, she massacred the English language. I suppose she had the fascination of ignorance for Brown. I've seen other young writers and artists fall for girls like that. I've been guilty of it myself, when I was in my pre-Freudian period." He added wryly: "That means before I got analyzed."

"Do you remember her name?"

"Mrs. Brown's name?" He shook his head. "Sorry. In the poem I botched I called her Stella Maris, star of the sea. But that doesn't help you, does it?"

"Can you tell me when you were there? It must have been toward the end of the year 1936."

"Yes. It was around Christmas, just before Christmas—I took along some bauble for the child. Young Brown was very pleased that I did." Bolling pulled at his chin, lengthening his face. "It's queer I never heard from him after that."

"Did you ever try to get in touch with him?"

"No, I didn't. He may have felt I'd brushed him off. Perhaps I did, without intending to. The woods were full of young writers; it was hard to keep track of them all. I was doing valid work in those days, and a lot of them came to me. Frankly, I've hardly thought of Brown from that day to this. Is he still living on the coast?"

"I don't know. What was he doing in Luna Bay, did he tell you?"

"He was trying to write a novel. He didn't seem to have a job, and I can't imagine what they were living on. They couldn't have been completely destitute, either. They had a nurse to look after the mother and child."

"A nurse?"

"I suppose she was what you'd call a practical nurse. One of those young women who take charge," he added vaguely.

"Do you recall anything about her?"

"She had remarkable eyes, I remember. Sharp black eyes which kept watching me. I don't think she approved of the literary life."

"Did you talk to her at all?"

"I may have. I have a distinct impression of her, that she was the only sensible person in the house. Brown and his wife seemed to be living in Cloud-Cuckoo-Land."

"How do you mean?"

"They were out of touch with the ordinary run of life. I don't mean that as a criticism. I've been out of touch enough in my own life, God knows. I still am." He gave me his clown grin. "You can't make a Hamlet without breaking egos. But let's not talk about me."

"Getting back to the nurse, do you think you can remember her name?"

"I know perfectly well I can't."

"Would you recognize it if I said it?"

"That I doubt. But try me."

"Marian Culligan," I said. "C-u-l-l-i-g-a-n."

"It rings no bell with me. Sorry."

Bolling finished his drink and looked around the bar as if he expected something to happen. I guessed that most of the things that can happen to a man had already happened to him. He changed expressions like rubber masks, but between the masks I could see dismay in his face.

"We might as well have another drink," he said. "This one will be on me. I'm loaded. I just made a hundred smackers at the Ear." Even his commercialism sounded phony.

While I lit a fire under the bartender, Bolling studied the photographs I'd left on the table:

"That's John all right. A nice boy, and perhaps a talented one, but out of this world. All the way out of this world. Where did he get the money for horses and tennis?"

49

"From his family. They're heavily loaded."

"Good Lord, don't tell me he's the missing heir. Is that why you're making a search for him?"

"That's why."

"They waited long enough."

"You can say that again. Can you tell me how to get to the house the Browns were living in when you visited them?"

"I'm afraid not. I might be able to *show* you, though."

"When?"

"Tomorrow morning if you like."

"That's good of you."

"Not at all. I *liked* John Brown. Besides, I haven't been to Luna Bay for years. Eons. Maybe I'll rediscover my lost youth."

"Maybe." But I didn't think it likely.

Neither did he.

chapter
9

IN THE morning I picked up Bolling at his Telegraph Hill apartment. It was one of those sparkling days that make up for all the fog in San Francisco. An onshore wind had swept the air clear and tessellated the blue surface of the Bay. A white ship cutting a white furrow was headed out toward the Golden Gate. White gulls hung above her on the air.

Bolling looked at all this with a fishy eye. He was frowsy and gray and shivering with hangover. He crawled into the back seat and snored all the way to our destination. It was a dingy, formless town sprawling along the coast highway. Its low buildings were dwarfed by the hills rising behind it, the broad sea spreading out in front.

I stopped beside a filling-station where the inland road met Highway 1, and told Bolling to wake up.

"Wha' for?" he mumbled from the depths of sleep. "Wha' happen?"

"Nothing yet. Where do we go from here?"

He groaned and sat up and looked around. The glare from the ocean made his eyes water. He shaded them with his hand. "Where are we?"

"Luna Bay."

50

"It doesn't look the same," he complained. "I'm not sure whether I can find the place or not. Anyway, we turn north here. Just drive along slowly, and I'll try to spot the road."

Almost two miles north of Luna Bay, the highway cut inland across the base of a promontory. On the far side of the promontory, a new-looking asphalt road turned off toward the sea. A billboard stood at the intersection: "Marvista Manor. Three bedrooms and rumpus room. Tile bathrooms. Built-in kitchens. All utilities in. See our model home."

Bolling tapped my shoulder. "This is the place, I think."

I backed up and made a left turn. The road ran straight for several hundred yards up a gentle slope. We passed a rectangle of bare adobe as big as a football field, where earth-movers were working. A wooden sign at the roadside explained their activity: "Site of the Marvista Shopping Center."

From the crest of the slope we looked down over the rooftops of a hundred or more houses. They stood along the hillside on raw earth terraces which were only just beginning to sprout grass. Driving along the winding street between them, I could see that most of the houses were occupied. There were curtains at the windows, children playing in the yards, clothes drying on the lines. The houses were painted different colors, which only seemed to emphasize their sameness.

The street unwound itself at the foot of the slope, paralleling the edge of the bluffs. I stopped the car and turned to look at Bolling.

"I'm sorry," he said. "It's changed so much, I can't be certain this is the place. There were some clapboard bungalows, five or six of them, scattered along the bluff. The Browns lived in one of them, if memory serves me."

We got out and walked toward the edge of the bluff. A couple of hundred feet below, the sea wrinkled like blue metal against its base, and burst in periodic white explosions. A mile to the south, under the shelter of the promontory, a cove of quiet water lay in a brown rind of beach.

Bolling pointed toward the cove. "This has to be the place. I remember Brown telling me that inlet was used as a harbor by rum-runners in the old Prohibition days. There used to be an old hotel on the bluff above it. You could see it from the Browns' front porch. Their bungalow must have stood quite near here."

"They probably tore it down when they put in the road. It wouldn't have done me much good to see it, anyway. I was

51

hoping I'd run across a neighbor who remembered the Browns."

"I suppose you could canvass the tradesmen in Luna Bay."

"I could."

"Oh well, it's nice to get out in the country."

Bolling wandered off along the edge of the bluff. Suddenly he said: "Whee!" in a high voice like a gull's screak. He began to flap his arms.

I ran toward him. "What's the matter?"

"Whee!" he said again, and let out a childish laugh. "I was just imagining that I was a bird."

"How did you like it?"

"Very much." He flapped his arms some more. "I can fly! I breast the windy currents of the sky. I soar like Icarus toward the sun. The wax melts. I fall from a great height into the sea. Mother Thalassa."

"Mother who?"

"Thalassa, the sea, the Homeric sea. We could build another Athens. I used to think we could do it in San Francisco, build a new city of man on the great hills. A city measured with forgiveness. Oh, well."

His mood sank again. I pulled him away from the edge. He was so unpredictable I thought he might take a flying leap into space, and I was beginning to like him.

"Speaking of mothers," I said, "if John Brown's wife had just had a baby, she must have been going to a doctor. Did they happen to mention where the baby was born?"

"Yes. Right in their house. The nearest hospital is in Redwood City, and Brown didn't want to take his wife there. The chances are she had a local doctor."

"Let's hope he's still around."

I drove back through the housing-tract until I saw a young woman walking a pram. She shied like a filly when I pulled up beside her. In the daytime the tract was reserved for women and children; unknown men in cars were probably kidnappers. I got out and approached her, smiling as innocuously as I could.

"I'm looking for a doctor."

"Oh. Is somebody sick?"

"My friend's wife is going to have a baby. They're thinking of moving into Marvista Manor, and they thought they'd better check on the medical situation."

"Dr. Meyers is very good," she said. "I go to him myself."

"In Luna Bay?"

"That's right."

"How long has he practiced there?"

"I wouldn't know. We just moved out from Richmond month before last."

"How old is Dr. Meyers?"

"Thirty, thirty-five, I dunno."

"Too young," I said.

"If your friend will feel safer with an older man, I think there is one in town. I don't remember his name, though. Personally I like a young doctor, they know all the latest wonder drugs and all."

Wonder drugs. I thanked her, and drove back to Luna Bay in search of a drugstore. The proprietor gave me a run-down on the three local doctors. A Dr. George Dineen was the only one who had practiced there in the thirties. He was an elderly man on the verge of retirement. I'd probably find him in his office if he wasn't out on a call. It was only a couple of blocks from the drugstore.

I left Bolling drinking coffee at the fountain, and walked to the doctor's office. It occupied the front rooms of a rambling house with green shingle walls which stood on a dusty side street. A woman of about sixty answered the door. She had blue-white hair and a look on her face you don't see too often any more, the look of a woman who hasn't been disappointed:

"Yes, young man?"

"I'd like to see the doctor."

"His office hours are in the afternoon. They don't start till one-thirty."

"I don't want to see him as a patient."

"If you're a pharmaceutical salesman, you'd better wait till after lunch. Dr. Dineen doesn't like his mornings to be disturbed."

"I'm only in town for the morning. I'm investigating a disappearance. He may be able to help me to find a missing man."

She had a very responsive face, in spite of its slack lines of age. Her eyes imagined what it would be like to lose a loved one. "Well, that's different. Come in, Mr.—"

"Archer. I'm a private detective."

"My husband is in the garden. I'll bring him in."

She left me in the doctor's office. Several diplomas hung on the wall above the old oak desk. The earliest stated that Dr. Dineen had graduated from the University of Ohio Medical School in 1914. The room itself was like a preserve of prewar

53

time. The cracked leather furniture had been molded by use into comfortable human shapes. A set of old chessmen laid out on a board stood like miniature armies stalled in the sunlight that fell slanting from the window.

The doctor came in and shook hands with me. He was a tall high-shouldered old man. His eyes were noncommittal under shaggy gray brows which hung like bird's-nests on the cliff of his face. He lowered himself into the chair behind his desk. His head was partly bald; a few strands of hair lay lankly across the top of his scalp.

"You mentioned a missing person to my wife. One of my patients, perhaps?"

"Perhaps. His name was John Brown. In 1936 he and his wife lived a few miles up the coast where the Marvista tract is now."

"I remember them very well," the doctor said. "Their son was in this office not so very long ago, sitting where you're sitting."

"Their son?"

"John, Junior. You may know him. He's looking for his father, too."

"No," I said, "I don't know him. But I'd certainly like to."

"I daresay that could be arranged." Dr. Dineen's deep voice rumbled to a stop. He looked at me intently, as if he was getting ready to make a diagnosis. "First, I'd want to know the reasons for your interest in the family."

"I was hired to make a search for the father, the senior John Brown."

"Has your search had any results?"

"Not until now. You say this boy who came to see you is looking for his father?"

"That is correct."

"What brought him to you?"

"He has the ordinary filial emotions. If his father is alive, he wants to be with him. If his father is dead, he wants to know."

"I mean what brought him here to your office specifically? Had you known him before?"

"I brought him into the world. In my profession, that constitutes the best possible introduction."

"Are you sure it's the same boy?"

"I have no reason to doubt it." The doctor looked at me with some distaste, as if I'd criticized some work he'd done with his hands. "Before we go any further, Mr. Archer, you

54

can oblige me with a fuller response to my question. You haven't told me who hired you."

"Sorry, I can't do that. I've been asked to keep my client's identity confidential."

"No doubt you have. I've been keeping such matters confidential for the past forty years."

"And you won't talk unless I do, is that it?"

The doctor raised his hand and brushed the thought away from his face, like an annoying insect. "I suggested no bargain. I simply want to know who I'm dealing with. There may be grave matters involved."

"There are."

"I think you ought to elucidate that remark."

"I can't."

We faced each other in a stretching silence. His eyes were steady, and bright with the hostility of a proud old man. I was afraid of losing him entirely, just as the case seemed to be breaking open. While I didn't doubt his integrity, I had my own integrity to think of, too. I'd promised Gordon Sable and Mrs. Galton to name no names.

Dr. Dineen produced a pipe, and began to pack its charred bowl with tobacco from an oilskin pouch. "We seem to have reached a stalemate. Do you play chess, Mr. Archer?"

"Not as well as you do, probably. I've never studied the book."

"I would have thought you had." He finished packing his pipe, and lit it with a kitchen match. The blue smoke swirled in the hollow shafts of sunlight from the window. "We're wasting both our times. I suggest you make a move."

"I thought this was a stalemate."

"New game." A flicker of interest showed in his eyes for the first time. "Tell me about yourself. Why would a man of your sort spend his life doing the kind of work you do? Do you make much money?"

"Enough to live on. I don't do it for the money, though. I do it because I want to."

"Isn't it dirty work, Mr. Archer?"

"It depends on who's doing it, like doctoring or anything else. I try to keep it clean."

"Do you succeed?"

"Not entirely. I've made some bad mistakes about people. Some of them assume that a private detective is automatically crooked, and they act accordingly, as you're doing now."

The old man emitted a grunt which sounded like a seal's

bark. "I can't act blindly in a matter of this importance."

"Neither can I. I don't know what makes it important to you—"

"I'll tell you," he said shortly. "Human lives are involved. A boy's love for his parents is involved. I try to handle these things with the care they deserve."

"I appreciate that. You seem to have a special interest in John Brown, Junior."

"I do have. The young fellow's had a rough time of it. I don't want him hurt unnecessarily."

"It's not my intention to hurt him. If the boy is acutally John Brown's son, you'd be doing him a favor by leading me to him."

"You're going to have to prove that to me. I'll be frank to say I've had one or two experiences with private detectives in my time. One of them had to do with the blackmailing of a patient of mine—a young girl who had a child out of wedlock. I don't mean that reflects on you, but it makes a man leery."

"All right. I'll put my position hypothetically. Let's say I'd been hired to find the heir to several million dollars."

"I've heard that one before. You'll have to invent a better gambit than that."

"I didn't invent it. It happens to be the truth."

"Prove it."

"That will be easy to do when the time comes. Right now, I'd say the burden of proof is on this boy. Can he prove his identity?"

"The question never came up. As a matter of fact, the proof of his identity is on his face. I knew whose son he was as soon as he stepped in here. His resemblance to his father is striking."

"How long ago did he turn up?"

"About a month. I've seen him since."

"As a patient?"

"As a friend," Dineen said.

"Why did he come to you in the first place?"

"My name is on his birth certificate. Now hold your horses, young man. Give me a chance to think." The doctor smoked in silence for a while. "Do you seriously tell me that this boy is heir to a fortune?"

"He will be, if his father is dead. His grandmother is still living. She has the money."

"But you won't divulge her name?"

56

"Not without her permission. I suppose I could call her long distance. But I'd rather have a chance to talk to the boy first."

The doctor hesitated. He held his right hand poised in the air, then struck the desk-top with the flat of it. "I'll take a chance on you, though I may regret it later."

"You won't if I can help it. Where can I find him?"

"We'll come to that."

"What did he have to say about his origins?"

"It would be more appropriate if you got that from him. I'm willing to tell you what I know about his father and mother from my own direct observation. And this has more relevance than you may think." He paused. "What precisely did this anonymous client of yours hire you to do?"

"Find John Brown, Senior," I said.

"I take it that isn't his real name."

"That's right, it isn't."

"I'm not surprised," Dineen said. "At the time I knew him, I did some speculating about him. It occurred to me he might be a remittance man—one of those ne'er-do-wells whose families paid them to stay away from home. I remember when his wife was delivered, Brown paid me with a hundred-dollar-bill. It didn't seem to suit with their scale of living. And there were other things, his wife's jewels, for example—diamonds and rubies in ornate gold settings. One day she came in here like a walking jewelry store.

"I warned her not to wear them. They were living out in the country, near the old Inn, and it was fairly raw territory in those days. Also, people were poor. A lot of them used to pay me for my services in fish. I had so much fish during the Depression I've never eaten it since. No matter. A public display of jewels was an incitement to robbery. I told the young lady so, and she left off wearing them, at least when I saw her."

"Did you see her often?"

"Four or five times, I'd say. Once or twice before the boy was born, and several times afterwards. She was a healthy enough wench, no complications. The main thing I did for her was to instruct her in the care of an infant. Nothing in her background had prepared her for motherhood."

"Did she talk about her background?"

"She didn't have to. It had left marks on her body, for one thing. She'd been beaten half to death with a belt buckle."

"Not by her husband?"

"Hardly. There had been other men in her life, as the phrase goes. I gathered that she'd been on her own from an early age. She was one of the wandering children of the thirties—quite a different sort from her husband."

"How old was she?"

"I think nineteen or twenty, perhaps older. She looked older. Her experiences hadn't hardened her, but as I said they left her unprepared for motherhood. Even after she was back on her feet, she needed a nurse to help her care for the child. Actually, she was a child herself in emotional development."

"Do you remember the nurse's name?"

"Let me see. I believe she was a Mrs. Kerrigan."

"Or Culligan?"

"Culligan, that was it. She was a good young woman, fairly well trained. I believe she took off at the same time the Brown family did."

"The Brown family took off?"

"They skipped, without a good-by or a thank-you to anybody. Or so it appeared at the time."

"When was this?"

"A very few weeks after the child was born. It was close to Christmas Day of 1936, I think a day or two after. I remember it so distinctly because I've gone into it since with the sheriff's men."

"Recently?"

"Within the last five months. To make a long story short, when they were clearing the land for the Marvista tract, a set of bones were unearthed. The local deputy asked me to look them over to see what I could learn from them. I did so. They were human bones, which had probably belonged to a man of medium height, in his early twenties.

"It's not unlikely, in my opinion, that they are John Brown's bones. They were found buried under the house he lived in. The house was torn down to make way for the new road. Unfortunately, we had no means of making a positive identification. The skull was missing, which ruled out the possibility of dental evidence."

"It rules in the possibility of murder."

Dineen nodded gravely. "There's rather more than a possibility of murder. One of the cervical vertebrae had been cut through by a heavy instrument. I'd say John Brown, if that is who he is, was decapitated with an ax."

10

BEFORE I left Dr. Dineen, he gave me a note of introduction to the deputy in charge of the local sheriff's office, written on a prescription blank; and the address of the gas station where John Brown, Jr., worked. I walked back to the drugstore in a hurry. Bolling was still at the fountain, with a grilled cheese sandwich in his left hand and a pencil in his right. He was simultaneously munching the sandwich and scribbling in a notebook.

"Sorry to keep you waiting—"

"Excuse me, I'm writing a poem."

He went on scribbling. I ate an impatient sandwich while he finished, and dragged him out to the car:

"I want to show you somebody; I'll explain who he is later." I started the car and turned south on the highway. "What's your poem about?"

"The city of man. I'm making a break-through into the affirmative. It's going to be good—the first good poem I've written in years."

He went on telling me about it, in language which I didn't understand. I found the place I was looking for on the southern outskirts of the town. It was a small independent station with three pumps, one attendant. The attendant was a young man in white drill coveralls. He was busy gassing a pickup truck whose bed was piled with brown fishermen's nets. I pulled in behind it and watched him.

There was no doubt that he looked like Anthony Galton. He had the same light eyes set wide apart, the same straight nose and full mouth. Only his hair was different; it was dark and straight.

Bolling was leaning forward in the seat. "For Christ's sake! Is it Brown? It can't be Brown. He's almost as old as I am."

"He had a son, remember."

"Is this the son?"

"I think so. Do you remember the color of the baby's hair?"

"It was dark, what there was of it. Like his mother's."

Bolling started to get out of the car.

"Wait a minute," I said. "Don't tell him who you are."

"I want to ask him about his father."

59

"He doesn't know where his father is. Besides, there's a question of identity. I want to see what he says without any prompting."

Bolling gave me a frustrated look, but he stayed in the car. The driver of the pickup paid for his gas and rattled away. I pulled up even with the pumps, and got out for a better look at the boy.

He appeared to be about twenty-one or -two. He was very good-looking, as his putative father had been. His smile was engaging.

"What can I do for you, sir?"

"Fill her up. It'll only take a couple of gallons. I stopped because I want you to check the oil."

"I'll be glad to, sir."

He seemed like a willing boy. He filled the tank, and wiped the windshield spotless. But when he lifted the hood to check the oil, he couldn't find the dip-stick. I showed him where it was.

"Been working here long?"

He looked embarrassed. "Two weeks. I haven't caught on to all the new cars yet."

"Think nothing of it." I looked across the highway at the windswept shore where the long combers were crashing. "This is nice country. I wouldn't mind settling out here."

"Are you from San Francisco?"

"My friend is." I indicated Bolling, who was still in the car, sulking. "I came up from Santa Teresa last night."

He didn't react to the name.

"Who owns the beach property across the highway, do you know?"

"I'm sorry, I wouldn't know. My boss probably would, though."

"Where is he?"

"Mr. Turnell has gone to lunch. He should be back pretty soon, if you want to talk to him."

"How soon?"

He glanced at the cheap watch on his wrist. "Fifteen or twenty minutes. His lunch-hour is from eleven to twelve. It's twenty to twelve now."

"I might as well wait for him. I'm in no hurry."

Bolling was in visible pain by this time. He made a con-spiratorial gesture, beckoning me to the car.

"Is it Brown's son?" he said in a stage whisper.

"Could be."

60

"Why don't you ask him?"

"I'm waiting for him to tell me. Take it easy, Mr. Bolling."

"May I talk to him?"

"I'd just as soon you didn't. This is a ticklish business."

"I don't see why it should be. Either he is or he isn't."

The boy came up behind me. "Is something the matter, sir? Anything more I can do?"

"Nothing on both counts. The service was fine."

"Thank you."

His teeth showed bright in his tanned face. His smile was strained, though. He seemed to sense the tension in me and Bolling. I said as genially as I knew how:

"Are you from these parts?"

"I could say I was, I guess. I was born a few miles from here."

"But you're not a local boy."

"That's true. How can you tell?"

"Accent. I'd say you were raised in the middle west."

"I was." He seemed pleased by my interest. "I just came out from Michigan this year."

"Have you had any higher education?"

"College, you mean? As a matter of fact I have. Why do you ask?"

"I was thinking you could do better for yourself than jockeying a gas pump."

"I hope to," he said, with a look of aspiration. "I regard this work as temporary."

"What kind of work would you like to do?"

He hesitated, flushing under his tan. "I'm interested in acting. I know that sounds ridiculous. Half the people who come to California probably want to be actors."

"Is that why you came to California?"

"It was one of the reasons."

"This is a way-stop to Hollywood for you, then?"

"I guess you could say that." His face was closing up. Too many questions were making him suspicious.

"Ever been to Hollywood?"

"No. I haven't."

"Had any acting experience?"

"I have as a student."

"Where?"

"At the University of Michigan."

I had what I wanted: a way to check his background, if he was telling the truth; if he was lying, a way to prove that he was lying. Universities kept full dossiers on their students.

"The reason I'm asking you all these questions," I said, "is this. I have an office on Sunset Boulevard in Hollywood. I'm interested in talent, and I was struck by your appearance."

He brightened up considerably. "Are you an agent?"

"No, but I know a lot of agents." I wanted to avoid the lie direct, on general principles, so I brought Bolling into the conversation: "My friend here is a well-known writer. Mr. Chad Bolling. You may have heard of him."

Bolling was confused. He was a sensitive man, and my underhanded approach to the boy troubled him. He leaned out of the car to shake hands:

"Pleased to meet you."

"I'm very glad to meet you, sir. My name is John Brown, by the way. Are you in the picture business?"

"No."

Bolling was tongue-tied by the things he wanted to say and wasn't supposed to. The boy looked from Bolling to me, wondering what he had done to spoil the occasion. Bolling took pity on him. With a defiant look at me, he said:

"Did you say your name was John Brown? I knew a John Brown once, in Luna Bay."

"That was my father's name. You must have known my father."

"I believe I did." Bolling climbed out of the car. "I met you when you were a very small baby."

I watched John Brown. He flushed up warmly. His gray eyes shone with pleasure, and then were moist with deeper feelings. I had to remind myself that he was a self-admitted actor.

He pumped Bolling's hand a second time. "Imagine your knowing my father! How long is it since you've seen him?"

"Twenty-two years—a long time."

"Then you don't know where he is now?"

"I'm afraid not, John. He dropped out of sight, you know, quite soon after you were born."

The boy's face stiffened. "And Mother?" His voice cracked on the word.

"Same story," I said. "Don't you remember either of your parents?"

He answered reluctantly: "I remember my mother. She left me in an orphanage in Ohio when I was four. She promised to come back for me, but she never did come back. I spent

62

nearly twelve years in that institution, waiting for her to come back." His face was dark with emotion. "Then I realized she must be dead. I ran away."

"Where was it?" I said. "What town?"

"Crystal Springs, a little place near Cleveland."

"And you say you ran away from there?"

"Yes, when I was sixteen. I went to Ann Arbor, Michigan, to get an education. A man named Lindsay took me in. He didn't adopt me, but he let me use his name. I went to school under the name of John Lindsay."

"Why the name change?"

"I didn't want to use my own name. I had good reason."

"Are you sure it wasn't the other way around? Are you sure John Lindsay wasn't your real name, and you took the name of Brown later?"

"Why would I do that?"

"Somebody hired you, maybe."

He flushed up darkly. "Who are you?"

"A private detective."

"If you're a detective, what was all that bushwa about Hollywood and Sunset Boulevard?"

"I have my office on Sunset Boulevard."

"But what you said was deliberately misleading."

"Don't worry about me so much. I needed some information, and I got it."

"You could have asked me directly. I have nothing to hide."

"That remains to be seen."

Bolling stepped between us, sputtering at me in sudden anger: "Leave the boy alone now. He's obviously genuine. He even has his father's voice. Your implications are an insult."

I didn't argue with him. In fact, I was ready to believe he was right. The boy stepped back away from us as if we'd threatened his life. His eyes had turned the color of slate, and there were white rims on his nostrils:

"What is this, anyway?"

"Don't get excited," I said.

"I'm not excited." He was trembling all over. "You come here and ask me a bunch of questions and tell me you knew my father. Naturally I want to know what it means."

Bolling moved toward him and laid an impulsive hand on his arm. "It could mean a great deal to you, John. Your father belonged to a wealthy family."

63

The boy brushed him off. He was young for his age in some ways. "I don't care about that. I want to see my father."

"Why is it so important?" Bolling said.

"I never had a father." His working face was naked to the light. Tears ran down his cheeks. He shook them off angrily.

I bought him, and made a down payment: "I've asked enough questions for now, John. Have you talked to the local police, by the way?"

"Yes, I have. And I know what you're getting at. They have a box of bones at the sheriff's station. Some of them claim that they're my father's bones, but I don't believe it. Neither does Deputy Mungan."

"Do you want to come down there with me now?"

"I can't," he said. "I can't close up the station. Mr. Turnell expects me to stay on the job."

"What time do you get off?"

"About seven-thirty, week nights."

"Where can I get in touch with you tonight?"

"I live in a boardinghouse about a mile from here. Mrs. Gorgello's." He gave me the address.

"Aren't you going to tell him who his father was?" Bolling said.

"I will when it's been proved. Let's go, Bolling."

He climbed into the car reluctantly.

chapter
11   THE Sheriff's substation was a stucco shoebox of a building across the street from a sad-looking country hotel. Bolling said he would stay in the car, on the grounds that skeletons frightened him:

"It even horrifies me to think that I contain one. Unlike Webster in Mr. Eliot's poem, I like to remain oblivious to the skull beneath the skin."

I never knew whether Bolling was kidding me.

Deputy Mungan was a very large man, half a head taller than I was, with a face like unfinished sculpture. I gave him my name and occupation, and Dineen's note of introduction. When he'd read it, he reached across the counter that divided his little office, and broke all the bones in my hand:

64

"Any friend of Doc Dineen's is a friend of mine. Come on in around behind and tell me your business."

I went on in around behind and sat in the chair he placed for me at the end of his desk:

"It has to do with some bones that were found out in the Marvista tract. I understand you've made a tentative identification."

"I wouldn't go so far as to say that. Doc Dineen thinks it was a man he knew—fellow by the name of John Brown. It fits in with the location of the body, all right. But we haven't been able to nail it down. The trouble is, no such man was ever reported missing in these parts. We haven't been able to turn up any local antecedents. Naturally we're still working on it."

Mungan's broad face was serious. He talked like a trained cop, and his eyes were sharp as tacks. I said: "We may be able to help each other to clarify the issue."

"Any help you can give me will be welcome. This has been dragging on for five months now, more like six." He threw out a quick hooked question: "You represent his family, maybe?"

"I represent a family. They asked me not to use their name. And there's still a question whether they are the dead man's family. Was there any physical evidence found with the bones? A watch, or a ring? Shoes? Clothing?"

"Nothing. Not even a stitch of clothing."

"I suppose it could rot away completely in twenty-two years. What about buttons?"

"No buttons. Our theory is he was buried the way he came into the world."

"But without a head."

Mungan nodded gravely. "Doc Dineen filled you in, eh? I've been thinking about that head myself. A young fellow came in here a few weeks ago, claimed to be John Brown's son."

"Don't you think he is?"

"He acted like it. He got pretty upset when I showed him the bones. Unfortunately, he didn't know any more about his father than I do. Which is nil, absolutely nil. We know this John Brown lived out on the old Bluff Road for a couple of months in 1936, and that's the sum-total of it. On top of that, the boy doesn't believe these are his father's bones. And he could just be right. I've been doing some thinking, as I said.

65

"This business about the head, now. We assumed when the body was first turned up, that he was killed by having his head cut off." Mungan made a snicking sound between tongue and palate, and sheared the air with the edge of his huge hand. "Maybe he was. Or maybe the head was chopped off after death, to remove identification. You know how much we depend on teeth and fillings. Back in the thirties, before we developed our modern lab techniques, teeth and fillings were the main thing we had to go on.

"If my hypothesis is right, the killer was a pro. And that fits in with certain other facts. In the twenties and thirties, the Bluff Road area was a stamping ground for hoods. It was until quite recently, as a matter of fact. In those days it was a real hotbed. A lot of the liquor that kept San Francisco going during Prohibition came in by sea and was funneled through Luna Bay. They brought in other things than liquor —drugs, for instance, and women from Mexico and Panama. You ever hear of the Red Horse Inn?"

"No."

"It stood on the coast about a mile south of where we found the skeleton. They tore it down a couple of years ago, after we put the stopper on it. That was a place with a history. It used to be a resort hotel for well-heeled people from the City and the Peninsula. The rum-runners took it over in the twenties. They converted it into a three-way operation: liquor warehouse in the basement, bars and gaming on the first floor, women upstairs. The reason I know so much about it, I had my first drink there back about 1930. And my first woman."

"You don't look that old."

"I was sixteen at the time. I think that's one of the reasons I went into law enforcement. I wanted to put bastards like Lempi out of circulation. Lempi was the boss hood who ran the place in the twenties. I knew him personally, but the law got to him before I grew up to his size. They got him for income tax in 1932, he died on the Rock a few years later. Some of his guns were sent up at the same time.

"I knew those boys, see, and this is the point I'm coming to. I knew what they were capable of doing. They killed for pay, and they killed because they enjoyed it. They bragged in public that nobody could touch them. It took a federal indictment to cool Lempi. Meantime a number of people lost their lives. Our Mr. Bones could be one of them."

66

"But you say Lempi and his boys were cleaned out in '32. Our man was killed in '36."

"We don't know that. We jumped to that conclusion on the basis of what Doc Dineen said, but we've got no concrete evidence to go on. The Doc himself admits that given the chemistry of that particular soil, he can't pinpoint time of burial closer than five years either way. Mr. Bones could have been knocked off as early as 1931. I say *could* have."

"Or as late as 1941?" I said.

"That's right. You see how little we have to go on."

"Do I get to take a look at what you have?"

"Why not?"

Mungan went into a back room and returned lugging a metal box about the size of a hope chest. He set it on top of his desk, unlocked it, lifted the lid. Its contents were jumbled like kindling. Only the vertebrae had been articulated with wire, and lay coiled on the heap like the skeleton of a snake. Mungan showed me where the neck bone had been severed by a cutting instrument.

The larger bones had been labeled: left femur, left fibula, and so on. Mungan picked out a heavy bone about a foot long; it was marked "right humerus."

"This is the bone of the upper arm," he said in a lecturer's tone. "Come along on over to the window here. I want to show you something."

He held the bone to the light. Close to one knobbed end, I made out a thin line filled and surrounded by deposits of calcium.

"A break?" I said.

"I hope in more senses than one. It's a mended fracture, the only unusual thing in the entire skeleton. Dineen says it was probably set by a trained hand, a doctor. If we could find the doctor that set it, it would answer some of our questions. So if you've got any ideas . . ." Mungan let his voice trail off, but his eyes stayed hard on my face.

"I'll do some telephoning."

"You can use my phone."

"A pay phone would suit me better."

"If you say so. There's one across the street, in the hotel."

I found the telephone booth at the rear of the dingy hotel lobby, and placed a call to Santa Teresa. Sable's secretary put him on the line.

"Archer speaking, the one-man dragnet," I said. "I'm in Luna Bay."

67

"You're where?"

"Luna Bay. It's a small town on the coast south of San Francisco. I have a couple of items for you: a dead man's bones, and a live boy. Let's start with the bones."

"Bones?"

"Bones. They were dug up by accident about six months ago, and they're in the sheriff's substation here. They're unidentified, but the chances are better than even that they belong to the man I'm looking for. The chances are also better than even that he was murdered twenty-two years ago."

The line was silent.

"Did you get that, Sable? He was probably murdered."

"I heard you. But you say the remains haven't been identified."

"That's where you can help me, if you will. You better write this down. There's a fracture in the right humerus, close to the elbow. It was evidently set by a doctor. I want you to check on whether Tony Galton ever had a broken right arm. If so, who was the doctor that looked after it? It may have been Howell, in which case there's no sweat. I'll call you back in fifteen minutes."

"Wait. You mentioned a boy. What's he got to do with all this?"

"That remains to be seen. He thinks he's the dead man's son."

"Tony's son?"

"Yes, but he isn't sure about it. He came here from Michigan in the hope of finding out who his father was."

"Do you think he's Tony's son?"

"I wouldn't bet my life savings on it. I wouldn't bet against it, either. He bears a strong resemblance to Tony. On the other hand, his story is weak."

"What story does he tell?"

"It's pretty long and complicated for the telephone. He was brought up in an orphanage, he says, went to college under an assumed name, came out here a month ago to find out who he really is. I don't say it couldn't have happened the way he says, but it needs to be proved out."

"What kind of a boy is he?"

"Intelligent, well spoken, fairly well mannered. If he's a con artist, he's smooth for his age."

"How old is he?"

"Twenty-two."

"You work very quickly," he said.

68

"I was lucky. What about your end? Has Trask got anything on my car?"

"Yes. It was found abandoned in San Luis Obispo."

"Wrecked?"

"Out of gas. It's in perfectly good shape, I saw it myself. Trask has it impounded in the county garage."

"What about the man who stole it?"

"Nothing definite. He probably took another car in San Luis. One disappeared late yesterday afternoon. Incidentally, Trask tells me that the Jaguar, the murder car, as he calls it, was another stolen car."

"Who was the owner?"

"I have no idea. The Sheriff is having the engine number traced."

I hung up, and spent the better part of fifteen minutes thinking about Marian Culligan Matheson and her respectable life in Redwood City which I was going to have to invade again. Then I called Sable back. The line was busy. I tried again in ten minutes, and got him.

"I've been talking to Dr. Howell," he said. "Tony broke his right arm when he was in prep school. Howell didn't set the break himself, but he knows the doctor who did. In any case, it was a fractured humerus."

"See if they can turn up the X-ray, will you? They don't usually keep X-ray pictures this long, but it's worth trying. It's the only means I can think of for making a positive identification."

"What about teeth?"

"Everything above the neck is missing."

It took Sable a moment to grasp this. Then he said: "Good Lord!" After another pause: "Perhaps I should drop everything and come up there. What do you think?"

"It might be a good idea. It would give you a chance to interview the boy."

"I believe I'll do that. Where is he now?"

"Working. He works at a gas station in town. How long will it take you to get here?"

"I'll be there between eight and nine."

"Meet me at the sheriff's substation at nine. In the meantime, is it all right if I take the local deputy into my confidence? He's a good man."

"I'd just as soon you didn't."

"You can't handle murder without publicity."

69

"I'm aware of that," Sable said acidly. "But then we don't know for certain that the victim was Tony, do we?"

Before I could give him any further argument, Sable hung up.

chapter

12

I PHONED the Santa Teresa courthouse. After some palaver, I got Sheriff Trask himself on the other end of the line. He sounded harried:

"What is it?"

"Gordon Sable just told me you traced the murder car in the Culligan case."

"A fat lot of good it did us. It was stolen in San Francisco night before last. The thief changed the license plates."

"Who owns it?"

"San Francisco man. I'm thinking of sending somebody up to talk to him. Far as I can make out, he didn't report the theft."

"That doesn't sound so good. I'm near San Francisco now, in Luna Bay. Do you want me to look him up?"

"I'd be obliged. I can't really spare anybody. His name is Roy Lemberg. He lives at a hotel called the Sussex Arms."

An hour later, I drove into the garage under Union Square. Bolling said good-by to me at the entrance:

"Good luck with your case."

"Good luck with your poem. And thanks."

The Sussex Arms was another side-street hotel like the one I had spent the night in. It was several blocks closer to Market Street, and several degrees more dilapidated. The desk clerk had large sorrowful eyes and a very flexible manner, as if he had been run through all the wringers of circumstance.

He said Mr. Lemberg was probably at work.

"Where does he work?"

"He's supposed to be a car salesman."

"Supposed to be?"

"I don't think he's doing so good. He's just on commission with a secondhand dealer. The reason I know, he tried to sell *me* a car." He snickered, as if he possessed the secret of a more advanced type of transportation.

"Has Lemberg lived here long?"

"A few weeks, more or less. This wouldn't happen to be a police matter?"

"I want to see him on personal business."

"Maybe Mrs. Lemberg is up in the room. She usually is."

"Try her, will you? My name is Archer. I'm interested in buying their car."

He went to the switchboard and relayed the message. "Mrs. Lemberg says come right on up. It's three-eleven. You can take the elevator."

The elevator jerked me up to the third floor. At the end of the dust-colored hallway, a blonde in a pink robe gleamed like a mirage. Closer up, her luster was dimmer. She had darkness at the roots of her hair, and a slightly desperate smile.

She waited until I was practically standing on her feet; then she yawned and stretched elastically. She had wine and sleep on her breath. But her figure was very good, lush-breasted and narrow-waisted. I wondered if it was for sale or simply on exhibition by the owner.

"Mrs. Lemberg?"

"Yeah. What's all this about the Jag? Somebody phones this morning and he tells them it was stole. And now you want to buy it."

"Was the car stolen?"

"That was just some of Roy's malarkey. He's full of it. You serious about buying?"

"Only if he has clear title," I said fussily.

My show of reluctance made her eager, as it was intended to. "Come in, we'll talk about it. The Jag is in his name, but I'm the one that makes the money decisions."

I followed her into the little room. At the chinks in the drawn blinds, daylight peered like a spy. She turned on a lamp and waved her hand vaguely toward a chair. A man's shirt hung on the back of it. A half-empty half-gallon jug of muscatel stood on the floor beside it.

"Siddown, excuse the mess. With all the outside work I do, I don't get time to houseclean."

"What do you do?"

"I model. Go ahead, siddown. That shirt is ready for the laundry, anyway."

I sat down against the shirt. She flung herself on the bed, her body falling automatically into a cheesecake pose:

"Were you thinking of paying cash?"

71

"If I buy."

"We sure could use a chunk of ready cash. What price did you have in mind? I'm warning you, I won't let it go too cheap. That's my chief recreation in life, driving out in the country. The trees and everything." Her own words seemed to bewilder her. "Not that he takes me out in it. I hardly ever see the car any more. That brother of his monopolizes it. Roy's so soft, he don't stick up for his rights the way he should. Like the other night."

"What happened the other night?"

"Just more of the same. Tommy comes up full of the usual. He's got another one of these big job opportunities that never pan out. All he needs is a car, see, and he'll be making a fortune in no time. So Roy lends him the car, just like that. Tommy could talk the fillings right out of his teeth."

"How long ago was this?"

"Night before last, I think. I lose count of the nights and days."

"I didn't know Roy had a brother," I prompted her.

"Yeah, he's got a brother." Her voice was flat. "Roy's all fixed up with a brother, till death doth us part. We'd still be in Nevada, living the life of O'Reilly, if it wasn't for that punk."

"How so?"

"I'm talking too much." But bad luck had dulled her brains, bad wine had loosened her tongue: "The Adult Authority said they'd give him a parole if he had somebody willing to be responsible. So back we move to California, to make a home for Tommy."

I thought: This is a home? She caught my look:

"We didn't always live here. We made a down payment on a real nice little place in Daly City. But Roy started drinking again, we couldn't hold onto it." She turned over onto her stomach, supporting her chin on her hand. Her china-blue eyes looked fractured in the light. "Not that I blame him," she added more softly. "That brother of his would drive a saint to drink. Roy never hurt nobody in his life. Except me, and you expect that from any man."

I was touched by her asphalt innocence. The long curve of her hip and thigh, the rich flesh of her bosom, were like the disguise of a frightened adolescent.

"What was Tommy in for?"

"He beat up a guy and took his wallet. The wallet had three bucks in it, and Tommy was in for six months."

"That works out to fifty cents a month. Tommy must be quite a mastermind."

"Yeah, to hear him tell it. It was supposed to be longer, but I guess he's good when he's in, with somebody watching him. It's just when he gets out." She cocked her head sideways, and her bright hair fell across her hand. "I don't know why I'm telling you all this. In my experience, the guys do most of the talking. I guess you have a talkable-attable face."

"You're welcome to the use of it."

"Sanctuary mucho. But you came here to buy a car. I was almost forgetting. I worry so much, I forget things." Her gaze slid down from my face to the muscatel jug. "I had a few drinkies, too, if the truth be knownst." She drew a lock of hair across her eyes and looked at me through it.

Her kittenish mood was depressing. I said: "When can I have a look at the Jaguar?"

"Any time, I guess. Maybe you better talk to Roy."

"Where can I find him?"

"Don't ask me. Tell you the truth, I don't even know if Tommy brought it back yet."

"Why did Roy say the car was stolen?"

"I dunno. I was half asleep when he left. I didn't ask him."

The thought of sleep made her yawn. She dropped her head and lay still. Traffic went by in the street like a hostile army. Then footsteps came down the corridor and paused outside the door. A man spoke softly through it:

"You busy, Fran?"

She raised herself on her arms like a fighter hearing a far-off count. "Is that you, hon?"

"Yeah. You busy?"

"Not so's you'd notice. Come ahead in."

He flung the door open, saw me, and hung back like an interloper. "Excuse me."

His dark eyes were quick and uncertain. He was still in his early thirties, but he had a look about him, intangible and definite as an odor. The look of a man who has lost his grip and is sliding. His suit was sharply pressed, but it hadn't been cleaned for too long. The very plumpness of his face gave it a lardlike inertness, as if it had stopped reacting to everything but crises.

His face interested me. Unless I was getting hipped on family resemblances, he was an older softer version of the boy who'd stolen my car. This one's dark curls were thinner

73

and limper. And the violence of the younger man was petulance in him. He said to his wife:

"You told me you weren't busy."

"I'm not. I'm only resting." She rolled over and sat up. "This gentleman wants to buy the Jaguar."

"It's not for sale." Lemberg closed the door behind him. "Who told you it was?"

"Grapevine."

"What else did you hear?"

He was quick on the uptake. I couldn't hope to con him for long, so I struck at his vulnerable spot:

"Your brother's in trouble."

His gaze went to my shoulder, my hands, my mouth, and then my eyes. I think in his extremity he would have liked to hit me. But I could have broken him in half, and he must have known it. Still, anger or frustration made him foolish:

"Did Schwartz send you to tell me this?"

"Who?"

"You needn't play dumb. Otto Schwartz." He gargled the words. "If he sent you, you can take a message back for me. Tell him to take a running jump in the Truckee River and do us all a favor."

I got up. Instinctively, one of Lemberg's arms rose to guard his face. The gesture told a lot about him and his background.

"Your brother's in very bad trouble. So are you. He drove down south to do a murder yesterday. You provided the car."

"I didn't know whah—" His jaw hung open, and then clicked shut. "Who are you?"

"A friend of the family. Show me where Tommy is."

"But I don't know. He isn't in his room. He never came back."

The woman said: "Are you from the Adult Authority?"

"No."

"Who are you?" Lemberg repeated. "What do you want?"

"Your brother, Tommy."

"I don't know where Tommy is. I swear."

"What's Otto Schwartz got to do with you and Tommy?"

"I don't know."

"You brought up his name. Did Schwartz give Tommy a contract to murder Culligan?"

"Who?" the woman said. "Who did you say got murdered?"

"Peter Culligan. Know him?"

74

"No," Lemberg answered for her. "We don't know him."

I advanced on him: "You're lying, Lemberg. You better let down your back hair, tell me all about it. Tommy isn't the only one in trouble. You're accessory to any crime he did."

He backed away until the backs of his legs were touching the bed. He looked down at his wife as if she was his only source of comfort. She was looking at me:

"What did you say Tommy did?"

"He committed a murder."

"For gosh sake." She swung her legs down and stood up facing her husband. "And you lent him the car?"

"I had to. It was his car. It was only in my name."

"Because he was on parole?" I said.

He didn't answer me.

The woman took hold of his arm and shook it. "Tell the man where he is."

"I don't know where he is." Lemberg turned to me: "And that's the honest truth."

"What about Schwartz?"

"Tommy used to work for him, when we lived in Reno. They were always asking him to come back to work."

"Doing what?"

"Any dirty thing they could dream up."

"Including murder?"

"Tommy never did a murder."

"Before this one, you mean."

"I'll believe it when I hear it from him."

The woman groaned. "Don't be an idiot all your life. What did he ever do for you, Roy?"

"He's my brother."

"Do you expect to hear from him?" I said.

"I hope so."

"If you do, will you let me know?"

"Sure I will," he lied.

I went down in the elevator and laid a ten-dollar bill on the counter in front of the room clerk. He raised a languid eyebrow:

"What's this for? You want to check in?"

"Not today, thanks. It's your certificate of membership in the junior G-men society. Tomorrow you get your intermediate certificate."

"Another ten?"

"You catch on fast."

"What do I have to do for it?"

"Keep track of Lemberg's visitors, if he has any. And any telephone calls, especially long-distance calls."

"Can do." His hand moved quickly, flicking the bill out of sight. "What about *her* visitors?"

"Does she have many?"

"They come and go."

"She pay you to let them come and go?"

"That's between me and her. Are you a cop?"

"Not me," I said, as if his question was an insult. "Just keep the best track you can. If it works out, I may give you a bonus."

"If what works out?"

"Developments. Also I'll mention you in my memoirs."

"That will be just ducky."

"What's your name?"

"Jerry Farnsworth."

"Will you be on duty in the morning?"

"What time in the morning?"

"Any time."

"For a bonus I can be."

"An extra five," I said, and went outside.

There was a magazine shop on the opposite corner. I crossed to it, bought a *Saturday Review*, and punched a hole in the cover. For an hour or more, I watched the front of the Sussex Arms, trusting that Lemberg wouldn't penetrate my literate disguise.

But Lemberg didn't come out.

chapter

13
IT WAS past five when I got to Redwood City. The commuting trains were running south every few minutes. The commuters in their uniforms, hat on head, briefcase in hand, newspaper under arm, marched wearily toward their waiting cars. The cop on traffic duty at the station corner told me how to get to Sherwood Drive.

It was in a junior-executive residential section, several cuts above the Marvista tract. The houses were set further apart, and differed from each other in architectural detail. Flowers bloomed competitively in the yards.

A bicycle lay on the grass in front of the Matheson house. A small boy answered my knock. He had black eyes like his mother's, and short brown hair which stuck up all over his head like visible excitement.

"I was doing pushups," he said, breathing hard. "You want my daddy? He ain't, I mean, he isn't home from the city yet."

"Is your mother home?"

"She went to the station to get him. They ought to be back in about eleven minutes. That's how old I am."

"Eleven minutes?"

"Eleven *years*. I had my birthday last week. You want to see me do some pushups?"

"All right."

"Come in, I'll show you."

I followed him into a living-room which was dominated by a large brick fireplace with a raised hearth. Everything in the room was so new and clean, the furniture so carefully placed around it, that it seemed forbidding. The boy flung himself down in the middle of the green broadloom carpet:

"Watch me."

He did a series of pushups, until his arms collapsed under him. He got up panting like a dog on a hot day:

"Now that I got the knack, I can do pushups all night if I want to."

"You wouldn't want to wear yourself out."

"Shucks, I'm strong. Mr. Steele says I'm very strong for my age, it's just my co-ordination. Here, feel my muscle."

He pulled up the sleeve of his jersey, flexed his biceps, and produced an egg-sized lump. I palpated this:

"It's hard."

"That's from doing pushups. You think I'm big for my age, or just average?"

"A pretty fair size, I'd say."

"As big as you when you were eleven?"

"Just about."

"How big are you now?"

"Six feet or so."

"How much do you weigh?"

"About one-ninety."

"Did you ever play football?"

"Some, in high school."

"Do you think, will I ever get to be a football player?" he said wistfully.

77

"I don't see why not."

"That's my ambition, to be a football player."

He darted out of the room and was back in no time with a football which he threw at me from the doorway.

"Y. A. Tittle," he said.

I caught the ball and said: "Hugh McElhenny."

This struck him as very funny. He laughed until he fell down. Being in position, he did a few pushups.

"Stop it. You're making me tired."

"I never get tired," he bragged exhaustedly. "When I get through doing pushups, I'm going to take a run around the block."

"Don't tell me. It wears me out."

A car turned into the driveway. The boy struggled to his feet:

"That's Mummy and Daddy now. I'll tell them you're here, Mr. Steele."

"My name is Archer. Who's Mr. Steele?"

"My coach in the Little League. I got you mixed up with him, I guess."

It didn't bother him, but it bothered me. It was a declaration of trust, and I didn't know what I was going to have to do to his mother.

She came in alone. Her face hardened and thinned when she saw me:

"What do you want? What are you doing with my son's football?"

"Holding it. He threw it to me. I'm holding it."

"We were making like Forty-niners," the boy said. But the laughter had gone out of him.

"Leave my son alone, you hear me?" She turned on the boy: "James, your father is in the garage. You can help him bring in the groceries. And take that football with you."

"Here." I tossed him the ball. He carried it out as if it was made of iron. The door closed behind him. "He's a likely boy."

"A lot you care, coming here to badger me. I talked to the police this morning. I don't have to talk to you."

"I think you want to, though."

"I can't. My husband—he doesn't know."

"What doesn't he know?"

"Please." She moved toward me rapidly, heavily, almost as though she was falling, and grasped my arm. "Ron will

78

be coming in any minute. You won't force me to talk in front of him?"

"Send him away."

"How can I? He wants his dinner."

"You need something from the store."

"But we just came from the store."

"Think of something else."

Her eyes narrowed to two black glittering slits. "Damn you. You come in here disrupting my life. What did I do to bring this down on me?"

"That's the question that needs answering, Mrs. Matheson."

"Won't you go away and come back later?"

"I have other things to do later. Let's get this over with."

"I only wish I could."

The back door opened. She pulled away from me. Her face smoothed out and became inert, like the face of someone dying.

"Sit down," she said. "You might as well sit down."

I sat on the edge of an overstuffed chesterfield covered with hard shiny green brocade. Footsteps crossed the kitchen, and paper rustled. A man raised his voice:

"Marian, where are you?"

"I'm in here," she said tightly.

Her husband appeared in the doorway. Matheson was a thin small man in a gray suit who looked about five years younger than his wife. He stared at me through his glasses with the belligerence of his size. It was his wife he spoke to:

"I didn't know you had a visitor."

"Mr. Archer is Sally Archer's husband. You've heard me speak of Sally Archer, Ron." In spite of his uncomprehending look, she rushed on: "I promised to send her a cake for the church supper, and I forgot to bake it. What am I going to do?"

"You'll have to skip it."

"I can't. She's depending on me. Ron, would you go downtown and bring me a cake for Mr. Archer to take to Sally? Please?"

"Now?" he said with disgust.

"It's for tonight. Sally's waiting for it."

"Let her wait."

"But I can't. You wouldn't want it to get around that I didn't do my share."

He turned out his hands in resignation. "How big a cake does it have to be?"

"The two-dollar size will do. Chocolate. You know the bakery at the shopping center."

"But that's way over on the other side of town."

"It's got to be good, Ron. You don't want to shame me in front of my friends."

Some of her real feeling was caught in the words. His eyes jabbed at me and returned to her face, searching it:

"Listen, Marian, what's the trouble? Are you okay?"

"Certainly I'm okay." She produced a smile. "Now run along like a good boy and bring me that cake. You can take Jimmy with you, and I'll have supper ready when you get back."

Matheson went out, slamming the door behind him in protest. I heard his car engine start, and sat down again:

"You've got him well trained."

"Please leave my husband out of this. He doesn't deserve trouble."

"Does he know the police were here?"

"No, but the neighbors will tell him. And then I'll have to do some more lying. I hate this lying."

"Stop lying."

"And let him know I'm mixed up in a murder? That would be just great."

"Which murder are you talking about?"

She opened her mouth. Her hand flew up to cover it. She forced her hand down to her side and stood very still, like a sentinel guarding her hearth.

"Culligan's?" I said. "Or the murder of John Brown?"

The name struck her like a blow in the mouth. She was too shaken to speak for a minute. Then she gathered her forces and straightened up and said:

"I don't know any John Brown."

"You said you hated lying, but you're doing it. You worked for him in the winter of 1936, looking after his wife and baby."

She was silent. I brought out one of my pictures of Anthony Galton and thrust it up to her face:

"Don't you recognize him?"

She nodded resignedly. "I recognize him. It's Mr. Brown."

"And you worked for him, didn't you?"

"So what? Working for a person is no crime."

80

"Murder is the crime we're talking about. Who killed him, Marian? Was it Culligan?"

"Who says anybody killed him? He pulled up stakes and went away. The whole family did."

"Brown didn't go very far, just a foot or two underground. They dug him up last spring, all but his head. His head was missing. Who cut it off, Marian?"

The ugliness rose like smoke in the room, spreading to its far corners, fouling the light at the window. The ugliness entered the woman and stained her eyes. Her lips moved, trying to find the words that would exorcise it. I said:

"I'll make a bargain with you, and keep it if I can. I don't want to hurt your boy. I've got nothing against you or your husband. I suspect you're material witness to a murder. Maybe the law would call it accessory—"

"No." She shook her head jerkily. "I had nothing to do with it."

"Maybe not. I'm not interested in pinning anything on you. If you'll tell me the whole truth as you know it, I'll do my best to keep you out of it. But it has to be the whole truth, and I have to have it now. A lot depends on it."

"How could a lot depend, after all these years?"

"Why did Culligan die, after all these years? I think that the two deaths are connected. I also think that you can tell me how."

Her deeper, cruder personality rose to the surface. "What do you think I am, a crystal ball?"

"Stop fooling around," I said sharply. "We only have a few minutes. If you won't talk to me alone, you can talk in front of your husband."

"What if I refuse to talk at all?"

"You'll be having another visit from the cops. It'll start here and end up at the courthouse. And everybody west of the Rockies will have a chance to read all about it in the papers. Now talk."

"I need a minute to think."

"You've had it. Who murdered Brown?"

"I didn't know he was murdered, not for sure. Culligan wouldn't let me go back to the house after that night. He said the Browns moved on, bag and baggage. He even tried to give me money he said they left for me."

"Where did he get it?"

After a silence, she blurted: "He stole it from them."

"Did he murder Brown?"

"Not Culligan. He wouldn't have the nerve."

"Who did?"

"There was another man. It must have been him."

"What was his name?"

"I don't know."

"What did he look like?"

"I hardly remember. I only saw him the once, and it was at night."

Her story was turning vague, and it made me suspicious. "Are you sure the other man existed?"

"Of course he did."

"Prove it."

"He was a jailbird," she said. "He escaped from San Quentin. He used to belong to the same gang Culligan did."

"What gang is that?"

"I wouldn't know. It broke up long before I married Culligan. He never talked about his gang days. I wasn't interested."

"Let's get back to this man who broke out of 'Q.' He must have had a name. Culligan must have called him something."

"I don't remember what."

"Try harder."

She looked toward the window. Her face was drawn in the tarnished light.

"Shoulders. I think it was Shoulders."

"No last name?"

"Not that I remember. I don't think Culligan ever told me his last name."

"What did he look like?"

"He was a big man, dark-haired. I never really saw him, not in the light."

"What makes you think he murdered Brown?"

She answered in a low voice, to keep her house from hearing: "I heard them arguing that night, in the middle of the night. They were sitting out in my car arguing about money. The other man—Shoulders—said that he'd knock off Pete, too, if he didn't get his way. I heard him say it. The walls of the shack we lived in were paper thin. This Shoulders had a kind of shrill voice, and it cut through the walls like a knife. He wanted all the money for himself, and most of the jewels.

"Pete said it wasn't fair, that he was the finger man and

should have an equal split. He needed money, too, and God knows that he did. He always needed money. He said that a couple of hot rubies were no good to him. That was how I guessed what happened. Little Mrs. Brown had these big red jewels, I always thought they were glass. But they were rubies."

"What happened to the rubies?"

"The other man took them, he must of. Culligan settled for part of the·money, I guess. At least he was flush for a while."

"Did you ever ask him why?"

"No. I was afraid."

"Afraid of Culligan?"

"Not him so much." She tried to go on, but the words stuck in her throat. She plucked at the skin of her throat as if to dislodge them. "I was afraid of the truth, afraid he'd tell me. I didn't want to believe what happened, I guess. That argument I heard outside our house—I tried to pretend to myself it was all a dream. I was in love with Culligan in those days. I couldn't face my own part in it."

"You mean the fact that you didn't take your suspicions to the police?"

"That would have been bad enough, but I did worse. I was the one responsible for the whole thing. I've lived with it on my conscience for over twenty years. It was all my fault for not keeping my loud mouth shut." She gave me an up-from-under look, her eyes burning with pain: "Maybe I ought to be keeping it shut now."

"How were you responsible?"

She hung her head still lower. Her eyes sank out of sight under her black brows. "I told Culligan about the money," she said. "Mr. Brown kept it in a steel box in his room. I saw it when he paid me. There must have been thousands of dollars. And I had to go and mention it to my hus—to Culligan. I would have done better to go and cut my tongue out instead." She raised her head, slowly, as if she was balancing a weight. "So there you have it."

"Did Brown ever tell you where *he* got the money?"

"Not really. He made a joke about it—said he stole it. But he wasn't the type."

"What type was he?"

"Mr. Brown was a gentleman, at least he started out to be a gentleman. Until he married that wife of his. I don't know what he saw in her outside of a pretty face. She didn't know

83

from nothing, if you ask me. But he knew plenty, he could talk your head off."

She gasped. The enormity of the image struck her. "God! They cut his head off?" She wasn't asking me. She was asking the dark memories flooding up from the basement of her life.

"Before death or after, we don't know which. You say you never went back to the house?"

"I never did. We went back to San Francisco."

"Do you know what happened to the rest of the family, the wife and son?"

She shook her head. "I tried not to think about them. What did happen to them?"

"I'm not sure, but I think they went east. The indications are they got away safe, at any rate."

"Thank God for that." She tried to smile, and failed. Her eyes were 'still intent on the guilty memory. She looked at the walls of her living-room as if they were transparent. "I guess you wonder what kind of a woman I am, that I could run out on a patient like that. Don't think it didn't bother me. I almost went out of my mind for a while that winter. I used to wake up in the middle of the night and listen to Culligan's breathing and wish it would stop. But I stuck to him for five more years after that. Then I divorced him."

"And now he's stopped breathing."

"What do you mean by that?"

"You could have hired a gun to knock him off. He was threatening to make trouble for you. You have a lot to lose." I didn't believe it, but I wanted to see what she would make of it.

Her two hands went to her breasts and grasped them cruelly. "Me? You think I'd do that?"

"To keep your husband and son, you would. Did you?"

"No. For God's sake, no."

"That's good."

"Why do you say that?" Her eyes were dull with the sickness of the past.

"Because I want you to keep what you have."

"Don't do me any favors."

"I'm going to, though. I'm going to keep you out of the Culligan case. As for the information you've given me, I'm going to use it for private reference only. It would be easier for me if I didn't—"

"So you want to be paid for your trouble, is that it?"

84

"Yes, but not in money. I want your confidence, and any other information you can give me."

"But there isn't any more. That's all there is."

"What happened to Shoulders?"

"I don't know. He must of got away. I never heard of him again."

"Culligan never mentioned him?"

"No. Honest."

"And you never brought the subject up?"

"No. I was too much of a coward."

A car entered the driveway. She started, and went to the window. The light outside was turning dusky gray. In the yard across the street, red roses burned like coals. She rubbed her eyes with her knuckles, as if she wanted to wipe out all her past experiences, live innocent in an innocent world.

The little boy burst through the door. Matheson came at his heels, balancing a cake box in his hands.

"Well, I got the darn thing." He thrust it into my hands. "That takes care of the church supper."

"Thanks."

"Don't mention it," he said brusquely, and turned to his wife: "Is supper ready? I'm starved."

She stood on the far side of the room, cut off from him by the ugliness. "I didn't make supper."

"You didn't make it? What is this? You said you'd have it ready when I got home."

Hidden forces dragged at her face, widening her mouth, drawing deep lines between her eyes. Suddenly her eyes were blind with tears. The tears ran in the furrows of her face. Sobbing, she sat on the edge of the hearth like an urchin on a curb.

"Marian? What's the matter? What's the trouble, kiddie?"

"I'm not a good wife to you."

Matheson went across the room to her. He sat on the hearth beside her and took her in his arms. She buried her face in his neck.

The boy started toward them, and then turned back to me. "Why is Mother crying?"

"People cry."

"I don't cry," he said.

chapter 14

I DROVE back across the ridge toward the last fading light in the sky. On the road that wound down to Luna Bay I passed an old man with a burlap bag on his back. He was one of the old-time hoboes who follow the sun like migratory birds. But the birds fly, and the men walk. The birds mate and nest; the old men have no nests. They pace out their lives along the roadsides.

I stopped and backed up and gave him the cake.

"Thank you very kindly." His mouth was a rent in shaggy fur. He put the cake in his bag. It was a cheap gift, so I gave him a dollar to go with it. "Do you want a ride into town?"

"No, thank you very kindly. I'd smell up your car."

He walked away from me with a long, slow, swinging purposeless stride, lost in a dream of timeless space. When I passed him, he didn't raise his bearded head. He was like a moving piece of countryside on the edge of my headlight beam.

I had fish and chips at a greasy spoon and went to the sheriff's substation. It was eight by the clock on the wall above Mungan's desk. He looked up from his paperwork:

"Where you been? The Brown kid's been looking for you."

"I want to see him. Do you know where he went?"

"Over to Doc Dineen's house. They're pretty good friends. He told me that the doc is teaching him how to play chess. That game was always a little over my head. Give me a hand of poker any time."

I went around the end of the counter and complied with his request, in a way:

"I've been doing some asking around. A couple of things came up that ought to interest you. You say you knew some of the hoods in these parts, back in the early thirties. Does the name Culligan mean anything to you?"

"Yeah. Happy Culligan, they called him. He was in the Red Horse mob."

"Who were his friends?"

"Let's see." Mungan stroked his massive chin. "There was Rossi, Shoulders Nelson, Lefty Dearborn—all of them

86

Lempi's guns. Culligan was more the operator type, but he liked to hang around with the guns."

"What about Shoulders Nelson?"

"He was about the hardest limb in the bunch. Even his buddies were afraid of him." A trace of his boyhood admiration showed in Mungan's eyes. "I saw him beat Culligan to a pulp one night. They both wanted the same girl."

"What girl?"

"One of the girls upstairs at the Red Horse. I didn't know her name. Nelson shacked up with her for a while, I heard."

"What did Nelson look like?"

"He was a big man, almost as big as me. The women went for him, he must have been good-looking to them. I never thought so, though. He was a mean-looking bastard, with a long sad face and mean eyes. Him and Rossi and Dearborn got sent up the same time as Lempi."

"To Alcatraz?"

"Lempi went there, when the Government took it over. But the others took the fall on a larceny charge. Highjacking. The three of them went to San Quentin."

"What happened to them after that?"

"I didn't keep any track of them. I wasn't in law enforcement at the time. Where is all this supposed to be leading?"

"Shoulders Nelson may be the killer you want," I said. "Would your Redwood City office have a dossier on him?"

"I doubt that. He hasn't been heard of around here in more than twenty-five years. It was a state case, anyway."

"Then Sacramento should have it. You could have Redwood City teletype them."

Mungan spread his hands on the desk-top and stood up, wagging his big head slowly from side to side. "If all you got is a hunch, you can't use official channels to test it out for you."

"I thought we were co-operating."

"I am. You're not. I've been doing the talking, you've been doing the listening. And this has been going on for quite some time."

"I told you Nelson's probably our killer. That's a fairly big mouthful."

"By itself, it doesn't do anything for me."

"It could if you let it. Try querying Sacramento."

"What's your source of information?"

"I can't tell you."

"Like that, eh?"

"I'm afraid so."

Mungan looked down at me in a disappointed way. Not surprised, just disappointed. We had had the beginning of a beautiful friendship, but I had proved unworthy.

"I hope you know what you're doing."

"I hope I do. You think about this Nelson angle. It's worth going into. You could earn yourself some very nice publicity."

"I don't give a damn about publicity."

"Good for you."

"And you can go to hell."

I didn't blame him for blowing off. It's tough to live with a case for half a year and then watch it elope with a casual pickup.

But I couldn't afford to leave him feeling sore. I didn't even want to. I went outside the counter and sat down on a wooden bench against the wall. Mungan resumed his place at his desk and avoided looking at me. I sat there like a penitent while the minute hand of the clock took little pouncing bites of eternity.

At eight-thirty-five Mungan got up and made an elaborate show of discovering me:

"You still here?"

"I'm waiting for a friend—a lawyer from down south. He said he'd be here by nine o'clock."

"What for? To help you to pick my brains?"

"I don't know why you're browned off, Mungan. This is a big case, bigger than you realize. It's going to take more than one of us to handle it."

"What makes it so big?"

"The people involved, the money, and the names. At this end we have the Red Horse gang, or what's left of it; at the other end, one of the richest and oldest families in California. It's their lawyer I'm expecting, a man named Sable."

"So what? I get down on my knees? I give everybody an even shake, treat 'em all alike."

"Mr. Sable may be able to identify those bones of yours."

Mungan couldn't repress his interest. "He the one you talked to on the phone?"

"He's the one."

"You're working on this case for him?"

"He hired me. And he may be bringing some medical data that will help us identify the remains."

88

Mungan went back to his paperwork. After a few minutes, he said casually:

"If you're working for a lawyer, it lets you off the hook. It gives you the same rights of privacy a lawyer has. You probably wouldn't know that, but I've made quite a study of the law."

"It's news to me," I lied.

He said magnanimously: "People in general, even law officers, they don't know all the fine points of the law."

His pride and his integrity were satisfied. He called the county courthouse and asked them to get a rundown on Nelson from Sacramento.

Gordon Sable walked in at five minutes to nine. He had on a brown topcoat and a brown Homburg, and a pair of yellow pigskin driving gloves. The lids of his gray eyes were slightly inflamed. His mouth was drawn down at the corners, and lines of weariness ran from them to the wings of his nose.

"You made a quick trip," I said.

"Too quick to suit me. I didn't get away until nearly three o'clock."

He looked around the small office as if he doubted that the trip had been worth making. Mungan rose expectantly.

"Mr. Sable, Deputy Mungan."

The two men shook hands, each of them appraising the other.

"Glad to meet you," Mungan said. "Mr. Archer tells me you've got some medical information about this—these remains we turned up last spring."

"That may be." Sable glanced sideways at me. "How much more detail did you go into?"

"Just that, and the fact that the family is important. We're not going to be able to keep them anonymous from here on in."

"I realize that," he snapped. "But let's get the identification established first, if we can. Before I left, I talked to the doctor who set the broken arm. He did have X-ray pictures taken, but unfortunately they don't survive. He has his written record, however, and he gave me the—ah—specifications of the fracture." Sable produced a folded piece of paper from an inner pocket. "It was a clean break in the right humerus, two inches above the joint. The boy sustained it falling off a horse."

Mungan said: "It figures."

Sable turned to him. "May we see the exhibit in question?"

Mungan went into the back room.

"Where's the boy?" Sable said in an undertone.

"At a friend's house, playing chess. I'll take you to him when we finish here."

"Tony was a chess-player. Do you really think he's Tony's son?"

"I don't know. I'm waiting to have my mind made up for me."

"By the evidence of the bones?"

"Partly. I've got hold of another piece of evidence that fits in. Brown has been identified from one of Tony Galton's pictures."

"You didn't tell me that before."

"I didn't know it before."

"Who's your witness?"

"A woman named Matheson in Redwood City. She's Culligan's ex-wife and Galton's ex-nurse. I've made a commitment to keep her name out of the police case."

"Is that wise?" Sable's voice was sharp and unpleasant.

"Wise or not, it's the way it is."

We were close to quarreling. Mungan came back into the room and cut it short. The bones rattled in his evidence box. He hoisted it onto the counter and raised the lid. Sable looked down at John Brown's leavings. His face was grave.

Mungan picked out the arm bone and laid it on the counter. He went to his desk and came back with a steel foot-rule. The break was exactly two inches from the end.

Sable was breathing quickly. He spoke in repressed excitement: "It looks very much as if we've found Tony Galton. Why is the skull missing? What was done to him?"

Mungan told him what he knew. On the way to the Dineen house I told Sable the rest of it.

"I have to congratulate you, Archer. You certainly get results."

"They fell into my lap. It's one of the things that made me suspicious. Too many coincidences came together—the Culligan murder, the Brown-Galton murder, the Brown-Galton boy turning up, if that's who he is. I can't help feeling that the whole business may have been planned to come out this way. There are mobsters involved, remember. Those boys look a long way ahead sometimes, and they're willing to wait for their payoff."

"Payoff?"

"The Galton money. I think the Culligan killing was a gang killing. I think it was no accident that Culligan came to work for you three months ago. Your house was a perfect hide-out for him, and a place where he could watch developments in the Galton family."

"For what possible purpose?"

"My thinking hasn't got that far," I said. "But I'm reasonably certain that Culligan didn't go there on his own."

"Who sent him?"

"That's the question." After a pause, I said: "How is Mrs. Sable, by the way?"

"Not good. I had to put her in a nursing home. I couldn't leave her by herself at home."

"I suppose it's the Culligan killing that got her down?"

"The doctors seem to think it's what triggered her breakdown. But she's had emotional trouble before."

"What sort of emotional trouble?"

"I'd just as soon not go into it," he said bleakly.

chapter
15

DR. DINEEN came to the door in an ancient smoking-jacket made of red velvet which reminded me of the plush in old railway coaches. His wrinkled face was set in a frown of concentration. He looked at me impatiently:

"What is it?"

"I think we've identified your skeleton."

"Really? How?"

"Through the mended break in the arm bone. Dr. Dineen, this is Mr. Sable. Mr. Sable's an attorney representing the dead man's family."

"Who were his family?"

Sable answered: "His true name was Anthony Galton. His mother is Mrs. Henry Galton of Santa Teresa."

"You don't say. I used to see her name on the society pages. She cut quite a swathe at one time."

"I suppose she did," Sable said. "She's an old woman now."

"We all grow older, don't we? But come in, gentlemen."

He stood back to let us enter. I turned to him in the hallway:

"Is John Brown with you?"

"He is, yes. I believe he was trying to locate you earlier in the evening. At the moment he's in my office studying the chessboard. Much good may it do him. I propose to beat him in six more moves."

"Can you give us a minute, Doctor, by ourselves?"

"If it's important, and I gather it is."

He steered us into a dining-room furnished in beautiful old mahogany. Light from a yellowing crystal chandelier fell on the dark wood and on the sterling tea set which stood in geometrical order on the tall buffet. The room recalled the feeling I'd had that morning, that the doctor's house was an enclave of the solid past.

He sat at the head of the table and placed us on either side of him. Sable leaned forward across the corner of the table. The events of the day and the one before it had honed his profile sharp:

"Will you give me your opinion of the young man's moral character?"

"I entertain him in my house. That ought to answer your question."

"You consider him a friend?"

"I do, yes. I don't make a practice of entertaining casual strangers. At my age you can't afford to waste your time on second-rate people."

"Does that imply that he's a first-rate person?"

"It would seem to." The doctor's smile was slow, and almost indistinguishable from his frown. "At least he has the makings. You don't ask much more from a boy of twenty-two."

"How long have you known him?"

"All his life, if you count your initial introduction. Mr. Archer may have told you that I brought him into the world."

"Are you certain this is the same boy that you brought into the world?"

"I have no reason to doubt it."

"Would you swear to it, Doctor?"

"If necessary."

"It may be necessary. The question of his identity is a highly important one. A very great deal of money is involved."

The old man smiled, or frowned. "Forgive me if I'm not overly impressed. Money is only money, after all. I don't believe John is particularly hungry for money. As a matter of fact, this development will be quite a blow to him. He came here in the hope of finding his father, alive."

"If he qualifies for a fortune," Sable said, "it ought to be some comfort to him. Were his parents legally married, do you know?"

"It happens that I can answer that question, in the affirmative. John has been making some inquiries. He discovered just last week that a John Brown and a Theodora Gavin were married in Benicia, by civil ceremony, in September 1936. That seems to make him legitimate, by a narrow margin."

Sable sat in silence for a minute. He looked at Dineen like a prosecutor trying to weigh the credibility of a witness.

"Well," the old man said. "Are you satisfied? I don't wish to appear inhospitable, but I'm an early riser, and it happens to be my bedtime."

"There are one or two other things, if you'll bear with me, Doctor. I'm wondering, for instance, just how you happen to be so close to the boy's affairs."

"I choose to be," Dineen said abruptly.

"Why?"

The doctor looked at Sable with faint dislike. "My motives are no concern of yours, Counselor. The young man knocked on my door a month ago, looking for some trace of his family. Naturally I did my best to help him. He has a moral right to the protection and support of his family."

"If he can prove that he's a member of it."

"There seems to be no question of that. I think you're being unnecessarily hard on him, and I see no reason why you should continue in that vein. Certainly there's no indication that he's an impostor. He has his birth certificate, which proves the facts of his birth. My name is on it as attending physician. It's why he came to me in the first place."

"Birth certificates are easy to get," I said. "You can write in, pay your money, and take your choice."

"I suppose you can, if you're a cheat and a scoundrel. I resent the implication that this boy is."

"Please don't." Sable moderated his tone. "As Mrs. Galton's attorney, it's my duty to be skeptical of these claims."

"John has been making no claims."

"Perhaps not yet. He will. And very important interests are involved, human as well as financial. Mrs. Galton is in uncertain health. I don't intend to present her with a situation that's likely to blow up in her face."

93

"I don't believe that's the case here. You asked me for my opinion, and now you have it. But no human situation is entirely predictable, is it?" The old man leaned forward to get up. His bald scalp gleamed like polished stone in the light from the chandelier. "You'll be wanting to talk to John, I suppose. I'll tell him you're here."

He left the room and came back with the boy. John was wearing flannel slacks and a gray sweater over an open-necked shirt. He looked like the recent college graduate that he was supposed to be, but he wasn't at ease in the situation. His eyes shifted from my face to Sable's. Dineen stood beside him in an almost protective posture.

"This is Mr. Sable," he said in a neutral tone. "Mr. Sable is an attorney from Santa Teresa, and he's very much interested in you."

Sable stepped forward and gave him a brisk handshake. "I'm glad to meet you."

"Glad to meet you." His gray eyes matched Sable's in watchfulness. "I understand you know who my father is."

"Was, John," I said. "We've identified those bones at the station, pretty definitely. They belonged to a man named Anthony Galton. The indications are that he was your father."

"But my father's name was John Brown."

"He used that name. It started out as a pen name, apparently." I looked at the lawyer beside me. "We can take it for granted, can't we, that Galton and Brown were the same man, and that he was murdered in 1936?"

"It appears so." Sable laid a restraining hand on my arm. "I wish you'd let me handle this. There are legal questions involved."

He turned to the boy, who looked as if he hadn't absorbed the fact of his father's death. The doctor laid an arm across his shoulders:

"I'm sorry about this, John. I know how much it means to you."

"It's funny, it doesn't seem to mean a thing. I never knew my father. It's simply words, about a stranger."

"I'd like to talk to you in private," Sable said. "Where can we do that?"

"In my room, I suppose. What are we going to talk about?"
"You."

He lived in a workingmen's boardinghouse on the other side of town. It was a ramshackle frame house standing among others which had known better days. The landlady intercepted us at the front door. She was a large-breasted Portuguese woman with rings in her ears and spice on her breath. Something in the boy's face made her say:

"Whatsamatter, Johnny? You in trouble?"

"Nothing like that, Mrs. Gorgello," he said with forced lightness. "These men are friends of mine. Is it all right if I take them up to my room?"

"It's your room, you pay rent. I cleaned it up today for you, real nice. Come right in, gentlemen," she said royally.

Not so royally, she jostled the boy as he passed her in the doorway. "Lift up the long face, Johnny. You look like judgment day."

His room was a small bare cubicle on the second floor at the rear. I guessed that it had been a servant's room in the days when the house was a private residence. Torn places and stains among the faded roses of the wallpaper hinted at a long history of decline.

The room was furnished with an iron cot covered by an army blanket, a stained pine chest of drawers topped by a clouded mirror, a teetery wardrobe, a kitchen chair standing beside a table. In spite of the books on the table, something about the room reminded me of the dead man Culligan. Perhaps it was the smell, compound of hidden dirt and damp and old grim masculine odors.

My mind skipped to Mrs. Galton's grandiose estate. It would be quite a leap from this place to that. I wondered if the boy was going to make it.

He was standing by the single window, looking at us with a sort of defiance. This was his room, his bearing seemed to say, and we could take it or leave it. He lifted the kitchen chair and turned it away from the table:

"Sit down if you like. One of you can sit on the bed."

"I'd just as soon stand, thanks," Sable said. "I had a long drive up here, and I'm going to have to drive back tonight."

The boy said stiffly: "I'm sorry to put you to all this trouble."

"Nonsense. This is my job, and there's nothing personal about it. Now I understand you have your birth certificate with you. May I have a look at it?"

"Certainly."

He pulled out the top drawer of the chest of drawers and produced a folded document. Sable put on horn-rimmed spectacles to read it. I read it over his shoulder. It stated that John Brown, Jr., had been born on Bluff Road in San Mateo County on December 2, 1936; father, John Brown; mother, Theodora Gavin Brown; attending physician, Dr. George T. Dineen.

Sable glanced up, snatching off his glasses like a politician:

"You realize this document means nothing in itself? Anyone can apply for a birth certificate, any birth certificate."

"This one happens to be mine, sir."

"I notice it was issued only last March. Where were you in March?"

"I was still in Ann Arbor. I lived there for over five years."

"Going to the University all that time?" I asked.

"Most of it. I attended high school for a year and a half, then I shifted over to the University. I graduated this spring." He paused, and caught with his teeth at his full lower lip. "I suppose you'll be checking all this, so I might as well explain that I didn't go to school under my own name."

"Why? Didn't you know your own name?"

"Of course I did. I always have. If you want me to go into the circumstances, I will."

"I think that's very much to be desiderated," Sable said.

The boy picked up one of the books from the table. Its title was *Dramas of Modernism.* He opened it to the flyleaf and showed us the name "John Lindsay" written in ink there.

"That was the name I used, John Lindsay. The Christian name was my own, of course. The surname belonged to Mr. Lindsay, the man who took me into his home."

"He lived in Ann Arbor?" Sable said.

"Yes, at 1028 Hill Street." The boy's tone was faintly sardonic. "I lived there with him for several years. His full name was Mr. Gabriel R. Lindsay. He was a teacher and counselor at the high school."

"Isn't it rather odd that you used his name?"

"I didn't think so, under the circumstances. The circumstances were odd—that's putting it mildly—and Mr. Lindsay was the one who took a real interest in my case."

"Your case?"

The boy smiled wryly. "I was a case, all right. I've come a long way in five years, thanks to Mr. Lindsay. I was a mess when I showed up at that high school—a mess in more ways than one. I'd been two days on the road, and I didn't have decent clothes, or anything. Naturally they wouldn't let

96

me in. I didn't have a school record, and I wouldn't tell them my name."

"Why not?"

"I was mortally scared that they'd drag me back to Ohio and put me in training-school. They did that to some of the boys who ran away from the orphanage. Besides, the superintendent didn't like me."

"The superintendent of the orphanage?"

"Yes. His name was Mr. Merriweather."

"What was the name of the orphanage?"

"Crystal Springs. It's near Cleveland. They didn't call it an orphanage. They called it a Home. Which didn't make it any more homelike."

"You say your mother put you there?" I said.

"When I was four."

"Do you remember your mother?"

"Of course. I remember her face, especially. She was very pale and thin, with blue eyes. I think she must have been sick. She had a bad cough. Her voice was husky, very low and soft. I remember the last thing she ever said to me: 'Your daddy's name was John Brown, too, and you were born in California.' I didn't know what or where California was, but I held on to the word. You can see why I had to come here, finally." His voice seemed to have the resonance of his life behind it.

Sable was unimpressed by his emotion. "Where did she say that to you?"

"In the Superintendent's office, when she left me there. She promised to come back for me, but she never did. I don't know what happened to her."

"But you remember her words from the age of four?"

"I was bright for my age," he answered matter-of-factly. "I'm bright, and I'm not ashamed of it. It stood me in good stead when I was trying to get into the high school in Ann Arbor."

"Why did you pick Ann Arbor?"

"I heard it was a good place to get an education. The teachers in the Home were a couple of ignorant bullies. I wanted an education more than anything. Mr. Lindsay gave me an aptitude test, and he decided that I deserved an education, even if I didn't have any transcript. He put up quite a battle for me, getting me into the high school. And then he had to fight the welfare people. They wanted to put me in

97

Juvenile, or find a foster-home for me. Mr. Lindsay convinced them that his home would do, even if he didn't have a wife. He was a widower."

"He sounds like a good man," I said.

"He was the best, and I ought to know. I lived with him for nearly four years. I looked after the furnace, mowed the lawn in the summer, worked around the house to pay for my board and room. But board and room was the least of what he gave me. I was a little bum when he took me in. He made a decent person out of me."

He paused, and his eyes looked past us, thousands of miles. Then they focused on me:

"I had no right today, to tell you that I never had a father. Gabe Lindsay was a father to me."

"I'd like to meet him," I said.

"So that you can check up on me?"

"Not necessarily. Don't take all this so hard, John. As Mr. Sable said, there's nothing personal about it. It's our business to get the facts."

"It's too late to get them from Mr. Lindsay. Mr. Lindsay died the winter before last. He was good to me right up to the end, and past it. He left me enough money to finish my studies."

"How much did he leave you?" Sable said.

"Two thousand dollars. I still have a little of it left."

"What did he die of?"

"Pneumonia. He died in the University Hospital in Ann Arbor. I was with him when he died. You can check that. Next question."

His irony was young and vulnerable. It failed to mask his feeling. I thought if his feeling was artificial, he didn't need the Galton money: he could make his fortune as an actor.

"What motivated you to come here to Luna Bay?" Sable said. "It couldn't have been pure coincidence."

"Who said it was?" Under the pressure of cross-questioning, the boy's poise was breaking down. "I had a right to come here. I was born here, wasn't I?"

"Were you?"

"You just saw my birth certificate."

"How did you get hold of it?"

"I wrote to Sacramento. Is there anything wrong with that? I gave them my birthdate, and they were able to tell me where I was born."

"Why the sudden interest in where you were born?"

"It wasn't a sudden interest. Ask any orphan how important it is to him. The only sudden part of it was my bright idea of writing to Sacramento. It hadn't occurred to me before."

"How did you know your birthdate?"

"My mother must have told the orphanage people. They always gave me a birthday present on December second." He grinned wryly. "Winter underwear."

Sable smiled, too, in spite of himself. He waved his hand in front of his face, as if to dissipate the tension in the room: "Are you satisfied, Archer?"

"I am for now. We've all had a long day. Why don't you lay over for the night?"

"I can't. I have an important probate coming up at ten tomorrow morning. Before that, I have to talk to the Judge in his chambers." He turned suddenly to the boy: "Do you drive a car?"

"I don't have one of my own, but I can drive."

"How would you like to drive me to Santa Teresa? Now."

"To stay?"

"If it works out. I think it will. Your grandmother will be eager to see you."

"But Mr. Turnell's counting on me at the station."

"He can get himself another boy," I said. "You better go, John. You're due for a big change, and this is the beginning of it."

"I'll give you ten minutes to pack," Sable said.

The boy seemed dazed for a minute. He looked around the walls of the mean little room as if he hated to leave it. Perhaps he was afraid to make the big leap.

"Come on," Sable said. "Snap into it."

John shook himself out of his apathy, and dragged an old leather suitcase from the wardrobe. We stood and watched him pack his mager belongings: a suit, a few shirts and socks, shaving gear, a dozen books, his precious birth certificate.

I wondered if we were doing him a favor. The Galton household had hot and cold running money piped in from an inexhaustible reservoir. But money was never free. Like any other commodity, it had to be paid for.

16

I SAT up late in my motel room, making notes on John Brown's story. It wasn't a likely story, on the face of it. His apparent sincerity made it plausible; that, and the fact that it could easily be checked. Some time in the course of the interview I'd made a moral bet with myself that John Brown was telling the truth. John Galton, that is.

In the morning I mailed my notes to my office in Hollywood. Then I paid a visit to the sheriff's substation. A young deputy with a crewcut was sitting at Mungan's desk.

"Yessir?"

"Is, Deputy Mungan anywhere around?"

"Sorry, he's off duty. If you're Mr. Archer, he left a message for you."

He took a long envelope out of a drawer and handed it across the counter. It contained a hurried note written on yellow scratch-pad paper:

R.C. phoned me some dope on Fred Nelson. Record goes back to S.F. docks in twenties. Assault with intent, nolle-prossed. Lempi gang enforcer 1928 on. Arrested suspicion murder 1930, habeas-corpused. Convicted grand theft 1932 sentenced "Q." Attempted escape 1933, extended sentence. Escaped December 1936, never apprehended.

Mungan.

I walked across the street to the hotel and phoned Roy Lemberg's hotel, the Sussex Arms. The desk clerk answered:

"Sussex Arms. Mr. Farnsworth speaking."

"This is Archer. Is Lemberg there?"

"Who did you say it was?"

"Archer. I gave you ten dollars yesterday. Is Lemberg there?"

"Mr. and Mrs. Lemberg both checked out."

"When?"

"Yesterday aft, right after you left."

"Why didn't I see them go?"

"Maybe because they went out the back way. They didn't

100

even leave a forwarding address. But Lemberg made a long-distance call before they took off. A call to Reno."

"Who did he call in Reno?"

"Car-dealer name of Generous Joe. Lemberg used to work for him, I think."

"And that's all there is?"

"That's all," Farnsworth said. "I hope it's what you want."

I drove across country to International Airport, turned in my rented car, and caught a plane to Reno. By noon I was parking another rented car in front of Generous Joe's lot.

A huge billboard depicted a smiling Santa Claus type scattering silver dollars. The lot had a kiosk on one corner, and a row of late-model cars fronting for half an acre of clunks. A big corrugated metal shed with a Cars Painted sign on the wall stood at the rear of the lot.

An eager young man with a rawhide tie cantered out of the kiosk almost before I'd brought my car to a halt. He patted and stroked the fender:

"Nice. Very nice. Beautiful condition, clean inside and out. Depending on your equity, you can trade up and still carry cash away."

"They'd put me in jail. I just rented this crate."

He gulped, performed a mental back somersault, and landed on his feet: "So why pay rent? On our terms, you can *own* a car for less money."

"You wouldn't be Generous Joe?"

"Mr. Culotti's in the back. You want to talk to him?"

I said I did. He waved me toward the shed, and yelled: "Hey, Mr. Culotti, customer!"

A gray-haired man came out, looking cheaply gala in an ice-cream suit. His face was swarthy and pitted like an Epstein bronze, and its two halves didn't quite match. When I got closer to him, I saw that one of his brown eyes was made of glass. He looked permanently startled.

"Mr. Culotti?"

"That's me." He smiled a money smile. "What can I do for you?" A trace of Mediterranean accent added feminine endings to some of his words.

"A man named Lemberg called you yesterday."

"That's right, he used to work for me, wanted his old job back. Nix." A gesture of his spread hand swept Lemberg into the dust-bin.

"Is he back in Reno? I'm trying to locate him."

101

Culotti picked at his nose and looked wise, in a startled way. He smiled expansively, and put a fatherly arm around my back. "Come in, we'll talk."

He propelled me toward the door. Hissing sounds came from the shed, and the sweet anesthetic odor of sprayed paint. Culotti opened the door and stepped back. A goggled man with a paint-gun turned from his work on a blue car.

I was trying to recognize him, when Culotti's shoulder caught me like a trunk-bumper in the small of the back. I staggered toward the goggled man. The paint-gun hissed in his hands.

A blue cloud stung my eyes. In the burning blue darkness, I recalled that the room clerk Farnsworth hadn't asked me for more money. Then I felt the sap's soft explosion against the back of my head. I glissaded down blue slopes of pain to a hole which opened for me.

Later there was talking.

"Better wash out his eyes," the first gravedigger said. "We don't want to blind him."

"Let him go blind," the second gravedigger said. "Teach him a lesson. I got a hook in the eye."

"Did it teach you a lesson, Blind-eye? Do what I tell you."

I heard Culotti breathe like a bull. He spat, but made no answer. My hands were tied behind me. My face was on cement. I tried to blink. My eyelids were stuck tight.

The fear of blindness is the worst fear there is. It crawled on my face and entered my mouth. I wanted to beg them to save my eyes. A persistent bright speck behind my eyes stared me down and shamed me into continued silence.

Liquid gurgled in a can.

"Not with gasoline, greaseball."

"Don't call me that."

"Why not? You're a blind-eye greaseball, hamburger that used to be muscle." This voice was light and featureless, without feeling, almost without meaning. "You got any olive oil?"

"At home, plenty."

"Go and get it. I'll keep store."

My consciousness must have lapsed. Oil ran on my face like tears. I thought of a friend named Angelo who made his own oil from the olives he grew on his hillside in the Valley. The Maffia had killed his father.

A face came into blurred focus, Culotti's face, hanging slack-mouthed over me. I twisted from my side onto my back, and lashed at him with both feet. One heel caught

102

him under the chin, and he went down. Something bounced and rolled on the floor. Then he stood one-eyed over me, bleeding at the mouth. He stamped my head back down into earthy darkness.

It was a bad afternoon. Quite suddenly it was a bad evening. Somebody had awakened me with his snoring. I listened to the snoring for a while. It stopped when I held my breath and started again when I let my breath out. For a long time I missed the significance of this.

There were too many other interesting things to do and think about. The staring speck was back again in the center of my mind. It moved, and my hands moved with it. They felt my face. It bored me. Ruins always bored me.

I was lying in a room. The room had walls. There was a window in one of the walls. Snow-capped mountains rose against a yellow sky which darkened to green, then blue. Twilight hung like blue smoke in the room.

I sat up; springs creaked under me. A man I hadn't noticed moved away from the wall he'd been leaning on. I dropped my feet to the floor and turned to face him, slowly and carefully, so as not to lose my balance.

He was a thick young man with shiny black curls tumbling over his forehead. One of his arms was in a sling. The other arm had a gun at the end of it. His hot eyes and the cold eye of the gun triangulated my breastbone.

"Hello, Tommy," I tried to say. It came out: "Huddo, Tawy."

My mouth contained ropes of blood. I tried to spit them out. That started a chain-reaction which flung me back on the bed retching and cawing. Tommy Lemberg stood and watched me.

He said when I was still: "Mr. Schwartz is waiting to talk to you. You want to clean up a little?"

"When do I do dat?" I said in my inimitable patois.

"There's a bathroom down the hall. Think you can walk?"

"I can walk."

But I had to lean on the wall to reach the bathroom. Tommy Lemberg stood and watched me wash my face and gargle. I tried to avoid looking into the mirror over the sink. I looked, though, finally, when I was drying my face. One of my front teeth was broken off short. My nose resembled a boiled potato.

All of this made me angry. I moved on Tommy. He stepped back into the doorway. I lost my footing and fell to my knees, took the barrel of his gun in the nape of my neck. Pain went through me so large and dull it scared me. I got up, supporting myself on the sink.

Tommy was grinning in an excited way. "Don't *do* things like that. I don't want to hurt you."

"Or Culligan, either, I bet." I was talking better now, but my eyes weren't focusing properly.

"Culligan? Who he? I never heard of any Culligan."

"And you've never been in Santa Teresa?"

"Where's that?"

He ushered me to the end of the corridor and down a flight of steps into a big dim room. In its picture windows, the mountains now stood black against the darkening sky. I recognized the mountains west of Reno. Tommy turned on lights which blotted them out. He moved around the room as if he was at home there.

I suppose it was the living-room of Otto Schwartz's house, but it was more like the lobby of a hotel or the recreation room of an institution. The furniture stood around in impersonal groupings, covered with plastic so that nothing could harm it. An antique bar and a wall of bottles took up one whole end. A jukebox, an electric player piano, a roulette layout, and several slot machines stood against the rear wall.

"You might as well sit down." Tommy waved his gun at a chair.

I sat down and closed my eyes, which still weren't focusing. Everything I looked at had a double outline. I was afraid of concussion. I was having a lot of fears.

Tommy turned on the player piano. It started to tinkle out a tune about a little Spanish town. Tommy did a few dance steps to it, facing me and holding the gun in his hand. He didn't seem to know what to do with himself.

I concentrated on wishing that he would put his gun away and give me some kind of chance at him. He never would, though. He loved holding the gun. He held it different ways, posturing in front of his reflection in the window. I began to draft a mental letter to my congressman advocating legislation prohibiting the manufacture of guns except for military purposes.

Mr. J. Edgar Hoover entered the room at this point. He must have been able to read minds, because he said that he approved of my plan and intended to present it to the President. I felt my forehead. It was hot and dry, like a heating-

104

pad. Mr. Hoover faded away. The player piano went on hammering out the same tune: music to be delirious by.

The man who came in next radiated chill from green glacial eyes. He had a cruel nose and under it the kind of mouth that smiles by stretching horizontally. He must have been nearly sixty but he had a well-sustained tan and a lean quick body. He wore a light fedora and a topcoat.

So did the man who moved a step behind him and towered half a foot over him. This one had the flat impervious eyes, the battered face and pathological nervelessness of an old-fashioned western torpedo. When his boss paused in front of me, he stood to one side in canine watchfulness. Tommy moved up beside him, like an apprentice.

"You're quite a mess." Schwartz's voice was chilly, too, and very soft, expecting to be listened to. "I'm Otto Schwartz, in case you don't know. I got no time to waste on two-bit private eyes. I got other things on my mind."

"What kind of things have you got on it? Murder?"

He tightened up. Instead of hitting me, he took off his hat and threw it to Tommy. His head was completely bald. He put his hands in his coat pockets and leaned back on his heels and looked down the curve of his nose at me:

"I was giving you the benefit, that you got in over your head without knowing. What's going to happen, you go on like this, talk about murder, crazy stuff like that?" He wagged his head solemnly from side to side. "Lake Tahoe is very deep. You could take a long dive, no Aqualung, concrete on the legs."

"You could sit in a hot seat, no cushion, electrodes on the bald head."

The big man took a step toward me, watching Schwartz with a doggy eye, and lunged around with his big shoulders. Schwartz surprised me by laughing, rather tinnily:

"You are a brave young man. I like you. I wish you no harm. What do you suggest? A little money, and that's that?"

"A little murder. Murder everybody. Then you can be the bigshot of the world."

"I am a bigshot, don't ever doubt it." His mouth pursed suddenly and curiously, like a wrinkled old wound: "I take insults from nobody! And nobody steals from me."

"Did Culligan steal from you? Is that why you ordered him killed?"

Schwartz looked down at me some more. His eyes had

105

dark centers. I thought of the depths of Tahoe, and poor drowned Archer with concrete on his legs. I was in a susceptible mood, and fighting it. Tommy Lemberg spoke up:

"Can I say something, Mr. Schwartz? I didn't knock the guy off. The cops got it wrong. He must of fell down on the knife and stabbed himself."

"Yah! Moron!" Schwartz turned his contained fury on Tommy: "Go tell that to the cops. Just leave me out of it, please."

"They wouldn't believe me," he said in a misunderstood whine. "They'd pin it on me, just because I tried to defend myself. I was the one got shot. He pulled a gun on me."

"Shut up! Shut up!" Schwartz spread one hand on top of his head and pulled at imaginary hair. "Why is there no intelligence left in the world? All morons!"

"The intelligent ones wouldn't touch your rackets with a ten-foot pole."

"I heard enough out of you."

He jerked his head at the big man, who started to take off his coat:

"Want me to work him over, Mr. Schwartz?"

It was the light and meaningless voice that had argued with Culotti. It lifted me out of my chair. Because Schwartz was handy, I hit him in the stomach. He jackknifed, and went down gasping. It doesn't take much to make me happy, and that gave me a happy feeling which lasted through the first three or four minutes of the beating.

Then the big man's face began to appear in red snatches. When the light in the room failed entirely, the bright staring speck in my mind took over for a while. Schwartz's voice kept making tinny little jokes:

"Just promise to forget it, that will be that."

"All you gotta do, give me your word. I'm a man of my word, you're another."

"Back to L.A., that's all you gotta do. No questions asked, no harm done."

The bright speck stood like a nail in my brain. It wouldn't let me let go of the room. I cursed it, but it wouldn't go away. It wrote little luminous remarks on the red pounding darkness: This is it. You take a stand.

Then it was a light surging away from me like the light of a ship. I swam for it, but it rose away, hung in the dark heaven still as a star. I let go of the pounding room, and swung from it up and over the black mountains.

106

chapter

17

I CAME to early next morning in the accident ward of the Reno hospital. When I had learned to talk with a packed nose and a wired jaw, a couple of detectives asked me who took my wallet. I didn't bother disturbing their assumption that I was a mugging victim.

Anything I told them about Schwartz would be wasted words. Besides, I needed Schwartz. The thought of him got me through the first bad days, when I doubted from time to time that I would be very active in the future. Everything was still fuzzy at the edges. I got very tired of fuzzy nurses and earnest young fuzzy doctors asking me how my head felt.

By the fourth day, though, my vision was clear enough to read some of yesterday's newspapers which the voluntary aides brought around for the ward patients. There was hardware in the sky, and dissension on earth. A special dispatch in the back pages told how a real-life fairy-tale had reached its happy ending when the long-lost John Galton was restored to the bosom of his grandmother, the railroad and oil widow. In the accompanying photograph, John himself was wearing a new-looking sports jacket and a world-is-my-oyster grin.

This spurred me on. By the end of the first week, I was starting to get around. One morning after my Cream of Wheat I sneaked out to the nurses' station and put in a collect call to Santa Teresa. I had time to tell Gordon Sable where I was, before the head nurse caught me and marched me back to the ward.

Sable arrived while I was eating my Gerber's-baby-food dinner. He waved a checkbook. Before I knew it I was in a private room with a bottle of Old Forester which Sable had brought me. I sat up late with him, drinking highballs through a glass tube and talking through my remaining teeth like a gangster in very early sound.

"You're going to need a crown on that tooth," Sable said comfortingly. "Also, plastic surgery on the nose. Do you have any hospital insurance?"

"No."

"I'm afraid I can't commit Mrs. Galton." Then he took another look at me, and his manner softened: "Well, yes, I think I can. I think I can persuade her to underwrite the expense, even though you did exceed your instructions."

"That's mighty white of you and her." But the words didn't come out ironic. It had been a bad eight days. "Doesn't she give a good goddam about who murdered her son? And what about Culligan?"

"The police are working on both cases, don't worry."

"They're the same case. The cops are sitting on their tails. Schwartz put the fix in."

Sable shook his head. "You're way off in left field, Lew."

"The hell I am. Tommy Lemberg's his boy. Have they arrested Tommy?"

"He dropped out of sight. Don't let it ride you. You're a willing man, but you can't take on responsibility for all the trouble in the world. Not in your present condition, anyway."

"I'll be on my feet in another week. Sooner." The whisky in the bottle was falling like a barometer. I was full of stormy optimism. "Give me another week after that and I'll break the case wide open for you."

"I hope so, Lew. But don't take too much on yourself. You've been hurt, and naturally your feelings are a bit exaggerated."

He was sitting directly under the light, but his face was getting fuzzy. I leaned out of bed and grabbed his shoulder. "Listen, Sable, I can't prove it, but I can feel it. That Galton boy is a phony, part of a big conspiracy, with the Organization behind it."

"I think you're wrong. I've spent hours on his story. It checks out. And Mrs. Galton is quite happy, for the first time in many years."

"I'm not."

He rose, and pushed me gently back against the pillows. I was still as weak as a cat. "You've talked enough for one night. Let it rest, and don't worry, eh? Mrs. Galton will take care of everything, and if she doesn't want to, I'll make her. You've earned her gratitude. We're all sorry this had to happen."

He shook my hand and started for the door.

"Flying back tonight?" I asked him.

108

"I have to. My wife's in bad shape. Take it easy, now, you'll hear from me. And I'll leave some money for you at the desk."

18

I SPRUNG myself out of the hospital three days later, and assembled myself aboard a plane for San Francisco. From International Airport I took a cab to the Sussex Arms Hotel.

The room clerk, Farnsworth, was sitting behind the counter at the rear of the dim little lobby, looking as if he hadn't moved in two weeks. He was reading a muscle magazine, and he didn't look up until I was close enough to see the yellow of his eyes. Even then he didn't recognize me right away: the bandages on my face made an effective mask.

"You wish a room, sir?"

"No. I came to see you."

"Me?" His eyebrows jumped, and then came down in a frown of concentration.

"I owe you something."

The color left his face. "No. No, you don't. That's all right."

"The other ten and the bonus. That makes fifteen I owe you. Excuse the delay. I got held up."

"That's too bad." He craned his neck around and looked behind him. There was nothing there but the switchboard, staring like a wall of empty eyes.

"Don't let it bother you, Farnsworth. It wasn't your fault. Was it?"

"No." He swallowed several times. "It wasn't my fault.".

I stood and smiled at him with the visible parts of my face.

"What happened?" he said after a while.

"It's a long sad story. You wouldn't be interested."

I took the creaking new wallet out of my hip pocket and laid a five and a ten on the counter between us. He sat and looked at the money.

"Take it," I said.

He didn't move.

"Go ahead, don't be bashful. The money belongs to you."

"Well. Thanks."

Slowly and reluctantly, he reached out for the bills. I caught his wrist in my left hand, and held it. He jerked convulsively, reached under the counter and came up with a gun in his left hand:

"Turn me loose."

"Not a chance."

"I'll shoot!" But the gun was wavering.

I reached for his gun wrist, and twisted it until the gun dropped on the counter between us. It was a .32 revolver, a little nickel-plated suicide gun. I let go of Farnsworth and picked it up and pointed it at the knot of his tie Without moving, he seemed to draw away from it. His eyes got closer together.

"Please. I couldn't help it."

"What couldn't you help?"

"I had orders to give you that contact in Reno."

"Who gave you the orders?"

"Roy Lemberg. It wasn't my fault."

"Lemberg doesn't give orders to anybody. He's the kind that takes them."

"Sure, he passed the word, that's what I meant."

"Who gave him the word?"

"Some gambler in Nevada, name of Schwartz." Farnsworth wet his mauve lips with his tongue. "Listen, you don't want to ruin me. I make a little book, lay off the heavy bets. If I don't do like the money boys say, I'm out of business. So have a heart, mister."

"If you level with me. Does Lemberg work for Schwartz?"

"His brother does. Not him."

"Where are the Lembergs now?"

"I wouldn't know about the brother. Roy took off like I said, him and his wife both. Put the gun down, mister. Jeez. I got a nervous stomach."

"You'll have a perforated ulcer if you don't talk. Where did the Lembergs go?"

"Los Angeles, I think."

"Where in Los Angeles?"

"I dunno." He spread his hands. They had a tremor running through them, like dry twigs in a wind. "Honest."

"You know, Farnsworth," I said in my menacing new lockjaw voice, "I'll give you five seconds to tell me."

He looked around at the switchboard again, as if it was

110

an instrument of execution, and swallowed audibly. "All right, I'll tell you. They're at a motor court on Bayshore, down by Moffett Field. The Triton Motor Court. At least, that's where they said they were going. Now will you put down the gun, mister?"

Before the rhythm of his fear ran down, I said: "Do you know a man named Peter Culligan?"

"Yeah. He roomed here for a while, over a year ago."

"What did he do for a living?"

"He was a horseplayer."

"That's a living?"

"I guess he hacked a little, too. Put the gun down, eh? I told you what you wanted to know."

"Where did Culligan go from here?"

"I heard he got a job in Reno."

"Working for Schwartz?"

"Could be. He told me once he used to be a stickman." I dropped the gun in my jacket pocket.

"Hey," he said. "That's my gun. I bought it myself."

"You're better off without it."

Looking back from the door, I saw that Farnsworth was halfway between the counter and the switchboard. He stopped in mid-motion. I went back across the lobby:

"If it turns out you're lying, or if you tip off the Lembergs, I'll come back for you. Is that clear?"

A kind of moral wriggle moved up his body from his waist to his fish-belly face. "Yeah. Sure. Okay."

This time I didn't look back. I walked up to Union Square, where I made a reservation on an afternoon flight to L.A. Then I rented a car and drove down Bayshore past the airport.

The hangars of Moffett Field loomed up through the smog like gray leviathans. The Triton Motor Court stood in a wasteland of shacks on the edge of the flight pattern. Its buildings were a fading salmon pink. Its only visible attraction was the $3.00 Double sign. Jets snored like flies in the sky.

I parked on the cinder driveway beside the chicken-coop office. The woman who ran it wore a string of fake pearls dirtied by her neck. She said that Mr. and Mrs. Lemberg weren't registered there.

"They may be going under their maiden name." I described them.

111

"Sounds like the girl in seven, maybe. She don't want to be disturbed, not in the daytime."

"She won't mind. I have no designs on her."

She bridled. "Who said you had? What kind of a place do you think this is, anyway?"

It was a tough question to answer. I said: "What name is she going under?"

"You from the cops? I don't want trouble with the cops."

"I was in an accident. She may be able to help me find the driver."

"That's different." The woman probably didn't believe me, but she chose to act as if she did. "They registered under the name Hamburg, Mr. and Mrs. Rex Hamburg."

"Is her husband with her?"

"Not for the last week. Maybe it's just as well," she added cryptically.

I knocked on the weathered door under the rusted iron seven. Footsteps dragged across the floor behind it. Fran Lemberg blinked in the light. Her eyes were puffed. The roots of her hair were darker. Her robe was taking on a grimy patina.

She stopped blinking when she recognized me.

"Go away."

"I'm coming in for a minute. You don't want trouble."

She looked past me, and I followed her look. The woman with the dirty pearls was watching us from the window of the office.

"All right, come in."

She let me come in past her, and slammed the door on daylight. The room smelled of wine and smoke, stale orange-peel and a woman's sleep, and a perfume I didn't recognize, Original Sin perhaps. When my eyes became night-adapted, I saw the confusion on the floor and the furniture: clothes and looped stockings and shoes and empty bottles, ashes and papers, the congealed remains of hamburgers and french fries.

She sat in a defensive posture on the edge of the unmade bed. I cleared a space for myself on the chair.

"What happened to you?" she said.

"I had a run-in with some of Tommy's playmates. Your husband set me up for the fall."

"Roy did?"

"Don't kid me, you were with him at the time. I thought

112

he was a straight joe trying to help his brother, but he's just another errandboy for mobsters."

"No. He isn't."

"Is that what he told you?"

"I lived with him nearly ten years, I ought to know. He worked one time for a crooked car-dealer in Nevada. When Roy found out about the crookedness, he quit. That's the kind of guy he is."

"If you mean Generous Joe, that hardly qualifies Roy as a boy scout."

"I didn't say he was. He's just a guy trying to get through life."

"Some of us make it harder for the others."

"You can't blame Roy for trying to protect himself. He's wanted for accessory in a murder. But it isn't fair. You can't blame him for what Tommy did."

"You're a loyal wife," I said. "But where is it getting you?"

"Who says I want to get any place?"

"There are better places than this."

"You're telling me. I've lived in some of them."

"How long has Roy been gone?"

"Nearly two weeks, I guess. I don't keep track of the time. It goes faster that way."

"How old are you, Fran?"

"None of your business." After a pause she added: "A hundred and twenty-eight."

"Is Roy coming back?"

"He says he is. But he always sides with his brother when the chips are down." Emotion flooded up in her eyes, but drained away again. "I guess I can't blame him. This time the chips are really down."

"Tommy's staying in Nevada," I said, trying to find the wedge that would open her up.

"Tommy's in Nevada?"

"I saw him there. Schwartz is looking after him. And Roy, too, probably."

"I don't believe you. Roy said they were leaving the country."

"The state, maybe. Isn't that what he said, that they were leaving the state?"

"The country," she repeated stubbornly. "That's why they couldn't take me along."

"They were stringing you. They just don't want a woman

113

in the way. So here you sit in a rundown crib on Bayshore. Hustling for hamburgers, while the boys are living high on the hog in Nevada."

"You're a liar!" she cried. "They're in Canada!"

"Don't let them kid you."

"Roy is going to send for me as soon as he can swing it."

"You've heard from him, then."

"Yeah, I've heard from him." Her loose mouth tightened, too late to hold back the words. "Okay, so you got it out of me. That's all you're going to get out of me." She folded her arms across her half-naked breasts, and looked at me grimly: "Why don't you beat it? You got nothing on me, you never will have."

"As soon as you show me Roy's letter."

"There was no letter. I got the message by word of mouth."

"Who brought it?"

"A guy."

"What guy?"

"Just a guy. Roy told him to look me up."

"He sent him from Nevada, probably."

"He did not. The guy drove a haulaway out from Detroit. He talked to Roy in Detroit."

"Is that where Roy and Tommy crossed the border?"

"I guess so."

"Where were they headed?"

"I don't know, and I wouldn't tell you if I did know."

I sat on the bed beside her. "Listen to me, Fran. You want your husband back, don't you?"

"Not in a convict suit, or on a slab."

"It doesn't have to be that way. Tommy's the one we're after. If Roy will turn him over to us, he'll be taking a long step out of trouble. Can you get that message to Roy from me?"

"Maybe if he phones me or something. All I can do is wait."

"You must have some idea where they went."

"Yeah, they said something about this town in Ontario near Windsor. Tommy was the one that knew about it."

"What's the name of the place?"

"They didn't say."

"Was Tommy ever in Canada before?"

"No, but Pete Culligan—"

She covered the lower part of her face with her hand and looked at me over it. Fear and distress hardened her eyes,

114

but not for long. Her feelings were too diffuse to sustain themselves.

I said: "Tommy did know Culligan, then?"

She nodded.

"Did he have a personal reason for killing Culligan?"

"Not that I know of. Him and Pete were palsy-walsy."

"When did you see them together?"

"Last winter in Frisco. Tommy was gonna jump parole until Roy talked him out of it, and Pete told him about this place in Canada. It's sort of an irony of fate like, now Tommy's hiding out there for knocking Pete off." .

"Did Tommy admit to you that he killed Culligan?"

"No, to hear him tell it he's innocent as an unborn babe. Roy even believes him."

"But you don't?"

"I swore off believing Tommy the day after I met him. But we won't go into that."

"Where is this hideout in Canada?"

"I don't know." Her voice was taking on an edge of hysteria. "Why don't you go away and leave me alone?"

"Will you contact me if you hear from them?"

"Maybe I will, maybe I won't."

"How are you fixed for money?"

"I'm loaded," she said. "What do you think? I park in this crib because I like the homey atmosphere."

I dropped a ten in her lap as I went out. Before my plane took off for Los Angeles, I had time to phone Sheriff Trask. I filled him in, with emphasis on Culligan's probable connection with Schwartz. In the rational light of day, I didn't want Schwartz all to myself.

chapter
19

IN THE morning, after a session with my dentist, I opened up my office on Sunset Boulevard. The mailbox was stuffed with envelopes, mostly bills and circulars. There were two envelopes mailed from Santa Teresa in the past few days.

The first one I opened contained a check for a thousand dollars and a short letter from Gordon Sable typed on the letterhead of his firm. Sad as was the fact of Anthony

Galton's death, his client and he both felt that the over-all outcome was better than could have been hoped for. He hoped and trusted that I was back in harness, and none the worse for wear, and would I forward my medical bills as I received them.

The other letter was a carefully hand-written note from John Galton:

Dear Mr. Archer—
Just a brief note to thank you for your labours on my behalf. My father's death is a painful blow to all of us here. There is tragedy in the situation, which I have to learn to face up to. But there is also opportunity, for me. I hope to prove myself worthy of my patrimony.

Mr. Sable told me how you "fell among thieves." I hope that you are well again, and Grandmother joins me in this wish. For what it's worth, I did persuade Grandmother to send you an additional check in token of appreciation. She joins me in inviting you to visit us when you can make the trip up this way.

I myself would like very much to talk to you.

> Respectfully yours,
> John Galton.

It seemed to be pure gratitude undiluted by commercialism, until I reflected that he was taking credit for the check Sable had sent me. His letter stirred up the suspicions that had been latent in my mind since I'd talked to Sable in the hospital. Whatever John was, he was a bright boy and a fast worker. I wondered what he wanted from me.

After going through the rest of my mail, I called my answering-service. The girl at the switchboard expressed surprise that I was still in the land of the living, and told me that a Dr. Howell had been trying to reach me. I called the Santa Teresa number he'd left.

A girl's voice answered: "Dr. Howell's residence."

"This is Lew Archer. Miss Howell?" The temporary crown I'd just acquired that morning pushed out against my upper lip, and made me lisp.

"Yes, Mr. Archer."

"Your father has been trying to get in touch with me."

"Oh. He's just leaving for the hospital. I'll see if I can catch him."

After a pause, Howell's precise voice came over the line:

116

"I'm glad to hear from you, Archer. You may recall that we met briefly at Mrs. Galton's house. I'd like to buy you a lunch."

"Lunch will be fine. What time and place do you have in mind?"

"The time is up to you—the sooner the better. The Santa Teresa Country Club would be the most convenient place for me."

"It's a long way for me to come for lunch."

"I had a little more than lunch in mind." He lowered his voice as though he suspected eavesdroppers. "I'd like to engage your services, if you're free."

"To do what?"

"I'd much prefer to discuss that in person. Would today be possible for you?"

"Yes. I'll be at the Country Club at one."

"You can't drive it in three hours, man."

"I'll take the noon plane."

"Oh, fine."

I heard the click as he hung up, and then a second click. Someone had been listening on an extension. I found out who it was when I got off the plane at Santa Teresa. A young girl with doe eyes and honey-colored hair was waiting for me at the barrier.

"Remember me? I'm Sheila Howell. I thought I'd pick you up."

"That was a nice thought."

"Not really. I have an ulterior motive."

She smiled charmingly. I followed her through the sunlit terminal to her car. It was a convertible with the top down.

Sheila turned to me as she slid behind the wheel: "I might as well be frank about it. I overheard what was said, and I wanted to talk to you about John before Dad does. Dad is a well-meaning person, but he's been a widower for ten years, and he has certain blind spots. He doesn't understand the modern world."

"But you do?"

She colored slightly, like a peach in the sun. "I understand it better than Dad does. I've studied social science at college, and people just don't go around any more telling other people who to be interested in. That sort of thing is as dead as the proverbial dodo. Deader." She nodded her small head, once, with emphasis.

"First-year social science?"

117

The color in her cheeks deepened. Her eyes were candid, the color of the sky. "How did you know? Anyway, I'm a sophomore now." As if this made all the difference between adolescence and maturity.

"I'm a mind reader. You're interested in John Galton."

Her pure gaze didn't waver. "I love John. I think he loves me."

"Is that what you wanted to say to me?"

"No." She was suddenly flustered. "I didn't mean to say it. But it's true." Her eyes darkened. "The things that Dad believes aren't true, though. He's just a typical patriarch type, full of prejudices against the boy I happen to like. He believes the most awful things against John, or pretends to."

"What things, Sheila?"

"I wouldn't even repeat them, so there. Anyway, you'll be hearing them from him. I know what Dad wants you to do, you see. He let the cat out of the bag last night."

"What does he want me to do?"

"Please," she said, "don't talk to me as if I were a child. I know that tone so well, and I'm so tired of it. Dad uses it on me all the time. He doesn't realize I'm practically grown up. I'm going to be nineteen on my next birthday."

"Wow," I said softly.

"All right, go ahead and patronize me. Maybe I'm not mature. I'm mature enough to know good people from bad people."

"We all make mistakes about people, no matter how ancient we are."

"But I couldn't be mistaken about John. He's the nicest boy I ever met in my life."

I said: "I like him, too."

"I'm so glad." Her hand touched my arm, like a bird alighting and then taking off again: "John likes you, or I wouldn't be taking you into our confidence."

"You wouldn't be planning on getting married?"

"Not just yet," she said, as if this was a very conservative approach. "John has a lot of things he wants to do first, and of course I couldn't go against Father's wishes."

"What things does John want to do?"

She answered vaguely: "He wants to make something of himself. He's very ambitious. And of course the one big thing in his life is finding out who killed his father. It's all he thinks about."

118

"Has he done anything about it?"

"Not yet, but I know he has plans. He doesn't tell me all he has on his mind. I probably wouldn't understand, anyway. He's much more intelligent than I am."

"I'm glad you realize that. It's a good thing to bear in mind."

"What do you mean?" she said in a small voice. But she knew what I meant: "It isn't true, what Father says, that John is an imposter. It can't be true!"

"What makes you so sure?"

"I know it here." Her hand touched her breast, ever so lightly. "He couldn't be lying to me. And Cassie says he's the image of his dad. So does Aunt Maria."

"Does John ever talk about his past to you?"

She regarded me with deepening distrust. "Now you sound just like Father again. You mustn't ask me questions about John. It wouldn't be fair to John."

"Give yourself some thought, too," I said. "I know it doesn't seem likely, but if he is an imposter, you could be letting yourself in for a lot of pain and trouble."

"I don't even care if he is!" she cried, and burst into tears.

A young man in airline coveralls came out of the terminal and glared at me. I was making a pretty girl cry, and there ought to be a law. I assumed a very legal expression. He went back inside again.

My plane took off with a roar. The roar diminished to a cicada humming in the northern sky. Sheila's tears passed like a summer shower. She started the engine and drove me into town, very efficiently, like a chauffeur who happened to be a deaf-mute.

John was a very fast worker.

chapter
20   BEFORE she deposited me in the main lounge of the clubhouse, Sheila apologized for her emotional outburst, as she called it, and said something inarticulate about not telling Daddy. I said that no apology was necessary, and that I wouldn't.

The windows of the lounge overlooked the golf course. The

players were a shifting confetti of color on the greens and fairways. I watched them until Howell came in at five minutes after one.

He shook my hand vigorously. "Good to see you, Archer. I hope you don't mind eating right away. I have to meet a committee shortly after two."

He led me into a huge dining-room. Most of the tables were roped off and empty. We took one by a window which looked out across a walled swimming-pool enclosure where young people were romping and splashing. The waiter deferred to Howell as if he was a member of the stewardship committee.

Since I knew nothing about the man, I asked him the first question that occurred to me: "What kind of a committee are you meeting?"

"Aren't all committees alike? They spend hours making up their collective mind to do something which any one of their members could accomplish in half the time. I'm thinking of setting up a committee to work for the abolition of committees." His smile was a rapid flash. "As a matter of fact, it's a Heart Association committee. We're laying plans for a fund campaign, and I happen to be chairman. Will you have something to drink? I'm going to have a Gibson."

"That will do for me."

He ordered two Gibsons from the hovering waiter. "As a medical man, I feel it's my duty to perpetuate the little saving vices. It's probably safer to overdrink than it is to overeat. What will you have to eat?"

I consulted the menu.

"If you like sea food," he said executively, "the lobster Newberg is easy to chew. Gordon Sable told me about your little accident. How's the jaw?"

"Mending, thanks."

"What precisely was the trouble about, if you don't object to the question?"

"It's a long story, which boils down to something like this: Anthony Galton was killed for his money by a criminal named Nelson who had just escaped from prison. Your original guess was very close to the truth. But there's more to the case. I believe Tony Galton's murder and Pete Culligan's murder are related."

Howell leaned forward across the table, his short gray hair bristling. "How related?"

"That's the problem I was trying to solve when I got my

jaw broken. Let me ask you a question, Doctor. What's your impression of John Galton?"

"I was going to ask you the same question. Since you got to it first, I'll take first turn in answering. The boy *seems* open and aboveboard. He's certainly intelligent, and I suppose prepossessing if you like obvious charm. His grand— Mrs. Galton seems to be charmed with him."

"She doesn't question his identity?"

"Not in the slightest, she hasn't from the beginning. For Maria, the boy is practically the reincarnation of her son Tony. Her companion, Miss Hildreth, feels very much the same way. I have to admit myself that the resemblance is striking. But such things can be arranged, when a great deal of money is involved. I suppose there's no man alive who doesn't have a double somewhere in the world."

"You're suggesting that he was searched out and hired?"

"Hasn't the possibility occurred to you?"

"Yes, it has. I think it should be explored."

"I'm glad to hear you say that. I'll be frank with you. It occurred to me when the boy turned up here, that you might be a part of the conspiracy. But Gordon Sable vouches for you absolutely, and I've had other inquiries made." His gray eyes probed mine. "In addition to which, you have the marks of honesty on your face."

"It's the hard way to prove you're honest."

Howell smiled slightly, looking out over the pool. His daughter, Sheila, had appeared at the poolside in a bathing-suit. She was beautifully made, but the fact seemed to give her no pleasure. She sat by herself, with a pale closed looked, undergoing the growing pains of womanhood. Howell's glance rested on her briefly, and a curious woodenness possessed his face.

The waiter brought our drinks, and we ordered lunch. When the waiter was out of hearing, Howell said:

"It's the boy's story that bothers me. I understand you were the first to hear it. What do you think about it?"

"Sable and I gave him quite a going-over. He took it well, and his story stood up. I made notes on it the same night. I've gone over the notes since I talked to you this morning, and couldn't find any self-contradictions."

"The story may have been carefully prepared. Remember that the stakes are very high. You may be interested to know that Maria is planning to change her will in his favor."

"Already?"

"Already. She may already have done. Gordon wouldn't agree to it, so she called in another attorney to draw up a will. Maria's half out of her mind—she's pent up her generous feelings for so long, that she's intoxicated with them."

"Is she incompetent?"

"By no means," he said hastily. "I don't mean to overstate the case. And I concede her perfect right to do what she wants to do with her own money. On the other hand, we can't let her be defrauded by a—confidence man."

"How much money is involved?"

He raised his eyes over my head as if he could see a mountain of gold in the distance. "I couldn't estimate. Something like the national debt of a medium-sized European country. I know Henry left her oil property that brings in a weekly income in the thousands. And she has hundreds of thousands in securities."

"Where does it all go if it doesn't go to the boy?"

Howell smiled mirthlessly. "I'm not supposed to know that. It happens that I do, but I'm certainly not supposed to tell."

"You've been frank with me," I said. "I'll be frank with you. I'm wondering if you have an interest in the estate."

He scratched at his jaw, violently, but gave no other sign of discomposure. "I have, yes, in several senses. Mrs. Galton named me executor in her original will. I assure you personal considerations are not influencing my judgment. I think I know my own motives well enough to say that."

It's a lucky man who does, I thought. I said: "Apart from the amount of money involved, what exactly is bothering you?"

"The young man's story. As he tells it, it doesn't really start till age sixteen. There's no way to go beyond that to his origins, whatever they may be. I tried, and came up against a stone wall."

"I'm afraid I don't follow you. The way John tells it, he was in an orphanage until he ran away at the age of sixteen. The Crystal Springs Home, in Ohio."

"I've been in touch with a man I know in Cleveland—chap I went to medical school with. The Crystal Springs Home burned to the ground three years ago."

"That doesn't make John a liar. He says he left there five and a half years ago."

"That doesn't make John a liar, no. But if he is, it leaves us

122

with no way to prove that he is. The records of the Home were completely destroyed in the fire. The staff was scattered."

"The Superintendent should be traceable. What was his name—Merriweather?"

"Merriweather died in the fire of a heart attack. All of this suggests the possibility—I'd say probability—that John provided himself with a story *ex post facto*. Or was provided with one. He or his backers looked around for a foolproof background to equip him with—one that was uncheckable. Crystal Springs was it—a large institution which no longer existed, which had no surviving records. Who knows if John Brown ever spent a day there?"

"You've been doing a lot of thinking about this."

"I have, and I haven't told you all of it. There's the question of his speech, for instance. He represents himself as an American, born and raised in the United States."

"You're not suggesting he's a foreigner?"

"I am, though. National differences in speech have always interested me, and it happens I've spent some time in central Canada. Have you ever listened to a Canadian pronounce the word 'about'?"

"If I did, I never noticed. 'About'?"

"You say aba-oot, more or less. A Canadian pronounces the word more like 'aboat.' And that's the way John Brown pronounces it."

"Are you certain?"

"Of course I'm certain."

"About the theory, I mean?"

"It isn't a theory. It's a fact. I've taken it up with specialists in the subject."

"In the last two weeks?"

"In the last two days," he said. "I hadn't meant to bring this up, but my daughter, Sheila is—ah—interested in the boy. If he's a criminal, as I suspect—" Howell broke off, almost choking on the words.

Both our glances wandered to the poolside. Sheila was still alone, sitting on the edge and paddling her feet in the water. She turned to look toward the entrance twice while I watched her. Her neck and body were stiff with expectancy.

The waiter brought our food, and we ate in silence for a few minutes. Our end of the dining-room was slowly filling up with people in sports clothes. Slice and sand-trap seemed to be the passwords. Dr. Howell glanced around independently from time to time, as if to let the golfers know that he resented their intrusion on his privacy.

"What do you intend to do, Doctor?"

"I propose to employ you myself. I understand that Gordon has terminated your services."

"So far as I know. Have you taken it up with him?"

"Naturally I have. He's just as keen as I am that there should be further investigation. Unfortunately Maria won't hear of it, and as her attorney he can't very well proceed on his own. I can."

"Have you discussed it with Mrs. Galton?"

"I've tried to." Howell grimaced. "She won't listen to a word against the blessed youth. It's frustrating, to say the least, but I can understand why she has to believe in him. The fact of her son Anthony's death came as a great shock to her. She had to hold on to something, and there was Anthony's putative son, ready and willing. Perhaps it was planned that way. At any rate, she's clinging to the boy as if her life depended on it."

"What will the consequences be if we prove he's crooked?"

"Naturally we'll put him in prison where he belongs."

"I mean the consequences to Mrs. Galton's health. You told me yourself that any great shock might kill her."

"That's true, I did."

"Aren't you concerned about that?"

His face slowly reddened, in blotches. "Of course I'm concerned. But there are ethical priorities in life. We can't sit still for a criminal conspiracy, merely because the victim has diseases. The longer we permit it to go on, the worse it will be in the long run for Maria."

"You're probably right. Anyway, her health is your responsibility. I'm willing to undertake the investigation. When do I begin?"

"Now."

"I'll probably have to go to Michigan, for a start. That will cost money."

"I understand that. How much?"

"Five hundred."

Howell didn't blink. He produced a checkbook and a fountain pen. While he was making out the check, he said:

"It might be a good idea if you talked to the boy first. That is, if you can do it without arousing suspicion."

124

"I think I can do that. I got an invitation from him this morning."

"An invitation?"

"A written invitation to visit the Galton house."

"He's making very free with Mrs. Galton's property. Do you happen to have the document with you?"

I handed him the letter. He studied it with growing signs of excitement. "I was right, by God!"

"What do you mean?"

"The dirty little hypocrite is a Canadian. Look here." He put the letter on the table between us, and speared at it with his forefinger. "He spells the word 'labor' l, a, b, o, u, r. It's the British spelling, still current in Canada. He isn't even American. He's an impostor."

"It's going to take more than this to prove it."

"I realize that. Get busy, man."

"If you don't mind, I'll finish my lunch first."

Howell didn't hear me. He was looking out of the window again, half out of his seat.

A dark-headed youth in a tan sport shirt was talking to Sheila Howell at the poolside. He turned his head slightly. I recognized John Galton. He patted the shoulder of her terrycloth robe familiarly. Sheila smiled up full into his face.

Howell's light chair fell over backwards. He was out of the room before I could stop him. From the front door of the clubhouse, I saw him striding across the lawn toward the entrance of the swimming-pool enclosure.

John and Sheila came out hand-in-hand. They were so intent on each other that they didn't see Howell until he was on top of them. He thrust himself between them, shaking the boy by the arm. His voice was an ugly tearing rent in the quietness:

"Get out of here, do you hear me? You're not a member of this club."

John pulled away and faced him, white and rigid. "Sheila invited me."

"I dis-invite you." The back of Howell's neck was carbuncle red.

Sheila touched his arm. "Please, Daddy, don't make a scene. There's nothing to be gained."

John was encouraged to say: "My grandmother won't like this, Doctor."

"She will when she knows the facts." But the threat had

taken the wind out of Howell's sails. He wasn't as loud as he had been.

"Please," Sheila repeated. "John's done no harm to anyone."

"Don't you understand, Sheila, I'm trying to protect you?"

"From what?"

"From corruption."

"That's silly, Dad. To hear you talk, you'd think John was a criminal."

The boy's head tilted suddenly, as if the word had struck a nerve in his neck. "Don't argue with him, Sheila. I oughtn't to've come here."

He turned on his heel and walked head down toward the parking-lot. Sheila went in the other direction. Molded in terrycloth, her body had a massiveness and mystery that hadn't struck me before. Her father stood and watched her until she entered the enclosure. She seemed to be moving heavily and fatally out of his control.

I went back to the dining-room and let Howell find me there. He came in pale and slack-faced, as if he'd had a serious loss of blood. His daughter was in the pool now, swimming its length back and forth with slow and powerful strokes. Her feet churned a steady white wake behind her.

She was still swimming when we left. Howell drove me to the courthouse. He scowled up at the barred windows of the county jail:

"Put him behind bars, that's all I ask."

chapter
21 SHERIFF TRASK was in his office. Its walls were hung with testimonials from civic organizations and service clubs; recruiting certificates from Army, Navy, and Air Force; and a number of pictures of the Sheriff himself taken with the Governor and other notables. Trask's actual face was less genial than the face in the photographs.

"Trouble?" I said.

"Sit down. You're the trouble. You stir up a storm, and then you drop out of the picture. The trouble with you private investigators is irresponsibility."

"That's a rough word, Sheriff." I fingered the broken bones in my face, thoughtfully and tenderly.

"Yeah, I know you got yourself hurt, and I'm sorry. But what can I do about it? Otto Schwartz is outside my jurisdiction."

"Murder raps cross state lines, or haven't you heard."

"Yeah, and I also heard at the same time that you can't extradite without a case. Without some kind of evidence, I can't even get to Schwartz to question him. And you want to know why I have no evidence?"

"Let me guess. Me again."

"It isn't funny, Archer. I was depending on you for some discretion. Why did you have to go and spill your guts to Roy Lemberg? Scare my witnesses clear out of the damn country?"

"I got overeager, and made a mistake. I wasn't the only one."

"What is that supposed to mean?"

"You told me Lemberg's car had been stolen."

"That's what switched license plates usually mean." Trask sat and thought about this for a minute, pushing out his lower lip. "Okay. We made mistakes. I made a medium-sized dilly and you made a peacheroo. So you took a beating for it. We won't sit around and cry. Where do we go from here?"

"It's your case, Sheriff. I'm just your patient helper."

He leaned toward me, heavy-shouldered and earnest. "You really mean to help? Or have you got an angle?"

"I mean to help, that's my angle."

"We'll see. Are you still working for Sable—for Mrs. Galton, that is?"

"Not at the moment."

"Who's bankrolling you. Dr. Howell?"

"News travels fast."

"Heck, I knew it before you did. Howell came around asking me to check your record with L.A. You seem to have some good friends down south. If you ever conned any old ladies, you never got caught."

"Young ones are more my meat."

Trask brushed aside the badinage with an impatient gesture. "I assume you're being hired to go into the boy's background. Howell wanted me to. Naturally I told him I couldn't move without some indication that law's been broken. You got any such indication?"

"Not yet."

"Neither have I. I talked to the boy, and he's as smooth as silk. He doesn't even make any definite claims. He merely says that people tell him he's his father's son, so it's probably so."

"Do you think he's been coached, Sheriff?"

"I don't know. He may be quarterbacking his own plays. When he came in to see me, it had nothing to do on the face of it with establishing his identity. He wanted information about his father's murder, if this John Brown was his father."

"Hasn't that been proved?"

"As close as it ever will be. There's still room for doubt, in my opinion. But what I started to say, he came in here to tell *me* what to do. He wanted more action on that old killing. I told him it was up to the San Mateo people, so what did he do? He made a trip up there to build a fire under the San Mateo sheriff."

"It's barely possible he's serious."

"Either that, or he's a psychologist. That kind of behavior doesn't go with consciousness of guilt."

"The Syndicate hires good lawyers."

Trask pondered this, his eyes withdrawing under the ledges of his brows. "You think it's a Syndicate job, eh? A big conspiracy?"

"With a big payoff, in the millions. Howell tells me Mrs. Galton's rewriting her will, leaving everything to the boy. I think her house should be watched."

"You honestly believe they'd try to knock her off?"

"They kill people for peanuts. What wouldn't they do to get hold of the Galton property?"

"Don't let your imagination run away. It won't happen, not in Santa Teresa County."

"It started to happen two weeks ago, when Culligan got it. That has all the marks of a gang killing, and in your territory."

"Don't rub it in. That case isn't finished yet."

"It's the same case," I said. "The Brown killing and the Culligan killing and the Galton impersonation, if it is one, all hang together."

"That's easy to say. How do we prove it?"

"Through the boy. I'm taking off for Michigan tonight. Howell thinks his accent originated in central Canada. That ties in with the Lembergs. Apparently they crossed the border into Canada from Detroit, and were headed for an

128

address Culligan gave them. If you could trace Culligan that far back—"

"We're working on it." Trask smiled, rather forbiddingly. "Your Reno lead was a good one, Archer. I talked long distance last night to a friend in Reno, captain of detectives. He called me back just before lunch. Culligan was working for Schwartz about a year ago."

"Doing what?"

"Steerer for his casino. Another interesting thing: Culligan was arrested in Detroit five-six years ago. The FBI has a rap sheet on him."

"What was this particular rap?"

"An old larceny charge. It seems he left the country to evade it, got nabbed as soon as he showed his face on American soil, spent the next couple of years in Southern Michigan pen."

"What was the date of his arrest in Detroit?"

"I don't remember exactly. It was about five-and-a-half years ago. I could look it up, if it matters."

"It matters."

"What's on your mind?"

"John Galton turned up in Ann Arbor five-and-a-half years ago. Ann Arbor is practically a suburb of Detroit. I'm asking myself if he crossed the Canadian border with Culligan."

Trask whistled softly, and flicked on the switch of his squawk-box:

"Conger, bring me the Culligan records. Yeah, I'm in my office."

I remembered Conger's hard brown face. He didn't remember me at first, then did a double take:

"Long time no see."

I quipped lamely: "How's the handcuff business?"

"Clicking."

Trask rustled the papers Conger had brought, and frowned impatiently. When he looked up his eyes were crackling bright:

"A little over five-and-a-half years. Culligan got picked up in Detroit January 7. Does that fit with your date?"

"I haven't pinned it down yet, but I will."

I rose to go. Trask's parting handshake was warm. "If you run into anything, call me collect, anytime day or night. And keep the hard nose out of the chopper."

"That's my aspiration."

"By the way, your car's in the county garage. I can release it to you if you want."

"Save it for me. And take care of the old lady, eh?"

The Sheriff was giving Conger orders to that effect before I reached the door.

chapter

22   I CASHED Howell's check at his bank just before it closed for business at three. The teller directed me to a travel agency where I made a plane reservation from Los Angeles to Detroit. The connecting plane didn't leave Santa Teresa for nearly three hours.

I walked the few blocks to Sable's office. The private elevator let me out into the oak-paneled anteroom.

Mrs. Haines looked up from her work, and raised her hand to smooth her dyed red hair. She said in maternal dismay:

"Why, Mr. Archer, you were *badly* injured. Mr. Sable *told* me you'd been hurt, but I had no idea—"

"Stop it. You're making me feel sorry for myself."

"What's the matter with feeling sorry for yourself? I do it all the time. It bucks me up no end."

"You're a woman."

She dipped her bright head as if I'd paid her a compliment. "What's the difference?"

"You don't want me to spell it out."

She tittered, not unpleasantly, and tried to blush, but her experienced face resisted the attempt. "Some other time, perhaps. What can I do for you now?"

"Is Mr. Sable in?"

"I'm sorry, he isn't back from lunch."

"It's three-thirty."

"I know. I don't expect he'll be in again today. He'll be sorry he missed you. The poor man's schedule has been all broken up, ever since that trouble at his house."

"The murder, you mean?"

"That, and other things. His wife isn't well."

"So I understand. Gordon told me she had a breakdown."

"Oh, did he tell you that? He doesn't do much talking about it to anyone. He's awfully sensitive on the subject."

She made a confidential gesture, raising her red-tipped hand vertically beside her mouth. "Just between you and me, this isn't the first time he's had trouble with her."

"When was the other time?"

"Times, in the plural. She came here one night in March when we were doing income tax, and accused me of trying to steal her husband. I could have told her a thing or two, but of course I couldn't say a word in front of Mr. Sable. I tell you, he's a living saint, what he's taken from that woman, and he goes right on looking after her."

"What did she do to him?"

Color dabbed her cheekbones. She was slightly drunk with malice. "Plenty. Last summer she took off and went rampaging around the country spending his good money like water. Spending it on other men, too, can you imagine? He finally tracked her down in Reno, where she was *living* with another man."

"Reno?"

"Reno," she repeated flatly. "She probably intended to divorce him or something, but she gave up on the idea. She'd have been doing him a favor, if you ask me. But the poor man talked her into coming back with him. He seems to be infatuated with her." Her voice was disconsolate. After a moment's thought, she said: "I oughtn't to be telling you all this. Ought I?"

"I knew she had a history of trouble. Gordon told me himself that he had to put her in a nursing home."

"That's right, he's probably there with her now. He generally goes over to eat lunch with her, and most of the time he stays the rest of the day. Wasted devotion, I call it. If you ask me, that's one marriage doomed to failure. I did a horoscope on it, and you never saw such antagonism in the stars."

Not only in the stars.

"Where is the nursing home she's in, Mrs. Haines?"

"It's Dr. Trenchard's, on Light Street. But I wouldn't go there, if that's what you're thinking of. Mr. Sable doesn't like to be disturbed when he's visiting Mrs. Sable."

"I'll take my chances. And I won't mention that I've been here. Okay?"

"I guess so," she said dubiously. "It's over on the west side, 235 Light Street."

I took a cab across town. The driver looked me over curiously as I got out. Perhaps he was trying to figure out if I was a patient or just a visitor.

131

"You want me to wait?"

"I think so. If I don't come out, you know what that will mean."

I left him having a delayed reaction. The "home" was a long stucco building set far back from the street on its own acre. Nothing indicated its specialness, except for the high wire fence which surrounded the patio at the side.

A man and a woman were sitting in a blue canvas swing behind the fence. Their backs were to me, but I recognized Sable's white head. The woman's blond head rested on his shoulder.

I resisted the impulse to call out to them. I climbed the long veranda, which was out of sight of the patio, and pressed the bellpush beside the front door. The door was unlocked and opened by a nurse in white, without a cap. She was unexpectedly young and pretty.

"Yes, sir?"

"I'd like to speak to Mr. Sable."

"And who shall I say is calling?"

"Lew Archer."

She left me in a living-room or lounge whose furniture was covered with bright chintz. Two old ladies in shawls were watching a baseball game on television. A young man with a beard squatted on his heels in a corner, watching the opposite corner of the ceiling. His lips were moving.

One of the half-curtained windows looked out across the sun-filled patio. I saw the young nurse cross to the blue swing, and Sable's face come up as if from sleep. He disengaged himself from his wife. Her body relaxed into an awkward position. Blue-shadowed by the canvas shade of the swing, her face had the open-eyed blankness of a doll's.

Sable dragged his shadow across the imitation flagstone. He looked small, oddly diminished, under the sky's blue height. The impression persisted when he entered the lounge. Age had fallen on him. He needed a haircut, and his tie was pulled to one side. The look he gave me was red-eyed; his voice was cranky.

"What brings you here, anyway?"

"I wanted to see you. I don't have much time in town."

"Well. You see me." He lifted his arms from his sides, and dropped them.

The old ladies, who had greeted him with smiles and nods, reacted like frightened children to his bitterness. One of them hitched her shawl high around her neck and slunk out of

132

the room. The other stretched her hand out toward Sable as if she wanted to comfort him. She remained frozen in that position while she went on watching the ball game. The bearded man watched the corner of the ceiling.

"How is Mrs. Sable?"

"Not well." He frowned, and drew me out into the corridor. "As a matter of fact, she's threatened with melancholia. Dr. Trenchard tells me she's had a similar illness before—before I married her. The shock she suffered two weeks ago stirred up the old trouble. Good Lord, was that only two weeks ago?"

I risked asking: "What sort of background does she have?"

"Alice was a model in Chicago, and she's been married before. She lost a child, and her first husband treated her badly. I've tried to make it up to her. With damn poor success."

His voice sank toward despair.

"I take it she's having therapy."

"Of course. Dr. Trenchard is one of the best psychiatrists on the coast. If she gets any worse, he's going to try shock treatment." He leaned on the wall, looking down at nothing in particular. His red eyes seemed to be burning.

"You should go home and get some sleep."

"I haven't been sleeping much lately. It's easy to say, sleep. But you can't will yourself to sleep. Besides, Alice needs me with her. She's much calmer when I'm around." He shook himself, and straightened. "But you didn't come here to discuss my woes with me."

"That's true, I didn't. I came to thank you for the check, and to ask you a couple of questions."

"You earned the money. I'll answer the questions if I can."

"Dr. Howell has hired me to investigate John Galton's background. Since you brought me into the case, I'd like to have your go-ahead."

"Of course. You have it, as far as I'm concerned. I can't speak for Mrs. Galton."

"I understand that. Howell tells me she's sold on the boy. Howell himself is convinced that he's a phony."

"We've discussed it. There seems to be some sort of romance between John and Howell's daughter."

"Does Howell have any other special motive?"

"For doing what?"

"Investigating John, trying to prevent Mrs. Galton from changing her will."

133

Sable looked at me with some of his old sharpness. "That's a good question. Under the present will, Howell stands to benefit in several ways. He himself is executor, and due to inherit a substantial sum, I really mustn't say how much. His daughter, Sheila, is in for another substantial sum, very substantial. And after various other bequests have been met, the bulk of the estate goes to various charities, one of which is the Heart Association. Henry Galton died of cardiovascular trouble. Howell is an officer of the Heart Association. All of which makes him a highly interested party."

"And highly interesting. Has the will been changed yet?"

"I can't say. I told Mrs. Galton I couldn't conscientiously draw up a new will for her, under the circumstances. She said she'd get someone else. Whether she has or not, I can't say."

"Then you're not sold on the boy, either."

"I was. I no longer know what to think. Frankly, I haven't been giving the matter much thought." He moved impatiently, and made a misstep to one side, his shoulder thudding against the wall. "If you don't mind, I think I'll get back to my wife."

The young nurse let me out.

I looked back through the wire fence. Mrs. Sable remained in the same position on the swing. Her husband joined her in the blue shadow. He raised her inert head and insinuated his shoulder behind it. They sat like a very old couple waiting for the afternoon shadows to lengthen and merge into night.

chapter
23

THE cab-driver stopped at the curb opposite the gates of the Galton estate. He hung one arm over the back of the seat and gave me a quizzical look:

"No offense, Mister, but you want the front entrance or the service entrance?"

"The front entrance."

"Okay. I just didn't want to make a mistake."

He let me off under the porte-cochere. I paid him, and told him not to wait. The Negro maid let me into the reception hall, and left me to cool my heels among the ancestors.

134

I moved over to one of the tall, narrow windows. It looked out across the front lawn, where the late afternoon sunlight lay serenely. I got some sense of the guarded peace that walled estates like this had once provided. In the modern world the walls were more like prison walls, or the wire fence around a nursing-home garden. When it came right down to it, I preferred the service entrance. The people in the kitchen usually had more fun.

Quick footsteps descended the stairs, and Cassie Hildreth came into the room. She had on a skirt and a sweater which emphasized her figure. She looked more feminine in other, subtler, ways. Something had happened to change her style.

She gave me her hand. "It's good to see you, Mr. Archer. Sit down. Mrs. Galton will be down in a minute."

"Under her own power?"

"Yes, isn't it remarkable? She's becoming much more active than she was. John takes her out for a drive nearly every day."

"That's nice of him."

"He actually seems to enjoy it. They hit it off from the start."

"He's the one I really came to see. Is he around?"

"I haven't seen him since lunch. Probably he's out in his car somewhere."

"His car?"

"Aunt Maria bought him a cute little Thunderbird. John's crazy about it. He's like a child with a new toy. He told me he's never had a car of his own before."

"I guess he has a lot of things he never had before."

"Yes. I'm so happy for him."

"You're a generous woman."

"Not really. I've a lot to be thankful for. Now that John's come home, I wouldn't trade my life for any other. It may sound like a strange thing to say, but life is suddenly just as it was in the old days—before the war, before Tony died. Everything seems to have fallen into harmony."

She sounded as if she had transferred her lifelong crush from Tony to John Galton. A dream possessed her face. I wanted to warn her not to bank too heavily on it. Everything could fall into chaos again.

Mrs. Galton was fussing on the stairs. Cassie went to the door to meet her. The old lady had on a black tailored suit

135

with something white at her throat. Her hair was marcelled in hard gray corrugations which resembled galvanized iron. She extended her bony hand:

"I'm most pleased to see you. I've been wanting to express my personal appreciation to you. You've made my house a happier one."

"Your check was a very nice expression," I said.

"The laborer is worthy of his hire." Perhaps she sensed that that wasn't the most tactful way to put it, because she added: "Won't you stay for tea? My grandson will want to see you. I expect him back for tea. He should be here now."

The querulous note was still in her voice. I wondered how much of her happiness was real, how much sheer will to believe that something good could happen to a poor old rich lady. She lowered herself into a chair, exaggerating the difficulty of her movements. Cassie began to look anxious.

"I think he's at the country club, Aunt Maria."

"With Sheila?"

"I think so," Cassie said.

"Is he still seeing a lot of her?"

"Just about every day."

"We'll have to put a stop to that. He's much too young to think of taking an interest in any one girl. Sheila is a dear sweet child, of course, but we can't have her monopolizing John. I have other plans for him."

"What plans," I said, "if you don't mind my asking?"

"I'm thinking of sending John to Europe in the fall. He needs broadening, and he's very much interested in the modern drama. If the interest persists, and deepens, I'll build him a repertory theater here in Santa Teresa. John has great talent, you know. The Galton distinction comes out in a different form in each generation."

As if to demonstrate this proposition, a red Thunderbird convertible careened up the long driveway. A door slammed. John came in. His face was flushed and sullen. He stood inside the doorway and pushed his fists deep in his jacket pockets, his head thrust forward in a peering attitude.

"Well!" he said. "Here we all are. The three fates, Clotho, Lachesis, and Mr. Archer."

"That isn't funny, John," Cassie said in a voice of warning.

"I think it's funny. Very, very funny."

He came toward us, weaving slightly, exaggerating the movements of his shoulders. I went to meet him:

136

"Hello, John."

"Get away from me. I know why you're here."

"Tell me."

"I'll tell you all right."

He threw a wild fist in my direction, staggering off balance. I moved in close, turned him with his back to me, took hold of his jacket collar with both hands and pulled it halfway down his arms. He sputtered words at me which smelled like the exhalations from a still. But I could feel the lethal force vibrating through him.

"Straighten up and quiet down," I said.

"I'll knock your block off."

"First you'll have to load yourself up with something solider than whisky."

Mrs. Galton breathed at my shoulder. "Has he been drinking?"

John answered her himself, in a kind of small-boy defiance: "Yes I have been drinking. And I've been thinking. Thinking and drinking. I say it's a lousy setup."

"What?" she said. "What's happened?"

"A lot of things have happened. Tell this man to turn me loose."

"Let him go," Mrs. Galton said commandingly.

"Do you think he's ready?"

"Damn you, let me go."

He made a violent lunge, and tore loose from the arms of his jacket. He whirled and faced me with his fists up:

"Come on and fight. I'm not afraid of you."

"This is hardly the time and place."

I tossed his jacket to him. He caught and held it, looking down at it stupidly. Cassie stepped between us. She took the jacket and helped him on with it. He submitted almost meekly to her hands.

"You need some black coffee, John. Let me get you some black coffee."

"I don't want coffee, I'm not drunk."

"But you've been drinking." Mrs. Galton's voice rose almost an octave and stayed there on a querulous monotone: "Your *father* started drinking young, you mustn't let it happen all over again. Please, you must promise me."

The old lady hung on John's arm, making anxious noises, while Cassie tried to soothe her. John's head swung around, his eyes on me:

137

"Get that man out of here! He's spying for Dr. Howell."

Mrs. Galton turned on me, the bony structure of her face pushing out through the seamed flesh:

"I trust my grandson is mistaken about you. I know Dr. Howell is incapable of committing disloyal acts behind my back."

"Don't be too sure of that," John said. "He doesn't want me seeing Sheila. There's nothing he wouldn't do to break it up."

"I'm asking you, Mr. Archer. Did Dr. Howell hire you?"

"I'll have to ask you to take it up with Howell."

"It is true, then?"

"I can't answer that, Mrs. Galton."

"In that case please leave my house. You entered it under false pretenses. If you trespass again, I'll have you prosecuted. I've a good mind to go to the authorities as it is."

"No, don't do that," John said. "We can handle it, Grandma."

He seemed to be sobering rapidly. Cassie chimed in:

"You mustn't get so excited about nothing. You know what Dr. Howell—"

"Don't mention his name in my presence. To be betrayed by an old and trusted friend—well, that's what it is to have money. They think they have a right to it simply because it's there. I see now what August Howell has been up to, insinuating himself and his chit of a daughter into my life. Well, he's not getting a cent of my money. I've seen to that."

"Please calm down, Aunt Maria."

Cassie tried to lead her back to her chair. Mrs. Galton wouldn't budge. She called hoarsely in my direction:

"You can go and tell August Howell he's overreached himself. He won't get a cent of my money, not a cent. It's going to my own kith and kin. And tell him to keep that daughter of his from flinging herself at my grandson. I have other plans for him."

The breath rustled and moaned in her head. She closed her eyes; her face was like a death mask. She tottered and almost fell. John held her around the shoulders.

"Get out," he said to me. "My grandmother is a sick woman. Can't you see what you're doing to her?"

"Somebody's doing it to her."

"Are you going to get out, or do I call the police?"

"You'd better go," Cassie said. "Mrs. Galton has a heart condition."

138

Mrs. Galton's hand went to her heart automatically. Her head fell loosely onto John's shoulder. He stroked her gray hair. It was a very touching scene.

I wondered as I went out how many more scenes like that the old lady's heart would stand. The question kept me awake on the night plane to Chicago.

chapter
24

I PUT in two days of legwork in Ann Arbor, where I represented myself as a personnel investigator for a firm with overseas contracts. John's account of his high school and college life checked out in detail. I established one interesting additional detail: He had enrolled in the high school under the name of John Lindsay five-and-a-half years before, on January 9. Peter Culligan had been arrested in Detroit, forty miles away, on January 7 of the same year. Apparently it had taken the boy just two days to find a new protector in Gabriel Lindsay.

I talked to friends of Lindsay's, mostly high-school teachers. They remembered John as a likely boy, though he had been, as one of them said: "A tough little egg to start with." They understood that Lindsay had taken him off the streets.

Gabriel Lindsay had gone in for helping young people in trouble. He was an older man who had lost a son in the war, and his wife soon after the war. He died himself in the University Hospital in February of the previous year, of pneumonia.

His doctor remembered John's constant attendance at his bedside. The copy of his will on file in the Washtenaw County courthouse left two thousand dollars to "my quasi-foster-son, known as John Lindsay, for the furtherance of his education." There were no other specific bequests in Lindsay's will; which probably meant it was all the money he had.

John had graduated from the University in June, as a Speech major, with honors. His counselor in the Dean's office said that he had been a student without any overt problems; not exactly popular perhaps: he seemed to have no close friends. On the other hand, he had been active in campus theatrical productions, and moderately successful as an actor in his senior year.

His address at the time of his graduation had been a rooming-house on Catherine Street, over behind the Graduate School. The landlady's name was Mrs. Haskell. Maybe she could help me.

Mrs. Haskell lived on the first floor of an old three-story gingerbread mansion. I guessed from the bundles of mail on the table inside the door that the rest of her house was given over to roomers. She led me along the polished parquetry hallway into a half-blinded parlor. It was a cool oasis in the heat of the Michigan July.

Somewhere over our heads, a typewriter pecked at the silence. The echo of a southern drawl twanged like a mandolin in Mrs. Haskell's voice:

"Do sit down and tell me how John is. And how is he doing in his position?" Mrs. Haskell clasped her hands enthusiastically on her flowered print bosom. The curled bangs on her forehead shook like silent bells.

"He hasn't started with us yet, Mrs. Haskell. The purpose of my investigation is to clear him for a confidential assignment."

"Does that mean the other thing has fallen through?"

"What other thing is that?"

"The acting thing. You may not know it, but John Lindsay's a very fine actor. One of the most talented boys I've ever had in my house. I never missed an appearance of his at the Lydia Mendelssohn. In *Hobson's Choice* last winter, he was rich."

"I bet he was. And you say he had acting offers?"

"I don't know about offers in the plural, but he had one very good one. Some big producer wanted to give him a personal contract and train him professionally. The last I heard, John had accepted it. But I guess he changed his mind, if he's going with your firm. Security."

"It's interesting about his acting," I said. "We like our employees to be well-rounded people. Do you remember the producer's name?"

"I'm afraid I never knew it."

"Where did he come from?"

"I don't know. John was very secretive about his private affairs. He didn't even leave a forwarding address when he left in June. All I really know about this is what Miss Reichler told me after he left."

140

"Miss Reichler?"

"His friend. I don't mean she was his girlfriend exactly. Maybe she thought so, but he didn't. I warned him not to get mixed up with a rich young lady like her, riding around in her Cadillacs and her convertibles. My boys come and go, but I try to keep them from overstepping themselves. Miss Reichler is several years older than John." Her lips moved over his name with a kind of maternal greed. The mandolin twang was becoming more pronounced.

"He sounds like the kind of young man we need. Socially mobile, attractive to the ladies."

"Oh, he was always that. I don't mean he's girl-crazy. He paid the girls no mind, unless they forced themselves on his attention. Ada Reichler practically beat a path to his door. She used to drive up in her Cadillac every second or third day. Her father's a big man in Detroit. Auto parts."

"Good," I said. "A high-level business connection."

Mrs. Haskell sniffed. "Don't count too much on that one. Miss Reichler was sore as a boil when John left without even saying good-by. She was really let down. I tried to explain to her that a young man just starting out in the world couldn't carry any excess baggage. Then she got mad at me, for some god-forsaken reason. She slam-banged into her car and ground those old Cadillac gears to a pulp."

"How long did they know each other?"

"As long as he was with me, at least a year. I guess she had her nice qualities, or he wouldn't have stuck with her so long. She's pretty enough, if you like the slinky type."

"Do you have her address? I'd like to talk to her."

"She might tell you a lot of lies. You know: 'Hell hath no fury like a woman scorned.'"

"I can discount anything like that."

"See that you do. John's a fine young man, and your people will be lucky if he decides to go with them. Her father's name is Ben, I think, Ben Reichler. They live over in the section by the river."

I drove on winding roads through a semi-wooded area. Eventually I found the Reichlers' mailbox. Their driveway ran between rows of maples to a low brick house with a sweeping roof. It looked small from a distance, and massive when I got up close to it. I began to understand how John could have made the leap from Mrs. Gorgello's boarding-house to the Galton house. He'd been training for it.

A man in overalls with a spraygun in his hands climbed up the granite steps of a sunken garden.

"The folks aren't home," he said. "They're never home in July."

"Where can I find them?"

"If it's business, Mr. Reichler's in his office in the Reichler Building three-four days a week."

"Miss Ada Reichler's the one I want."

"Far as I know, she's in Kingsville with her mother. Kingsville, Canada. They have a place up there. You a friend of Miss Ada's?"

"Friend of a friend," I said.

It was early evening when I drove into Kingsville. The heat hadn't let up, and my shirt was sticking to my back. The lake lay below the town like a blue haze in which white sails hung upright by their tips.

The Reichlers' summer place was on the lakeshore. Green terraces descended from the house to a private dock and boathouse. The house itself was a big old lodge whose brown shingled sides were shaggy with ivy. The Reichlers weren't camping out, though. The maid who answered the door wore a fresh starched uniform, complete with cap. She told me that Mrs. Reichler was resting and Miss Ada was out in one of the boats. She was expected back at any time, if I cared to wait.

I waited on the dock, which was plastered with No Trespassing signs. A faint breeze had begun to stir, and the sailboats were leaning shoreward. Mild little land-locked waves lapped at the pilings. A motorboat went by like a bird shaking out wings of white water. Its wash rocked the dock. The boat turned and came in, slowing down. A girl with dark hair and dark glasses was at the wheel. She pointed a finger at her brown chest, and cocked her head questioningly.

"You want me?"

I nodded, and she brought the boat in. I caught the line she threw and helped her onto the dock. Her body was lean and supple in black Capris and a halter. Her face, when she took off her glasses, was lean and intense.

"Who are you?"

I had already decided to discard my role. "My name is Archer. I'm a private detective from California."

"You came all this way to see me?"

"Yes."

"Why on earth?"

142

"Because you knew John Lindsay."

Her face opened up, ready for anything, wonderful or otherwise.

"John sent you here?"

"Not exactly."

"Is he in some kind of trouble?"

I didn't answer her. She jerked at my arm like a child wanting attention.

"Tell me, is John in trouble? Don't be afraid, I can take it."

"I don't know whether he is or not, Miss Reichler. What makes you jump to the conclusion that he is?"

"Nothing, I don't mean that." Her speech was staccato. "You said that you're a detective. Doesn't that indicate trouble?"

"Say he is in trouble. What then?"

"I'd want to help him, naturally. Why are we talking in riddles?"

I liked her rapid, definite personality, and guessed that honesty went along with it:

"I don't like riddles any more than you do. I'll make a bargain with you, Miss Reichler. I'll tell you my end of the story if you'll tell me yours."

"What is this, true confession hour?"

"I'm serious, and I'm willing to do my talking first. If you're interested in John's situation—"

"Situation is a nice neutral word."

"That's why I used it. Is it a bargain?"

"All right." She gave me her hand on it, as a man would have. "I warn you in advance, though, I won't tell you anything against him. I don't *know* anything against him, except that he treated me—well, I was asking for it." She lifted her high thin shoulders, shrugging off the past. "We can talk in the garden, if you like."

We climbed the terraces to a walled garden in the shadow of the house. It was crowded with the colors and odors of flowers. She placed me in a canvas chair facing hers. I told her where John was and what he was doing.

Her eyes were soft and black, lit tremulously from within. Their expression followed all the movements of my story. She said when I'd finished:

"It sounds like one of Grimm's fairy tales. The goatherd turns out to be the prince in disguise. Or like Œdipus. John had an Œdipus theory of his own, that Œdipus killed his father because he banished him from the kingdom. I thought it was very clever." Her voice was brittle. She was marking time.

"John's a clever boy," I said. "And you're a clever girl, and you knew him well. Do you believe he's who he claims to be?"

"Do you?" When I failed to answer, she said: "So he has a girl in California, already." Her hands lay open on her slender thighs. She hugged them between her thighs.

"The girl's father hired me. He thinks John is a fraud."

"And you do, too?"

"I don't like to think it, but I'm afraid I do. There are some indications that his whole story was invented to fit the occasion."

"To inherit money?"

"That's the general idea. I've been talking to his landlady in Ann Arbor, Mrs. Haskell."

"I know her," the girl said shortly.

"Do you know anything about this offer John had from a producer?"

"Yes, he mentioned it to me. It was one of these personal contacts that the movie producers give to promising young actors. This man saw him in *Hobson's Choice*."

"When?"

"Last February."

"Did you meet the man?"

"I never did. John said he flew back to the coast. He didn't want to discuss it after that."

"Did he mention any names before he dried up?"

"Not that I recall. Do you think John was lying about him, that it wasn't an acting job he was offered?"

"That could be. Or it could be John was sucked in. The conspirators made their approach as movie producers or agents, and later told him what was required of him."

"Why would John fall in with their plans? He's not a criminal."

"The Galton estate is worth millions. He stands to inherit all of it, any day. Even a small percentage of it would make him a rich man."

"But he never cared about money, at least not the kind you inherit. He could have married me: Barkis was willing. My father's money was one of the reasons he didn't. At least that's what he said. The real reason, I guess, was that he didn't love me. Does he love her?"

144

"My client's daughter? I couldn't say for sure. Maybe he doesn't love anybody."

"You're very honest, Mr. Archer. I gave you an opening, but you didn't try to use her on me as a wedge. You could have said that he was crazy about her, thus fanning the fires of jealousy." She winced at her own self-mockery.

"I try to be honest with honest people."

She gave me a flashing look. "That's intended to put me on the spot."

"Yes."

She turned her head and looked out over the lake as if she could see all the way to California. The last sails were converging toward shore, away from the darkness falling like soot along the horizon. As light drained from the sky, it seemed to gather more intensely on the water.

"What will they do to him if they find out he's an impostor?"

"Put him in jail."

"For how long?"

"It's hard to say. It'll be easier on him if we get it over with soon. He hasn't made any big claims yet, or taken any big money."

"You really mean, really and truly, that I'd be doing him a favor by puncturing his story?"

"That's my honest opinion. If it's all a pack of lies, we'll find out sooner or later. The sooner the better."

She hesitated. Her profile was stark. One cord in her neck stood out under the skin. "You say that he claims that he was brought up in an orphanage in Ohio."

"Crystal Springs, Ohio. Did he ever mention the place to you?"

She shook her head in a quick short arc. I said:

"There are some indications that he was raised here in Canada."

"What indications?"

"Speech. Spelling."

She rose suddenly, walked to the end of the garden, stooped to pick a snapdragon, threw it away with a spurning gesture. She came back toward me and stood with her face half-averted. She said in a rough dry voice:

"Just don't tell him I was the one that told you. I couldn't bear to have him hate me, even if I never see him again. The poor damn silly fool was born and raised right here in

145

Ontario. His real name is Theodore Fredericks, and his mother runs a boardinghouse in Pitt, not more than sixty miles from here."

I stood up, forcing her to look at me. "How do you know, Miss Reichler?"

"I talked to Mrs. Fredericks. It wasn't a very fortunate meeting. It didn't do anything for either of us. I should never have gone there."

"Did he take you to meet his mother?"

"Hardly. I went to see her myself a couple of weeks ago, after John left Ann Arbor. When I didn't hear from him I got it into my head that perhaps he'd gone home to Pitt."

"How did you learn about his home in Pitt? Did he tell you?"

"Yes, but I don't believe he intended to. It happened on the spur of the moment, when he was spending a week-end here with us. It was the only time he ever came to visit us here in Kingsville, and it was a bad time for me—the worst. I hate to think of it."

"Why?"

"If you have to know, he turned me down. We went for a drive on Sunday morning. I did the driving, of course. He'd never touch the wheel of my car. That's the way he was with me, so proud, and I had no pride at all with him. I got carried away by the flowers and the bees, or something, and I asked him to marry me. He gave me a flat refusal.

"He must have seen how hurt I was, because he asked me to drive him to Pitt. We weren't too far from there, and he wanted to show me something. When we got there he made me drive down a street that runs along by the river on the edge of the Negro section. It was a dreadful neighborhood, filthy children of all colors playing in the mud, and slatternly women screaming at them. We stopped across from an old red brick house where some men in their undershirts were sitting on the front steps passing around a wine jug.

"John asked me to take a good look, because he said he belonged there. He said he'd grown up in that neighborhood, in that red house. A woman came out on the porch to call the men in for dinner. She had a voice like a kazoo, and she was a hideous fat pig of a woman. John said that she was his mother.

"I didn't believe him. I thought he was hoaxing me, putting me to some kind of silly test. It was a test, in a way, but not in the way I imagined. He wanted to be *known*, I

146

think. He wanted me to accept him as he actually was. But by the time I understood that, it was too late. He'd gone into one of his deep freezes." She touched her mournful mouth with the tips of her long fingers.

"When did this happen?"

"Last spring. It must have been early in March, there was still some snow on the ground."

"Did you see John after that?"

"A few times, but it wasn't any good. I think he regretted telling me about himself. In fact I know he did. That Sunday in Pitt was the end of any real communication between us. There were so many things we couldn't talk about, finally we couldn't talk at all. The last time I saw him was humiliating, for him, and for me, too. He asked me not to mention what he'd said about his origins, if anyone ever brought it up."

"Who did he expect to bring it up? The police?"

"The immigration authorities. Apparently there was something irregular about his entry into the United States. That fitted in with what his mother told me afterwards. He'd run away with one of her boarders when he was sixteen, and apparently crossed over into the States."

"Did she give you the boarder's name?"

"No. I'm surprised Mrs. Fredericks told me as much as she did. You know how the lower classes are, suspicious, but I gave her a little money, and that loosened her up." Her tone was contemptuous, and she must have overheard herself: "I know, I'm just what John said I was, a dollar snob. Well, I had my comeuppance. There I was prowling around the Pitt slums on a hot summer day like a lady dog in season. And I might as well have stayed at home. His mother hadn't laid eyes on him for over five years, and she never expected to see him again, she said. I realized that I'd lost him, for good."

"He was easy to lose," I said, "and no great loss."

She looked at me like an enemy. "You don't know him. John's a fine person at heart, fine and deep. I was the one who failed in our relationship. If I'd been able to understand him that Sunday, say the right thing and hold him, he mightn't have gone into this fraudulent life. I'm the one who wasn't good for anything."

She screwed up her face like a monkey and tugged at her hair, making herself look ugly.

"I'm just a hag."

147

"Be quiet."

She looked at me incredulously, one hand flat against her temple. "Who do you think you're talking to?"

"Ada Reichler. You're worth five of him."

"I'm not. I'm no good. I betrayed him. Nobody could love me. *Nobody* could."

"I told you to be quiet." I'd never been angrier in my life. "Don't you dare speak to me like that. Don't you dare!"

Her eyes were as bright and heavy as mercury. She ran blind to the end of the garden, knelt at the edge of the grass, and buried her face in flowers.

Her back was long and beautiful. I waited until she was still, and lifted her to her feet. She turned toward me.

The last light faded from the flowers and from the lake. Night came on warm and moist. The grass was wet.

chapter
25

THE town of Pitt was dark except for occasional street lights and the fainter lights that fell from the heavily starred sky. Driving along the street Ada Reichler had named, I could see the moving river down between the houses. When I got out of the car, I could smell the river. A chanting chorus of frogs made the summer night pulsate at its edges.

On the second floor of the old red house, a bleary light outlined a window. The boards of the veranda groaned under my weight. I knocked on the alligatored door. A card offering "Rooms for Rent" was stuck inside the window beside the door.

A light went on over my head. Moths swirled up around it like unseasonable snow. An old man peered out, cocking his narrow gray head at me out of a permanent stoop.

"Something you want?" His voice was a husky whisper.

"I'd like to speak to Mrs. Fredericks, the landlady."

"I'm Mr. Fredericks. If it's a room you want, I can rent you a room just as good as she can."

"Do you rent by the night?"

"Sure, I got a nice front room you can have. It'll cost you —let's see." He stroked the bristles along the edge of his

148

jaw, making a rasping noise. His dull eyes looked me over with stupid cunning. "Two dollars?"

"I'd like to see the room first."

"If you say so. Try not to make too much noise, eh? The old woman—Mrs. Fredericks is in bed."

He must have been just about to go himself. His shirt was open so that I could have counted his ribs, and his broad striped suspenders were hanging down. I followed him up the stairs. He moved with elaborate secrecy, and turned at the top to set a hushing finger to his lips. The light from the hall below cast his hunched condor shadow on the wall.

A woman's voice rose from the back of the house: "What are you creeping around for?"

"Didn't want to disturb the boarders," he said in his carrying whisper.

"The boarders aren't in yet, and you know it. Is somebody with you?"

"Nope. Just me and my shadow."

He smiled a yellow-toothed smile at me, as if he expected me to share the joke.

"Come to bed then," she called.

"In a minute."

He tiptoed to the front of the hallway, beckoned me through an open door, and closed the door quietly behind me. For a moment we were alone in the dark, like conspirators. I could hear his emotional breathing.

Then he reached up to pull on a light. It swung on its cord, throwing lariats of shadow up to the high ceiling, and shifting gleam and gloom on the room's contents. These included a bureau, a washstand with pitcher and bowl, and a bed which had taken the impress of many bodies. The furnishings reminded me of the room John Brown had had in Luna Bay.

John Brown? John Nobody.

I looked at the old man's face. It was hard to imagine what quirk of his genes had produced the boy. If Fredericks had ever possessed good looks, time had washed them out. His face was patchily furred leather, stretched on gaunt bones, held in place by black nailhead eyes.

"The room all right?" he said uneasily.

I glanced at the flowered paper on the walls. Faded morning-glories climbed brown lattices to the watermarked ceiling. I didn't think I could sleep in a room with morning-glories crawling up the walls all night.

149

"If it's bugs you're worried about," he said, "we had the place fumigated last spring."

"Oh. Good."

"I'll let in some fresh air." He opened the window and sidled back to me. "Pay me cash in advance, and I can let you have it for a dollar and a half."

I had no intention of staying the night, but I decided to let him have the money. I took out my wallet and gave him two ones. His hand trembled as he took them:

"I got no change."

"Keep it. Mr. Fredericks, you have a son."

He gave me a long slow cautious look. "What if I have?"

"A boy named Theodore."

"He's no boy. He'll be grown up now."

"How long is it since you've seen him?"

"I dunno. Four-five years, maybe longer. He ran away when he was sixteen. It's a tough thing to have to say about your own boy, but it was good riddance of bad rubbish."

"Why do you say that?"

"Because it's the truth. You acquainted with Theo?"

"Slightly."

"Is he in trouble again? Is that why you're here?"

Before I could answer, the door of the room flew open. A short stout woman in a flannelette nightgown brushed past me and advanced on Fredericks: "What you think you're doing, renting a room behind my back?"

"I didn't."

But the money was still in his hand. He tried to crumple it in his fist and hide it. She grabbed for it:

"Give me my money."

He hugged his valuable fist against his washboard chest. "It's just as much my money as it is yours."

"Aw no it isn't. I work myself to the bone keeping our heads above water. And what do you do? Drink it up as fast as I can make it."

"I ain't had a drink for a week."

"You're a liar." She stamped her bare foot. Her body shook under the nightgown, and her gray braids swung like cables down her back. "You were drinking wine last night with the boys in the downstairs bedroom."

"That was free," he said virtuously. "And you got no call to talk to me like this in front of a stranger."

She turned to me for the first time. "Excuse us, mister.

150

It's no fault of yours, but he can't handle money." She added unnecessarily: "He drinks."

While her eyes were off him, Fredericks made for the door. She intercepted him. He struggled feebly in her embrace. Her upper arms were as thick as hams. She pried open his bony fist and pushed the crumpled bills down between her breasts. He watched the money go as though it represented his hope of heaven:

"Just give me fifty cents. Fifty cents won't break you."

"Not one red cent," she said. "If you think I'm going to help you get the d.t.'s again, you got another think coming."

"All I want is one drink."

"Sure, and then another and another. Until you feel the rats crawling up under your clothes, and I got to nurse you out of it again."

"There's all different kinds of rats. A woman that won't give her lawful husband four bits to settle his stomach is the worst kind of rat there is."

"Take that back."

She moved on him, arms akimbo. He backed into the hallway:

"All right, I take it back. But I'll get a drink, don't worry. I got good friends in this town, they know my worth."

"Sure they do. They feed you stinking rotgut across the river, and then they come to me asking for money. Don't you set foot outside this house tonight."

"You're not going to order me around, treat me like a has-been. It ain't my fault I can't work, with a hole in my belly. It ain't my fault I can't sleep without a drink to ease the pain."

"Scat," she said. "Go to bed, old man."

He shambled away, trailing his slack suspenders. The fat woman turned to me.

"I apologize for my husband. He's never been the same since his accident."

"What happened to him?"

"He got hurt bad." Her answer seemed deliberately vague. Under folds of fat, her face showed traces of her son's stubborn intelligence. She changed the subject: "I notice you paid with American money. You from the States?"

"I just drove over from Detroit."

"You live in Detroit? I never been over there, but I hear it's an interesting place."

"It probably is. I was just passing through on my way from California."

"What brings you all the way from California?"

"A man named Peter Culligan was murdered there several weeks ago. Culligan was stabbed to death."

"Stabbed to death?"

I nodded. Her head moved slightly in unison with mine. Without shifting her eyes from my face, she moved around me and sat on the edge of the bed.

"You know him, don't you, Mrs. Fredericks?"

"He boarded with me for a while, years ago. He had this very room."

"What was he doing in Canada?"

"Don't ask me. I don't ask my boarders where their money comes from. Mostly he sat in this room and studied his racing sheets." She looked up shrewdly from under frowning brows. "Would you be a policeman?"

"I'm working with the police. Are you sure you don't know why Culligan came here?"

"I guess it was just a place like any other. He was a loner and a drifter—I get quite a few of them. He probably covered a lot of territory in his time." She looked up at the shadows on the ceiling. The light was still now, and the shadows were concentric, spreading out like ripples on a pool. "Listen, mister, who stabbed him?"

"A young hoodlum."

"My boy? Was it my boy that done it? Is that why you come to me?"

"I think your son is involved."

"I knew it." Her cheeks shuddered. "He took a knife to his father before he was out of high school. He would of killed him, too. Now he really is a murderer." She pressed her clenched hands deep into her bosom; it swelled around her fists like rising dough. "I didn't have enough trouble in my life. I had to give birth to a murderer."

"I don't know about that, Mrs. Fredericks. He committed fraud. I doubt that he committed murder." Even as I said it, I was wondering if he had been within striking distance of Culligan, and if he had an alibi for that day. "Do you have a picture of your son?"

"I have when he was in high school. He ran away before he graduated."

"May I have a look at the picture, Mrs. Fredericks? It's barely possible we're talking about two different people."

152

But any hope of this died a quick death. The boy in the snapshot she brought was the same one, six years younger. He stood on the riverbank, his back to the water, smiling with conscious charm into the camera.

I gave the picture back to Mrs. Fredericks. She held it up to the light and studied it as if she could re-create the past from its single image.

"Theo was a good-looking boy," she said wistfully. "He was doing so good in school and all, until he started getting those ideas of his."

"What kind of ideas did he have?"

"Crazy ideas, like he was the son of an English lord, and the gypsies stole him away when he was a baby. When he was just a little tyke, he used to call himself Percival Fitzroy, like in a book. That was always his way—he thought he was too good for his own people. I worried about where all that daydreaming was going to land him."

"He's still dreaming," I said. "Right now he's representing himself as the grandson of a wealthy woman in Southern California. Do you know anything about that?"

"I never hear from him. How would I know about it?"

"Apparently Culligan put him up to it. I understand he ran away from here with Culligan."

"Yeah. The dirty scamp talked him into it, turned him against his own father."

"And you say he knifed his father?"

"That very same day." Her eyes widened and glazed. "He stabbed him with a butcher knife, gave him an awful wound. Fredericks was on his back for weeks. He's never got back on his feet entirely. Neither have I, to think my own boy would do a thing like that."

"What was the trouble about, Mrs. Fredericks?"

"Wildness and willfulness," she said. "He wanted to leave home and make his own way in the world. That Culligan encouraged him. He pretended to have Theo's welfare at heart and I know what you're thinking, that Theo did right to run away from home with his old man a bum and the kind of boarders I get. But the proof of the pudding is in the eating. Look at how Theo turned out."

"I have been, Mrs. Fredericks."

"I knew he was headed for a bad end," she said. "He didn't show natural feelings. He never wrote home once since he left. Where has he been all these years?"

"Going to college."

153

"To college? He went to college?"

"Your son's an ambitious boy."

"Oh, he always had an ambition, if that's what you want to call it. Is that what he learned in college, how to cheat people?"

"He learned that someplace else."

Perhaps in this room, I thought, where Culligan spun his fantasies and laid a long-shot bet on an accidental resemblance to a dead man. The room had Culligan's taint on it.

The woman stirred uncomfortably, as if I'd made a subtle accusation:

"I don't claim we were good parents to him. He wanted more than we could give him. He always had a dream of himself, like."

Her face moved sluggishly, trying to find the shape of truth and feeling. She leaned back on her arms and let her gaze rest on the swollen slopes of her body, great sagging breasts, distended belly from which a son had struggled headfirst into the light. Over her bowed head, insects swung in eccentric orbits around the hanging bulb, tempting hot death.

She managed to find some hope in the situation: "At least he didn't murder anybody, eh?"

"No."

"Who was it that knifed Culligan? You said it was a young hoodlum."

"His name is Tommy Lemberg. Tommy and his brother Roy are supposed to be hiding out in Ontario—"

"Hamburg, did you say?"

"They may be using that name. Do you know Roy and Tommy?"

"I hope to tell you. They been renting the downstairs room for the last two weeks. They told me their name was Hamburg. How was I to know they were hiding out?"

chapter
26

I WAITED for the Lembergs on the dark porch. They came home after midnight, walking a bit unsteadily down the street. My parked car attracted their attention, and

they crossed the street to look it over. I went down the front
steps and across the street after them.

They turned, so close together that they resembled a single
amorphous body with two white startled faces. Tommy
started toward me, a wide lopsided shape. His arm was still
in a white sling under his jacket.

Roy lifted his head with a kind of hopeless alertness.
"Come back here, kid."

"The hell. It's old man trouble himself." He walked up
to me busily, and spat in the dust at my feet.

"Take it easy, Tommy." Roy came up behind him. "Talk
to him."

"Sure I'll talk to him." He said to me: "Didn't you get
enough from Mr. Schwartz? You came all this way looking
for more?"

Without giving the matter any advance thought, I set myself on my heels and hit him with all my force on the point
of the jaw. He went down and stayed. His brother knelt
beside him, making small shocked noises which resolved
themselves into words:

"You had no right to hit him. He wanted to talk to you."

"I heard him."

"He's been drinking, and he was scared. He was just
putting on a big bluff."

"Put away the violin. It doesn't go with a knifing rap."

"Tommy never knifed anybody."

"That's right, he was framed. Culligan framed him by
falling down and stabbing himself. Tommy was just an innocent bystander."

"I don't claim he was innocent. Schwartz sent him there
to throw his weight around. But nobody figured he was
going to run into Culligan, let alone Culligan with a knife
and a gun. He got shot taking the gun away from Culligan.
Then he knocked Culligan out, and that's the whole thing
as far as Tommy's concerned."

"At which point the Apaches came out of the hills."

"I thought maybe you'd be interested in the truth," Roy
said in a shaking voice. "But your thinking is the same as
all the others. Once a fellow takes a fall, he's got no human
rights."

"Sure, I'm unfair to organized crime."

The wisecrack sounded faintly tinny, even to me. Roy
made a disgusted sound in his throat. Tommy groaned as

if in response. His eyes were still turned up, veined white between half-closed lids. Roy inserted one arm under his brother's head and lifted it.

Peering down at the dim face, unconscious and innocent-looking, I had a pang of doubt. I knew my bitterness wasn't all for Tommy Lemberg. When I hit him I was lashing out at the other boy, too, reacting to a world of treacherous little hustlers that wouldn't let a man believe in it.

I scraped together a nickel's worth of something, faith or gullibility, and invested it:

"Lemberg, do you believe this yarn your brother told you?"

"Yes."

"Are you willing to put it to the test?"

"I don't understand you." But his white face slanted up fearfully. "If you're talking about him going back to California, no. They'd put him in the gas chamber."

"Not if his story is true. He could do a lot to back it up by coming back with me voluntarily."

"He can't. He's been in jail. He has a record."

"That record of his means a lot to you, doesn't it? More than it does to other people, maybe."

"I don't dig you."

"Why don't you dissolve the brother act? Commit yourself where there's some future. Your wife could do with a piece of you. She's in a bad way, Lemberg."

He didn't answer me. He held his brother's head possessively against his shoulder. In the light of the stars they seemed like twins, mirror images of each other. Roy looked at Tommy in a puzzled way, as if he couldn't tell which was the real man and which was the reflection. Or which was the possessor and which was the possessed.

Footfalls thudded in the dust behind me. It was Mrs. Fredericks, wearing a bathrobe and carrying a pan of water.

"Here," was all she said.

She handed me the pan and went back into the house. She wanted no part of the trouble in the street. Her house was well supplied with trouble.

I sprinkled some water on Tommy's face. He snorted and sat up blinking. "Who hit me?" Then he saw me, and remembered: "You sucker-punched me. You sucker-punched a cripple."

He tried to get up. Roy held him down with both hands on his shoulders:

"You had it coming, you know that. I've been talking to Mr. Archer. He'll listen to what you have to say."

"I'm willing to listen to the truth," I said. "Anything else is a waste of time."

With his brother's help, Tommy got onto his feet. "Go ahead," Roy prompted him. "Tell him. And no more kid stuff."

"The whole truth, remember," I said, "including the Schwartz angle."

"Yeah. Yeah." Tommy was still dazed. "Schwartz was the one hired me in the first place. He sent one of his boys to look me up, promised me a hundred bucks to put a fear into this certain party."

"A little death, you mean?"

He shook his head violently. "Nothing like that, just a little working over."

"What did Schwartz have against Culligan?"

"Culligan wasn't the one. He wasn't supposed to be there, see. He got in the picture by mistake."

"I told you that," Roy said.

"Be quiet. Let Tommy do the talking."

"Yeah, sure," Tommy said. "It was this beast that I was supposed to put on a little show for. I wasn't supposed to hurt her, nothing like that, just put the fear of God in her so she'd cough up what she owed Schwartz. It was like a collection agency, y'unnerstan'? Legit."

"What was her name?"

"Alice Sable. They sent me because I knew what she looked like. Last summer in Reno she used to run around with Pete Culligan. But he wasn't supposed to be there at her house, for God sake. The way they told it to me, she was alone by herself out there all day. When Culligan came marching out, armed up to the teeth, you could of knocked me over with a 'dozer.

"I moved in on him, very fast, very fast reflexes I got, talking all the time. Got hold of the gun but it went off, the slug plowed up my arm, same time he dropped the gun. I picked it up. By that time he had his knife out. What could I do? He was going to gut me. I slammed him on the noggin with the gun and chilled him. Then I beat it."

"Did you see Alice Sable?"

"Yeah, she came surging out and yelled at me. I was starting the Jag, and I couldn't hear what she said over the en-

157

gine. I didn't stop or turn around. Hell, I didn't want to rough up no beast, anyway."

"Did you pick up Culligan's knife before you left, and cut him with it?"

"No sir. What would I do that for? Man, I was hurt. I wanted out."

"What was Culligan doing when you left?"

"Laying there." He glanced at his brother. "Lying there."

"Who coached you to say that?"

"Nobody did."

"That's true," Roy said. "It's just the way he told it to me. You've got to believe him."

"I'm not the important one. The man he has to convince is Sheriff Trask of Santa Teresa County. And planes are taking off for there all the time."

"Aw, no." Tommy's gaze swiveled frantically from me to Roy. "They'll throw the book at me if I go back."

"Sooner or later you have to go back. You can come along peaceably now, or you can force extradition proceedings and make the trip in handcuffs and leg-chains. Which way do you want it, hard or easy?"

For once in his young life, Tommy Lemberg did something the easy way.

chapter
27
I PHONED Sheriff Trask long distance. He agreed to wire me transportation authorization for the Lemberg brothers. I picked it up at Willow Run, and the three of us got aboard an early plane. Trask had an official car waiting to meet the connecting plane when it landed in Santa Teresa.

Before noon we were in the interrogation room in the Santa Teresa courthouse. Roy and Tommy made statements, which were recorded by a court reporter on steno and tape-machine. Tommy seemed to be awed by the big room with its barred windows, the Sheriff's quiet power, the weight of the law which both man and building represented. There were no discrepancies in the part of his statement I heard.

Trask motioned me out before Tommy was finished. I followed him down the corridor to his office. He took off his coat and opened the neck of his shirt. Blotches of sweat spread from his armpits. He filled a paper cup with water from a cooler, drained the cup, and crushed it in his fist.

"If we buy this," he said at last, "it puts us back at the beginning. You buy it, don't you, Archer?"

"I've taken an option on it. Naturally I think it should be investigated. But that can wait. Have you questioned Theo Fredericks about the Culligan killing?"

"No."

"Is Fredericks doing any talking at all?"

"Not to me he isn't."

"But you picked him up last night?"

Trask's face had a raw red look. I thought at first that he was on the verge of a heart attack. Then I realized that he was painfully embarrassed. He turned his back on me, walked over to the wall, and stood looking at a photograph of himself shaking hands with the Governor.

"Somebody tipped him off," he said. "He flew the coop five minutes before I got there." He turned to face me: "The worst part of it is, he took Sheila Howell with him."

"By force?"

"You kidding? She was probably the one who tipped him off. I made the mistake of phoning Dr. Howell before I moved on the little rat. In any case, she went along with him willingly—walked out of her father's house and drove away with him in the middle of the night. Howell's been on my back ever since."

"Howell's very fond of his daughter."

"Yeah, I know how he feels, I have a daughter of my own. I was afraid for a while that he was going to take off after her with a shotgun, and I mean literally. Howell's a trap-shooter, one of the best in the county. But I got him calmed down. He's in the communications room, waiting to hear some word of them."

"They're traveling by car?"

"The one Mrs. Galton bought for him."

"A red Thunderbird should be easy to spot."

"You'd think so. But they've been gone over eight hours without a trace. They may be in Mexico by now. Or they may be cuddled up in an L.A. motel under one of his aliases." Trask scowled at the image. "Why do so many nice young girls go for the dangerous ones?"

The question didn't expect an answer, and that was just as well. I hadn't any.

Trask sat down heavily behind his desk. "Just how dangerous is he? When we talked on the telephone last night, you mentioned a knifing he did before he left Canada."

"He stabbed his father. Apparently he meant to kill him. The old man is no saint, either. In fact, the Fredericks' boardinghouse is a regular thieves' kitchen. Peter Culligan was staying there at the time of the knifing. The boy ran away with him."

Trask took up a pencil and broke it in half, abstractedly, dropping the pieces on his blotter. "How do we know the Fredericks boy didn't murder Culligan? He had a motive: Culligan was in a position to call his bluff and tell the world who he really was. And M.O. figures, with his knifing record."

"We've been thinking the same thing, Sheriff. There's even a strong likelihood that Culligan was his partner in the conspiracy. That would give him a powerful motive to silence Culligan. We've been assuming that Fredericks was in Luna Bay that day. But has his alibi ever been checked?"

"There's no time like the present."

Trask picked up his phone and asked the switchboard to put through a call to the San Mateo County sheriff's office in Redwood City.

"I can think of one other possibility," I said. "Alice Sable was involved with Culligan last year in Reno, and maybe since. Remember how she reacted to his death. We put it down to nervous shock, but it could have been something worse."

"You're not suggesting that she killed him?"

"As a hypothesis."

Trask shook his head impatiently. "Even putting it hypothetically, it's pretty hard to swallow about a lady like her."

"What kind of a lady is she? Do you know her?"

"I've met her, that's about all. But hell, Gordon Sable's one of the top lawyers in the city."

The politician latent in every elected official was rising to the surface and blurring Trask's hard, clear attitudes. I said:

"That doesn't put his wife above suspicion. Have you questioned her?"

"No." Trask became explanatory, as though he felt that he had missed a move: "I haven't been able to get to her. Sable was opposed, and the head-shrinkers backed him up. They say she shouldn't be questioned on painful subjects. She's been borderline psychotic since the killing, and any more pressure might push her over the edge."

"Howell's her personal doctor, isn't he?"

"He is. As a matter of fact, I tried to get to her through Howell. He was dead set against it, and as long as it looked like an open-and-shut case, I didn't press the point."

"Howell should be ready to change his mind. Did you say he's somewhere around the courthouse?"

"Yeah, he's down in Communications. But wait a minute, Archer." Trask rose and came around the desk. "This is a touchy business, and you don't want to hang too much weight on the Lemberg brothers' story. They're not disinterested witnesses."

"They don't know enough to invent the story, either."

"Schwartz and his lawyers do."

"Are we back on the Schwartz kick again?"

"You were the one that got me on it in the first place. You were convinced that the Culligan killing was a gang killing."

"I was wrong."

"Maybe. We'll let the facts decide when they all come out. But if you were wrong, you could be wrong again." Trask punched me in the stomach in a friendly way. "How about that, Archer?"

His telephone chirped, and he lifted the receiver. I couldn't make out the words that came scratchily over the wire, but I saw their effect on Trask. His body stiffened, and his face seemed to grow larger.

"I'll use my Aero Squadron," he said finally, "and I ought to be there in two hours. But don't sit around waiting for me." He slammed down the receiver and reached for the coat draped over the back of his chair.

"They made the red Thunderbird," he said. "Fredericks abandoned it in San Mateo. They were just going to put the word on the teletype when they got my call."

"Where in San Mateo?"

"Parking-lot of the S.P. station. Fredericks and the girl probably took a train into San Francisco."

"Are you flying up?"

"Yeah, I've had a volunteer pilot standing by all morning. Ride along with us if you want. He has a four-passenger Beechcraft."

"Thanks, I've had enough flying to last me for a while. You didn't ask them to check Fredericks's alibi."

"I forgot," Trask said lightly. "I'll take it up with Fredericks personally."

He seemed glad to be leaving Alice Sable in my lap.

chapter
28
THE communications center of the courthouse was a windowless room on the basement level, full of the chatter and whine of short-wave radio signals. Dr. Howell was sitting with his head down in front of a quiet teletype machine. He raised his head abruptly when I spoke to him. His face was gray in the white overhead light:

"So here you are. While you've been junketing around the country at my expense, she's gone away with him. Do you understand what that means?"

His voice rose out of control. The two deputies monitoring the radios looked at him and then at each other. One of them said: "If you two gentlemen want to talk in private, this is no place to do it."

"Come outside," I said to Howell: "You're not accomplishing anything here. They'll be picked up soon, don't worry."

He sat in inert silence. I wanted to get him away from the teletype machine before the message from San Mateo hit it. It would send him off to the Bay area, and I had a use for him here:

"Doctor, is Alice Sable still under your care?"

He looked up questioningly. "Yes."

"Is she still in the nursing home?"

"Yes. I should try to get there today." He brushed his forehead with his fingertips. "I've been neglecting my patients, I'm afraid."

"Come out there with me now."

"What on earth for?"

"Mrs. Sable may be able to help us terminate this case, and help us reach your daughter."

He rose, but stood irresolute beside the teletype machine. Sheila's defection had robbed him of his force. I took hold of his elbow and steered him out into the basement corridor. Once moving, he went ahead of me up the iron stairs into the hot white noon.

His Chevrolet was in the county parking-lot. He turned to me as he started the engine:

"How can Mrs. Sable help us to find Sheila?"

"I'm not certain she can. But she was involved with Culligan, the Fredericks boy's probable partner in the conspiracy. She may know more about Theo Fredericks than anyone else does."

"She never said a word about him to me."

"Has she been talking to you about the case?"

He said after some hesitation: "Not being a practicing psychiatrist, I haven't encouraged that line of discussion with her. The matter has come up, however. Unavoidably so, since it's part and parcel of her mental condition."

"Can you be more specific?"

"I prefer not to. You know the ethics of my profession. The doctor-patient relationship is sacrosanct."

"So is human life. Don't forget a man was murdered. We have evidence that Mrs. Sable knew Culligan before he came to Santa Teresa. She was also a witness to his death. Anything she has to say about it may be very significant."

"Not if her memory of the event is delusional."

"Does she have delusions on the subject?"

"She has indeed. Her account doesn't agree with the actual event as we know it. I've gone into this with Trask, and there's no doubt whatever that a thug named Lemberg stabbed the man."

"There's a good deal of doubt," I said. "The Sheriff just took a statement from Lemberg. A Reno gambler sent Lemberg to collect money from Alice Sable, and maybe rough her up a bit. Culligan got in the way. Lemberg knocked him out, was shot in the process, left him unconscious on the ground. He claims that somebody else did the knifing after he left."

Howell's face underwent a curious change. His eyes became harder and brighter. He wasn't looking at me, or at anything external. The lines around his eyes and at the corners of his mouth curved and deepened, as if he was being forced to look against his will at something horrible.

"But Trask said Lemberg was undeniably guilty."

"Trask was wrong. We all were."

"Do you honestly mean to say that Alice Sable has been speaking the truth all along?"

"I don't know what she's been saying, Doctor. You do."

163

"But Trenchard and the other psychiatrists were convinced that her self-accusations were fantasies. They had me convinced."

"What does she accuse herself of? Does she blame herself for Culligan's death?"

Howell sat over the wheel in silence. He had been shaken, and wide open, for a few minutes. Now his personality closed up again:

"You have no right to cross-examine me about the intimate affairs of one of my patients."

"I'm afraid I have to, Doctor. If Alice Sable murdered Culligan, there's no way you can cover up for her. I'm surprised you want to. You're not only breaking the law, you're violating the ethics you set such store by."

"I'll be the judge of my own ethics," he said in a strained voice.

He sat and wrestled with his unstated problem. His gaze was inward and glaring. Sweat-drops studded his forehead. I got some sense of the empathy he felt for his patient. Even his daughter was forgotten.

"She has confessed the murder to you, Doctor?"

Slowly his eyes remembered me again. "What did you say?"

"Has Mrs. Sable confessed Culligan's murder?"

"I'm going to ask you not to question me further."

Abruptly he released the emergency brake. I kept quiet all the way to the nursing home, hoping my patience might earn me an interview with Alice Sable herself.

A gray-haired nurse unlocked the front door, and smiled with special intensity at Howell. "Good morning, Doctor. We're a little late this morning."

"I'm having to skip my regular calls today. I do want to see Mrs. Sable."

"I'm sorry, Doctor, she's already gone."

"Gone where, for heaven's sake?"

"Mr. Sable took her home this morning, didn't you know? He said it was all right with you."

"It certainly is not. You don't release disturbed patients without specific orders from a doctor. Haven't you learned that yet, nurse?"

Before she could answer, Howell turned on his heel and started back to his car. I had to run to catch him.

"The man's a fool!" he cried above the roar of the engine. "He can't be permitted to take a chance like this with his wife's safety. She's dangerous to herself and other people."

I said when we were underway: "Was she dangerous to Culligan, Doctor?"

His answer was a sigh which seemed to rise from the center of his body. The outskirts of Santa Teresa gave place to open country. The hills of Arroyo Park rose ahead of us. With his eyes on the green hills, Howell said:

"The poor wretch of a woman told me that she killed him. And I didn't have sense enough to believe her. Somehow her story didn't ring true to me. I was convinced that it was fantasy masking the actual event."

"Is that why you wouldn't let Trask talk to her?"

"Yes. The present state of the law being what it is, a doctor has a duty to protect his patients, especially the semi-psychotic ones. We can't run off to the police with every sick delusion they come up with. But in this case," he added reluctantly, "it seems I was mistaken."

"You're not sure."

"I'm no longer sure about anything."

"Exactly what did she say to you?"

"She heard the sounds of a struggle, two men fighting and calling each other names. A gun went off. She was terrified, of course, but she forced herself to go to the front door. Culligan was lying on the lawn. The other man was just driving away in the Jaguar. When he was out of sight, she went out to Culligan. Her intention was to help him, she said, but she saw his knife in the grass. She picked it up and—used it."

We had reached the foot of Sable's hill. Howell wrestled his car up the climbing curves. The tires shuddered and screeched like lost souls under punishment.

chapter
29
SABLE must have heard the car, and been waiting behind the door for Howell's knock. He opened the door at once. His bloodshot eyes began to water in the strong sunlight, and he sneezed.

"Where is your wife?" Howell said.

"In her own room, where she belongs. There was so much noise and confusion in the nursing home—"

"I want to see her."

165

"I don't think so, Doctor. I understand you've been grilling her about the unfortunate crime that occurred on our premises. It's been most disturbing to Alice. You told me yourself that she shouldn't be forced to talk about it."

"She brought up the subject of her own accord. I demand to be allowed to see her."

"Demand, Doctor? How can you do that? I should make it clear, I suppose, that I'm terminating your services as of now. I intend to hire a new crew of doctors, and find a place where Alice can rest in peace."

The phrase set up whispering echoes which Howell's voice cut through:

"You don't hire doctors, Sable, and you don't fire them."

"Your law is rusty. Perhaps you should hire a lawyer. You're certainly going to need one if you try to force your way into my house." Sable's voice was controlled, but queerly atonal.

"I have a duty to my patient. You had no right to remove her from nursing care."

"From your third-degree methods, you mean? Let me remind you, if you need reminding, that anything Alice has said to you is privileged. I employed you and the others in my capacity as her lawyer in order to have your assistance in determining certain facts. Is that clear? If you communicate these facts or alleged facts to anyone, official or unofficial, I'll sue you for criminal libel."

"You're talking doubletalk," I said. "You won't be suing anybody."

"Won't I, though? You're in roughly the same position as Dr. Howell. I employed you to make a certain investigation, and ordered you to communicate the results orally to me. Any further communication is a breach of contract. Try it out, and by God I'll have your license."

I didn't know if he was legally right. I didn't care. When he started to swing the door shut, I set my foot against it:

"We're coming in, Sable."

"I think not," his queer new voice said.

He reached behind the door and stepped back with a gun in his hands. It was a long, heavy gun, a deer rifle with a telescopic sight. He raised it deliberately. I looked directly into the muzzle, at the clean, glinting spiral of the rifling.

Sable curled his finger on the trigger, and cuddled the polished stock against his cheek. His face had a fine glaze on it, like porcelain. I realized that he was ready to kill me.

166

"Put it down," Howell said.

He moved ahead of me into the doorway, taking my place in the line of fire:

"Put it down, Gordon. You're not yourself, you're feeling upset, you're terribly worried about Alice. But we're your friends, we're Alice's friends, too. We want to help you both."

"I have no friends," Sable said. "I know why you're here, why you want to talk to Alice. And I'm not going to let you."

"Don't be silly, Gordon. You can't look after a sick woman by yourself. I know you don't care about your personal safety, but you have to consider Alice's safety. She needs looking after, Gordon. So put it down now, let me in to see her."

"Get back. I'll shoot."

Sable's voice was a high sharp yell. His wife must have heard it. From deep inside the house, she cried out in answer: "No!"

Sable blinked against the light. He looked like a sleepwalker waking up on the verge of a precipice. Behind him his wife's crying went on, punctuated by resounding blows and then a crash of glass.

Caught between impossible pressures, Sable half-turned toward the noise. The rifle swung sideways with his movement. I went in past Howell and got one hand on the gun-barrel and the other on the knot of Sable's tie. I heaved. Man and rifle came apart.

Sable thudded against the wall and almost fell. He was breathing hard. His hair was in his eyes. He bore a strange resemblance to an old woman peering out through the fringes of a matted white wig.

I opened the breech of the rifle. While I was unloading it, running feet slapped the pavement of the inner court. Alice Sable appeared at the end of the hallway. Her light hair was ruffled, and her nightgown was twisted around her slender body. Blood ran down over her naked foot from a cut in her leg.

"I hurt myself on the window," she said in a small voice. "I cut myself on the glass."

"Did you have to break it?" Sable made an abrupt, threatening movement toward her. Then he remembered us, and sweetened his tone: "Go back to your room, dear. You don't want to run around half-dressed in front of visitors."

"Dr. Howell isn't a visitor. You came to fix it where I hurt myself, didn't you?"

She moved uncertainly toward the doctor. He went to meet her with his hands out. "Of course I did. Come back to your room with me and we'll fix it now."

"But I don't want to go back in there. I hate it in there, it depresses me. Peter used to visit me in there."

"Be quiet!" Sable said.

She moved behind the doctor, making her body small as if to claim a child's irresponsibility. From the protection of Howell's shoulder, she peered sadly at her husband:

"Be quiet is all you say to me. Be quiet, hush it up. But what's the use, Gordon? Everybody knows about me and Peter. Dr. Howell knows. I made a clean breast of it to him." Her hand went to her breast, and fingered the rosebuds embroidered on her nightgown. Her heavy gaze swung to me. "This man knows about me, too, I can see it in his face."

"Did you kill him, Mrs. Sable?"

"Don't answer," Sable said.

"But I want to confess. I'll feel better then, won't I?" Her smile was bright and agonized. It faded, leaving its lines in her face and her teeth bare: "I did kill him. The fellow in the black car knocked him out, and I went out and stabbed him."

Her hand jerked downward from her breast, clenched on an imaginary knife. Her husband watched her like a poker-player.

"Why did you do it?" I said.

"I don't know. I guess I just got sick of him. Now it's time for me to take my punishment. I killed, and I deserve to die."

The tragic words had an unreal quality. She spoke them like a life-size puppet activated by strings and used by a voice that didn't belong to her. Only her eyes were her own, and they contained a persistent stunned innocence.

"I deserve to die," she repeated. "Don't I, Gordon?"

He flushed up darkly. "Leave me out of this."

"But you said—"

"I said nothing of the sort."

"You're lying, Gordon," she chided him. Perhaps there was an undertone of malice in her voice. "You told me after all my crimes that I deserved to die. And you were right. I lost your good money gambling and went with another man and now on top of it all I'm a murderer."

Sable appealed to Howell: "Can't we put an end to this? My wife is ill and hurt. It's inconceivable that you should let her be questioned. This man isn't even a policeman—"

168

"I'll take the responsibility for what I do," I said. "Mrs. Sable, do you remember stabbing Peter Culligan?"

She raised one hand to her forehead, pushing back her hair as if it got in the way of her thoughts. "I don't remember exactly, but I must have."

"Why do you say you must have, if you don't remember?"

"Gordon saw me."

I looked at Sable. He wouldn't look at me. He stood against the wall, trying to merge with the wall.

"Gordon wasn't here," I said. "He was at Mrs. Galton's house when you telephoned."

"But he came. He came right over. Peter was lying there on the grass for a long time. He was making a funny noise, it sounded like snoring. I unbuttoned the top of his shirt to help him breathe."

"You remember all this, but you don't remember stabbing him?"

"I must have blanked out on that part. I'm always blanking out on things, ask Gordon."

"I'm asking you, Mrs. Sable."

"Let me think. I remember, I slid my hand down under his shirt, to see if his heart was beating properly. I could feel it there thumping and jumping. You'd think it was a little animal trying to get out. The hair on his chest was scratchy, like wire."

Sable made a noise in his throat.

"What did you do then?" I said.

"I—nothing. I just sat for a while and looked at him and his poor old beatup face. I put my arms around him and tried to coax him awake. But he went on snoring at me. He was still snoring when Gordon got there. Gordon was angry, catching me with him like that. I ran into the house. But I watched from the window."

Suddenly her face was incandescent. "I didn't kill him. It wasn't me out there. It was Gordon, and I watched him from the window. He picked up Peter's knife and pushed it into his stomach." Her clenched hand repeated its downward gesture, striking her own soft abdomen. "The blood spurted out and ran red on the grass. It was all red and green."

Sable thrust his head forward. The rest of his body, even his arms and hands, remained stuck to the wall:

"You can't believe her. She's hallucinating again."

His wife seemed not to hear him. Perhaps she was tuned to

169

a higher frequency, singing like salvation in her head. Tears streamed from her eyes:

"I didn't kill him."

"Hush now." Howell quieted her face against his shoulder.

"This is the truth, isn't it?" I said.

"It must be. I'm certain of it. Those self-accusations of hers were fantasy after all. This account is much more circumstantial. I'd say she's taken a long step toward reality."

"She's crazier than she ever was," Sable said. "If you think you can use this against me, you're crazier than she is. Don't forget I'm a lawyer—"

"Is that what you are—a lawyer?" Howell turned his back on Sable and spoke to his wife: "Come on, Alice, we'll put a bandage on that cut and you can get some clothes on. Then we'll take a little ride, back to the nice place with the other ladies."

"It isn't a nice place," she said.

Howell smiled down at her. "That's the spirit. Keep saying what you really think and know, and we'll get you out of there to stay. But not for a while yet, eh?"

"Not for a while yet."

Holding her with one arm, Howell stretched out his other hand to Sable. "The key to your wife's room. You won't be needing it."

Sable produced a flat brass key which Howell accepted from him without a word. The doctor walked Alice Sable down the hallway toward the court.

chapter
30
GORDON SABLE watched them go with something approaching relief. The bright expectancy had left his eyes. He had done it.

"I wouldn't have done it," he said, "if I'd known what I know now. There are factors you don't foresee—the factor of human change, for example. You think you can handle anything, that you can go on forever. But your strength wears away under pressure. A few days, or a few weeks, and everything looks different. Nothing seems worth struggling for. It all goes blah." He made a loose bumbling sound with his lips: "All gone to bloody blah. So here we are."

170

"Why did you kill him?"

"You heard her. When I got back here she was crying and moaning over him, trying to wake him up with kisses. It made me sick to death."

"Don't tell me it was a sudden crime of passion. You must have known about them long before."

"I don't deny that." Sable shifted his stance, as if to prepare himself for a shift in his story. "Culligan picked her up in Reno last summer. She went there to divorce me, but she ended up on a gambling spree with Culligan egging her on. No doubt he collected commissions on the money she lost. She lost a great deal, all the ready money I could raise. When it was gone, and her credit was exhausted, he let her share his apartment for a while. I had to go there and beg her to come home with me. She didn't want to come. I had to pay him to send her away."

I didn't doubt the truth of what he was saying. No man would invent such a story against himself. It was Sable who didn't seem to believe his own words. They fell weightlessly from his mouth, like a memorized report of an accident he didn't understand, which had happened to people in a foreign country:

"I never felt quite the same about myself after that. Neither of us did. We lived in this house I'd built for her as if there were always a glass partition between us. We could see each other, but we couldn't really speak. We had to act out our feelings like clowns, or apes in separate cages. Alice's gestures became queerer, and no doubt mine did, too. The things we acted out got uglier. She would throw herself on the floor and strike herself with her fist until her face was bruised and swollen. And I would laugh at her and call her names.

"We did such things to each other," he said. "I think we were both glad, in a strange way, when Culligan turned up here in the course of the winter. Anthony Galton's bones had been unearthed, and Culligan had read about it in the papers. He knew who they belonged to, and came to me with the information."

"How did he happen to pick you?"

"It's a good question. I've often asked myself that good question. Alice had told him that I was Mrs. Galton's lawyer, of course. It may have been the source of his interest in her. He knew that her gambling losses had put me in financial straits. He needed expert help with the plan he had; he wasn't

171

clever enough to execute it alone. He was just clever enough to realize that I was infinitely cleverer."

And he knew other things about you, I thought. You were a loveless man who could be bent and finally twisted.

"How did Schwartz get in on the deal?"

"Otto Schwartz? He wasn't in on it." Sable seemed offended by the notion. "His only connection with it was the fact that Alice owed him sixty thousand dollars. Schwartz had been pressing for payment, and it finally reached the point where he was threatening both of us with a beating. I had to raise money somehow. I was desperate. I didn't know which way to turn."

"Leave out the drama, Sable. You didn't go into this conspiracy on the spur of the moment. You've been working on it for months."

"I'm not denying that. There was a lot of work to be done. Culligan's idea didn't look too promising at first. He'd been carrying it around ever since he ran into the Fredericks boy in Canada five or six years ago. He'd known Anthony Galton. in Luna Bay, and was struck by the boy's resemblance to him. He even brought Fredericks into the States in the hope of cashing in on the resemblance in some way. But he ran into trouble with the law, and lost track of the boy. He believed that if I'd stake him, he could find him again.

"Culligan did find him, as you know, going to school in Ann Arbor. I went east myself in February, and saw him in one of the student plays. He was a fairly good actor, with a nice air of sincerity about him. I decided when I talked to him that he could carry the thing off if anyone could. I introduced myself as a Hollywood producer interested in his talent. Once he was hooked on that, and had taken money from me, he wasn't too hard to talk around to the other.

"I prepared his story for him, of course. It required considerable thought. The most difficult problem was how to lead investigation of his actual Canadian background into a blind alley. The Crystal Springs orphanage was my inspiration. But I realized that the success of the imposture depended primarily on him. If he did succeed in bringing it off, he would be entitled to the lion's share. I was modest in my own demands. He simply gave me an option to buy, at a nominal price, a certain amount of producing oil property."

I watched him, trying to understand how a man with so much foresight could have ended where Sable was. Something had cut off the use of his mind from constructive purposes.

172

Perhaps it was the shallow pride which he seemed to take in his schemes, even at this late date.

"They talk about the crime of the century," he said. "This would have been the greatest of all—a multi-million-dollar enterprise with no actual harm done to anyone. The boy was simply to let himself be discovered, and let the facts speak for themselves."

"The facts?" I said sharply.

"The apparent facts, if you like. I'm not a philosopher. We lawyers don't deal in ultimate realities. Who knows what they are? We deal in appearances. There was very little manipulation of the facts in this case, no actual falsification of documents. True, the boy had to tell one or two little lies about his childhood and his parents. What did a few little lies matter? They made Mrs. Galton just as happy as if he was her real grandson. And if she chose to leave him her money, that was her affair."

"Has she made a new will?"

"I believe so. I had no part in it. I advised her to get another lawyer."

"Wasn't that taking a chance?"

"Not if you know Maria Galton as I know her. Her reactions are so consistently contrary that you can depend on them. I got her to make a new will by urging her not to. I got her interested in looking for Tony by telling her it was hopeless. I persuaded her to hire you by opposing the whole idea of a detective."

"Why me?"

"Schwartz was prodding me, and I had to get the ball rolling. I couldn't take the chance of finding the boy for myself. I had to have someone to do it for me, someone I could trust. I thought, too, if we could get past you, we could get past anyone. And if we failed to get past you, I thought you'd be—more flexible, shall we say?"

"Crooked, shall we say?"

Sable winced at the word. Words meant more to him than the facts they stood for.

A door opened at the end of the corridor, and Alice Sable and Dr. Howell came toward us. She hung on the doctor's arm, dressed and freshly groomed and empty-faced under her makeup. He was carrying a white leather suitcase in his free hand.

"Sable has made a full confession," I said to Howell. "Phone the Sheriff's office, will you?"

"I already have. They ought to be here shortly. I'm taking Mrs. Sable back where she'll be properly attended to." He added in an undertone: "I hope this will be a turning-point for her."

"I hope so, too," Sable said. "Honestly I do."

Howell made no response. Sable tried again:

"Good-by, Alice. I really do wish you well, you know."

Her neck stiffened, but she didn't look at him. She went out leaning on Howell. Her brushed hair shone like gold in the sunlight. Fool's gold. I felt a twinge of sympathy for Sable. He hadn't been able to carry her weight. In the stretching gap between his weakness and her need, Culligan had driven a wedge, and the whole structure had fallen.

Sable was a subtle man, and he must have noticed some change in my expression:

"You surprise me, Lew. I didn't expect you to bear down so hard. You have a reputation for tempering the wind to the shorn lamb."

"Stabbing Culligan to death wasn't exactly a lamblike gesture."

"I had to kill him. You don't seem to understand."

"On account of your wife?"

"My wife was only the beginning. He kept moving in on me. He wasn't content to share my wife and my house. He was very hungry, always wanting more. I finally saw that he wanted it all to himself. Everything." His voice trembled with indignation. "After all my contributions, all my risks, he was planning to shut me out."

"How could he?"

"Through the boy. He had something on Theo Fredericks. I never learned what it was, I couldn't get it out of either of them. But Culligan said that it was enough to ruin my whole plan. It was his plan, too, of course, but he was irresponsible enough to wreck it unless he got his way."

"So you killed him."

"The chance offered itself, and I took it. It wasn't premeditated."

"No jury will believe that, after what you did to your wife. It looks as premeditated as hell. You waited for your chance to knock off a defenseless man, and then tried to push the guilt onto a sick woman."

"She asked for it," he said coldly. "She wanted to believe that she killed him. She was half-convinced before I talked

174

to her, she felt so guilty about her affair with him. I only did what any man would do under the circumstances. She'd seen me stab him. I had to do something to purge her mind of the memory."

"Is that what you've been doing on your long visits, pounding guilt into her mind?"

He struck the wall with the flat of his hand. "She was the cause of the trouble. She brought him into our life. She deserved to suffer for it. Why should I do all the suffering?"

"You don't have to. Spread it around a little. Tell me how to get to the Fredericks boy."

He glanced at me from the corners of his eyes. "I'd want a quid pro quo." The legal phrase seemed to encourage him. He went on in quickening tempo until he was almost chattering: "As a matter of fact, he should take the blame for most of this frightful mess. If it will help to clear up the matter, I'm willing to turn state's evidence. Alice can't be made to testify against me. You don't even know that what she said was true. How do you know her story is true? I may be simply covering up for her." His voice was rising like a manic hope.

"How do you know you're alive, Sable? I want your partner. He was in San Mateo this morning. Where is he headed for?"

"I haven't the faintest idea."

"When did you see him last?"

"I don't know why I should co-operate with you if you won't co-operate with me."

I still had his empty rifle in my hands. I reversed it and raised it like a club. I was angry enough to use it if I had to.

"This is why."

He pulled his head back so sharply it rapped the wall. "You can't use third-degree methods on me. It isn't legal."

"Stop blowing bubbles, Sable. Was Fredericks here last night?"

"Yes. He wanted me to cash a check for him. I gave him all the cash I had in the house. It amounted to over two hundred dollars."

"What did he want it for?"

"He didn't tell me. Actually, he wasn't making too much sense. He talked as if the strain had been too much for him."

"What did he say?"

"I can't reproduce it verbatim. I was upset myself. He asked me a lot of questions, which I wasn't able to answer, about Anthony Galton and what happened to him. The imposture must have gone to his head; he seemed to have himself convinced that he actually was Galton's son."

"Was Sheila Howell with him?"

"Yes, she was present, and I see what you mean. He may have been talking for her benefit. If it was an act, she was certainly taken in by it. But as I said, he seemed to be taken in by it himself. He became very excited, and threatened me with force unless I told him who murdered Galton. I didn't know what to tell him. I finally thought of the name of that woman in Redwood City—the Galtons' former nurse."

"Mrs. Matheson?"

"Yes. I had to tell him something, get rid of him somehow."

A patrol car whined up the hill and stopped in front of the house. Conger and another deputy climbed out. Sable was going to have a hard time getting rid of them.

chapter
31 THEY dropped me at the airport, and I got aboard a plane. It was the same two-engine bucket, on the same flight, that had taken me north three weeks ago. Even the stewardess was the same. Somehow she looked younger and more innocent. Time had stood still for her while it had been rushing me along into premature middle age.

She comforted me with Chiclets and coffee in paper cups. And there was the blessed Bay again, and the salt flats.

The Matheson house was closed up tight, with the drapes pulled over the windows, as if there was sickness inside. I asked my cab-driver to wait and knocked on the front door. Marian Matheson answered it herself.

She had been living on my time-schedule, and growing old rapidly. There was more gray in her hair, more bone in her face. But the process of change had softened her. Even her voice was gentler:

"I've been sort of expecting you. I had another visitor this morning."

"John Galton?"

"Yes. John Galton—the little boy I looked after in Luna Bay. It was quite an experience meeting him after all these years. And his girl, too. He brought his girl along." She hesitated, then opened the door wider. "Come in if you want."

She took me into the darkened living-room and placed me in a chair.

"What did they come to you for, Mrs. Matheson?"

"The same thing you did. Information."

"What about?"

"That night. I thought he had a right to know the truth, so I told him all I told you, about Culligan and Shoulders." Her answer was vague; perhaps she was trying to keep the memory vague in her mind.

"What was his reaction?"

"He was very interested. Naturally. He really pricked up his ears when I told him about the rubies."

"Did he explain his interest in the rubies?"

"He didn't explain anything. He got up and left in a hurry, and they rocketed off in that little red car of his. They didn't even wait to drink the coffee I was brewing."

"Were they friendly?"

"To me, you mean? Very friendly. The girl was lovely to me. She confided they were going to get married as soon as her young man worked his way out of the darkness."

"What did she mean by the darkness?"

"I don't know, that was just the phrase she used." But she squinted at the sunlight filtering through the drapes, like someone who understood what darkness meant. "He seemed to be very concerned about his father's death."

"Did he say what he was going to do next, or where he was going?"

"No. He did ask me how to get to the airport—if there were buses running. It seemed kind of funny, him asking about buses when he had a brand-new sports car standing out front."

"He's evading arrest, Mrs. Matheson. He knew his car would be spotted right away if he parked it at the airport."

"Who wants to arrest him?"

"I do, for one. He isn't Galton's son, or Brown's son. He's an impostor."

"How can that be? Why, he's the spitting image of his father."

"Appearances can be deceiving, and you're not the first one to be taken in by his appearance. His real name is Theo Fredericks. He's a small-time crook from Canada with a record of violence."

Her hand went to her mouth. "From Canada, did you say?"

"Yes. His parents run a boardinghouse in Pitt, Ontario."

"But that's where they're going, Ontario. I heard him say to her, when I was out in the kitchen, that there were no direct flights to Ontario. That was just before they took off from here."

"What time were they here?"

"It was early in the morning, just past eight. They were waiting out front when I got back from driving Ron to the station."

I looked at my watch. It was nearly five. They had had almost nine hours. With the right connections, they could be in Canada by now.

And with the right connections, I could be there in another eight or nine hours.

Mrs. Matheson followed me to the door. "Is this trouble going to go on forever?"

"We're coming to the end of it," I said. "I'm sorry I couldn't keep you out of it after all."

"It's all right. I've talked it out with Ron. Whatever comes up—if I have to testify in court or anything—we can handle it together. My husband is a very good man."

"He has a good wife."

"No." She shook the compliment off her fingers. "But I love him and the boy, and that's something. I'm glad it all came out between me and Ron. It's a big load off my heart." She smiled gravely. "I hope it works out some way for that young girl. It's hard to believe that her boy is a criminal. But I know how these things can be in life."

She looked up at the sun.

On the way to International Airport my taxi passed the Redwood City courthouse. I thought of stopping and getting in touch with Trask. Then I decided not to. It was my case, and I wanted to end it.

Perhaps I had a glimmering of the truth.

chapter

32

I DROVE my rented car into Pitt at three o'clock, the darkest hour of the night. But there were lights in the red house on the riverbank. Mrs. Fredericks came to the door fully dressed in rusty black. Her heavy face set stubbornly when she saw me.

"You got no call coming here again. What do you think you're after? I didn't know those Hamburg fellows were wanted by the police."

"They're not the only ones. Has your son been here?"

"Theo?" Her eyes and mouth sought obtusely for an answer. "He hasn't come near me for years."

A husky whisper rose from the shadows behind her. "Don't believe her, mister." Her husband came forward, supporting himself with one hand against the wall. He looked and sounded very drunk: "She'd lie her false heart out for him."

"Hold your tongue, old man."

Dark anger filled her eyes like a seepage of ink: I'd seen the same thing happen to her son. She turned on Fredericks, and he backed away. His face looked porous and moist like a deliquescent substance. His clothes were covered with dust.

"Have you seen him, Mr. Fredericks?"

"No. Lucky for him I was out, or I'd of shown him what's what." His hatchet profile chopped the air. "She saw him, though."

"Where is he, Mrs. Fredericks?"

Her husband answered for her: "She told me they went to check in at the hotel, him and the girl both."

Some obscure feeling, guilt or resentment, made the woman say: "They didn't have to go to the hotel. I offered them the use of my house. I guess it isn't good enough for muckymucks like her."

"Is the girl all right?"

"I guess so. Theo's the one that's got me worried. What did he want to come here for, after all these years? I can't figure him out."

"He always did have crazy ideas," Fredericks said. "But he's crazy like a fox, see. Watch him close when you go to nab him. He talks smooth, but he's a real snake-in-the-grass."

"Where is this hotel?"

"Downtown. The Pitt Hotel—you can't miss it. Just keep us out of it, eh? He'll try to drag us into his trouble, but I'm a respectable man—"

His wife cried: "Shut up, you. I want to see him again if you don't."

I left them locked in the combat which seemed the normal condition of their nights.

The hotel was a three-story red brick building with one lighted window on the second floor corner. One other light was burning in the lobby. I punched the hand-bell on the desk. A middle-aged little man in a green eyeshade came yawning out of a dark room behind it.

"You're up early," he said.

"I'm up late. Can you rent me a room?"

"Sure can. I got more vacancies than you can shake a stick at. With or without bath?"

"With."

"That will be three dollars." He opened the heavy leather-cornered register, and pushed it across the desk. "Sign on the line."

I signed. The registration above my signature was: Mr. and Mrs. John Galton, Detroit, Michigan.

"I see you have some other Americans staying here."

"Yeah. Nice young couple, checked in late last night. I believe they're honeymooners, probably on their way to Niagara Falls. Anyway, I put them in the bridal chamber."

"Corner room on the second floor?"

He gave me a sharp dry look. "You wouldn't want to disturb them, mister."

"No, I thought I'd say hello to them in the morning."

"Better make it late in the morning." He took a key from a hook and dropped it on the desk. "I'm putting you in two-ten, at the other end. I'll show you up if you want."

"Thanks, I can find it by myself."

I climbed the stairs that rose from the rear of the lobby. My legs were heavy. In the room, I took my .32 automatic out of my overnight bag and inserted one of the clips I had brought for it. The carpet in the dim corridor was threadbare, but it was thick enough to silence my footsteps.

There was still light in the corner room, spilling over through the open transom. A sleeper's heavy breathing came over, too, a long sighing choked off and then repeated. I tried the door. It was locked.

Sheila Howell spoke clearly from the darkness: "Who is that?"

I waited. She spoke again:

"John. Wake up."

"What is it?" His voice sounded nearer than hers.

"Somebody's trying to get in."

I heard the creak of bed springs, the pad of his feet. The brass doorknob rotated.

He jerked the door open, stepped out with his right fist cocked, saw me and started to swing, saw the gun and froze.

180

He was naked to the waist. His muscles stood out under his pale skin.

"Easy, boy. Raise your hands."

"This nonsense isn't necessary. Put the gun down."

"I'm giving the orders. Clasp your hands and turn around, walk slowly into the room."

He moved reluctantly, like stone forced into motion. When he turned, I saw the white scars down his back, hundreds of them, like fading cuneiform cuts.

Sheila was standing beside the rumpled bed. She had on a man's shirt which was too big for her. The shirt and the lipstick smudged on her mouth gave her a dissolute air.

"When did you two have time to get married?"

"We didn't. Not yet." A blush mounted like fire from her neck to her cheekbones. "This isn't what you think. John shared my room because I asked him to. I was frightened. And he slept across the foot of the bed, so there."

He made a quelling gesture with his raised hands. "Don't tell him anything. He's on your father's side. Anything we say he'll twist against us."

"I'm not the twister, Theo."

He turned on me, so suddenly I almost shot him. "Don't call me by that name."

"It belongs to you, doesn't it?"

"My name is John Galton."

"Come off it. Your partner, Sable, made a full confession to me yesterday afternoon."

"Sable is not my partner. He never was."

"Sable tells a different story, and he tells it very well. Don't get the idea that he's covering up for you. He'll be turning state's witness on the conspiracy charge to help him with the murder charge."

"Are you trying to tell me that Sable murdered Culligan?"

"It's hardly news to you, is it? You sat on the information while we were wasting weeks on a bum lead."

The girl stepped between us. "Please. You don't understand the situation. John had his suspicions of Mr. Sable, it's true, but he wasn't in any position to go to the police with them. He was under suspicion himself. Won't you put that awful gun away, Mr. Archer? Give John a chance to explain?"

Her blind faith in him made me angry. "His name isn't John. He's Theo Fredericks, a local boy who left Pitt some years ago after knifing his father."

181

"The Fredericks person is not his father."

"I have his mother's word for it."

"She's lying," the boy said.

"Everybody's lying but you, eh? Sable says you're a phony, and he ought to know."

"I let him think it. The fact is, when Sable first approached me I didn't know who I was. I went into the deal he offered me partly in the hope of finding out."

"Money had nothing to do with it?"

"There's more than money to a man's inheritance. Above everything else, I wanted to be sure of my identity."

"And now you are?"

"Now I am. I'm Anthony Galton's son."

"When did this fortunate revelation strike you?"

"You don't want a serious answer, but I'll give you one anyway. It grew on me gradually. I think it began when Gabe Lindsay saw something in me I didn't know was there. And then Dr. Dineen recognized me as my father's son. When my grandmother accepted me, too, I thought it must be true. I didn't know it was true until these last few days."

"What happened in the last few days?"

"Sheila believed me. I told her everything, my whole life, and she believed me."

He glanced at her, almost shyly. She reached for his hand. I began to feel like an intruder in their room. Perhaps he sensed this shift in the moral balance, because he began to talk about himself in a deeper, quieter tone:

"Actually, it goes back much further. I suspected the truth about myself, or part of it, when I was a little kid. Nelson Fredericks never treated me as if I belonged to him. He used to beat me with a belt-buckle. He never gave me a kind word. I knew he couldn't possibly be my father."

"A lot of boys feel like that about their real fathers."

Sheila moved closer to him, in a tender protective movement, pressing his hand unconsciously to her breast. "Please let him tell his story. I know it sounds wild, but it's only as wild as life. John's telling you the honest truth, so far as he knows it."

"Assuming that he is, how far does he know it? Some very earnest people have fantastic ideas about who they are and what they've got coming to them."

I expected him to flare up again. He surprised me by saying: "I know, it's what I was scared of, that I was hipped on the subject. I really used to be hipped when I was a boy. I

182

imagined I was the prince in the poorhouse, and so on. My mother encouraged me. She used to dress me up in velvet suits and tell me I was different from the other kids.

"Even before that, though, long before, she had a story that she used to tell me. She was a young woman then. I remember her face was thin, and her hair hadn't turned gray. I was only a toddler, and I used to think it was a fairytale. I realize now it was a story about myself. She wanted me to know about myself, but she was afraid to come right out with it.

"She said that I was a king's son, and we used to live in a palace in the sun. But the young king died and the bogeyman stole us away to the caves of ice where nothing was nice. She made a sort of rhyme of it. And she showed me a gold ring with a little red stone set in it that the king had left her for a remembrance."

He gave me a curious questioning look. Our eyes met solidly for the first time. I think the reality formed between us then.

"A ruby?" I said.

"It must have been. I talked to a woman named Matheson yesterday in Redwood City. You know her, don't you, and you've heard her story? It made sense of some of the things that had puzzled me, and it confirmed what Culligan told me long before. He said that my stepfather was an ex-convict whose real name was Fred Nelson. He had taken my mother out of a place called the Red Horse Inn and made her his—lover. She married my father after Nelson was sent to prison. But he escaped, and found them, and murdered my father." His voice had sunk almost out of hearing.

"When did Culligan tell you this?"

"The day I ran away with him. He'd just had a fight with Fredericks about his board bill. I listened to it from the cellar stairs. They were always fighting. Fredericks was older than Culligan, but he gave him an awful lacing, worse than usual, and left him unconscious on the kitchen floor. I poured water on Culligan's face and brought him to. It was then he told me that Fredericks killed my father. I got a butcher knife out of the drawer, and hid it upstairs in my room. When Fredericks tried to lock me in, I stabbed him in the guts.

"I thought I'd killed him. By the time I saw a newspaper and found out that I hadn't, I was across the border. I rode through the Detroit tunnel under the burlaps in an empty truck-trailer. The border police didn't find me, but they caught Culligan. I didn't see him again until last winter. Then he claimed that he'd been lying to me. He said that Fredericks had nothing to do with my father's death, that he'd simply blamed Fredericks to get back at him, through me.

"You can see why I decided to play along with Culligan and his scheme. I didn't know which of his stories was true, or if the truth was something else again. I even suspected that Culligan had killed my father himself. How else would he know about the murder?"

"He was involved in it," I said. "It's why he changed his story when he wanted to use you again. It's also the reason he couldn't admit to other people, even Sable, that he knew who you were."

"How was he involved?"

How wasn't he? I thought. His life ran through the case like a dirty piece of cord. He had marked Anthony Galton for the ax and Anthony Galton's murderer for the knife. He had helped a half-sane woman to lose her money, then sold her husband a half-sane dream of wealth. Which brought him to the ironic day when his half-realities came together in a final reality, and Gordon Sable killed him to preserve a lie.

"I don't understand," John said. "What did Culligan have to do with my father's death?"

"Apparently he was the finger man. Have you talked to your mother about the circumstances of the killing? She was probably a witness."

"She was more than that." The words almost strangled him. Sheila turned to him anxiously. "John?" she said. "Johnny?"

He made no response to her. His gaze was dark and inward:
"Even last night she was lying to me, trying to pretend that I was Fredericks's son, that I never had another father. She's stolen half my life away already. Isn't she satisfied?"

"You haven't seen Fredericks?"

"Fredericks has gone away, she wouldn't tell me where. But I'll find him."

"He can't be far. He was at home an hour ago."

"Damn you! Why didn't you say so?"

"I just did. I'm wondering now if I made a mistake."

John got the message. He didn't speak again until we were a few blocks from his mother's house. Then he turned in the seat and said across Sheila:

"Don't worry about me. There's been enough death and violence. I don't want any more of it."

184

Along the riverside street the rooftops thrust their dark angles up against a whitening sky. I watched the boy as he got out of the car. His face was pinched and pale as a revenant's. Sheila held his arm, slowing his abrupt movements.

I knocked on the front door. After a long minute, the door was unlocked from the inside. Mrs. Fredericks peered out at us.

"Yes? What now?"

John brushed past me, and faced her on the threshold:

"Where is he?"

"He went away."

"You're a liar. You've lied to me all your life." His voice broke, and then resumed on a different, higher note. "You knew he killed my father, you probably helped him. I know you helped him to hush it up. You left the country with him, changed your name when he did."

"I'm not denying that much," she said levelly.

His whole body heaved as if in nausea. He called her an ugly name. In spite of his promise to me, he was on the thin edge of violence. I laid one hand on his shoulder, heavily:

"Don't be too hard on your mother. Even the law admits mitigation, when a woman is dominated or threatened by a man."

"But that isn't the case. She's still trying to protect him."

"Am I?" the woman said. "Protect him from what?"

"From punishment for murder."

She shook her head solemnly. "It's too late for that, son. Fredericks has took his punishment. He said he would rather have digger get him than go back behind walls. Fredericks hung himself, and I didn't try to argue him out of doing it."

We found him in a back room on the second floor. He was on an old brass bed, in a half-sitting position. A piece of heavy electrical cord was tied to the head of the bed and wrapped several times around his neck. The free end of the cord was clenched in his right hand. There was no doubt that he had been his own executioner.

"Get Sheila out of here," I said to John.

She stood close to him. "I'm all right. I'm not afraid."

Mrs. Fredericks came into the doorway, heavy and panting. She looked at her son with her head up:

"This is the end of it. I told him it was him or you, and which it was going to be. I couldn't go on lying for him, and let you get arrested instead of him."

He faced her, still the accuser. "Why did you lie for so long? You stayed with him after he killed my father."

"You got no call to judge me for doing that. It was to save your life that I married him. I saw him cut off your daddy's head with an ax, fill it with stones, and chunk it in the sea. He said that if I ever told a living soul, that he would kill you, too. You were just a tiny baby, but that wouldn't of stopped him. He held up the bloody ax over your crib and made me swear to marry him and keep my lips shut forever. Which I have done until now."

"Did you have to spend the rest of your life with him?"

"That was my choice," she said. "For sixteen years I stood between you and him. Then you ran away and left me alone with him. I had nobody else left in my life excepting him. Do you understand what it's like to have nobody at all, son?"

He tried to speak, to rise to the word, but the gorgon past held him frozen.

"All I ever wanted in my life," she said, "was a husband and a family and a place I could call my own."

Sheila made an impulsive movement toward her. "You have us."

"Aw, no. You don't want me in your life. We might as well be honest about it. The less you see of me, the better you'll like it. Too much water flowed under the bridge. I don't blame my son for hating me."

"I don't hate you," John said. "I'm sorry for you, Mother. And I'm sorry for what I said."

"You and who else is sorry?" she said roughly. "You and who else?"

He put his arm around her, awkwardly, trying to comfort her. But she was past comforting, perhaps beyond sorrow, too. Whatever she felt was masked by unfeeling layers of flesh. The stiff black silk she was wearing curved over her breast like armor.

"Don't bother about me. Just take good care of your girl."

Somewhere outside, a single bird raised its voice for a few notes, then fell into abashed silence. I went to the window. The river was white. The trees and buildings on its banks were resuming their colors and shapes. A light went on in one of the other houses. As if at this human signal, the bird raised its voice again.

Sheila said: "Listen."

John turned his head to listen. Even the dead man seemed to be listening. THE END

186

THE BLUE HAMMER

To William Campbell Gault

I DROVE UP to the house on a private road that widened at the summit into a parking apron. When I got out of my car I could look back over the city and see the towers of the mission and the courthouse half submerged in smog. The channel lay on the other side of the ridge, partly enclosed by its broken girdle of islands.

The only sound I could hear, apart from the hum of the freeway which I had just left, was the noise of a tennis ball being hit back and forth. The court was at the side of the house, enclosed by high wire mesh. A thick-bodied man in shorts and a linen hat was playing against an agile blonde woman. Something about the trapped intensity of their game reminded me of prisoners in an exercise yard.

The man lost several points in a row and decided to notice my presence. Turning his back on the woman and the game, he came towards the fence.

'Are you Lew Archer?'

I said I was.

'You're late for our appointment.'

'I had some trouble finding your road.'

'You could have asked anybody in town. Everybody knows where Jack Biemeyer lives. Even the planes coming in use my home as a landmark.'

I could see why. The house was a sprawling pile of white stucco and red tile, set on the highest point in Santa Teresa. The only things higher were the mountains standing behind the city and a red-tailed hawk circling in the bright October sky.

The woman came up behind Biemeyer. She looked much younger than he did. Both her narrow blonde head and her pared-down middle-aged body seemed to be hyperconscious of my eyes. Biemeyer didn't introduce us. I told her who I was.

'I'm Ruth Biemeyer. You must be thirsty, Mr Archer. I know I am.'

'We won't go into the hospitality routine,' Biemeyer said. 'This man is here on business.'

'I know that. It was my picture that was stolen.'

'I'll do the talking, Ruth, if you don't mind.'

He took me into the house, his wife following us at a little distance. The air was pleasantly cool inside, though I could feel the weight of the structure surrounding me and hanging over me. It was more like a public building than a house—the kind of place where you go to pay your taxes or get a divorce.

We trekked to the far side of a big central room. Biemeyer pointed at a white wall, empty except for a pair of hooks on which he said the picture had been hung.

I got out my notebook and ball-point pen. 'When was it taken?'

'Yesterday.'

'That was when I first noticed that it was missing,' the woman said. 'But I don't come into this room every day.'

'Is the picture insured?'

'Not specifically,' Biemeyer said. 'Of course everything in the house is covered by some insurance.'

'Just how valuable is the picture?'

'It's worth a couple of thousand, maybe.'

'It's worth a lot more than that,' the woman said. 'Five or six times that, anyway. Chantry's prices have been appreciating.'

'I didn't know you'd been keeping track of them,' Biemeyer said in a suspicious tone. 'Ten or twelve thousand? Is that what you paid for that picture?'

'I'm not telling you what I paid for it. I bought it with my own money.'

'Did you have to do it without consulting me? I thought you'd gotten over being hipped on the subject of Chantry.'

She became very still. 'That's an uncalled-for remark. I haven't seen Richard Chantry in thirty years. He had nothing to do with my purchase of the picture.'

'I hear you saying so, anyway.'

Ruth Biemeyer gave her husband a quick bright look, as if she had taken a point from him in a harder game than tennis. 'You're jealous of a dead man.'

He let out a mirthless laugh. 'That's ridiculous on two counts. I know bloody well I'm not jealous, and I don't believe he's dead.'

The Biemeyers were talking as though they had forgotten me, but I suspected they hadn't. I was an unwilling referee who let them speak out on their old trouble without the danger that it would lead to something more immediate, like violence. In spite of his age Biemeyer looked and talked like a violent man, and I was getting tired of my passive role.

'Who is Richard Chantry?'

The woman looked at me in surprise. 'You mean you've never heard of him?'

'Most of the world's population have never heard of him,' Biemeyer said.

'That simply isn't true. He was already famous before he disappeared, and he wasn't even out of his twenties.'

Her tone was nostalgic and affectionate. I looked at her husband's face. It was red with anger, and his eyes were confused. I edged between them, facing his wife.

'Where did Richard Chantry disappear from?'

'From here,' she said. 'From Santa Teresa.'

'Recently?'

'No. It was over twenty-five years ago. He simply decided to walk away from it all. He was in search of new horizons, as he said in his farewell statement.'

'Did he make the statement to you, Mrs Biemeyer?'

'Not to me, no. He left a letter which his wife made public. I never saw Richard Chantry again after our early days in Arizona.'

'It's not for want of trying,' her husband said. 'You wanted me to retire here because this was Chantry's town. You got me to build a house right next to his house.'

'That isn't true, Jack. It was your idea to build here. I simply went along with it, and you know it.'

His face lost its flush and became suddenly pale. There was a stricken look in his eyes, as he realized that his mind had slipped a notch.

'I don't know anything any more,' he said in an old man's voice, and left the room.

His wife started after him and then turned back, pausing beside a window. Her face was hard with thought.

'My husband is a terribly jealous man.'

'Is that why he sent for me?'

'He sent for you because I asked him to. I want my picture back. It's the only thing I have of Richard Chantry's.'

I sat on the arm of a deep chair and reopened my notebook. 'Describe it for me, will you?'

'It's a portrait of a youngish woman, rather conventionalized. The colours are simple and bright, Indian colours. She has yellow hair, a red and black serape. Richard was very much influenced by Indian art in his early period.'

'Was this an early painting?'

'I don't really know. The man I bought it from couldn't date it.'

'How do you know it's genuine?'

'I think I can tell by looking at it. And the dealer vouched for its authenticity. He was close to Richard back in the Arizona days. He only recently came here to Santa Teresa. His name is Paul Grimes.'

'Do you have a photograph of the painting?'

'I haven't, but Mr Grimes has. I'm sure he'd let you have a look at it. He has a small gallery in the lower town.'

'I better talk to him first. May I use your phone?'

She led me into a room where her husband was sitting at an old rolltop desk. The scarred oak sides of the desk contrasted with the fine teakwood panelling that lined the walls. Biemeyer didn't look around. He was studying an aerial photograph that hung above the desk. It was a picture of the biggest hole in the ground I'd ever seen.

He said with nostalgic pride, 'That was my copper mine.'

'I've always hated that picture,' his wife said. 'I wish you'd take it down.'

'It bought you this house, Ruth.'

'Lucky me. Do you mind if Mr Archer uses the phone?'

'Yes. I do mind. There ought to be some place in a four-hundred-thousand-dollar building where a man can sit down in peace.'

He got up abruptly and left the room.

RUTH BIEMEYER leaned on the doorframe, exhibiting the profile of her body. It wasn't young any longer, but tennis and possibly anger had kept it thin and taut.

'Is your husband always like this?'

'Not always. He's worried these days.'

'About the missing picture?'

'That's part of it.'

'What's the rest?'

'It may be connected with the picture, as a matter of fact.' She hesitated. 'Our daughter, Doris, is an undergraduate at the university and it's brought her into contact with some people we wouldn't normally choose for her. You know how it is.'

'How old is Doris?'

'Twenty. She's a sophomore.'

'Living at home?'

'Unfortunately not. Doris moved out last month at the start of the fall semester. We got her an apartment in Academia Village on the edge of the campus. I wanted her to stay here, of course, but she said she had a right to her own life-style, just as Jack and I have a right to ours. She's always been very critical of Jack's drinking. Mine, too, if you want the exact truth.'

'Is Doris into drugs?'

'I wouldn't say that. Not deeply, anyway.' She was silent for a while, imagining her daughter's life, which seemed to frighten her. 'I'm not too crazy about some of the people she goes around with.'

'Anyone in particular?'

'There's a boy named Fred Johnson, whom she's brought to the house. Actually he's a pretty ancient boy; he must be at least thirty. He's one of those perpetual students who hang around the university because they like the atmosphere, or the pickings.'

'Do you suspect he could have stolen your picture?'

'I wouldn't put it that strongly. But he is interested in art. He's a docent at the art museum, and taking college courses in that field. He was familiar with Richard Chantry's name, in fact he seemed quite knowledgeable about him.'

'Wouldn't that be true of local art students in general?'

'I suppose so. But Fred Johnson showed unusual interest in the picture.'

'Can you give me a description of Fred Johnson?'

'I can try.'

I opened my notebook again and leaned on the rolltop desk. She sat in the swivel chair facing me.

'Colour of hair?'

'Reddish blond. He wears his hair quite long. It's already thinning a bit on top. But he compensates for that with his moustache. He has one of those big bristly shoebrush moustaches. His teeth aren't very good. His nose is too long.'

'What colour are his eyes? Blue?'

'More greenish. It's his eyes that really bother me. He never looks straight at you, at least he didn't at me.'

'Tall or short?'

'Medium size. Five foot nine, perhaps. Quite slender. On the whole he isn't bad-looking, if you like the type.'

'And Doris does?'

'I'm afraid so. She likes Fred Johnson much too well to suit me.'

'And Fred liked the missing picture?'

'He more than liked it. He was fascinated by it. He gave it a lot more attention than he gave my daughter. I sort of got the impression that he came here to visit the picture instead of her.'

'Did he say anything about it?'

She hesitated. 'He said something to the effect that it looked like one of Chantry's memory pictures. I asked him just what he meant. He said it was probably one of several Chantrys that hadn't been painted directly from a model, but from memory. He seemed to think that added to its rarity and its value.'

'Did he mention its value?'

'He asked me how much I paid for it. I wouldn't tell him
—that's my own little secret.'

'I can keep a secret.'

'So can I.' She opened the top drawer of the rolltop desk
and brought out a local telephone directory. 'You wanted to
call Paul Grimes, didn't you? Just don't try to get the price
out of him, either. I've sworn him to secrecy.'

I made a note of the dealer's number and his address in the
lower town. Then I called the number. A woman's voice
answered, faintly exotic, faintly guttural. She said that Grimes
was busy with a client but would be free shortly. I gave her
my name and said I would drop in later.

Ruth Biemeyer whispered urgently in my free ear, 'Don't
mention me to her.'

I hung up. 'Who is she?'

'I believe her name is Paola. She calls herself his secretary.
I think their relationship may be more intimate than that.'

'Where's her accent from?'

'Arizona. I believe she's part Indian.'

I glanced up at the picture of the hole that Jack Biemeyer
had made in the Arizona landscape. 'This seems to be turning
out to be an Arizona case. Didn't you say Richard Chantry
came from there?'

'Yes, he did. We all did. But we all ended up here in
California.'

Her voice was flat, betraying no regret for the state she had
left nor any particular pleasure with the state she lived in
now. She sounded like a disappointed woman.

'Why did you come to California, Mrs Biemeyer?'

'I suppose you're thinking about something my husband
said. That this is Dick Chantry's town, or was, and that was
why I wanted to settle here.'

'Is that true?'

'I suppose there's some truth in it. Dick was the only good
painter I ever knew really well. He taught me to see things.
And I liked the idea of living in the place where he did his
best work. He did it all in seven years, you know, and then he
disappeared.'

'When?'

'If you want the exact date of his departure, it was 4 July 1950.'

'Are you sure he went of his own accord? He wasn't murdered, or kidnapped?'

'He couldn't have been. He left a letter to his wife, remember.'

'Is she still in town?'

'Very much so. As a matter of fact you can see her house from our house. It's just across the barranca.'

'Do you know her?'

'I used to know Francine quite well, when we were young. She and I were never close, though. I've hardly seen her at all since we moved here. Why?'

'I'd like to have a look at the letter her husband left behind.'

'I have a copy. They sell photostats of it at the art museum.'

She went and got the letter. It was framed in silver. She stood above me reading it to herself. Her lips moved as if she was repeating a litany.

She handed it over with some reluctance. It was typewritten except for the signature and dated 4 July 1950, at Santa Teresa.

Dear Francine,

This is a letter of farewell. It breaks my heart to leave you, but I must. We have often talked about my need to discover new horizons beyond which I may find the light that never was on sea or land. This lovely coast and its history have told me what they had to tell me, as Arizona once did.

But as in Arizona the history is shallow and recent, and cannot support the major work that I was born to do. I must seek elsewhere for other roots, a more profound and cavernous darkness, a more searching light. And like Gauguin I have decided that I must seek it alone. For it is not just the physical world I have to explore, but the mines and chambers of my own soul.

I take nothing with me but the clothes on my back, my talent, and my memory of you. Please remember me with

affection, dear wife, dear friends, and wish me well. I only
do what I was born to do.

Richard Chantry

I handed the framed letter back to Ruth Biemeyer.

She held it against her body. 'It's beautiful, isn't it?'

'I'm not sure. Beauty is in the eye of the beholder. It must
have come as quite a shock to Chantry's wife.'

'She seems to have stood up to it very well.'

'Have you ever discussed it with her?'

'No. I have not.' I gathered from the sharpness of her tone
that she and Mrs Chantry were not friends. 'But she seems to
enjoy all that inherited fame. Not to mention the money he
left her.'

'Was Chantry suicidal? Did he ever talk about suicide?'

'No, of course not.' But she added after a silence, 'You must
remember I knew Dick when he was very young. I was even
younger. Actually I haven't seen him or talked to him for over
thirty years. But I've got a very strong feeling that he's still
alive.'

She touched her breast, as if at least he was alive there.
Droplets of sweat grew on her upper lip. She brushed them
away with her hand.

'I'm afraid this is getting me down a little. All of a sudden
the past rears up and smacks you. Just when I thought I
finally had it under control. Does that ever happen to you?'

'Not so much in the daytime. At night, just before I go to
sleep—'

'Aren't you married?' She was a quick woman.

'I was, about twenty-five years ago.'

'Is your wife still alive?'

'I hope so.'

'Haven't you tried to find out?'

'Not recently. I prefer to find out about other people's
lives. Right now I'd like to talk to Mrs Chantry.'

'I don't see why that's necessary.'

'Still I think I'll give it a try. She can help me fill in the
background.'

The woman's face stiffened with disapproval. 'But all I want you to do is get my picture back.'

'You also seem to want to tell me how to do it, Mrs Biemeyer. I've tried to work that way with other clients, and it didn't turn out too well.'

'Why do you want to talk to Francine Chantry? She isn't exactly a friend of ours, you know.'

'And I'm only supposed to interview your friends?'

'I didn't mean that.' She was silent for a moment. 'You plan to talk to several people, do you?'

'As many as I have to. This case looks a bit more complex to me than it does to you. It may take me several days, and cost you several hundred dollars.'

'Our credit is perfectly good.'

'I don't doubt that. What I'm not certain of is your and your husband's intentions.'

'Don't worry, I'll pay you if he doesn't.'

She took me outside and showed me the Chantry house. It was a turreted neo-Spanish mansion with several outbuildings, including a large greenhouse. It lay far down the hill from where we stood, on the other side of a barranca that separated the two estates like a deep wound in the earth.

III

I FOUND MY circuitous way to the bridge that crossed the barranca and parked in front of the Chantry house. A large hook-nosed man in a white silk shirt opened the door before I could knock. He stepped outside and shut the door behind him.

'What can I do for you?' He had the voice and look of a spoiled servant.

'I'd like to see Mrs Chantry.'

'She isn't here. I'll take a message for her if you want.'

'I'd like to speak to her personally.'

'What about?'

'I'll tell her, okay? If you'll tell me where she is.'

'I guess she's at the museum. This is her day for that.'

I decided to call on the dealer Paul Grimes first. I drove
along the waterfront towards the lower town. There were
white sails on the water, and gulls and terns in the air like
their small flying counterparts. I stopped on impulse and
checked in at a motel that faced the harbour.

The lower town was a blighted area standing above the
waterfront about ten blocks deep. There were blighted men
wandering along the main street or leaning against the fronts
of the secondhand stores.

Paul Grimes's shop was a block off the main street between
a liquor store and a soul-food restaurant. It wasn't impressive
—no more than a dingy stucco storefront with what looked
like living quarters above it. Inscribed across the front window
in gilt was the legend *Paul Grimes—Paintings and Decorations*. I
parked at the green curb in front of it.

A bell tinkled over the door as I went in. The interior had
been disguised with painted plyboard screens and grey cloth
hangings. A few tentative-looking pictures had been attached
to them. On one side a dark woman in a loose multicoloured
costume sat behind a cheap desk and tried to look busy.

She had deep black eyes, prominent cheekbones, prominent
breasts. Her long hair was unflecked black. She was very
handsome, and quite young.

I told her my name. 'Mr Grimes is expecting me.'

'I'm sorry, he had to go out.'

'When will he be back?'

'He didn't say. I think he was going out of town on business.'

'Are you his secretary?'

'You could call me that.' Her smile was like the flash of a
half-concealed knife. 'You the man that called about a picture?'

'Yes.'

'I can show you some pictures.' She gestured towards those
on display. 'Most of these are pretty abstract, but we have
some representational ones in the back.'

'Do you have any of Richard Chantry's paintings?'

'I don't think so. No.'

'Mr Grimes sold a Chantry painting to some people named Biemeyer. They told me he could show me a photograph of it.'

'I wouldn't know about that.'

She spread her hands in front of her, palms upward, and her loose sleeves fell away from her round brown arms. The light growth of hair on her arms looked like clinging smoke.

'Can you give me Mr Grimes's home address?'

'He lives upstairs. He isn't in.'

'When do you expect him back?'

'I wouldn't know. Sometimes he goes away for a week. He doesn't tell me where he's going, and I don't ask him.'

I thanked her and went into the liquor store next door. The middle-aged black man behind the counter asked if he could help me.

'I hope so. Do you know Mr Grimes?'

'Who?'

'Paul Grimes, the art dealer in the next building.'

'Older man with a grey goatee?' He shaped a pointed beard with his fingers. 'Wears a white sombrero?'

'That sounds like Mr Grimes.'

He shook his head. 'Can't say I know him. I don't believe he drinks. Never does any business with me, anyway.'

'What about his girl?'

'She came in for a six-pack once or twice. Paola, I think her name is. Has she got Indian blood, do you know?'

'I wouldn't be surprised.'

'I thought so.' The idea seemed to please him. 'She's a sharp-looking chick. I don't know how a man his age holds on to a chick like that.'

'Neither do I. I'd like to know when Mr Grimes gets back here.' I put two dollar bills on the counter between us and laid one of my cards on top of them. 'Could I check back with you?'

'Why not?'

I drove up the main street to the chaste white building that housed the art museum. The young man at the turnstile said that Fred Johnson had left the building an hour or so before.

'Did you wish to see him about a personal matter? Or something connected with the museum?'

'I understand he's interested in the painter Richard Chantry.'

His smile brightened. 'We all are. Are you from out of town, sir?'

'Los Angeles.'

'Have you seen our permanent Chantry collection?'

'Not yet.'

'You came at a good time. Mrs Chantry is here now. She gives us one afternoon a week.'

He directed me through a room where a group of classical sculptures stood pale and serene, to a quite different kind of room. The first pictures I looked at resembled windows into an alternative world, like the windows that jungle travellers use to watch the animals at night. But the animals in Chantry's paintings seemed to be on the verge of becoming human. Or perhaps they were human beings devolving into animals.

A woman came into the room behind me and answered my unspoken question:

'These are known as the Creation pictures—the artist's imaginative conception of evolution. They represent his first great creative burst. He painted them in a period of six months, incredible as it may seem.'

I turned to look at the woman. In spite of her conservative dark blue suit and her rather stilted patter, she gave an impression of rough strength. Her chastely trimmed greying hair seemed to glisten with vitality.

'Are you Mrs Chantry?'

'Yes.' She seemed pleased to be recognized. 'I really shouldn't be here. I'm giving a party tonight. But it's hard for me to stay away from the museum on my day.'

She led me to a farther wall on which were hung a series of figure studies of women. One of them stopped me. A young woman was sitting on a rock that was partly hidden, as she was, by a buffalo robe around her waist. Her fine breasts and shoulders were bare. Behind her and above her in the picture, the mounted head of a buffalo bull hung in space.

'He called it *Europa*,' Mrs Chantry said.

I turned to her. She was smiling. I looked again at the girl in the picture.

'Is that you?'

'In a sense. I used to model for Richard.'

We looked at each other more sharply for a moment. She was about my age or a little younger, with *Europa*'s body holding firm under her blue suit. I wondered what kind of compulsion, what pride in her husband or in herself, made her serve as a museum guide to his pictures.

'Had you ever seen any of his paintings before? They seemed to take you by surprise.'

'They did. They do.'

'His work has that effect on most people seeing it for the first time. Tell me, what got you interested in it?'

I told her I was a private detective employed by the Biemeyers to investigate the theft of their picture. I wanted to get her reaction.

She went pale under her make-up. 'The Biemeyers are ignorant people. That picture they bought from Paul Grimes is a fake. He offered it to me long before they saw it. I wouldn't touch it. It's an obvious imitation of a style which Richard abandoned long ago.'

'How long ago?'

'About thirty years. It belonged to his Arizona period. Paul Grimes may have painted it himself.'

'Does Grimes have that kind of a reputation?'

I'd asked her one question too many. 'I can't discuss his reputation with you, or anyone. He was Richard's friend and teacher in the Arizona days.'

'But not a friend of yours?'

'I prefer not to go into that. Paul was helpful to my husband when it counted. But people change over the years. Everything changes.' She looked around her, scanning her husband's paintings as if even they had become unfamiliar, like half-remembered dreams. 'I try to guard my husband's reputation, keep the canon pure. All sorts of people try to cash in on his work.'

'Would Fred Johnson be one of them?'

The question seemed to surprise her. She shook her head, setting her hair swinging like a flexible grey bell.

'Fred is fascinated by my husband's work. But I wouldn't

say he's trying to cash in on it.' She was silent for a moment. 'Did Ruth Biemeyer accuse him of stealing her lousy picture?'

'His name came up.'

'Well, it's nonsense. Even if he were dishonest, which he shows no signs of being, Fred has too much taste to be taken in by a poor imitation like that.'

'I'd still like to talk to him. Do you happen to know where he lives?'

'I can find out.' She went into the front office and came out a minute later. 'Fred lives with his parents at 2024 Olive Street. Be nice to him. He's a sensitive young man, and a very great Chantry enthusiast.'

I thanked her for the information. She thanked me for my interest in her husband. She seemed to be playing a complex role, part salesperson and part guardian of a shrine, and part something else. I couldn't help wondering if the undefinable part was an angry widowed sexuality.

IV

THE JOHNSON house was one of a block of three-storey frame houses that appeared to date from the early years of the century. The olive trees that gave the street its name were even older. Their leaves looked like tarnished silver in the afternoon sunlight.

This part of the city was a mixed neighbourhood of rooming houses and private residences, doctors' offices and houses half-converted into offices. A large modern hospital, whose fenestration made it look like a giant honeycomb, rose in the middle of the area and seemed to have absorbed most of its energy.

The Johnson house was particularly run-down. Some of its boards were loose, and it needed paint. It stood like a grey and gabled ghost of a house in a yard choked with yellow grass and brown weeds.

I rattled the rusty screen door with my fist. The house seemed to stir into slow, reluctant life. I could hear lagging footsteps coming down the inside stairs.

A heavy old man opened the door and peered out at me through the screen. He had dirty grey hair and a short growth of moth-eaten grey beard. His voice was querulous.

'What's up?'

'I'd like to see Fred.'

'I don't know if he's home. I've been sacked out.' He leaned towards me, his face against the screen, and I could smell wine on his breath. 'What do you want with Fred?'

'Just to talk to him.'

His red little eyes scanned me up and down. 'What do you want to talk to him about?'

'I'd prefer to tell Fred.'

'You better tell me. My son is a busy young man. His time is worth money. Fred's got expertise'—he rolled the word on his tongue—'and that's worth more money.'

The old man was probably out of wine, I thought, and getting ready to put the bite on me. A woman in a nurse's uniform came out from under the stairs. She carried herself with a certain clumsy authority, but her voice was small and girlish.

'I'll talk to the man, Gerard. You don't have to trouble your poor head with Fred's comings and goings.'

She laid her open hand against the furred side of his face, peered sharply into his eyes like a diagnostician, and gave him a little slap of dismissal. He didn't argue with her but made his way back up the stairs.

'I'm Mrs Johnson,' she said to me. 'Fred's mother.'

She had grey-streaked black hair drawn back from a face whose history and meaning were obscured, like her husband's face, by an inert layer of flesh. Her heavy body was strictly girdled, though, and her white uniform was clean.

'Is Fred here?'

'I don't believe so.' She looked past me into the street. 'I don't see the car.'

'When do you expect him back?'

'It's hard to say. Fred is a student at the university.' She reported the fact as if it were the one great pride of her life. 'They keep shifting his class hours around, and he works part-time besides at the art museum. They really depend on him there. Was it anything I could help you with?'

'It may be. Is it all right if I come in?'

'I'll come *out*,' she said brightly. 'The house isn't fit to be seen on the inside. Since I went back to full-time nursing, I haven't had the time to keep it up.'

She removed a heavy key from the inside keyhole and used it to lock the door as she came out. It made me wonder if she kept her husband under lock and key when he had been drinking.

She led me off the porch and looked up at the peeling façade of the house. 'It isn't fit to be seen on the outside, either. But I can't help that. The house belongs to the clinic—all these houses do—and they're planning to tear them down next year. This whole side of the street is going to be a parking lot.' She sighed. 'I don't know where we're going to go from here, with rents going up the way they are, and my husband no better than an invalid.'

'I'm sorry to hear that.'

'About Jerry, you mean? Yeah, I'm sorry, too. He used to be a fine strong man. But he had a nervous breakdown a while ago—it all goes back to the war—and he's never been the same since. And of course he has a drinking problem, too. So many of them do,' she added meditatively.

I liked the woman's candour, even though it sounded slightly carnivorous. I wondered idly how it was that nurses so often ended up with invalid husbands.

'So what's your problem?' she said in a different tone.

'No problem. I'd simply like to talk to Fred.'

'What about?'

'A picture.'

'That's his field, all right. Fred can tell you anything you want to know about pictures.' But she dropped the subject suddenly, as though it frightened her, and said in still a third voice, hesitant and low, 'Is Fred in some kind of trouble?'

'I hope not, Mrs Johnson.'

'So do I. Fred is a good boy. He always has been. I ought to know, I'm his mother.' She gave me a long dubious look. 'Are you a policeman?'

I had been when I was younger, and apparently it still showed to a cop-sensitive eye. But I had my story ready: 'I'm a journalist. I'm thinking of doing a magazine piece on the artist Richard Chantry.'

Her face and body tightened as if in response to a threat. 'I see.'

'I understand your son is an expert on Chantry.'

'I wouldn't know about that,' she said. 'Fred is interested in a lot of different artists. He's going to make that his career.'

'As a dealer?'

'That's what he'd like to be. But it takes capital. And we don't even own the house we live in.'

She looked up at the tall grey house as if it were the source of all her trouble. From a window high up under the roof, her husband was watching us like a prisoner in a tower. She made a pushing gesture with her open hand, as if she were putting the shot. Johnson receded into the dimness.

'I'm haunted by the thought,' she said, 'that he'll tumble out of one of those windows. The poor man never got over his war injuries. Sometimes, when it takes him really bad, he falls right down on the floor. I keep wondering if I ought to put him back in the veterans' hospital. But I don't have the heart to. He's so much happier here with us. Fred and I would really miss him. And Fred is the kind of boy who needs a father.'

Her words were full of feeling, but the voice in which she said them was emotionless. Her eyes were peering coldly into mine, assessing my reaction. I guessed that she was afraid for her son, trying in a hurry to put together a protective family nest.

'Where can I find Fred, do you know?'

'I *don't* know. He may be out on campus, or he could be down at the art museum, or any place in town. He's a very busy young man, and he keeps moving. He'll be taking his degree next spring, if all goes well. And it will.'

She nodded emphatically several times. But there seemed to be a stubborn hopelessness in the gesture, like a woman knocking her head against a wall.

As if in response, an old blue Ford sedan came down the

street past the hospital. It slowed as it approached us, turning
in towards the curb behind my car. The young man behind the
wheel had long hair and a moustache, both reddish blond.

Out of the corner of my eye I saw Mrs Johnson shake her
head, once, in such a short arc that she hardly seemed to have
moved. The young man's eyes flickered. Without having
brought it to a full stop, he turned the Ford back in to the
road, barely missing my left rear fender. The car accelerated
sluggishly, leaving a trail of oil smoke on the air.

'Is that Fred, Mrs Johnson?'

She answered after a brief hesitation: 'That's Fred. I
wonder where he thinks he's going.'

'You signalled him not to stop.'

'*I* did? You must be seeing things.'

I left her standing there and followed the blue Ford. It
caught a yellow light at the entrance to the freeway and
turned off to the right in the direction of the university. I sat
behind a long red light and watched the spoor of oil smoke
dissipating, mixing with the general smog that overlay this
part of the city.

When the light changed, I drove on out to the campus,
where Fred's friend Doris Biemeyer lived.

V

THE UNIVERSITY had been built on an elevated spur of land
that jutted into the sea and was narrowed at its base by a tidal
slough. Almost surrounded by water and softened by blue
haze, it looked from the distance like a medieval fortress
town.

Close up, the buildings shed this romantic aspect. They
were half-heartedly modern, cubes and oblongs and slabs that
looked as if their architect had spent his life designing business
buildings. The parking attendant at the entrance told me that
the student village was on the north side.

I followed a winding road along the edge of the campus,
looking for Fred Johnson. There weren't many students in

sight. Still the place seemed crowded and jumbled, like something thrown at a map in the hope that it would stick there.

Academia Village was even more haphazard than the campus proper. Loose dogs and loose students roamed the narrow streets in about equal numbers. The buildings ranged from hamburger stands and tiny cottages and duplexes to giant apartment buildings. The Sherbourne, where Doris Biemeyer lived, was one of the big ones. It was six storeys high and occupied most of a block.

I found a parking place behind a camper painted to simulate a log cabin on wheels. No sign of the old blue Ford. I went into the Sherbourne and took an elevator to the third floor.

The building was fairly new but its interior smelled old and used. It was crowded with the odours of rapid generations, sweat and perfume and pot and spices. If there were human voices they were drowned out by the music from several competing sources along the third-floor hallway, which sounded like the voices of the building's own multiple personality.

I had to knock several times on the door of Apartment 304. The girl who opened the door looked like a smaller version of her mother, prettier but vaguer and less sure of herself.

'Miss Biemeyer?'

'Yes?'

Her eyes looked past me at something just beyond my left shoulder. I sidestepped and looked behind me, half expecting to be hit. But there was nobody there.

'May I come in and talk to you for a minute?'

'I'm sorry. I'm meditating.'

'What are you meditating about?'

'I don't really know.' She giggled softly and touched the side of her head, where her light hair hung straight like raw silk. 'It hasn't come together yet. It hasn't materialized, you know?'

She looked as though she hadn't quite materialized, herself. She had the kind of blondeness you can almost see through. She swayed gently like a curtain at a window. Then she lost her balance and fell quite hard against the doorframe.

I took hold of both her arms and pulled her upright. Her hands were cold, and she seemed slightly dazed. I wondered what she had swallowed or sipped or imbibed.

With one arm around her shoulders, I propelled her into her living-room. On its far side a screen door opened on a balcony. The room was almost as bare as a coolie's hut: a few plain chairs, a pallet on a metal frame, a card table, fibre mats. The only decoration was a large butterfly made of spangled red tissue paper on a wire skeleton. It was almost as big as she was, and it hung on a string from the central ceiling fixture and very slowly rotated.

She sat on one of the floor mats and looked up at the paper butterfly. Under the long cotton gown, which seemed to be her only garment, she tried to arrange her legs and feet in the lotus position, and failed.

'Did you make the butterfly, Doris?'

She shook her head. 'No. I don't make things. It was one of the decorations at the dance when I got out of boarding school. It was my mother's idea to hang it in here. I hate it.' Her soft little voice seemed out of sync with the movements of her mouth. 'I don't feel very well.'

I went down on one knee beside her. 'What have you been taking?'

'Just some pills to calm my nerves. They help me meditate.' She began to struggle again with her feet and knees, trying to force them into position. The soles of her feet were dirty.

'What kind of pills?'

'The red ones. Just a couple. The trouble with me is I haven't eaten, not since some time yesterday. Fred said he'd bring me something to eat from home, but I guess his mother won't let him. She doesn't like me—she wants Fred all to herself.' The girl added in her gentle sibilant voice, 'She can go to hell and copulate with spiders.'

'What about your own mother, Doris?'

She let go of her feet. Her legs straightened out in front of her. She pulled her long dress down over them.

'What about her?' she said.

'If you need food or any kind of help, can't you get it from her?'

She shook her head with sudden startling violence. Her hair streamed over her eyes and mouth. She flung it back in an angry two-handed movement, like someone peeling off a rubber mask.

'I don't want her kind of help. She wants to take away my freedom—lock me up in a nursing home and throw away the key.' She got up clumsily on to her knees, so that her blue eyes were on a level with mine. 'Are you a shrink?'

'Not me.'

'Are you sure? She threatened to turn the shrinks loose on me. I almost wish she would—I could tell them a thing or two.' She nodded vengefully, chopping at the air with her soft chin.

'Like what?'

'Like the only thing they ever did in their lives was fight and argue. They built themselves that great big hideous house and all they ever did was fight in it. When they weren't giving each other the silent treatment.'

'What were they fighting about?'

'A woman named Mildred—that was one of the things. But the basic thing was they didn't—they don't love each other, and they blamed each other for that. Also they blamed me, at least they acted that way. I don't remember much of what happened when I was a little girl. But one of the things I do remember is their yelling at each other over my head—yelling like crazy giants without any clothes on, with me in between them. And he was sticking out about a foot. She picked me up and took me into the bathroom and locked the door. He broke the door down with his shoulder. He went around with his arm in a sling for a long time after that. And,' she added softly, 'I've been going around with my mind in a sling.'

'Downers won't cure that.'

She narrowed her eyes and stuck out her lower lip like a stubborn child on the verge of tears. 'Nobody asked you for your advice. You are a shrink, aren't you?' She sniffed. 'I can smell the dirt on you, from people's dirty secrets.'

I produced what felt from the inside like a lopsided smile. The girl was young and foolish, perhaps a little addled, by her own admission drugged. But she was young, and had clean hair. I hated to smell dirty to her.

I stood up and lightly hit my head on the paper butterfly.

I went to the screen door and looked out across the balcony. Through the narrow gap between two apartment buildings I could see a strip of bright sea. A trimaran crossed it, running before a light wind.

The room seemed dim when I turned back to it, a transparent cube of shadow full of obscure life. The paper butterfly seemed to move in some sort of actual flight. The girl rose and stood swaying under it.

'Did my mother send you here?'

'Not exactly. I've talked to your mother.'

'And I suppose she told you all the terrible things I've done. What a rotten egg I am. What a rotten ego.' She giggled nervously.

'No. She is worried about you, though.'

'About me and Fred?'

'I think so.'

She nodded, and her head stayed down. 'I'm worried about us, too, but not for the same reason. She thinks that Fred and I are lovers or something. But I don't seem to be able to relate to people. The closer I get to them, the colder I feel.'

'Why?'

'They scare me. When he—when my father broke down the bathroom door, I climbed into the laundry hamper and pulled the lid down on top of me. I'll never forget the feeling it gave me, like I was dead and buried and safe for ever.'

'Safe?'

'They can't kill you after you're dead.'

'What are you so afraid of, Doris?'

She looked up at me from under her light brows. 'People.'

'Do you feel that way about Fred?'

'No, I'm not afraid of him. He makes me terribly mad sometimes. He makes me want to—' she bit off the sentence. I could hear her teeth grind together.

'Makes you want to what?'

She hesitated, her face taut, listening to the secret life behind it. 'Kill him, I was going to say. But I didn't really mean it. Anyway, what would be the use? Poor old Fred is dead and buried already, the way I am.'

I felt an angry desire to disagree, to tell her that she was too pretty and young to be talking in that way. But she was a witness, and it was best not to argue with her.

'What happened to Fred?'

'A lot of things. He comes from a poor family and it took him half his life just to get where he is now, which is practically nowhere. His mother's some kind of a nurse, but she's fixated on her husband. He was crippled in the war and doesn't do much of anything. Fred was meant to be an artist or something like that, but I'm afraid he's never going to make it.'

'Has Fred been in trouble?'

Her face closed. 'I didn't say that.'

'I thought you implied it.'

'Maybe I did. Everybody's been in some kind of trouble.'

'What kind has Fred been in?'

She shook her head. 'I'm not going to tell you. You'd go back to my mother with it.'

'No, I wouldn't.'

'Yes, you would.'

'You care about Fred, don't you?'

'I've got a right to care about somebody in this world. He's a nice boy—a nice man.'

'Sure he is. Did the nice man steal the nice picture from your nice parents?'

'You don't have to get sarcastic.'

'But I do sometimes. It comes from everybody being so nice. You haven't answered my question, Doris. Did Fred steal the picture?'

She shook her head. 'It wasn't stolen.'

'You mean it climbed down off the wall and walked away?'

'No. I don't mean that.' Tears overflowed her eyes and ran down her face. 'I took it.'

'Why?'

'Fred told me—Fred asked me to.'

'Did he give a reason?'

'He had a good reason.'

'What reason?'

'He told me not to tell anybody.'

'Did Fred keep the picture?'

'I guess he did. He hasn't brought it back yet.'

'Did he say he was going to bring it back?'

'Yes, and he will, too. He wanted to make an examination of it, he said.'

'An examination for what?'

'To see if it was genuine.'

'Did he think it was a fake?'

'He wanted to find out.'

'Did he have to steal it to do that?'

'He didn't steal it. I let him take it. And you're not very nice.'

VI

I WAS BEGINNING to agree with her. I left her and walked down the stairs and out to my car. For over an hour, while the afternoon shadows of the buildings lengthened across me, I sat and watched the main entrance of the Sherbourne.

There was a natureburger place in a geodesic dome up the block, and now and then the uncertain wind brought me the smell of food. Eventually I went and had a natureburger. The atmosphere in the place was dim and inert. The bearded young customers made me think of early cave men waiting for the ice age to end.

I was back in my car when Fred Johnson finally came. He parked his blue Ford directly behind me and looked up and down the street. He went into the Sherbourne and took the elevator up. I took the stairs, fast. We met in the third-floor hallway. He was wearing a green suit and a wide yellow tie.

He tried to retreat into the elevator, but its door closed in his face and it started down. He turned to face me. He was pale and wide-eyed.

'What do you want?'

'The picture you took from the Biemeyers.'

'What picture?'

'You know what picture. The Chantry.'

'I didn't take it.'

'Maybe not. But it came into your hands.'

He looked past me down the hall towards the girl's room. 'Did Doris tell you that?'

'We could leave Doris out of this. She's in enough trouble now, with her parents and with herself.'

He nodded as if he understood and agreed. But his eyes had a separate life of their own, and were searching for a way out. He looked to me like one of those tired boys who go from youth to middle age without passing through manhood.

'Who are you, anyway?'

'I'm a private detective.' I told him my name. 'The Biemeyers hired me to reclaim their picture. Where is it, Fred?'

'I don't know.'

He wagged his head despondently. As if I had taken hold of his head and squeezed it with my hands, clear drops of sweat stood out on his forehead.

'What happened to it, Fred?'

'I took it home, I admit that. I had no intention of stealing it. I only wanted to study it.'

'When did you take it home?'

'Yesterday.'

'Where is it now?'

'I don't know. Honestly. Somebody must have stolen it from my room.'

'From the house on Olive Street?'

'Yes, sir. Somebody broke into the house and stole it while I was sleeping. It was there when I went to bed and when I woke up it was gone.'

'You must be a heavy sleeper.'

'I guess I am.'

'Or a heavy liar.'

His slender body was shaken by a flurry of shame or anger. I thought he was going to take a swing at me, and I set myself for that. But he made a dash for the stairs. I was too slow to head him off. By the time I got down to the street, he was driving away in his old blue Ford.

I bought a natureburger in a paper bag and took the elevator back up to the third floor. Doris let me into her apartment, looking disappointed that it was me.

I handed her the sandwich. 'Here's something to eat.'

'I'm not hungry. Fred promised to bring me something, anyway.'

'You better eat that. Fred may not be coming today.'

'But he said he would.'

'He may be in trouble, Doris, about that picture.'

Her hand closed, squeezing the sandwich in the bag. 'Are my parents trying to get him?'

'I wouldn't put it that strongly.'

'You don't know my parents. They'll make him lose his job at the museum. He'll never become a college graduate. And all because he tried to do them a favour.'

'I don't quite follow that.'

She nodded her head emphatically. 'He was trying to authenticate their painting. He wanted to examine the paint for age. If it was fresh paint, it would probably mean that it wasn't genuine.'

'Wasn't a genuine Chantry?'

'That's correct. Fred thought when he first looked at it that it wasn't genuine. At least he wasn't sure. And he doesn't trust the man my parents bought it from.'

'Grimes?'

'That's right. Fred said he has a bad reputation in art circles.'

I wondered what kind of a reputation Fred was going to have, now that the picture had been stolen. But there was no use worrying the girl about it. The meaning of her face was still as diffuse as a cloud. I left her with her dilapidated sandwich and drove back down along the freeway to the lower town.

The door of Paul Grimes's shop was locked. I knocked and got no answer. I rattled the knob and raised my voice. No answer. Peering into the dim interior, I could see nothing but emptiness and shadows.

I went into the liquor store and asked the black man if he had seen Paola.

'She was out in front an hour or so ago, loading some pictures into her van. As a matter of fact, I helped her.'

'What kind of pictures?'

'Framed pictures. Weird junk, gobs of colour. I like a picture to look like something real. No wonder they couldn't sell 'em.'

'How do you know they couldn't sell 'em?'

'It stands to reason. She said they were giving up on the shop.'

'Was Paul Grimes with her—the man with the beard?'

'Nope, he didn't show. I haven't seen him since I saw you.'

'Did Paola say where she was going?'

'I didn't ask. She took off in the direction of Montevista.' He pointed south-west with his thumb.

'What kind of a van is she driving?'

'Old yellow Volkswagen. Is she in some kind of trouble?'

'No. I wanted to talk to her about a picture.'

'To buy?'

'Maybe.'

He looked at me incredulously. 'You like that kind of stuff?'

'Sometimes.'

'Too bad. If they knew they had a buyer, they might of stayed in business to accommodate you.'

'They might. Will you sell me two half-pints of Tennessee whisky?'

'Why not a whole pint? It's cheaper that way.'

'Two half-pints are better.'

VII

ON MY WAY uptown I stopped at the art museum, intending to ask for Fred. But the place was closed for the night.

I drove on up to Olive Street. Darkness had spread like a branching tree across the lawns and yards, and lights were coming on in the old houses. The hospital was a great pierced box of light. I parked near the gabled house where the Johnsons lived and made my way up its broken steps to the front door.

Fred's father must have been listening on the other side of

the door. He spoke before I had a chance to knock: 'Who is that?'

'Archer. I was here earlier today, looking for Fred.'

'That's right. I remember.' He sounded proud of the feat.

'May I come in and talk to you for a minute, Mr Johnson?'

'Sorry, no can do. My wife locked the door.'

'Where's the key?'

'Sarah took it with her to the hospital. She's afraid I'll go out in the street and get run over. But the fact is I'm completely sober. I'm so sober that it's making me physically sick. She's supposed to be a nurse, but little does she care.' His voice was fogged with self-pity.

'Is there any way you can let me in? Through a window, maybe?'

'She'd crucify me.'

'How would she know? I've got some whisky with me. Could you use a couple of snorts?'

His tone brightened. 'Could I not. But how are you going to get in?'

'I have some keys.'

It was a simple old lock, and the second key that I tried opened it. I closed the door behind me, moving into the cramped hallway with some difficulty. Johnson's thick body crowded mine. In the light of a dim overhead bulb, I could see that his face was working with excitement.

'You said you had some whisky for me.'

'Hold on for a minute.'

'But I'm sick. You can see that I'm sick.'

I opened one of my half-pint bottles. He drained it in one continuous shuddering swallow, and licked the mouth of the empty bottle.

I felt like a pander. But the strong jolt of whisky didn't seem to bother him at all. Instead of making him drunker, it seemed to improve his diction and delivery.

'I used to drink Tennessee whisky in my palmy days. I drank Tennessee whisky and rode a Tennessee Walking Horse. That is Tennessee whisky, is it not?'

'You're right, Mr Johnson.'

'Just call me Jerry. I know a friend when I see one.' He set down the empty bottle on the first step of the staircase, put his hand on my shoulder, and leaned his weight on it. 'I won't forget this. What did you say your name was?'

'Archer.'

'And what do you do for a living, Mr Archer?'

'I'm a private investigator.' I opened my wallet and showed Johnson a photostat of my state licence. 'Some people in town hired me to trace a painting that they lost. It's a portrait of a woman, probably by a well-known local painter named Richard Chantry. You've heard of him, I suppose.'

He scowled with concentration. 'I can't say I have. You should take it up with my son Fred. That's his department.'

'I already have. Fred took the picture and brought it home.'

'Here?'

'So he told me this afternoon.'

'I don't believe it. Fred wouldn't do a thing like that. He's a good boy, he always has been. He never stole anything in his life. The people at the art museum trust him. Everybody trusts him.'

I interrupted Johnson's alcoholic flow of words: 'He claims he didn't steal it. He said he brought it home to make some tests on it.'

'What kind of tests are you talking about?'

'I'm not sure. According to Fred, his idea was to find out how old the picture was. The artist who was supposed to have painted it disappeared a long time ago.'

'Who was that?'

'Richard Chantry.'

'Yeah, I guess I have heard of him. They've got a lot of his pictures in the museum.' He rubbed his grey scalp as if to warm his memory. 'Isn't he supposed to be dead?'

'Dead or missing. One way or the other, he's been gone for twenty-five years. If the paint on the picture is comparatively fresh, he probably didn't paint it.'

'Sorry, I don't quite follow that.'

'It doesn't matter. The point is that Fred brought the picture here, and he says it was stolen from his room last night.

Do you know anything about that?'

'Hell, no.' His whole face wrinkled as if old age had fallen on him suddenly. 'You think I took it?'

'I don't mean that at all.'

'I hope not. Fred would kill me if I touched any of his sacred things. I'm not even supposed to go into his room.'

'What I'm trying to find out—did Fred say anything about a painting being stolen from his room last night?'

'Not that I know of.'

'Did you see him this morning?'

'I certainly did. I dished up his porridge for him.'

'And he didn't mention the missing painting?'

'No, sir. Not to me.'

'I'd like to take a look at Fred's room. Would it be possible?'

The suggestion seemed to frighten him. 'I don't know. I don't think so. *She* hates to have anybody in her house. She'd even like to get rid of me if she could.'

'Didn't you say she's gone to the hospital?'

'That's right, she went to work.'

'Then how would she know?'

'I don't know *how* she knows, but she always does. I guess she worms it out of me or something. It's *hard* on me, hard on my nerves.' He giggled shamefacedly. 'You wouldn't have any more of that Tennessee walking whisky?'

I got out the other half-pint and showed it to him. He reached for it. I held it away from him.

'Let's go upstairs, Jerry. Then I'll leave this with you.' I put it back in my pocket.

'I don't know.'

He glanced up the stairs as if his wife might be there listening. She wasn't, of course, but her invisible presence seemed to fill the house. Johnson was trembling with fear of her, or with desire for the whisky.

The desire won out. He switched on a light and led me up the stairs. The second floor was in much poorer condition than the first. The ancient paper on the walls was discoloured and peeling. The carpetless floor was splintered. A panel was missing from one of the bedroom doors, and had been replaced with the side of a cardboard carton.

I had seen worse houses in the slums and barrios, places that looked as if a full-scale infantry battle had passed through them. The Johnsons' house was the scene of a less obvious disaster. But it suddenly seemed quite possible to me that the house had hatched a crime; perhaps Fred had stolen the picture in the hope of improving his life.

I felt a certain sympathy for Fred. It would be hard to come back to this house from the Biemeyers' house, or from the art museum.

Johnson opened the door with the missing panel and switched on a light that hung by a cord from the ceiling.

'This is Fred's little room.'

It contained an iron single bed covered with a US Army blanket, a bureau, a torn canvas deck chair, a bookcase almost full of books, and in one corner by the blinded window an old kitchen table with various tools arranged on it, hammers and shears and saws of varying sizes, sewing equipment, pots of glue and paint.

The light over the bed was still swinging back and forth, its reflection climbing the walls alternately. For a moment, I had the feeling that the whole house was rocking on its foundations. I reached up and held the light still. There were pictures on the walls, modern classics like Monet and Modigliani, most of them cheap reproductions that looked as though they had been clipped from magazines. I opened the closet door. It contained a jacket and a couple of shirts on hangers, and a pair of shiny black boots. For a man in his early thirties, Fred had very few possessions.

I went through the bureau drawers, which contained some underwear and handkerchiefs and socks and a high school senior class picture for the year 1961. I couldn't find Fred in the picture.

'This is him,' Johnson said at my shoulder. He pointed out a teenage boy's face that from this distance in time looked touchingly hopeful.

I looked over the books in the bookcase. Most of them were paperbacks on art and culture and technology. There were a few books about psychiatry and psychoanalysis. The only ones I had read myself were *The Psychopathology of Everyday Life* and *Gandhi's Truth*—unusual background reading for a thief, if that's what Fred was.

I turned to Johnson. 'Could someone have gotten into the house and taken the picture from this room?'

He lifted his heavy shoulders and dropped them. 'I guess anything is possible. *I* didn't hear anybody. But then I generally sleep the sleep of the dead.'

'You didn't take the picture yourself, Jerry?'

'No, sir.' He shook his head violently. 'I know enough not to mess with Fred's stuff. I may be an old nothing man but I wouldn't steal from my own boy. He's the only one of us with any future, in this house.'

'Just the three of you live here—you and Fred and Mrs Johnson?'

'That's correct. We had roomers at one time, but that was long ago.'

'Then what happened to the picture Fred brought home?'

Johnson lowered his head and swung it from side to side like a sick old bull. 'I never saw the picture. You don't understand how it is with me. I spent six, seven years after the war in a veterans' hospital. Most of the time I was in a daze, most of the time I still am. The days go by, and half the time I don't know what day it is and I don't want to. I'm a sick man. Now why don't you leave me alone?'

I left him alone and made a cursory search of the upstairs rooms. Only one other was occupied, a room containing a double bed that Johnson evidently shared with his wife. There was no painting under the mattress, nothing incriminating in the closet or chest of drawers, no evidence of any crime but that of poverty.

One narrow door at the end of the upstairs hallway was closed and padlocked. I stopped in front of it.

Johnson came up behind me. 'That goes up to the attic. I don't have a key for it. Sarah's always afraid I'll fall down the stairs. Anyway, there isn't anything up there. Like me,' he added foolishly, tapping the side of his head. 'Nobody home upstairs.'

He gave me a broad idiot smile. I gave him the other half-pint. It was an ugly transaction, and I was glad to leave him. He closed the front door behind me like a trusty shutting himself into his own prison. I locked the door.

VIII

I LEFT MY car where it was and walked towards the hospital. I hoped to get some further information about Fred from Mrs Johnson. The night was almost fully dark, the streetlights scattered sparsely among the trees. On the sidewalk ahead of me I noticed a spillage of oil drops that became more frequent as I moved along.

I dipped my finger in one of the spilled drops and held it up to the light. It had a reddish tinge. It didn't smell like oil.

On the grass beside the sidewalk ahead of me someone was snoring. It was a man lying face down. I ran to him and got down on my knees beside him. The back of his head was dark and lustrous with blood. I moved him just enough to look at his face. It was bloody, too.

He groaned and tried to raise himself in a sad and helpless parody of a push-up, then fell on his face again. I turned his head to one side so that he could breathe more freely.

He opened one eye and said, 'Chantry? Leave me alone.'

Then he relapsed into his broken-faced snuffling. I could see that he was very badly hurt. I left him and ran to the emergency entrance of the hospital.

Seven or eight adults and children were waiting inside on collapsible chairs. A harassed young nurse behind a counter was manning it like a barricade.

I said, 'There's an injured man just up the street.'

'So bring him in.'

'I can't. He needs an ambulance.'

'How far up the street?'

'Next block.'

'There's no ambulance here. If you want to call one, that's a public phone in the corner there. Do you have a dime?'

She gave me a number to call. In less than five minutes an ambulance pulled up outside. I got in with the driver and directed him to the bleeding man in the grass.

His snoring was less regular now, and less loud. The ambulance attendant turned a flashlight on him. I took a closer look. He was a man of sixty or so, with a pointed grey beard and a lot of bloody grey hair. He looked like a dying sea-lion, and his snoring sounded like a sea-lion's distant barking.

'Do you know him, sir?'

I was thinking that he fitted the liquor-store proprietor's description of the art dealer Paul Grimes.

I said, 'No. I've never seen him before.'

The ambulance man lifted him gently on to a stretcher and drove him to the emergency entrance. I rode along and was there when they carried him out. He raised himself on his arms, almost overturning the stretcher, and looked at me from his blind broken glistening face.

He said, 'I know you, you bastard.'

He fell back and lay still. The ambulance man rushed him into the hospital. I waited outside for the inevitable police.

They came in an unmarked car, a pair of youngish detective-sergeants wearing light summery clothes and dark wintry faces. One went into the hospital, and the other, a Sergeant Leverett, stayed with me.

'You know the injured man?'

'I never saw him before. I found him on the street.'

'How did you happen to call an ambulance for him?'

'It seemed like the logical thing to do.'

'Why didn't you call us?'

'I knew somebody would.'

Leverett reddened slightly. 'You sound like a smart bastard. Who in hell are you, anyway?'

I swallowed my anger and told him that I was a private detective doing a job for the Biemeyers. Leverett knew the name and it altered his voice and manner.

'May I see your identification?'

I showed it to him. He asked me to stick around, if I would be so good. I promised that I would.

Interpreting my promise loosely, I wandered back into the

next block and found the place on the sidewalk where the
drippings of blood had started. They were already drying in
the warm air.

Parked at the adjacent curb was an old black convertible
with a ragged top. Its key was in the ignition. A square white
envelope was stuck between the black plastic seat and the
back cushion. On the shelf behind the seat were a pile of
smallish oil paintings and a white sombrero.

I turned on the dashboard light and examined the square
envelope. It was an invitation to cocktails addressed to Mr
Paul Grimes, on Mrs Richard Chantry's stationery, and
signed 'Francine Chantry'. The party was tonight at eight
o'clock.

I looked at my watch: just past eight. Then I examined
the stack of paintings behind the seat. Two of them were
framed in old-fashioned gilt, the rest unframed. They didn't
resemble any of the Chantrys I had seen.

They didn't look like much of anything. There were a few
seascapes and beach scenes, which looked like minor accidents,
and a small portrait of a woman, which looked like a major
one. But I didn't entirely trust my eye or my judgement.

I took one of the seascapes and put it in the trunk of my
own car. Then I started back towards the hospital.

Leverett and the other detective-sergeant met me on the
way. They were accompanied by a captain of detectives
named Mackendrick, a heavy powerful-looking middle-aged
man in a crumpled blue suit that went with his crumpled face.
He told me that the man I had found was dead. I told him
who the man probably was.

Mackendrick absorbed my information quickly and made
a few scrawlings in a black notebook. He was particularly
interested in the fact that Grimes had mentioned Richard
Chantry before he died.

'I remember Chantry,' he said. 'I was a rookie when he
pulled his big disappearance.'

'You think he disappeared deliberately?'

'Sure. There was plenty of evidence of that.'

He didn't tell me what the evidence was. I didn't tell him
where I was going.

I DROVE through the lower town, past Grimes's lightless and uninhabited little building. I could taste the salty tang of the sea long before I got to it, and feel its cool breath. A seaside park stretched along the shore for more than a mile. Below it waves foamed on the beach, preternaturally white against the darkness. There were pairs of lovers here and there in the grass instead of dead men, and that was good.

Channel Road ascended a cliff that overlooked and partly enclosed the harbour. Suddenly I was looking down at its masts. The road climbed away over the shoulder of the cliff, wound past a Coast Guard colony, and skirted a deep barranca that opened out on to the sea. Beyond the barranca was the hill on which the Biemeyers' house stood.

Mrs Chantry's house was perched between the barranca and the water. It was built of stone and stucco, with many arches and several turrets. There was a glass-roofed greenhouse on one side, and between me and the house was a walled flagstone parking area holding about twenty cars. A white-coated attendant came up to the side of my car and offered to park it for me.

A uniformed black maid greeted me pleasantly at the open front door. She didn't ask me for my invitation or any identification. She didn't even allow herself to notice that I wasn't wearing party clothes or a party look on my face.

Piano music drew me past her into a central room of the house, a wide high room that rose two storeys to the roof. A woman with short black hair was playing 'Someone to Watch Over Me' on a grand piano that was dwarfed by the room. A couple of dozen men and women stood around in party clothes with drinks. It looked like a scene recovered from the past, somehow less real than the oil paintings hanging on the walls.

Mrs Chantry came towards me from the far end of the room. She was wearing a blue evening dress with a lot of skirt and not much top, which displayed her arms and shoulders. She didn't seem to recognize me at first, but then she lifted both her hands in a gesture of happy surprise.

'How good of you to come. I was hoping I'd mentioned my little party to you, and I'm so glad I did. It's Mr Marsh, isn't it?' Her eyes were watching me carefully. I couldn't tell if she liked me or was afraid of me.

'Archer,' I said. 'Lew Archer.'

'Of course. I never could remember names. If you don't mind, I'll let Betty Jo Siddon introduce you to my other guests.'

Betty Jo Siddon was a level-eyed brunette of about thirty. She was well-shaped but rather awkward in her movements, as if she weren't quite at home in the world. She said she was covering the party for the local paper, and clearly wondered what I was doing there. I didn't tell her. She didn't ask.

She introduced me to Colonel Aspinwall, an elderly man with an English accent, an English suit, and a young English wife who looked me over and found me socially undesirable. To Dr Ian Innes, a cigar-chomping thick-jowled man, whose surgical eyes seemed to be examining me for symptoms. To Mrs Innes, who was pale and tense and fluttering, like a patient. To Jeremy Rader, the artist, tall and hairy and jovial in the last late flush of his youth. To Molly Rader, a statuesque brunette of about thirty-nine, who was the most beautiful thing I'd seen in weeks. To Jackie Pratt, a spare little long-haired man in a narrow dark suit, who looked like a juvenile character out of Dickens but on second glance had to be fifty, at least. To the two young women with Jackie, who had the looks and the conversation of models. To Ralph Sandman and Larry Fallon, who wore black silk jackets and ruffled white shirts, and appeared to comprise a pair. And to Arthur Planter, an art collector so well known that I had heard of him.

Betty Jo turned to me when we had finished our rounds. 'Would you like a drink?'

'Not really.'

She looked at me more closely. 'Are you feeling all right? You look a little peaked.'

I caught it from a dead man I just found on Olive Street.

What I said was, 'I don't believe I've eaten for a while.'

'Of course. You look hungry.'

'I *am* hungry. I've had a big day.'

She took me into the dining-room. Its wide uncurtained windows looked out over the sea. The room was uncertainly lit by the tall candles on the refectory table.

Standing behind the table with the air of a proprietor was the large dark hook-nosed man, whom the girl addressed as Rico, I had met on my earlier visit. He cut some slices off a baked ham and made me a sandwich with which he offered me wine. I asked for beer instead, if he didn't mind. He strutted towards the back of the house, grumbling.

'Is he a servant?'

Betty Jo answered me with deliberate vagueness: 'More or less.' She changed the subject. 'A big day doing what?'

'I'm a private detective. I was working.'

'Policeman was one of the thoughts that occurred to me. Are you on a case?'

'More or less.'

'How exciting.' She squeezed my arm. 'Does it have to do with the picture the Biemeyers had stolen?'

'You're very well informed.'

'I try to be. I don't intend to write a social column for the rest of my life. Actually I heard about the missing picture in the newsroom this morning. I understand it's a conventional-ized picture of a woman.'

'So I've been told. I haven't seen it. What else was the newsroom saying?'

'That the picture was probably a fake. Is it?'

'The Biemeyers don't think so. But Mrs Chantry does.'

'If Francine says it's a fake, it probably is. I think she knows by heart every painting her husband did. Not that he did so many—fewer than a hundred altogether. His high period only lasted seven years. And then he disappeared. Or some-thing.'

'What do you mean, "Or something"?'

'Some old-timers in town here think he was murdered. But that's pure speculation, so far as I can find out.'

'Murdered by whom?'

She gave me a quick bright probing look. 'Francine Chantry. You won't quote me, will you?'

'You wouldn't have said it if you thought I would. Why Francine?'

'He disappeared so suddenly. People always suspect the spouse, don't they?'

'Sometimes with good reason,' I said. 'Are you professionally interested in the Chantry disappearance?'

'I'd like to write about it, if that's what you mean.'

'That's what I mean. I'll make a deal with you.'

She gave me another of her probing looks, this one edged with sexual suspicion. 'Oh?'

'I don't mean that. I mean this. I'll give you a hot tip on the Chantry case. You tell me what you find out.'

'How hot?'

'This hot.'

I told her about the dead man at the hospital. Her eyes became narrower and brighter. She pushed out her lips like a woman expecting to be kissed, but kissing was not what was on her mind.

'That's hot enough.'

Rico came back into the room carrying a foaming glass.

'It took me a long time,' he said in a complaining tone. 'The beer wasn't cold. Nobody else drinks beer. I had to chill it.'

'Thanks very much.'

I took the cold glass from his hand and offered it to Betty Jo.

She smiled and declined. 'I have to work tonight. Will you forgive me if I run off now?'

I advised her to talk to Mackendrick. She said she would, and went out the back door. Right away I found myself missing her.

I ate my ham sandwich and drank my beer. Then I went back into the room where the music was. The woman at the piano was playing a show tune with heavy-handed professional assurance. Mrs Chantry, who was talking with Arthur Planter, caught my eye and detached herself from him.

'What happened to Betty Jo? I hope you didn't do away with her.'

She meant the remark to be light, but neither of us smiled. 'Miss Siddon had to leave.'

Mrs Chantry's eyes became even more unsmiling. 'She didn't tell me that she was going to leave. I hope she gives my party proper coverage—we're raising money for the art museum.'

'I'm sure she will.'

, 'Did she tell you where she was going?'

'To the hospital. There's been a murder. Paul Grimes was killed.'

Her face opened, almost as if I'd accused her, then closed against the notion. She was quiet but internally active, re-arranging her face from the inside. She drew me into the dining-room, reacted to the presence of Rico, and took me into a small sitting-room.

She closed the door and faced me in front of a dead and empty fireplace. 'How do you know Paul Grimes was murdered?'

'I found him dying.'

'Where?'

'Near the hospital. He may have been trying to get there for treatment, but he died before he made it. He was very badly smashed up around the head and face.'

The woman took a deep breath. She was still very handsome, in a cold silvery way, but the life seemed to have gone out of her face. Her eyes had enlarged and darkened.

'Could it have been an accident, Mr Archer?'

'No. I think he was murdered. So do the police.'

'Who is in charge of the case, do you know?'

'Captain Mackendrick.'

'Good.' She gave an abrupt little nod. 'He knew my husband.'

'How does your husband come into this? I don't understand.'

'It's inevitable that he should. Paul Grimes was close to Richard at one time. His death is bound to stir up all the old stories.'

'What old stories?'

'We don't have time for them now. Perhaps another day.'
Her hand came out and encircled my wrist, like a bracelet of
ice. 'I'm going to ask you to do something for me, Mr Archer.
Two things. Please don't tell Captain Mackendrick or anyone
else what I said to you about poor dear Paul today. He was a
good friend to Richard, to me as well. I was angry when I said
what I did. I shouldn't have said it, and I'm terribly sorry.'

She released my wrist and leaned on the back of a straight
chair. Her voice was veering up and down the scale, but her
eyes were steady and intense. I could almost feel them tangibly
on my face. But I didn't really believe in her sudden kindly
feeling for Paul Grimes, and I wondered what had happened
between them in the past.

As if the past had slugged her from behind, she sat down
rather suddenly on the chair.

She said in a wan voice, 'Will you get me a drink, please?'

'Water?'

'Yes, water.'

I brought her a glassful from the dining-room. Her hands
were shaking. Holding the glass in both hands, she sipped at
the water and then drank it down and thanked me.

'I don't know why I'm thanking you. You've ruined my
party.'

'I'm sorry. But it really wasn't me. Whoever killed Paul
Grimes ruined your party. I'm just the flunky who brought
the bad tidings and gets put to death.'

She glanced up at my face. 'You're quite an intelligent
man.'

'Do you want to talk to me?'

'I thought I had been.'

'I mean really talk.'

She shook her head. 'I have guests in the house.'

'They'll do all right on their own, as long as the drinks hold
out.'

'I really can't.' She rose to leave the room.

I said, 'Wasn't Paul Grimes supposed to be one of your
guests tonight?'

'Certainly not.'

'He was carrying an invitation to your party. Didn't you send it to him?'

She turned to face me, leaning on the door. 'I may have. I sent out quite a few invitations. Some were sent out by other members of my committee.'

'But you must know whether Paul Grimes was invited.'

'I don't think he was.'

'But you're not sure?'

'That's right.'

'Has he ever been here to your house?'

'Not to my knowledge. I don't understand what you're trying to prove.'

'I'm trying to get some idea of your relationship with Grimes.'

'There wasn't any.'

'Good or bad, I mean. This afternoon you practically accused him of faking the Biemeyers' painting. Tonight you invite him to your party.'

'The invitations went out early last week.'

'You admit that you sent him one.'

'I may have. I probably did. What I said to you this afternoon about Paul wasn't intended for the record. I confess he gets on my nerves.'

'He won't any more.'

'I know that. I'm sorry. I'm sorry he's been killed.' She hung her pretty grey head. 'And I did send him that invitation. I was hoping for a reconciliation. We hadn't been friends for some time. I thought he might respond to a show of warmth on my part.'

She looked at me from under the wings of her hair. Her eyes were cold and watchful. I didn't believe what she was telling me, and it must have showed.

She said with renewed insistence, 'I hate to lose friends, particularly friends of my husband's. There are fewer and fewer survivors of the Arizona days, and Paul was one of them. He was with us when Richard made his first great breakthrough. Paul really made it possible, you know. But he never succeeded in making his own breakthrough.'

'Were there hard feelings between them?'

'Between my husband and Paul? Certainly not. Paul was one of Richard's teachers. He took great pride in Richard's accomplishment.'

'How did your husband feel about Paul?'

'He was grateful to him. They were always good friends, as long as Richard was with us.' But she gave me a long and doubting look. 'I don't know where this is leading.'

'Neither do I, Mrs Chantry.'

'Then what's the purpose of it? You're wasting my time and your own.'

'I don't think so. Tell me, is your husband still alive?'

She shook her head. 'I can't answer that. I don't know. I honestly don't know.'

'How long is it since you've seen him?'

'He left in the summer of 1950. I haven't seen him since then.'

'Were there indications that something had happened to him?'

'On the contrary. He wrote me a wonderful letter. If you'd like to see it—'

'I've seen it. As far as you know, then, he's still alive.'

'I hope and pray he is. I believe he is.'

'Have you heard from him since he took off?'

'Never.'

'Do you expect to?'

'I don't know.' She turned her head to one side, the cords of her white neck taut. 'This is painful for me.'

'I'm sorry.'

'Then why are you doing it?'

'I'm trying to find out if there's any possibility that your husband killed Paul Grimes.'

'That's an absurd idea. Absurd and obscene.'

'Grimes didn't seem to think so. He spoke Chantry's name before he died.'

She didn't quite faint, but she seemed to come close to it. She turned white under her make-up, and might have fallen. I held her by the upper arms. Her flesh was as smooth as marble, and almost as cold.

Rico opened the door and shouldered his way in. I realized

how big he was. The room hardly contained him.

'What goes on?'

'Nothing,' the woman said. 'Please go away, Rico.'

'Is he bothering you?'

'No, he's not. But I want both of you to go away. Please.'

'You heard her,' Rico said to me.

'So did you. Mrs Chantry and I have something to discuss.'
I turned to her. 'Don't you want to know what Grimes said?'

'I suppose I have to. Rico, do you mind leaving us alone
now? It's perfectly all right.'

It wasn't all right with Rico. He gave me a black scowl that
at the same time managed to look hurt, like the scowl of a
little boy who has been told to stand in the corner. He was a
big good-looking man, if you liked the dark florid type. I
couldn't help wondering if Mrs Chantry did.

'Please, Rico.' She sounded like the mistress of a barely
controllable watchdog or a jealous stud.

The big man moved sideways out of the room. I closed the
door behind him.

Mrs Chantry turned to me. 'Rico's been with me a long
time. He was devoted to my husband. When Richard left, he
transferred his allegiance to me.'

'Of course,' I said.

She coloured faintly, but didn't pursue the subject. 'You
were going to tell me what Paul Grimes said to you before he
died.'

'So I was. He thought I was your husband, apparently. He
said: "Chantry? Leave me alone." Later he said: "I know you,
you bastard." It naturally gave me the idea that it may have
been your husband who beat him to death.'

She dropped her hands from her face, which looked pale
and sick. 'That's impossible. Richard was a gentle person.
Paul Grimes was his good friend.'

'Do I resemble your husband?'

'No. Richard was much younger—' She caught herself.
'But of course he'd be a great deal older now, wouldn't he?'

'We all are. Twenty-five years older.'

'Yes.' She bowed her head as if she suddenly felt the weight
of the years. 'But Richard didn't look at all like you. Perhaps

there's some similarity of voices.'

'But Grimes called me Chantry before I spoke. I never did say anything to him directly.'

'What does that prove? Please go away now, won't you? This has been very hard. And I have to go out there again.'

She went back into the dining-room. After a minute or two I followed her. She and Rico were standing by the candlelit table with their heads close together, talking in intimate low tones.

I felt like an intruder and moved over to the windows. Through them I could see the harbour in the distance. Its masts and cordage resembled a bleached winter grove stripped of leaves and gauntly beautiful. The candle flames reflected in the windows seemed to flicker like St Elmo's fire around the distant masts.

X

I WENT OUT to the big front room. The art expert Arthur Planter was standing with his back to the room, in front of one of the paintings on the wall. When I spoke to him, he didn't turn or answer me, but his tall narrow body stiffened a little.

I repeated his name. 'Mr Planter?'

He turned unwillingly from the picture, which was a head-and-shoulders portrait of a man. 'What can I do for you, sir?'

'I'm a private detective—'

'Really?' The pale narrow eyes in his thin face were looking at me without interest.

'Did you know Paul Grimes?'

'I wouldn't say I *know* him. I've done some business with him, a very little.' He pursed his lips as if the memory had a bitter taste.

'You won't do any more,' I said, hoping to shock him into communication. 'He was murdered earlier this evening.'

'Am I a suspect?' His voice was dry and bored.

'Hardly. Some paintings were found in his car. Would you be willing to look at one of them?'

'With what end in view?'

'Identification, maybe.'

'I suppose so,' he said wearily. 'Though I'd much rather look at this.' He indicated the picture of the man on the wall.

'Who is it?'

'You mean you don't know? It's Richard Chantry—his only major self-portrait.'

I gave the picture a closer look. The head was a little like a lion's head, with rumpled tawny hair, a full beard partly masking an almost feminine mouth, deep eyes the colour of emeralds. It seemed to radiate force.

'Did you know him?' I said to Planter.

'Indeed I did. I was one of his discoverers, in a sense.'

'Do you believe he's still alive?'

'I don't know. I earnestly hope he is. But if he is alive, and if he's painting, he's keeping his work to himself.'

'Why would he take off the way he did?'

'I don't know,' Planter repeated. 'I think he was a man who lived in phases, like the moon. Perhaps he came to the end of this phase.' Planter looked around a little contemptuously at the other people in the crowded room. 'This painting you want me to look at, is it a Chantry?'

'I wouldn't know. Maybe you can tell me.'

I led him out to my car and showed him in my headlights the small seascape I had taken from Paul Grimes's convertible. He lifted it out of my hands with delicate care, as if he were showing me how to handle a painting.

But what he said was, 'I'm afraid it's pretty bad. It's certainly not a Chantry, if that's your question.'

'Do you have any idea who might have painted it?'

He considered the question. 'It could be the work of Jacob Whitmore. If so, it's very early Whitmore—purely and clumsily representational. I'm afraid poor Jacob's career recapitulated the history of modern art a generation or so late. He'd worked his way up to surrealism and was beginning to discover symbolism, when he died.'

'When did he die?'

'Yesterday.' Planter seemed to take pleasure in giving me this mild shock. 'I understood he went for a dip in the sea off

Sycamore Point and had a heart attack.' He looked down musingly at the picture in his hands. 'I wonder what Paul Grimes thought he could do with this. A good painter's prices will often go up at his death. But Jacob Whitmore was not a good painter.'

'Does his work resemble Chantry's?'

'No. It does not.' Planter's eyes probed at my face. 'Why?'

'I've heard that Paul Grimes may not have been above selling fake Chantrys.'

'I see. Well, he'd have had a difficult time selling this as a Chantry. It isn't even a passable Whitmore. As you can see for yourself, it's no more than half finished.' Planter added with elaborate cruel wit, 'He took his revenge on the sea in advance by painting it badly.'

I looked at the blurred and swirling blues and greens in the unfinished seascape. However bad the painting was, it seemed to be given some depth and meaning by the fact that the painter had died in that sea.

'Did you say he lived at Sycamore Point?'

'Yes. That's on the beach north of the campus.'

'Did he have any family?'

'He had a girl,' Planter said. 'As a matter of fact, she called me up today. She wanted me to come and look at the paintings he left behind. She's selling them off cheap, I understand. Frankly I wouldn't buy them at any price.'

He handed the picture back to me and told me how to find the place. I got into my car and drove northward past the university to Sycamore Point.

The girl that Jacob Whitmore had left behind was a mournful blonde in a rather late stage of girlhood. She lived in one of half a dozen cottages and cabins that sprawled across the sandy base of the point. She held her door almost completely closed and peered at me through the crack as if I might be bringing a second disaster.

'What do you want?'

'I'm interested in pictures.'

'A lot of them are gone. I've been selling them off. Jake drowned yesterday—I suppose you know that. He left me without a sou.'

Her voice was dark with sorrow and resentment. The darkness appeared to have seeped up from her mind into the roots of her hair. She looked past me out to sea where the barely visible waves were rolling in like measured instalments of eternity.

'May I come in and look?'

'I guess so. Sure.'

She opened the door and swung it shut behind me against the wind. The room smelled of the sea, of wine and pot and mildew. The furniture was sparse and broken-down. It looked like a house that had barely survived a battle—an earlier stage of the same desultory battle against poverty and failure that had passed through the Johnson house on Olive Street.

The woman went into an inner room and emerged with a stack of unframed paintings in her arms. She set them down on the warped rattan table.

'These'll cost you ten apiece, or forty-five for five of them. Jake used to get more for his paintings at the Saturday art show on Santa Teresa beach. A while ago, he sold one of them to a dealer for a good price. But I can't afford to wait.'

'Was Paul Grimes the dealer?'

'That's right.' She looked at me with some suspicion. 'Are you a dealer, too?'

'No.'

'But you know Paul Grimes?'

'Slightly.'

'Is he honest?'

'I don't know. Why?'

'*I* don't think he is. He put on quite an act about how much he liked Jake's work. He was going to publicize it on a big scale and make our fortune. I thought that Jake's big dream had come true at last. The dealers would be knocking on our door, Jake's prices would skyrocket. But Grimes bought two measly pictures and that was that. One of them wasn't even Jake's—it was somebody else's.'

'Who painted the other picture?'

'I don't know. Jake didn't discuss his business with me. I think he took the picture on consignment from one of his friends on the beach.'

'Can you describe the picture?'

'It was a picture of a woman—maybe a portrait, maybe imaginary. She was a beautiful woman, with hair the same colour as mine.' She touched her own bleached hair; the action seemed to arouse her fear or suspicion. 'Why is everybody so interested in that picture? Was it worth a lot?'

'I don't know.'

'I think it was. Jake wouldn't tell me what he got for it, but I know we've been living on the money for the last couple of months. The money ran out yesterday. And so,' she added in a toneless voice, 'did Jake.'

She turned away and spread out the unframed paintings on the table. Most of them were unfinished-looking small seascapes like the one in my car that I'd shown to Arthur Planter. The drowned man had clearly been obsessed by the sea, and I couldn't help wondering if his drowning had been entirely accidental.

I said, 'Were you suggesting that Jake drowned himself?'

'No, I was not.' She changed the subject abruptly: 'I'll give you all five of them for forty dollars. The canvases alone are worth that much. You know that if you're a painter.'

'I'm not a painter.'

'I sometimes wonder if Jake was. He painted for over thirty years and ended up with nothing to show for it but this.' The gesture of her hand took in the paintings on the table, the house and its history, Jake's death. 'Nothing but this and me.'

She smiled, or grimaced with half of her face. Her eyes remained cold as a sea-bird's, peering down into the roiled and cloudy past.

She caught me watching her and recoiled from the look on my face. 'I'm not as bad as you think I am,' she said. 'If you want to know why I'm selling these things, I want to buy him a coffin. I don't want the county to bury him in one of those pine boxes. And I don't want to leave him lying in the basement of the county hospital.'

'Okay, I'll take the five pictures.'

I handed her two twenties, wondering if I'd ever get the money back from Biemeyer.

She took it with some distaste and held it. 'That wasn't a

sales pitch. You don't have to buy them just because you know why I need the money.'

'I need the pictures.'

'What for? *Are* you a dealer?'

'Not exactly.'

'That means you are. I knew you weren't a painter.'

'How did you know?'

'I've lived with a painter for the last ten years.' She moved the position of her hips, resting her weight against the corner of the table. 'You don't look like a painter or talk like one. You don't have a painter's eyes. You don't smell like a painter.'

'What do I smell like?'

'A cop, maybe. I thought when Paul Grimes bought those two pictures from Jake that maybe there was something funny about them. Is there?'

'I don't know.'

'Then why are you buying these?'

'Because Paul Grimes bought the others.'

'You mean if he put out money for them, they must be worth something?'

'I'd certainly like to know why he wanted them.'

'So would I,' she said. 'Why do *you* want the pictures?'

'Because Paul Grimes wanted them.'

'You mean you do everything he does?'

'I hope not everything.'

She gave me her cold half-smile and nodded. 'Yeah, I heard he's slightly crooked on occasion. I shouldn't say that, though. I've got nothing against him. And his daughter's kind of a friend of mine.'

'Paola? Is she his daughter?'

'Yeah. You know her?'

'We've met. How do you happen to know her?'

'I met her at a party in the barrio. She told me her mother was part Spanish and part Indian. Paola's a beautiful woman, don't you think? I love those Spanish types.'

She hunched her shoulders and rubbed her palms together as if she were warming herself at Paola's heat.

I drove back to Santa Teresa and paid a visit to the morgue in the basement of the hospital. A young deputy coroner named Henry Purvis, whom I knew, told me that Jacob Whitmore had drowned while swimming. He pulled out a drawer and showed me the blue body with its massive hairy head and shrunken sex. I walked out of the cold room shivering.

XI

As IF HE were feeling lonely, the deputy coroner, Purvis, followed me into the anteroom, letting the heavy metal door swing shut behind him. He was almost as hairy as the dead man, and almost young enough to be his son.

I said, 'Is there any official doubt that Whitmore died by accident?'

'I don't think so. He was getting too old for the kind of surf they have at Sycamore Point. The coroner put it down as an accident. He hasn't even ordered an autopsy.'

'I think he should, Henry.'

'Do you have a reason?'

'Whitmore and Grimes had a business connection. It's probably not a coincidence that they're in here together. Of course there'll be an autopsy on Grimes, won't there?'

Purvis nodded. 'It's set for first thing in the morning. But I did a preliminary examination, and I can tell them what the probable results will be. He was beaten to death with a heavy weapon, probably a tyre iron.'

'The weapon hasn't been found?'

'Not that I know of. You should ask the police. The weapon is their department.' He looked me over carefully. 'Did you know Grimes?'

'Not really. I knew he was an art dealer in town.'

'Was he an addict at one time?' Purvis said.

'I didn't know him that well. What kind of addiction do you have in mind?'

'Heroin, probably. He's got old needle marks on his arms and thighs. I asked the woman about them, but she wouldn't talk. The way she blew her top, she may be an addict herself.

There's a lot of it around, even right in the hospital here.'

'What woman are we talking about?'

'Dark woman—Spanish type. When I showed her the body, she did everything but climb the wall. I put her in the chapel and tried to call a priest for her but I couldn't raise one, not at this time of night. I called the police, and they want to talk to her.'

I asked him where the chapel was. It was a narrow little room on the first floor, with a single small stained-glass window denoting its function. It was furnished with a lectern and eight or ten padded chairs. Paola was sitting on the floor head down, hugging her knees, her black hair almost covering her face. She was hiccuping. When I approached her, she raised a bent arm over her head as if I might be planning to murder her.

'Get away from me.'

'I won't hurt you, Paola.'

She tossed back her mane of hair and stared at me narrow-eyed, without recognition. She had an aura of fierce forlorn sexuality. 'You're no priest.'

'You can say that again.'

I sat near her on the carpeted floor, which repeated the design of the stained-glass window. There were times when I almost wished I was a priest. I was growing weary of other people's pain and wondered if a black suit and a white collar might serve as armour against it. I'd never know. My grandmother in Contra Costa County had marked me for the priesthood, but I had slipped away under the fence.

Looking into Paola's opaque black eyes, I thought that the grief you shared with women was most always partly desire. At least sometimes you could take them to bed, I thought, and exchange a temporary kindness, which priests were denied. But not Paola. Both she and the woman at Sycamore Point belonged to dead men tonight. Chapel thoughts.

'What happened to Paul?' I asked her.

She looked at me with her chin on her shoulder, her lower lip protruding, her eyes defensive. 'You haven't told me who you are. Are you a policeman?'

'No. I run a small business.' I winced at the half-lie: the chapel was getting to me. 'I heard that Paul was in the market for pictures.'

'Not any more. He's dead.'

'Aren't you going to carry on the business?'

She raised her shoulders and shook her head fiercely, as if she were being violently threatened. 'Not me. You think I want to be killed like my father was?'

'Was Paul really your father?'

'Yes, he was.'

'Who killed him?'

'I'm not saying. You're not saying much, either.' She leaned towards me. 'Didn't you come into the shop today?'

'Yes.'

'It was something about the Biemeyers' picture, wasn't it? What kind of business are you in? Are you a dealer?'

'I'm interested in pictures.'

'I can see that. But whose side are you on?'

'The good guys.'

'There are no good guys. If you don't know that, you're no use to me.' She rose on her knees and swept her arm between us in a gesture of angry dismissal. 'So why don't you get lost?'

'I want to help you.' It wasn't entirely a lie.

'Sure you do. You want to help me. Then you want me to help you. Then you want to take the profits and run. That's the story, isn't it?'

'What profits? All you've got is a double handful of grief.'

She was silent for a while. Her eyes stayed on my face. Through them I could sense the movements of her mind almost as tangibly as if she were playing chess or checkers on a board, asking herself what she had to lose to me in order to take a greater amount away.

'I admit I'm in trouble.' She turned her hands palms upward on her knees, as if to offer me a share of her grief. 'Only I think you're worse trouble. Who are you, anyway?'

I told her my name and what I did for a living. Her eyes changed but she didn't speak. I told her that the Biemeyers had hired me to find their stolen painting.

'I don't know anything about it. I told you that this afternoon at the shop.'

'I believe you,' I said with a mental reservation. 'The point is that the theft of the painting and the killing of your father may be connected.'

'How do you know that?'

'I don't know it, but it seems likely. Where did that painting come from, Miss Grimes?'

She winced. 'Just call me Paola. I never use my father's name. And I can't tell you where he got the picture. He just used me for front; he never told me his business.'

'You can't tell me, or you won't?'

'Both.'

'Was the picture genuine?'

'I don't know.' She was silent for an interval, during which she hardly seemed to breathe. 'You say you want to help me, but all you do is ask questions. I'm supposed to supply the answers. How does it help me if I talk myself into jail?'

'Your father might have been better off in jail.'

'Maybe you're right. But I don't want to end up there. Or in a hole in the ground, either.' Her gaze was restless and inward, lost in the convolutions of her mind. 'You think whoever painted that picture killed my father, too.'

'That may be true. I have a feeling it is.'

She said in a thin voice, 'Is Richard Chantry still alive?'

'He may be. What makes you think he is?'

'That picture. I'm no expert like my father was, but it looked like a Chantry to me, the real McCoy.'

'What did your father say about it?'

'I'm not telling you. And I don't want to talk about that picture any more. You're still asking all the questions, and I'm doing all the answering, and I'm tired. I want to go home.'

'Let me take you.'

'No. You don't know where I live, and I'm not telling you, either. That's my secret.'

She got up from her knees, staggering a little. I supported her with my arm. Her breast touched my side. She leaned on me, breathing deeply for a moment, then pulled away. Some of her heat migrated through my body to my groin. I felt less tired than I had.

'I'll take you home.'

'No, thanks. I have to wait here for the police. Anyway, all I need right now is a private cop in my life.'

'You could do worse, Paola. Your father was murdered, remember, possibly by the man who painted that picture.'

She took hold of my left arm above the elbow. 'So you keep telling me, but do you know it?'

'No. I don't know it.'

'Then stop trying to scare me. I'm scared enough already.'

'I think you should be. I got to your father before he died. It happened just a couple of hundred yards from here. It was dark, and he was badly hurt, and he thought I was Chantry. In fact, he called me Chantry. And what he said implied that Chantry killed him.'

Her eyes dilated. 'Why would Richard Chantry kill my father? They were good friends in Arizona. My father often talked about him. He was Chantry's first teacher.'

'That must have been a long time ago.'

'Yes. Over thirty years.'

'And people can change in thirty years.'

She nodded in assent, and her head stayed down. Her hair swung forward so that it poured like black water over her face.

'What happened to your father in those years?'

'I don't know much about it. I didn't see a lot of my father until recently—until he had a use for me.'

'Was he on heroin?'

She was silent for a time. Her hair was still over her face, and she didn't push it back. She looked like a woman without a face.

Finally she said, 'You know the answer to that question, or you wouldn't ask it. He used to be an addict. They sent him to federal prison, and he licked it there, cold turkey.' She separated her hair with her hands and looked at me between it, probably to see if I believed her. 'I wouldn't have come here with him if he had been on drugs. I saw what it did to him when I was a kid in Tucson and Copper City.'

'What did it do to him?'

'He used to be a good man, an important man. He even

taught a course at the university once. Then he turned into something else.'

'What did he turn into?'

'I don't know. He started running after boys. Or maybe he was always like that. I don't know.'

'Did he kick that habit, too, Paola?'

'I guess he did.' But her voice was uncertain, full of pain and doubt.

'Was the Biemeyers' painting genuine?'

'I don't know. *He* thought it was, and he was the expert.'

'How do you know that?'

'He talked to me about it the day he bought it on the beach. He said it had to be a Chantry, nobody else could have painted it. He said it was the greatest find he ever made in his life.'

'Did he say this to you?'

'Yes. Why would he lie to me? He had no reason.' But she was watching my face as if my reaction might resolve the question of her father's honesty.

She was frightened, and I was tired. I sat down on one of the padded chairs and let my mind fray out for a couple of minutes. Paola went to the door but she didn't go out. She leaned on the doorframe, watching me as if I might steal her purse, or already had.

'I'm not your enemy,' I said.

'Then don't press me so hard. I've had a rough night.' She averted her face, as if she were ashamed of what she was about to say. 'I liked my father. When I saw him dead, it was a terrible thing for me.'

'I'm sorry, Paola. I hope tomorrow will be better.'

'I hope so,' she said.

'I understand your father had a photograph of the painting.'

'That's right. The coroner has it.'

'Henry Purvis?'

'Is that his name? Anyway, he has it.'

'How do you know?'

'He showed it to me. He said he found it in my father's clothes, and he wanted to know if I recognized the woman. I told him I didn't.'

'You recognized the painting?'

'Yes.'

'It was the painting your father sold to the Biemeyers?'

'Yes, it was.'

'How much did they pay him for it?'

'My father never told me. I think he needed the money to pay off a debt, and he didn't want me to know. I can tell you something that he did say, though. He knew the woman in the painting, and that was how he authenticated it as a Chantry.'

'It is an authentic Chantry, then?'

'Yes. My father said it was.'

'Did he tell you the woman's name?'

'It was Mildred. She was a model in Tucson when he was young—a beautiful woman. He said it must be a memory painting, because she's an old woman now, if she's alive at all.'

'Do you remember her last name?'

'No. I think she took the names of the men she lived with.'

I left Paola in the chapel and went back to the cold room. Purvis was in the anteroom, but he no longer had the photograph of the painting. He told me that he had given it to Betty Jo Siddon.

'What for?'

'She wanted to take it down to the newspaper building and have it photographed.'

'Mackendrick will like that, Henry.'

'Hell, it was Mackendrick who told me to let her have it. The chief of police is retiring this year, and it's made Captain Mackendrick publicity-conscious.'

I started out of the hospital. A sense of unfinished business brought me to a full stop before I left the building. When Paul Grimes fell and died in my path, I had been on my way to talk to Fred's mother, Mrs Johnson.

XII

I WENT TO the nurses' station at the front and asked where I could find Mrs Johnson. The nurse in charge was a middle-aged woman with a sallow bony face and an impatient manner.

'We have several Mrs Johnsons working in the hospital. Is her Christian name Sarah?'

'Yes. Her husband's name is Jerry or Gerard.'

'Why didn't you say so in the first place? I'm afraid Mrs Gerard Johnson is no longer employed in this hospital.' She spoke with deliberate formal emphasis, like a court official pronouncing sentence on Mrs Johnson.

'She told me that she worked here.'

'Then she lied to you.' The woman overheard the harshness of her words, and softened them: 'Or it's possible you misunderstood her. She *is* presently employed at a convalescent home down by the highway.'

'Do you know the name of it?'

'It's called the La Paloma,' she said with distaste.

'Thank you. Why was she fired here?'

'I didn't say she was fired. She was allowed to leave. But I'm not authorized to discuss it.' At the same time, she seemed unwilling to let me go. 'Are you from the police?'

'I'm a private detective co-operating with the police.'

I got out my wallet and showed her my licence photostat. She smiled into it as though it were a mirror. 'She's in trouble again, is she?'

'I hope not.'

'Stealing drugs again?'

'Let's just say I'm investigating Mrs Johnson. How long ago did she leave her employment here?'

'It happened last week. The administration let her go without a black mark on her record. But they gave her no choice about leaving. It was an open-and-shut case. She had some of the pills in her pocket—and I was there when they searched her. You should have heard the language she used to the superintendent.'

'What language did she use?'

'Oh, I couldn't repeat it.'

Her wan face flamed red, as if I had made an indecent proposal to her. She looked at me with sudden dislike, perhaps embarrassed by her own excitement. Then she turned on her heel and walked away.

It was past midnight. I had been in the hospital so long that I was beginning to feel like a patient. I left by a route different from the one I had come in by. I didn't want to see Captain Mackendrick or Purvis or Paola or either of the dead men again.

I had noticed the La Paloma sign from the freeway and had some idea of where the convalescent home was. Driving towards it from the hospital, I passed a dark row of doctors' offices, a nurses' residence and several blocks of lower-middle-class houses, all one-storeyed and built before the war. Between the houses and the freeway was a narrow park studded with oak trees. In their shelter a few late lovers were parked with fog on their windshields.

The one-storeyed stucco complex of the La Paloma was almost as close to the freeway as a filling station. Once I had stepped inside and closed the heavy front door, the noises of late-night traffic dwindled to a far-off irregular sound like that of distant surf. I could hear the more immediate sounds of the place, snores and sighs and vague indecipherable demands.

A nurse's muted footsteps came up behind me. She was young and black and pretty.

'It's too late for visiting,' she said. 'We're all closed down for the night.'

'I want to see a member of the staff—Mrs Johnson?'

'I'll see if I can find her. She's getting very sought after. You're the second visitor she's had tonight.'

'Who was the other one?'

She paused, then said, 'Would you be Mr Johnson?'

'No. I'm just a friend.'

'Well, the other one was her son—dude with a red moustache. He stirred up quite a hassle before I got him out of here.' She gave me a hard but not unfriendly look. 'I hope you're not planning to stir up another hassle.'

'Nothing could be farther from my thoughts. I want to stir one down.'

'All right, I'll get her. But keep it quiet, eh? People are sleeping.'

'Sure. What was the hassle about?'

'Money. Isn't it always?'

'Not always,' I said. 'Sometimes it's love.'

'*That* comes into it, too. He had a blonde in the car.'

'Not all of us are so lucky.'

She hardened her look a little in order to deflect a pass, if that was what I had offered her. 'I'll get Sarah.'

Mrs Johnson came unwillingly. She had been crying, and her eyes were swollen.

'What do you want?' She made it sound as if she had very little left to give.

'I'd like to talk to you for a couple of minutes.'

'I'm behind in my work already. Are you trying to get me fired?'

'No. I do happen to be a private detective, though.'

Her gaze veered around the dark little anteroom and rested on the outside door. Her thick body tensed as if she were getting ready to run out on to the highway.

I stepped between her and the door. 'Is there some place we can sit down in private for a few minutes?'

'I guess so. But if I lose my job it's on your head.'

She led me into a visiting room that was crowded with mismatched furniture, and turned on a dim standing lamp. We sat down facing each other under the lamp, our knees almost touching. As though the touch of mine might contaminate hers, she pulled down her white nylon skirt.

'What do you want with me? And don't give me any more guff about being a newspaperman. I thought you were a policeman from the beginning.'

'I want your son, Fred.'

'So do I.' She lifted her heavy shoulders and dropped them. 'I'm getting worried about Fred. I haven't heard from him all day.'

'He was here tonight. What was he after?'

She was silent for a moment, but not inactive. Her face worked as if she were swallowing her lie and possibly planning another.

'He needed money. That's nothing new. And it's no crime to ask your own mother for money. This isn't the first time that I've helped him out. He always pays me back as soon as he can.'

I cut through her smoke screen of words. 'Come off it, Mrs Johnson. Fred's in trouble. A stolen picture is bad enough. A stolen girl compounds the felony.'

'He didn't steal the girl. That's a lie, a snivelling lie. She went along with him of her own free will. In fact, it was probably her idea in the first place—she's been after Fred for some time. And if that little spade said something different, she's lying.' The woman shook her fist at the door where the black nurse had disappeared.

'What about the picture, Mrs Johnson?'

'What picture?'

'The painting that Fred stole from the Biemeyers' house.'

'He didn't steal it. He simply borrowed it to make some tests on it. He took it down to the art museum, and it was stolen from there.'

'Fred told me it was taken from your house.'

She shook her head. 'You must have misunderstood him. It was taken from the basement of the art museum. They're responsible.'

'Is that the story you and Fred have agreed on?'

'It's the truth, so naturally we agree on it. Fred is as honest as the day is long. If you can't see that, it's because your own mind is twisted. You've had too much to do with dishonest people.'

'That's true enough,' I said. 'I think you're one of them.'

'I don't have to sit here and listen to your insults.'

She tried to evoke her own anger but somehow it wouldn't come. The day had been too much for her, and the night hung over her like a slowly gathering wave. She looked down into her cupped and empty hands, then put her face into them. She didn't sob or cry or say a word. But her silence in the midst of the muffled freeway noises sounded like desolation itself.

After a time she sat up and looked at me quite calmly. 'It's time I got back to work.'

'Nobody's watching you.'

'Maybe not, but they'll blame me if things are in a mess in the morning. There are only the two of us on in this crummy place.'

'I thought you worked at the hospital.'

'I used to. I had a misunderstanding with one of the supervisors there.'

'Do you want to tell me about it?'

'It wasn't important.'

'Then tell me about it, Mrs Johnson.'

'Why should I? I've got enough on my mind without you bullying me.'

'And enough on your conscience?'

'That's between me and my conscience. I don't need any help from you in straightening out my conscience.'

She sat as still as stone. I admired her as I might have admired a statue without concern for its history. But I wasn't content to let her stay silent. The case, which had begun with a not very serious theft, was beginning to draw human lives into its vortex. Two men were dead, and the Biemeyers' girl had been spun off into the darkness.

'Mrs Johnson, where is Fred going with Miss Biemeyer?'

'I don't know.'

'Didn't you ask him? You wouldn't give him money without finding out what he intended to do with it.'

'I did, though.'

'I think you're lying.'

'Think away,' she said almost cheerfully.

'Not for the first time, either. You've lied to me already more than once.'

Her eyes brightened with interest, and with the superiority that liars feel towards the people they lie to.

'For instance, you left the hospital because they caught you stealing drugs. You told me you left because you had a misunderstanding with a supervisor.'

'Over drugs,' she added quickly. 'There was a discrepancy in the count. They blamed me.'

'You weren't responsible?'

'Certainly not. What do you think I am?'

'A liar.'

She stirred threateningly, but didn't get up. 'Go ahead and call me names. I'm used to it. You can't prove anything.'

'Are you on drugs now?'

'I don't take drugs.'

'Not of any kind?'

'Not of any kind.'

'Then who did you steal them for? Fred?'

She mimed laughter, and managed to produce a high tone-less giggle. If I had heard the giggle without seeing its source, I might have taken her for a wild young girl. And I wondered if this was how she felt in relationship to her son.

'Why did Fred take the picture, Mrs Johnson? To sell it and buy drugs?'

'He doesn't use drugs.'

'To buy drugs for Miss Biemeyer?'

'That's a silly idea. She's independently wealthy.'

'Is that why Fred is interested in her?'

She leaned forward with her hands on her knees, sober and dead serious. The woman who had giggled a moment ago had been swallowed up like a ghostly emanation by her body.

'You don't know Fred. You never will—you don't have the understanding. He's a good man. The way he feels about the Biemeyer girl is like a brother, an older brother.'

'Where is the older brother taking his little sister?'

'You don't have to get snotty.'

'I want to know where they are, or where they're going. Do you know?'

'No, I don't.'

'You wouldn't give them travelling money unless you knew where they were going.'

'Who says I did?'

'I say.'

She clenched her fists and used them to strike both of her white nylon knees simultaneously several times. 'I'll kill that little spade.'

'I wouldn't, Mrs Johnson. They'll put you in Corona if you do.'

She grinned unpleasantly. 'I was just kidding.'

'You picked a bad subject and a bad time. A man named Paul Grimes was murdered earlier tonight.'

'Murdered?'

'Beaten to death.'

Mrs Johnson pitched sideways on to the floor. She didn't move until the black girl, whom I called to help me, came and poured water on her head. Then she got up gasping and feeling her hair.

'What did you do that for? You've ruined my hairdo.'

'You passed out,' I said.

She swung her head from side to side, staggering a little. The other nurse put her arm around her shoulders and held her still. 'Better sit down, hon. You were really out.'

But Mrs Johnson stayed on her feet. 'What happened? Did somebody hit me?'

'I hit you with a piece of news,' I said. 'Paul Grimes was beaten to death tonight. I found him on the street not very far from here.'

Mrs Johnson's face went completely blank for a moment, then set in a scowling mask of ignorance. 'Who's he?'

'An art dealer from Arizona. He sold that picture ⌐ the Biemeyers. Don't you know him?'

'What did you say his name was?'

'Paul Grimes.'

'I never heard of him.'

'Then why did you faint when I told you he'd been murdered?'

'I didn't. I have these fainting spells is all. They don't mean anything.'

'You better let me take you home.'

'No! I'd lose my job. I can't afford that—it's the only thing that keeps us going.'

Head down and weaving slightly, she turned and moved away towards the wards.

I followed her. 'Where is Fred taking the Biemeyer girl?'

She didn't answer the question or even acknowledge it.

I FOLLOWED THE freeway into the centre of town, which was almost deserted. A cruising police car overtook me. Its driver gave me a quick once-over as he passed, and went on.

There were lights on the second floor of the newspaper building. It faced on a grassy square fringed with tall palms. The trees stood still and silent in the calm post-midnight air.

I parked my car by the square and climbed the stairs to the lighted newsroom. A clacking typewriter led me across the large unpeopled room to a partitioned space where Betty Jo Siddon was working. She looked up with a start when I spoke her first two names.

'You shouldn't *do* that. You scared me.'

'I'm sorry.'

'That's all right. As a matter of fact, I'm glad you came by. I'm trying to make some kind of sense out of this murder story.'

'May I read it?'

'In tomorrow's paper, if they use it. They don't always print my stuff. The news editor is a male chauvinist and he tries to keep me segregated in the women's pages.' She was smiling but her dark eyes were rebellious.

'You can tell me what your theory is.'

'I'm afraid I don't have a theory. I'm trying to build a story around the question of who the woman in the painting was, and who painted the picture, and of course who stole it. Actually it's a triple mystery, isn't it? Do you know who stole it?'

'I think so, but I wouldn't want to be quoted.'

'I won't quote you,' she said. 'This is just for background.'

'Okay. According to my witnesses, who frankly aren't worth much, the picture was stolen twice in quick succession. An art student by the name of Fred Johnson took it from the Biemeyers' house—'

'Fred Johnson from the museum? I wouldn't have thought he was the type.'

'He may not be. He claims he took it to make some tests on it and try to authenticate it as a Chantry. But somebody stole it from his parents' house, or from the art museum—there are two versions.'

Betty Jo was making pencilled notes on a sheet of typewriter paper. 'Where's Fred now? Do you think I can talk to him?'

'If you can find him. He's taken off for parts unknown with the Biemeyer girl. As for your other questions, I don't know who painted the picture. It may be a Chantry and it may not. Maybe Fred Johnson knows. I did get a partial identification of the woman in the picture. Her name is Mildred.'

'Is she in town here?'

'I doubt it. She was a model in Tucson a generation ago. Paul Grimes, the man who was killed, knew her. He thought the painting of her had probably been done from memory. She was much younger in it than she could be in real life.'

'Does that mean it was painted recently?'

'That's one of the questions Fred was trying to answer, apparently. He was trying to date the picture to determine if Chantry could have painted it.'

Betty Jo looked up brightly from her notes. 'Do you think Chantry could have?'

'My opinion isn't worth anything. I haven't seen the picture or the photograph of it.'

'Why didn't you say so? I'll get it.'

She rose quickly and disappeared through the door marked 'Photography Department'. Her passage left vibrations on the air. The vibrations lingered in my body.

I was feeling lonely and late but I felt dubious about jumping the generation gap. It could open up like a chasm and swallow you, or close on you like pincers. I tried to focus my excitement on the woman in the picture that I hadn't seen yet.

Betty Jo brought it and laid it down on her desk. It was a coloured photograph of a painting, measuring about four by six inches. I held it up in the fluorescent light. The pictured

woman was beautiful, as Paola had said. She had classical
features, delicate blonde colouring. The whole painting held
a sense of distance that centred in her ice-blue eyes and seemed
to suggest that she was watching me, or I was watching her,
from a long way off. Perhaps the suggestion came from what
Paola had relayed from her father, that the woman who sat for
the picture would be old or dead, her beauty only remembered.

But it seemed to have the power to focus the case for me.
I wanted to reclaim the picture, meet the woman if she was
alive. I wanted to find out where and when and by whom she
had been painted.

'Will you be running this in tomorrow's paper?'

'I doubt it,' Betty Jo said. 'The photographer said the
picture he took wouldn't reproduce too well.'

'Even a bad print of it would be useful to me. The original
has to go back to the police.'

'I suppose you could ask Carlos for a copy.'

'You ask him, will you? You know him. It could help me to
track down Fred and the Biemeyer girl.'

'And if you do you'll give me the details, right?'

'I won't forget you.' The words held a double meaning for
my inner ear.

Betty Jo took the picture back into the photography department. I sat down in her chair and rested my arms on her desk
and my head on my arms, and slid off into sleep. I must have
dreamed about violence, or the expectation of violence. When
the girl's hand touched my shoulder, I lunged to my feet
reaching for a gun in a shoulder holster that I wasn't wearing.

Betty Jo backed away from me with her hands half raised
and fingers spread. 'You frightened me.'

'I'm sorry.'

'Carlos is making you a picture. In the meantime, I'm afraid
I have to use my typewriter. I want to have my story ready
for the noon edition. Incidentally, is it all right if I mention
you in it?'

'Not by name, please.'

'You're modest.'

'Hardly. I'm a private detective. I want to stay private.'

I retreated to the city editor's desk and put my head down

on my arms again. It was some time since I had gone to sleep in the same room with a girl. Of course the room was large and reasonably well lighted, and the girl had other things than me on her mind.

This time she woke me by voice, standing well back. 'Mr Archer?'

She had a young black with her. He showed me the black-and-white copy that he had made. It was rather blurred and grimy, as if the blonde woman had slipped away still farther into time, out of sight of the sun. Still her features were identifiable.

I thanked the photographer and offered to pay him for the copy. He deplored the suggestion, pushing air towards me with his hands. He retreated into his workroom, and the girl sat down at her typewriter again. She typed a few words and stopped, withdrawing her hands from the keys and dropping them in her lap.

'I don't know whether I can do this piece after all. I can't name Fred Johnson or the girl. It doesn't really make for much of a story, does it?'

'It will.'

'But when? I don't really know enough about the people. If the woman in the picture is alive and reachable, that would make all the difference. I could hang the whole story on her.'

'You can anyway.'

'It would be so much better if I could say definitely who and where she is. And that she's alive if she is alive. I might even do a follow-up interview.'

'The Biemeyers might know,' I said. 'They may have had a personal reason for buying that picture of her.'

She looked at her watch. 'It's after midnight. I wouldn't dare to call them at this time of night. Anyway, the chances are that they don't know anything. Ruth Biemeyer does a lot of talking about her relationship with Richard Chantry, yet I doubt that she was ever very close to him.'

I didn't argue. I didn't want to talk to my clients right now. The case had enlarged enormously since they had hired me, and I had no immediate hope of being able to explain it to them. But I did want another crack at Mrs Chantry.

'Chantry's wife was very close to him,' I said.

'You think Francine Chantry would be willing to talk to me?'

'She can hardly refuse, since there's a murder involved. Which she's taking pretty hard. She may know all about the woman in the picture. Didn't she used to model for her husband herself?'

'How do you know that?' Betty Jo said.

'She told me.'

'She never told *me*.'

'You're not a man.'

'You noticed.'

XIV

I DROVE BETTY JO along the deserted waterfront to the Chantry house. It was dark and silent. The parking area was empty. The party was over.

Perhaps not entirely over. I could hear a faint sound, the sound of a woman moaning in pain or pleasure, which ended abruptly as we approached the front door. Betty Jo turned to me.

'Who was that?'

'It could have been Mrs Chantry. But women all sound the same under certain circumstances.'

She let out her breath, making a small impatient angry noise, and knocked on the door. A light went on above it.

After what seemed a long wait, the door was opened and Rico looked out at us. Lipstick was smeared on one side of his mouth. He saw me looking at it, and wiped his mouth with the back of his hand. It dragged the red smear down across his chin. His black eyes were unfriendly.

'What do you want?'

'We have a couple of questions to ask Mrs Chantry,' I said.

'She's in bed asleep.'

'You'd better wake her up.'

'I can't do that. She's had a big day. A big day and a big

night.' The lipstick smear on Rico's face touched his words
with comic lewdness.

'Ask her if she'll see us. We're investigating a murder, as
you possibly know.'

'Mr Archer and Miss Siddon,' Betty Jo said.

'I know who you are.'

Rico let us into the long front room and turned on the light.
With his dark bald-eagle head jutting out of his long brown
dressing gown, he looked like some kind of wild medieval
monk. There was stale smoke in the deserted room. Through
it I could almost hear the remembered buzzing hum of party
conversation. Empty and half-empty glasses stood on most of
the horizontal surfaces, including the keyboard of the grand
piano. Except for the paintings on the walls—quiet windows
into a more orderly world, which even murder didn't seem
to have changed—the room was like a visible hangover.

I moved around the room inspecting the portraits and trying in an amateurish way to tell if the same hand had painted
the Biemeyers' picture. I couldn't tell, and neither, she said,
could Betty Jo.

But I found that the murder of Grimes, and the possible
murder of Whitmore, had after all subtly changed the portraits
or my perceptions of them. Their eyes seemed to regard me
with suspicion and a kind of fearful resignation. Some looked
at me like prisoners, some like jurors, and some like quiet
animals in a cage. I wondered which, if any, reflected the
mind of the man who had painted them.

'Did you know Chantry, Betty Jo?'

'Not really. He was before my time. Actually I did see him
once.'

'When?'

'Right here in this room. My father, who was a writer,
brought me to meet him. It was a very special occasion. He
hardly saw anybody, you know. All he did was work.'

'How did he strike you?'

She considered the question. 'He was very remote and shy,
as shy as I was. He held me on his knee but he didn't really
want to. He got rid of me as soon as he could, I think. And
that suited me. Either he didn't like little girls at all, or he

liked them too much.'

'Did you really think that at the time?'

'I believe I did. Little girls are quite aware of such things, at least I was.'

'How old were you?'

'I must have been four or five.'

'How old are you now?'

'I'm not saying.' She said it with a slightly defensive smile.

'Under thirty?'

'Barely. It was roughly twenty-five years ago, if that's what you're getting at. Chantry disappeared soon after I visited him. I often seem to have that effect on men.'

'Not on me.'

A little colour invaded her cheeks and made her prettier. 'Just don't try to hold me on your knee. You could disappear.'

'Thanks for the warning.'

'Don't mention it. Seriously,' she added, 'it gives me a funny feeling to be in this same room prying into Richard Chantry's life. It makes me wonder if certain things aren't fated. Do you think they are?'

'Of course. By the place and the time and the family you're born into. Those are the things that fate most people.'

'I'm sorry I asked. I don't really like my family. I don't like the place and time too well, either.'

'So react against them.'

'Is that what you do?'

'I try.'

Betty Jo's eyes shifted to a point behind me. Mrs Chantry had quietly entered the room. Her hair was brushed, her face looked newly washed. She was wearing a white robe that moulded her figure from neck to knee and swept the floor.

'I do wish you'd find another place to react, Mr Archer. And by all means another time. It's dreadfully late.' She gave me a long-suffering smile, which hardened when she turned to Betty Jo. 'What is this all about, dear?'

The younger woman was embarrassed. Her mouth moved, trying to find the right words.

I got out my black-and-white photograph of the stolen painting. 'Do you mind taking a look at this, Mrs Chantry?

It's a photograph of the Biemeyers' picture.'

'I have nothing to add to what I told you earlier. I'm sure it's a fake. I'm familiar with all of my husband's paintings, I believe, and this isn't one of them.'

'Look at it anyway, will you?'

'I've already seen the painting itself, as I told you.'

'Did you recognize the model who sat for it?'

Her eyes met mine in an instant of shared knowledge. She had recognized the model.

,'No,' she said.

'Will you take a look at this photo and try again?'

'I don't see the point.'

'Try anyway, Mrs Chantry. It may be important.'

'Not to me.'

'You can't be sure,' I said.

'Oh, very well.'

She took the photograph from my hand and studied it. Her hand was shaking, and the picture fluttered like something in a high wind from the past. She handed it back to me as if she were glad to get rid of it.

'It does bear some resemblance to a woman I knew when I was a young girl.'

'When did you know her?'

'I didn't really *know* her. I met her at a party in Santa Fe before the war.'

'What was her name?'

'I honestly can't say. I don't believe she had a definite surname. She lived with various men and took their names.' Her eyes came up abruptly. 'No, my husband wasn't one of those men.'

'But he must have known her if he painted the picture.'

'He didn't paint this picture. I told you that.'

'Who did, Mrs Chantry?'

'I have no idea.'

Impatience had been rising in her voice. She glanced towards the door. Rico was leaning there with his hand in the pocket of his robe; and something larger than a hand, shaped like a gun. He moved towards me.

I said, 'Call off your dog, Mrs Chantry. Unless you want

this written up in the paper.'

She gave Betty Jo an icy look, which Betty Jo managed to return. But she said, 'Go away, Rico, I can take care of this.'

Rico moved reluctantly into the hallway.

I said to Mrs Chantry, 'How do you know your husband didn't paint it?'

'I would have known if he had. I know all his paintings.'

'Does that mean you still keep in touch with him?'

'No, of course not.'

'Then how do you know he didn't paint this some time in the last twenty-five years?'

The question stopped her for a moment. Then she said, 'The woman in the painting is too young. She was older than this when I saw her in Santa Fe in 1940. She'd be a really old woman now, if she's alive at all.'

'But your husband could have painted her from memory, any time up to the present. If *he's* alive.'

'I see what you mean,' she said in a small flat voice. 'But I still don't think he painted it.'

'Paul Grimes thought he did.'

'Because it paid him to think so.'

'Did it, though? I think this picture got him killed. He knew the model who sat for it, and she told him your husband had painted it. For some reason the knowledge was dangerous. Dangerous to Paul Grimes, obviously, and dangerous to whoever killed Grimes.'

'Are you accusing my husband?'

'No. I have nothing to go on. I don't even know if your husband is alive. Do you know, Mrs Chantry?'

She took a deep breath, her breasts rising like fists under her robe. 'I haven't heard from him since the day he left. I warn you, though, Mr Archer, his memory is all I live for. Whether Richard is dead or alive, I'll fight for his reputation. And I'm not the only one in this city who will fight you. Please get out of my house now.'

She included Betty Jo in the invitation. Rico opened the front door and slammed it behind us.

Betty Jo was shaken. She crept into my car like a refugee from trouble.

I said, 'Was Mrs Chantry ever an actress?'

'An amateur one, I think. Why?'

'She reads her lines like one.'

The girl shook her head. 'No. I think Francine meant what she said. Chantry and his work are all she cares about. And I feel small about doing what I just did. We hurt her and made her angry.'

'Are you afraid of her?'

'No, but I thought we were friends.' She added as we drove away from the house, 'Maybe I am a little afraid of her. But also I'm sorry that we hurt her.'

'She was hurt long ago.'

'Yes, I know what you mean.'

I meant Rico.

I checked into a waterfront motel. Betty Jo came in with me to compare notes. We compared not only notes.

The night was sweet and short. Dawn slipped in like something cool and young and almost forgotten.

XV

WHEN I WOKE up in the morning, she was gone. A pang that resembled hunger went through me a little higher than my stomach. The phone beside the bed rang.

'This is Betty Jo.'

'You sound very cheerful,' I said. 'Painfully cheerful.'

'You had that effect on me. Also my editor wants me to do a feature on the Chantry case. He says he'll give me all the time I need. The only drawback is that they may not print it.'

'Why not?'

'Mrs Chantry talked to Mr Brailsford first thing this morning. He owns the paper. So they're going to have an editorial conference in Mr Brailsford's office. In the meantime, I'm supposed to go on digging. Do you have any suggestions?'

'You might try the art museum. Take along your photograph of the painting. There may be somebody in the museum who can identify the model who sat for it. And if we're very lucky the model may be able to tell us who painted it.'

'That's exactly what I was planning to do.'

'Good for you.'

She lowered her voice. 'Lew?'

'What do you want?'

'Nothing. I mean, do you mind about my thinking of it first? I mean, you're older than I am, and maybe not quite so liberated.'

I said, 'Cheer up, I'll probably see you at the art museum. You'll find me among the old masters.'

'I did hurt your feelings, didn't I?'

'On the contrary. I never felt better. I'm going to hang up now before you hurt my feelings.'

She laughed and hung up on me. I shaved and had a shower and went out for breakfast. An early wind was blowing on the water. A few small craft were out in it. But most of the boats in the harbour danced in place at their moorings, naked-masted.

I found a clean-looking restaurant and took a seat by the front window so that I could watch the boats. They gave me the emphatic feeling that I was in motion, too, scudding along under complex pressures and even more complex controls towards the open sea.

I had ham and eggs with potatoes and toast and coffee. Then I drove uptown and parked in the lot behind the art museum.

Betty Jo met me at the front entrance.

I said, 'We seem to be synchronized, Betty Jo.'

'Yes.' But she didn't sound too happy about it.

'What's the matter?'

'You just said it. My name. I hate my name.'

'Why?'

'It's a silly name. A double name always sounds like a child's name. It's immature. I don't like either of my names separately, either. Betty is such a plain name, and Jo sounds like a boy. But I suppose I have to settle for one of them. Unless you can suggest something better.'

'How about Lew?'

She didn't smile. 'You're making fun of me. This is serious.'

She was a serious girl, and more delicate in her feelings than I'd imagined. It didn't make me sorry that I had slept with her, but it lent a certain weight to the event. I hoped she wasn't getting ready to fall in love, especially not with me. But I kissed her, lightly, philanthropically.

A young man had appeared at the entrance to the classical sculpture exhibit. He had a wavy blond head and a tapered torso. He was carrying the coloured photograph of the memory painting.

'Betty Jo?'

'I've changed my name to Betty,' she said. 'Please just call me Betty.'

'Okay, Betty.' The young man's voice was precise and rather thin. 'What I was going to say is, I matched up your picture with one of the Lashman pictures in the basement.'

'That's marvellous, Ralph. You're a genius.' She took his hand and shook it wildly. 'By the way, this is Mr Archer.'

'The non-genius,' I said. 'Nice to meet you.'

Ralph flushed. 'Actually it was terribly easy to do. The Lashman painting was sitting out on one of the worktables, propped up against the wall. You'd almost think it was looking for me instead of I for it. It virtually leaped right out at me.'

Betty turned to me. 'Ralph has found another painting of that same blonde model. One by a different painter.'

'So I gathered. May I see it?'

'You certainly may,' Ralph said. 'The beauty of it is that Simon Lashman should be able to tell you who she is.'

'Is he in town?'

'No. He lives in Tucson. We should have a record of his address. We've bought several of his paintings over the years.'

'Right now, I'd rather look at the one in the basement.'

Ralph unlocked a door. The three of us went downstairs and along a windowless corridor that reminded me of jails I had known. The workroom where Ralph took me was also windowless, but whitely lit by fluorescent tubes in the ceiling.

The picture on the table was a full-length nude. The woman looked much older than she had in the Biemeyer painting. There were marks of pain at the corners of her eyes and mouth. Her breasts were larger, and they drooped a little. Her entire body was less confident.

Betty looked from the sorrowful painted face to mine, almost as if she were jealous of the woman.

She said to Ralph, 'How long ago was this painted?'

'Over twenty years. I checked the file. Lashman called it *Penelope*, by the way.'

'She'd be really old now,' Betty said to me. 'She's old enough in the picture.'

'I'm no spring chicken myself,' I said.

She flushed and looked away as if I'd rebuffed her.

I said to Ralph, 'Why would the picture be sitting out on the table like this? It isn't where it's usually kept, is it?'

'Of course not. One of the staff must have set it out.'

'This morning?'

'That I doubt. There wasn't anyone down here this morning before me. I had to unlock the door.'

'Who was down here yesterday?'

'Several people, at least half a dozen. We're preparing a show.'

'Including this picture?'

'No. It's a show of Southern California landscapes.'

'Was Fred Johnson down here yesterday?'

'As a matter of fact, he was. He put in quite a lot of time sorting through the paintings in the storage room.'

'Did he tell you what he was after?'

'Not exactly. He said he was looking for something.'

'He was looking for this,' Betty said abruptly.

She had forgotten her jealousy of the painted woman, if that is what it had been. Excitement coloured her cheekbones. Her eyes were bright.

'Fred is probably on his way to Tucson.' She clenched her fists and shook them in the air like an excited child. 'Now if I could get Mr Brailsford to pay my travel expenses—'

I was thinking the same thing about Mr Biemeyer. But before I approached Biemeyer I decided to try to make a phone call to the painter Lashman.

Ralph got me the painter's number and address out of the file, and left me alone at the desk in his own office.

I dialled Lashman's house in Tucson direct.

A hoarse reluctant voice answered, 'Simon Lashman speaking.'

'This is Lew Archer calling from the Santa Teresa Art Museum. I'm investigating the theft of a picture. I understand you painted the picture of Penelope in the museum.'

There was a silence. Then Lashman's voice creaked like an old door opening: 'That was a long time ago. I'm painting better now. Don't tell me someone thought that picture was worth stealing.'

'It hasn't been stolen, Mr Lashman. Whoever painted the stolen picture used the same model as you used for *Penelope*.'

'Mildred Mead? Is she still alive and kicking?'

'I was hoping you could tell me.'

'I'm sorry, I haven't seen her in some years. She'd be an old woman by now. We're all getting older.' His voice was becoming fainter. 'She may be dead.'

'I hope not. She was a beautiful woman.'

'I used to think that Mildred was the most beautiful woman in the South-west.' His voice had become stronger, as if the thought of her beauty had stimulated him. 'Who painted the picture you're talking about?'

'It's been attributed to Richard Chantry.'

'Really?'

'The attribution isn't certain.'

'I'm not surprised. I never heard that he used Mildred as a model.' Lashman was silent for a moment. 'Can you describe the picture to me?'

'It's a very simple nude in plain colours. Someone said it showed the influence of Indian painting.'

'A lot of Chantry's stuff did, in his Arizona period. But none of it is particularly good. Is this one any good?'

'I don't know. It seems to be causing a lot of excitement.'

'Does it belong to the Santa Teresa museum?'

'No. It was bought by a man named Biemeyer.'

'The copper magnate?'

'That's correct. I'm investigating the theft for Biemeyer.'

'To hell with you, then,' Lashman said, and hung up.

I dialled his number again. He said, 'Who is that?'

'Archer. Please hold on. There's more involved than the

theft of a picture here. A man named Paul Grimes was murdered in Santa Teresa last night. Grimes was the dealer who sold the picture to Biemeyer. The sale and the murder are almost certainly connected.'

Lashman was silent again. Finally he said, 'Who stole the picture?'

'An art student named Fred Johnson. I think he may be on his way to Tucson with it now. And he may turn up on your doorstep.'

'Why me?'

'He wants to find Mildred and see who painted her. He seems to be obsessed with the painting. In fact, he may be off his rocker entirely, and he has a young girl travelling with him.' I deliberately omitted the fact that she was Biemeyer's daughter.

'Anything else?'

'That's the gist of it.'

'Good,' he said. 'I am seventy-five years old. I'm painting my two-hundred-and-fourteenth picture. If I stopped to attend to other people's problems, I'd never get it finished. So I am going to hang up on you again, Mr whatever-your-name-is.'

'Archer,' I said. 'Lew Archer. L-E-W A-R-C-H-E-R. You can always get my number from Los Angeles information.'

Lashman hung up again.

XVI

THE MORNING wind had died down. The air was clear and sparkling. Like a flashing ornament suspended from an infinitely high ceiling, the red-tailed hawk swung over the Biemeyer house.

Jack and Ruth Biemeyer both came out to meet me. They were rather conservatively dressed, like people on their way to a funeral, and they looked as if the funeral might be their own.

The woman reached me first. She had dark circles under

her eyes, which she hadn't quite succeeded in covering with
make-up.

'Is there any word about Doris?'

'I think she left town with Fred Johnson last night.'

'Why didn't you stop her?'

'She didn't give me notice that she was leaving. I couldn't
have stopped her if she had.'

'Why not?' Ruth Biemeyer was leaning towards me, her
handsome head poised like a tomahawk.

'Doris is old enough to be a free agent. She may not be
smart enough, but she's old enough.'

'Where have they gone?'

'Possibly Arizona. I have a little bit of a lead in Tucson, and
I think they may be heading there. I don't know if they have
the picture with them. Fred claims it was stolen from *him*.'

Jack Biemeyer spoke for the first time. 'That's horse manure.'

I didn't argue with him. 'You're probably right. If you want
me to go to Tucson, it's going to cost you more, naturally.'

'Naturally.' Biemeyer looked past me at his wife. 'I told
you there would be another bite. There always is.'

I felt like hitting him. Instead I turned on my heel and
walked to the far end of the driveway. It wasn't far enough.
A five-foot wire fence stopped me.

The hill slanted sharply downward to the edge of the
barranca. On the far side stood the Chantry house, miniatured by distance like a building in a bell jar.

The greenhouse behind it had a half-painted glass roof.
Through its flashing multiple panes I could make out dim
movements inside the building, which was choked with
greenery. There seemed to be two people facing each other
and making wide sweeping motions, like duelists too far apart
to hurt each other.

Ruth Biemeyer spoke in a quiet voice behind me. 'Please
come back. I know Jack can be difficult—God knows I know
it. But we really need you.'

I couldn't resist that, and I said so. But I asked her to wait
a minute, and got a pair of binoculars out of my car. They
gave me a clearer view of what was going on in the Chantry

greenhouse. A grey-headed woman and a black-haired man, whom I identified as Mrs Chantry and Rico, were standing among the masses of weeds and overgrown orchid plants, and using long hooked knives to cut them down.

'What is it?' Ruth Biemeyer said.

I handed her my binoculars. Standing on tiptoe, she looked over the fence.

'What are they doing?'

'They seem to be doing some gardening. Is Mrs Chantry fond of gardening?'

'She may be. But I never saw her doing any actual work, until now.'

We went back to her husband, who all this time had been standing in a silent stony anger beside my car, like some kind of picket.

I said to him, 'Do you want me to go to Tucson for you?'

'I suppose so. I have no choice.'

'Sure you have.'

Ruth Biemeyer interrupted, glancing from her husband to me and back again like a tennis referee. 'We want you to go on with the case, Mr Archer. If you need some money in advance, I'll be glad to give it to you out of my own savings.'

'That won't be necessary,' Biemeyer said.

'Good. Thank you, Jack.'

'I'll take five hundred dollars from you,' I said.

Biemeyer yelped and looked stricken. But he said he would write me a cheque, and went into the house.

I said to his wife, 'What made him that way about money?'

'Getting some, I think. Jack used to be quite different when he was a young mining engineer and had nothing. But lately he's been making a lot of enemies.'

'Including his own daughter.' And his own wife. 'What about Simon Lashman?'

'The painter? What about him?'

'I mentioned your husband's name to him this morning. Lashman reacted negatively. In fact, he told me to go to hell and hung up on me.'

'I'm sorry.'

'It doesn't matter to me personally. Still I may need Lashman's co-operation. Are you on good terms with him?'

'I don't know him. Naturally I know who he is.'

'Does your husband know him?'

She hesitated, then spoke haltingly. 'I believe he does. I don't want to talk about it.'

'You might as well, though.'

'No. This is really painful for me.'

'Why?'

'There's so much old history involved.' She shook her head, as if it were still encumbered by the past. Then she spoke in a smaller voice, watching the doorway through which her husband had disappeared. 'My husband and Mr Lashman were rivals at one time. She was an older woman than my husband—actually she belonged to Lashman's generation —but Jack preferred her to me. He bought her away from Lashman.'

'Mildred Mead?'

'You've heard of her, have you?' Her voice grew coarse with anger and contempt. 'She was a notorious woman in Arizona.'

'I've heard of her. She sat for that picture you bought.'

She gave me a vague disoriented look. 'What picture?'

'The one we're looking for. The Chantry.'

'No,' she said.

'Yes. Didn't you know it was a picture of Mildred Mead?'

She put her hand over her eyes and spoke blindfolded. 'I suppose I may have known. If I did know, I'd blanked out on the fact. It was a terrible shock to me when Jack bought a house for her. A better house than I was living in at the time.' She dropped her hand and blinked at the high harsh light. 'I must have been crazy to bring that picture and hang it in the house. Jack must have known who it was. He never said a word, but he must have wondered what I was trying to do.'

'You could ask him what he thought.'

She shook her head. 'I wouldn't dare. I wouldn't want to open that can of worms.' She looked behind her as if to see if her husband was listening, but he was still out of sight in the house.

'You did open it, though. You bought the picture and brought it home.'

'Yes, I did. I must be going out of my mind—do you think I am?'

'You'd know better than I would. It's your mind.'

'Anybody else would be welcome to it.' There was a faint rising note of excitement in her voice: she had surprised herself with her own complexity.

'Did you ever see Mildred Mead?'

'No, I never did. When she—when she became important in my life, I was careful not to see her. I was afraid.'

'Of her?'

'Of myself,' she said. 'I was afraid I might do something violent. She must have been twenty years older than I, at least. And Jack, who had always been such a skinflint with me, bought her a house.'

'Is she still living in it?'

'I don't know. She may be.'

'Where is the house?'

'In Chantry Canyon in Arizona. It's on the New Mexico border, not too far from the mine. In fact it was the original Chantry house.'

'Are we talking about Chantry the painter?'

'His father, Felix,' she said. 'Felix Chantry was the engineer who first developed the mine. He was in charge of operations until he died. It's why it was such an insult to me when Jack bought the house from the old man's estate and gave it to that woman.'

'I don't quite follow you.'

'It's perfectly simple. Jack took over the mine from Felix Chantry. Actually he was related to Felix Chantry. Jack's mother was Chantry's cousin. Which was all the more reason why he should have bought the Chantry house for me.' She spoke with an almost childish bitterness.

'Is that why you bought the Chantry picture?'

'Maybe it is. I never thought of it in that way. I bought it really because I was interested in the man who painted it. Don't ask me how interested, it's a moot question now.'

'Do you still want the picture back?'

'I don't know,' she said. 'I want my daughter back. We shouldn't be standing here wasting time.'

'I know that. I'm waiting for your husband to bring me my cheque.'

Mrs Biemeyer gave me an embarrassed look and went into the house. She didn't come out right away.

I still had my binoculars hanging around my neck, and I carried them down the driveway to the edge of the slope again. The black-haired man and the grey-haired woman were still cutting weeds in the greenhouse.

Mrs Biemeyer came out of the house by herself. Angry tears were spilling from her eyes. The cheque she handed me was signed with her name, not her husband's.

'I'm going to leave him,' she said to me and the house. 'As soon as we get through this.'

XVII

I DROVE downtown and cashed the Biemeyers' cheque before either of them could cancel it. Leaving my car in the parking lot behind the bank, I walked a block to the newspaper building on the city square. The newsroom, which had been almost deserted in the early morning, was fully alive now. Nearly twenty people were working at typewriters.

Betty saw me and stood up behind her desk. She walked towards me smiling, with her stomach pulled in.

'I want to talk to you,' I said.

'I want to talk to *you*.'

'I mean seriously.'

'So do I mean seriously.'

'You look too happy,' I said.

'I'm seriously happy.'

'I'm not. I have to leave town.' I told her why. 'There's something you can do for me in my absence.'

She said with her wry intense smile, 'I was hoping there was something I could do for you in your presence.'

'If you're going to make verbal passes, isn't there some-place private where we can talk?'

'Let's try here.'

She knocked on a door marked 'Managing Editor', and got no answer. We went inside and I kissed her. Not only my temperature rose.

'Hey,' she said. 'He still likes me.'

'But I have to leave town. Fred Johnson is probably in Tucson now.'

She tapped me on the chest with her pointed fingers, as if she were typing out a message there. 'Take care of yourself. Fred is one of those gentle boys who could turn out to be dangerous.'

'He isn't a boy.'

'I know that. He's the fair-haired young man at the art museum but he's very unhappy. He unburdened himself to me about his ghastly family life. His father's an unemployable drunk and his mother's in a constant state of eruption. Fred's trying to work his way out of all this, but I think in his quiet way he's pretty desperate. So be careful.'

'I can handle Fred.'

'I know you can.' She put her hands on my upper arms. 'Now what do you want me to do?'

'How well do you know Mrs Chantry?'

'I've known Francine all my life, since I was a small child.'

'Are you friends?'

'I think so. I've been useful to her. Last night was embarrassing, though.'

'Keep in touch with her, will you? I'd like to have some idea of what she does today and tomorrow.'

The suggestion worried her. 'May I ask why?'

'You may ask but I can't answer. I don't know why.'

'Do you suspect her of doing something wrong?'

'I'm suspicious of everybody.'

'Except me, I hope.' Her smile was serious and questioning.

'Except thee and me. Will you check on Francine Chantry for me?'

'Of course. I was intending to call her anyway.'

I left my car at the Santa Teresa airport and caught a commuter plane to Los Angeles. The next plane to Tucson didn't leave for forty minutes. I had a quick sandwich and a glass of beer, and checked in with my answering service.

Simon Lashman had called me. I had time to call him back.

His voice on the line sounded still older and more reluctant than it had that morning. I told him who and where I was, and thanked him for calling.

'Don't mention it,' he said drily. 'I'm not going to apologize for my show of impatience. It's more than justified. The girl's father once did me a serious disservice, and I'm not a forgiving man. Like father, like daughter.'

'I'm not working for Biemeyer.'

'I thought you were,' he said.

'I'm working for his wife. She's very much concerned about her daughter.'

'She has a right to be. The girl acts as if she's on drugs.'

'You've seen her, then?'

'Yes. She was here with Fred Johnson.'

'May I come and talk to you later this afternoon?'

'I thought you said you were in Los Angeles.'

'I'm catching a flight to Tucson in a few minutes.'

'Good. I prefer not to discuss these things on the telephone. When I was painting in Taos, I didn't even have a telephone on the place. Those were the happiest days of my life.' He pulled himself up short: 'I'm maundering. I detest old men who maunder. I'll say goodbye.'

XVIII

His house was on the edge of the desert, near the base of a mountain, which had loomed up on my vision long before the plane landed. The house was one-storeyed and sprawling, surrounded by a natural wood fence that resembled a miniature stockade. It was late in the day but still hot.

Lashman opened a gate in the fence and came out to meet me. His face was deeply seamed, and his white hair straggled down on to his shoulders. He had on faded blue denims and flat-soled buckskin slippers. His eyes were blue, faded like his clothes by too much light.

'Are you Mr Archer?'

'Yes. It's good of you to let me come.'

Informal as he seemed to be, something about the old man imposed formality on me. The hand he gave me was knobbed with arthritis and stained with paint.

'What kind of shape is Fred Johnson in?'

'He seemed very tired,' Lashman said. 'But excited, too. Buoyed up by excitement.'

'What about?'

'He was very eager to talk to Mildred Mead. It had to do with the attribution of a painting. He told me he works for the Santa Teresa Art Museum. Is that correct?'

'Yes. What about the girl?'

'She was very quiet. I don't remember that she said a word.' Lashman gave me a questioning look, which I didn't respond to. 'Come inside.'

He led me through an inner courtyard into his studio. One large window looked out across the desert to the horizon. There was a painting of a woman on an easel, unfinished, perhaps hardly begun. The swirls of paint looked fresh, and the woman's half-emerging features looked like Mildred Mead's face struggling up out of the limbo of the past. On a table beside it, which was scaly with old paint, was a rectangular palette containing daubs of glistening colour.

Lashman came up beside me as I examined the painting. 'Yes, that's Mildred. I only just started it, after we talked on the phone. I had an urge to paint her one more time. And I'm at the age where you have to put all your sudden urges to work.'

'Are you painting her from the life?'

He gave me a shrewd look. 'Mildred hasn't been here, if that's what you want to know. She hasn't been here in nearly twenty years. I believe I mentioned that to you on the phone,' he said precisely.

'I gather you've painted her often?'

'She was my favourite model. She lived with me off and on for a long time. Then she moved to the far end of the state. I haven't seen her since.' He spoke with pride and nostalgia and regret. 'Another man made her what she considered a better offer. I don't blame her. She was getting old. I have to confess I didn't treat her too well.'

His words set up a vibration in my mind. I'd had a woman and lost her, but not to another man. I'd lost her on my own.

I said, 'Is she still living in Arizona?'

'I think so. I had a Christmas card from her last year. That's the last I've heard from Mildred.' He looked out across the desert. 'Frankly, I'd like to be in touch with her again, even if we're both as old as the hills.'

'Where is Mildred living now?'

'In Chantry Canyon, in the Chiricahua Mountains. That's near the New Mexico border.' He drew a rough map of Arizona with a piece of charcoal and told me how to get to Chantry Canyon, which was in the state's south-eastern corner. 'Biemeyer bought her the Chantry house about twenty years ago, and she's been in it ever since. It was the house she always wanted—the house more than the man.'

'More than Jack Biemeyer, you mean?'

'And more than Felix Chantry, who built the house and developed the copper mine. She fell in love with Felix Chantry's house and his copper mine long before she fell in love with Felix. She told me it was her lifelong dream to live in Chantry's house. She became his mistress and even bore him an illegitimate son. But he never let her live in the house in his lifetime. He stuck with his wife and the son he had by her.'

'That would be Richard,' I said.

Lashman nodded. 'He grew up into a pretty good painter. I have to admit that, even if I hated his father. Richard Chantry had a real gift, but he didn't use it to the full. He lacked the endurance to stay the course. In this work, you really need endurance.' Leaning into the afternoon light from the window, his face bunched, he looked like a metal monument to that quality.

'Do you think Richard Chantry is alive?'

'Young Fred Johnson asked me the same question. I'll give you the same answer I gave him. I think Richard is probably dead—as dead as his brother is—but it hardly matters. A painter who gives up his work in mid-career, as Richard apparently did—he might as well be dead. I expect to die myself the day that I stop working.' The old man's circling mind kept returning with fascination and disgust to his own mortality. 'And that will be good riddance to bad rubbish, as we used to say when I was a boy.'

'What happened to Felix Chantry's other son by Mildred —the illegitimate brother?'

'William? He died young. William was the one I knew and cared about. He and his mother lived with me, off and on, for some years. He even used my name while he was going to art school here in Tucson. But he took his mother's name when he went into the army. He called himself William Mead, and that was the name he was using when he died.'

'Was he killed in the war?'

Lashman said quietly, 'William died in uniform, but he was on leave when it happened. He was beaten to death and his body left in the desert, not very far from where his mother lives now.'

'Who killed him?'

'That was never established. If you want more information, I suggest you get in touch with Sheriff Brotherton in Copper City. He handled the case, or mishandled it. I never did get the full facts of the murder. When Mildred came back from identifying William's body, she didn't say a word for over a week. I knew how she felt. William wasn't my son, and I hadn't seen him for a long time, but he felt like a son to me.'

The old man was silent for a moment, and then went on: 'I was on my way to making a painter of William. As a matter of fact, his early work was better than his half-brother Richard's, and Richard paid him the compliment of imitation. But it was William who became food for worms.'

He swung around to face me, angrily, as if I had brought death back into his house. 'I'll be food for worms myself before too long. But before I am, I intend to paint one more picture of Mildred. Tell her that, will you?'

'Why don't you tell her yourself?'

'Perhaps I will.'

Lashman was showing signs of wanting to be rid of me before the afternoon light failed. He kept looking out the window. Before I left, I showed him my photograph of the picture that Fred had taken from the Biemeyers.

'Is that Mildred?'

'Yes, it is.'

'Can you tell who painted it?'

'I couldn't be sure. Not from a small black-and-white photo-graph.'

'Does it look like Richard Chantry's work?'

'I believe it does. It looks something like my early work, too, as a matter of fact.' He glanced up sharply, half serious, half amused. 'I didn't realize until now that I might have influenced Chantry. Certainly whoever did this painting had to have seen my early portraits of Mildred Mead.' He looked at the painted head on the easel as if it would confirm his claim.

'You didn't paint it yourself, did you?'

'No. I happen to be a better painter than that.'

'A better painter than Chantry?'

'I think so. I didn't disappear, of course. I've stayed here and kept at my work. I'm not as well known as the disappear-ance artist. But I've outstayed him, by God, and my work will outstay his. This picture I'm doing now will outstay his.'

Lashman's voice was angry and young. His face was flushed. In his old age, I thought, he was still fighting the Chantrys for the possession of Mildred Mead.

He picked up a brush and, holding it in his hand as if it were a weapon, turned back to his unfinished portrait.

XIX

I DROVE SOUTH and then east across the desert, through blow-ing curtains of evening. The traffic was comparatively thin and I made good time. By nine o'clock I was in Copper City, driving past Biemeyer's big hole in the ground. It looked in the fading evening light like the abandoned playground of a race of giants or their children.

I found the sheriff's station and showed my photostat to the captain in charge. He told me that Sheriff Brotherton could be found in a substation north of the city, near his mountain home. He got out a map and showed me how to get there.

I drove north towards the mountains. They had been built by bigger giants than the ones who dug Biemeyer's hole. As I approached the mountains, they took up more and more of the night sky.

I skirted their south-eastern end on a winding road that ran between the mountains on my left and the desert on my right. Other traffic had dwindled away. I had begun to wonder if I was lost when I came to a cluster of buildings with lights in them.

One was the sheriff's substation. The others were a small motel and a grocery store with a gas pump in front of it. There were a number of cars, including a couple of sheriff's cars, parked on the paved area in front of the buildings.

I added my rented car to the line of parked cars and went into the substation. The deputy on duty looked me over carefully and finally admitted that the sheriff was next door in the grocery store. I went there. The back of the store was dim with cigar smoke. Several men in wide-brimmed hats were drinking beer from cans and playing pool on a table with a patched and wrinkled top. The heat in the place was oppressive.

A sweating bald man in a once-white apron came towards me. 'If it's groceries you want, I'm really closed for the night.'

'I could use a can of beer. And a wedge of cheese?'

'I guess I can handle that. How much cheese?'

'Half a pound.'

He brought me the beer and cheese. 'That will be a dollar and a half.'

I paid him. 'Is Chantry Canyon anywhere near here?'

He nodded. 'Second turn to the left—that's about a mile north of here. Go on up about four miles until you hit a crossroads. Turn left, another couple of miles or so, and you'll be in the canyon. Are you with the people that's taken it over?'

'What people do you mean?'

'I forget what they call themselves. They're fixing up the old house, planning to make it some kind of religious settlement.' He turned towards the back of the store and raised his voice: 'Sheriff? What do those people call themselves that took over Chantry Canyon?'

One of the pool players leaned his cue against the wall and came towards us, his polished boots kicking his shadow ahead of him. He was a man in his late fifties, with a grey military-style moustache. A sheriff's badge glinted on his chest. His eyes had a matching glint.

'Society of Mutual Love,' he said to me. 'Is that who you're looking for?'

'I wasn't. I was looking for Mildred Mead.' I showed him my photostat.

'You're in the wrong state, Mister. Mildred sold out about three months ago and took off for California. She told me she couldn't stand the loneliness any more. I told her she had friends here, and she has, but she wanted to spend her last days with her folks in California.'

'Where in California?'

'She didn't say.' The sheriff looked uneasy.

'What was the name of her folks?'

'I don't know.'

'Did she mean relatives?'

'Mildred didn't tell me. She was always close-mouthed about her family. I had to tell the same thing to the young couple that came through here earlier today.'

'Young man and a girl in a blue Ford sedan?'

The sheriff nodded. 'That's them. Are they with you?'

'I'm hoping to join them.'

'You'll probably find them up there in the canyon. They went up about sunset. I warned them they were running the risk of getting themselves converted. I don't know what those Mutual Love people believe in, but the belief they have is certainly powerful. One of the converts told me he turned over everything he had to the organization, and they worked him hard besides. Looks to me like they're coining money. I know they paid Mildred over a hundred thousand for the place. Of course that includes the acreage. So hold on to your wallet with both hands.'

'I'll do that, Sheriff.'

'My name is Brotherton, by the way.'

'Lew Archer.'

We shook hands. I thanked him and turned towards the door. He followed me outside. The night was clear and high, after the smoky interior of the store. We stood in silence for a minute. I found myself liking the man's company, in spite of his rather artificial folksiness.

'I don't want to pry,' he said, 'but I'm kind of fond of Mildred. Quite a few of us are. She was always generous with her money *and* her favours. Maybe too generous, I don't know. I hope she isn't in any kind of trouble in California.'

'I hope not.'

'You're a private detective there. Right?'

I said I was.

'Do you mind telling me what your business is with Mildred?'

'It isn't really Mildred I want to see. It's the young man and the girl who were asking for her earlier. They haven't come down the mountain again, have they?'

'I don't believe so.'

'Is this the only way out?'

'They could get out the other side if they had to, towards Tombstone. But, as I told them, it's a hard road to drive at night. They on the run from something?'

'I can tell you better after I talk to them.'

Brotherton's look hardened. 'You're close-mouthed, Mr Archer.'

'The girl's parents hired me.'

'I asked myself if she was a runaway.'

'That's putting it a little strong. But I expect to take her home with me.'

He let me go up the mountain by myself. I followed the storekeeper's directions, and they brought me to the head of a canyon whose open end framed the distant lights of Copper City. There were several lighted buildings in the canyon. The highest and largest was a sprawling stone house with a peaked shingled roof and a wide porch shelving out in front.

The road that led to the stone house was blocked by a wire gate. When I got out to open it, I could hear the people singing on the porch, singing a kind of song that I'd never heard before. Their refrain was something about Armageddon and the end of the world. Raising their voices on the prowlike porch, they made me think of passengers singing hymns on a sinking ship.

Fred Johnson's old blue Ford was parked in the gravel lane ahead of me. Its engine was dripping oil like something wounded. As I approached it, Fred got out and walked uncertainly into the wash of my headlights. His moustache was wet and spiky and he had a beard of blood. He didn't know me.

'Are you in some kind of trouble?'

He opened his swollen mouth. 'Yeah. They've got my girl inside. They're trying to convert her.'

The hymn had died in mid-phrase, as if the sinking ship had gone down abruptly. The hymn-singers were coming off the porch in our direction. From somewhere out of sight in the building, a girl's voice was raised in what sounded like fear.

Fred's head jerked. 'That's her now.'

I started for the gun in the trunk of my car, then remembered that I was driving a rented car. By that time, Fred and I were surrounded by half a dozen bearded men in overalls. Several long-skirted women stood to one side and watched us with cold eyes in long faces.

The oldest man was middle-aged, and he spoke to me in a monotone. 'You're disturbing our evening service.'

'Sorry. I want Miss Biemeyer. I'm a licenced private detective employed by her parents. The sheriff of the county knows I'm here.'

'We don't recognize his authority. This is holy ground, consecrated by our leader. The only authority we bow down to is the voice of the mountains and the sky and our own consciences.'

'Tell your conscience to tell you to go and get your leader.'

'You must be more respectful. He's performing an important ceremony.'

The girl raised her voice again. Fred started towards it, and I went along. The overalled men came together and formed a solid phalanx blocking our way.

I stood back and shouted at the top of my voice: 'Hey, leader! Get the hell out here!'

He came out on to the porch, a white-haired man in a black

robe who looked as if he had been dazzled or struck by lightning. He walked towards us, smiling a wide cold smile. His followers made way for him.

'Blessings,' he said to them, and to me: 'Who are you? I heard you reviling and cursing me. I resent it, not so much for myself as for the Power I represent.'

One of the women moaned in awe and delight. She got down on her knees in the gravel and kissed the leader's hand. I said, 'I want Miss Biemeyer. I work for Miss Biemeyer's father. He used to own this house.'

'I own it now,' he said, and then corrected himself: '*We* own it now. You're trespassing.'

The bearded men let out an assenting growl in unison. The oldest one of them said, 'We paid good money for this place. It's our refuge in time of trouble. We don't want it desecrated by cohorts of the devil.'

'Then bring Miss Biemeyer out here.'

'The poor child needs my help,' the leader said. 'She's been taking drugs. She's drowning in trouble, going down for the third time.'

'I'm not leaving her here.'

Fred let out a sob of frustration and grief and rage. 'That's what I told them. But they beat me up.'

'You gave her drugs,' the leader said. 'She told me you gave her drugs. It's my responsibility to purge her of the habit. Nearly all of my flock took drugs at one time. I was a sinner myself, in other ways.'

'I'd say you still are,' I said. 'Or don't you believe that kidnapping is wrong?'

'She's here of her own free will.'

'I want to hear her tell me that herself.'

'Very well,' he said to me, and to his followers: 'Let them approach the dwelling place.'

We went down the lane to the house. The bearded men crowded around Fred and me without exactly touching us. I could smell them, though. They stank of curdled hopes and poisonous fears and rancid innocence and unwashed armpits.

We were kept outside on the porch. I could see through the open front door that there was reconstruction work going on inside. The central hallway was being converted into a dormitory lined with bunks two high along the walls. I wondered how large a congregation the leader hoped to gather, and how much each of them might pay him for his bunk and his overalls and his salvation.

He brought Doris out of an inner room into the hallway. His followers let me go as far as the open door, and she and I faced each other there. She looked pale and scared and sane.

She said, 'Am I supposed to know you?'

'My name is Archer. We met in your apartment yesterday.'

'I'm sorry, I don't remember. I think I was stoned yesterday.'

'I think you were, Doris. How are you feeling now?'

'Sort of woozy,' she said. 'I hardly got any sleep in the car last night. And ever since we got here they've been at me.' She yawned deeply.

'At you in what way?'

'Praying for me. They want me to stay with them. They won't even charge me. My father would like that, not having to pay for me.' She smiled dispiritedly on one side of her mouth.

'I don't think your father feels that way about you.'

'You don't know my father.'

'I do, though.'

She frowned at me. 'Did my father send you after me?'

'No. I sort of came on my own. But your mother is paying me. She wants you back. So does he.'

'I don't really think they do,' the girl said. 'Maybe they think they do, but they don't really.'

Fred spoke up behind me. 'I do, Doris.'

'Maybe you do, and maybe you don't. But maybe I don't want you.' She looked at him in cold unfriendly coquetry. 'I wasn't what you wanted, anyway. You wanted the picture that my parents bought.'

Fred looked down at the porch floor. The leader stepped between the girl and us. His face was a complex blend of exalted mystic and Yankee trader. His hands were shaking with nervousness.

'Do you believe me now?' he said to me. 'Doris wants to stay with us. Her parents have neglected and rejected her.

Her friend is a false friend. She knows her true friends when
she sees them. She wants to live with us in the brotherhood of
spiritual love.'

'Is that true, Doris?'

'I guess so,' she said with a dubious half-smile. 'I might as
well give it a try. I've been here before, you know. My father
used to bring me here when I was a little girl. We used to
come up and visit Mrs Mead. They used to—' She broke off
the sentence and covered her mouth with her hand.

'They used to what, Doris?'

'Nothing. I don't want to talk about my father. I want to
stay here with them and get straightened out. I'm spiritually
unwell.' The self-diagnosis sounded like a parroting of something that she had recently been told. Unfortunately it also
sounded true.

I had a strong urge to take her away from the brothers. I
didn't like them or their leader. I didn't trust the girl's judgement. But she knew her own life better than I could possibly
know it for her. Even I could see that it hadn't been working
out.

I said, 'Remember that you can always change your mind.
You can change it right now.'

'I don't want to change it right now. Why would I want to
change it?' she asked me glumly. 'This is the first time in a
week that I even knew what I was doing.'

'Bless you, my child,' the leader said. 'Don't worry, we'll
take good care of you.'

I wanted to break his bones. But that made very little sense.
I turned and started back to my rented car. I felt very small,
dwarfed by the mountains.

XX

I LOCKED THE blue Ford and left it standing in the lane. Fred
didn't look fit to drive it, and if he had been I wouldn't have
trusted him not to run out on me. He climbed into my car like
a poorly working automaton and sat with his head hanging on

his blood-spotted chest.

He roused himself from his lethargy when I backed out on to the road: 'Where are we going?'

'Down the mountain to talk to the sheriff.'

'No.'

He turned away from me and fumbled with the door latch on his side. I took hold of his collar and pulled him back into the middle of the seat.

'I don't want to turn you in,' I said. 'But that's on condition that you answer some questions. I've come a long way to ask them.'

He answered after a thinking pause: 'I've come a long way, too.'

'What for?'

Another pause. 'To ask some questions.'

'This isn't a word game, Fred. You'll have to do better than that. Doris told me you took her parents' painting and you admitted it to me.'

'I didn't say I stole it.'

'You took it without their permission. What's the difference?'

'I explained all that to you yesterday. I took the picture to see if I could authenticate it. I took it down to the art museum to compare it with their Chantrys. I left it there overnight and somebody stole it.'

'Stole it from the art museum?'

'Yes, sir. I should have locked it up, I admit that. But I left it in one of the open bins. I didn't think anyone would notice it.'

'Who did notice it?'

'I have no way of knowing. I didn't tell anyone. You've got to believe me.' He turned his dismayed face to me. 'I'm not lying.'

'Then you were lying yesterday. You said the painting was stolen from your room at home.'

'I made a mistake,' he said. 'I got confused. I was so upset I forgot about taking it down to the museum.'

'Is that your final story?'

'It's the truth. I can't change the truth.'

I didn't believe him. We drove down the mountain in unfriendly silence. The repeated cry of a screech owl followed us.

'Why did you come to Arizona, Fred?'

He seemed to consider his answer, and finally said, 'I wanted to trace the picture.'

'The one you took from the Biemeyers' house?'

'Yes.' He hung his head.

'What makes you think it's in Arizona?'

'I don't think that. I mean, I don't know whether it is or not. What I'm trying to find out is who painted it.'

'Didn't Richard Chantry paint it?'

'I think so, but I don't know when. And I don't know who or where Richard Chantry is. I thought perhaps that Mildred Mead could tell me. Mr Lashman says she was the model all right. But now she's gone, too.'

'To California.'

Fred straightened up in his seat. 'Where in California?'

'I don't know. Maybe some of the local people can give us the information.'

Sheriff Brotherton was waiting in his car, which was parked in the lighted lot outside the substation. I parked beside it, and we all climbed out. Fred was watching me intently, wanting to hear what I would tell the authorities.

'Where's the young lady?' the sheriff said.

'She decided to stay with the society overnight. Maybe longer.'

'I hope she knows what she's doing. Are there any sisteren around?'

'I saw a few. This is Fred Johnson, Sheriff.'

Brotherton shook the younger man's hand and looked closely into his face. 'Did they attack you?'

'I took a swing at one of them. He took a swing at me.' Fred seemed proud of the incident. 'That was about it.'

The sheriff seemed disappointed. 'Don't you want to lodge a complaint?'

Fred glanced at me. I gave him no sign, one way or the other.

'No,' he said to the sheriff.

'You better think it over. That nose of yours is still bleeding. While you're here, you better go into the station and get

Deputy Cameron to give you first aid.'

Fred moved towards the substation as if, once inside, he might never get out again.

When he was beyond hearing, I turned to the sheriff: 'Did you know Mildred Mead well?'

His face was stony for a moment. His eyes glittered. 'Better than you think.'

'Does that mean what I think it means?'

He smiled. 'She was my first woman. That was around forty years ago, when I was just a kid. It was a great favour she did me. We've been friends ever since.'

'But you don't know where she is now?'

'No. I'm kind of worried about Mildred. Her health isn't the best, and she isn't getting any younger. Mildred's had a lot of hard blows in her life, too. I don't like her going off by herself like this.' He gave me a long hard contemplative look.

'Are you going back to California tomorrow?'

'I plan to.'

'I'd appreciate it if you'd look Mildred up, see how she's doing.'

'California's a big state, Sheriff.'

'I know that. But I can ask around, and see if anyone here has heard from her.'

'You said she went to California to stay with relatives.'

'That's what she told me before she left. I didn't know she had any relatives, there or anywhere else. Except for her son William.' Brotherton's voice had dropped so low that he seemed to be talking to himself.

'And William was murdered in 1943,' I said.

The sheriff spat on the ground, and then withdrew into silence. I could hear the murmur of voices from the substation, and the screech owl's cry high on the mountainside. It sounded like an old woman's husky titter.

'You've been doing some research into Mildred's life,' he said.

'Not really. She's the subject of a painting that I was hired to recover. But the case keeps sliding off into other cases. Mostly disaster cases.'

'Give me a for-instance.'

'The disappearance of Richard Chantry. He dropped out of sight in California in 1950, and left behind some paintings which have made him famous.'

'I know that,' the sheriff said. 'I knew him when he was a boy. He was the son of Felix Chantry, who was chief engineer of the mine in Copper City. Richard came back here after he got married. He and his young wife lived in the house up the mountain, and he started painting there. That was back in the early forties.'

'Before or after his half-brother William was murdered?'

The sheriff walked away from me a few steps, then came back. 'How did you know that William Mead was Richard Chantry's half-brother?'

'It came up in conversation.'

'You must have some pretty wide-ranging conversations.' He stood perfectly still for a moment. 'You're not suggesting that Richard Chantry murdered his half-brother William?'

'The suggestion is all yours, Sheriff. I didn't even know about William's death until today.'

'Then why are you so interested?'

'Murder always interests me. Last night in Santa Teresa there was another murder—also connected with the Chantry family. Did you ever hear of a man named Paul Grimes?'

'I knew him. He was Richard Chantry's teacher. Grimes lived with him and his wife for quite some time. I never thought too much of Grimes. He lost his job at the Copper City high school and married a half-breed.' The sheriff averted his head and spat on the ground again.

'Don't you want to know how he was murdered?'

'It doesn't matter to me.' He seemed to have a supply of anger in him, which broke out at unexpected points. 'Santa Teresa is way outside my territory.'

'He was beaten to death,' I said. 'I understand that William Mead was also beaten to death. Two murders, in two different states, over thirty years apart, but the same *m.o.*'

'You're reaching,' he said, 'with very little to go on.'

'Give me more, then. Was Paul Grimes living with the Chantrys when William Mead was killed?'

'He may have been. I think he was. That was back in 1943, during the war.'

'Why wasn't Richard Chantry in uniform?'

'He was supposed to be working in the family's copper mine. But I don't think he ever went near it. He stayed at home with his pretty young wife and painted pretty pictures.'

'What about William?'

'He was in the army. He came here on leave to visit his brother. William was in uniform when he was killed.'

'Was Richard ever questioned about William's death?'

The sheriff answered after some delay, and when he did answer he spoke with difficulty: 'Not to my knowledge. I wasn't in charge then, you understand. I was just a junior deputy.'

'Who conducted the investigation?'

'I did, for the most part. I was the one that found the body, not too far from here.' He pointed east towards the New Mexico desert. 'Understand, we didn't find him right away. He'd been dead for several days, and the varmints had been at him. There wasn't much left of his face. We weren't even sure that he'd been killed by human hands until we got the medical examiner out from Tucson. By that time it was too late to do much.'

'What would you have done if you'd had the chance?'

The sheriff became quite still again, as if he were listening to voices from the past that I couldn't hear. His eyes were shadowed and remote.

Finally he said, with too much angry certainty, 'I wouldn't have done anything different. I don't know what you're trying to prove. I don't know why I'm talking to you at all.'

'Because you're an honest man, and you're worried.'

'What am I worried about?'

'Mildred Mead, for one thing. You're afraid that something has happened to her.'

He took a deep breath. 'I don't deny that.'

'And I think you're still worried about that body you found in the desert.'

He looked at me sharply but made no other response. I said,

'Are you certain that it was her son William's body?'

'Absolutely certain.'

'Did you know him?'

'Not that well. But he was carrying his official papers. In addition to which, we brought Mildred out from Tucson. I was there when she made the identification.' He went into another of his silences.

'Did Mildred take the body back to Tucson with her?'

'She wanted to. But the army decided that after we got finished with it the body should go to Mead's wife. We packed the poor remains into a sealed coffin and shipped them back to the wife in California. At first none of us knew he had a wife. He hadn't been married very long. He married her after he entered the service, a friend of his told me.'

'Was this a local friend?'

'No. He was an army buddy. I disremember his name—something like Wilson or Jackson. Anyway, he was very fond of Mead and he wangled a leave to come out here and talk to me about him. But he couldn't tell me much, except that Mead had a wife and a baby boy in California. I wanted to go and see them, but the county wouldn't put up the expense money for me. Mead's army buddy got shipped out in a hurry, and I never saw him again, though later, after the war, he sent me a postcard from a vets' hospital in California. One way and another, I never did make a case.' The sheriff sounded faintly apologetic.

'I don't understand why Richard Chantry wasn't questioned.'

'It's simple enough. Richard was out of the state before the body was found. I made a real effort to have him brought back —you understand, I'm not saying he was guilty, in any way— but I couldn't get any support from higher authorities. The Chantrys still had a lot of political power, and the Chantry name was kept out of the William Mead case. It wasn't even publicized that Mildred Mead was his mother.'

'Was old Felix Chantry still alive in 1943?'

'No. He died the year before.'

'Who was running the copper mine?'

'A fellow named Biemeyer. He wasn't the official head at

the time, but he was making the decisions.'

'Including the one not to question Richard Chantry?'

'I wouldn't know about that.'

His voice had changed. He had started to lie, or to withhold the truth. Like every sheriff in every county, he would have his political debts and his unspeakable secrets.

I wanted to ask him who he was trying to protect, but decided not to. I was far out of my own territory, among people I didn't know or entirely understand, and there was a sense of unexpended trouble in the air.

XXI

THE SHERIFF was leaning towards me slightly, almost as if he could overhear my thoughts. He was as still as a perching hawk, with some of a hawk's poised threat.

'I've been open with you,' he said. 'But you've been holding back on me. You haven't even told me who you represent.'

'Biemeyer,' I said.

The sheriff smiled broadly without showing any teeth at all. 'You're kidding me.'

'No, I'm not. The girl is Biemeyer's daughter.'

Without any obvious change, his smile turned into a grin of shock and alarm. He must have become aware that he was revealing himself. Like a hostile fist relaxing, his face smoothed itself out into blandness. Only his sharp grey eyes were hostile and watchful. He jerked a thumb towards the mountain behind him.

'The girl you left up there is Biemeyer's daughter?'

'That's right.'

'Don't you know he's majority owner of the copper mine?'

'He makes no secret of it,' I said.

'But why didn't you tell me?'

It was a question I couldn't answer easily. Perhaps I'd let myself imagine that Doris might possibly be better off in a world quite different from her parents' world, at least for a while. But this world belonged to Biemeyer, too.

The sheriff was saying, 'The copper mine is the biggest employer at this end of the state.'

'Okay, we'll put the girl to work in the copper mine.'

He stiffened. 'What in hell do you mean by that? Nobody said anything about putting her to work.'

'It was just a joke.'

'It's not funny. We've got to get her out of that funny farm before some harm comes to her. My wife and I can put her up for the night. We have a nice spare room—it used to be our own daughter's room. Let's get going, eh?'

The sheriff left Fred in the deputy's custody and drove me up the mountain in his official car. He parked it in the lane behind Fred's old blue Ford. A dented white moon watched us over the mountain's shoulder.

The big house in the canyon was dark and silent, its stillness hardly broken by a man's random snore, a girl's faint crying. The crying girl turned out to be Doris. She came to the door when I called her name. She had on a white flannelette nightgown that covered her like a tent from the neck down. Her eyes were wide and dark and her face was wet.

'Get your clothes on, honey,' the sheriff said. 'We're taking you out of this place.'

'But I like it here.'

'You wouldn't like it if you stayed. This is no place for a girl like you, Miss Biemeyer.'

Her body stiffened and her chin came up. 'You can't make me leave.'

The leader came up behind her, not too close. He didn't speak. He seemed to be watching the sheriff with the detachment of a spectator at somebody else's funeral.

'Don't be like that, now, will you?' the sheriff said to Doris. 'I've got a daughter of my own, I know how it is. We all like a little adventure. But then it comes time to get back to normal living.'

'I'm not normal,' she said.

'Don't worry, you will be, honey. What you need is to find the right young man. The same thing happened to my girl. She went and lived in a commune in Seattle for a year. But then she came back and found Mr Right, and they've got two children now and everybody's happy.'

'I'm never going to have any children,' she said.

But she put on her clothes and went out to the sheriff's car with him. I lingered behind with the leader. He stepped out on to the porch, moving rather uncertainly. In the light from the sky, his eyes and his white hair seemed faintly phosphorescent.

'She would have been welcome to stay with us.'

'For a price?'

'We all contribute as we can. We practise tithing, each paying according to his ability. My own contribution is largely spiritual. Some of us earn our keep at humbler tasks.'

'Where did you study theology?'

'In the world,' he said. 'Benares, Camarillo, Lompoc. I admit I don't have a degree. But I've done a great deal of counselling. I find myself able to help people. I could have helped Miss Biemeyer. I doubt that the sheriff can.' He reached out and touched my arm with his long thin hand. 'I believe I could help you.'

'Help me do what?'

'Do nothing, perhaps.' He spread his arms wide in an actorish gesture. 'You seem to be a man engaged in an endless battle, an endless search. Has it ever occurred to you that the search may be for yourself? And that the way to find yourself is to be still and silent, silent and still?' He dropped his arms to his sides.

I was tired enough to be taken by his questions, and to find myself repeating them in my mind. They were questions I had asked myself, though never in just those terms. Perhaps, after all, the truth I was looking for couldn't be found in the world. You had to go up on a mountain and wait for it, or find it in yourself.

But even as I was taking a short-term lease on a piece of this thought, I was watching the lights of Copper City framed in the canyon mouth, and planning what I would do there in the morning.

'I don't have any money.'

'Neither do I,' he said. 'But there seems to be enough for everyone. Money is the least of our worries.'

'You're lucky.'

He disregarded my irony. 'I'm glad you see that. We're very lucky indeed.'

'Where did you get the money to buy this place?'

'Some of our people have income.' The idea seemed to please him, and he smiled. 'We may not go in for worldly show, but this isn't exactly a poorhouse. Of course it isn't all paid for.'

'I'm not surprised. I understand it cost you over a hundred thousand dollars.'

His smile faded. 'Are you investigating us?'

'I have no interest in you at all, now that the girl is out of here.'

'We did her no harm,' he said quickly.

'I'm not suggesting you did.'

'But I suppose the sheriff will be bothering us now. Simply because we gave shelter to Biemeyer's daughter.'

'I hope not. I'll put in a word with him, if you like.'

'I would like, very much.' He relaxed visibly and then audibly, letting out a long sighing breath.

'In return for which,' I said, 'you can do something for me.'

'What is it?' He was suspicious of me again.

'Help me to get in touch with Mildred Mead.'

He spread his hands, palms up. 'I wouldn't know how. I don't have her address.'

'Aren't you making payments to her for this house?'

'Not directly. Through the bank. I haven't seen her since she went to California. That was several months ago.'

'Which bank is handling the account?'

'The Copper City branch of Southwestern Savings. They'll tell you I'm not a swindler. I'm not, you know.'

I believed him, provisionally. But he had two voices. One of them belonged to a man who was reaching for a foothold in the spiritual world. The other voice, which I had just been listening to, belonged to a man who was buying a place in the actual world with other people's money.

It was an unstable combination. He could end as a con man, or a radio preacher with a million listeners, or a bartender with a cure of souls in Fresno. Perhaps he had already been some of those things.

But I trusted him up to a point. I gave him the keys to the blue Ford and asked him to keep it for Fred, just in case Fred ever came back that way.

XXII

WE DROVE BACK down the mountain to the substation and found Fred sitting inside with the deputy. I couldn't tell at first glance whether he was a prisoner or a patient. He had an adhesive bandage across the bridge of his nose and cotton stuffed up his nostrils. He looked like a permanent loser.

The sheriff, who was a small winner, went into the inner office to make a phone call. His voice was a smooth blend of confidence and respect. He was making arrangements to fly Doris home in a copper-company jet.

He lifted his head, flushed and bright-eyed, and offered me the receiver. 'Mr Biemeyer wants to talk to you.'

I didn't really want to talk to Biemeyer, now or ever. But I took the receiver and said into it, 'This is Archer.'

'I've been expecting to hear from you,' he said. 'After all, I'm paying you good money.'

I didn't remind him that his wife had paid me. 'You're hearing from me now.'

'Thanks to Sheriff Brotherton. I know how you private dicks operate. You let the men in uniform do the work and then you step in and take the credit.'

For a hotheaded instant, I was close to hanging up on Biemeyer. I had to remind myself that the case was far from over. The stolen painting was still missing. There were two unsolved murders, Paul Grimes's and now William Mead's.

'There's credit enough for everybody,' I said. 'We have your daughter and she's in reasonably good shape. I gather she'll be flying home tomorrow in one of your planes.'

'First thing in the morning. I was just finalizing the arrangement with Sheriff Brotherton.'

'Could you hold that plane until late morning or so? I have

some things to do in Copper City, and I don't think your daughter should travel unaccompanied.'

'I don't like the delay,' he said. 'Mrs Biemeyer and I are very eager to see Doris.'

'May I speak to Mrs Biemeyer?'

'I suppose you can,' he said reluctantly. 'She's right here.'

There was some indistinct palaver at the other end, and then Ruth Biemeyer's voice came over the line. 'Mr Archer? I'm relieved to hear from you. Doris hasn't been arrested, has she?'

'No. Neither has Fred. I want to bring them both home with me tomorrow on the company plane. But I may not be able to get out of here much before noon. Is that all right with you?'

'Yes.'

'Thanks very much. Good night, Mrs Biemeyer.'

I hung up and told the sheriff that the plane would leave at noon tomorrow with me and Doris and Fred. Brotherton didn't argue. My telephone conversation had invested me with some of the Biemeyer charisma.

On the strength of this, I put in a word for the people in Chantry Canyon, as I had promised, and offered to assume responsibility for Fred. The sheriff agreed. Doris, he said, would be spending the night at his house.

Fred and I checked into a double room in the motel. I needed a drink, but the store was closed and not even beer was available. I had no razor or toothbrush. I was as tired as sin.

But I sat on my bed and felt surprisingly good. The girl was safe. The boy was in my hands.

Fred had stretched out on his bed with his back to me. His shoulders moved spasmodically, and he made a repeated noise that sounded like hiccuping. I realized he was crying.

'What's the matter, Fred?'

'You know what's the matter. My career is over and done with. It never even started. I'll lose my job at the museum. They'll probably put me in jail, and you know what will happen to me then.' His voice was dulled by the cotton in his nose.

'Do you have a record?'

'No. Of course I don't.' The idea seemed to shock him. 'I've never been in trouble.'

'Then you should be able to stay out of jail.'

'Really?' He sat up and looked at me with wet red eyes.

'Unless there's something that I don't know about. I still don't understand why you took the picture from the Biemeyer house.'

'I wanted to test it. I told you about that. Doris even suggested that I should take it. She was just as interested as I was.'

'Interested in what, exactly?'

'In whether it was a Chantry. I thought I could put my expertise to work on it.' He added in a muffled voice, 'I wanted to show them that I was good for something.'

He sat up on the edge of the bed and put his feet on the floor. He was young for his age, in his thirties and still a boy, and foolish for a person of his intelligence. It seemed that the sad house on Olive Street hadn't taught him much about the ways of the world.

Then I reminded myself that I mustn't buy too much of Fred's queer little story. After all, he was a self-admitted liar.

I said, 'I'd like your expert opinion on that picture.'

'I'm not really an expert.'

'But you're entitled to an informed opinion. As a close student of Chantry, do you think he painted the Biemeyer picture?'

'Yes, sir. I do. But my statement has to be qualified.'

'Go ahead and qualify it.'

'Well. It certainly doesn't go back any twenty-five years. The paint is much too new, applied maybe as recently as this year. And the style has changed, of course. It naturally would. I think it's Chantry's style, his *developed* style, but I couldn't swear to it unless I saw other late examples. You can't base a theory or an opinion on a single work.'

Fred seemed to be talking as an expert, or at least an informed student. He sounded honest and for once forgetful of himself. I decided to ask him a harder question.

'Why did you say in the first place that the painting had

been stolen from your house?'

'I don't know. I must have been crazy.' He sat looking down at his dusty shoes. 'I guess I was afraid to involve the museum.'

'In what way?'

'In any way. They'd fire me if they knew I'd taken the picture myself the way I did. Now they'll fire me for sure. I have no future.'

'Everybody has a future, Fred.'

The words didn't sound too encouraging, even to me. A lot of futures were disastrous, and Fred's was beginning to look like one of those. He hung his head under the threat of it.

'The most foolish thing you did was to bring Doris with you.'

'I know. But she wanted to come along.'

'Why?'

'To see Mildred Mead if I found her. She was the main source of the trouble in Doris's family, you know. I thought it might be a good idea if Doris could talk to her. You know?'

I knew. Like other lost and foolish souls, Fred had an urge to help people, to give them psychotherapy even if it wrecked them. When he was probably the one who needed it most. Watch it, I said to myself, or you'll be trying to help Fred in that way. Take a look at your own life, Archer.

But I preferred not to. My chosen study was other men, hunted men in rented rooms, ageing boys clutching at manhood before night fell and they grew suddenly old. If you were the therapist, how could you need therapy? If you were the hunter, you couldn't be hunted. Or could you?

'Doris is having a hard time maintaining,' Fred said. 'I've been trying to help her out of it.'

'By taking her on a long drive to nowhere?'

'She wanted to come. She insisted. I thought it was better than leaving her where she was, sitting in an apartment by herself and gobbling drugs.'

'You have a point.'

He managed to give me a quick shy smile that twitched and cowered in the shadow of his moustache. 'Besides, you have to remember that this isn't nowhere for Doris. She was born in Copper City and spent at least half of her life here in

Arizona. This is home for her.'

'It hasn't been a very happy homecoming.'

'No. She was terribly disappointed. I guess you can't go home again, as Thomas Wolfe says.'

Remembering the gabled house where Fred lived with his father and mother, I wondered who would want to.

'Have you always lived in Santa Teresa?'

He was thoughtful for a moment. Then he said, 'Since I was a little boy, we've lived in the same house on Olive Street. It wasn't always the wreck that it is now. Mother kept it up much better—I used to help her—and we had roomers, nurses from the hospital and such.' He spoke as if having roomers was a privilege. 'The best times were before my father came home from Canada.' Fred looked past me at my hunched shadow on the wall.

'What was your father doing in Canada?'

'Working at various jobs, mostly in British Columbia. He liked it then. I don't think he and Mother got along too well, even in those days. I've realized since that he probably stayed away from her for that reason. But it was a bit rough on me. I don't remember ever seeing my father until I was six or seven.'

'How old are you now, Fred?'

'Thirty-two,' he said reluctantly.

'You've had long enough to get over your father's absence.'

'That isn't what I meant at all.' He was flustered and angry, and disappointed in me. 'I wasn't offering him as an excuse.'

'I didn't say you were.'

'As a matter of fact, he's been a good father to me.' He thought this statement over, and amended it. 'At least he was in those early days when he came back from Canada. Before he started drinking so hard. I really loved him in those days. Sometimes I think I still do, in spite of all the awful things he does.'

'What awful things?'

'He rants and roars and threatens Mother and smashes things and cries. He never does a stroke of work. He sits up there with his crazy hobbies and drinks cheap wine, and it's all he's good for.' His voice had coarsened and rose and fell like an angry wife's ululation. I wondered if Fred was unconsciously imitating his mother.

'Who brings him the wine?'

'Mother does. I don't know why she does it, but she keeps on doing it. Sometimes,' he added in a voice that was almost too low to hear, 'sometimes I think she does it in revenge.'

'Revenge for what?'

'For ruining himself and his life, and ruining *her* life. I've seen her stand and watch him staggering from wall to wall as if she took pleasure in seeing him degraded. At the same time, she's his willing slave and buys him liquor. That's another form of revenge—a subtle form. She's a woman who refuses to be a full woman.'

Fred had surprised me. As he reached deeper into the life behind his present trouble, he lost his air of self-deprecating foolishness. His voice deepened. His thin and long-nosed boyish face almost supported his moustache. I began to feel faint stirrings of respect for him, and even hope.

'She's a troubled woman,' I said.

'I know. They're both troubled people. It's really too bad they ever got together. Too bad for both of them. I believe my father once had the makings of a brilliant man, before he turned into a lush. Mother isn't up to him mentally, of course, and I suppose she resents it, but she isn't a negligible person. She's a registered nurse and she's kept up her profession and looked after my father, both at the same time. That took some doing.'

'Most people do what they have to.'

'She's done a bit more than that. She's been helping me through college. I don't know how she makes the money stretch.'

'Does she have any extracurricular income?'

'Not since the last roomer left. That was some time ago.'

'And I heard last night that she lost her job at the hospital.'

'Not exactly. She gave it up.' Fred's voice had risen, and lost its masculine timbre. 'They made her a much better offer at the La Paloma nursing home.'

'That doesn't sound very likely, Fred.'

'It's true.' His voice rose higher, his eyes were too bright, his moustache was ragged. 'Are you calling my mother a liar?'

'People make mistakes.'

'You're making one now, running down my mother like that. I want you to take it back.'

'Take what back?'

'What you said about my mother. She doesn't peddle drugs.'

'I never said she did, Fred.'

'But you implied it. You implied that the hospital let her go because she was stealing drugs and peddling them.'

'Is that what the hospital people said?'

'Yes. They're a bunch of sadistic liars. My mother would never do a thing like that. She's always been a good woman.' Tears formed in his eyes and left snail-tracks on his cheeks. 'I haven't been a good man,' he said. 'I've been living out a fantasy, I see that now.'

'What do you mean, Fred?'

'I was hoping to pull off a coup that would make me famous in art circles. I thought if I could get to Miss Mead, she could help me find the painter Chantry. But all I've done is make an ass of myself and get the whole family into deeper trouble.'

'It was a fair try, Fred.'

'It wasn't. I'm a fool!'

He turned his back on me. Gradually his breathing slowed down. I felt mine slowing down with it. I realized just before I fell asleep that I was beginning to like him.

I woke up once in the middle of the night and felt the weight of the mountains squatting over me. I turned on the light at the head of my bed. There were old watermarks on the walls like the indistinct traces of bad dreams.

I didn't try to read them. I turned off the light and fell back into sleep, breathing in unison with my foolish pseudo-son.

XXIII

WHEN I GOT up in the morning, Fred was still sleeping. One arm was over his eyes as if he dreaded the new day and its light. I asked the deputy on duty in the substation to keep track of Fred. Then I drove my rented car into Copper City, guided by the plume of smoke over the smelter.

A barber sold me a shave for four dollars. For a similar amount, I got a small breakfast and directions on how to find my way to Southwestern Savings.

It was in a downtown shopping centre, which looked like a piece of Southern California that had broken loose and blown across the desert. The little city that surrounded it seemed to have been drained of energy by the huge wound of the copper mine in its side, the endless suspiration of the smelter. The smoke blew over the city like a great ironic flag.

The sign on the glass front door of Southwestern Savings said that the building didn't open until ten. It was not quite nine by my watch. It was getting hotter.

I found a phone booth and looked for Paul Grimes in the directory. His name wasn't listed but there were two listings for Mrs Paul Grimes, one for a residence and the other for Grimes Art & School Supplies. The latter turned out to be in the downtown area, within easy walking distance.

It was a small store on a side street, full of paper goods and picture reproductions, empty of customers. The deep dim narrow room reminded me of an ancient painted cave, but most of the modern pictures on the walls weren't quite as lifelike as the cave paintings.

The woman who emerged from a door at the back looked like Paola's sister. She was broad-shouldered and full-breasted, and she had the same dark colouring and prominent cheekbones. She was wearing an embroidered blouse, beads that jangled, a long full skirt, and open sandals.

Her eyes were black and bright in her carved brown face. She gave the impression of saved-up force that wasn't being used.

'Can I help you?'

'I hope so. I'm a friend of your daughter's.' I told her my name.

'Of course. Mr Archer. Paola mentioned you on the phone. You were the one who found Paul's body.'

'Yes. I'm sorry.'

'And you are a detective, is that correct?'

'I work at it.'

She gave me a hard black look. 'Are you working at it now?'

'It seems to be a full-time job, Mrs Grimes.'

'Am I under suspicion?'

'I don't know. Should you be?'

She shook her handsome head. 'I haven't seen Paul for over a year. We've been divorced for a good many years. Once Paola was out of her childhood, there was nothing to stay together for. It was all burnt out long ago.'

Mrs Grimes spoke with a direct emotional force that impressed me. But she must have realized that she was telling me more than she needed to. She put her left hand over her mouth. I noticed that her red fingernails were bitten down to the quick, and I felt sorry that I had frightened her.

'I don't think anybody suspects you of anything.'

'They shouldn't, either. I didn't do anything to Paul except try to make a man of him. Paola might tell you different—she always took his side. But I did my best for Paul whenever he let me. The truth is—the truth was, he was never meant to be married to any woman.'

Her hidden life, the memories of her marriage, seemed to be very near the surface, boiling cold behind her smooth dark face.

Remembering what Paola had once told me, I asked her bluntly, 'Was he homosexual?'

'Bi,' she said. 'I don't believe he had much to do with men while I was married to him. But he always loved the company of young men, including his high school boys when he was a teacher. It wasn't a bad thing entirely. He loved to teach.

'He taught me a lot, too,' she added thoughtfully. 'The most important thing, he taught me to speak correct English. That changed my life. But something went wrong with his life. Maybe it was me. He couldn't handle me.' She moved her body impatiently from the waist down. 'He always said it was my fault that his life went off the track. Maybe it was.'

She lowered her handsome head and clenched her fists. 'I used to have a bad temper. I used to fight him hard, physically.

I used to love him, too, very much. Paul didn't really love me. At least not after I became his wife and stopped being his pupil.'

'Who did he love?'

She thought about the question. 'Paola. He really loved Paola—not that it did her much good. And he loved some of his students.'

'Does that include Richard Chantry?'

Her black gaze turned inward towards the past. She nodded almost imperceptibly. 'Yes, he loved Richard Chantry.'

'Were they lovers in the technical sense?'

'I think they were. Young Mrs Chantry thought so. In fact, she was considering divorce.'

'How do you know?'

'After Paul moved in with them, she came to me. She wanted me to break up their relationship, at least that was the way she put it to me. I think now she was trying to use me as a witness against her husband, in case it came to divorce. I told her nothing.'

'Where did the conversation take place, Mrs Grimes?'

'Right here in the shop.'

She tapped the floor with her toe, and her whole body moved. She was one of those women whose sex had aged into artiness but might still flare up if given provocation. I kept my own feet still.

'What year did you have that talk with Mrs Chantry?'

'It must have been 1943, the early summer of '43. We'd only just opened this shop. Paul had borrowed quite a lot of money from Richard to fix the place up and stock it. The money was supposed to be an advance on further art lessons. But Richard never got his money's worth. He and his wife moved to California before the summer was out.' She let out a snort of laughter so explosive that it jangled her beads. 'That was a desperation move if I ever saw one.'

'Why do you say so?'

'I'm absolutely certain it was her idea. She pushed it through in a hurry, practically overnight—anything to get Richard out of the state and away from my husband's influence. I was glad to see the twosome broken up myself.' She raised her spread hands and lifted her shoulders in a large gesture of relief, then let them slump.

'But they both ended up in Santa Teresa, after all,' I said. 'I wonder why. And why did your ex-husband and Paola go to Santa Teresa this year?'

She repeated the gesture with her arms and shoulders, but this time it seemed to mean that she didn't have any answers. 'I didn't know they were going there. They didn't tell *me*. They just went.'

'Do you think Richard Chantry had anything to do with it?'

'Anything is possible, I guess. But it's my opinion—it has been for a long time—that Richard Chantry is dead.'

'Murdered?'

'It could be. It happens to homosexuals—bisexuals—whatever he is or was. I see a lot of them in this business. Some of them go in for the rough trade almost as if they wanted to be killed. Or they wander away by themselves and commit suicide. That may be what Richard Chantry did. On the other hand, he may have found a soul mate and is living happily ever after in Algiers or Tahiti.'

She smiled without warmth but so broadly that I could see that one of her molars was missing. Both physically and emotionally, I thought, she was a bit dilapidated.

'Did your ex-husband go for the rough trade?'

'He may have. He spent three years in federal prison—did you know that? He was a heroin addict on top of everything else.'

'So I was told. But I heard he'd kicked the habit.'

She didn't answer my implied question, and I didn't put it to her more directly. Grimes hadn't died of heroin or any other drug. He had been beaten to death, like William Mead.

I said, 'Did you know Richard Chantry's half-brother William?'

'Yes. I knew him through his mother, Mildred Mead. She was a famous model in these parts.' She narrowed her eyes as if she had remembered something puzzling. 'You know, she's gone to California, too.'

'Where in California?'

'Santa Teresa. She sent me a card from there.'

'Did she mention Jack Biemeyer? He lives in Santa Teresa.'

She knitted her black brows. 'I don't think so. I don't think she mentioned anybody by name.'

'Are she and Biemeyer still friends?'

'I doubt it. As you probably know, he inherited Mildred from old Felix Chantry. He stashed her in a house in the mountains and lived with her for years. But I think he broke off with her long before he retired. Mildred was quite a lot older than Jack Biemeyer. For a long time she didn't show her age, but she's feeling it now. She made that clear in the card she sent me.'

'Did she give you her address?'

'She was staying in a motel in Santa Teresa. She said she was looking for a more permanent place.'

'Which motel?'

Her face went vague in thought. 'I'm afraid I don't remember. But it's on the front of the card. I'll see if I can find it.'

XXIV

SHE WENT TO her office in the back of the store and returned brandishing a postcard. On the front was a coloured picture of Siesta Village, which was one of the newer waterfront motels in Santa Teresa. A shaky hand had written on the back, beside Juanita Grimes's name and address in Copper City:

Dear Nita:

Am staying here temporarily till I find a better place. The foggy weather does not agree with me, in fact am not feeling too well. The Calif. climate is not what it's cracked up to be. Don't quote me but am looking for a nursing home where I can stay temporarily and get back on my feet. Not to worry—I have friends here.

Mildred

I handed the card back to Mrs Grimes. 'It sounds as if Mildred's in some trouble.'

She shook her head, perhaps not so much in denial as in resistance to the thought. 'She may be. It isn't like Mildred to complain about her health. She's always been a hardy soul. She must be over seventy by now.'

'When did you get this card from her?'

'A couple of months ago. I wrote her an answer and sent it to the motel, but I haven't heard from her since.'

'Do you know who her friends in Santa Teresa are?'

'I'm afraid I don't. Mildred was pretty close-mouthed about her friends. She lived a very full life, to put it mildly. But old age finally caught up with her.' She looked down along the slopes of her own body. 'Mildred had a lot of trouble in her time. She didn't go out of her way to avoid it, either. She's always had more guts than she could use.'

'Were you close to Mildred?'

'As close as any other woman in town. She wasn't—she isn't a woman's woman. She's a man's woman who never married.'

'So I gather. Wasn't William an illegitimate son?'

Mrs Grimes nodded. 'She had a long love affair with Felix Chantry, the man who developed the copper mine. William was his son.'

'How well did you know William, Mrs Grimes?'

'Paul and I saw quite a lot of him. He was a budding painter, too, before the army took him. Paul thought he had more potential talent than his brother Richard. He didn't live to develop it. He was murdered by an unknown hand in the summer of '43.'

'The same summer that Richard and his wife went to California.'

'The same summer,' she repeated solemnly. 'I'll never forget that summer. Mildred drove over from Tucson—she was living with a painter in Tucson then—and she drove over from there to view poor William's body in the morgue. Afterwards she came to my adobe, and as it turned out she spent the night. She was strong and healthy in those days, no more than forty, but the death of her son came as a terrible shock to her. She walked into my house like an old woman. We sat in the kitchen and killed a quart of bourbon between us. Mildred was a lively conversationalist most of the time, but that night she hardly said a word. She was completely used up. William was her only child, you know, and she really loved him.'

'Did she have any idea who had killed him?'

'If she had, she didn't tell me. I don't think she had. It was an unsolved killing. It stayed that way.'

'Do you have any thoughts on the subject, Mrs Grimes?'

'I thought at the time it was one of those senseless killings. I still do. Poor William hitched a ride with the wrong party, and he was probably killed for the money in his pockets.' She was looking intently into my face as if it were a clouded window. 'I can see you don't believe that.'

'It may be true. But it seems too easy. William may have hitched a ride with the wrong people, but I doubt that they were unknown to him.'

'Really?' She leaned closer. The part in her hair was white and straight as a desert road. 'You think William was deliberately murdered by someone he knew. What do you base that on?'

'Two things, mainly. Talking to the authorities about it, I got a feeling that they knew more than they were saying, that there may have been a deliberate or half-deliberate cover-up. I know that's vague. The other thing on my mind is even vaguer. However, I think I give it more weight. I've worked on several dozen murder cases, many of them involving multiple murders. And in nearly every case the murders were connected in some way. In fact, the deeper you go into a series of crimes, or any set of circumstances involving people who know each other, the more connectedness you find.'

Her eyes were still intent on my face; I felt as if she were trying to look directly into my mind. 'You believe that Paul's death the other night was connected with William Mead's death in 1943?'

'Yes. I'm working on that theory.'

'Connected in what way?'

'I'm not sure.'

'You think the same person killed both of them?' In spite of her age, she sounded like a young girl frightening herself with a story whose ending might frighten her more. 'Who do you think it was?'

'I don't want to lead you. You seem to have known all the suspects.'

'You mean you have more than one suspect?'

'Two or three.'

'Who are they?'

'You tell me, Mrs Grimes. You're an intelligent woman. You're probably acquainted with all the people involved, and you know more about them than I ever will.'

Her breasts rose and fell rapidly with her breathing. In some way, I had touched and excited her. Perhaps she was feeling that something she said or did might after all make a difference to the world, or to her dead husband.

'Will I be quoted?' she said.

'Not by me.'

'All right. I know something that very few people know. I got it from Mildred Mead.'

'On the night when the two of you killed the bottle of bourbon?'

'No. Some time before that, not long after her son William was drafted. It must have been back in 1942. He got a girl pregnant and had to marry her, Mildred told me. But he was really in love with Richard Chantry's wife. And she was in love with William.'

'Are you suggesting that Richard murdered William?'

'I'm telling you he had a motive, anyway.'

'I thought you said that Richard Chantry was homosexual.'

'Bisexual, like my husband. It doesn't rule anything out— I learned that the hard way.'

'Do you think Richard killed your husband, too?'

'I don't know. He may have.' She peered past me into the bright empty street. 'Nobody seems to know where Richard is or what he's doing. As all the world knows, he's been gone for twenty-five years.'

'Gone where? Do you have any ideas, Mrs Grimes?'

'I have one. It struck me when I heard that Paul had been killed. I wondered if Richard was hiding out in Santa Teresa. And whether Paul had seen him, and been silenced.' She hung her head, wagging it dolefully from side to side. 'Those are terrible thoughts to have, but I've been having them.'

'So have I,' I said. 'What does your daughter Paola think about all this? You said you talked to her on the phone.'

Mrs Grimes closed her teeth over her lower lip and looked away. 'I'm afraid I don't know what she thinks. Paola and I don't communicate too well. Has she talked to you?'

'Soon after the murder. She was in shock to some extent.'

'I'm afraid she still is. Would you be good enough to look her up when you go back to Santa Teresa?'

'I was planning to.'

'Good. Would you take her some money from me? She says she's completely broke.'

'I'll be glad to. Where is she staying?'

'The Monte Cristo Hotel.'

'That sounds like swank.'

'It isn't, though.'

'Good.' She gave me two twenties and a ten out of the cash register. 'This should at least cover her rent for a couple of days.'

The morning was running out. I went back to Southwestern Savings, which I found open now, and approached a bright-looking woman who sat at a desk by herself. The nameplate on the desk identified her as Mrs Conchita Alvarez.

I told her my name. 'I'm looking for a friend named Mildred Mead. I understand she does her banking here.'

Mrs Alvarez gave me a hard look that was almost tangible. She must have decided I wasn't a con man, because she nodded her shiny dark head and said, 'Yes. She did. But she's moved to California.'

'Santa Teresa? She often talked about moving there.'

'Well, now she has.'

'Can you give me an address for Mrs Mead? I happen to be on my way to Santa Teresa. Mr Biemeyer is flying me over in one of the company planes.'

Mrs Alvarez stood up. 'I'll see what I can find.'

She went through a door and was gone for some time. She came back looking rather disappointed.

'The only address I have for Miss Mead is a motel called Siesta Village. But that address is two months old.'

'Is that where you're sending her mortgage payments?'

'No. I checked into that. She rented a PO box.' Mrs Alvarez looked at a slip of paper in her hand. 'Number 121.'

'In Santa Teresa?'

'In the main post office in Santa Teresa, yes.'

I drove out to the airport and turned in my rented car. The company jet was already warming up, and Doris and Fred were in it. They were sitting in separate seats, Doris in the front behind the pilot's compartment and Fred in the back. There seemed to be no communication between them, perhaps because the sheriff was standing guard at the door.

He seemed relieved to see me. 'I was afraid you weren't going to make it. I thought I'd have to make the trip to California myself.'

'Has there been any trouble?'

'No.' He cast a cold eye on Fred, who winced away. 'I've got so I don't trust anybody under forty.'

'I'm afraid I qualify for your trust.'

'Yeah, you're more like fifty, aren't you? And I'll be sixty on my next birthday. I never thought it would happen, but I've started to look forward to retirement. The world is changing, you know.'

But not fast enough, I thought. It was still a world where money talked, or bought silence.

XXV

THE JET CLIMBED in a long straight slant. It was a clear day. The long dry savannahs of Mexico extended themselves on my left. On my right I could see the ten-thousand-foot peak standing above Tucson. It gradually moved backward like a drifting pyramid as we flew west.

Fred kept his head turned away from me, his eyes on the scenery sliding away underneath us. The girl in the seat behind the pilot seemed equally oblivious and remote. The high sierra rose in the faded distance.

Fred looked at the mountains ahead as if they constituted

the walls of a jail where he was going to be confined.

He turned to me: 'What do you think they'll do to me?'

'I don't know. It depends on two things. Whether we recover the picture, and whether you decide to tell the whole story.'

'I told you the whole story last night.'

'I've been thinking about that, and I wonder if you did. It seems to me you left out some pertinent facts.'

'That's your opinion.'

'Isn't it yours, too?'

He turned his head away and looked down at the great sunlit world into which he had escaped for a day or two. It seemed to be fleeing backward into the past. The mountain walls loomed ahead, and the jet whined louder as it climbed to vault over them.

'What got you so interested in Mildred Mead?' I asked him.

'Nothing. I wasn't interested in her. I didn't even know who she was until Mr Lashman told me yesterday.'

'And you didn't know that Mildred moved to Santa Teresa a few months ago?'

He turned towards me. He badly needed a shave, and it made him look both older and more furtive. But he seemed honestly confused.

'I certainly didn't. What is she doing there?'

'Looking for a place to live, apparently. She's a sick old woman.'

'I didn't know that. I don't know anything about her.'

'Then what was it that got you interested in the Biemeyers' painting?'

He shook his head. 'I can't tell you. Chantry's work has always fascinated me. It isn't a crime to be interested in paintings.'

'Only if you steal them, Fred.'

'But I didn't *plan* to steal it. I simply borrowed it overnight. I meant to return it next day.'

Doris had turned in her seat. She was up on her knees, watching us over the back.

'That's true,' she said. 'Fred *told* me he borrowed the

picture. He wouldn't do that if he planned to steal it, would he?'

Unless, I thought, he planned to steal you, too. I said, 'It doesn't seem to make sense. But nearly everything does when you understand it.'

She gave me a long cold appraising look. 'You really believe that, that everything makes sense?'

'I work on that principle, anyway.'

She lifted her eyes in sardonic prayer and smiled. It was the first time I had seen her smile.

'Would you mind if I sat with Fred for a while?' she said.

His sensitive little smile peeked out from under his heavy moustache. He flushed with pleasure.

I said, 'I don't mind, Miss Biemeyer.'

I traded seats with her, and pretended to go to sleep. Their conversation was steady and low, too low to be overheard through the sound of the engine. Eventually I did go to sleep.

When I woke up, we were turning over the sea, back towards the Santa Teresa airport. We landed with a gentle bump and taxied towards the small Spanish Mission terminal.

Jack Biemeyer was waiting at the gate. His wife broke past him as we climbed out. She folded Doris in her arms.

'Oh, Mother,' the girl said in embarrassment.

'I'm so glad you're all right.'

The girl looked at me over her mother's shoulder like a prisoner peering over a wall.

Biemeyer began to talk to Fred. Then he began to shout. He accused Fred of rape and other crimes. He said that he would have Fred put away for the rest of his life.

Fred's eyes were watering. He was close to tears. He bit at his moustache with his lower teeth. People were coming out of the terminal to watch and listen from a distance.

I was afraid of something more serious happening. Biemeyer might talk himself into an act of violence, or scare Fred into one.

I took Fred by the arm and marched him through the terminal into the parking lot. Before I could get him out of there, an official car drove up. Two policemen climbed out and arrested Fred.

The Biemeyer family came out of the terminal in time to see him leave. In what looked like a parody of Fred's arrest, Biemeyer took his daughter by the elbow and hustled her into the front seat of his Mercedes. He ordered his wife to get in. She refused with gestures. He drove away.

Ruth Biemeyer stood by herself in the parking lot, stiff with embarrassment and blanched by anger. She didn't appear to recognize me at first.

'Are you all right, Mrs Biemeyer?'

'Yes, of course. But my husband seems to have driven away without me.' She produced a frantic smile. 'What do you think I should do?'

'It depends on what you want to do.'

'But I never do what I want to do,' she said. 'Nobody ever does what he really wants to do.'

Wondering what Ruth Biemeyer really wanted to do, I opened the right-hand door of my car for her. 'I'll drive you home.'

'I don't want to go home.' But she got in.

It was a strange situation. The Biemeyers, for all their protestations and all their efforts, didn't really seem to want their daughter back. They didn't know how to treat her, or what to do about Fred. Well, neither did I, unless we could invent an alternative world for the people who didn't quite fit into this one.

I closed the door on Ruth Biemeyer, walked around the car, and got in behind the wheel. The air was hot and stuffy in the car, which had sat all day in the parking lot. I rolled down the window on my side.

It was a blank and desolate patch of earth, squeezed between the airport and the road and littered with empty cars. The blue sea winked and wrinkled in the distance.

Like a blind date trying to make conversation, Mrs Biemeyer said, 'This is a strange world we live in nowadays.'

'It always was.'

'I didn't used to think so. I don't know what will happen to Doris. She can't live at home and she can't make it on her own. I don't know what she can do.'

'What did you do?'

'I married Jack. He may not have been the greatest choice in the world but at least we got through life.' She spoke as if her life were already over. 'I was hoping Doris would find some eligible young man.'

'She has Fred.'

The woman said coldly, 'He isn't possible.'

'At least he's a friend.'

She cocked her head as if she was surprised that anyone should befriend her daughter. 'How do you know that?'

'I've talked to him. I've seen them together.'

'He's simply been using her.'

'I don't believe that. One thing I'm pretty sure of, Fred didn't take your painting with any idea of selling it, or cashing in. No doubt he's a little hipped on it, but that's another matter. He's been trying to use it to solve the Chantry problem.'

She gave me a sharp inquiring look. 'Do you believe that?'

'Yes, I do. He may be emotionally unstable. Anybody with his family background would be likely to be. He's not a common thief, or an uncommon one, either.'

'So what happened to the picture?'

'He left it in the museum overnight and it was stolen.'

'How do you know?'

'He told me.'

'And you believe him?'

'Not necessarily. I don't know what happened to the picture. I doubt that Fred does, either. But I don't believe he belongs in jail, though.'

She lifted her head. 'Is that where they took him?'

'Yes. You can get him out if you want to.'

'Why should I?'

'Because as far as I know, he's your daughter's only friend. And I think she's just as desperate as Fred is, if not more so.'

She looked around at the parking lot and the surrounding flatlands. The battlements of the university loomed on the horizon beyond the tidal slough.

She said, 'What has Doris got to be so desperate about? We've given her everything. Why, when I was her age I was in secretarial school and working part-time on the side. I even enjoyed it,' she said with nostalgia and some surprise. 'In fact, those were the best days of my life.'

'These aren't Doris's best days.'

She pulled away in the seat, turning in my direction. 'I don't understand you. You're a peculiar detective. I thought detectives ran down thieves and put them behind bars.'

'I just did that.'

'But now you want to undo it. Why?'

'I've already told you. Fred Johnson isn't a thief, no matter what he did. He's your daughter's friend, and she needs one.'

The woman turned her face away and bowed her head. The blonde hair fell away from her vulnerable neck.

'Jack will kill me if I interfere.'

'If you mean that literally, maybe Jack is the one who belongs in jail.'

She gave me a shocked look, which gradually changed into something more real and humane. 'I'll tell you what I'll do. I'll take it up with my lawyer.'

'What's his name?'

'Roy Lackner.'

'Is he a criminal lawyer?'

'He's in general practice. He was a public defender for a while.'

'Is he your husband's lawyer as well as yours?'

She hesitated, glancing at my face and away. 'No. He isn't. I went to him to find out where I stood if I divorced Jack. And we've also discussed Doris.'

'When was this?'

'Yesterday afternoon. I shouldn't be telling you all these things.'

'You should, though.'

'I hope so,' she said. 'I also hope you're discreet.'

'I try to be.'

We drove downtown to Lackner's office, and I told her what I knew about Fred as we went. I added in summation, 'He can go either way.'

That went for Doris, too, but I didn't think it was necessary to say so.

Lackner's offices were in a rehabilitated frame cottage on the upper edge of the downtown slums. He came to the front door to meet us, a blue-eyed young man with a blond beard and lank yellow hair that came down almost to his shoulders. His look was pleasant, and his grip was hard.

I would have liked to go in and talk to him, but Ruth Biemeyer made it plain that she didn't want me. Her attitude was proprietorial and firm, and I wondered in passing if there was some attachment between the young man and the older woman.

I gave her the name of my motel. Then I went down to the waterfront to give Paola her mother's fifty dollars.

XXVI

THE MONTE CRISTO was a three-storey stucco hotel that had once been a large private residence. Now it advertised 'Special Rates for Weekenders'. Some of the weekenders were drinking canned beer in the lobby and matching coins to see who was going to pay for it. The desk clerk was a little doll-faced man with an anxious look that intensified when he saw me. I think he was trying to decide whether I was a cop.

I didn't tell him whether I was or not. Sometimes I didn't even tell myself. I asked him if Paola Grimes was in. He gave me a puzzled look.

'She's a dark girl with long black hair. Good figure.'

'Oh. Yeah. Room 312.' He turned and examined her key slot. 'She isn't in.'

I didn't bother asking him when to expect Paola. He wouldn't be likely to know. I kept her fifty dollars in my wallet and made a mental note of her room number. Before I left the hotel, I looked into the bar. It was a kind of post-historic ruin. All the girls waiting there were blonde. Outside, along the beach front, there were a number of women with long black hair but none of them was Paola.

I drove uptown to the newspaper building and left my car at a fifteen-minute curb in front of it. Betty was at her type-writer in the newsroom. Her hands were quiet on the keys. She had faint blue circles under her eyes, no lipstick on her mouth. She looked dispirited, and she failed to brighten appreciably when she saw me.

'What's the matter, Betty?'

'I haven't been making good progress on the Mildred Mead thing. I can't seem to find out enough about her.'

'Why don't you interview her?'

She screwed up her face as if I'd threatened to slap her. 'That isn't funny.'

'It wasn't meant to be. Mildred Mead has a box in the Santa Teresa post office, number 121 in the main branch. If you can't get to her through that, she's probably in one of the local nursing homes.'

'Is she sick?'

'Sick and old.'

Betty's eyes, her whole face, changed and softened. 'What on earth is she doing here in Santa Teresa?'

'Ask her. And when she tells you, you tell me.'

'But I don't know which nursing home she's in.'

'Call all of them.'

'Why don't *you*?'

'I want to talk to Captain Mackendrick. Besides, you can do a better job on a phone check. You know the people in this town and they know you. If you locate her, don't say anything to scare her off. I wouldn't mention that you work for a newspaper.'

'What *shall* I say?'

'As little as possible. I'll check back with you.'

I drove across the centre of town to the police station. It was a stucco oblong that lay like a dingy sarcophagus in the middle of an asphalt parking lot. I talked my way past an armed and uniformed woman guard into Mackendrick's office, which was small and bleak. It contained a wall of files, a desk and three chairs, one of which was occupied by Mackendrick. Across the single window there were bars.

Mackendrick was studying a typed sheet that lay flat on the desk in front of him. He was slow in looking up. I wondered if this was meant to imply that he was more important than I was, but not important enough. He finally raised his impervious eyes to mine.

'Mr Archer? I thought you'd left town for good.'

'I went to Arizona to pick up the Biemeyer girl. Her father flew us back in one of his company's jets.'

Mackendrick was impressed, and slightly startled, as I had meant him to be. He massaged the side of his crumpled face with his hand, as if to reassure himself of its solidity.

'Of course,' he said, 'you're working for the Biemeyers. Right?'

'Right.'

'Does he have some special interest in the Grimes killing?'

'He bought a picture from Grimes. There's some question whether it's a phony or a genuine new Chantry.'

'If Grimes had anything to do with it, it probably is a phony. Is that the picture that was stolen?'

'It wasn't exactly stolen,' I said, 'at least not the first time around. Fred Johnson took it to make some tests on it at the art museum. Somebody stole it from there.'

'Is that Johnson's story?'

'Yes, and I believe it.' But even to me the story had sounded weak in my retelling.

'I don't. Neither does Biemeyer. I've just been talking to him on the phone.' Mackendrick smiled in cold pleasure. He had taken a point from me in the endless game of power that complicated his life. 'If you want to go on working for Biemeyer, you better check with him about some of those little details.'

'He isn't my only source. I've talked to Fred Johnson at some length, and I don't believe he's a criminal type.'

'Nearly everybody is,' Mackendrick said. 'All they need is the opportunity. And Fred Johnson had that. He may even have been in cahoots with Paul Grimes. That would be quite a trick, to sell a phony Chantry, then steal it back before it could be detected.'

'I thought of that possibility. But I doubt that it happened. Fred Johnson isn't capable of planning and carrying out an action like that. And Paul Grimes is dead.'

Mackendrick leaned forward with his elbows on his desk, his left palm and his right fist forming a ball joint under his chin. 'There may be others involved. There almost certainly are. We may be dealing with an art-theft ring of queers and addicts. It's a crazy world.' He disengaged his hands and waved his fingers in front of his face, miming the wildness of the world. 'Did you know Grimes was a queer?'

'Yes. His wife was telling me that this morning.'

The captain's eyes widened in astonishment. 'He has a wife?'

'He had. She told me they've been separated for years. She runs an art shop in Copper City under her married name.'

Mackendrick pencilled a note on a yellow pad. 'Is Fred Johnson queer?'

'I doubt it. He has a girl.'

'You just got finished telling me that Grimes had a wife.'

'It's true, Fred could be bisexual. But I've spent a fair amount of time with him now, and haven't seen any evidence of it. Even if he is, it doesn't make him a thief.'

'He stole a picture.'

'He took it with the knowledge and permission of the owner's daughter. Fred is a budding art expert. He wanted to test the picture for age and authenticity.'

'So he says now.'

'I believe him. I honestly don't think he belongs in jail.'

Mackendrick's palm and fist came together again like parts of a machine. 'Is Fred Johnson paying you to say this?'

'Biemeyer is paying me to recover his picture. Fred Johnson says he hasn't got it. I think it's time we looked elsewhere. In fact, that's what I've been doing, more or less accidentally.'

Mackendrick waited. I told him what I had learned about Paul Grimes's early life in Arizona, and about his relationship with Richard Chantry. I also told him about the death of Mildred Mead's illegitimate son William, and the quick departure of Richard Chantry from Arizona in the summer of 1943.

Mackendrick picked up his pencil and began to draw connected squares across the yellow paper, a series of squares like a random chessboard representing the precincts of the city or his mind.

'This is new information to me,' he admitted finally. 'Are you sure that it's good information?'

'I got most of it from the sheriff who handled the William Mead killing. You can check with him if you want to.'

'I'll do that. I was in the army when Chantry came here and bought that house on the ocean. But I got out and joined the force in 1945 and I was one of the few people who got to know him personally.' Mackendrick spoke as if his own experience and the history of the city had become almost synonymous to him. 'I patrolled the beach front there for several years, until I made sergeant. That was how I became acquainted with Mr Chantry. He was very security-conscious. He did a lot of complaining about people loitering around his house. You know how the beach and the ocean always attract out-of-towners.'

'Was he nervous?'

'I guess you'd say that. He was a loner, anyway. I never knew him to give a party, or even invite friends into his house. As far as I knew, he had no friends. He kept himself locked up in that house with his wife and a man called Rico, who cooked for them. And he worked. As far as I know, all he did was work. Sometimes he'd be up painting all night and I'd see the lights still burning in his house when I cruised by on the early-morning shift.' Mackendrick lifted his eyes, which had been emptied of the present and now became filled and perplexed by it again. 'Are you sure that Mr Chantry was a homo? I never knew one of them who liked hard work.'

I didn't mention Leonardo for fear of confusing the issue. 'I'm fairly certain. You could ask around.'

Mackendrick shook his head abruptly. 'Not in this town I couldn't. He's Santa Teresa's claim to fame—gone for twenty-five years, and still our leading citizen. And *you* be careful what you say about him.'

'Is that a threat?'

'It's a warning. I'm doing you a favour giving it. Mrs Chantry could sue you, and don't think she wouldn't. She's got the local paper so bulldozed that they let her read it ahead of time whenever they mention her husband. Especially when they mention his disappearance, it has to be handled with kid gloves.'

'What do you think happened to him, Captain? I've told

you what I know.'

'And I appreciate it. If he was a homo, as you say he was, then there's your answer right there. He stayed with his wife for seven years and couldn't stick it any longer. It's one thing I've often noticed about homos. Their lives run in cycles; they can't stay the course. And they have a tougher course to run than most of us.'

Mackendrick had succeeded in surprising me. There was a vein of tolerance in his granite after all.

I said, 'Is that the official theory, Captain? That Chantry simply took off of his own accord. No murder? No suicide? No blackmailing pressure?'

Mackendrick took in a deep whistling breath through his nose, and blew it out through his lips. 'I wouldn't attempt to tell you how many times I've been asked that question. It's just about my favourite question by now,' he said with irony. 'And I always give the same answer. We never came up with any evidence at all that Chantry had been killed, or forced to leave. As far as we were able to establish the facts, Chantry left here because he wanted to start a new life. And what you tell me about his sexual background only confirms it.'

'I assume his farewell letter was checked out in every way.'

'Every way possible. Handwriting, fingerprints, source of stationery—everything. The writing and the prints and the stationery were all Chantry's. There was no evidence that the letter was written under duress, either. And no new evidence has come up in the twenty-five years since then. I've had a special interest in the case from the beginning, because I knew Chantry, and you can take my word for all this. For some reason, he got sick and tired of his life here in Santa Teresa, and he dropped out.'

'He may have dropped in again, Captain. Fred Johnson seems to think that the stolen picture is a Chantry, and a fairly recent one.'

Mackendrick made an impatient flinging gesture with his left hand. 'I'd want a better opinion than Fred Johnson's. And I don't buy his story that the picture was stolen from the museum. I think he's got it stashed some place. If it is a genuine Chantry, it's worth real money. And in case you don't know it, Fred Johnson's family is on the rocks financially. His father's a hopeless drunk who hasn't worked for years; his mother lost her job at the hospital under suspicion of stealing drugs. And no matter whether he lost it or sold it or gave it away, Fred is criminally responsible for the loss of that picture.'

'Not until he's proved responsible.'

'Don't give me that, Archer. Are you a lawyer?'

'No.'

'Then stop trying to act the part of one. Fred is where he belongs. You're not. And I have an appointment with the deputy coroner.'

I thanked Mackendrick for his patience, without irony. He had told me a number of things I needed to know.

Leaving the police station, I passed my friend Purvis coming in. The young deputy coroner had the bright glazed look of a dedicated public servant on his way to get his picture in the paper. He didn't even break stride as he went by.

I waited beside his official station wagon. Squad cars came and went. A flock of starlings flew over in a twittering cloud, and the first early shadow of evening followed them across the sky. I was worried about what might happen to Fred in jail, and regretful that I hadn't been able to spring him.

Purvis came out of the station eventually, walking more slowly, with a certain weight of confidence.

I said, 'What's the word?'

'Remember the cadaver I showed you last night in the morgue?'

'I'm not likely to forget him. Jacob Whitmore, the painter.'

Purvis nodded. 'He wasn't drowned in the ocean after all. We completed a very careful autopsy this afternoon. Whitmore was drowned in fresh water.'

'Does that mean he was murdered?'

'Probably. Mackendrick seems to think so. Drowned in somebody's bathtub and chucked into the ocean afterwards.'

XXVII

I DROVE OUT to Sycamore Point and knocked on the door of Jacob Whitmore's cottage. It was opened by the girl he had left behind. The low sun touched her face with a rosy glow and made her narrow her eyes. She didn't appear to recognize me.

I had to remind her who I was. 'I was here the night before last. I bought some of Jake's pictures from you.'

She shaded her eyes and studied my face. Hers was pale and unfocused. Her blonde hair was uncombed, and it was lifted by the sundown wind pouring down the draw.

She said, 'Are the pictures okay?'

'They're okay.'

'I have some more if you want them.'

'We'll talk about it.'

She let me into her front room. Nothing in it had changed essentially, but it had lapsed into more extreme disorder. A chair was lying on its back. There were bottles on the floor, fragments of enchilada on the table.

She sat at the table. I picked up the fallen chair and sat facing her. 'Have you heard from the coroner this afternoon?'

She shook her head. 'I haven't heard from anybody; not that I remember, anyway. Excuse the condition of the room, will you, please? I drank too much wine last night and I must have had a tantrum. It seemed—it seems so unfair that Jake had to drown.' She was silent for a time, and then said, 'They asked my permission to do an autopsy yesterday.'

'They did it today. Jake drowned in fresh water.'

She shook her bleached head again. 'No, he didn't. He drowned in the ocean.'

'His body was found in the ocean, but the water that killed him was fresh water. You can take the coroner's word for it.'

She looked at me dimly through her half-closed eyes. 'I don't understand. Does that mean he drowned in a creek and his body was washed down into the sea?'

'That isn't likely. The creeks are low in the summer. It probably means that he was drowned in a bathtub or a swimming pool, and whoever did it dumped his body here in the ocean.'

'I don't believe it.' She looked around the room as if the murderer might be lurking behind the furniture. 'Who would do that to Jake?'

'You tell me, Mrs Whitmore.'

She shook her head. 'We weren't married. My name is Jessie Gable.' The sound of her name brought tears to her eyes. She blinked and the tears ran down her cheeks. 'You're telling me that Jake was murdered, aren't you?'

'Yes.'

'I don't understand. He never hurt a living soul. Except me. But I forgave him.'

'Murder victims don't usually deserve it.'

'But he had nothing worth stealing.'

'Maybe he had. Didn't Paul Grimes buy some of his pictures?'

She nodded. 'That's true, he did. But it wasn't really the pictures that he wanted. I was here in the room when Grimes was talking to Jake. He was trying to get some information out of him, and he bought Jake's pictures just to get him talking.'

'Talking about what?'

'The other picture. The picture that Jake had sold him at the beach art show, the day before.'

'And did Jake tell him what he wanted to know?'

'I don't know. They went outside to talk about it. They didn't want me to hear what they were saying.'

I got out my photograph of the Biemeyers' stolen painting and showed it to her in the light from the window. 'Is this the picture that Jake sold to Grimes the day before?'

She took the picture and nodded. 'It certainly looks like it. It's a really good picture and Jake got a lot of money for it. He didn't tell me how much, but it must have been several hundred, anyway.'

'And Grimes probably sold it for several thousand.'

'Really?'

'I'm not fooling, Jessie. The people who bought the picture

from Grimes had it stolen from them. I was hired to recover it.'

She sat up straight and crossed her legs. 'You don't think *I* stole it, do you?'

'No. I doubt you ever stole anything.'

'I didn't,' she said firmly. 'I never did. Except Jake from his wife.'

'That isn't a felony.'

'I don't know,' she said. 'I'm being punished like it was. And so was Jake punished.'

'Everybody dies, Jessie.'

'I hope that I die soon.'

I waited. 'Before you do,' I said, 'I want you to do Jake a favour.'

'How can I? He's already dead.'

'You can help me find the person or persons who killed him.' I took the photograph from her limp hands. 'I think he was killed over this.'

'But why?'

'Because he knew or figured out who painted it. I'm winging, you understand. I don't know for certain that that's true. But I think it is. This picture was the connecting link between the two men who were killed, Jake and Paul Grimes.'

I remembered as I said it that a third man had been killed: William Mead, whose body was found in the Arizona desert in 1943, and whose mother was the subject of the picture. These facts coming together in my mind gave me a kind of subterranean jolt, like an earthquake fault beginning to make its first tentative move. I was breathing quickly and my head was pounding.

I leaned across the littered table. 'Jessie, do you have any idea where Jake got this picture?'

'He bought it.'

'How much did he pay for it?'

'Fifty dollars at least—probably more. He wouldn't tell me how much more. He took the fifty dollars I had in my safety fund—that's money I kept in case we couldn't pay the rent. I told him he was crazy to put out cash for the picture, that he should take it on consignment. But he said he had a chance to make a profit. And I guess he did.'

'Did you ever see the person he bought it from?'

'No, but it was a woman. He let that slip.'

'How old a woman?'

Jessie spread her hands like someone feeling for rain. 'Jake didn't tell me, not really. He said that it was an older woman but that doesn't mean it was. She could be seventeen and he'd still tell me she was an older woman. He knew that I was jealous of the chicks. And I had reason to be.'

Tears rose in her eyes. I didn't know whether they stood for anger or grief. Her feelings seemed to be fluctuating between those two emotions. So did mine. I was weary of questioning the widows of murdered men. But I still had questions to ask.

'Did the woman bring the picture here to the house?'

'No. I never saw her. I told you that. She took it down to the waterfront on a Saturday. These last years, Jake had a sideline buying and selling pictures at the Saturday art show. He bought the picture there.'

'How long ago was that?'

She was slow in answering, perhaps looking back over a flickering passage of days that seemed all the same: sun and sea, wine and pot and grief and poverty.

'It must have been a couple of months ago. It's at least that long since he took my safety fund. And when he sold the picture to Paul Grimes he didn't replace my fund. He kept the money himself. He didn't want me to know how much it was. But we've been living on it ever since.' She scanned the room. 'If you can call this living.'

I got a twenty out of my wallet and dropped it on the table. She scowled at it and then at me.

'What's that for?'

'Information.'

'I couldn't give you much. Jake was secretive about this deal. He seemed to think he was on to something big.'

'I think he was, too, or trying to get on to it. Do you want to try and dig up some more information for me?'

'What kind of information?'

'Where this picture came from.' I showed her the portrait

of Mildred Mead again. 'Who Jake bought it from. Anything else that you can find out about it.'

'Can I keep that photo?'

'No. It's the only one I have. You'll have to describe it.'

'Who to?'

'The dealers at the Saturday art show. You know them, don't you?'

'Most of them.'

'Okay. If you come up with anything usable, I'll give you another twenty. If you can give me the name or address of the woman who sold Jake this picture, I'll give you a hundred.'

'I could use a hundred.' But she looked at me as if she didn't expect to see it in this life. 'Jake and I had bad luck. He's had nothing but bad luck since he joined up with me.' Her voice was harsh. 'I wish I could of died instead of him.'

'Don't wish it,' I said. 'We all die soon enough.'

'It can't come too soon for me.'

'Just wait awhile. Your life will start again. You're a young woman, Jessie.'

'I feel as old as the hills.'

Outside, the sun had just gone down. The sunset spread across the sea like a conflagration so intense that it fed on water.

XXVIII

THE RED SKY was darkening when I got downtown. The stores were full of light and almost empty of customers. I parked near the newspaper building and climbed the stairs to the newsroom. There was nobody there at all.

A woman in the hall behind me spoke in a husky tentative voice: 'Can I help you, sir?'

'I hope so. I'm looking for Betty.'

She was a small grey-haired woman wearing strong glasses that magnified her eyes. She looked at me with sharp friendly curiosity.

'You must be Mr Archer.'

I said I was.

The woman introduced herself as Mrs Fay Brighton, the librarian of the paper. 'Betty Jo asked me to relay a message to you. She said she'd be back here by half past seven at the latest.' She looked at the small gold watch on her wrist, holding it close to her eyes. 'It's almost that now. You shouldn't have long to wait.'

Mrs Brighton went back behind the counter of the room that housed her files. I waited for half an hour, listening to the evening sounds of the emptying city. Then I tapped on her door.

'Betty may have given up on me and gone home. Do you know where she lives?'

'As a matter of fact, I don't. Not since her divorce. But I'll be glad to look it up for you.'

She opened a directory and transcribed Betty's number and address on to a slip of paper: 'Seabrae Apartments, number 8, phone 967-9152.' Then she brought out a phone from under the counter. Her eyes clung to my face as I dialled and listened. Betty's phone rang twelve times before I hung up.

'Did she give you any idea where she was going?'

'No, but she made a number of calls. She used this phone for some of them, so that I couldn't help hearing. Betty was calling various nursing homes in town, trying to locate a relative of hers. Or so she said.'

'Did she mention the name?'

'Mildred Mead, I think it was. In fact, I'm sure of it. I think she found her, too. She took off in a hurry, and she had that light in her eyes—you know?—a young news hen on a breaking story.' She let out a sighing breath. 'I used to be one myself.'

'Did she tell you where she was going?'

'Not Betty Jo.' The woman smiled with shrewd pleasure. 'When she's on a story, she wouldn't give her best friend the time of day. She started late in the game, you know, and the virus really got to her. But you probably know all that if you're a friend of hers.'

The unspoken question hung in the air between us.

'Yes,' I said. 'I am a friend of hers. How long ago did she leave here?'

'It must have been two hours ago, or more.' She looked at her watch. 'I think she took off about five-thirty.'

'By car?'

'I wouldn't know that. And she didn't give me any hint at all as to where she was heading.'

'Where does she eat dinner?'

'Various places. Sometimes I see her in the Tea Kettle. That's a fairly good cafeteria just down the street.' Mrs Brighton pointed with her thumb in the direction of the sea.

'If she comes back here,' I said, 'will you give her a message for me?'

'I'd be glad to. But I'm not staying. I haven't eaten all day, and I really only waited for you to give you Betty's message. If you want to write one to her, I'll put it on her desk.'

She slid a small pad of blank paper across the counter to me. I wrote: 'Sorry I missed you. I'll check back in the course of the evening. Later you can get me at the motel.'

I signed the message 'Lew'. Then, after a moment's indecision, I wrote the word 'Love' above my name. I folded the note and gave it to Mrs Brighton. She took it into the newsroom.

When she came back, she gave me a slightly flushed and conscious look that made me wonder if she had read my message. I had a sudden cold urge to recall it and cross out the word I had added. So far as I could remember, I hadn't written the word, or spoken it to a woman, in some years. But now it was in my mind, like a twinge of pain or hope.

I walked down the block to the Tea Kettle's red neon sign and went in under it. It was nearly eight o'clock, which was late for cafeteria patrons, and the place looked rather desolate. There was no line at the serving counter, and only a few scattered elderly patrons at the tables.

I remembered that I hadn't eaten since morning. I picked up a plate, had it filled with roast beef and vegetables, and carried it to a table from which I could watch the whole place. I seemed to have entered another city, a convalescent city where the wars of love were over and I was merely one of the ageing survivors.

I didn't like the feeling. When Mrs Brighton came in, she did nothing to relieve it. But when she brought her tray into the dining-room, I stood up and asked her to share my table.

'Thank you. I hate eating alone. I spend so much time alone as it is, since my husband died.' She gave me an anxious half-smile as if in apology for mentioning her loss. 'Do you live alone?'

'I'm afraid I do. My wife and I were divorced some years ago.'

'That's too bad.'

'I thought so. But she didn't.'

Mrs Brighton became absorbed in her macaroni and cheese. Then she added milk and sugar to her tea. She stirred it and raised it to her lips.

'Have you known Betty long?'

'I met her at a party the night before last. She was covering it for the paper.'

'She was supposed to be. But if you're talking about the Chantry party she never did submit any usable copy. She got wound up in a murder case, and she hasn't thought about anything else in two days. She's a terribly ambitious young woman, you know.'

Mrs Brighton gave me one of her large-eyed impervious looks. I wondered if she was offering me a warning or simply making conversation with a stranger.

'Are you involved in that murder case?' she said.

'Yes. I'm a private detective.'

'May I ask who has employed you?'

'You may ask. But I better not answer.'

'Come on.' She gave me a roguish smile that wrinkled up her face yet somehow improved it. 'I'm not a reporter any more. You're not talking for print.'

'Jack Biemeyer.'

Her pencilled eyebrows rose. 'Mr Bigshot's involved with a murder?'

'Not directly. He bought a picture which was later stolen. He hired me to get it back.'

'And did you?'

'No. I'm working on it, though. This is the third day.'

'And no progress?'

'Some progress. The case keeps growing. There's been a second murder—Jacob Whitmore.'

Mrs Brighton leaned towards me suddenly. Her elbow spilled the rest of her tea. 'Jake was drowned three days ago, accidentally drowned in the ocean.'

'He was drowned in fresh water,' I said, 'and put into the ocean afterwards.'

'But that's terrible. I knew Jake. I've known him since he was in high school. He was one of our delivery boys. He was the most harmless soul I ever knew.'

'It's often the harmless ones that get killed.'

As I said that, I thought of Betty. Her face was in my mind, and her firm harmless body. My chest felt hot and tight, and I took a deep breath and let it out, without intending to, in a barely audible sigh.

'What's the matter?' Mrs Brighton said.

'I hate to see people die.'

'Then you picked a strange profession.'

'I know I did. But every now and then I have a chance to prevent a killing.'

And every now and then I precipitated one. I tried to keep that thought and the thought of Betty from coming together, but the two thoughts nudged each other like conspirators.

'Eat your vegetables,' Mrs Brighton said. 'A man needs all the vitamins he can get.' She added in the same matter-of-fact tone: 'You're worried about Betty Jo Siddon, aren't you?'

'Yes, I am.'

'So am I. Particularly since you told me Jake Whitmore was murdered. Somebody I've known half my life—that's striking close to home. And if something happened to Betty—' Her voice broke off and started again in a lower register: 'I'm fond of that girl, and if anything happened to her—well, there's nothing I wouldn't do.'

'What do you think happened?'

She looked around the room as if for a portent or a prophet. There was no one there but a few old people eating.

'Betty's hooked on the Chantry case,' she sighed. 'She hasn't been talking about it much lately but I know the signs. I had it myself at one time, over twenty years ago. I was going to track Chantry down and bring him back alive and become the foremost lady journalist of my time. I even wangled my way to Tahiti on a tip. Gauguin was one of Chantry's big influences, you know. But he wasn't in Tahiti. Neither was Gauguin.'

'But you think Chantry's alive?'

'I did then. Now I don't know. It's funny how you change your views of things as you get older. You're old enough to know what I mean. When I was a young woman, I imagined that Chantry had done what I would have liked to do. He thumbed his nose at this poky little town and walked away from it. He was only thirty or so, you know, when he dropped out of sight. He had all the time in the world ahead of him— time for a second life. Now that my own time is running short, I don't know. I think it's possible that he was murdered all those years ago.'

'Who had reason to kill him?'

'I don't know. His wife, perhaps. Wives often do have reason. Don't quote me, but I wouldn't put it past her.'

'Do you know her?'

'I know her quite well, at least I did. She's very publicity-conscious. When I stopped being a reporter, she lost all interest in me.'

'Did you know Chantry himself?'

'I never did. He was a recluse, you know. He lived in this town for seven or eight years, and you could count on the fingers of one hand the number of people who knew him to speak to.'

'Can you name any of them?'

'I can think of one,' she said. 'Jake Whitmore knew Chantry. He used to deliver their paper. I think it was knowing Chantry that made a painter of him.'

'I wonder if it was knowing Chantry that killed him.'

Mrs Brighton took off her glasses and wiped them with a lace-edged handkerchief. She put them on again and studied me through them.

'I'm not sure I follow you. Could you tell me just what you

mean by that, in words of one syllable? I've had a long hard day.'

'I have a feeling that Chantry may be here in town. It's something more than a feeling. Jack Biemeyer's stolen painting was probably a Chantry. It passed through two pairs of hands on its way to Biemeyer—Jake Whitmore's and Paul Grimes's. Both Whitmore and Grimes are dead. I guess you know that.'

She bowed her grey head under the weight of the knowledge. 'You think Betty's in real trouble, don't you?'

'She may be.'

'Can I help? Do you want me to start phoning the nursing homes?'

'Yes. But please be careful. Don't mention any names. You have an aged aunt who needs custodial care. Get them to describe the facilities. Listen for sounds of guilt or any sign of trouble.'

'I'm good at that,' she said drily. 'I hear a lot of those kinds of sounds in the office. But I'm not sure that that's the best approach.'

'What do you suggest?'

'I don't have anything specific in mind. It depends on what theory we're working on. Is it your idea that Betty located the nursing home where Mildred Mead is staying, was inveigled into going there, and got snatched? Isn't that a little melodramatic?'

'Melodramatic things are happening all the time.'

She sighed. 'I suppose you're right. I hear a lot of *them* in the office, too. But isn't it just as likely that Betty simply took off on the track of something, and she'll be turning up again any time?'

'It may be just as likely,' I said. 'But don't forget that Jake Whitmore turned up drowned. Paul Grimes turned up beaten to death.'

Her face absorbed the knowledge and grew heavy with it, like an old sponge absorbing water. 'You're right, of course. We have to do what we can. But shouldn't we be going to the police?'

'As soon as we have something definite to take to them.

Mackendrick is hard to convince.'

'Is he not. Okay. I'll be in the office if you want me.'

She gave me the number, and I wrote it down. I asked her further to make me a list of the nursing homes and their numbers as she called them.

XXIX

I DROVE UP the dark hill to Biemeyer's house feeling angry and powerless. The house was blazing with lights but entirely silent.

Biemeyer answered the door with a drink held securely in his hand. He gave the impression that the drink was holding him up. Everything else about him, shoulders and knees and face, seemed to be sagging.

'What in the hell do you want?' His voice was husky and frayed, as if he had been doing a lot of shouting.

'I'd like to have a serious talk with you, Mr Biemeyer.'

'I can translate that. You want more money.'

'Forget about the money for a change. I don't care about your money.'

His face lengthened. He had hoisted his money up the mast, but I had failed to salute it. Slowly his face came together again, wrinkling around his dark hostile eyes.

'Does that mean you won't be sending me a bill?'

I was tempted to turn my back on him and leave, perhaps taking a swing at him first. But Biemeyer and his household possessed knowledge that I had to have. And working for them gave me standing with the police that I couldn't get in any other way.

'Please take it easy,' I said. 'The money you've advanced will probably cover it. If it doesn't, I'll send you a bill. After all, I did recover your daughter.'

'But not the picture.'

'I'm working on the picture, getting closer to it. Is there some place we could have a private talk?'

'No,' he said. 'There is not. All I'm asking you to do is to respect the sanctity of my home. If you won't do that, to hell with you.'

Now even the glass in his hand was no longer steady. He waved it in a declamatory gesture and sloshed some liquor on the polished floor. Mrs Biemeyer appeared behind him, as if the spilling of liquor was an understood signal in the family. Much farther back, half hidden by the edge of a partition, Doris stood still and silent.

'I think you should talk to him, Jack,' Ruth Biemeyer said. 'We've been through quite a lot in the last couple of days. And thanks in good part to Mr Archer, we've survived it.'

Her face was calm and smooth, and she was dressed for evening. Her voice was resigned. I guessed that she had made a bargain with whatever fates she recognized: bring Doris home and I'll put up with Jack. Well, Doris was there, standing like a Chirico figure in the receding distances of the house.

Biemeyer failed to put up an argument. He didn't even acknowledge his wife's remarks. He simply turned on his heel and led me through the house to his study. Doris gave me a small propitiatory smile as we went by. Her eyes were bright and scared.

Biemeyer sat down at his desk in front of the picture of his copper mine. He set down his drink and swivelled his chair towards me. 'All right. What do you want from me now?'

'I'm looking for a pair of women. I think they may be together. One of them is Betty—Betty Jo Siddon.'

Biemeyer leaned forward. 'The society reporter? Don't tell me she's turned up missing.'

'Just tonight. But she may be in danger. You may be able to help me find her.'

'I don't see how. I haven't seen her in weeks. We don't go to many parties.'

'She didn't get lost at a party, Mr Biemeyer. I'm not sure how it happened, but I think she went to a nursing home in town here and got waylaid. That's the theory I have to work on, anyway.'

'Where do I come in? I've never been in a nursing home

in my life.' He gave me a macho look and reached for his drink.

'Miss Siddon was looking for Mildred Mead.'

His hand jerked and closed on his drink, spilling part of it on his trousers. 'I never heard of her,' he said without conviction.

'She was the subject of the painting I've been looking for. You must have recognized her.'

'How?' he said. 'I never met the woman in my life. What did you say her name was?'

'Mildred Mead. You bought her a house in Chantry Canyon quite a few years ago. That was a generous gift to a woman you say you never met. Incidentally, your daughter, Doris, ended up in that house the night before last. It's been taken over by a commune. Mildred sold them the house a few months ago and moved here. Don't tell me this is news to you.'

'I'm not telling you anything.'

Biemeyer's face had turned fiery red. He got to his feet. I expected him to take a swing at me. Instead he rushed out of the room.

I thought that was the end of our conversation. But he came back with a fresh drink and sat down opposite me again. His face had turned pale in blotches.

'Have you been researching me?'

'No.'

'I don't believe you. How did you find out about Mildred Mead?'

'Her name came up in Arizona, together with yours.'

He sighed. 'They hate me there. There were times when I had to close down the smelter and put half of Copper City out of work. I know how it feels—I'm a Copper City boy myself. Back before the war, my family didn't have two nickels to rub against each other. I worked my way through high school and played football to stay in college. But I suppose you know all that already?'

I gave him a knowing look, which didn't come hard. I knew now.

'Have you talked to Mildred?' he said.

'No. I haven't seen her.'

'She's an old woman now. But she was something to see in the old days. A beautiful thing.' He opened and closed his free hand and gulped part of his drink. 'When I finally got hold of her, it made everything worthwhile—all the work and the goddam football games getting my bones beaten. But she's old now. She finally got old.'

'Is she here in town?'

'You know she is, or you wouldn't ask me the question. Or she was.' He reached out with his free hand and grasped my shoulder. 'Just don't tell Ruth. She's insanely jealous. You know how women are.'

Just beyond the open door of the study the light stirred. Ruth Biemeyer moved into the doorway, trampling on the heels of her own shadow.

She said, 'It isn't true that I'm insanely jealous. I may have been jealous at times. But it gives you no right to speak like that.'

Biemeyer stood facing her, not quite as tall as she was on her heels. His face was set in creases of bitter loathing that gave it the character it had lacked.

'You were eaten up with jealousy,' he said. 'You have been all your life. You wouldn't give me normal sex, but when I got it from another woman you couldn't stand it. You did your dirty damnedest to break it up. And when you couldn't, you ran her out of town.'

'I was ashamed for you,' she said with acid sweetness. 'Chasing after that poor old woman, when she was so sick and tired she could hardly walk.'

'Mildred isn't so old. She's got more sex in her little finger than you ever had in your body.'

'What would you know about sex? You were looking for a mother, not a wife.'

'Wife?' He swept the room with an exaggerated glance. 'I don't see any wife, I see a woman who cut me off when I was in my prime.'

'Because you chose that old hag.'

'Don't call her that!'

Their quarrel had had from the start a self-conscious dramatic aspect. They looked sideways at me as they spoke, as if I were their judge or referee. I thought of their daughter, Doris, and wondered if she had been used in this way as the audience and fulcrum of their quarrels.

I remembered Doris's memory of the scene when she had hidden in the clothes hamper in the bathroom, and I began to get angry again. This time I kept my anger hidden. Doris's parents were telling me some of the things I had to know. But both of them were looking at me now, perhaps wondering if they had lost their audience.

I said to Ruth Biemeyer, 'Why did you buy that picture of Mildred Mead and hang it on the wall?'

'I didn't know it was Mildred Mead. It's an idealized portrait, and she's a wrinkled old crone by now. Why should I connect her with the picture?'

'You did, though,' Biemeyer said. 'And she still was better-looking than you ever were on your best day. That was the thing you couldn't stand.'

'*You* were the thing I couldn't stand.'

'At least you're admitting it now. You used to pretend that all the trouble originated with me. I was the King Kong of Copper City and you were the delicate maiden. You're not so bloody delicate, *or* maidenly.'

'No,' she said. 'I've grown scar tissue. I've needed it.'

I was getting sick of them. I had gone through quarrels like theirs myself, when my own marriage was breaking up. Eventually the quarrels reached a point where nothing hopeful, and nothing entirely true, was being said.

I could smell the sour animal anger of their bodies, and hear them breathing quickly, out of phase. I stepped between them, facing Biemeyer.

'Where is Mildred? I want to talk to her,' I said.

'I don't know. Honestly.'

'He's lying,' the woman said. 'He brought her to town and set her up in an apartment on the beach. I have friends in this town, I know what's going on. They saw him beating a path to her door, visiting her every day.' She turned on her husband.

'What kind of a creep are you, anyway, sneaking away from your lawful home to make love to a crazy old woman?'

'I wasn't making love to her.'

'Then what were you doing?'

'Talking. We'd have a few drinks and some conversation. That's all it amounted to.'

'Just an innocent friendship, eh?'

'That's right.'

'And that's all it ever was,' she said sardonically.

'I don't claim that.'

'What do you claim?'

He pulled himself together and said, 'I loved her.'

She looked at him in a lost way. It made me wonder if he had ever told her that before. She burst into tears and sat down in his chair, bending her streaming face close to her knees.

Biemeyer seemed upset, almost disoriented. I took him by the arm and led him to the far end of the room.

'Where is Mildred now?'

'I haven't seen her for weeks. I don't know where she went. We got into an argument about money. I was looking after her, of course, but she wanted more. She wanted me to set her up in a house with a staff of servants and a nurse to look after her. Mildred always did have big ideas.'

'And you didn't want to pay for them?'

'That's right. I was willing to pay my share. But she wasn't penniless. And she was getting old—she's in her seventies. I told her a woman has to adjust when she gets into her seventies. She can't expect to go on living like a queen.'

'Where did she go?'

'I can't tell you. She moved out several weeks ago without telling me anything. She said she was going some place to move in with relatives.'

'In town here?'

'I don't know.'

'You didn't try to find her?'

'Why should I?' Biemeyer said. 'Why the hell should I? There wasn't anything going on between us any more. With the money from the house in Chantry Canyon, she had enough to live on for the rest of her life. I didn't owe her anything. Frankly, she was turning into a nuisance.'

So was Biemeyer, but I stayed with him. 'I need to get in touch with her, and you may be able to help me. Do you have any contacts at the Southwestern Savings branch in Copper City?'

'I know the resident manager. Delbert Knapp.'

'Can you find out from him where Mildred Mead has been cashing her mortgage cheques?'

'I guess I can try.'

'You can do better than try, Mr Biemeyer. I hate to press you, but this could be a matter of life or death.'

'Whose death? Mildred's?'

'Possibly. But I'm more immediately concerned with Betty Siddon. I'm trying to trace her through Mildred. Will you get in touch with Delbert Knapp?'

'I may not be able to do it tonight. He wouldn't have the information at home with him, anyway.'

'What about Mildred's local contacts? Can you help me with those?'

'I'll think about it. But you understand I don't want my name in the paper. I don't want my name mentioned at all in connection with Mildred. In fact, the more I think about it, the less I like the whole idea of getting involved.'

'A woman's life may be at stake.'

'People die every day,' he said.

I stood up and spoke down to him. 'I got your daughter back. Now I want some help from you. And if I don't get it, and something happens to Miss Siddon, I'll fix you.'

'That sounds like a threat.'

'It is. There's enough crap in your life to make you fixable.'

'But I'm your client.'

'Your wife is.'

My voice sounded calm in my ears, a little distant. But my eyes felt as if they had shrunk, and I was shaking.

'You must be crazy,' he said. 'I could buy and sell you.'

'I'm not for sale. Anyway, that's just talk. You may have money, but you're too tight to use it. The other day you were bellyaching about five hundred measly bucks to get your daughter back. Half the time you're the king of the world, and the other half you talk like poor white trash.'

He stood up. 'I'm going to report you to Sacramento for threatening to blackmail me. You're going to regret this for the rest of your life.'

I was already regretting it. But I was too angry to try to conciliate him. I walked out of the study and headed for the front door.

Mrs Biemeyer caught me before I reached it. 'You shouldn't have said what you did.'

'I know that. I'm sorry. May I use your phone, Mrs Biemeyer?'

'Don't call the police, will you? I don't want them here.'

'No. I'm just calling a friend.'

She led me into the huge bricked kitchen, seated me at a table by the window, and brought me a telephone on a long cord. The window overlooked the distant harbour. Closer, near the foot of the hill, the Chantry house had lights on in it. While I was dialling the number Fay Brighton had given me, I took a second, longer look and saw that some of the lights were in the greenhouse.

I got a busy signal, and dialled again.

This time Mrs Brighton answered on the first ring: 'Hello?'

'This is Archer speaking. Have you had any luck?'

'Yes, sir, but all of it was bad. The trouble is that a whole lot of the people sound suspicious. It may be something in *my* voice that does it to them. I'm sort of scared sitting here by myself, you know. And I don't seem to be accomplishing anything.'

'How far down the list are you?'

'Maybe halfway. But I feel that I'm not accomplishing anything. Is it all right with you if I quit for the night?'

I didn't answer her right away. Before I did, she let out an apologetic snuffling sob and hung up.

XXX

I SWITCHED OFF the kitchen lights and took another look at the Chantry place. There were definitely movements in the greenhouse. But I couldn't make out their significance.

I went out to the car for my binoculars, and ran into Ruth Biemeyer for the second time.

'Have you seen Doris?' she said. 'I'm getting a little concerned about her.'

She was more than a little concerned. Her voice was thin. Her eyes were dark and craterous in the brilliant outside lights. I said, 'Has Doris left the house?'

'I'm afraid she has, unless she's hiding somewhere. She may have run away with Fred Johnson.'

'How could she? Fred's in jail.'

'He was,' she said. 'But my lawyer got him out today. I'm afraid I made a mistake. Please don't tell Jack about it, will you? He'd never let me forget it.'

She was a woman in trouble, sinking still deeper into trouble. She had lost her poise and started to lose her hope.

'I'll tell your husband what I have to—no more. Where is Fred? I want to talk to him.'

'We dropped him off at his parents' home. I'm afraid it wasn't a good idea, was it?'

'It isn't a good idea,' I said, 'for you and me to be standing here with all the outside lights on. There's something funny going on at the Chantry place.'

'I know there is. It's been going on a good part of the day. Today they were cutting down weeds in there. Tonight they've been digging a hole.'

'What kind of a hole?'

'Go and look for yourself. They're still at it.'

I went down the driveway to the edge of the slope, where the wire fence stopped me. The lights went out behind me. I leaned on the fence and focused my binoculars on the greenhouse. A dark man and a woman with shining grey hair—

Rico and Mrs Chantry—were working inside the building. They seemed to be filling in a hole with shovels, using a pile of dirt that stood between them.

Rico slid down into the half-filled hole and jumped up and down, packing the loose dirt. He appeared to be sinking upright into the earth, like a damned soul sinking into hell by his own volition. Mrs Chantry stood and watched him.

I caught her face in my binoculars. She looked rosy and rough and dangerous. There was dirt on her face, and her hair curved like glistening grey hawk wings over her temples.

She reached a hand down to Rico and helped him out of the hole. They teetered together on its edge and then returned to their task of filling it in. The earth fell soundlessly from their spades.

A black thought bit at the edge of my mind and gradually eclipsed it. The people in the greenhouse had dug a grave and now they were filling it in. It didn't seem quite possible. But if it was, then it was possible that Betty Siddon's body was under the dirt.

I went back to the car for my gun and had it in my hand when Ruth Biemeyer said behind me, 'What are you planning to do with that?'

'I want to know what's happening down there.'

'For God's sake, don't take a gun with you. So many innocent people get shot. And I still haven't found my daughter.'

I didn't argue. But I slipped the gun, a medium-calibre automatic, into my jacket pocket. I went back to the fence and climbed over it and started down the slope to the barranca. It had been planted and overgrown with succulent plants that felt rubbery under my feet.

Farther down, the succulents gave way to sage and other native bushes. Nestled among the bushes, like a giant golden egg, was a girl's blonde head. Doris was crouched there, watching what was going on in the greenhouse.

'Doris?' I said. 'Don't be scared.'

But she jumped like a fawn and went crashing down the slope. I caught her and told her to be quiet. She was trembling and breathing hard. Her body kept making unwilled or half-willed movements, trying to jerk away from me. I held her with both arms around her shoulders.

'Don't be afraid, Doris. I won't hurt you.'

'You're hurting me now. Let me go.'

'I will if you promise to stay where you are and keep quiet.'

The girl quieted down a bit, but I could still hear her breathing.

The couple in the greenhouse had stopped filling in the hole and were standing together in listening attitudes. Their eyes ranged up the dark hillside. I got down among the sage-brush and pulled Doris down with me. After a long tense minute, the people in the greenhouse resumed their work. It looked like gravediggers' work.

'Did you see what they were burying, Doris?'

'No, I didn't. It was already covered when I got here.'

'What brought you here?'

'I saw the light in the greenhouse; then I came down the hill and saw the big pile of dirt. Do you think they're burying a body?'

There was awe in her voice. There was also familiarity, as if her nightmares were coming true at last.

'I don't know,' I said.

We moved across the slope to the corner of the wire fence and along it to her parents' driveway. Ruth Biemeyer was waiting at the top.

'What do you think we ought to do?' she said.

'I'll phone Captain Mackendrick.'

She left me in the kitchen. I kept my eye on the greenhouse through the window. All I could see was barred light crossed by occasional shadows.

Mackendrick wasn't in his office, and the police operator couldn't locate him right away. I had time to remember that he had known Chantry when he was a young cop, and to wonder if he was going to see him again shortly.

I got Mackendrick at home. His phone was answered by a woman with a semi-official voice who sounded both impatient and resigned. After a certain amount of explanation, I per-suaded her to let me talk to her husband. I told him what was happening in the greenhouse.

'Digging in your own greenhouse isn't a crime,' he said.

'I can't do anything about it officially. Hell, they could sue the city.'

'Not if they buried a body.'

'Did you see them bury a body?'

'No.'

'Then what do you expect me to do?'

'Think about it,' I said. 'People don't dig grave-sized holes and fill them up just for the fun of it.'

'You'd be surprised at what they do. Maybe they're looking for something.'

'Such as?'

'A leaky water main. I've seen people dig up a whole yard looking for a water pipe with a hole in it.'

'People like Mrs Chantry?'

He was slow in answering. 'I don't think we better continue this conversation. If you decide to take any action, I don't want to know about it.'

'There's something else you don't want to know about,' I said. 'But I want to tell you.'

Mackendrick sighed, or grunted. 'Make it fast, eh? I've got a lot on my agenda, and it's late.'

'You know a young woman named Betty Siddon.'

'That I do. She's been in my hair.'

'You haven't seen her tonight, have you?'

'No.'

'She seems to be missing.'

'What does that mean?'

'She's dropped out of sight. I haven't been able to contact her.'

'For how long?'

'Several hours.'

Mackendrick shouted at me, in a voice that was half angry and half jocose, 'For God's sake, that doesn't mean anything. If she'd been gone for a week or two, you might say she was missing.'

'Let's wait twenty years,' I said. 'Then we'll all be dead.'

My voice sounded strange in my own ears, high and angry.

Mackendrick lowered his voice, as if to set me an example.

'What's the trouble, Archer, are you stuck on the girl or something?'

'I'm worried about her.'

'Okay, I'll tell my people to be on the lookout for her. Good night.'

I sat with the dead receiver in my hand, feeling an angry pain that I had felt before. I lived at the intersection of two worlds. One was the actual world where danger was seldom far from people's lives, where reality threatened them with its cutting edge. The other was the world where Mackendrick had to operate in a maze of tradition and a grid of rules—a world where nothing officially happened until it was reported through channels.

From where I sat in the dark kitchen, I could see the gravediggers putting the final touches to the hole they had filled in. They seemed to be gathering up armfuls of cuttings and scattering them over the raw dirt. Finally Rico picked up a brown sack, swung it over his shoulder, and carried it out to a car standing in the courtyard. He opened the trunk of the car and slung the brown sack in.

Mrs Chantry turned out the lights in the greenhouse and followed Rico into the main house.

I went out to my car and drove it down the hill, parking just around the corner from Mrs Chantry's street. Though the movements of the night and its people were far beyond the range of my understanding, I was beginning to pick up some of the smaller rhythms. In less than fifteen minutes, there was a glow of headlights from the direction of the Chantry house. The Chantry car, with Rico driving alone in the front seat, passed me and turned towards the freeway.

I followed at a distance, but close enough to see him enter the northbound lane. There was fairly heavy traffic at this mid-evening hour, crawling like an endless luminescent worm into the tunnelled darkness. We passed the university's lighted towers, the crowded buildings of the student annex where I had first met Doris the day before, the narrow entrance to the dark beach where Jake Whitmore's body had been found.

Rico stayed on the freeway, and so did I. The traffic was dwindling down to its intercity components, trucks and night-driving tourists and the like. I let the distance between us lengthen out, and almost lost him. He made an unexpected right turn off the freeway, then a quick left through an underpass. I left the highway and waited out of sight for a minute, then followed him down to the sea with my car lights out.

The object of his journey was a wooden pier that extended out over the water for a couple of hundred yards. Three or four miles beyond the end of the pier, a half-dozen oil platforms blazed with lights like leafless Christmas trees. And off to the north, like a menacing West Coast Statue of Liberty, a giant gas flame flared.

Against the several lights I could see Rico approaching the foot of the pier, hunchbacked by the sack he had slung across his shoulder. I left my car and followed him on foot, walking softly and narrowing my distance. By the time Rico had reached the seaward end, I was close behind him.

'Drop it, Rico,' I said. 'Get your hands up.'

He made a move to heave the sack overside. It struck the top rail and fell clanking on the deck of the pier. Rico turned on me swinging. I moved inside his flailing arms and hit him several times in the belly, then once on the jaw. He went down and stayed for a while. I searched his clothes. No gun.

I untied the twine that closed the mouth of his sack, and spilled some of its contents on the planking. There were human bones caked with dirt, a damaged human skull, rusted engine parts from an old car.

Rico sighed and rolled over. Then he was on me, heavy and strong but dull in his reactions. His head swung loose and undefended. I didn't hit him again. I backed away and got out my gun and told him to calm down.

Instead he turned and ran staggering to the outer end of the pier. He started to climb over the railing, or try to. His feet kept slipping. The tide was low and the water was a long way down.

For some reason, it became important to me that Rico shouldn't make it into the black water. I pocketed my gun and got my arms around his waist. Dragged him back on to the deck and held him down.

As I marched Rico back to my car and got him safely inside of it, I understood one source of my satisfaction. Twenty-odd years ago, near an oil-stained pier like this, I had fought in the water with a man named Puddler and drowned him.

Rico, whatever his sins, had served as an equalizer for one of mine.

XXXI

CAPTAIN MACKENDRICK was glad to see Rico, too. The three of us convened in Mackendrick's office with a male police stenotypist ready to record what was said. Rico didn't say anything at all until we brought in the sack of bones and iron. Mackendrick held it up in front of Rico's face and shook it. It made a strange dull clatter.

Mackendrick brought out the damaged skull and placed it on his desk. It looked empty-eyed at Rico. Rico returned the stare for a long moment. He tried to wet his lips with his dry tongue. Then he tried to scratch his head, but his fingers got tangled in the bandages he was now wearing.

'You used to be a pretty good young fellow,' Mackendrick said. 'I remember when you used to play volleyball on the beach, you liked good clean sport. You liked good clean work —mowing the lawn, washing the car. You thought Mr Chantry was the greatest boss a young fellow ever had. You said so to me, remember?'

Tears had begun to roll from Rico's eyes and find twin downward channels on either side of his nose.

He said, 'I'm sorry.'

'What are you sorry for, Rico? Did you kill him?'

He shook his head, and the tears flew out from his face. 'I don't even know who he is.'

'Then why did you dig up his poor bones and try to get rid of them?'

'I don't know.'

'You mean you do things without knowing why?'

'Sometimes. When people tell me.'

'Who told you to get rid of these bones, weight them with iron, and chuck them in the sea? Who told you to do that?' Mackendrick said.

'I don't remember.'

'Was it your own idea?'

The man recoiled from the suggestion. 'No.'

'Whose idea was it?'

Rico stared into the empty eyes of the skull. His face became even more sober, as if he had looked into a mirror and recognized his own mortal condition. He raised his hands and touched his cheeks with his fingertips, feeling the skull behind them.

'Is this Mr Richard Chantry's skull?' Mackendrick said.

'I don't know. Honest to God, I don't know.'

'What do you know?'

He looked at the floor. 'Nothing much. I always was a dumbhead.'

'That's true, but not that dumb. You used to look out for yourself in the old days, Rico. You went for the girls, but you didn't let them lead you around by the nose. You didn't go out and commit a crime because a woman jiggled her hips at you. You used to have more sense than to do that.'

The stenotypist's fingertips danced a rapid minuet on the keys of his machine. Rico was watching them as if they were miming a dance of death, telling his past or perhaps foretelling his future. His mouth opened and closed several times in an effort to find words. Then he began to whisper to himself, too low to be heard.

Mackendrick leaned forward, speaking quietly: 'What did you say, Rico? Speak up, man, it may be important.'

Rico nodded. 'It is important. I had nothing to do with it.'

'Nothing to do with the murder, you mean?'

'That's right. It was all her doing. My conscience is clear on that. She told me to bury him, which I did. Then twenty-five years later she told me to dig him up. That's all I did.'

Rico was looking into the empty eyes of the skull. They seemed to be draining all the life from his own eyes.

'All you did.' Mackendrick echoed him softly and sardoni-

cally. 'All you did was bury a murdered man and later dig
him up and try to dispose of his bones in the sea. Why would
you do that if you didn't kill him?'

'Because she told me to.'

'Who told you to?'

'Mrs Chantry.'

'She told you to bury her husband's body?'

Mackendrick had risen and stood over Rico, who moved his
head from side to side, trying to evade the weight of Mackendrick's shadow.

'It isn't her husband's body.'

'Who is it, then?'

'It was just a guy that came to the door one day about
twenty-five years ago. He wanted to see Mr Chantry. I told
him that Mr Chantry was working in his studio and anyway
he didn't see people without an appointment. But the guy
said Mr Chantry would see *him* if I gave him his name.'

'What *was* his name?' Mackendrick said.

'I'm sorry. I don't remember.'

'What did he look like?'

'He just looked ordinary. Kind of pale and flabby, not in
good shape. The most outstanding thing about him, he didn't
talk too good. I mean, he talked like he had a stroke or something. He sounded like an old bum, only he wasn't that old.'

'How old was he?'

'Early thirties, maybe. Older than I was, anyway.'

'How was he dressed?'

'Not too good. He had on a kind of brown suit that didn't
fit too well. I remember thinking at the time, it looked like
he got it at the Starvation Army.'

'Did you take him in to see Mr Chantry?'

'*She* did. They were in the studio talking for quite a while,
all three of them.'

'What were they talking about?' I said.

'I didn't listen in. They closed the door, and that's a solid
oak door about three inches thick. After a while, she brought
him out and sent him on his way.'

Mackendrick made a contemptuous dry spitting sound.
'You just got through telling us that you buried him. Are you

withdrawing that statement?'

'No, sir. That was later in the week, when he came back with the woman and the little boy.'

'What woman? What little boy?'

'She was a woman around thirty, I'd say. Pretty good figure, otherwise nothing much to look at—kind of a blah brunette. Her little boy was around seven or eight. He was very quiet. He didn't ask questions the way kids usually do. In fact, I didn't hear him say a word the whole time he was there. And no wonder. He must have been right there when it happened.'

'What did happen?'

Rico answered slowly, 'I don't know for sure. I didn't *see* it happen. But after it was all over, there was this body in the greenhouse scrunched up in a big old sack. She said he had a stroke and fell and hit his head and died on her. She said she didn't want any trouble, so I should bury him. She said if I would be nice to her and bury him, then she would be nice to me.'

'So you've been in her bed for the last twenty-five years,' Mackendrick said with distaste. 'And this poor bastard has been in the ground feeding her orchids. Isn't that right?'

Rico lowered his head and looked at the scarred floor between his feet. 'I guess it is. But I didn't kill him.'

'You covered up for whoever did. Who did?'

'I don't know. I didn't see it happen.'

'In the course of twenty-five years in her bed, did you ever think of asking her who killed him?'

'No, sir. It wasn't my business.'

'It is now. You're all in this together, I guess you know that—you and Mr Chantry and Mrs Chantry and the brunette with the little boy.' Mackendrick picked up the skull again and held it, like a *memento mori*, close to Rico's face. 'Are you sure this isn't Mr Chantry?'

'No, sir. I mean yes, sir, I'm sure it isn't.'

'What makes you sure? You buried him in a sack.'

'She said it was the other man—the man in the brown suit.'

'But all you have is her word for it?'

'Yes, sir.'

'Mrs Chantry's word for it?'

'Yes, sir.'

Mackendrick gave the skull a long sad look, which he transferred to me. 'Do you have any questions you want to ask him?'

'Thanks, I do, Captain.' I turned back to Rico. 'Assuming this skull isn't Richard Chantry's, what do you think happened to Richard Chantry?'

'I always thought he just walked away.'

'Why?'

'I don't know why.'

'Did you ever see him again, or hear from him?'

'No, sir. He left this letter behind—you've probably seen it in the art museum.'

'I've seen it. When did he write it?'

'I don't know.'

'Between the time he killed this man and the time he walked away?'

'I don't know when he wrote it. I never saw him or talked to him after that day.'

'Did Mrs Chantry tell you where he went?'

'No, sir. I don't believe she knew.'

'Did he take anything with him?'

'Not that I know of. *She* looked after his things after he left.'

'Was Mrs Chantry unhappy about his leaving?'

'I don't know. She didn't talk to me about it.'

'Not even in bed?'

Rico flushed. 'No, sir.'

'What about the dark-haired woman and the little boy? Did you ever see them again?'

'No, sir. I didn't go out looking for them, either. They were none of my business.'

'What is your business, Rico?'

'Looking after the house and the people. I do the best I can.'

'There's only one person left in the house, isn't that right?'

'I guess so. Mrs Chantry.'

I turned to Mackendrick. 'Do you think she'll answer questions?'

'I'm not ready to ask them,' Mackendrick said in a strained voice. 'I have to check with the higher-ups on this.'

I wanted to go on checking with the lower-downs, but I needed Mackendrick's co-operation. I waited until Rico had been taken out and placed in a holding cell. When Mackendrick and I were alone in his office with the skull and bones, I told him briefly what had happened, or what I thought had happened, to Betty Siddon.

Mackendrick fidgeted at his desk. His face flushed and became obtuse, as if his circuits were getting overloaded.

Finally he broke in: 'I can't do anything about the Siddon woman tonight. I wouldn't even if I had the men. Women are always taking off on their own little business. She's a good-looking piece; she's probably sacked out in her boy-friend's apartment.'

I came close to taking a swing at Mackendrick. I sat and contained my rage, which boiled cold in my head like liquid gas. I told myself to watch it. If I let myself go out of control, as I had been threatening to do all evening, I could find myself locked out of the case, or possibly locked into a holding cell, like Rico.

I concentrated on the skull on the desk, reminding myself that men were supposed to calm down as they got older. When I had myself in hand, I said, 'I sort of am her boy-friend.'

'I thought so. I still don't have the men to go around knocking on doors. You don't have to worry about her, take my word for it. She's a smart girl and this is her town. If she doesn't turn up overnight, we'll reassess the situation in the morning.'

He was beginning to talk like a chief of police. I caught myself hoping that he would never make it. But I seemed to have been elected to help him on his way.

'May I make a couple of suggestions, Captain? And a couple of requests?'

He cast an impatient glance at the electric clock on the wall: it registered close to midnight. 'You've earned the right to that.'

'We should try to pinpoint the date of this man's death. It

probably coincides with the date of Chantry's disappearance. That date should be checked for other disappearances, here and in the whole Southern California area, particularly the hospitals and asylums. This man sounds like a possible mental patient.' I reached out and touched the poor broken skull.

'We do all that as a matter of routine,' Mackendrick said.

'Sure. But this isn't a routine situation. I think you should start burning up the wires.'

'Because you're worried about your girl?'

·'I'm worried about her and several other people. This isn't just past history that we're dealing with. There are crimes in the present, too, including the crime of murder. And I have a feeling that they're all connected.'

'How?'

'Probably through the disappearance of Chantry. That seems to be the central event in the series.' I briefly rehearsed the others, beginning with the apparent murder of William Mead in Arizona thirty-two years before, and concluding with the deaths of the art dealers Paul Grimes and Jacob Whitmore.

'What makes you so certain that they're connected?'

'Because the people are connected. Grimes was Chantry's teacher and very good friend. Grimes bought the picture of Mildred Mead from Whitmore. William Mead was Chantry's half-brother, and incidentally the son of Mildred Mead. Mildred seems to be one of the two central women in the case. The other one is Mrs Chantry, of course. If we could get hold of those women and get them talking—'

'Mrs Chantry is out,' Mackendrick said, 'at least for the present. I can't bring her in for questioning on Rico's say-so.' He looked at me as if he were about to say more, but fell silent.

'What about Mildred Mead?'

Mackendrick reddened in anger or embarrassment. 'Who is this Mildred Mead? I never heard of her before.'

I showed him my photograph of her picture and told him the story that went with it. 'She probably knows more about the background of this case than anybody else. With the possible exception of Mrs Chantry.'

'Where can we find Mildred Mead? Does she live here in town?'

'She did until recently. She probably still does, in one of the nursing homes. She's the woman that Betty Siddon was looking for.'

Mackendrick sat and looked at me. His face passed moon-like through a number of phases, from anger and disgust to acceptance touched with heavy humour.

'Okay,' he said, 'you win. We'll make the rounds of the nursing homes and see if we can find those two women.'

'May I come?'

'No. I'm going to supervise this search myself.'

XXXII

I TOLD MYSELF that it was time I talked to Fred again. It was Mrs Chantry I really wanted to talk to. But Mackendrick had placed her off-limits and I didn't want to cross him just as he was beginning to co-operate.

I drove across town and parked on Olive Street. The shadows under the trees were as thick and dark as old blood. The tall grey gabled house looked cheerful by comparison, with lights on all three storeys. There was an interplay of voices behind the front door.

My knocking silenced the voices. Mrs Johnson came to the door in her white uniform. Her eyes were bright with emotions I couldn't read. Her face was grey and slack. She looked like a woman who had been pushed to her limit and might break down under further pressure.

'What is it?' she said.

'I thought I'd come by and see how Fred is doing. I just found out that he'd been released.'

'Thanks to Mr Lackner.' Her voice had risen, as if I weren't the only one she was talking to. 'Do you know Mr Lackner? He's in the front room with Fred.'

The long-haired young lawyer gave me a grip that seemed to have become more powerful in the course of the day. He smiled and called me by name and said that it was nice to see me again. I smiled and congratulated him on his quick work.

Even Fred was smiling for a change, but rather dubiously, as if he had no established right to feel good. The room itself had a tentative air, like a stage set for a play that had closed down soon after opening, a long time ago. The old chesterfield and matching chairs sagged almost to the floor. The curtains at the windows were slightly tattered. There were threadbare places in the carpet where the wooden floor almost showed through.

Like a ghost who haunted the ruined house, Mr Johnson appeared at the doorway. His face—including his eyes—was red and moist. His breath was like an inconstant wind that had lost its way in a winery. He looked at me without recognition but with dislike, as if I had done him a bad turn in his unremembered past.

'Do I know you?'

'Of course you do,' Mrs Johnson said. 'Certainly you know him. This is Mr Archer.'

'I thought so. You're the man who put my boy in jail.'

Fred jumped up white and shaking. 'That isn't so, Dad. Please don't say things like that.'

'I'll say them when they're true. Are you calling me a liar?'

Lackner stepped between the father and son. 'This is no time for family quarrels,' he said. 'We're all happy here—all together and all happy, isn't that right?'

'I'm not happy,' Johnson said. 'I'm miserable, and you want to know why? Because this sneaking bastard here—' he pointed a waving forefinger at me — 'is lousing up the atmosphere in my front room. And I want it clearly understood that if he stays one minute longer I'll bloody well kill him.' He lurched towards me. 'Do you understand that, you bastard? You bastard that brought my son home and put him in jail.'

'I brought him home,' I said. 'I didn't put him in jail. That was somebody else's idea.'

'But you masterminded it. I know that. You know that.'

I turned to Mrs Johnson. 'I think I better leave.'

'No. Please.' She pressed her doughy face with her fingers.

'He isn't himself tonight. He's been drinking heavily all day. He's terribly sensitive; he can't stand all these pressures. Can you, dear?'

'Stop snivelling,' he said. 'You've been sneaking and snivelling all your life, and that's all right when there's no one around but us chickens. Just don't let down your guard when this man is in the house. He means us no good, you know that. And if he doesn't get out of here while I count to ten, I'll throw him out bodily.'

I almost laughed in his face. He was a stout unsteady man whose speech was fed by synthetic energy. Perhaps there had been a time, many years ago, when he was capable of carrying out his threats. But he was fat and flaccid, prematurely aged by alcohol. His face and frame were so draped with adipose tissue that I couldn't imagine what he had looked like as a young man.

Johnson began to count. Lackner and I looked at each other and left the room together. Johnson came stumbling after us, still counting, and slammed the front door behind us.

'Gosh,' Lackner said. 'What makes a man act that way?'

'Too much to drink. He's a far-gone alcoholic.'

'I can see that for myself. But why does he drink like that?'

'Pain,' I said. 'The pain of being himself. He's been cooped up in that run-down house for God knows how many years. Probably since Fred was a boy. Trying to drink himself to death and not succeeding.'

'I still don't understand it.'

'Neither do I, really. Every drunk has his own reason. But all of them tend to end up the same, with a soft brain and a diseased liver.'

As if we were both looking for someone to blame, Lackner and I glanced up at the sky. Above the dark olive trees that marched in single file along this side of the street, the sky was clouded and the stars were hidden.

'The fact is,' Lackner said, 'I don't know what to make of the boy, either.'

'Do you mean Fred?'

'Yes. I realize I shouldn't call him a boy. He must be almost as old as I am.'

'I believe he's thirty-two.'

'Really? Then he's a year older than I am. He seems terribly immature for his age.'

'His mental growth has been stunted, too, living in this house.'

'What's so much the matter with this house? Actually, if it were fixed up, it could be quite elegant. It probably was at one time.'

'The people in it are the matter,' I said. 'There are certain families whose members should all live in different towns— different states, if possible—and write each other letters once a year. You might suggest that to Fred, provided you can keep him out of jail.'

'I think I can do that. Mrs Biemeyer isn't feeling vindictive. In fact, she's a pretty nice woman when you talk to her outside of the family circle.'

'It's another one of those families that should write letters once a year,' I said. 'And forget to mail them. It's really no accident that Fred and Doris got together. Neither of their homes is broken, exactly, but they're both badly bent. So are Fred and Doris.'

Lackner wagged his coiffed and bearded head. In the dim clouded moonlight, I felt for a moment that some ancient story was being repeated, that we had all been here before. I couldn't remember exactly what the story was or how it ended. But I felt that the ending somehow depended on me.

I said to Lackner, 'Did Fred ever explain to you why he took that picture in the first place?'

'Not in any satisfactory way, no. Has he talked to you about it?'

'He wanted to demonstrate his expertise,' I said. 'Prove to the Biemeyers that he was good for something. Those were his conscious reasons, anyway.'

'What were his unconscious reasons?'

'I don't really know. It would take a panel of psychiatrists to answer that, and they won't tell. But, like a lot of other people in this town, Fred seems to have a fixation on Richard Chantry.'

'Do you think the painting was really Chantry's work?'

'Fred thinks so, and he's the expert.'

'He doesn't claim to be,' Lackner said. 'He's just a student.'

'Fred's entitled to an opinion, though. And I think it's his opinion that Chantry painted the picture recently, maybe some time this year.'

'How could he know?'

'By the condition of the paint. He says.'

'Do you believe that, Mr Archer?'

'I didn't until tonight. I was pretty well taking it for granted that Richard Chantry was long dead.'

'But now you don't.'

'Now I don't. I think Chantry is alive and kicking.'

'Where?'

'Possibly here in town,' I said. 'I don't go in much for hunches. But I've got a funny feeling tonight, as if Chantry was breathing on the back of my neck and looking over my shoulder.'

I was on the verge of telling Lackner about the human remains that Mrs Chantry and Rico had dug up in her greenhouse. It wasn't public knowledge yet, and it would have been a violation of my basic rule. Never tell anyone more than he needs to know, because he'll tell somebody else.

At this point, Gerard Johnson came out on to the porch and staggered down the uneven steps. He looked like a dead man walking blind, but his eyes or his nose or his alcoholic's radar picked me up and dragged him through the weeds in my direction.

'Are you still here, you bastard?'

'I'm still here, Mr Johnson.'

'Don't "mister" me. I know how you feel. You treat me with disrespect. You think I'm a stinking old drunk. But I'm here to tell you with my last breath that I'm a better man—right here as I stand, I'm a better man than you ever were and I'm ready to prove it.'

I didn't ask him how. I didn't have to. He thrust his right hand into the sagging pocket of his pants and brought it out holding a nickel-plated revolver, the kind cops like to call a 'Saturday-night special'. I heard the click of the hammer, and dived for Johnson's legs. He went down.

I climbed rapidly up his recumbent body and took the gun away from him. It was empty. My hands were shaking.

Gerard Johnson struggled to his feet and began to shout. He shouted at me and at his wife and son as they came out on the porch. The words he used were mostly scatological. He raised his voice and shouted at his house. He shouted at the houses across the road and down the street.

More lights came on in those houses, but no one appeared at the windows or opened the doors. Perhaps if someone had appeared, Johnson might have felt less lonely.

It was his son Fred who took pity on him. Fred came down off the porch and put his arms around Johnson from behind, encircling his labouring chest.

'Please act like a human being, Dad.'

Johnson struggled and surged and swore, and gradually left off shouting. Fred's face was wet with tears. The sky tore like a net and the moon swam out.

Suddenly the night had changed its weather. It was higher and brighter and stranger. Holding Johnson around the shoulders, Fred walked him up the steps and into the house. It was a sad and touching thing to see the lost son fathering his father. There was no real hope for Johnson, but there was still hope for Fred. Lackner agreed. I turned the gun over to him before he drove away in his Toyota.

Fred had left the front door open, and after a moment Mrs Johnson came out and down the steps. Her body moved aimlessly, like a stray animal. The light from the sky silvered her uniform.

'I want to apologize.'

'For what?'

'Everything.'

She flung out her arm in an awkward sideways gesture, as much a brushing away as an embracing. It seemed to take in the gabled house and everyone and everything in it, her family and the neighbours, and the street, the thick dark olive trees and their darker shadows, the moon that drenched her in its cold light and deeply scored her face.

'Don't apologize to me,' I said. 'I chose this job, or it chose me. There's a lot of human pain involved in it, but I'm not looking for another job.'

'I know what you mean. I'm a nurse. I may be an unemployed nurse by tomorrow. I just had to come home on account of Fred getting out, and I walked off my shift. It's about time I walked back on.'

'Can I offer you a lift?'

She gave me a quick suspicious look, as if I might have designs on her heavy middle-aged body. But she said, 'You're very kind, sir. Fred left our car some place in Arizona. I don't know if it's even worth bringing back.'

I opened the door for her. She reacted as if this hadn't happened to her for some time.

When we were both in the car, I said, 'There's a question I'd like to ask you. You don't have to answer it. But if you do, I don't plan to pass your answer on to anybody.'

She stirred in her seat and turned towards me. 'Has somebody been bad-mouthing me?'

'About those drugs that were missing at the hospital, do you want to discuss it some more?'

She said, 'I admit I took a few sample pills. But I didn't take them for myself, or for any wrong purpose. I wanted to try them out on Gerard, and see if I could get him to cut down on his drinking. I guess they could get me on a technical charge of prescribing medicine without being a doctor. But nearly every nurse I ever knew does that.' She gave me an anxious look. 'Are they thinking about bringing charges?'

'Not to my knowledge.'

'Then how did the subject come up?'

'One of the nurses at the hospital mentioned it. She was explaining why you'd been fired.'

'That was the excuse they used. But I'll tell you why I was fired. There were people in that institution that didn't like me.' We were passing the hospital, and she pointed an accusing finger at the great lighted building. 'I may not be the easiest person to get along with. But I am a good nurse, and they had no right to fire me. You had no right to bring it up with them, either.'

'I think I had, Mrs Johnson.'

'What gives you the right?'

'I'm investigating a couple of murders, as well as the missing picture. You know that.'

'You think I know where the picture is? I don't. Fred doesn't either. We're not thieves. We may have problems in the family, but we're not that kind of people.'

'I never said you were. People can change, though, if they get involved with drugs. It gives other people a handle to use on them.'

'Nobody's got that kind of a handle on me. I took a few pills, I admit it. I gave them to Gerard. And now I'm paying for it. I'll be spending the rest of my working days in under-staffed nursing homes. That is, if I'm lucky enough to hold any job at all.'

She fell into a glum silence that lasted most of the way to the La Paloma. Before she left the car, I told her about the women I was looking for, Mildred Mead and Betty Siddon.

She listened gravely. 'I'll do what I can. I won't have much time for phoning on *this* night shift. But I'll pass the word along to some nurses I know in the other nursing homes.' She added haltingly, as if it cost her a moral effort to acknowledge any debt: 'Fred told me how you treated him in Arizona. I appreciate that. After all, I'm his mother,' she said in something like surprise.

She stepped out on to the asphalt and moved heavily to-wards the half-lighted building. Beyond the wall that enclosed the parking lot, cars went by in unceasing flight and pursuit on mourning tyres. Mrs Johnson turned as she reached the doorway and lifted her hand to me.

A moment after she entered, Mrs Johnson backed out of the doorway. She was closely followed by two cops. One was in uniform. The other was Captain Mackendrick. I heard her complaining as I approached that they had no right to jump on her in the dark, she was an innocent woman on her way to work.

Mackendrick scanned her angry frightened face. 'You're Mrs Johnson, aren't you? Fred Johnson's mother?'

'That is correct,' she said coldly. 'It doesn't give you any licence to scare me out of my wits.'

'I didn't mean to do that, ma'am. I'm sorry.'

'You ought to be sorry.' Mrs Johnson was pressing her advantage. 'You have no right to harry me and harass me. We've got a good lawyer working on our behalf, and you'll be hearing from him if you don't look out.'

Mackendrick gazed helplessly at the sky and then at me. 'Look, did I do anything wrong? I bumped into a woman accidentally in the dark. I apologized. Do I have to get down on my knees?'

'Mrs Johnson is a little nervous tonight.'

She nodded approvingly in my direction. 'You bet I am. What are you doing here, anyway, Captain?'

'We're making a search for a woman.'

'Miss Siddon?'

'That's correct, ma'am.' Mackendrick gave her a sharp inquiring look. 'Who told you about Miss Siddon?'

'Mr Archer here. He asked me to phone some of my friends in the other nursing homes. I said I would if I got the time, and I will. May I go now?'

'Please do,' Mackendrick said. 'Nobody's interfering with your movements in any way, shape, or form. But it may not be a good idea to call the other nursing homes. We'd rather surprise 'em.'

Mrs Johnson went into the building for a second time, and didn't reappear.

'She's a tough old babe,' Mackendrick said.

'She's had a tough couple of days. Could you and I have a word in private, Captain?'

He jerked his head at the man in uniform, who climbed into the police car. We walked to the far corner of the lot, as far as possible from the building and the highway. A native oak that had somehow kept itself alive in this waste of pavement extended its faint moon-shadow to us.

I said, 'What brought you here?'

'We got a tip. Someone phoned in and said we should look here for Miss Siddon. That's why I came over myself. We went through the place with a fine-toothed comb and found no trace of her or anybody like her.'

'Who provided the tip?'

'It was anonymous—evidently some woman trying to stir

up trouble. Mrs Johnson's the kind who makes enemies. She got herself fired from the hospital, you know.'

'So she was telling me. You don't need my opinion, Captain, but I'll give it to you anyway. I think I gave you a bum steer on this search of nursing homes. I'm not suggesting you call it off entirely. But I think it's time to concentrate your own energies on something else.'

Mackendrick was slow to answer. 'You mean Mrs Chantry, don't you?'

'She seems to be at the centre of this case.'

'We don't know that.'

'I think we do.'

'What you think isn't good enough, Archer. I can't move against that woman without enough evidence to sink her.'

XXXIII

I PARKED AT the head of Mrs Chantry's street and walked down to her house. Fog was crawling up the barranca behind it. On the hill above, the Biemeyers' place was full of cold light. But Mrs Chantry's house was dark and still.

I knocked on the front door. I must have half expected to find her dead, or gone, because her immediate response took me by surprise.

As if she'd been waiting there all night, she said through the door, 'Who is that? Rico?'

I didn't answer her. We stood on opposite sides of the door in a long waiting silence. It was unevenly filled by the noise of the waves that mounted the beach like giant blundering footsteps and then slid back again.

'Who is that?' she said on a rising note.

'Archer.'

'Go away.'

'Should I go and get Captain Mackendrick?'

There was another silence, measured by the thumping, slumping footsteps of the sea. Then she unlocked the door and opened it.

There were no lights in the hallway or, so far as I could see, in the house. Against the interior darkness, her hair and her face were the same silvery colour. She had on a high-necked dark dress, which suggested that she was a widow and made me wonder if she was.

'Come in if you must,' she said in a small cold voice.

I followed her into the main room where her party had been held. She switched on a floor lamp above an armchair and stood beside it waiting. We faced each other in dead silence. Her party had left no echoes in the room.

Finally she said, 'I know your type. You're one of these self-elected experts who can't keep his sharp little nose out of other people's business. You just can't bear to see them live their lives without your horning in, can you?'

She flushed, perhaps partly in anger. But what she was saying seemed to have other pressures behind it, too.

I said, 'You call this a life that you're living? Covering up a murder for a man you haven't seen in twenty-five years. Sleeping with a boy-man like Rico to keep him quiet.'

As if the lighting in the room had changed drastically, the colour left her face and her eyes darkened.

'Nobody talks to me like that.'

'You might as well get used to it. When the DA's men make their case in Superior Court, they won't be mincing their words.'

'The case will never get to court. There is no case.' But her eyes were strained and questioning, trying to see over the sharp edge of the present.

'Come off it, Mrs Chantry. Twenty-five years ago, a man was killed in this house. I don't know who he was but you probably do. Rico buried him in the greenhouse. Tonight, with some help from you, he dug up his bones and put them in a weighted sack. Unfortunately for both of you, I caught him before he threw them in the sea. Do you want to know where they are now?'

She turned her face away. She didn't want to know. Suddenly, as if her legs had collapsed, she sat down in the armchair. She covered her face with her hands and appeared to be trying to cry.

I stood and listened to her painful noises. Handsome as she was, and deep in trouble, I couldn't feel much sympathy for her. She had built her life on a dead man's bones, and death had taken partial possession of her.

As if our minds had been tracking each other, she said, 'Where are the bones now?'

'Captain Mackendrick has them. He has your friend Rico, too. And Rico's been talking.'

She sat and absorbed the knowledge. It seemed to make her physically smaller. But the hard intelligence in her eyes didn't fade.

'I think I can handle Mackendrick. He's ambitious. I'm not so sure about you. But you do work for money, don't you?'

'I have all the money I need.'

She leaned forward, her ringed fists on her knees. 'I'm thinking about quite a lot of money. More than you can ever accumulate in a lifetime. Enough to retire on.'

'I like my work.'

She made a bitter face, and succeeded in looking quite ugly. She struck her knees with her fists. 'Don't play with me. I'm serious.'

'So am I. I don't want your money. But you could try bribing me with information.'

'Bribe you to do what, exactly?'

'Give you an even break if you've got one coming.'

'All you want to do is play God, right?'

'Not exactly. I would like to understand why a woman like you, with everything going for her, would try to cover up a lousy murder.'

'It wasn't a murder. It was an accident.'

'Who committed the accident?'

'You don't believe me, do you?'

'You haven't given me anything to believe, or not to believe. All I know is that you and Rico dug up a dead man's bones; then you sent Rico to sink them in the sea. That was a foolish thing to do, Mrs Chantry. You should have left them underground in the greenhouse.'

'I don't think so. My mistake was getting Rico to handle it. I should have disposed of the body myself.'

'Whose body was it, Mrs Chantry?'

She shook her head as if the past were swarming like bees around her. 'He was a stranger to me. He came to the house asking to see my husband. Richard shouldn't have seen him, and normally wouldn't have. But evidently the man's name meant something to him. He told Rico to send the man into his studio. And when I saw the man again, he was dead.'

'What was the dead man's name?'

'I don't remember.'

'Were you there when the dead man talked to Rico?'

'Yes, at least part of the time.'

'And later when Rico buried the body?'

'I knew what was being done. I didn't participate in the burial.'

'Rico said you ordered it.'

'I suppose I did, in a sense. I was relaying my husband's wish.'

'Where was your husband at the time of the burial?'

'He was in his studio, writing his farewell letter. It's a strange thing,' she added after a moment. 'He'd often spoken of taking off in that way. Dropping everything, starting a new, unencumbered life. And then the occasion came up, and he did just that.'

'Do you know where he went?'

'No. I haven't heard from him since. Neither has anyone else, to my knowledge.'

'Do you think he's dead?'

'I hope he isn't. He was—he is a great man, after all.'

She let herself cry a little. She seemed to be trying to regain lost emotional ground, rebuilding the Chantry myth with the materials that came to hand, partly old and partly new.

'Why did he kill the man in the brown suit?'

'I don't know that he did. It may have been an accident.'

'Did your husband claim it was an accident?'

'I don't know. We didn't talk about it. He wrote his letter and went.'

'You have no idea how or why the man was killed?'

'None whatever.'

'Your husband gave you no explanation at all?'

'No. Richard left in such a hurry there was no time for explanations.'

'That isn't the way I heard it, Mrs Chantry. According to Rico, you and your husband and the man in the brown suit did some talking in the studio. What were you talking about?'

'I don't remember that,' she said.

'Rico does.'

'He's a liar.'

'Most men are, when they get into real trouble. So are most women.'

She was losing her self-assurance, and anger seemed to be taking its place again. 'Could you possibly spare me your generalizations? I've been through quite a lot in the last twenty-four hours and I don't have the strength to listen to a cheap private detective mouthing moral maxims.'

Her voice was high, and she looked tormented.

I said, 'You've been through quite a lot in the last twenty-five years. It'll go on and get worse unless you do something to end it.'

She sat in silence for a while, her gaze turned inward on the unburied past. 'End it, how?' she said finally.

'Tell me what actually happened, and why.'

'I have been.'

'Not really, Mrs Chantry. You've left out some of the most important things. Who the man in the brown suit was, and why he came here. The fact that he came here twice, and when he came here the second time—the time that he was killed—he had a woman and a small boy with him. The fact that you told Rico the man had a stroke and died more or less by accident.'

She sat and absorbed this, too, like someone undergoing a rapid ageing process. She didn't try to evade it or push it away. In a sense, it appeared to be what she had been waiting for.

'So Rico did a lot of talking,' she said.

'All he had time for. You picked a lousy co-conspirator.'

'I didn't pick him. He simply happened to be here.' She looked me over carefully, as if perhaps I might be used to take Rico's place in her life. 'I had no choice.'

'People always have some kind of choice.'

She hung her pretty head and brushed it with her hand in a desolate twisting gesture. 'That's easy to say. Not so easy to act on.'

'You have a choice to make now,' I said. 'You can co-operate with me—'

'I thought I had been.'

'Some. But you're holding back. You can help me to sort out this case. And if you do, I'll make it as easy for you as I can.'

'Don't do me any favours.' But she was studying my face for the exact meaning of what I had said.

'You wouldn't be well advised,' I said, 'to go on trying to cover up for your husband. You could end up with your own share of a murder rap.'

'It wasn't a murder. It was an accident. The man was in poor shape. My husband may have struck or pushed him. He had no intention of killing him.'

'How do you know?'

'He told me. He wasn't lying.'

'Did he tell you who the man was?'

'Yes.'

'What was his name?'

She shook her head in a quick distracted movement. 'I don't remember. He was simply a man my husband had known in the army. The man had been wounded in the Pacific, and spent some years in a veterans' hospital. When they finally released him, he came here to see my husband. Apparently he'd heard of Richard's success as a painter and came here to bask in reflected glory.'

'Who were the woman and the little boy?'

'They were the man's wife and son. The second time he came, he brought them to meet my husband.'

'Were they aware that your husband killed the man?'

'I don't know. I'm not even certain that that's what happened.'

'But you assumed it.'

'Yes. I had to. I kept waiting to hear from the woman. I

hardly slept for weeks. But I never did hear from her. Sometimes I wonder if I imagined the whole thing.'

'The bones Rico dug up aren't imaginary.'

'I know that. I meant the woman and the little boy.'

'What happened to them?'

'They simply went away—I don't know where. And I went on with my life as best I could.'

There was self-pity in her voice, but she was watching me in cold surmise. The contours of her body appeared to be aware of me, more in resignation than anything else.

Below the house, the sea thumped and fumbled and slid like a dead man trying clumsily to climb back into life. I shivered. She touched my knee with her tapered fingers.

'Are you cold?'

'I suppose I am.'

'I suppose I could turn on the heat.'

The smile that went with the offer lent it a double meaning, but it was forced.

'I won't be staying, Mrs Chantry.'

'I'll be all alone here.'

She uttered a mock sigh, which ended on a note of genuine desolation. She seemed to be realizing how completely alone she was.

'You'll be having visitors before long.'

Her hands came together and clenched. 'You mean the police, don't you?'

'You can probably expect Mackendrick in the morning, if not before.'

'I thought you were going to help me,' she said in a small voice.

'I will if you let me. You haven't told me enough. And some of the things you've told me aren't true.'

She gave me an angry look, but it was calculated and controlled. 'I haven't been lying.'

'Maybe not consciously. When you live a phony life for twenty-five years, it's possible to get a bit out of touch.'

'Are you telling me I'm out of my mind?'

'More likely you're simply lying, to yourself as well as me.'

'What did I say that wasn't true?'

'You said the dead man was an old army friend of your husband's. I happen to know that Chantry was never in the army. That one discrepancy casts doubt on your whole story.'

She flushed and bit her lower lip and looked at me like a thief. 'I was just talking loosely. I meant that the dead man had been in the army at the time they met. But of course Richard wasn't.'

'Do you want to make some other corrections in your account?'

'If you'll tell me where I went wrong.'

A spurt of anger went through me. 'It isn't so funny, Mrs Chantry. Several people have been killed. Others are in danger.'

'Not from me. I've never injured anyone in my life.'

'You've stood by and let it happen.'

'Not by choice.' She tried to project a look of candour, which failed to come off. 'I don't know what happened between Richard and the dead man. I have no idea what their relationship actually was.'

'I've been told your husband was bisexual.'

'Really? This is the first I've heard of it.'

'Are you telling me he wasn't?'

'The question never came up. Why is it so important to you?'

'It may be an essential part of the case.'

'I doubt it. Richard wasn't a very sexual man at all. He was more excited by his work than he ever was by me.'

She made a doleful mouth and looked at me to measure its effect. For some reason, it made me angrier. I had had enough of the woman and her lies, enough of her truth as well. While I sat trading words with her, a woman I cared about was lost in the dangerous night.

'Do you know where Betty Siddon is?'

She shook her silver head. 'I'm afraid I don't. Has something happened to Betty Jo?'

'She went looking for Mildred Mead and got lost herself. Do you know where I can find Mildred Mead?'

'No. I don't. She phoned me a few months ago, when she'd

just come to town. But I didn't want to see her. I didn't want to stir up all the old memories.'

'Then you should never have dug up those bones,' I said.

She swore at me violently, damning me to hell. But the wish rebounded, almost as if she'd meant it for herself in the first place. A grey look of self-loathing dropped like a veil across her face. She covered it with her hands.

'Why did you dig them up?' I said.

She was silent for a while. Then she said behind her hands, 'I simply panicked.'

'Why?'

'I was afraid the place would be searched, and I would be blamed for the man's death.'

She was watching me between her fingers, like a woman behind bars.

'Did somebody threaten you with exposure?'

She didn't answer. I took this to mean yes. 'Who was it, Mrs Chantry?'

'I'm not sure. She didn't come here. She phoned me last night and threatened to go to the police with what she knew. I think it was the woman who came here with the little boy the day the man was killed.'

'What did she want from you?'

'Money.' She dropped her hands: her mouth was twisted and her eyes were hard.

'How much?'

'She didn't specify. A large amount, I gather.'

'When does she want it?'

'Tomorrow. She said she'd call me again tomorrow, and meanwhile I should raise all the money I could.'

'Do you plan to do that?'

'I had planned to. But there's no point in it now, is there? Unless you and I can come to some arrangement.'

She thrust her hands into her hair and held her head between them, chin high, like a work of art that she was offering for lease or outright sale.

I said, 'I'll do what I can. But you can't keep Mackendrick out of this. If you can help him to close the case, he'll be grateful. I think you should get in touch with him right away.'

'No. I need time to think. Will you give me until morning?'

'I will on one condition. Don't do anything rash.'

'Like run away, you mean?'

'Like kill yourself.'

She shook her head in a short angry movement. 'I'm going to stay here and fight. I hope you'll be on my side.'

I didn't commit myself. As I got up to leave the eyes of Chantry's portraits seemed to be watching me from the shadowed walls.

Mrs Chantry followed me to the door. 'Please don't judge me harshly. I know I appear to be a wicked person. But I've really had very little choice about the things I've done, or left undone. My life wasn't easy even before my husband took off. And since then it's been a kind of shabby hell.'

'With Rico.'

'Yes. With Rico. I said I had no real choice.'

She was standing close to me, her eyes hooded and calculating, as if she might be getting ready to make another unfortunate choice.

I said, 'A young soldier named William Mead was murdered in Arizona over thirty years ago. He was the illegitimate son of Felix Chantry by Mildred Mead—your husband's half-brother.'

She reacted as though I had struck her and she was about to cry out. Her eyebrows rose and her lower lip dropped. For a moment, her face was open. But she didn't make a sound.

'Your husband left Arizona immediately afterwards, and there was some suspicion that he had killed William Mead. Did he?'

'Certainly not. What reason would he have?'

'I was hoping you could tell me. Weren't you quite close to William at one time?'

'No. Of course not.'

But there was no conviction in her denial.

XXXIV

I LEFT HER and drove south along the waterfront. The traffic was still fairly heavy. It wasn't really late, but I was tired. The long indeterminate conversation with Mrs Chantry had drained my energy. I checked in at my motel, hoping that Betty might have left a message for me.

She hadn't. But there was one from Paola Grimes, who wanted me to call her at the Monte Cristo Hotel. I got the front desk of the hotel after some difficulty.

Paola answered her room phone on the first ring: 'Hello?'

'This is Archer.'

'It's about time.' Her voice was flat and angry. 'My mother told me she gave you some money for me. Fifty dollars. I need it. I can't get out of this flea-trap without it, and my van won't start, either.'

'I'll bring you your fifty now. I tried to deliver it earlier.'

'You could have left it at the desk.'

'Not that desk. I'll see you, Paola.'

I found her waiting for me in the Monte Cristo lobby. She had evidently brushed her hair and washed her face and put on fresh lipstick. But she looked sad and out of place among the night-blooming girls and their followers.

I handed her the fifty dollars. She counted and rolled the bills and thrust them into her brassière.

I said, 'Will that cover your hotel bill?'

'Up until now I guess it will. I don't know about tomorrow. The police want me to stick around but they won't release any of my father's money. He was carrying quite a lot of money.'

'You'll get it back, or your mother will.'

'Or my great-grandchildren will,' she said bitterly. 'I don't trust cops and I don't like this town. I don't like the people here. They killed my father and I'm afraid they'll kill me.'

Her fear was contagious. I followed the movements of her eyes and began to see the place as she was seeing it, an anteroom where lost souls waited for a one-night stand that was never going to end.

'Who killed your father?'

She shook her head, and her black hair fell like night around her face. 'I don't want to talk about it. Not here.'

'We could talk in your room.'

'No, thanks.' She gave me a sharp dark paranoid look, like a frightened animal peering out from the cover of her hair. 'The room may be bugged. That's one reason I can't stay in it.'

'Who would bug it?'

'Maybe the cops. Maybe the killers. What difference does it make? They're all in this together.'

'Come out and sit in my car.'

'No, thanks.'

'Then let's take a walk, Paola.'

Surprisingly she agreed. We went out and joined the people on the sidewalk. Across the road, a line of palms tossed their plumes above the empty booths of the weekly art show. Beyond them the phosphorescent white waves broke and rose and receded as if they had been set the eternal task of marking time and measuring space.

Gradually, as we moved along the sidewalk, Paola became less tense. Our movements seemed to relate to the natural rhythms of the sea. The sky opened out above us, poorly lit by the low sinking moon on the horizon.

Paola touched my arm. 'You asked me who killed my father.'

'Yes.'

'You want to know what I think?'

'Tell me what you think.'

'Well, I've been going over in my mind everything my father said. You know, he believed that Richard Chantry was alive and staying here in town under a different name. And he thought that Chantry actually painted that picture of Mildred Mead. I thought so, too, when I saw it. I don't claim to be an expert, like my father, but it looked like a Chantry to me.'

'Are you sure your father's opinion was honest, Paola? The picture was worth a lot more to him if it was a Chantry.'

'I know that, and so did he. That's why he did his best to authenticate it. He spent the last days of his life trying to locate Chantry and trace the picture to him. He even looked up Mildred Mead, who is living here in town. She was Chantry's favourite model, though of course she didn't actually sit for that particular portrait. She's an old woman now.'

'Have you seen her?'

She nodded. 'My father took me to see her a couple of days before he was killed. Mildred was a friend of my mother's in Arizona, and I've known her ever since I was a child. My father probably thought that having me there would get her talking. But Mildred didn't say much the day we visited her.'

'Exactly where was this?'

'She has a little place in a court. She was just moving in. I think it's called Magnolia Court. There's a big magnolia tree in the middle of it.'

'In town here?'

'Yes. It's in the downtown section. She said she took it because she couldn't do much walking any more. She didn't talk much, either.'

'Why not?'

'I think she was scared. My father kept pressing her about Richard Chantry. Was he alive or dead? Did he paint that picture? But she didn't want to talk about him. She said she hadn't seen him in over thirty years and he was probably dead, and she hoped he was. She sounded very bitter.'

'I'm not surprised. Chantry may have killed her son William.'

'And he may have killed my father, too. My father could have traced the picture to him and got himself killed for his trouble.'

Her voice was low and frightened. She looked around suspiciously at the palms and the low moon, as if they were parts of a shabby stage set hiding the actual jungle life of the world. Her hands grasped at each other and pulled in opposing directions.

'I've got to get out of this town. The police say I have to stick around, they need me for a witness. But they're not even protecting me.'

'Protecting you from what?' I said, though I knew the answer.

'Chantry. Who else? He killed my father – I know that in my bones. But I don't know who he is or where he is. I don't even know what he looks like any more. He could be any man I meet on the street.'

Her voice was rising. Other people on the sidewalk had begun to notice us. We were approaching a restaurant-bar that was spilling jazz through its open front door. I steered her in and sat her at a table. The room was narrow and deep, resembling a tunnel, and the band at its far end was like a train coming.

'I don't like that music,' she said.

'No matter. You need a drink.'

She shook her dark head. 'I can't drink. Alcohol drives me crazy. It was the same with my father. He told me that was why he went on drugs.' She covered her ears with her hands and closed her eyes. 'I've got to get out of here.'

I took her hand and drew her to her feet. Pulling and jerking against me, out of phase with my movements, she followed me out. She stared at the people on the street in profound distrust, ready to yell if anyone looked twice at her. She was on the narrow edge of hysteria or something worse.

I gripped her arm and walked her quickly in the direction of the hotel.

She hung back. 'I don't want to go back there. I don't like it there. They kept me up all night, knocking and fooling around and whispering. They think that any woman is their meat.'

'Then check out of the place.'

'I wouldn't know where to go. I guess I could go back to the gallery. I have a little room in the back there. But I'm afraid to.'

'Because your father isn't there?'

'No.' She hugged herself and shuddered. 'Because he might come back.'

That sent a chill through me. I didn't quite believe that the woman was losing her mind, but she was trying hard to. If she went on like this, she might succeed before morning.

For various reasons, I felt responsible for her. I made a kind of superstitious bargain with the controlling forces of the world, if any. If I tried to look after Paola, then maybe Betty would be looked after.

I took Paola into the Monte Cristo and paid her bill and helped her pack her suitcase and carried it out to my car.

She trotted along beside me. 'Where are we going?'

'I'll get you a room in my motel. It's across from the yacht harbour, and it's quieter. There's an all-night restaurant on the corner if you get hungry.'

'I'm hungry now,' she said. 'I haven't been eating.'

I took her to the restaurant for a sandwich, then got her checked into the motel. Biemeyer could pay for her room. She was a witness.

I left the motel without going into my own room. But when I was out in the parking lot getting into my car, I had a sudden wild idea that Betty might be waiting for me in that room. I went and looked. The room was empty, the bed unslept-in.

There was only one thing I could do: follow my case until it took me to her. Not too late. Please.

XXXV

THE MAGNOLIA TREE hung like a tethered cloud over the court to which it had given its name. There was light in only one of the small cottages, shining dimly through drawn blinds. I tapped on the screen door.

I heard a movement behind it, and then a breathing silence. A woman's voice finally said, 'Who is that?'

'My name is Archer. I'm a private detective working for Jack Biemeyer.'

'Then you can go plumb to hell,' she said quietly. 'But

before you do you can go back and tell Jack Biemeyer to do the same.'

'I'll be glad to, Miss Mead. I don't like that s.o.b. either.'

She opened the inner door, a small and dainty figure against the light. 'What did you say your name was?'

'Lew Archer.'

'Did Jack Biemeyer send you here?'

'Not exactly. He had a picture stolen—a painting of you. I thought you might be able to help me trace it.'

'How did Jack know I was here? I haven't told a living soul.'

'Paola Grimes sent me.'

'I see. I should have known better than to let her into my house.' Her body had stiffened as if she were getting ready to slam the door in my face. 'She's a bad-luck member of a bad-luck family.'

'I talked to her mother, Juanita, this morning in Copper City. She sent her best wishes to you.'

'Did she? That's nice.'

I had said the right thing. She moved to unlatch the outer door. Until then, she hadn't shown her age. She was lame, and her hips moved awkwardly. I was reminded of certain kinds of pelagic birds that move at ease in the air or on the ocean, but have a hard time walking.

Her white head was like a bird's. It was sparse and elegant, with hollow cheeks, a thin straight nose, eyes that still had distance and wildness. She caught me looking at her, and smiled. One of her front teeth was missing. It gave her a gamine touch.

'Do you like my looks? I can't say they've improved with age.'

'That's true.'

She went on smiling. 'Who would want them to? My looks got me into more trouble. I don't mean to complain. A woman can't have everything in her life. I travelled a lot— first class a good deal of the time. I knew some talented and famous men.'

'I met one of them in Tucson yesterday.'

'Lashman?'

'Yes.'

'How is he?'

'Getting old. But he's still painting. As a matter of fact, when I left him he was working on another portrait of you.'

She was silent for a moment. Her head was poised and her eyes were empty. 'The way I am now, or the way I was?'

'The way you were.'

'Of course, it would have to be. He hasn't seen me since I got really old.' She talked about herself as if she were an object of art that unfortunately hadn't been made to last—a Japanese flower arrangement or a song by a composer who didn't know musical notation. 'But that's enough about me. Tell me about Juanita.'

She sat in an armchair under a standing lamp, and I sat facing her. I gave her a brief report on Juanita Grimes, then on Juanita's ex-husband, Paul, and his death.

She seemed shocked by the knowledge. 'I can't believe Paul Grimes is dead. He was here just the other day, with his daughter.'

'So she told me. I understand he wanted you to authenticate a painting of you.'

'That was the general idea. Unfortunately I couldn't place it. All he had was a small photograph of it, and I've been painted so many times I lost track long ago. As a matter of fact, I've got very bored with pictures, especially pictures of my own face. I haven't hung any pictures since I moved in, though I've got a ton of them in the back room.' She waved her fingers at the bare walls. 'It's no fun being reminded of what you've lost.'

'I know that. But would you mind taking another look at a photograph of a picture?'

'A picture of me?'

'I think so. It's the same picture that Paul Grimes was interested in.'

I got out my photograph of the painting and handed it to her. She held it up to the light and studied it. Then she let out a little wordless grunt of recognition.

'Have you seen it before, Miss Mead?'

'This is the third time I've seen it. The second time tonight.

But I still can't say for sure who painted it, or when. It looks like a Chantry, all right, but I don't remember him painting it.'

'It's been suggested that it was a memory picture, one you never sat for—maybe done quite recently.'

'That's what the young woman was saying this evening.'

'What young woman?'

'The girl from the local paper. I told her I don't give interviews. But she was very persistent and I finally let her come. I must admit she was nice enough. I wasn't much help to her, though.'

'Was her name Betty Siddon?'

'That's it. Betty Siddon. Do you know her?'

'I've been trying to get in touch with her. Did she tell you where she was going from here?'

'She said something about a beach—Sycamore Beach?'

'Sycamore Point?'

'I guess that was it. Anyway, the man who sold the picture to Paul Grimes drowned in the ocean there the other day. What was his name?'

'Jake Whitmore. He didn't drown in the ocean, though. He was drowned in fresh water, probably in somebody's bathtub.'

Without intending to, I had succeeded in shocking her. The life and colour drained from her face. Its bones still made it handsome, though her eyes had gone as dead as any statue's.

Her pale mauve mouth said: 'This Whitmore was murdered, too?'

'The police and the coroner think so.'

'Jesus.' She was breathing like a runner.

'Can I get you some water, Miss Mead?'

'Got something better than that.' She pointed at a cabinet against the wall. 'There's a fifth of Jack Daniels in there. And glasses. Pour yourself one, too. I take mine straight. Double.'

I got out the whisky and poured her a double shot and myself a single. She took hers in a single gulp. She asked for another double. I poured it, and she drank it. I watched the colour rise in her face.

'Drink yours down,' she said. 'I hate to drink alone.'

I wondered if she was an alcoholic, and decided she probably was.

'Why are you looking at me like that?' she said. 'Do I look funny? Do my eyes look funny?'

'No. They look fine.'

'Then quit staring at me like that.'

'I'm sorry. I have to leave, anyway.'

'You're interested in that Siddon girl, aren't you?'

'Yes, I am. You're a mind reader.'

'I know men,' she said. 'Isn't she a little young for you?'

'Maybe. How long ago was she here?'

'I didn't look at the time. It was early in the evening.'

'How did she find you?'

'She called the—' The old woman's mouth clamped shut. After a short period of strained silence, she said, 'I have no idea.'

'You were going to say she called somewhere.'

'Was I? Then you know more than I do. I must have been thinking about something else. Don't let me keep you—you say you have to go. Just leave that bottle where I can reach it, will you?'

She touched the table beside her chair with one of her wrinkled white hands.

I said, 'I'm not leaving yet.'

'I wish you would. I'm very tired. Anyway, I've told you all I know.'

'I seriously doubt that, Miss Mead. When I was in Arizona, I stumbled into some very interesting facts. Back in the early forties, your natural son William was killed by someone and left in the desert.'

Her face grew paler and longer. 'Juanita Grimes always did talk a lot.'

'She wasn't my main source. Your son's murder was and is public knowledge. I talked to the man who discovered his body and investigated his death. Sheriff Brotherton.'

'So?'

'Aren't you interested in who killed your son?'

'It doesn't matter now,' she said. 'What difference can it possibly make? He's dead. He's been dead for over thirty-two years.'

'But I think the man who killed him is still alive.'

'How can you know that?'

'I feel it in my bones. Not that there isn't plenty of evidence. There have been other deaths. Paul Grimes, Jacob Whitmore. And the man whose remains were dug up tonight in Richard Chantry's greenhouse.'

She tried to speak, and succeeded on her second attempt. 'What man?'

'He hasn't been identified yet, but he will be. He came to Chantry's house about twenty-five years ago with a woman and a little boy. There was an argument, and a fight between him and Chantry. According to the account I heard, the man fell down and hit his head and died. The Chantrys buried him.'

'Did Mrs Chantry tell you this?' she said.

'Some of it.'

Her eyes widened while the rest of her face had tightened and thinned. She looked like a kestrel or some other small bird of prey.

'What else did Mrs Chantry tell you?'

'That was the gist of it. What else was there to tell?'

'I'm asking you,' she said.

'But I think you're the one who knows the answer. Why did Jack Biemeyer buy you the house in Chantry Canyon?'

'Because I asked him to.'

'Jack Biemeyer isn't that generous.'

'He was to me, in those days.' A little colour came into her face and gathered on her cheekbones. 'I admit he hasn't improved with age. But then neither have I.'

'I suggest that Biemeyer bought you that house on behalf of the Chantry family. Or possibly they gave it to you, by way of him, for nothing.'

'What reason would they have to do that?'

'To keep you quiet about your son William's murder.'

'William's death was public knowledge. What was there to be quiet about?'

'Who killed him. I think it was Richard Chantry. He left Arizona for California right after the murder and never went back. The case against him was quashed, or never developed. If you had any suspicions, you kept them to yourself.'

She shook her head. 'You don't know me. I loved my son. When they showed me William's body, I almost died myself. And don't forget he was a Chantry, too. Felix Chantry was his natural father. And there was no bad blood between William and Richard.'

'Then why did Richard leave Arizona immediately after William's death?'

'I don't know. Perhaps he was afraid of being murdered, too.'

'Did he say that?'

'I never discussed it with him. As a matter of fact, I haven't seen Richard since then.'

'Since William's death?'

'That's right. I haven't seen Richard once in thirty-two years. Nobody's seen him in the last twenty-five years. And I didn't find out why until tonight, from you.' She moved restlessly, and looked at the bottle beside her. 'If you're planning to stay around for a while, you might as well pour me another. And yourself, too.'

'No, thanks. I have a few more questions, and that should do it. I understand that when your son William was killed he left behind a wife and a small son.'

Her eyes changed as if she were looking inward and downward into the past. 'I believe he did.'

'You mean you don't know?'

'I've been told about them. I've never seen them.'

'Why not?'

'It wasn't through any wish of mine. They simply dropped out of sight. I did hear a rumour that the woman, William's widow, married another man and changed the boy's name to his.'

'Do you know the name?'

'I'm afraid I don't. They never contacted me.'

'Do you think they contacted Richard Chantry?'

She looked away. 'I wouldn't know about that.'

'The woman and the little boy who came to Chantry's house twenty-five years ago—could they have been William's widow and son?'

'I don't know. It seems to me you're really reaching.'

'I have to. It's all a long way back in the past. Do you have any idea who the man was—the man who got himself killed and buried in the greenhouse?'

'I haven't the slightest.'

'Could it have been your son William?'

'You must be crazy. William was killed in Arizona in 1943 —seven years before that.'

'Did you see his body?'

'Yes.'

'I understand it was pretty chewed up. Were you able to make a positive identification?'

'Yes. I was. My son William died thirty-two years ago.'

'What happened to his body after you identified it?'

'I don't know exactly.'

'That's surprising.'

'Is it? He had a wife in California, you know. She wanted his body shipped back here for final burial. And I had no objections. Once a man is dead, he's dead. It doesn't matter where he's finally planted.'

Her voice was rough and careless, and I got the impression that she was deliberately violating her own feelings.

As if she realized this, she added, 'I want my own body cremated—it won't be long now—and the ashes scattered on the desert near Tucson.'

'Near Lashman's?'

She looked at me with irritation, and renewed interest. 'You know too damn much.'

'You tell me too damn little, Mildred. Where *was* your son William buried?'

'Some place in California, I was told.'

'Did you ever visit his grave?'

'No. I don't know where it is.'

'Do you know where his widow lives now?'

'No. I never was much interested in family. I left my own family in Denver when I was fourteen years old, and never went back. I never looked back, either.'

But her eyes were in long focus now, looking back over the continent of her life. She may have been feeling what I felt, the subterranean jolt as the case moved once again, with enough force to throw a dead man out of his grave.

XXXVI

IT WAS NEARLY three by my car clock when I got out to Sycamore Point. At the foot of the beach, the sea was coughing in its sleep. My own tides were at a low ebb and I was tempted to go to sleep sitting up in the front seat.

But there was a light in Jacob Whitmore's cottage. I let myself hope for a minute that Betty was there. But Jessie Gable turned out to be alone.

I noticed the difference in Jessie as soon as she let me into the lighted room. Her movements were more assured, her eyes more definite. There was wine on her breath, but she didn't seem to be drunk.

She offered me a chair and said, 'You owe me a hundred dollars. I found out the name of the woman who sold Jake the picture.'

'Who was it?'

She reached across the table and laid her hand on my arm. 'Wait a minute, now. Don't be in such a hurry. How do I know you *have* a hundred dollars?'

I counted out the money on to the table. She reached for the stack of bills. I picked them up again from under her hands.

'Hey,' she said, 'that's my money.'

'You haven't told me the woman's name yet.'

She tossed her blonde hair. It fell like a soiled silk shawl over her shoulders. 'Don't you trust me?'

'I did until you started not trusting me.'

'You sound like Jake. He was always turning things around and upside down.'

'Who sold Jake the picture?'

'I'll tell you when you give me the money.'

I dealt fifty on to the table. 'There's half. I'll give you the other half when you tell me who she is.'

'It's worth more than that. This is an important case. I was told I should get a big reward.'

I sat and studied her face. Two days before, when I had first come here, she hadn't seemed to care about money.

'Who's going to pay the reward?' I said.

'The newspaper.'

'Did Betty Siddon tell you that?'

'More or less. She said I'd be well paid for my information.'

'Did you tell Betty who the woman was?'

She disengaged her eyes from mine and looked away into a shadowed corner of the room. 'She said it was important. And I didn't know if you were coming back or not. You know how it is. I really need the money.'

I knew how it was. She was selling Jake Whitmore's bones, as survivors often do, and I was buying them. I dealt the rest of the hundred on to the table-top.

Jessie reached for the bills, but her hand fell on the table short of them. She looked at me as if I might interfere, or possibly hit her.

I was sick of the game. 'Go ahead and take it.'

She picked up the tens and twenties, and put them inside her shirt against her breast. She looked at me guiltily, close to tears.

I said, 'Let's not waste any more time, Jessie. Who was the woman?'

She said in a low hesitant voice, 'Her name is Mrs Johnson.'

'Fred's mother?'

'I don't know whose mother she is.'

'What's her first name?'

'I don't know. All I got from Stanley Meyer was her last name.'

'Who is Stanley Meyer?'

'He's a hospital orderly who paints in his spare time. He sells his stuff at the beach art show. His booth is right next to Jake's. He was there when Jake bought the picture from her.'

'You're talking about the portrait of a woman that Jake later sold to Paul Grimes.'

She nodded. 'That's the one you're interested in, isn't it?'

'Yes. Did your informer Stanley Meyer describe the woman to you?'

'Sort of. He said she was a middle-aged woman, maybe in her fifties. A big woman, broad in the beam. Dark hair with some grey in it.'

'Did he say how she was dressed?'

'No.'

'How did he happen to know her name?'

'He knew her from the hospital. This Mrs Johnson worked there as a nurse, until they fired her.'

'Why did they fire her?'

'Meyer said he didn't know. He said that the last he heard she was working at the La Paloma nursing home.'

'What else did he tell you about Mrs Johnson?'

'That's about all I remember.'

'Did you tell all this to Betty Siddon?'

'Yes.'

'How long ago?'

'I don't really know. Jake didn't believe in clocks. He thought that we should tell time by the sun, like the Chumash Indians.'

'Was it before or after sundown that Betty Siddon was here?'

'After sundown. I remember now—it was right after you were here.'

'Did you tell her you'd seen me?'

'No.'

'Did she say where she was going when she left?'

'She didn't say it in so many words. But she asked me about the La Paloma nursing home. She wanted to make sure she had it straight that that was where Mrs Johnson was working now.'

I drove back down the highway, which was empty except for a few long-distance trucks. I felt as though I had climbed the ridge between the late dead middle of the night and chilly early morning. I could go on now, for another day if I had to.

I parked in the La Paloma lot and rang the bell at the service entrance. Someone inside groaned and muttered in reply. I rang again and heard rapid quiet footsteps. The door was opened six inches on a chain, and the young black nurse peered out at me.

'I was here the other night,' I said.

'I remember you. If it's Mrs Johnson you're after, she isn't here. It's the second time tonight she left me to handle the whole place by myself. I'm just about beat now and I've got hours to go yet. Talking to you isn't getting my work done, either.'

'I know how you feel. I've been working all night, too.'

She gave me an incredulous look. 'What at?'

'I'm a detective. May I come in and talk to you for a minute, Miss?'

'Mrs—Mrs Holman.' She sighed and unlatched the chain. 'I guess so. But make it fast, please.'

We leaned against the wall in the dark hallway. The breathings and groans of the patients and the intermittent sounds from the highway made a late-night undersong. Her face merged with the darkness so that her eyes appeared to be the night's own glowing eyes.

'What do you want to know?' she said.

'Why Mrs Johnson went home.'

'Well, she got a call from Fred. Fred is her son. He said the old man was on the rampage again. He's a terrible drunk—she's the only one who can handle him when he's that way. So she took a taxi home. I don't hold it against her, because you gotta do what you gotta do.' She took a big breath and let it out: I could feel the warm exhalation in the darkness. 'I don't mean to bear down hard on Mrs Johnson. There are drinkers in my family, too.'

'Did you ever visit the Johnson house?'

'No,' she said abruptly. 'If that's all you want to know, you're wasting my time.'

'It isn't, though. This is very important, Mrs Holman—a matter of life and death.'

'Whose life?' she said. 'Whose death?'

'A woman named Betty Siddon. She works for the local paper.'

I heard the woman draw in her breath.

'Do you recognize the name.'

'Yeah. I do. She called here from the newspaper office right after I came on duty. She wanted to know if we had a patient here named Mildred Mead. I said we did have but not any more; Miss Mead got independent and moved out to Magnolia Court. The only reason she came here in the first place was on account of her connection with Mrs Johnson.'

'What connection?'

'Her—Miss Mead and Mrs Johnson were relatives.'

'What kind of relatives?'

'I never got that straight.'

'Did you mention Miss Siddon's call to Mrs Johnson?'

'No. I didn't want to get her stirred up. She didn't like it at all, you know, when old Miss Mead moved out of here. She took it personally, you might say. They had quite an argument when Miss Mead left. As a matter of fact, they almost came to blows. They're both a couple of blowtops, if you want my opinion.'

I got the impression that the woman was talking too freely, sending up a smoke screen of words between me and the thing I wanted to know.

I said, 'Has Miss Siddon been here tonight?'

'No.' Her answer was firm. But her eyes seemed to flicker a little, as if a counter-thought had moved behind them.

'If she has been, you better tell me. She may be in serious danger.'

'I'm sorry about that. I haven't seen her.'

'Is that the honest truth, Mrs Holman?'

She flared up. 'Why don't you stop bugging me? I'm sorry there's trouble in the air, and that your friend's in trouble. But I'm not responsible. And I've got work to do, if you haven't.'

I left her reluctantly, feeling that she knew more than she was willing to tell. The atmosphere of the nursing home, compounded of age and sickness and blurred pain, followed me across town to the Johnson house.

XXXVII

THE HIGH OLD house was completely dark. It seemed to hang over me like a dismal past piled generation on generation against the stars. I knocked on the front door, knocked repeatedly and got no answer.

I felt like shouting at the house as Gerard Johnson had done, and I wondered if I was going crazy, too. I leaned on the wall and looked out at the quiet street. I had parked my car around the corner, and the road was empty. Above the dense masses of the olive trees, a pallor was slowly spreading up the sky.

The dawn chill made my bones ache. I threw off my lethargy and pounded on the door and skinned my knuckles and stood in the grey dark sucking them.

Gerard Johnson spoke through the door: 'What is it?'

'Archer. Open the door.'

'I can't. She went away and locked me in.' His voice was a hoarse whine.

'Where did she go?'

'Probably the La Paloma—that's the nursing home. She's supposed to be on night duty.'

'I just came from there. Mrs Johnson walked off the job again.'

'She shouldn't do that. She'll lose that job, too. We'll have to go on welfare. I don't know what will happen to us.'

'Where's Fred?'

'I don't know.'

There were other questions I wanted to ask him, about his wife and the missing picture, but I despaired of getting useful answers. I gave Johnson a curt good night through the door and drove to the police station.

Mackendrick was in his office, looking not much different from the way he had looked seven or eight hours before. There were tender-looking blue patches under his eyes, but the eyes themselves were stern and steady, and he was freshly shaven.

'You look as if you didn't get much sleep,' he said.

'I didn't get any. I've been trying to catch up with Betty Siddon.'

Mackendrick drew in a long breath that made the chair creak under him. He let it out with a sigh.

'Why is it so important? We can't keep twenty-four-hour tabs on every reporter in town.'

'I know that. This is a special case. I think the Johnson house ought to be searched.'

'Do you have any reason to think Miss Siddon's in there?'

'Nothing definite, no. But there's a possibility, more than a possibility, that the missing picture is hidden in that house. It passed through Mrs Johnson's hands once before, and then through her son Fred's.'

I reminded Mackendrick of the facts of the case: Fred Johnson's theft or borrowing of the picture from the Biemeyer house; its subsequent theft from the art museum or, according to Fred's original story, from the Johnson house. I added what Jessie Gable had told me, that Whitmore had bought the picture from Mrs Johnson in the first place.

'All this is very interesting,' Mackendrick said in a flat voice. 'But I haven't got time to look for Miss Siddon right now. And I haven't got time to look for a lost or stolen or mislaid picture which probably isn't worth very much anyway.'

'The girl is. And the picture is the key to the whole bloody case.'

Mackendrick leaned heavily forward across his desk. 'She's your girl, right?'

'I don't know yet.'

'But you're interested in her?'

'Very interested,' I said.

'And the picture is the one you were hired to reclaim?'

'I guess so.'

'And that makes it the key to the case, right?'

'I didn't say that, Captain. My personal connection with the girl and the picture aren't the reasons they're important.'

'You may not think so. I want you to go into my washroom and take a good look at your face in the mirror. Incidentally, while you're in there, you can use my electric razor. It's in the cabinet behind the mirror. The light switch is to the left inside the door.'

I went into the little room and looked at my face. It was drawn and pale. I grimaced to bring it to life but my eyes didn't change. They were at the same time dull and glaring.

I shaved and washed. It made some improvement in my looks. But it didn't touch the anxiety and fatigue that I was carrying inside my head and body.

When I came back into Mackendrick's office, he gave me a hard stare.

'Are you feeling any better?'

'Some.'

'How long is it since you've eaten?'

I looked at my watch. It was ten to seven. 'About nine or ten hours.'

'No sleep?'

'No.'

'Okay, let's get some breakfast. Joe's opens at seven.'

Joe's was a working man's restaurant whose booths and bar were already filling up with customers. There was a low-key half-kidding kind of hopefulness in the smoky atmosphere, as if the day might turn out to be not so bad after all.

Mackendrick and I sat across from each other in one of the booths. We discussed the case over coffee while we waited for our breakfasts to arrive. I was becoming painfully aware that I hadn't told Mackendrick about my interview with Mrs Chantry. I was going to have to tell him before he found out for himself, if he hadn't already. I was going to have to tell him very soon. But I put it off until I had fortified myself with some solid food.

Both Mackendrick and I had ham and eggs and fried potatoes and toast. On top of that, he ordered a piece of apple pie with vanilla ice cream on the side.

When he had eaten it and ordered a fresh cup of coffee, I said, 'I went to see Mrs Chantry last night.'

His face hardened, cracking at the corners of the mouth

and eyes. 'I asked you not to.'

'It seemed necessary. We work under different rules, Captain.'

'You can say that again.'

I had meant that he had to work under special political constraints. He was the iron fist of the city, embodying all its crushing force, but he had to listen to what the city told him to do with it. He seemed to be listening now to the city's multitudinous voices, some of which were speaking in the big smoky room where we sat.

Gradually his face smoothed out and lost its cracked-cement look. His eyes remained impassive.

'What did you find out from Mrs Chantry?'

I told him in some detail, with special emphasis on the man in the brown suit whose bones Mrs Chantry and Rico had dug up. By this time, Mackendrick's face was flushed with interest.

'Did she tell you where the man came from?'

'Apparently he'd been in a veterans' hospital.'

Mackendrick hit the table once with his hand. The dishes jumped and rattled. Everyone at our end of the restaurant was probably aware of this, but nobody turned to look.

'I wish to hell,' he said, 'that you'd told me about this earlier. If the man was ever in a veterans' hospital, we should be able to trace him through his bones.'

Mackendrick laid three dollar bills on the table and got up and walked out.

I put down my own money and went outside. It was past eight, and the city was coming to life. I walked down the main street, hoping that I would come to life along with it, and ended up at the newspaper building.

She hadn't been seen or heard from.

I walked back to the parking lot and reclaimed my car and drove it down to the waterfront. I was guided by a half-admitted half-unconscious fantasy: if I went back to the room where Betty and I had started, she would be there.

She wasn't. I threw myself down on the bed and tried to turn my mind off. But it was invaded by dreams of the angry dead.

I woke up clear-minded in strong daylight. It was nearly twelve by my watch. I looked out the window at the harbour, sliced into long bright sizzling strips by the partly closed Venetian blinds. A few sailors were taking their boats out in the light noon wind. And my mind released the memory I needed.

When I was in Arizona, Sheriff Brotherton had told me about a soldier whose name was 'something like Wilson or Jackson', and who had been a friend of Mildred Mead's murdered son, William. The sheriff had had a postcard from the soldier after the war, sent from a veterans' hospital in California.

I picked up the room phone and placed a call to Sheriff Brotherton's office in Copper City. After a period of waiting, Brotherton himself came on the line.

'I'm glad you caught me, Archer. I was just going out to lunch. How's everything with the little Biemeyer girl? I take it she's home safe with her family.'

'She's home. I don't know how safe she is.'

'Isn't she safe with her own family?' Brotherton seemed to resent the implication that his rescue of Doris had not been permanent, like an ascent into heaven.

'She's a troubled girl, and she isn't too happy with her father. Speaking of whom, and forgive me if I've asked you this before, did Biemeyer have anything to do with shutting off the investigation of William Mead's death?'

'You have asked me that before. I said I didn't know.'

'What are the probabilities?'

'It wouldn't make sense for Biemeyer to do that. He was very close to William Mead's mother at that time. I'm not telling you anything that isn't generally known.'

'Did Mildred Mead want the investigation pressed?'

'I don't know whether she did or not. She did her talking to the higher echelons.' Brotherton's voice was stiff, on the point of freezing up completely.

'Did Mildred want Richard Chantry brought back from California for questioning?'

'I don't remember that she did. What are you looking for, Archer?'

'I may not know till I see it. But one of the things you told me about the Mead case may be important. You mentioned that an army friend of Mead's came out to Arizona and talked to you about his death.'

'That's correct. As a matter of fact, I've been thinking about him. I heard from him after the war, you know. He sent me a postcard from a veterans' hospital in L.A. He wanted to know if there were any further developments in the Mead case. I wrote him back that there weren't.'

'Do you remember how he signed his postcard?'

The sheriff hesitated, and then said, 'Jackson, I think. Jerry Jackson. His writing wasn't too clear.'

'Could the name have been Jerry Johnson?'

The sheriff was silent for a while. I could hear faint voices talking somewhere on the line, like half-forgotten memories coming home to roost.

'It could have been,' he said. 'The postcard may still be in my files. I hoped that some day I could write and give that poor buddy of Mead's a positive answer. But I never did.'

'You may be able to do it yet.'

'I keep hoping, anyway.'

'Do you have a suspect, Sheriff?'

'Do you?'

'No. But it wasn't my case.'

I had touched a nerve. 'It wasn't mine either,' he said with some bitterness. 'It was taken out of my hands.'

'Who did that?'

'The powers that be. I'm not naming any names.'

'Was Richard Chantry a suspect in his half-brother's death?'

'That's no secret. I told you how they hustled Richard out of the state. He never came back, to my knowledge.'

'Was there trouble between the two brothers?'

'I don't know if you could call it trouble. Healthy rivalry, anyway. Competition. They both wanted to be painters. They both wanted to marry the same girl. I guess you could say that Richard won on both counts. He even ended up with the family money.'

'But his luck only lasted seven years.'

'So I heard.'

'Do you have any idea what happened to him?'

'No, I don't. It's away outside my territory. And incidentally I have to talk to some people and you're making me late. Goodbye.'

The sheriff hung up abruptly. I went down the hall and tapped on the door of Paola's room. I heard her moving quietly inside.

She said through the door, 'Who is it?'

I told her. She opened the door. She looked as though she'd been having bad dreams like mine, and hadn't fully awakened.

'What do you want?'

'A little more information.'

'I've already told you everything.'

'I doubt that.'

She made an effort to close the door. I held it open. Each of us could feel the other's weight and the presence of an opposing will.

'Aren't you interested in who killed your father, Paola?'

Her dark eyes searched my face, not very hopefully. 'Do you know for certain?'

'I'm working on it. But I need your help. May I come in?'

'I'll come out.'

We sat in a pair of basket chairs beside a window at the end of the hall. Paola moved her chair away from the window.

'What are you afraid of, Paola?'

'That's a stupid question. My father was killed the other night. And I'm still here in this same lousy town.'

'Who are you afraid of?'

'Richard Chantry. Who else? He seems to be a hero around here. That's because people don't know what an s.o.b. he was.'

'Did you know him?'

'Not really. He was before my time. But my father knew him very well; so did my mother. There were some queer stories floating around about him in Copper City. About him and his half-brother William Mead.'

'What stories?'

Two deep clefts formed between her black eyebrows. 'The

way I heard it, Richard Chantry stole his brother's work. They were both serious painters, but William Mead was the one with the real talent. Richard imitated him, and after William was drafted Richard grabbed his drawings and some of his paintings, and passed them off as his own. He grabbed William's girl, too.'

'Is that the present Mrs Chantry?'

'I guess so.'

Gradually she had leaned towards the window, like a heliotropic plant that loved the light. Her eyes remained sullen and fearful. She pulled back her head as if she had spotted snipers in the street.

She followed me into my room and stood just inside the door while I called Mackendrick. I told him the two main facts that I had learned that morning: Richard Chantry had stolen and misrepresented as his own some of his half-brother William's work; and after William's death an army buddy of his who called himself Jerry Johnson had turned up in Arizona.

Mackendrick stopped me. 'Johnson's a common name. But I wouldn't be surprised if that's our Gerard Johnson on Olive Street.'

'Neither would I. If Gerard was injured in the war and spent time in a hospital, it could explain some of his peculiarities.'

'Some of them, anyway. All we can do is ask him. First I want to put out an additional query to the vets' hospitals.'

'An additional query?'

'That's right. Your friend Purvis has been examining those bones you brought in last night. He found traces of what looked like shrapnel wounds, and apparently they were given expert treatment. So Purvis has been getting in touch with the hospitals on his own hook.'

'What are you doing about Betty Siddon?'

'Hasn't she turned up yet?'

Mackendrick sounded bored. I slammed the receiver down. Then I sat regretting my show of anger and wondering what to do next.

XXXVIII

I DROVE UPTOWN to the newspaper office. Betty had not been heard from. Her friend Fay Brighton was red-eyed. She told me she had had one call that had made her suspicious, but the woman who called had left neither name nor number.

'Was it a threatening call?'

'I wouldn't say that exactly. The woman sounded worried. She wanted to know if Betty was all right. I asked her why she wanted to know, and she hung up on me.'

'When did the call come in?'

'This morning about ten o'clock. I shouldn't have let the woman rattle me. If I'd handled her with more tact, she might have told me more.'

'Did you get the impression she knew something?'

She thought about the question. 'Yes, I did. She sounded scared—guilty, maybe.'

'What kind of a woman was she?'

'I've been trying to figure that out. She talked intelligently, like a professional woman. But her voice was a little different.' She hesitated, in a listening attitude. 'She may have been a black woman, an educated black.'

It took me a minute to remember the name of the black nurse at the La Paloma. Mrs Holman. I borrowed Miss Brighton's phone directory and looked for the name Holman, but there was no listing under it.

I needed a black connection. The only one I could think of in the city was the proprietor of the liquor store where I had bought two half-pints of whisky for Jerry Johnson. I went there, and found him on duty behind the counter.

'Some Tennessee whisky?' he said.

'I can always use some.'

'Two half-pints?' he smiled indulgently over my eccentricity.

'I'll try a whole pint this time.'

While he was putting the bottle in a bag, I asked him if he

knew a nurse named Mrs Holman. He gave me an interested look that was careful not to stay on my face too long.

'I may have heard of her. I wouldn't say I know her. I know her husband.'

'She's been looking after a friend of mine,' I said. 'At the La Paloma nursing home. I was thinking of giving her a little present.'

'If you mean this'— he held the bottle up—'I can deliver it.'

'I'd rather do that in person.'

'Whatever you say. Mrs Holman lives near the corner of Nopal and Martinez. Third house up from the corner— there's a big old pepper tree in front of it. That's five blocks south of here and one block over towards the ocean.'

I thanked him and paid him for the whisky and drove south. The pepper tree was the only spot of green in a block of one-storey frame houses. Under its lacy shadow, several small black children were playing in the wheelless body of a 1946 Chevrolet sedan.

Mrs Holman was watching them from the porch. She started when she saw me and made an involuntary movement towards the door. Then she stood with her back to it and tried to smile at me, but her eyes were sombre.

'Good morning,' I said.

'Good morning.'

'Are these your children?'

'One of them is.' She didn't tell me which one. 'What can I do for you, sir?'

'I'm still looking for Miss Siddon. I'm worried about her. I thought maybe you were, too.'

'I don't know where you got that idea,' she said blankly.

'Didn't you call the newspaper office this morning?'

She looked past me at the children. They were silent and still, as if the feathery shadow of the pepper tree had become oppressive.

'What if I did?' she said.

'If you can do that, you can talk to me. I'm not trying to pin anything on you. I'm trying to find Betty Siddon. I think she may be in danger, and you seem to think so, too.'

'I didn't say that.'

'You don't have to. Did you see Miss Siddon last night at the La Paloma?'

She nodded slowly. 'I saw her.'

'When was that?'

'It was still the early part of the evening. She came to visit Mrs Johnson, and the two of them went into a huddle in one of the empty rooms. I don't know what they were talking about, but it ended up with both of them walking out of there together. They drove off in Miss Siddon's car without a word to me.'

'So Mrs Johnson went home twice last night?'

'I guess she did.'

'The police were at the La Paloma when Mrs Johnson came back there. Isn't that right?'

'I guess they were.'

'You know very well they were. And they must have told you what they were looking for.'

'Maybe they did. I don't remember.' Her voice was low. She was still, and very ill at ease.

'You must remember, Mrs Holman. The cops were looking for Mildred Mead and Betty Siddon. They must have asked you about them.'

'Maybe they did. I'm tired. I've got a lot on my mind and I had a rough night.'

'You could have a rougher day.'

She flared up. 'Don't you dare threaten me.'

The children in the Chevrolet were still and frightened. One of them, a little girl whom I guessed to be Mrs Holman's, began to weep quietly into her hands.

I said to the little girl's mother, 'Don't you dare lie to me. I've got nothing against you. I don't want to put you in the slammer. But that's where you'll end up if you don't tell the truth.'

She looked past me at the weeping child. 'Okay,' she said, 'okay. Mrs Johnson asked me not to tell the police about either of them being there—Miss Mead *or* Miss Siddon. I knew then there was trouble coming up. I might have known it would end up on my doorstep.'

She brushed past me and climbed into the Chevrolet. I left her there with her daughter in her lap, and the other children silent around her.

XXXIX

I WENT BACK to Olive Street. In the full white blast of noon, the Johnson house looked grim and strange, like a long old face appalled by the present.

I parked across the street and tried to imagine what had happened inside the house, and what was happening now. If Betty was there, she might not be easy to find. The house was old and rambling and largely unknown to me.

A small Toyota sedan went by in the street, moving in the direction of the hospital. The man at the wheel looked like Fred Johnson's attorney, Lackner. He stopped up the block, not far from the place where Paul Grimes had been murdered. I heard one of the Toyota's doors open and close quietly, but if anyone got out he was hidden by the trees.

I took the pint of whisky and my gun out of the glove compartment and put them in the pockets of my jacket. Then I crossed the street and knocked on the front door of the Johnson house.

There was a slight noise at the corner of the house. I flattened myself against the wall and made my gun ready to fire. At the end of the porch, the overgrown bushes stirred. Fred Johnson's voice came quietly out of them: 'Mr Archer?'

'Yes.'

Fred vaulted over the railing. He moved like a man who had spent his boyhood dodging trouble. His face was pale.

'Where have you been, Fred?'

'At Mr Lackner's office. He just dropped me off.'

'You feel you still need an attorney?'

He ducked his head so that I couldn't read his face. 'I suppose I do.'

'What for?'

'Mr Lackner told me not to discuss it with anybody.'

'You're going to have to, Fred.'

'I know that. Mr Lackner told me that. But he wants to be present when I do.'

'Where did he go?'

'To talk to Captain Mackendrick.'

'What about?'

He lowered his voice as if the house might hear him: 'I'm not supposed to say.'

'You owe me something, Fred. I helped to keep you out of jail. You could be in a cell in Copper City now.'

'I owe something to my mother and father, too.'

I took hold of him by the shoulders. He was trembling. His moustache drooped across his mouth like an emblem of his limp and injured manhood.

I said as gently as I knew how, 'What have your mother and father been doing, Fred?'

'I don't know.' He swallowed painfully, and his tongue moved between his lips like a small blind creature searching for a way out.

'Do they have a woman in the house?'

He nodded dismally. 'I heard a woman in the attic.'

'What was she doing up there?'

'I don't know. My father was up there with her.'

'When was this?'

'Early this morning. Before dawn. I guess she's been up there all night.'

I shook him. His head bobbed back and forth in meaningless assent. I stopped for fear of breaking his neck.

'Why didn't you tell me that before?'

'I didn't know what was going on up there. I thought I recognized her voice. I didn't know for sure it was Miss Siddon until I went around to the back just now and found her car.'

'Who did you think it was?'

'Just some woman he brought in off the street, maybe a woman from the hospital. He used to con them into the house and get them to take off their clothes for him. That was when my mother started to lock him in.'

'How bad a mental case is he?'

'I don't know.' Fred's eyes had filled with tears and shifted away from my face. 'Mr Lackner thinks he's really dangerous. He thinks the police should take him and put him in a safe place.'

So did I, but I didn't trust them to do it with a minimum of danger to others. I wanted Betty, if she was still alive, to survive her rescue.

'Do you have a key to the house, Fred?'

'Yes. I had one made.'

'Let me in.'

'I'm not supposed to. I'm supposed to wait for Mr Lackner and the police.'

'Okay, wait for them. Just give me the key.'

He took it out of his pocket and handed it over, reluctantly, as though he was surrendering some essential part of himself. When he spoke again his voice had deepened, as if the loss of that essential part had somehow been a gain.

'I'll go in with you. You don't know your way around in there like I do.'

I gave him back the key and he thrust it into the door. Mrs Johnson was waiting just inside, standing at the bottom of the stairs. She offered me a ghastly embarrassed smile, the kind you see on dead faces before the undertaker does his work.

'What can I do for you?'

'You can get out of my way. I want your husband.'

Her false smile clenched into a fierce grimace, which she turned on Fred. 'What have you been telling this man?'

'We have to stop him, Mother.'

Her face changed, groping for an expression that could accommodate the doubleness of her life. I thought she might spit at her son, or curse him, then perhaps that she might break down in tears.

'I've never been able to handle that crazy man.'

I said, 'Will you come up with me and talk to him?'

'I tried that in the course of the night. He said he'd shoot her, and then himself, if I didn't leave them alone.'

'He has another gun up there?'

'He always has had. More than one, I think. I've searched the whole place for them when he was blotto, but I've never been able to find them.'

'Has he ever used them on anyone?'

'No. He's just a talker.' Her face had taken on a frightened questioning look.

'How did he get Miss Siddon to go up there?'

Her heavy dark eyes veered away from mine. 'I don't know.'

'Did you take her up there?'

'No. I wouldn't do that.'

'You did, though,' her son said.

'So what if I did? She asked for it. She said she wanted to talk to him, and that was where he was. I'm not responsible for every newspaper reporter that inveigles her way into my house.'

I pushed her to one side and went up past her, with Fred at my heels. I paused in the dim upstairs hall, trying to get my bearings. Fred moved past me and turned on the light. The padlock was in place on the attic door.

'Did your mother lock him in?'

'I guess she must have. She has this phobia about his getting away from her, like when he went to British Columbia.'

'Go down and get the key from her.'

Fred ran downstairs.

Johnson's voice came through the attic door. 'Who is that out there?' He sounded hoarse and frightened.

'Archer. I'm a friend of yours.'

'I have no friends.'

'I brought you some Tennessee walking whisky the other day.'

There was a silence. 'I could use some of that now. I've been up all night.'

Fred came up the stairs two at a time, holding up a small key like a trophy.

'Who is that?' Johnson said.

Fred gave me a look that suggested I do the answering. At the same time, he handed me the padlock key. It gave me a feeling that whatever authority was left in the house was coming to me.

I said, 'It's your son Fred.'

'Tell him to go away,' Johnson said. 'And if you can let me have a sup of whisky, I'd appreciate it very much.'

But it was too late for such amenities. A siren had screamed in the distance, and now I could hear it dying in the street. Acting on strong impulse, I unlocked the padlock and got my gun out and held it cocked.

'What are you doing out there?' Johnson said.

'Bringing you your whisky.'

Heavy footsteps were mounting the porch below. I removed the padlock with my left hand and pulled the door open.

Johnson was sitting at the foot of the attic stairs. There was a small revolver, another Saturday-night special, on the wooden step beside him. He was slow in reaching for it.

I stamped on his hand, and scooped up the skittering gun. He put his hurt fingers in his mouth and looked at me as if I had betrayed him.

I pushed him out of the way and went up past him to his makeshift studio in the attic. Betty Siddon was sitting in a plain chair, wearing nothing except the piece of smooth clothesline that held her upright. Her face was pale and dull, her eyes were closed. I thought for a moment that she was dead. The world staggered under my feet like a top that had lost its spin.

But when I knelt down and cut the ropes, Betty came alive into my arms. I held her close. After a while she stirred and spoke to me.

'You were a long time getting here.'

'I was stupid.'

'I was the stupid one,' she said. 'I should never have come here alone. He held a gun on me and made me take off my clothes. Then he tied me into the chair and painted my picture.'

The unfinished picture was on a paint-spotted easel facing us. It reminded me of the other pictures I had seen in the last few days, in the art museum, in Mrs Chantry's house, at Mildred Mead's. Though I found it hard to believe, all the evidence seemed to indicate that the loud complaining drunk whom Mackendrick had just arrested at the foot of the attic stairs was the lost painter Chantry.

While Betty was putting on her clothes, I searched the attic. I found other pictures, most of them pictures of women, in various stages of completion. The last one I found, wrapped in a piece of burlap and covered with an old mattress, was the memory portrait of Mildred Mead that Jack Biemeyer had hired me to reclaim. Under the burlap wrapping was a set of keys which confirmed that Johnson's imprisonment in his house had not been complete.

I carried the picture down the attic stairs and found Fred lingering at their foot.

'Where's your father?'

'If you mean Gerard, Captain Mackendrick took him downstairs. But I don't believe he is my father.'

'Who is he, then?'

'That's what I've been trying to find out. I took—I borrowed that picture from the Biemeyer house because I suspected that Gerard had painted it. I wanted to try and determine its age, and also compare it with the Chantrys in the museum.'

'It wasn't stolen from the museum, was it?'

'No, sir. I lied about that. He took it from my room here in this house. That's when I suspected that Gerard had painted it. And then I began to suspect that he really was Richard Chantry, and not my father at all.'

'Then why did you try to protect him? Because you thought your mother was involved?'

Fred moved restlessly and looked past me up the stairs. Sitting at the top was Betty Siddon, taking pencilled notes in a sketch pad held on her knee. My heart jumped. She was incredible. She had been up all night, been threatened and mistreated by a suspected murderer, and all she wanted to do was catch her breaking story as it broke.

'Where is your mother, Fred?'

'Down in the front room with Mr Lackner and Captain Mackendrick.'

The three of us went down the steps. Betty stumbled once, and I felt her weight on my arm. I offered to drive her home.

She said she would see me in hell first.

Nothing much was going on in the drab living-room. The questioning had reached a near impasse, with both Gerard and Mrs Johnson refusing to answer Mackendrick's questions and the attorney Lackner reminding them of their rights. They were talking—or, rather, refusing to talk—about the murder of Paul Grimes.

'I have a theory,' I said. 'By now it's become a little more than a theory. Both Grimes and Jacob Whitmore were killed because they discovered the source of the Biemeyers' missing picture. Which incidentally isn't missing any more.' I showed it to them. 'I just found it in the attic, where Johnson probably painted it in the first place.'

Johnson sat with his head down. Mrs Johnson gave him a bitter look, at the same time worried and vengeful.

Mackendrick turned to me. 'I don't understand what makes the picture so important.'

'It seems to be a Chantry, Captain. And Johnson painted it.'

Mackendrick got the message by degrees, like a man becoming aware that he has an illness. He turned and looked at Gerard Johnson and his eyes gradually widened.

Gerard returned the captain's look in dim fear and dejection. I tried to penetrate the puffed discoloured flesh that overlay the original contours of his face. It was hard to imagine that he had ever been handsome, or that the mind behind his dull reddened eyes had created the world of his paintings. It occurred to me that his essential life might have gone into that world and left him empty.

Still there must have been vestiges of his younger self in his face, because Mackendrick said, 'You're Richard Chantry, aren't you? I recognize you.'

'No. My name is Gerard Johnson.'

That was all he would say. He stood silent while Mackendrick advised him of his rights and put him under arrest.

Fred and Mrs Johnson were not arrested but Mackendrick asked them to come to the station for questioning. They crowded into his official car under the eyes of a young detective-sergeant who kept his hand on his gun butt.

Betty and I were left standing on the sidewalk in front of the empty house. I put the Biemeyers' picture in the trunk of my car and opened the front door for her.

She hung back. 'Do you know where my car is?'

'Behind the house. Just leave it there for now. I'll drive you home.'

'I'm not going home. I have to write my story.'

I looked closely into her face. It seemed unnaturally bright, like an electric light which was about to burn out.

'Let's go for a little walk. I've got work to do, too, but it can wait.'

She came along with me under the trees, leaning with carefully controlled lightness on my arm. The old street seemed beautiful and formal in the morning light.

I told her a story that I remembered from childhood. There had been a time, it said, when men and women were closer than twins and shared the same mortal body. I told her that when the two of us came together in my motel room, I felt that close to her. And when she dropped out of sight, I felt the loss of part of myself.

She pressed my arm. 'I knew you'd find me.'

We walked slowly around the block, as if we had inherited the morning and were looking for a place to spend it. Later I drove her downtown and we had lunch together at the Tea Kettle. We were contented and grave, like two people performing a ceremony. I could see the life flowing back into her face and body.

I dropped her off at the newspaper office. She ran up the stairs towards her typewriter.

XL

I WENT BACK to the police station. There was a coroner's wagon in the parking lot, and I ran into Purvis coming out of Mackendrick's office. The young deputy coroner was flushed with excitement.

'I got a positive identification on those bones.'

'Where?'

'Skyhill Veterans' Hospital, in the Valley. He was a patient there for several years after the war. His name was Gerard Johnson.'

'Please repeat that.'

'Gerard Johnson. He was badly wounded in the Pacific. They practically had to rebuild him from the ground up. He was released from Skyhill about twenty-five years ago. He was supposed to go back for regular checks on his condition, but he never did. Now we know why.' Purvis drew in a deep satisfied breath. 'Incidentally, I have to thank you for helping me with the lead. Remind me to do something for you some day.'

'You can do something for me now.'

Purvis looked slightly startled. 'Okay. Just name it.'

'You better write this down.'

He got out an official pad and a ball-point pen. 'Shoot.'

I shot, at a distant target. 'Gerard Johnson had a friend in the army named William Mead. Mead was murdered in Arizona in the summer of 1943. Sheriff Brotherton of Copper City is familiar with the case. He was the one who found Mead's body in the desert and shipped it home to California for burial. I'd like to know where it was shipped to, and where it was buried. It might be a good idea to dig it up and examine it.'

Purvis looked up from his pad and squinted into the sun. 'Examine it for what?'

'Cause of death. Identity. The works. Also, Mead had a wife. It would help if we could trace her.'

'That's a big order.'

'It's a big case.'

I found Mackendrick alone in his office, looking glum and shaken.

'Where's your prisoner, Captain?'

'The DA took him over to the courthouse. Lackner advised him to stand mute. The rest of the family isn't talking either. I was hoping to wrap this up today.'

'Maybe we still can. Where are Fred and his mother?'

'I had to let them go home. The DA didn't want to bring

charges against them, at least not yet. He's fairly new on the job, and still feeling his way. According to him, all we have against the Johnson woman is that she's been living with Richard Chantry and passing him off as her husband, which isn't a felony.'

'It is if she was helping him to cover up a murder.'

'You mean the murder of the real Gerard Johnson?'

'That's right, Captain. As you know, Purvis has established that the real Johnson was the man in the brown suit whose body was buried in the Chantry greenhouse. It looks as though Chantry murdered Johnson and stole his identity and moved in with Johnson's wife and son.'

Mackendrick shook his head ponderously and sadly. 'That's what I thought. But I've just got through checking Johnson out with the DA and the people at Skyhill Hospital. Johnson wasn't married, and had no son. The whole bloody family is a fake.'

'Including Fred?'

'Including Fred.' Mackendrick must have seen the pain in my face, because he added, 'I know you made an emotional investment in Fred. It'll give you some idea of how I feel about Chantry. I really looked up to that man when I was a young patrolman. The whole town did, even if they never saw him. Now I have to tell them that he's a half-crazy drunk and a killer into the bargain.'

'You're absolutely certain that Johnson is Chantry?'

'Absolutely. I knew him personally, remember. I was one of the few who did. He's changed, of course, changed a hell of a lot. But he's the same man. I know him, and he knows I know him. But he isn't admitting anything at all.'

'Have you thought of confronting him with his real wife?'

'Naturally I have. I went to her house to talk to her first thing this morning. She'd already flown the coop, probably for keeps. She'd emptied her safe-deposit box and she was last seen headed south on the freeway.' Mackendrick gave me a grim look. 'You're partly to blame for that, when you took it on yourself to question her prematurely.'

'Maybe. I'm also partly to blame for solving your case.'

'It isn't solved. Sure, we've got Chantry. But there's a lot left unexplained. Why did he take the name Johnson, the name of the man he killed?'

'To cover up the fact that the real Johnson was missing.'

Mackendrick shook his head. 'That doesn't make much sense.'

'Neither did the murder of Johnson. But he committed it, and the woman knew it. She used the knowledge to take him over completely. He was virtually a prisoner in that house on Olive Street.'

'But why did she want him?'

I admitted I didn't know. 'There may have been a previous connection between them. We should look into the possibility.'

'That's easier said than done. Johnson's been dead for twenty-five years. The woman isn't talking. Neither is Chantry.'

'May I have a try at him?'

'It's out of my hands, Archer. It's a big case, and the DA wants all of it. Chantry's the most famous man we ever had in this town.' He struck his desk-top with his fist, heavily and repeatedly and slowly, like a dead march. 'Jesus, what a comedown that man has had.'

I went out to my car and drove the few blocks to the county courthouse. Its square white clock tower was the tallest structure in the downtown area. Above the giant four-sided clock was an observation platform surrounded by a black wrought-iron fence.

There was a family of tourists on the platform, and a little boy chinned himself on the wrought-iron fence and smiled down at me. I smiled back.

That was just about my last smile of the afternoon. I waited for nearly two hours in the outer reaches of the DA's wing. I finally got to see him, but not to talk to. He went out through the waiting-room, a bold-eyed young man with dark sweeping moustaches that seemed to bear him along like the wings of his ambition.

I tried to talk my way in to see one of his assistants. They were all busy. I never got past the outer circle of assistant assistants. I finally gave up and went downstairs to the coroner's office.

Purvis was still waiting for a return phone call from Copper

City. I sat and helped him wait. Towards the end of the afternoon, he got his call.

He took it at his desk and made notes as he listened. I tried to read them over his shoulder but they were indecipherable.

'Well?' I said when he finally hung up.

'The army assumed the responsibility and expense of shipping Mead's body home from Arizona in 1943. The cadaver was transported in a sealed coffin because it was in bad shape, unfit for viewing. They buried it in a local cemetery.'

'A local cemetery where?'

'Right here in Santa Teresa,' Purvis said. 'This is where Mead lived with his wife. Their address when the army took him was 2136 Los Bagnos Street. She could still be living there, if we're really lucky.'

As I followed Purvis's wagon across town into the hospital area, I felt that the thirty-two-year case was completing a long curve back to its source. We drove up Olive Street past the Johnson house, then past the place where I had found Paul Grimes dying.

Los Bagnos Street ran parallel to Olive, a block farther north of the highway. The old stucco house at 2136 had long since been denatured, converted into doctors' offices. On the east it was overshadowed by a tall new medical complex. But on the west there was a pre-war frame house with a cardboard 'Room to Let' sign in one of the front windows.

Purvis climbed out of his wagon and rattled the rusty screen door of the house with his fist. An old man answered the knock and peered out at us. The pouched and corded neck thrust up from his collarless shirt seemed to throb with suspicion.

'What is it?'

'My name is Purvis. I'm a deputy coroner.'

'Nobody died here. Not since my wife died, anyway.'

'What about Mr William Mead? Was he a neighbour of yours?'

'That's right, he was for a little while. He died, too. That was back during the war. Mead got himself murdered in Arizona. I heard that from his wife. I don't take the local paper, I never have. All·they ever print in it is bad news.' He squinted at us through the screen as if we were carriers of bad news, too. 'Is that what you wanted to know?'

'You've been very helpful,' Purvis said. 'Do you happen to know what happened to Mead's wife?'

'She didn't go far. She eventually remarried and moved to a house over here on Olive Street. But her luck didn't change.'

'How do you mean?' Purvis said.

'On her second go-round, she married a drunk. Don't quote me. And she's been working ever since to support his drinking habit.'

'Where does she work?'

'In the hospital. She's a nurse.'

'Is her husband's name Johnson?'

'That's right. If you know, why ask?'

XLI

WE DROVE between the dense ranks of the trees that had stood on Olive Street for a century or more. As Purvis and I moved up the walk into the afternoon shadow of the house, I felt the weight of the past like an atmosphere constricting my breathing.

The woman who called herself Mrs Johnson answered the door immediately, as if she had been expecting us. I could feel her sombre gaze like a tangible pressure on my face.

'What do you want?'

'May we come in? This is Deputy Coroner Purvis.'

'I know.' She said to Purvis, 'I've seen you at the hospital. I don't know what you want to come in for. There's nobody home but me, and everything's happened that's going to happen.' It sounded less like a statement of fact than a dubious hope.

I said, 'We want to talk about some of the things that happened in the past. One of them is the death of William Mead.'

She answered without blinking: 'I never heard of him.'

'Let me refresh your recollection,' Purvis said quietly and

formally. 'According to my information, William Mead was your husband. When he was murdered in Arizona in 1943, his body was shipped back here for burial. Is my information incorrect?'

Her black gaze didn't waver. 'I guess I kind of forgot all that. I always had a pretty good forgettery. And these awful things that I've been living through sort of wiped out everything, you know?'

'May we come in and sit down with you,' Purvis said, 'and talk about it?'

'I guess so.'

She moved to one side and let us enter the narrow hallway. There was a large worn canvas suitcase standing at the foot of the stairs. I lifted it. It was heavy.

'Leave that alone,' she said.

I set it down again. 'Are you planning to leave town?'

'What if I am? I haven't done anything wrong. I'm still a free agent. I can go where I like, and I might as well. There's nobody left here but me. My husband's gone, and Fred's moving out.'

'Where is Fred going?'

'He won't even tell me. Off with that girl of his, probably. After all the work I've put into this house, twenty-five years of hard work, I end up all alone in it. Alone and without a nickel and owing money. Why shouldn't I get out?'

I said, 'Because you're under suspicion. Any move you make is likely to trigger your arrest.'

'What am I under suspicion for? I didn't kill Will Mead. It happened in Arizona. I was nursing here in Santa Teresa at the time. When they told me he was dead, it was the biggest shock of my life. I haven't got over it yet. I'll never get over it. And when they buried him out in the cemetery, I wanted to crawl in with him.'

I felt a twinge of compassion for the woman but kept it under control. 'Mead isn't the only one who's been killed. There are also Paul Grimes and Jacob Whitmore, men that you and your husband were doing business with. Grimes was killed here in your street. Whitmore may have been drowned in your bathtub.'

She gave me a sudden shocked look. 'I don't know what you're talking about.'

'I'll be glad to explain. It may take a little time. Could we go into the living-room and sit down?'

'No,' she said. 'I don't want to. They've been firing questions at me most of the day. Mr Lackner advised me not to do any more talking.'

Purvis spoke up in a dubious voice: 'I'd better give her her rights, don't you think, Archer?'

His nervousness encouraged her, and she turned on him. 'I know my rights. I don't have to talk to you or anybody else. Speaking of rights, you have no right to force your way into my house like this.'

'No force was employed, ma'am. You invited us in.'

'I certainly did not. You invited yourself. You bullied your way in.'

Purvis turned to me. He had gone pale with the bureaucratic terror of making an attributable mistake.

'We better leave it for now, Archer. Questioning witnesses isn't my field anyway. For all I know, the DA will want to grant her immunity. I wouldn't want to ruin the case by making a mistake at this late date.'

'What case?' she said with renewed vigour. 'There is no case. You have no right to come here hustling me and harrying me. Just because I'm a poor woman without any friends and a mentally ill husband who doesn't even know who he is, he's so far gone.'

'Who is he?' I said.

She gave me a startled look, and fell silent.

I said, 'Incidentally, why do you call yourself Mrs Johnson? Were you ever married to Gerard Johnson? Or did Chantry simply change his name to Johnson after he murdered the real Gerard?'

'I'm not talking,' she repeated. 'You two get out of here now.'

Purvis was already out on the porch, dissociating himself from my unorthodox questioning. I followed him out and we parted on the sidewalk.

I sat in my car in the failing afternoon and tried to straighten out the case in my mind. It had started with the trouble between two brothers, Richard Chantry and his illegitimate half-brother William Mead. It appeared that Richard had stolen William's work and William's girl and eventually murdered him, leaving his body in the Arizona desert.

Richard came to Santa Teresa with the girl and, despite the fact that murder was an extraditable offence, was never brought back to Arizona for questioning. He prospered in California and, as if his talent had fed on William's death, developed in just seven years into an important painter. Then his world collapsed. An army friend of William's, Gerard Johnson, got out of the veterans' hospital and came to visit Richard.

Gerard made two visits to Richard, the second accompanied by William's widow and son. That was Gerard's last visit to anyone. Richard killed him and buried him in his own greenhouse. Then, as if in penance, Richard stepped down from his own place in the world and took Gerard's name and William's place. He had come to this house on Olive Street and lived as a drunken recluse for twenty-five years.

In the first years, before he put on the disguises of age and alcoholism, he must have lived in close confinement, like an insane relative in a nineteenth-century attic. But he hadn't been able to stay away from painting. In the end the persistence of his talent had helped to destroy him.

Fred must have become aware of his father's secret life as a painter and taken the first unconscious steps towards identifying him with the lost painter Chantry. This would explain Fred's overpowering interest in Chantry's work, culminating in his theft or borrowing of the Biemeyers' painting. When Fred brought that painting home to study it, his father took it from Fred's room and hid it in his own—the attic where he had painted it in the first place.

The missing painting was in the trunk of my car. Chantry was in jail. I should be feeling happy and successful but I wasn't. The case hung heavy on my hands and stillborn in my mind. It kept me sitting here under the olive trees as the afternoon slowly faded.

I told myself that I was waiting for the woman to come out. But I doubted that she would as long as I was parked there. Twice I saw her face at the living-room window. The first time she looked frightened. The second time she was angry, and shook her fist at me. I smiled at her reassuringly. She pulled down the frayed blind.

I sat there trying to imagine the life of the couple who had lived in the gabled house for twenty-five years. Chantry had been a moral prisoner as well as a physical one. The woman he had been living with under the name of Johnson must have known that he had killed the original Johnson. She probably knew that he had killed her legal husband, Mead, as well. Their cohabitation was more like a prison sentence than any kind of marriage.

Their secret, their multiple guilty secret, had been guarded by further crimes. Paul Grimes had been beaten to death in the street, and Jacob Whitmore probably drowned in this house, simply in order to preserve Chantry's cover. It was hard for me to sit still with such knowledge. But I felt that I had to wait.

Behind the rooftops to the west, the sun had died and suffused the sky with red. Now even that was fading, and the first grey chill of night was coming on.

A yellow cab pulled up behind my car. Betty Siddon got out. She said as she paid the driver, 'Do you mind waiting for a minute? I want to be sure my car is where I think it is.'

The driver said he would wait if she didn't take too long. Without noticing me, or looking in my direction, she started to wade through the weeds towards the back of the house. She seemed a little unsteady on her feet. So far as I knew, she hadn't slept since she had slept with me. The memory hit me like an arrow that had been in the air since then.

I followed her around to the back of the house. She was bent over the door of her car, trying to unlock it. The Johnson woman was watching her from the kitchen window.

Betty stood up and leaned on the car door. She greeted me without animation: 'Hello, Lew.'

'How are you, Betty?'

'Tired. I've been writing all day, to no avail. The publisher wanted to cut my story down to nothing, for legal reasons. So I walked out.'

'Where are you going now?'

'I'm on a mission,' she said with faint irony. 'But I can't seem to get this car door open.'

I took the keys from her hand and opened the door. 'You were using the wrong key.'

Being able to correct her on this point made me happy, for some reason.

It made Betty more tired. Her face was pale and heavy-eyed, half dissolved in twilight.

'What kind of a mission?' I asked her.

'Sorry, it's top secret, Lew.'

The Johnson woman opened the back door and stepped outside. Her voice rose like a stormy wind: 'You two get out of here. You've no right to harass me. I'm an innocent woman who took up with the wrong man. I should have left him years ago and I would have, too, if it hadn't been for the boy. I've lived with a crazy drunk for twenty-five years. If you think it's easy, try it some time.'

Betty cut her off. 'Shut up. You knew I was in your attic last night. You talked me into going up there yourself. You let me stay there all night with him, and you didn't lift a finger to help me. So shut up.'

Mrs Johnson's face began to twist and work like some amorphous sea creature trying to dodge an enemy, perhaps evade reality itself. She turned and went back into the kitchen, closing the door behind her carefully.

Betty yawned profoundly, her eyes streaming.

I put my arm around her shoulders. 'Are you all right?'

'I will be in a minute.' She yawned again, and waited, and yawned again. 'It did me good to tell that woman off. She's one of those wives who can watch a man commit murder and feel nothing. Nothing but her own moral superiority. Her whole life's been devoted to covering up. Her motto is save the surface and you save all. But nothing got saved. The whole thing went to rot, and people got killed while she stood by and let it happen. I almost got killed myself.'

'By Chantry?'

She nodded. 'That woman doesn't have the nerve to act
out her own fantasies. She stands to one side and lets the man
do it for her, so she can have her dim little sadistic orgasms.'

'You really hate her, don't you?'

'Yes. I do. Because I'm a woman, too.'

'But you don't hate Chantry, after what he did to you?'

She shook her head, and her short hair blurred in the twilight. 'The point is that he didn't do it. He was thinking about
killing me. He even talked about it. But then he changed his
mind. He painted my picture instead. I'm grateful to him—
for not killing me, and for painting my picture.'

'So am I.'

I tried to put both arms around her. But she wasn't ready
for that.

'Do you know why he took pity on me? Naturally you
don't. Remember the time I told you about, when my father
took me to visit Chantry? When I was just a little girl?'

'I remember.'

'Well, he remembered, too. I didn't have to remind him.
He actually remembered me from the time I was a child. He
said my eyes hadn't changed since then.'

'I'm afraid he has.'

'Has he not. Don't worry, Lew, I'm not getting sentimental
about Chantry. I'm simply glad to be alive. Very glad.'

I said that I was glad she was alive, too.

'There's only one thing I'm sorry about,' she added. 'All
through this thing, I've kept hoping that somehow it would
turn out that he wasn't Chantry. You know? That it had all
been a horrible mistake. But it wasn't. The man who painted
those pictures is a murderer.'

'I know.'

XLII

BETTY'S CAB-DRIVER appeared at the corner of the house,
looking unhappy. 'You've kept me waiting a long time, Miss,
I'm going to have to charge you.'

Betty paid him off. But when she got into her own car it wouldn't start. I tried it. The engine didn't turn over for me either.

I lifted the hood. The battery was gone.

'What am I going to do now? I have to go on an errand.'

'I'll be glad to drive you.'

'But I have to go by myself. I promised I would.'

'Who did you promise?'

'I can't tell you. I'm sorry.'

She seemed to be drawing away from me. I stepped closer and looked at her face. It was scarcely more than a pale oval now, dark-eyed, dark-mouthed. Night was flowing between the high old houses like a turbid river. I was afraid she would be swept away, this time beyond my reach.

She touched my arm. 'Will you lend me your car, Lew?'

'For how long?'

'Overnight.'

'For what purpose?'

'You don't have to cross-question me. Just give me a yes or no.'

'All right. The answer is no.'

'Please. This is important to me.'

'The answer is still no. I'm not going through another night like last night, wondering what's happened to you.'

'All right. I'll find someone who is willing to help me.'

She started to walk towards the street, stumbling a little among the weeds. I was shaken by the idea that I might lose her and went after her.

She turned at the sidewalk. 'Are you going to lend me your car?'

'No. I'm not letting you out of my sight. If you rent a car or borrow one, I'll follow you.'

'You can't bear to see me get ahead of you, is that it?'

'No. You were way ahead of me last night. You put yourself in an exposed position. I don't want that to happen again. There's such a thing as having too much nerve.' I took a deep breath. 'Have you had any rest today?'

She answered evasively, 'I forget.'

'That means you haven't. You can't take a long night drive

without any sleep. God knows what you might run into at the far end.'

'God and Archer,' she said bitterly, 'they know everything. Don't you and God ever make a mistake?'

'God did. He left off Eve's testicles.'

Betty let out a cry of pure sharp female rage, which somehow diminuendoed into mirth. She finally settled for both the car and me, on condition that she be allowed to do at least half the driving. I opted for the first shift.

'Where are we going?' I said as I started the engine.

'Long Beach. I assume you know where that is.'

'I ought to. I was born there. What's in Long Beach?'

'I promised not to tell anyone.'

'Promised who?' I said. 'Mrs Chantry?'

'Since you know everything,' Betty said clearly and carefully, 'it would seem superfluous to answer any of your questions.'

'So it's Francine Chantry. What is she doing in Long Beach?'

'Apparently she had a car accident.'

'Is she in hospital?'

'No. She's at a place called the Gilded Galleon.'

'That's a waterfront bar. What's she doing there?'

'I think she's drinking. I've never known her to drink much, but she seems to be breaking down.'

'Why did she call you?'

'She said she needed my advice and help. We're not really close but I suppose I'm as close to her as anyone is. She wants my advice in a public relations capacity, she said. Which probably means that she wants me to help her out of the mess she's got herself into by running away.'

'Did she say why she did that?'

'She simply panicked.'

I thought as I turned on to the freeway that Francine Chantry had some reason to panic. She had guilty knowledge of the death of Gerard Johnson, and possibly of the death of William Mead.

I drove hard. Betty slept against my shoulder. The combination of the speeding car and the sleeping woman made me feel almost young, as if my life might have a new beginning after all.

In spite of the early-evening traffic, we were in Long Beach in two hours. It was my home territory, as I had said, and the lights along the waterfront shone with remembered promise, even if all it had led to was the present.

I remembered the Galleon from the days when my marriage had been breaking up and I was looking for ways to pass the long nights. The place had changed surprisingly little since then, much less than I had. It was what was known as a family tavern, which meant that it accommodated drunks of all ages and sexes. I stood just inside the door, washed by waves of human sound, while Betty made her way around the horseshoe-shaped bar. Everybody seemed to be talking at once, including the barmaids. I could understand why the loud factitious family atmosphere might appeal to a woman as lonely as Francine Chantry probably was.

I saw her at the far end of the bar, sitting with her silver head drooping over an empty glass. She seemed to be slow in recognizing Betty. Then she threw her arms around her, and Betty responded. Though I felt some sympathy for Mrs Chantry, and some pleasure in Betty's warmth, I didn't like to see the two women embracing. Betty was young and clean. Francine Chantry had been living for decades deep in the knowledge of murder.

It was beginning to show in her face and body, reaching up for her from the earth like gravity. She stumbled before she got to me, and had to be supported by the younger woman. She had a cut on her forehead. Her jaw was slack and grim, her eyes dull. But she held on to her bag the way a plunging fullback holds the ball.

'Where's your car, Mrs Chantry?'

She roused herself from her apathy. 'The garageman said it was totalled. I think that means that it isn't worth repairing. I doubt that I am, either.'

'Were you in an accident?'

'I don't really know what happened. I was trying to get off the freeway, and things went out of control all of a sudden. That seems to be the story of my life.' Her laughter was like a dry compulsive cough.

'I'm interested in the story of your life.'

'I know you are.' She turned to Betty. 'Why did you have to bring *him* along? I thought we could have a constructive talk about the future. I thought you and I were good friends.'

'I hope we are,' Betty said. 'But I didn't think I could handle this by myself.'

'Handle what? I'm no problem.'

But there was a note of terror in Francine Chantry's voice. She sounded like a woman who had stepped off the edge of the world and discovered too late that she could never step back. When we got into my car and entered the freeway, the sense of moving through empty space stayed with me. We seemed to be flying above the rooftops of the tract houses that lined the freeway on both sides.

Betty was driving too fast, but I was content to have her do her stint. She had had some recent sleep; and I wanted a chance to talk to Francine Chantry.

'Speaking of your future,' I said, 'your husband may be hard to convict.'

'My husband?' She sounded confused.

'Richard Chantry alias Gerard or Jerry Johnson. It may not be too easy to pin these murders on him. I gather he isn't talking. And so much of it happened so long ago. I wouldn't be surprised if the prosecutor was willing to make a deal with you. I doubt that he'll want to bring any major charges. Of course that depends on him, and on what you have to offer.'

She let out another burst of dry laughter. 'My dead body? Would he accept my dead body?'

'He'll want you alive and talking. You know more about this case than anyone.'

She was silent for a minute. 'If I do, it's not by choice.'

'So you were telling me the other night. But you really made your choices long ago. When you dropped William Mead and took up with his half-brother Chantry. When you left Arizona with Chantry, even though you must have known that he was a major suspect in the murder of William Mead. Seven years later, you made a final choice, when you decided to cover up the murder of Gerard Johnson.'

'Who?'

'Gerard Johnson. The man in the brown suit. It turns out he was a friend of William Mead's. He'd just got out of five years in a veterans' hospital when he came to Santa Teresa to see your husband. I think he had evidence involving Chantry in William Mead's death.'

'How?'

'Perhaps William Mead had been threatened by Chantry and they had quarrelled over you, or over Mead's pictures, which Chantry stole. And Mead told his army buddy Gerard about it some time before Chantry killed him. When Gerard Johnson turned up in Santa Teresa with William's widow and little boy, it marked the end of Chantry's freedom. He killed Gerard in an effort to stay free, but it only made him more completely unfree. It was a final choice for Chantry as well as you.'

'I had no part in the choice,' she said.

'You went along with it. You let a man be killed in your house and buried there, and you kept quiet. It was a bad choice for you and your husband. He's been living out its consequences. The murder of Gerard Johnson put him in the hands of William Mead's widow, the woman who calls herself Mrs Johnson. I don't know why she wanted him. There may have been something between them in the past. Or perhaps the Johnson woman was simply interested in driving a hard primitive bargain with Chantry. He'd killed her husband, now he had to take her husband's place. I don't know why Chantry accepted the bargain, do you?'

Francine Chantry was slow in answering. Finally she said, 'I don't know anything about it. I've had no idea that Richard was living in town. I didn't even know if he was alive. I didn't hear from him once in twenty-five years.'

'Have you seen him recently?'

'No. I have no desire to see him.'

'You're going to have to. They'll be wanting you to identify him. Not that there's much doubt about who he is. He's deteriorated physically and mentally. I think he must have had an emotional breakdown after he murdered Johnson, perhaps before. But he can still paint. His paintings may not be as good as they were, but nobody else could have painted them.'

She said with some irony, 'Apparently you're an art critic as well as a detective.'

'Hardly. But I do have one of his recent paintings in the trunk of my car. And I'm not the only one who thinks that it's a Chantry.'

'Are you talking about the painting of Mildred Mead?'

'Yes. I found it this morning in Johnson's attic, where it originated. Where the whole current case originated. That picture seems to be the central thing in the case. Certainly it brought me into it. And it was the painting of it that got Chantry into his present trouble and led him to commit these new murders.'

'I don't quite follow that,' Francine Chantry said. But she sounded interested, as if this talk of her husband's work had acted on her like a stimulant.

'It's a fairly complex chain of events,' I said. 'The woman he's been living with on Olive Street—call her Mrs Johnson—sold the painting to the artist-dealer Jacob Whitmore. That blew Chantry's cover. Whitmore sold the painting to Paul Grimes, and that blew it wider.

'Grimes recognized it as Chantry's work and evidently used the knowledge to blackmail Mrs Johnson into stealing drugs for him. And he probably demanded more new pictures from Chantry. Grimes had sold the picture of Mildred Mead to Ruth Biemeyer, who had her own reasons for being interested in Mildred. As you probably know, Mildred was Jack Biemeyer's mistress.'

'Everybody in Arizona knew it,' Francine Chantry said. 'What wasn't so generally known was that Ruth Biemeyer had a crush on Richard when they were both young. I think that's the essential reason why she talked Jack into moving to Santa Teresa.'

'That's what he says, anyway. It made for a tight family situation which was made still tighter when Mildred Mead came to town. I think Chantry may have seen Mildred some time in the last few months and been moved to paint that memory picture of her.'

'I wouldn't know.'

'Haven't you seen him recently?'

'No. Certainly not.' She didn't look at me. She was peering through the windshield into the broken darkness. 'I haven't seen Richard, or heard from him, in twenty-five years. I had no idea that he was living in town.'

'Not even when you got a phone call from the woman he was living with?'

'She didn't mention him. She said something about the— the burial in the greenhouse, and she let me know that she needed money. She said if I would help her out she'd go on keeping the whole thing quiet. Otherwise she'd tell the world the real reason for my husband's disappearance.'

'Did you give her money?'

'No. I wish now I had. And I very much wish he had never painted that memory portrait of Mildred. You'd almost think he was trying to be found out.'

'Perhaps he was, unconsciously,' I said. 'Certainly Fred was doing his best to find him out. No doubt Fred borrowed the painting from the Biemeyers partly for professional reasons. He wanted to establish whether it really could be a Chantry. But he had personal reasons, too. I think he may have connected it with pictures he had seen in the past in the Johnson house on Olive Street. But he failed to make the final conscious connection between his foster father, Johnson, and the painter Chantry. Before he could do that, Johnson-Chantry took the painting from Fred's bedroom. And the Biemeyers hired me to get it back for them.'

Betty tapped the horn. We were moving down the long inland slope behind Camarillo. There were no cars immediately ahead of us. I looked at her and she looked back. She raised her right hand from the wheel and touched her mouth. I got the message. I had talked more than enough, and I subsided.

A few minutes later, Mrs Chantry said, 'It wasn't his first memory picture of Mildred. He painted several others, long ago, in our days together. One of them was a pietà.'

She was silent for a long time, until we were on the outskirts of Santa Teresa. Then I heard her crying softly. There was no way to tell if she was crying for Chantry or herself, or perhaps for the long-dead partnership that had held their young lives together and spawned his work. When I looked sideways at her face, I could see the bright tears on it.

'Where do we go from here?' Betty said.

'The police station.'

Francine Chantry let out a cry that subsided into a groan. 'Can't I even spend the night in my own house?'

'You can go back there and pack a bag if you want to. Then I think you should go to the police, with your lawyer.'

Much later, in the pre-dawn chill, I woke in a dark bed. I could feel Betty's heart and hear her breathing like the quiet susurrus of a summer ocean.

A harsher bedroom scene came into my mind. I had last seen Francine Chantry in a hospital room with specially screened windows and an armed guard outside the door. And just outside the half-open door of my partly sleeping mind another woman seemed to be waiting, a short lame white-haired women who had been beautiful.

The word 'pietà' came back into my mind. I woke Betty up with my hand on the curve of her hip. She sighed and turned over.

'Lew?'

'What's a pietà?'

She yawned deeply. 'You ask the darnedest questions at the darnedest times.'

'Does that mean you don't know?'

'Of course I know what a pietà is. It's a traditional picture of the Virgin Mary mourning over the body of her son. Why?'

'Francine Chantry said her husband painted one of Mildred Mead. I assume she was Mary.'

'Yes. I've seen the picture. They have it in the local gallery, but they don't exhibit it publicly. It's slightly embarrassing, or so some people think. Chantry painted the dead man as a self-portrait.'

Betty yawned and went to sleep again. I lay awake and watched her face emerging in the slow dawn. After a while I could see the steady blue pulse in her temple, the beating of the silent hammer which meant that she was alive. I hoped that the blue hammer would never stop.

XLIII

WHEN I WOKE up a second time, Betty had gone out. She had left four things for me on the kitchenette table: a carton of Granola, a bottle of milk, a safety razor, and a cryptic note, which said: 'Had funny dream—Mildred Mead Chantry's mother—is this possible?'

I ate my breakfast food and drove across town to Magnolia Court. Mildred Mead failed to answer my repeated knocking on her door. An old man came out of the next cottage and looked me over from the distance of a generation. Eventually he volunteered the information that Mrs Mead, as he called her, had gone out.

'Do you know where she went?'

'She told the taxi-driver to take her to the courthouse.'

I followed Mildred there, but she wasn't easy to find. The courthouse and its landscaped grounds occupied a city block. I soon decided that I was wasting my time walking up and down its gravelled paths and tiled corridors looking for a small old limping woman.

I checked in at the coroner's suite of offices and found Henry Purvis there. Mildred had come to his office within the past half-hour.

'What did she want from you?'

'Information about William Mead. He was her natural son, apparently. I told her he was buried in the Santa Teresa cemetery, and I offered to take her out to visit his grave. She didn't seem interested in that. She got off on the subject of Richard Chantry. She claimed she had been his model at one time, and she wanted to get in to see him. I told her it simply wasn't possible.'

'Where is Chantry being held?'

'District Attorney Lansing has him here in a special cell with round-the-clock guards. I couldn't even get in there myself—not that I particularly want to. Apparently he's gone completely off the rails. They have to sedate him to keep him quiet.'

'What happened to Mildred?'

'She walked out. I sort of hated to let her go. She seemed pretty upset, and she'd been drinking. But I had no reason to hold her.'

I went outside and made another circuit of the grounds and courtyards. No Mildred. I was getting nervous. Whether or not there was truth in Betty's dream, I felt that Mildred was in some way central to the case. But I was losing her, and losing the morning.

I looked up at the four-sided clock on the courthouse tower. It was ten. There was only one person visible on the observation platform, a white-headed woman whose rather clumsy movements caught my eye. Mildred. She paused and turned and gripped the black iron fence. It was almost up to her chin. She peered over it, down into the stone-paved courtyard.

She was extraordinarily still. She looked like a woman staring down into her grave. The life of the city seemed to freeze in widening circles around her.

I was nearly a hundred yards away and a hundred feet below. If I raised an alarm, it might only trigger the action she seemed to have in mind. I walked to the nearest door and took the tower elevator up.

When I stepped out on the observation platform, she had turned to face me, her back against the iron fence. She turned again and tried to clamber over the fence into empty space. Her lame old body failed in the attempt.

I put my arms around her and held her securely. She was breathing as if she had climbed the tower hand over hand. The frozen life of the city resumed, and I began to hear its sounds again.

She struggled in my arms. 'Let me go.'

'I don't think so, Mildred. Those flagstones are a long way down and I wouldn't want you to take a fall on them. You're too pretty.'

'I'm the hag of the universe.' But she gave me an up-from-under look, the automatic mannerism of a woman who had once been small and beautiful and was still handsome. 'Will you give me a break?'

'If I can.'

'Just take me down and turn me loose. I won't do anything —not to myself or anybody else.'

'I can't take a chance on that.'

I could feel the heat of her body through her clothes. Sweat gathered on her upper lip and in the blued hollows of her eyes.

'Tell me about your son William.'

She didn't answer me. Her make-up was eroding, and her grey face peered at me through it like a death mask.

'Did you trade in your son's dead body on that big house in Chantry Canyon? Or was it somebody else's dead body?'

She spat in my face. Then she went into a fit of passionate weeping. Then she was still. She didn't speak as I took her down in the elevator, or when I handed her over to the DA's men and women.

I told them that she should be carefully searched and kept under observation as a determined potential suicide. It was just as well I did. District Attorney Lansing told me later that the woman who searched her found a brightly honed stiletto wrapped in a silk stocking and tucked under her girdle.

'Did they find out what she was carrying it for?'

The DA shook his head. 'Presumably,' he said, 'she intended to use it on Chantry.'

'What was her motive?'

Lansing pulled alternately at the ends of his handlebar moustaches, as if he were using them to steer his mind through the complexities of the case. 'This isn't generally known, and I'll have to ask you to keep it to yourself. Chantry seems to have murdered Miss Mead's son in Arizona, thirty years ago. To give credit where credit is due, I got that from Captain Mackendrick. He's been doing some excellent spadework in this case. I think he'll be our next chief of police.'

'Good for him. But how does the revenge theory fit in with her suicide attempt?'

'Are you certain it was a real attempt?'

'It looked real to me. Mildred wanted out, and the only thing that stopped her was that iron fence. That and the fact that I happened to see her up there.'

'Well, it's not inconsistent with the revenge motif. She was thwarted in her attempt at revenge, so she turned her anger against herself.'

'I don't quite follow that, Mr DA.'

'No? You're probably not as familiar as some of us are with recent developments in criminal psychology.' There was an edge on his smile.

I gave him a soft answer because I wanted something from him. 'It's true I never went to law school.'

'But you've been of real assistance in spite of that,' he said reassuringly. 'And we're certainly grateful for your suggestions.'

His eyes went distant on me, and he stood up behind his desk. I stood up, too. I had a nightmare vision of my case moving inexorably away from me.

'Could I possibly have a minute with your prisoner, Mr DA?'

'Which one?'

'Chantry. I want to ask him a couple of questions.'

'He isn't answering questions. The public defender has advised him not to.'

'The questions I have in mind aren't connected with these murders, at least not directly.'

'What are they?' Lansing said.

'I want to ask him what his real name is, and get his reaction. And I want to ask him why Mildred Mead tried to kill herself.'

'We don't really know that she did.'

'I know that she did, and I want to know why.'

'What makes you so sure that Chantry might possess the information?'

'I think he and Mildred are closely connected. Incidentally, I feel sure that Jack Biemeyer will be interested. Biemeyer hired me, you know.'

Lansing said in a voice that seemed to be testing itself for firmness, 'If Mr Biemeyer has any suggestions, or any questions, I think he should communicate them to me directly.'

'I'll tell him that.'

The Biemeyer house had a deserted look, like a public

building that had been emptied by a bomb scare. I got the painting of Mildred Mead out of the trunk of my car and carried it up the flagstone walk to the front door. Just before I got to it, Ruth Biemeyer came out. She put a finger to her lips.

'My husband is very tired. I've been trying to get him to rest.'

'I'm afraid I have to talk to him, Mrs Biemeyer.'

She turned towards the door, but all she did was pull it closed. 'You can talk freely to me. I'm really your principal in this case. The picture that was stolen belongs to me. That is my picture that you have there, isn't it?'

'Yes. I wouldn't say it was stolen, though. Let's say Fred borrowed it, for scientific and biographical purposes. He wanted to establish who painted it, and when, and who the subject was. It's true the answers to these questions had personal meaning for Fred. But that doesn't make him a criminal exactly.'

She nodded. Her hair shifted in the wind and made her suddenly prettier, as if light had blown into her head.

'I can understand why Fred did what he did.'

'You should be able to. You had your own personal reasons for buying the painting. Mildred Mead had moved to town, and your husband was seeing her again. Didn't that have something to do with your hanging that picture of her in your house? As a reproach to him, perhaps, or a kind of threat?'

She frowned. The light in her eyes shifted, turning inward like a flashlight exploring a dark room.

'I don't know why I bought it. I didn't even realize at the time that it was Mildred.'

'Your husband must have.'

There was a silence between us. I could hear the sea marking time far down at the foot of the hill.

'My husband isn't in very good shape. He's aged in the last few days. If all this got out it would destroy his reputation. And maybe destroy him.'

'He assumed that risk, when he did what he did a long time ago.'

'Exactly what did he do?'

'I think he made the Chantry imposture possible.'

'The Chantry imposture? What do you mean by that?'

'I think you know what I mean. But I'd rather discuss it with your husband.'

She bit her lower lip. With her incisors bared, she looked a little like a watchdog at the door. Then she picked up the painting and led me through the house to her husband's study.

He was sitting in front of the photograph of his copper mine. His face had come apart. He pulled it together and smiled uncertainly with one side of his mouth.

'What do you want from me? More money?'

'More information. This case started in 1943. It's time it was closed.'

Ruth Biemeyer turned to me. 'Exactly what happened in 1943?'

'I can't tell you all of it. I think it started when William Mead went home to Arizona on leave from the army. Home isn't exactly the word. Mead had a young wife and an infant son waiting for him here in Santa Teresa. But his mother was still living in Arizona. Where exactly was Mildred living, Mr Biemeyer?'

He pretended not to hear me. His wife answered for him. 'She was living in Tucson but spending the weekends in the mountains with my husband.'

Biemeyer gave her a shocked look. It made me wonder if his affair with Mildred had ever been directly spoken of till now. I said:

'That probably came as no surprise to William. His mother had lived with other men, notably the painter Lashman. Lashman had been a father to him, and taught him to paint. When William came home to Arizona on leave he found that his so-called half-brother Richard had taken some of his work and assumed the credit for it. The Chantry imposture really started with Richard Chantry himself, when he stole William's paintings and drawings, and incidentally married William's girl Francine.

'The two young men had a fight over these matters. They fought to the death. William killed Richard and left his body in the desert, dressed in William's own army uniform. He was an illegitimate son who had probably dreamed all his life of taking Richard's place. This was his chance to do it, and incidentally to get out of the army and out of a forced marriage.

'But he couldn't have done it without the help of other people, three other people to be exact. First he had the help of Francine Chantry. She was obviously in love with him in spite of his marriage to Sarah and his killing of Francine's husband. She may even have incited that killing. In any case it didn't prevent her from coming to Santa Teresa with him and living here as his wife for seven years.

'I don't know why he took the risk of coming back here. Perhaps he had some idea of keeping an eye on his son. But so far as I can tell, he didn't see Fred in all that time. It may be that his living here, so close to his wife and son but invisible to them, was part of the game of doubleness he was playing. He may have needed that kind of tension to keep him in orbit and sustain the Chantry illusion and his art.

'The main thing was to get out of Arizona free and clear, and it was his mother who made that possible for him. What Mildred did was probably the most difficult thing of all. She looked at young Richard Chantry's dead body and identified it as the body of her own son William. It was a bold action, and not her last. She loved her bastard son, no matter what he was guilty of. But it was a fierce and tragic love she had for him. This morning she tried to reach him with a stiletto.'

'To kill him?' Ruth Biemeyer said.

'Or to let him kill himself. I don't think it would have made much difference to Mildred. Her own life is pretty well finished.'

Jack Biemeyer let out an involuntary sigh.

His wife turned to me. 'You said William had help from three people.'

'At least three.'

'Who was the third?'

'I think you know. William Mead never would have gotten out of Arizona, or succeeded in staying out, without some help. Somebody had to turn off Sheriff Brotherton's investigation and see that the case was closed.'

Ruth Biemeyer and I looked at her husband. He lifted his heavy arms as though our eyes were guns.

'I wouldn't do a thing like that.'

'You would if she told you to,' his wife said. 'She's been telling you what to do ever since I can remember. You'll be going down to the county jail to ask her what to do next. And she'll tell you to spend a fortune defending her murdering son, and you'll do it for her.'

'Maybe I will at that.'

He was watching her face. She looked at him in surprise and sudden fear.

Biemeyer stood up slowly, as if he was lifting a great weight on his shoulders. 'Will you drive me down there, Archer? I'm feeling a bit shaky.'

I said I would. Biemeyer started out of the room ahead of me. He turned at the open door and faced his wife.

'There's something you need to know, Ruth. William is my son, too. My illegitimate son by Mildred. I was just a kid in my teens when he was born.'

Desolation crept over her face. 'Why didn't you tell me before? It's too late now.'

She looked at her husband as if she was seeing him for the last time. He took me out through the empty echoing spaces of the house. He walked uncertainly, staggering a little. I helped him into my car and started down the hill.

'It was an accident,' he said, 'just one of those accidents that happen to people. I met Mildred after a high school football game. Old Felix Chantry threw a party in his mountain house. I was invited because my mother was his cousin. You know, a poor relation.'

He sat for a while with his head down, then spoke in a stronger voice. 'I scored three touchdowns that day, four if you count Mildred. I was seventeen when William was conceived, eighteen when he was born. There wasn't much I could do for him. I had no money. I was trying to make it through college. Mildred told Felix Chantry that the child was his, and he believed her. He let the boy use his name and gave her money for the boy's support until she broke with Chantry and went to Simon Lashman.

'She did what she could for me, too. She helped me get a football scholarship and when I graduated she saw that Felix gave me a job at the smelter. She helped me up the ladder. I owe her a great deal.'

But there was no warmth of gratitude in his voice. Perhaps he sensed that his life had been mislaid when he was young, and even at his age was still loose in his grasp. He peered out at the city we were driving through as though its shadowed streets were alien.

I felt the strangeness, too. The halls of the courthouse were like catacombs. After an elaborate proceeding that reminded me of the initiation rite into a tribe of aborigines, the DA's men ushered us into the presence of the man I had taken.

He didn't look like a mass murderer, in spite of the armed guards who stood one on each side of him. He looked pale and weak and worried, as violent men so often do after the event.

'William?' I said.

He nodded once. Tears had begun to form in his eyes and run down his cheeks, slowly, like the sparse blood from stiletto wounds.

Jack Biemeyer stepped forward and touched his son's wet face.